INTERSTELLAR
PATROL II:
THE FEDERATION OF HUMANITY

COMPILED & EDITED BY ERIC FLINT
CHRISTOPHER ANVIL

D1092704

INTERSTELLAR PATROL II: THE FEDERATION OF HUMANITY

Copyright © 2005 by Christopher Anvil. Afterword copyright © 2005 by Eric Flint.

A Baen Books Original

Baen Publishing Enterprises
P.O. Box 1403
Riverdale, NY 10471
www.baen.com

ISBN: 0-7434-9892-5

Cover art by Jeff Easley

First printing, March 2005

Library of Congress Cataloging-in-Publication Data

Anvil, Christopher.
    Interstellar patrol II : the federation of humanity / Christopher Anvil ; compiled & edited by Eric Flint.
        p. cm.
    "A Baen Books original"--T.p. verso.
    ISBN 0-7434-9892-5 (hc)
    1. Life on other planets--Fiction. 2. Space warfare--Fiction. 3. Space ships--Fiction. I. Title: Intersteller patrol 2. II. Title: Intersteller patrol two. III. Flint, Eric. IV. Title.

PS3551.N9I59 2005
13'.54--dc22   2004027041

Distributed by Simon & Schuster
1230 Avenue of the Americas
New York, NY 10020

Production by Windhaven Press, Auburn, NH (www.windhaven.com)
Printed in the United States of America

10   9   8   7   6   5   4   3   2   1

EDITOR'S NOTE:

Interstellar Patrol II: The Federation of Humanity is a companion volume to Christopher Anvil's *Interstellar Patrol* (published by Baen Books in April, 2003). In this volume, the later adventures of the Interstellar Patrol agents Vaughan Roberts and his associates are recounted. Included also are all the various other stories which Anvil wrote in the same Federation of Humanity setting.

CONTENTS

THE INTERSTELLAR PATROL

THE CLAW AND THE CLOCK

Iadrubel Vire glanced over the descriptive documents thoughtfully.

"A promising world. However, considering the extent of the Earthmen's possessions, and the size of their Space Force, one hesitates to start trouble."

Margash Grele bowed deferentially.

"Understood, Excellency. But there is a significant point that we have just discovered. We have always supposed this planet was a part of their Federation. It is not. It is *independent*."

Vire got his two hind ripping claws up onto their rest.

"Hm-m-m . . . How did we come by this information?"

"One of their merchant ships got off-course, and Admiral Arvast Nade answered the distress signal." Grele gave a bone-popping sound, signifying wry humor. "Needless to say, the Earthmen were more distressed after the rescue than before."

Vire sat up.

"So, contrary to my specific instructions, Nade has given the Earthmen pretext to strike at us?"

"Excellency, restraint of the kill-instinct requires high moral development when dealing with something as helpless as these Earthmen. Nade, himself, did not take part in the orgy, of course, but he was unable to restrain his men. It was the Earthlings' fault, because they were not armed. If they had been in full battle armor, with their tools of war—Well, who wants to crack his claws on a thing like that? But they presented themselves as defenseless offerings. The temptation was too great."

3

"Were the Earthmen aware of the identity of the rescue craft?"

Grele looked uneasy.

"Admiral Nade feared some trap, and . . . ah . . . undertook to forestall treachery by using an Ursoid recognition signal."

Vire could feel the scales across his back twitch. This fool, Nade, had created out of nothing the possibility of war with both Earth *and* Ursa.

Vire said shortly, "Having given the Ursoid recognition signal, the Earthmen naturally would not be prepared. Therefore Nade would naturally be unable to restrain his men. So, what—"

Grele gave his bone-grinding chuckle, and suddenly Vire saw it as amusement at the ability of Nade to disobey Vire's orders, and get away with it.

Vire's right-hand battle-pincer came up off its rest, his manipulators popped behind his bony chest armor, three death-dealing stings snicked into position in his left-hand battle pincer—

Grele hurtled into a corner, all claws menacingly thrust out, but screaming, "Excellency, I meant no offense! Forgive my error! I mean only respect!"

"Then get to the point! Let's have the *facts!"*

Grele said in a rush, "Admiral Nade saved several Earthlings, to question them. They saw him as their protector, and were frank. It seems the Earthmen on this planet have a method for eliminating war-like traits from their race, and—"

"From their race *on this planet alone?"*

"Yes. The planet was settled by very stern religionists, who believe in total peace unless attacked. They eliminate individuals who show irrepressible warlike traits."

Vire settled back in his seat. "They believe in 'Total peace, unless attacked.' *Then* what?"

"Apparently, they believe in self-defense. A little impractical, if proper precautions have not been made."

"Hm-m-m. How did the crewmen know about this?"

"They had made many delivery trips to the planet. It seems that the Earthmen call this planet, among themselves, 'Storehouse.' The code name is given in the documents there, and it is formally named 'Faith.' But to the Earthmen, it is 'Storehouse.'"

"Why?"

"These religious Earthlings have perfected means to preserve provisions with no loss whatever. Even live animals are in some way frozen, gassed, irradiated—or somehow treated—so they are just as good when they come out as when they went in. This is handy for shippers who have a surplus due to a temporary glut on the market, or because it's a bad year for the buyers. So, within practicable shipping distance, Storehouse does a thriving business, preserving goods from time of surplus to a time of need."

Vire absently grated his ripping claws on their rests.

"Hm-m-m . . . And the basis of this process is not generally known?"

"No, sir. They have a monopoly. Moreover, they use their monopoly to enforce codes of conduct on the shippers. Shippers who employ practices they regard as immoral, or who deal in goods they disapprove of, have their storage quotas cut. Shippers they approve of get reduced rates. And they are incorruptible, since they are religious fanatics—like our Cult of the Sea, who resist the last molt, and stick to gills."

"Well, well, this *does* offer possibilities. But, would the Earthmen be willing to lose this valuable facility, even if it is not a member of their Federation? On the other hand—I wonder if the fanatics have antagonized the Earthmen as the cursed sea cult antagonizes us? That collection of righteous clams."

Grele nodded. "From what Admiral Nade learned, it certainly seems so. The crew of the distressed ship, for instance, had just had their quota cut because they had been caught 'shooting craps,' a form of gambling—while on their own ship waiting to unload."

"Yes, that sounds like it. Nade, I suppose, has his fleet in position?"

"Excellency, he chafes at the restraints."

"No doubt."

Vire balanced the possibilities.

"It is rumored that some who have attacked independent Earth-settled planets have not enjoyed the experience."

"The Earthlings would be bound to spread such rumors. But what can mere religious fanatics do against the guns of our men? The fanatics are skilled operators of a preserving plant; of what use is *that* in combat?"

Vire settled back. Either the Earthmen were truly unprepared, in which case he, Vire, would receive partial credit for a valuable acquisition; or else the Earthmen were prepared, and Nade would get such a dent in his shell that his reputation would never recover.

"All right," said Vire cheerfully, "but we must have a pretext—these religious fanatics must have delivered some insult that we want to avenge, and it must fit in with their known character. If possible, it must rouse sympathy, even, for us. Let's see . . ."

Elder Hugh Phillips eyed the message dourly.

"These lobsters have their gall. Look at this."

Deacon Bentley adjusted his penance shirt to make the bristles bite in better, and took the message. He read aloud in a dry methodical voice:

" 'Headquarters, the Imperial Hatchery, Khlaftschffran'—lot of heathenish gabble there, I'll skip all that. Let's see ' . . . Pursuant to the blessings of the' . . . heh . . . 'fertility god Fflahvritschtsvri . . . Pursuant to the blessings of the fertility god, What's-His-Name, the Royal Brood has exceeded expectations this season, all praise to So-and-So, et cetera, et cetera, and exceeds the possibility of the Royal Hatchery to handle. We, therefore, favor you with the condescension of becoming for the next standard year an Auxiliary Royal Hatchery, consecrated according to the ritual of Fflahvrit . . . et cetera . . . and under due direction of the Imperial Priesthood, and appropriate Brood Masters, you to receive in addition to the honor your best standard payment for the service of maintaining the Royal Brood in good health, and returning same in time for the next season, undamaged by the delay, to make up the deficiency predicted by the Brood Masters. The fertility god, What's-His-Name, directs us through his Priesthood to command your immediate notice of compliance, as none of the precious Brood must be endangered by delay.' "

Deacon Bentley looked up.

"To make it short, we're supposed to store the royal lobsters for a year, is that it?"

"Evidently."

"There's no difficulty there." Bentley eyed the message coldly. "As for being consecrated according to the lobster's fertility god, *there* we part company."

Elder Phillips nodded.

"They *do* offer good pay, however."

"All worldly money is counterfeit. The only reward is in Heaven."

"Amen. But from their own heathen viewpoint, the offer is fair. Obviously, we can't accept it. But we must be fair in return, even to lobsters. We will take care of the Royal Brood, but as for their Priesthood"—he cleared his throat—"with due humility, we must decline that provision. Now, who writes the answer?"

"Brother Fry would be ideal for it."

"He's on a fast. How about Deacon Fenell?"

"No good. He went into a cell on Tuesday. Committed himself for a month."

"He did, eh? Able's boy, Wilder, would have been good at this. Too bad."

Phillips nodded.

"Unfortunately, not all can conquer their own nature. Some require grosser enemies." He sighed. "Let's see. How do we start the thing off?"

"Let's just say, 'We will put up your brood for so-and-so much per year. We decline the consecration.' That's the gist of the matter. Then we nail some diplomacy on both ends of it, dress it up a little, and there we are."

"I wish Brother Fry were here. This nonsense can eat up time. However, he's *not* here, so let's get at it."

Iadrubel Vire read the message over again intently:

> From:
> Central Contracting Office
> Penitence City
> Planet of Faith
>
> To:
> Headquarters
> The Imperial Hatchery
> Khlaftschiffranzitschopendischkla
>
> Dear Sirs:
> We are in receipt of your request of the 22nd instant that we put the excess of the Royal Brood in storage for a period approximating one standard year.
> We agree to do this, in accord with our standard rate schedule "D" appended, suitable for nonpreferred

live shipments. Kindly note that these rates apply from date of delivery to the storehouse entrance, to date of reshipment from the same point.

We regret that we must refuse your other terms, to wit:

a) Accompaniment of the shipment by priests and broodmasters.

b) Consecration to the fertility god, referred to in your communication.

In reference to a), no such accompaniment is necessary or allowed.

In reference to b), the said god, so-called, is, of course, nonexistent.

In view of the fact that your race is known to be heathen, these requests will not be held against you in determining the rate schedule, beyond placing you in the nonpreferred status.

We express our appreciation for this order, and trust that our service will be found satisfactory in every respect.

Truly yours,

Hugh Bentley
Chief Assistant
Central Contracting Office

Vire sat back, absently scratched his ripping claws on their rest, reached out with a manipulator, and punched a call-button.

A door popped open, and Margash Grele stepped in and bowed.

"Excellency?"

"Read this."

Grele read it, and looked up.

"These people are, as I told you, sir, like our sea cult—only worse."

"They certainly take an independent line for an isolated planet dealing with an interstellar empire—and on a sensitive subject, at that."

"Not so, Excellency. It is independent from *our* viewpoint. If you read between the lines, you can see that, for *them,* they are bent over backwards."

Vire absently squeaked the sharp tips of his right-hand battle claw together.

"Maybe. In any case, I don't think we would be quite justified by this reply in doing anything drastic. However, I think we can improve on this. Tell Nade to get his claws sharpened up, and we'll see what happens with the next message."

Hugh Phillips handed the message to Deacon Bentley.

"There seems to have been something wrong with our answer to these crabs."

"What, did we lose the order? Let's see."

Bentley's eyebrows raised.

"Hm-m-m. . . .'Due to your maligning the religious precepts of our Race, we must demand a full retraction and immediate apology . . .'When did we do that?"

"There was something about that part where we said they were heathens."

"They *are* heathens."

"I know."

"Truth is Truth."

"That is so. Nevertheless—well, Brother Fry would know how to handle this."

"Unfortunately, he is not here. Well, what to do about this?"

Phillips looked at it.

"What is there to do?"

Bentley's look of perplexity cleared away.

"True. We can't have lobsters giving us religious instruction." He looked wary. "On the other hand, we mustn't fall into the sin of pride, either."

"Here, let's have a pen." Phillips wrote rapidly, frowned, then glanced at Bentley. "How is your sister's son coming along? Her next-to-eldest?"

Bentley shook his head.

"I fear he is not meant for righteousness. He has refused to do his penances."

Phillips shook his head, then looked at what he had written. After a moment, he glanced up. "If the truth were told, some of us shaved by pretty close, ourselves. I suppose it's to be expected. The first settlers were certainly descended from a rough lot." He cleared his throat. "I am not so sure my eldest is going to make it."

Bentley caught his breath.

"Perhaps you judge too harshly."

"No. As a boy, he did not *play* marbles. He lined them up in ranks, and studied the formations. We would find him with his mother's pie plate and a pencil, holding them to observe how a space fleet in disk might destroy one in column. I have tried to . . ." Phillips cleared his throat. "Here, read this. See if you can improve it. We must be strictly honest, and must not truckle to these heathens. It would be bad for them as well as us."

"Amen, Elder. Let's see, now—"

Iadrubel Vire straightened up in his seat, reread the message, and summoned Margash Grele.

Margash bowed deferentially.

"Excellency?"

"This is incredible. Read this."

Grele read aloud:

"'Sirs: We acknowledge receipt of yours of the 28th instant, and are constrained, in all truth, to reply that you *are* heathen; that your so-called fertility god is no god at all; that your priests are at best misled, and at worst representatives of the devil; and that we can on no account tolerate priests of heathen religions on this planet. As these are plain facts, there can be no retraction and no apology, as there is no insult, but only a plain statement of truth. As a gesture of compromise, and to prove good will, we will allow one (1) brood master to accompany the shipment, provided he is not a priest of any godless 'religion,' so-called. We will not revise the schedule of charges on this occasion, but warn you plainly that this is our final offer. Truly yours . . .'"

Grele looked up blankly.

Vire said, "There is a tone to this, my dear Grele, that does not appear consistent with pacifism. Not with pacifism as *I* understand the word."

"I certainly see what you mean, sir. Nevertheless, they *are* pacifists. We have carefully checked our information."

"And we are *certain* they are not members of the Federation?"

"Absolutely certain."

"Well, there is *something* here that we do not understand. This message could not be better planned if it were a bait to draw us to the attack."

"It is certainly an insulting message, but one well suited to our purpose."

"That, too, is suspicious. Events rarely fall into line so easily."

"Excellency, they are religious fanatics. There is the explanation."

"Nevertheless, we must draw the net tighter before we attempt to take them. Such utter fearlessness usually implies either a formidable weapon, or a formidable protector. We must be certain the Federation does not have some informal agreement with this planet."

"Excellency, Admiral Nade grows impatient."

Vire's right-hand claw quivered. "We will give him the chance to do the job, once we have done ours. We must make certain we do not send our troops straight into the jaws of a trap. There is a strong Space Force fleet so situated that it *might* intervene."

General Larssen, of the Space Force, looked up from copies of the messages. "The only place in this end of space where we can store supplies with *no* spoilage, and they have to wind up in a fight with the lobsters over royal lobster eggs. And we aren't allowed to do anything about it."

"Well, sir," said Larssen's aide, "they *were* pretty insulting about it. And they've had every chance to join the Federation. It's hard to see why the Federation should take on all Crustax for them now."

"'All Crustax,' nuts. The lobsters would back down if we'd ram a stiff note down their throat. Do we have any reply from the . . . er . . . 'court of last resort' on this?"

"No, sir, they haven't replied yet."

"Much as I dislike them, they don't pussyfoot around, anyway. Let's hope—"

There was a quiet rap, and Larssen looked up.

"Come in!"

The communications officer stepped in, looking serious.

"I wanted to bring you this myself, sir. The Interstellar Patrol declines to intervene, because it feels that the locals can take care of themselves."

Larssen stared. "They're a bunch of pacifists! All *they're* strong at is fighting off temptation!"

"Yes, sir. We made that point. All we got back was, 'Wait and see.'"

"Well, we tried, at least. Now we've got a ringside seat for the slaughter."

Admiral Nade was in his bunk when the top priority message came in. His aide entered the room, approached the bunk, and hesitated. Nade was completely covered up, out of sight.

The aide looked around nervously. The chief was a trifle peevish when roused out of a sound sleep.

The aide put the message on the admiral's cloak of rank on the nightstand near the bunk, retraced his steps to the hatch, opened it wide, then returned to the bunk. Hopefully, he waited, but Nade didn't stir.

The aide spoke hesitantly: "Ah . . . a message, sir." Nothing happened. He tried again.

Nade didn't move.

The aide climbed over the raised lip of the catch tray, took hold of the edge of the bunk, dug several claws into the wood in his nervousness, and cautiously scratched back a little of the fine white sand. The admiral was in there *somewhere*. He scratched a little more urgently. A few smooth pebbles rattled into the tray.

Just then, he bumped something.

Claws shot up. Sand flew in all directions.

The aide fell over the edge of the tray, scrabbled violently, and hurled himself through the doorway.

The admiral bellowed, "WHO DARES—"

The aide rounded corners, and shot down cross-corridors as the admiral grabbed his cloak of rank, then spotted the message.

Nade seized the message, stripped off various seals the message machine had plastered on it, growled: "The fool probably wants *more* delay." Then he tore open the lightproof envelope that guaranteed no one would see it but him, unfolded the message itself, and snarled, "' . . . received your message #4e67t3fs . . . While I agree—' Bah! ' . . . extreme caution is advised . . . ' That clawless wonder! Let's see, what's this? ' . . . Provided due consideration is given to these precautions, you are hereby authorized to carry out the seizure by force of the aforesaid planet, its occupation, its annexation, and whatever ancillary measures may appear necessary or desirable. You are, however, warned on no account to engage forces of the Federation in battle, the operation to be strictly limited to the seizure, et cetera, of the aforesaid planet. If possible, minimum damage is to be done to the planet's storage equipment, as possession of this equipment should prove extremely valuable . . . ' Well, he's a hard-shell, after all! Let's see . . . 'Security against surprise by Federation forces will be employed without however endangering success of the operation by undue dividing of the attacking force . . . ' That doesn't hurt anything. Now, the quicker we take them, the better."

He whipped his cloak of rank around him, tied it with a few quick jerks of his manipulators, strode into the corridor, and headed for the bridge, composing an ultimatum as he went.

Elder Phillips examined the message, and cleared his throat. "We appear to have a war on our hands."

Deacon Bentley made a clucking noise. "Let's see."

Phillips handed him the message. Bentley sat back.

"Ha-hm-m-m. 'Due to your deliberately insulting references to our religion, to your slandering of our gods, and to your refusal to withdraw the insult, we are compelled to extend claws in battle to defend our honor. I hereby authorize the Fleet of Crustax to engage in lawful combat, and have notified Federation authorities as the contiguous independent power in this region that a state of war exists. Signed, Iadrubel Vire, Chief Commander of the Forces.' Well, it appears, Elder, that our message was not quite up to Brother Fry's level. Hm-m-m, there's more to this. Did this all come in at once?"

"It did, Deacon. The first part apparently authorizes the second part."

"Quite a different style, this. 'I, Arvast Nade, Commander Battle Fleet IV, hereby demand your immediate surrender. Failure to comply within one hour, your time, following receipt of this ultimatum, as determined by my communications center, will open your planet to pillage by my troops. Any attempt at resistance will be crushed without mercy, and your population decimated in retaliation. Any damage, or attempted damage, by you to goods or facilities of value on the planet will be avenged by execution of leading citizens selected at my command. By my fiat as conqueror, your status, retroactive to the moment of transmission of this ultimatum, is that of bond-sleg to the conquering race. Any lack of instantaneous obedience will be dealt with accordingly. Signed, Arvast Nade, Battle Fleet Commander.' "

Deacon Bentley looked up.

"What do we do with this?"

"I see no alternative to activating War Preventive Measures, as described in Chapter XXXVIII of the Lesser Works."

"I was afraid of that. Well . . . so be it."

"We can't have a war here. As soon as we saw a few of these heathen loose on the planet, we'd all revert to type. You know what *that* is."

"Well, let's waste no time. You take care of that, and I'll answer the ultimatum. Common courtesy requires that we answer it, I suppose."

Arvast Nade got the last of his battle armor on, and tested the joints.

"There's a squeak somewhere."

"Sir?" said his aide blankly.

"There's a squeak. Listen."

It could be heard plainly:

Squeak, squeak, squeak, squeak, squeak.

The aide got the oil can. "Work your claws one at a time, sir . . . Let's see . . . Again. *There* it is!"

"Ah, good," said Nade, working everything soundlessly. "That's what comes of too long a peace. And this stuff is supposed to be rustproof!"

There was a polite rap at the door. The aide leaned outside, and came back with a message. "For you, sir. It's from the Storehousers."

"Good. Wait till I get a hand out through this . . . uh . . . the thing is stiff. There, let's have it."

Reaching out with a manipulator through a kind of opened trapdoor in the armor, and almost knocking loose a hand-weapon clamped to the inside, Nade took hold of the message, which was without seals or embellishments, as befitted the mouthings of slegs.

Behind the clear visor, Nade's gaze grew fixed as he read.

From:
Central Contracting Office

Penitence City
Planet of Faith

To:
Arvast Nade
Commander
Battle Fleet IV
Crustax

Dear Sir:

We regret to inform you that we must decline the conditions mentioned in your message of the 2nd instant. As you may be aware, the planetary government of the planet Faith does not recognize war, and can permit no war to be waged on, or in the vicinity of, this planet. Our decision on this matter is final, and is not open to discussion.

Truly yours,

Hugh Bentley
Chief Assistant
Central Contracting Office

Nade dazedly handed the message to his aide.

"And just how," he demanded, "are they going to enforce *that?*"

Elder Phillips's hand trembled slightly as he reached out to accept the proffered hand of the robed figure.

"Judge Archer Goodwin," said the dignitary politely. "Elder, I bring you tidings of your eldest son, and I fear you will not find them happy tidings."

Phillips kept his voice level.

"I suspected as much, Judge."

"With due allowance for the fallibility of human judgment, Lance appears unsuited to a life of peace. Study bores him. Conflict and its techniques fascinate him. He is pugnacious, independent. He sees life in terms of conflict. He is himself authoritative, though subject to subordination to a superior authority. He is not dull. The acquisitions of useful skills, and even a quite deep knowledge, are well within his grasp, potentially. However, his basic bent is in another direction. On a different planet, we might expect him to shine in some limited but strategically-placed field, using it as a springboard to power and rank. Here, to allow him to pass into the populace would require us, out of fairness, to allow others to do the same. But the proportions of such traits are already so high that our way of living could not endure the shock. You see, he not only possesses these traits, plus a lust to put them in action, but *he sees nothing wrong with this.* Accordingly, he will not attempt to control his natural tendencies. Others of even greater combativeness have entered our population, but have recognized the sin of allowing such tendencies sway, unless the provocation is indeed serious. Then—" Judge Goodwin's face for an instant bent into a chilling smile, which he at once blinked away. He cleared his throat. "I am sorry to have to bring you this news."

Elder Phillips bowed his head. Somehow, somewhere, he had failed in proper discipline, in stern counsel. But, defiant, the boy always—

He put down the thoughts with an effort. Others took their place. People would talk. He would never live this down, would never know if a word, or a tone of voice, was a sly reference.

His fists clenched. For an instant, everything vanished in rage. Sin of sins, in a blur of mental pictures, he saw himself seek similarly afflicted parents—the planet teemed with them—rouse them to revolt, saw himself outwit the guards, seize the armory, arm the disaffected, and *put this unholy law to the test of battle!*

So real was the illusion that for an instant he felt the sword in his hand, saw the Council spring to their feet as he stepped over the bodies of the guards; his followers, armed to the teeth, were right behind him as he entered—

With a sob, he dropped to his knees.

The judge's hand gripped his shoulder. "Be steadfast. With the aid of the Almighty, you will conquer this. You can do it. Or you would not be here."

Arvast Nade studied the green and blue sphere swimming in the viewscreen.

"Just as I thought. They lack even a patrol ship."

"Sir," said the aide, "another message from the Storehousers."

Nade popped open his hatch, and reached out.

Gaze riveted to the page, he read:

From:
Office of the Chief
War Prevention Department
Level VI
Penitence City
Planet of Faith

To:
Arvast Nade
Commander
Battle Fleet IV
Crustax

Sir:

We hereby deliver final warning to you that this Department will not hesitate to use all measures necessary to bar the development of war on this planet or in its contiguous regions.

You are warned to signify peaceful intent by immediately altering course away from our planet. If this is impossible, signal the reason at once.

Hiram Wingate
Chief
War Prevention Dept.

Nade lowered the message. He took another look at the screen. He looked back at the message, then glanced at his aide.

"You've read this?"

"Certainly, sir. Communications from slegs have no right of privacy."

"How did it seem to you?"

The aide hesitated. "If I did not know they were disarmed pacifists, who destroy every warlike son born to them—well, I would be worried, sir."

"There is certainly a very hard note to this message. There is even a tone of command that can be heard in it. I find it difficult to believe this could have been written by one unfamiliar with and unequipped for war."

Nade hesitated, then activated his armored-suit communicator.

"Alter course ten girids solaxially outward of the planet Storehouse."

Nade's aide looked shocked.

The admiral said, "War is not unlimited heroics, my boy. We lose nothing from this maneuver but an air of omnipotence that has a poor effect on tactics, anyway. Conceivably, there are warships on the far side of that planet. But if these softshells are just putting up a smudge with no claws behind it, we will gobble them up, and I will add an additional two *skrads* free pillage to what they have already earned. The Storehouse regions being off-limits, of course."

The aide beamed, and clashed his claws in anticipation.

Admiral Nade adjusted the screen to a larger magnification.

Elder Phillips formally shook hands with his son, Lance, who was dressed in battle armor, with sword and pistol, and a repeater slung across his back.

"Sorry, Dad," said the younger Phillips, "I couldn't take this mush-mouthed hypocrisy, that's all. It's a trap, and the fact that you and the rest of your generation let themselves get caught in it is no reason why *I* should."

Tight-lipped, the elder said nothing.

His son's lip curled. Then he shrugged. "Wish me luck, at least, Dad."

"Good luck, son." The elder began to say more, but caught himself.

A harsh voice boomed over the gathering.

"Those who have been found unsuitable for life on this planet, do now separate from those who will remain, and step forward to face each other in armed combat. Those who will do battle on the physical level, assemble by the sign of the sword. Those who will give battle on the level of tactics, assemble by the stacked arms. Those who will give battle on the plane of high strategy, assemble by the open book. You will now be matched one with another until but one champion remains in each group. Those champions will have earned the right to life, but must still prove themselves against an enemy of the race or of the Holy Word. In any case, settlement shall not be here amongst the scenes of your childhood. Let any who have second thoughts speak out. Though a—"

A shrill voice interrupted. "Overthrow them! We have the guns!"

There was an instantaneous *crack!* One of the armored figures collapsed.

The harsh voice went on, a little lower-pitched:

"Anyone else who wants to defy regulations is free to try. The punishment is instantaneous death. I was about to say that anyone who has second thoughts should speak up, though a courage test will be required to rejoin your family, and you must again submit to judgment later. The purpose of the Law is not to raise a race of cowards, but a race capable of controlling its warlike instincts. Naturally, anyone who backs out of *this*, and fails the courage test, will be summarily killed. Does anyone on mature consideration regret the stand he has taken?"

There was a silence.

The armored figures, their faces through the raised visors expressing surprise, glanced at the outstretched rebel, then at each other.

Elder Phillips's son turned, and his gaze sought out his father. He grinned and raised the naked sword in salute. The elder, startled, raised his hand. Now, what was that about?

"Very well," said the harsh voice. "Take your positions by your respective emblems."

Elder Phillips, watching, saw his son hesitate, and then walk toward the open book. The elder was surprised; after all, some fool might think him cowardly, not realizing the type of courage the test would involve.

The voice said, "After a brief prayer, we will begin . . ."

Arvast Nade glanced at the ranked screens in the master control room.

"There is no hidden force off that planet. It was a bluff." He activated his armored-suit communicator, and spoke briskly: "Turn the Fleet by divisions, and land in the preselected zones."

Hiram Wingate, Chief, War Prevention Department, watched the maneuver on the screen, turned to a slanting console bearing ranks of numbered levers and redly-glowing lights, and methodically pulled down levers. The red lights winked off, to be replaced by green. On a second console, a corresponding number of blue lights went out, to be replaced by red.

Near the storage plant, huge camouflaged gates swung wide. An eager voice shouted over the communicator. "Men! Squadron A strikes the first blow! Follow me!"

Arvast Nade, just tuning from the screen, jerked back to take another look.

Between his fleet and the planet, a swarm of blurs had materialized.

The things were visibly growing large on the screen, testifying to an incredible velocity.

Abruptly the blurred effect vanished, and he could see what appeared to be medium-sized scout ships, all bearing some kind of angular symbol that apparently served as a unit identification.

Now again they blurred.

Nade activated his suit communicator.

"Secondary batteries open fi—"

The deck jumped underfoot. A siren howled, changed pitch, then faded out. Across the control room, a pressure-monitor needle wound down around its dial, then the plastic cover of the instrument blew off.

The whole ship jumped.

A tinny voice spoke in Nade's ear. "Admiral, we are being attacked by small ships of the Storehousers!"

"Fire back!" shouted Nade.

"They're too fast, sir! Fire control can't keep up with them! *Look out!* HERE COMES—"

Nade raised his battle pincers.

Before him, the whole scene burst into one white-hot incandescence.

General Larssen, watching on the long-range pickup, sat in shock as glare from the viewer lit his face.

"And they don't believe in war! Look at *that!*"

"Sir," said a dazed subordinate, "that *isn't* war."

"It isn't? What do *you* call it?"

"Extermination, sir. Pest control. War assumes some degree of equality between opponents."

✣   ✣   ✣

Lance Phillips, feeling dazed and drained, but with a small warm sense of achievement, straightened from the battle computer.

"I didn't do too badly?"

"Best of the lot," said the examiner cheerfully. "Your understanding of the geometrical aspects of space strategy is outstanding."

"I had a sense of drag—as if I couldn't get the most out of my forces."

"You didn't. You aren't dealing with pure abstract force, but with human beings. You made no allowance for that."

"But I did well enough to survive?"

"You did."

"What about the others?"

"They had their opportunity. Those who conquered will be saved. Any really outstanding fighters who lost because of bad luck, or superb opposition, will also be saved."

"We get a chance to do battle later?"

"Correct."

"We fight for our own planet?"

"That's right."

"But—how long since the planet was attacked?"

"Yesterday, when this trial began. Prior to that, not for about a hundred years."

"*Yesterday!* What are we doing here? We should—"

The examiner shook his head.

"The attack never amounted to anything. Just a fleet of lobsters wiped out in fifteen minutes."

Lance Phillips looked dizzy.

"I thought we didn't believe in war!"

"Of course not," said the examiner. "War, of the usual kind, has a brutalizing effect. As likely as not, the best are sent to slaughter each other, so at least the physical level of the race is lowered. The conquered are plundered of the fruits of their labor, which is wrong, while the conquerors learn to expect progress by pillage instead of work; they become a burden on everyone around them; *that* leads to a desire to exterminate them. The passions aroused do not end with the conflict, but go on to make more conflict. We *don't* believe in war. Unfortunately, not everyone is equally enlightened. Should we, because we recognize the truth, be at the mercy of every sword-rattler and egomaniac? Of course not. But how are we to avoid it? By simultaneously understanding the evils of war, and being prepared to wage it defensively on the greatest scale."

"But that's a contradiction! You can't distinguish between offensive and defensive weapons! And we have too small a planet to support a large-scale war!"

The examiner looked him over coolly.

"With due respect to your logic, your understanding is puny. Now, we have something here we call 'discipline.' Think carefully before you tell me again to my face that I am a fool, or a liar. I repeat, 'How do we avoid war? By simultaneously understanding the evils of war, and being prepared to wage it defensively on the greatest scale.'"

Lance Phillips felt the objections well up, felt the overpowering certainty, the determination to brush aside nonsense.

Simultaneously, he felt something else.

He opened his mouth. No words came out.

Could this be fear?

Not exactly.

What was it?

Suddenly he recognized it.

Caution.

Warily, he said, "In that case . . . ah . . . *how—*"

Iadrubel Vire scanned the fragmentary reports, and looked at Margash Grele. Grele's normally iridescent integument was a muddy gray.

"This is all?" said Vire.

"Yes, sir."

"No survivors?"

"Not one, so far as we know. It was a slaughter."

Vire sat back, dazed. A whole battle fleet wiped out—just like that. This would alter the balance of force all along the frontier.

"What word from the Storehousers?"

"Nothing, sir."

"No demands?"

"Not a word."

"After a victory like this, they could—" He paused, frowning. They were *pacifists, who believed in self-defense.*

That sounded fine, in principle, but—how had they reduced it to practice? After all, they were only one planet. Their productive capacity and manpower did not begin to approach that of Crustax and—

Vire cut off that line of thought. *This* loss, with enough patience and craft, could be overcome. Two or three more like it would be the finish. There was just not enough potential gain to risk further attempts on that one little planet. He had probed the murk with a claw, and drawn back a stub. Best to avoid trouble while that grew back, and just keep away from the place in the future.

"Release the announcement," said Vire slowly, "that Fleet IV, in maneuvers, has been caught in a meteor storm of unparalleled intensity. Communications have been temporarily cut off, and there is concern at headquarters over the fate of the fleet. It will be some time before we will know with certainty what has happened, but it is feared that a serious disaster may have occurred. As this fleet is merely a reserve fleet on maneuvers in the region of the border with the Federation, with which we have friendly relations, this, of course, in no way imperils our defenses, but . . . h'm-m-m . . . we are deeply concerned for the crewmen and their loved ones."

Grele made swift notes, and looked up.

"Excellency, might it not be wise to let this information out by stages? First, the word of the meteor shower—but our experts doubt the accuracy of the report. Next, a substantiating report has come in. Then—"

"No, because in the event of a real meteor shower, we would make no immediate public announcements. We have to be liars in this, but let's keep it to the minimum."

Grele bowed respectfully, and went out.

"Damned gravitor," said Squadron A's 2nd-Flight leader over the communicator, "cut out just as we finished off the lobster fleet. I was signaling for assembly on my ship, and aimed to cut a little swath through crab-land before going home. Instead, we've been streaking off on our own for the last week, and provisions are slim on these little boats, I'll tell you that! *What* outfit did you say you are?"

The strange, roughly minnow-shaped ship, not a great deal bigger than the scout, answered promptly:

"Interstellar Patrol. We have a few openings for recruits who can qualify. Plenty of chance for adventure, special training, top-grade weapons, good food, the pay's O.K., no bureaucrats to tangle things up. If you can qualify, it's a good outfit."

"Interstellar Patrol, huh? Never heard of it. I was thinking of the Space Force."

"Well, you *could* come in that way. We get quite a few men from the Space Force. It's a fair outfit, but they have to kowtow to Planetary Development. Their weapons aren't up to ours; but their training isn't so tough, either. They'd be *sure* to let you in, where we're a little more selective. You've got a point, all right. It would be a lot easier—if you want things easy."

"Well, I didn't mean—"

"We could shoot you supplies to last a couple of weeks, and *maybe* a Space Force ship will pick you up. If not, we could help—if we're still in the region. Of course, if not—"

The flight leader began to perspire. "Listen, tell me a little more about this Interstellar Patrol."

Lance Phillips stared at rank on rank of mirrorlike glittering forms stretching off into the distance, and divided into sections by massive pillars that buttressed the ceiling.

"*This* is part of the storage plant?"

"It is. Naturally, foreigners know nothing of this, and our own people have little cause to learn the details. You say a small planet can't afford a large striking force. It can, *if* the force is accumulated slowly, and requires no maintenance whatever. Bear in mind, we make our living by *storing* goods, with no loss. How can there be *no* loss? Obviously, if, from the viewpoint of the observer, *no time passes for the stored object.*"

"How could that be unless the object were moving at near the velocity of light?"

"How does an object increase its speed to near the velocity of light?"

"It *accelerates.*"

The examiner nodded. "When you see much of this, you have a tendency to speculate. Now, we regularly add to our stock of fighting men and ships, and our ability to control the effects of time enables us to operate, from the observer's viewpoint, either very slowly, or very fast. *How* is not in my department, and this knowledge is not handed out to satisfy curiosity. But—it's natural to speculate. The only way we know to slow time, from the observer's viewpoint, is to accelerate, and increase velocity to near the speed of light. A great ancient named Einstein said there is no way, without outside references, to distinguish the *force of gravity* from acceleration. So, I think some wizardry with gravitors is behind this." He looked thoughtfully at Lance Phillips. "The main thing is, you see what you have to know to be one of our apprentice strategists. We accumulate strength slowly, take the toughest, most generally uncivilizable of each generation, provided they have certain redeeming qualities. *These* are our fighting men. We take a few standard types of ships, improve them as time goes on, and when we are attacked, we accelerate our response, to strike with such speed that the enemy cannot react. We obliterate him. He, mortified, blames the defeat on something else. His fleet was caught in a nova, the gravitors got in resonating synchrony, *something* happened, but it didn't have anything to do with *us*. Nevertheless, he leaves us alone."

"Why not use our process to put his whole fleet in stasis, and use it as a warning?"

"*That* would be an insult he would have to respond to, and we are opposed to war. In the second place, we agreed to give you an opportunity to fight for the planet, and then live your life elsewhere. There has to be some outlet somewhere. We can't just keep stacking ships and warriors in here indefinitely."

"After we get out—*then* what happens?

"It depends on circumstances. However, fighting men are in demand. If, say, a properly keyed signal cut power to the engines, and after some days of drifting, the warrior were offered the opportunity to enlist in some outfit that meets our standards—"

"Yes, that fits." He hesitated, then thrust out his jaw. "I know I'm not supposed to even think about this, but—"

The Examiner looked wary: "Go ahead."

"With what we have here, we could rival the whole works—Federation, Crustax Empire—the lot. Well—why not? We could be the terror of all our opponents!"

The examiner shook his head in disgust.

"After what you've experienced, you can still ask *that*. Let's go at it from another direction. Consider what you know about the warlike character of our populace, and what we have to do to restrain it. Now, just ask yourself: What could such a stock as this be descended *from?*"

A great light seemed to dawn on Lance Phillips.

"You see," said the examiner, "we've already *done* that. We had to try something a little tougher."

RIDDLE ME THIS...

Roberts eyed the bristling model of the huge space station with no great happiness.

"And," said the Colonel, rotating it to bring another rank of fusion turrets into view, "three battalions of crabs are on internal guard duty in this place."

"Hm-m-m," said Roberts, studying the big metal gate below the latest set of turrets. "We're sure two of our men are alive in there?"

"Positive. We're still getting random signals from the deep implants. They're alive. Under torture."

Roberts turned the rim of a little wheel that rolled the model over, and rapid-fire guns and missile snouts protecting the gate came into view.

"Naturally," said Roberts, "if we blow the place up, we kill our own men."

The Colonel nodded. "As a matter of fact, there are quite a few things we *could* do. We have a distinct advantage in technology over these crabs. But if we're not careful, the prisoners will get killed."

"Yet, if we leave the place alone, they'll continue to get tortured?"

"Exactly."

"Suppose," said Roberts, "we put a stiff threat to the crabs to let them go, or else?"

"The diplomats have already done it. The crabs deny any human is in there. That's as far as the diplomats are prepared to go for us. Earth isn't going to declare war on Crustax for two apparently ordinary spacemen, and Crustax knows it."

Roberts turned the model slowly around, and watched the successive ranks of gun turrets swing into view.

The Colonel said, "Normally, an entire Crustaxan fleet is within easy reach of this strong point. But the crabs are minus one fleet since they tried to gobble up Storehouse. They're shorthanded, and they're shuttling fleets around to try to hide it. This place was covered last month, and it may be covered again next month. Right now, there's nothing between us and it but a few light scout ships and an outdated cruiser."

"What's behind that gate?"

The Colonel pushed a button, and on the model, the huge doors rolled back, to disclose a vast lighted interior with big ships at docks, or floating free inside.

"All the guns," said Roberts slowly, "are on the *out*side?"

"The big guns. But don't forget, the three battalions of guards are on the *in*side."

"How good are they at torture?"

"They have a natural talent for it."

"Where are the captives from?"

"Paradise," said the Colonel. He added dryly, "I'm referring to the planet by that name, of course."

Roberts blinked. "Where Hammell, Morrissey, and I were marooned?"

"The same, Roberts. As a matter of fact, these men volunteered out of loyalty to you. They were newly trained technicians on the planet, and after studying the last exchange of messages, they came to the conclusion that the Interstellar Patrol is actually the 'Royal Guard.' Don't ask me to explain their reasoning. That want-generator you used on the planet had a powerful effect. At any rate, they're good men."

Roberts swallowed, and with an effort, relaxed. When the Colonel had said, "these men volunteered out of loyalty to you," this for some reason had made it a personal matter for Roberts. Roberts was, therefore, going to free them—or the crabs were going to pay a steep price in blood. Roberts wasn't sure this was the right way to think, but it was the way he *did* think.

The Colonel glanced seriously at Roberts.

"You see the problem. If we destroy the place, we destroy the men. If we don't destroy it, we leave the men to be tortured. But there's more to it than that. If we go there in an unarmed ship, we can very likely get inside; the commander of this fortress would be delighted to have some more Earth prisoners. But even assuming that you get in, surprise them, and free the prisoners, how do you get away afterward in an unarmed ship? There are those weapons on the outside to deal with. The likelihood of capturing all those turrets from inside is very small. On the other hand, you can go there in a ship that can handle the weapons—and then the crabs will never let you near the place without a fight. That would defeat our purpose."

"Suppose it's a heavily armed ship camouflaged to look harmless?"

"Fine—except that the Crustax Fleet goes in for camouflage in a big way. They have dreadnoughts rigged out to look like big supply ships. Their larger supply ships often look like dreadnoughts. You can't tell who is what without the best instruments. The natural result is that they are suspicious of other people's ships, and if we go in there in a battleship fixed up to look exactly like a large spaceliner, they will automatically suspect what it really is. Their detecting instruments are nothing special; but where trickery is concerned, their naturally deceitful character gives them a running start."

Roberts considered it, frowning. "And what do they gain by all that?"

"It's ingrained in their character to start with. Until the adult molt, their whole life is spent *in the sea*. The ocean on Crustax sounds at least as bad as the ocean back on Earth. Only the toughest and most wary survive. Since a lot of the things in the sea are bigger and faster than they are, they find deception very handy. Once they get out into space, that's just a bigger ocean from their viewpoint, and they use deception there, too. It's automatic."

Roberts looked at the model thoughtfully.

"What kind of individual is in charge of that fortress? Assuming we know."

"A fanatic by the name of Garvast Nade. Garvast Nade is the 'son,' so-called, of Arvast Nade."

Roberts said, "Arvast Nade—"

"Was blown to bits, with his whole fleet, in the attempt to capture Storehouse."

"Hm-m-m. Therefore, Garvast Nade—"

"Garvast Nade has had his career wrecked by the obliteration of his 'father's' fleet and reputation. As nearly as we can follow it, a 'family' on Crustax is strictly a voluntary matter of an adult selecting promising young who have survived to the adult molt, with the young, in turn, hunting for a strong adult sponsor."

"Therefore, Garvast Nade has reason to seek revenge on humans? Assuming that is, the crabs have emotions."

"Oh," said the Colonel, "they have emotions, all right. If anything, they have more emotions than we have. You're right, Roberts—Garvast Nade, a fanatic selected by a power-hungry conqueror, has plenty of reasons to seek revenge on humans."

"How *smart* is he?"

"*That* we don't know. Supposedly he has brains, or Arvast Nade wouldn't have sponsored him."

Roberts eyed the dark-gray model with its yawning gate and ranked turrets, and suddenly had a sensation like a cold wind on the back of his neck.

The Colonel sat back, and cleared his throat.

"Our men are very seldom captured. These two were caught while serving on the crew of a fast freighter belonging to a small outfit that handles some of the toughest shipping jobs in this end of the universe. Our men were there to try to track down a very peculiar recent shipment, but we now think we had the wrong ship. The head of this shipping company changes the names of the ships arbitrarily, and shifts the officers around at will, which can make it exasperating to try to decipher what happened. At any rate, the ship got off course, and Arvast Nade captured it. When he got through with the prisoners, he passed the survivors over to Garvast."

The Colonel thought a moment. "As I say, Roberts, we don't have many of our men taken prisoner. But if they are captured by a humane opponent—and particularly if we have no reason to believe they are known to *be* our men—then we usually make no special attempt to free them. Sometimes, their friends get them out. Usually they can manage it themselves. But this, you see, is a little different."

Roberts nodded.

The Colonel said, "We aren't going to leave them there. We will either get them out, or something unfortunate is going to happen to this space station." The Colonel looked at Roberts. "This strikes me, Roberts, as being suited to your special talents, and I am turning it over to you."

"Thank you, sir," said Roberts, ugly sensations alternating with the chill at the back of his neck. "And what can I have to do this job?"

"Whatever you can lay your hands on," said the Colonel, eyeing the model with no very pleasant expression. "Whatever isn't already nailed down tight by somebody else is yours."

Roberts smiled at the wording of that stroke of generosity. That meant that things were so tied up already that the Colonel could think of no adequate force to give Roberts, and so he, therefore, left it up to Roberts to scrape one together by himself. On the other hand, that particular wording might prove to be useful. At any rate, it placed no limitation in material on him.

"Yes, sir," said Roberts. "I'll get started right away."

Roberts saluted, and went out immediately.

The first thing to do, he told himself, on the way down the corridor, was to get hold of his men. They, at least, would not have been assigned to some other job without Roberts knowing about it.

Roberts shoved open the corridor door to the room they shared while on the dreadnought, passed the bunks and desks to pause at a hatch-like door beyond the thick window of which the sun shone brightly on dazzling sand stretching down to blue and white water. Roberts frowned, momentarily distracted.

The gigantic dreadnought that served as an approximation of home contained a number of features Roberts didn't understand. The door from the corridor invariably and without delay listed who was assigned to the room—but Roberts never saw anyone put the names on the door. The door apparently put the names there *itself*. The hatchlike door here at the opposite end of the room, whose window looked out on a sandy beach, was sometimes brightly sunlit, and sometimes looked out on terrific storms. It was obvious to Roberts that the dreadnought didn't carry a private ocean around inside of it, and also didn't have its own internal sun. Which of Roberts' theories explained the situation, he didn't know, but he looked out exasperatedly, then shrugged, and changed into a swimsuit. He stepped out the door, felt the sunlight hot on his skin, and pulled the door shut behind him. As he walked out, scanning the dazzling beach, with its march of white-capped waves rolling in, a strongly built figure burst from the water and plunged ashore.

At the same moment, Roberts' feet got the message to him that he had walked out onto the equivalent of a bed of hot coals. He sprinted across the dazzling beach, his feet sinking deep in the burning sand, and was down the slope till suddenly he was on dark wet sand, and then he dove headlong into the water. The icy shock slid over him, taking away his breath. He surfaced, shook his head, and saw the powerful figure of Hammell standing on the wet sand, watching him with a smile.

Roberts swam back, and waded out onto the shore, the water curling around his feet as it ran far up the beach. Roberts called to Hammell.

"Where are Morrissey and Bergen?"

Hammell grinned, and pointed seaward. "They're racing me to shore."

Roberts glanced out, to see the flash of an arm a hundred feet or so from shore. An instant later, he saw, still further out, another swimmer.

Roberts shook his head wryly, and waited.

Hammell picked up a towel, dried himself briskly, and spread the towel neatly on the hot sand. He lay down, stretched out comfortably, and assumed a drowsy air as if he had spent the last half hour sunbathing.

Dan Bergen, chest heaving, short hair plastered to his skull, staggered ashore. An instant later, he was followed by Morrissey.

"This time," Bergen gasped, nodding to Roberts, then glancing around, "we *beat* him." He paused abruptly, looking past Roberts. Behind Bergen, Morrissey shook his head ruefully. "When he hits the water, he turns into twins. One drowns in our wake. The other materializes at the finish line."

Bergen glanced at Roberts. "Can you beat him?"

"Not me," said Roberts. "He's got a little submarine hidden around here, somewhere. You can't win."

Morrissey waded out, grinning. "What did the Colonel have to say?"

"Plenty," said Roberts.

Hammell opened one eye.

"I hope you told him we were looking forward to a long drowsy vacation."

"Strange to say," said Roberts, "I forgot that. He was busy telling me about a couple of guys who are prisoners of Crustax. It seems that the crabs have them locked up in a space fortress with three battalions of guards, and enough guns and launchers on the outside to stand off a Space Force battleship."

Hammell frowned and sat up. Morrissey and Bergen stood breathing deeply, and listened closely as Roberts described the situation. At the end, Hammell lay back, frowning.

"How do we get to them?"

"It seems to me," said Roberts, "that the situation has to be so arranged that the crabs *gladly* take us in because they *want* to."

Morrissey cleared his throat. "They'll *want* to, all right. This Garvast Nade will be happy to have us."

"Sure," said Bergen. "He could use more material."

Morrissey nodded. "The more information he can get, the better the crab high command will like it, and him. To say nothing of the personal gratification."

Hammell frowned. "Has it occurred to you that this thing has the elements of a baited trap? These two prisoners are the bait. This space fort is the trap. We go in the open door, the door closes behind us—and then what?"

Roberts said, "It seems to me there are possibly four times when we could be trapped. First, on approaching this fort, when the Crustax fleet could show up, and catch us between their ships and the fort itself. Second, we could be trapped with our ship inside the fort's spaceport, when those gates shut behind us. Third, we could be trapped when we leave the ship to get the prisoners. And, fourth, after we pass out through the gates, again their fleet could turn up."

Hammell nodded. "Then, on top of that, they might get on our ship while we're in their fort, and where does that leave *us?*"

Bergen said hesitantly, "Could we possibly disguise our ship to look like one of them, and slip in unnoticed?"

"Maybe," said Roberts. "But we couldn't fool them for long, especially once we got inside."

Morrissey said, "What do we have in the line of captured recognition signals, code books, and so on?"

"Only a few outdated ones turned over to us by the Space Force in repayment for past services. They'd give us more, but they don't have them."

Hammell said, "The more I think about trying to camouflage our ship to look like theirs, the less I like it. On top of everything else, how do we fool Garvast Nade when we don't know how Garvast's mind works?"

Morrissey said, "We know he's *hostile*."

"And," said Roberts, "naturally good at detecting camouflage."

"Suppose," said Bergen, "we camouflage our ship as a freighter— that is, a human-style freighter?"

Morrissey shrugged. "He'll spot the fakery."

"But then," said Roberts suddenly, "suppose we camouflage the imitation freighter as a warship. Knowing, of course, that *they will detect the harmless freighter underneath*."

Bergen looked surprised, then nodded enthusiastically.

Hammell sat up. "Not bad. They'd figure we were easy to take."

"Hm-m-m," said Morrissey. "A subtle approach. But what if the outer camouflage job fools them, and they don't let us in?"

Roberts said, "We can't take that chance. There has to be a flaw."

Morrissey shook his head. "They may not detect the flaw. Remember, they aren't as familiar with our warship designs as we are. And then, if they *do* detect it, how do they explain that we put the flaw there? The trick will be obvious."

"Not," said Roberts, "if it is a *Crustax* warship."

Hammell and Morrissey glanced at each other. Bergen looked impressed.

"But," said Hammell, "how do we explain our own reliance on the out-of-date recognition signals? How do we talk with the fort? How do we convince the other side that we even *thought* we had a chance to fool them in the first place? We have to reasonably *think* we're convincing, or they'll look for some trick in our arrangements."

"We can talk to them by message machine only. Our ship, you see, will have been heavily damaged. Everything but the message machine was smashed *in the attack on Storehouse,* and that is the only means of communication we can use."

The other three men looked briefly intent, then Hammell cleared his throat. "In other words, they detect that we are trying to gain entrance by disguising ourselves as Crustaxan survivors? So they rub their hands, and say, 'Step right into my parlor.'"

Morrissey said, "That might work. That is to say, it might get us *in* there. *Then* what?"

"In an operation like this," said Roberts, "a certain amount of improvisation is unavoidable. It seems to me that the main thing is to get in."

"O.K., let's try it for size. I'm the crab general and I see this wrecked dreadnought show up. It flashes the outdated recognition signal. For an instant, I don't know what to think. The message comes in, explaining that nearly all their communications are knocked out. Suddenly I spot an obvious flaw on this battleship—"

"Dreadnought," said Roberts. "Inside, under two layers of camouflage, we want something no smaller than a battleship. It follows that the outside has to be *big*."

"Dreadnought," corrected Hammell. "Suddenly I spot an obvious flaw on this dreadnought, check my detectors carefully, and realize an Earth ship is underneath. O.K.—what *kind* of Earth ship?"

"Hm-m-m." said Roberts. "It should be something harmless. Preferably, something they'll be delighted to let in."

"How about a colonization liner? One of the big ones that takes colonists from the colonization centers out on the first leg of the trip?"

"Yes. They'd like that. With enough cunning, they could use the ship later for deception of their own."

"So far so good," said Hammell.

"Now," said Roberts. "About this error that has to be obvious to them and not us?"

There was a silence, then Morrissey suggested.

"Could we make this ship a mirror-image of what it's supposed to be?

Roberts said, "Or suppose the *scale* of the ship were slightly wrong?"

Hammell nodded. "There is something they would spot that we, supposedly working from photographs, rough readings of mass, and so on, might have wrong. However, there's still a slight hole in this plan. What do we do after we get inside that fort?"

Bergen said, "We could pound it to pieces from inside."

Morrissey suggested, "What if we tell them we're packed solid with atomite. Release the prisoners or we'll blow the whole place up."

"Great," said Hammell. "This fanatic, Garvast, might tell us to go ahead. Then where are we?"

"It seems to me," said Roberts, "that we've got to risk landing on this place. From past experience, I think our battle armor will protect us in close fighting."

"What about the three battalions of guards? You know we aren't going to get any army to transport with us. It's bound to work out that the four of us have to do the whole job."

"If," suggested Roberts, "we could first get them to board *our* ship—"

Hammell looked thoughtful.

Bergen beamed. "Trap them!"

Morrissey looked uncomfortable. "And suppose they capture the ship?"

Hammell's gaze was remote and calculating. "Personally, I'd hate to capture even an Interstellar Patrol scout ship. A *battleship*, now—"

Bergen's eyes shone in creative effort. "We can put in false walls, and line the corridors with mines and automatic guns. Nothing will fire till they're well inside."

Hammell cast a fishy look at Bergen, and glanced at Roberts, who said, "We'll leave that end of it to you, then, Bergen. But we're going to have to do a little more work on this thing. A possible plan is only the first step. Next we have to work out the alternatives in case the crabs don't cooperate with us at any given point."

Hammell said, "Let's allow enough alternatives so we don't have to improvise too much after we get in there. It isn't healthy to rely on having strokes of genius when you get in a tight spot."

"Unfortunately," said Roberts, "we don't know for sure what they've got in there, so we can't help improvising. But we'll eliminate it so far as possible."

"Just so it's a well-planned operation," said Hammell, looking uneasy again. "Otherwise it could be a mess."

"We'll do our best," said Roberts.

✦   ✦   ✦

From the relay center in the interior of the imitation space liner, the view from the imitation wreck's forward pickups flashed onto Roberts' viewscreen in the battleship. A brief winking of lights was all that visually showed the existence of the Crustax space fortress as they approached. All that is, except for the blotting out of the stars by the looming bulk of the place.

There was a clacking noise, and Roberts watched the message as it slowly came out of the machine. Across the room, a small language computer clicked and hummed, apparently laboring to keep up with the incoming signals. These noises, Roberts thought, could not be a result of the computer's actual operation: they must have been added as a guide for the user. If so, the computer wasn't having an easy time with the message. The clicks came slowly, then in brief bursts, and the computer's hum sounded high-pitched and strained. Then, with a final burst of clicks and a corresponding series of clacks from the printer, the message wound up out of the printer. Roberts pulled it free, to read:

Seal Ready
Stamp-Emblem Ready
Number One Paper
Strike: Embossing Master Emblem Number Two
 ****Border

Begin Message
From:
Commander
Space Fortress *Ironclaw*
To:
Commander
Unidentified Damaged Warship
Sir:
 Your ****-signal received and acknowledged herewith. This is the correct signal for the ****. However, we require the following information:
 1) Who are you?
 2) What is the name of your ship?
 3) What are the circumstances surrounding the **** of your ship?

This information must be forwarded at once, or we must refuse entry. Stand off while replying.

Cordial claw-claspings,

Gratz Ialwo,
Commander
Space Fortress *Ironclaw*

Fold Message and Glue Shut
Stick Seal
Stamp Great Claw on Front
Eject

Roberts looked up blankly.

Who was Gratz Ialwo?

Across the room, Morrissey straightened from the visual display, as the battery of detectors labored to unravel the details of the fortress.

"Still clear as mud," growled Morrissey.

Roberts turned to the printer. How would the message he was about to send, which was slanted for the fanatical Garvast Nade, affect "Gratz Ialwo"?

A hatch came open, and Hammell stepped in. "Everything's set," he said, then glanced again at Roberts. "What's wrong?"

"Gratz Ialwo."

Hammell glanced at the printer, then at the message, but kept his mouth shut.

Roberts decided to send the original message. He snapped a little spool into the sending device. The printer clacked. Across the room, the translator labored, to produce a translation of the message just sent. Roberts ignored the coded instructions for the receiving printer, and read the message:

From:
Arvast Nade
Commander, Fleet ****
To:
Garvast Nade
Commander Fortress ****
Sir:

I **** survived the **** suffering **** this ship severe damage, **** and **** receiving apparatus out of order.

No ****. Vital information relative Earth **** at **** **** without delay. We ****enter Fortress. Vital **** **** surprise **** coming, urgent **** at once.
 Signed,

Arvast Nade
**** Fleet ****

Roberts glanced back at the screen, and saw nothing but a huge blackness, with stars showing around the edges. He glanced around the control room, seeing Morrissey at the forward detection screen, and Hammell now by the manual fire-control bank, the big manual-override lever shoved back in the "off" position. Roberts was by the pilot seat, the printer to his right, and the seat to his left, with the screen above the curving control panel before the seat.

Roberts, looking around, had the sensations of a frontier-raised colonist, seeing a miniature power-unit for the first time.

Roberts' Space Force training told him that this little room could not even be the control room of his own patrol ship, much less of a full-size battleship. And yet, as he'd seen clearly enough when he first boarded it, it *was* a battleship, full-size, armed to the teeth, and deadly.

Morrissey said, "That monster gate is starting to open. It's like a big metal curtain sliding up from the center, while another half slides down below it."

"Good," said Roberts.

Hammell said, "Have they answered the message?"

"Not yet. Where's Bergen?"

"Still improving his traps."

Roberts slid into the control seat, and reached out to reset the screen. A slightly different model from that on his own ship, this screen's differences bothered him. Yet when Roberts punched the split-screen button that was awkwardly located just above the course display, the button refused to depress. Irritated, Roberts pushed harder. The button yielded slightly, then shoved up against his finger, to recover its original position.

Roberts growled to himself, stood up, leaned forward, put his thumb on the button, and shoved down hard. The button resisted, then went *click*. The screen divided into two sections, the external viewscreen to the left, the battle screen to the right.

"Good," growled Roberts, at once feeling more at home.

There was a loud *clack!* from the printer, and just then Morrissey called, "Look at that gate!"

There was a *click* as the split-screen button depressed by itself, and a *snap* as a stubby lever below the screen jumped into a new position.

Roberts, just reaching out to take the message as it came from the printer, caught the motion, and realized that the ship had just canceled his directions. Instead of providing both battle and viewscreen, it chose to provide a single larger battlescreen view. There was another *snap*, and a small auxiliary screen to the left came on to provide a small external view, apparently to placate him.

Roberts irritatedly tore the message from the printer, noticing at the same time what Morrissey was pointing out—an iris-of-the-eye effect that followed the separation of the two sliding gates. Behind the big sliding gates, there remained a separate gate, like the shutter of a huge camera, and this gate had moved only enough to show a relatively small opening at the center. This mechanism hadn't been present in the model the Colonel had shown Roberts, which at once raised the question what else might be different? Unlike some other organizations, the Patrol didn't hesitate to use very advanced—but somewhat bug-ridden—techniques. This generally gave good results—but it could also give surprises. How had they got the information on that fortress? Then Roberts shrugged and read the message:

From:
Commander
Space Fortress *Ironclaw*
To:
Arvast Nade, Commander
Survivor of Meteor Storm
Sir:
    Welcome, survivors! Your ***** fleet believed lost without *****. You may enter ***** gates at once.
    Sad news must ***** *****, the death of Garvast Nade following your reported loss. I, Gratz Ialwo, the closest ***** of Garvast Nade, welcome you as a *****.
    Reverent lowering of antennae,
                                    Gratz Ialwo, Commander
                                    Space Fortress *Ironclaw*

Roberts glanced from the message to the screen, where the inner gate was steadily opening wider. Apparently, despite everything, Ialwo was fooled so far. Now Roberts' detectors picked up a transparent membrane that ballooned out as the gate opened, apparently to prevent the loss of an internal atmosphere through the opened gates.

Roberts leaned across to the printer, tapped out the usual heading, and then the message, hitting the "garble" button frequently:

Sir:

Our ***** severely ***** by damage and reception is *****.

We wish to enter, and request assistance ***** *****. Severe ***** of ***** causing recurrent difficulties which urgently need ***** without delay.
***** *****

Arvast Nade, Commander
Fleet *****

Morrissey called, "The gate is almost wide open."

Roberts glanced at his screen. "It took them long enough."

"Crab technology seems to leave a little something to be desired."

Roberts aimed the ship at the center of the opening, and guided it toward the interior.

Hammell looked at the scene of the gigantic interior that was opening up on Morrissey's screen, as the camouflaged battleship glided in. He murmured, "Quite an effort to save just two men. I hope they appreciate it."

Morrissey said uneasily, "We haven't saved them yet."

Roberts snapped a communicator switch, and said, "Personnel Monitor—locate Dan Bergen, and tell him to come to the control room."

Bergen's voice at once came out a small speaker to the right of the screen.

"Be right there, sir. Where are we?"

"Almost inside."

Roberts was studying the view on the battle screen in puzzlement.

The screen was blinking, switching rapidly from one view to another. The first view showed the spaceport facilities as seen by their own lights, and by the light floating globes or lightships that drifted in the interior. The second view, apparently taken from the same viewpoint as the first, showed ranks of guns and odd shieldlike objects in a somewhat larger space than the first view showed.

Slowly, the wrecked imitation dreadnought entered the spaceport. Now it moved slowly ahead, completely inside, the transparent membrane pressed tightly around it by the artificial atmosphere of the spaceport.

Roberts alertly studied the screen.

Morrissey said sharply, "The inner gate's *closed!* It *snapped* shut!"

Roberts glanced at a small auxiliary screen which showed the view to the rear. Where the open gate had been, there was now a solid surface with a massive grille sliding quickly down across it.

With a puff of briefly visible vapor, the membrane expanded, came free at one edge, and drifted away from the ship.

The printer clacked.

Roberts read:

No Seal
No Stamp
Shoddy paper
No Embossing
Tide-Dregs Border
Begin Message
From:
Commander
Space Fortress *Ironclaw*
To:
Most Honorable
High Admiral
Arvast Nade
Commander
Battle Fleet IV
Most Honored Sir:
    ***** abasements before your noble self as you enter, crowned with victory.

We beg you to emerge from your victorious vessel in order that we may properly welcome you.

Servile clutchings of sand before you.

Gratz Ialwo, Commander
Space Fortress *Ironclaw*

Fold Message Without Glue
No Seal
No Stamp
Eject

Roberts glanced quickly at the screen.

Several of the glowing spheres were coming closer, to illuminate the hulk. A small plain vessel of some kind was starting out from a distant dock.

Roberts reread the message.

"We seem to have made the wrong approach to this outfit somewhere."

Hammell was studying the fort through the master-control viewscope. He growled, "It looks to me as if this place is well armed, but the weapons are hidden behind all this loading equipment." He looked up. "What's wrong?"

"Take a glance at this message."

Hammell read it, grunted, and passed it to Morrissey. Morrissey and Bergen read it together. Bergen whistled.

"Shoddy paper, and 'Most Honored Sir,'" said Morrissey. "It sounds as if they want to carve Nade up the middle."

Hammell looked into the viewscope. "That boat must be coming out to get him. They seem heavily armed."

Roberts glanced at his viewscreen again. Suddenly the scene readjusted. The approaching boat filled the screen, and an abrupt shift in focus showed the still further magnified interior through a large viewport in the front of the boat. This showed what looked like large lobsters in space-armor, carrying guns, moving into position behind the side hatch of the vessel, while other lobsters looked grimly out the front.

Somewhere in Roberts' ship, there was a low rumble, then a voice spoke quietly but firmly:

"The four volunteers will prepare to don armor and enter the Crustaxan fortress."

Hammell looked grim. Morrissey winced, as Bergen nodded and

looked pleased. Roberts glanced around moodily as four lockers opened up. He studied irritatedly the four suits of battle armor that slid out into view.

"It won't work," he said. "They're too clever."

The battle armor had two large upper arms, with room for big pinching claws, along with what looked like a kind of trapdoor in the chest. The lower half looked relatively normal save for a kind of thick tail or extension of some kind in back. A quick glance at the viewscreen showed Roberts that this much was "normal" for the inhabitants of the fortress. But the business did not stop there.

On the chest of Roberts' armor was emblazoned a weird-looking monster like an octopus with the head of a shark. Hammell's armor bore a kind of big intertwined snake with large teeth. Morrissey's had a giant sea horse with a nasty look on its face, two impressively muscled scaly arms, a dagger in hand, and large sharp teeth. Only Bergen's looked like the regulation Crustaxan armor on the screen. Bergen's armor was considerably dented, blackened in places, and bore long scars and marks where the metal looked almost as if it had boiled and frozen in succession, to leave rings of beaded metal around an uneven surface.

Roberts strained his mind to try to encompass what was behind this, and failed.

"Listen," he said, "instead of this, whatever it is, what do you say you make the armor look like those things marked on it? Then we'll be aliens, and it will throw all their plans out of gear. We need a little room to improvise."

There was no answer.

Roberts shrugged, and headed for the armor. Each of these Interstellar Patrol ships had its own "symbiotic computer," and he had discovered that there was no point arguing with the things, though *sometimes* they would take suggestions.

Hammell, the same look of moody resignation on his face, started for his armor.

Before either man could reach it, three of the suits of armor—excepting only Bergen's—trundled back into the lockers. The lockers shut, and there was a rumbling noise.

The voice of the symbiotic computer said, "Not a bad idea. One moment . . . Volunteer Bergen, you may put on your armor. There will be a brief delay for the others."

Hammell looked at Roberts.

Roberts said intently, "Make sure we can move in that armor. We don't want to get in there and be helpless."

"Don't worry. These forms are suited to combat. You will adapt to them readily."

There was another rumble and the three lockers came open.

Roberts winced, and Hammell took a step backward. Bergen, struggling to get into his unfamiliar armor, made an abortive grab for his gun.

The armor now matched the creatures emblazoned on the front, but, in three dimensions, they were far more hideous than Roberts could have imagined.

Roberts' armor had various sizes and shapes of metal tentacles absently coiling and uncoiling, while Hammell's came out of the locker followed by some fifteen feet of sinuous flexing metal snakelike body. Morrissey's rolled into the room on caterpillar treads, the upper part of each arm as big around as the trunk of a sizable tree.

Bergen inside his suit, extended big claws, and laughed. "I'm the only human here."

Roberts cautiously avoided the metal tentacles, walked around to the rear of his armor, and snapped open the backplate.

"No," said Hammell, looking around irritatedly, "this is too much. How do I walk inside this thing? How do I handle anything? There are no arms or legs on it. It won't work. Let's have something a little more reasonable."

"The volunteer," said the symbiotic computer placidly, "will kindly refrain from criticism. The boarding craft is approaching. The armor will be found highly satisfactory—unless you would rather go out without it."

Roberts climbed in, to find the interior looked the same as usual. He got the back plate shut, and—

—Suddenly he was flexing giant tentacles, eager to get the enemy in his grasp and snap him in half.

Roberts blinked.

The thoughts died down, but the sensation that he possessed a variety of powerful flexible limbs persisted. He could, in fact, seem to *feel* with them.

Roberts cleared his throat, and wondered if the computer would hear him.

"No offense, friend," said Roberts, "but the illusion of control of all these tentacles is likely to be hard to maintain. It might work for an octopus, but someone with just two pairs of actual limbs—"

The complacent voice replied, "One dozen pairs of limbs, Volunteer."

"How do you count—"

"The fact of ten separate individually-controlled digits is not to be dismissed merely because they are activated at the ends of another set of jointed appendages."

Roberts frowned. "O.K., *maybe*. Where are there any weapons?"

"An excellent point. While carrying out a truly creative masterpiece, the artist sometimes loses sight of mere necessities."

There was a further rumble and *clank,* and the armor was jerked back into the locker, with Roberts inside it. The door of the locker shut. A weird intense light flickered briefly. Then the door opened up again.

"Weapons," said the symbiotic computer, "will be found in the usual place—attached to the weapons belt. Now, prepare to leave with your prisoner."

"What prisoner?"

"Admiral Nade, obviously, is your prisoner."

A small voice spoke in Roberts' ear, and Roberts recognized Dan Bergen, who said exasperatedly, "Does anyone understand what's going on?"

Hammell's voice, similarly small but clear, said, "All I know is, I'm inside armor that's shaped just about right for a boa constrictor that's thick through the chest. Nobody has explained anything to *me*. The funny thing is, I think I sense how to work the thing."

Roberts said, "If I can follow it correctly, the symbiotic computer wants us to act as if we've captured Nade."

"Who is *we*?" Hammell demanded. "So far as I know, there's no intelligent creature in the known universe that matches the shape of this armor."

Roberts said, "That ought to confuse the Crustaxans. I don't like the way that last message went. We want to get them off-balance."

"That's nice for a start, but where do we go from there?"

"We get the prisoners loose from the Crustaxans."

"How? You've skipped a few steps. What do we do *next?"*

"Don't ask me. But we've obviously got to get in that fort somehow. We'll have to see what turns up, and move fast."

"Yes, but . . . for the love of—"

"Bergen," said Roberts, taking a glance at the outside view-screen.

"Sir?" said Bergen unhappily.

"Lead the way to the nearest hatch onto the outside of this hulk. That boatload of armored crabs is getting close. Let's see—They look like they're heading for the wreckage of that armored bridge in back of the main turrets."

"O.K.," said Bergen. "We can go though in back of the false wall. But we don't dare get out in the corridor, or we'll get blown up."

"Lead the way," said Roberts.

Bergen went out the aft hatch. Roberts stood back to wave Hammell and Morrissey ahead, and involuntarily jumped back as they started to move. They looked like a giant armored python followed by an armored tank with a muscular sea horse inside of it.

Roberts growled to himself, watched Hammell's armor slither up through the hatch, while Morrissey's rose up on a kind of hydraulic jack arrangement that boosted him to where the treads could get a grip. In the corridor, Hammell slid along close behind Bergen, while Morrissey bumped and rumbled along behind Hammell.

Roberts shuddered at the sight, took hold of the hatchway with half-a-dozen tentacles, vaulted through, and strolled along the corridor behind Morrissey.

The voice of the symbiotic computer spoke in Roberts' ear:

"Communications spy-pickups are now moderately well distributed throughout the spaceport itself. We are processing large numbers of official and personal messages."

"What good does that do us? Have you found any trace of the prisoners?"

"Two references suggest that they are in the 'tank.' We have no indication yet as to where the 'tank' is located."

"That's a real help," said Roberts dryly.

"The principal benefit, however, is an improvement of language ability. We now have many cross-checks on previously uncertain words and phrases."

Bergen said, "Watch you don't bang anything going through here." He led the way through a narrow passage lined with squat guns on tripod mounts, connected by cables with small boxes hung on the bulkheads, this passage being one that paralleled one of the main corridors of the imitation dreadnought, the guns set to sweep the corridors after the Crustaxans were well inside the ship.

Bergen stopped. "Here we are." He undid a heavy fastener, slid a thick panel out of the way, and stood back to let Roberts, Hammell, and Morrissey go through the opening into what looked like the patched-up remains of a warship's bridge.

From somewhere came a clang, and Hammell said, "That's the outer hatch of the air lock. They're coming in."

Roberts noticed that Hammell's voice sounded clear, and as loud as usual, and realized that he was now hearing him "normally"—that is, by way of the speaker in Hammell's battle armor, which made sound vibrations in the air, and were picked up by Roberts' armor, and reproduced loud and clear so that he would know he was not hearing Hammell over the communicator.

Roberts turned, in order to face the inside hatch of the air lock.

Slowly, this hatch began to open.

Roberts turned his head and used his chin to fully depress a short broad lever inside the helmet of his suit. This snapped on the armored suit's communicator, and shut off its external speaker.

"Hammell," said Roberts. "Try your communicator."

"Here," said a small voice.

"Bergen," said Roberts, "step out in front of the rest of us. We want them to see you first."

The inner air-lock door was steadily coming open. Now a set of armored claws reached in.

Bergen's small, somewhat plaintive voice said, "Now what do I do?"

The inner air-lock door swung heavily open.

Eight or nine space-armored figures, carrying long-muzzled guns, stepped in.

Hammell's small voice spoke urgently in Roberts' ear. "Listen, what's the picture? What do we *do*?"

"Just follow my lead," said Roberts, "and don't worry. The general idea, for now, is that we are a collection of aliens who have captured Arvast Nade. We're here to stick a red-hot poker into the Crustaxans. As for the prisoners, our only interest in *them* is that we'd like to have them to wring some information out of them for ourselves."

Hammell's voice said uncertainly, "O.K. Lead on."

So far, so good. But for the moment, Roberts was not sure just what do next.

The Crustaxans, looking around, now spotted "Arvast Nade."

Roberts strained his mind for the right move to make next.

Abruptly, Roberts' voice boomed out, though his mouth was tightly shut:

"Gar trak no clagg bar ke ia tu dek holben—"

Suddenly, Roberts began to hear it differently:

"—by right of conquest. We also claim this prisoner here enslaved. You may step aboard this ship alone at our goodwill. We are masters of this great starry sea. How is it that we know not the like of you?"

Half in and half out of the air lock, the Crustaxans stood paralyzed.

Roberts' voice went on by itself, as he listened admiringly.

"We are come to split the stars between us, to say who owns here and who there. Have you no speech? Know you not the mighty of the realms of space? In your own tongue we conjure you to lead at once to your chiefs!"

The collection of frozen shapes at the air lock jarred into a semblance of disorganized motion.

Several with insignia on their spacesuits contended to thrust each other forward, and a large individual with claws like giant nutcrackers received the honor.

"Aaah," came his reply, "we . . . eh . . . hah . . . we welcome you to *Ironclaw* Fortress with . . . ah . . . cordial feelings of fellowship. But let's not stand talking here. Let us escort you to the commander. Admiral Ialwo is eager to see your, ah, *prisoner*."

Roberts attempted without success to unravel the undertones and innuendos of this speech. His job was made no simpler by the translation process. Where the symbiotic computer was itself uncertain how to render tone or emphasis, it gave various renderings simultaneously. The effect was like hearing a chorus of identical people simultaneously recite the same words in different tones of voice.

Roberts, however, did not hesitate. When the armor remained silent, he spoke in a loud firm voice. Now that things were moving, he aimed to keep them moving.

"We accept your cordial welcome," he said, "and we return it in the exact spirit in which you offer it." He glanced at the two armored monsters beside him. "Let us go, gentlemen."

He then glanced sharply at the battered armor inside which was Bergen.

"You, *slave!* Move!"

Roberts' battle armor added its own bit gratuitously, tacking the words on so neatly that there was no delay between Roberts' words and its own:

"*Move,* I say! Ha, ill-formed beast, dost wish another winding on the rack?"

A kick from Roberts sent the clawed figure staggering, to land with a crash against the base of the hatch opening.

Hammell was gliding along beside Roberts, the scales of his armor against the metal underfoot making a noise like the continuous riffling of a deck of steel cards. Hammell's voice came out in a loud guffaw.

"It doth entertain me greatly to see the clumsy figure stagger. You recall the arrogance with which it entered into our presence?"

Morrissey was rolling along beside Hammell, tracks clanking.

"We must remember to give it fodder ere too many more days pass. "'Tis best to keep it alive. I misdoubt we have drained the dregs of its secret knowledge as yet. A few more turns of the screw—Who knows?"

Roberts, alarmed, watched the shifting of guns amongst the Crustaxans. One of them swung his gun toward Roberts as Roberts entered the lock. Roberts, without thinking, reached for his sword.

It occurred to him belatedly that if he drew the sword, the whole situation, already shaky enough, might come unstrung.

One of the armored suit's larger limbs, however, obeyed his impulse instantly, and whipped out the sword. There was a glittering arc in the air. The Crustaxan's gun landed on the deck in two pieces. The suit thrust the point of the sword into the Crustaxan's armor at the midsection. Roberts' voice spoke casually.

"A little more respect to your betters, my lad, or you have a short life in front of you. Well, do we want to spend the whole day here? What's all this?"

Hammell had one of the Crustaxans battered off his feet, and another wound up in the coils of his armor. The tail of the armor was twining and untwining menacingly. Hammell's voice was a low rumble:

"This churl did menace me."

Morrissey had one of Crustaxans upside down by one foot, and jerked its gun away with his free hand.

"This fellow tried to pry at my treads as I passed. Why not slaughter the lot?"

"Come, come," said Roberts' voice, "we are here to be friends. 'Tis the nature of a crawfish to be a crawfish, and we should be philosophic about it. For now, anyway."

Morrissey promptly dropped the Crustaxan on his head, bent his gun into a pretzel, and courteously returned it. Hammell loosened the coils of his armor, and the Crustaxan inside fell out on the deck. Roberts observed that he himself had absently taken three or four of them around the neck by various tentacles, and now let them loose after a final squeeze.

The biggest Crustaxan, by the air-lock door, stared around, hesitated, and then shut the air-lock door.

Roberts had a sense of something missing, and realized he didn't see Bergen anywhere. He looked all around.

Bergen was huddled behind a couple of paralyzed Crustaxans, big-clawed arms over his face, his armor clanking against the air lock as he shook.

Apparently what had happened so far had induced some respect in the Crustaxans, as the transfer from the lock to the shuttle, and from the shuttle to the spaceport itself, took place without incident.

Roberts, Hammell, and Morrissey—along with Bergen, who cringed in Morrissey's grip—found themselves standing on a thing like a four-sided dock, which, with many others like it, was thrust out into empty space enclosed by the spaceport. The dock apparently had an axial gravitic field, as work was going on all its four sides, with Crustaxans striding back and forth at angles of ninety and one hundred eighty degrees from what Roberts' instincts considered "up."

The spokesman of the party that had taken Roberts and his

companions from the ship had the helmet of his armor off, and was talking in a low voice to the leader of a platoon of guards waiting on the dock. Roberts was too far away to hear what was said, but this didn't bother the battle armor, which selectively amplified the Crustaxans' murmurs, until they were louder than the shouts of laborers on the dock, *their* voices being moderated till they were merely sounds in the background.

"Impossible," the leader of the guards was saying. "Their Excellencies know something about that ship which you do *not* know."

"I don't doubt it," said the spokesman for the shuttle party. "But what I say is true, just the same. Don't take my word for it. Ask anyone who was out there with me."

"You seem straightforward. I'll take your word that you *think* it's so. Now, let's be sure I follow this. First, you're satisfied that isn't Nade's command ship?"

"Bah! It's anything *but*. Not only is size-scale off, but the inside of the air lock is wrong. The pressure was about right, but not quite. The bridge itself is like nothing you ever saw. Grant that it's a shambles, still—"

"Be specific."

"Well, there isn't a claw rest anywhere. And the switch-stalks are all too short. You'd have to stick your pincers into the control board up to your elbow to get close enough to get your manipulators onto the switches. The read-outs are too low, and the pilot's seat is solid in back. How are you going to sit in it? At a first glance, yes, it looks plausible. But then the details hit you."

"Now, how about Nade himself?"

"I don't know about that. The armor is nonstandard design, but you can't be sure. It's got fittings in all the right places. But if that's Nade, he's sure got his claws in the mud."

"Pretty much beat down, eh?"

"He feels it coming before they hit him."

There was a peculiar grating crunching noise that came across untranslated, and then the guard leader said, "Well, we'll even up the score when we give this bunch the thin-slice treatment. You still think all these fakes are real, eh?"

"I tell you, fakes *couldn't* act this way! They come across as fake as a force-10 meteor storm!"

"They're just faking on a deeper level. But I'll bear that in mind."

The guard commander left the shuttle-party spokesman, and walked over to Roberts. He clashed his claws together.

"Honored guests, accompany me. You will be taken directly to the audience."

Hammell growled, "Your Grace, another half dozen of those shuttles are heading for our ship."

"No bother," said Roberts. "We can use some more specimens."

The guard leader paused, then bellowed a command. The guards, bristling with weapons, formed a double line along the edges of the dock. One of the guards, carrying a thing like an overgrown washtub, with the flat bottom of it turned up, raised a kind of mallet, and hit the tub a mighty blow. The top of the tub vibrated with a rhythmic *thump-thump-thump* sound. The nearest of the guards marched off in unison between the lines on the dock.

The guard leader said sharply to Morrissey. "Stay right with me. If you fall behind, my officers may mistake it for disrespect, or even an attempt to escape, and use strong measures on you without thinking."

Morrissey promptly rotated on his treads, to look across the interior at the far side of the spaceport.

"If you will pardon me, Your Grace, I think I will admire the view for a few moments."

Hammell coiled himself into a sizable heap with a tip of armored tail sticking out the bottom.

"Ho-hum. I think I shall ease the fatigue of the day with a little snooze."

The guard commander, just briskly starting off, stopped and turned as Roberts reached out, took Bergen, who was just starting after the guard commander, and jerked him off his feet.

"My sincere and humble apologies," said Roberts dryly to the guard officer. "We could not agree to accompany you until it is understood that your officers will accommodate themselves to our pace. Otherwise, some momentary lapse of restraint on our part might lead us to unintentionally dismember your officers."

"Ah!" said the guard commander silkily. "Is that so?" He bellowed a new order.

The guards whirled, guns leveled, and approached at a run.

Morrissey reached out a tree-trunk arm, and with a loud

snapping noise bent up fifteen feet of thick L-shaped angle-iron that protected the edge of the dock.

Hammell unfolded from his coil like a streak of metallic glitter, and flashed into the ranks of approaching soldiery, hitting them below knee-level. Using these numerous legs as a snake uses twigs, rocks, and blades of grass, this equivalent of a tool-steel boa constrictor flashed in and out amongst them, the soldiers thrown in all direction like logs afloat in a rapids. Morrissey, like a giant spooning soup, reached methodically into the tangled heaving mass with his length of massive angle iron, to flip members of the guard off the dock and out into the void.

Roberts, meanwhile, casually held the guard commander with a few pairs of tentacles, switching grips on him from time to time to put him in the path of any angry guard that happened momentarily to get past Hammell and Morrissey. This way, the guard commander received the blows meant for Roberts.

Quickly wearying of this, the guard commander bawled a new order.

The tumult subsided. Hammell raised up, and looked out of the tangled heaps of soldiers.

Morrissey knocked loose a few more clinging to the edges of the dock and trying to take aim at Hammell, then propped his angle-iron upright, leaned on it, and waited.

Roberts had let go of the guard commander, save for one long slender tentacle, like a snare made of wire, that had him by what served for a foot.

"It would be appropriate," said Roberts judiciously, "since your armed strength is so inferior to ours, to avoid any action which we might mistakenly interpret as a discourtesy. Should we come to feel that there has been any serious provocation, we might find it necessary to wipe out the stain by dismantling the whole installation."

The guard commander was apparently making efforts to speak, and finally achieved it.

"I—You—We will adjust the rate of march to . . . to avoid any difficulty with the officers."

"Proceed," said Roberts, cheerfully.

The commander bellowed orders.

The guards, breastplates dented, weapons bent, many of the guards nursing injured limbs, fell in in two long lines.

With Roberts, Hammell, and Morrissey setting the pace, they headed for the audience.

The audience chamber proved to be a huge room; the near end was a blank wall, and the far end another blank wall. Roberts had the impression he was standing on the bottom of a giant's empty swimming pool. From a heavily glassed-in platform overhead, a creature well equipped with large claws and pincers looked down, holding a microphone in a set of comparatively small appendages at its chest.

"Pleasant greetings," purred the creature's amplified voice. "It is certainly a rare treat to have helpless victims present themselves as you have, both incapable of sustained resistance and yet sufficiently arrogant to add zest to the situation. Allow me to acquaint you with my identity. I am Gratz Ialwo—formerly Garvast Nade—Commander of Fortress *Ironclaw.*"

Roberts silently digested the face that, with one sponsor finished off, a promising Crustaxan might get another sponsor.

"I," said Roberts, "shall return the favor, and acquaint you with *my* identity. I am Rasgaard Seraak, Adjunct-Coordinate to the Empire, Galactic East."

That sounded good to Roberts. What it meant, he didn't know, but that was Ialwo's problem, not his.

"Uh—" came Ialwo's voice after a pause. "And your companions?"

"I," said Hammell, offhandedly, "am Prince Gdazzrik of the March."

"And I," growled Morrissey, "am known as Sarkonnian the Second, Lord Auxiliary of the Realm to the West."

There followed a further silence. Ialwo, when he did speak, sounded somewhat hesitant.

"And the other individual, who accompanies you?"

"His identity," said Roberts, trying to unravel the significance of the peculiar sound of Ialwo's voice, "must remain for the moment undisclosed."

"There has been a suggestion that he is in reality Arvast Nade, Admiral of Crustax."

"I am," said Roberts candidly, "aware of the suggestion."

"You are also aware that you are in a hopeless position."

Roberts had been looking over the walls of the place as he

talked, noting that they were apparently metal, with a number of small openings high up, below which were long, nearly-vertical brownish stains. The door that had shut behind them had fit into the wall in such a way as to leave no visible trace. Knowing the strength of the battle armor, Roberts was not prepared to say they were helpless; but he was inclined to think they would have some trouble getting out of here.

Roberts laughed, as if he had just heard an unusually funny joke. The armor eliminated some little imperfections in the laugh, which boomed around the smooth-walled chamber as a explosion of rare good humor.

Hammell and Morrissey chortled appreciatively.

Bergen trembled all over.

Ialwo's voice murmured, "So, this is the sound our interrogators identify as meaning 'entertainment, skepticism, or good cheer'? We'll adjust *that* attitude."

Abruptly there was a hiss.

From one of the holes high up across the room, a liquid jet reached out and arced toward the floor, but flashed into vapor before it hit.

Ialwo said pleasantly, "One of the most difficult engineering feats is the disposal of excess heat. The answer, nearly always, is to somehow conduct it to the external environment. But—when the external environment is itself far hotter than the . . . say . . . armored suit which needs to be cooled . . . what then, eh?"

There was another hiss, and a further spurt of sizzling vapor, this time from another hole.

Roberts considered the situation. Possibly the best solution was to take a shot at Ialwo, then see if he could cut his way out of this place. But—could he cut through fast enough?

Roberts relaxed. The armor made his casual reply even more cool and unconcerned. "Such an attempt would constitute a serious provocation. A person in an inferior position might well think carefully before venturing such a provocation."

"And in what way do you punish a provocation when the provocation succeeds in creating your demise?"

"Very easily, if serious preparations have been made beforehand."

"You will not escape this room. Whatever powers you may possess, the walls of this tank constitute an obstacle which will require a measurable pause for you to get through. *That is all that is necessary.* Your first motion at attempted escape will result in an instantaneous molten discharge that will cook you inside your armor. Again I ask: In what way do you punish a provocation when the provocation succeeds in creating your demise?"

There was a tone of barely suppressed jubilation in Ialwo's voice that Roberts didn't care for. However, he still had the possibility of creating unease in Ialwo's mind, since Ialwo's information came from prisoners thoroughly convinced of the reality of one of Roberts' earlier masquerades.

"I will tell you a story," said Roberts, his voice calm and unconcerned, "and at the end of this story, you will not only release us from this chamber unharmed—something which you will do anyway, as you have no choice—but you will also find a suitable way to make amends. *The Empire looks after its own, and does not treat such insults lightly.*"

There was a lengthy pause. A lack-of-breath sound was back in Ialwo's voice when he spoke.

"What Empire do you speak of?" Ialwo demanded.

"*The* Empire."

"Uh—" said Ialwo. "This . . . ah . . . is some governmental organization allied with Earth?"

"Earth," said Roberts, "acts on a basis of relatively short-range profit and loss. The Empire arranges its accounts somewhat differently, on a more long-range basis."

"Crustax," said Ialwo cautiously, "has had no formal contact with the Empire of which you speak. We have heard only *rumors*. Rumors prove nothing."

"Each and every Citizen of the Empire," said Roberts, "may rely—if his conduct be good, and his pursuits proper—upon each and every other Citizen of the Empire for protection against outsiders. In fact, the provision of such protection by one who is not a Citizen is often sufficient to move His Majesty to grant Citizenship to mere allies and associates—a boon for which many crave, and which is hard to gain."

There was a prolonged silence, during which Roberts seemed to hear Ialwo thinking.

"And," Ialwo said craftily, "if the rescue attempt *fails?*"

Roberts groped for an answer to the question, and with his mouth still shut heard his voice answer cheerfully:

"Why, all depends upon the manner of such a failure. There is failure, and then again failure. If failure ends in base cowardice, what is there to say? That is disgrace. But if it ends in glorious searing of a more powerful foe, and even if its failure doth rock him on his throne, perhaps cast him down into disorder and ruin—why, there is vengeance, if not success. 'Tis then a glorious failure. If known, it will be sung by the minstrels to the King himself. If unknown, yet it will be recorded on the Great Books, and seen aloft in Heaven. What is done cannot be undone, and glory once gained, though it rust on Earth, is immutable in the Great Records of Time. It is far best to succeed, but Honor may require—even unsure of success—that the attempt be made."

There followed a very lengthy delay, then Ialwo murmured, "This proves nothing at all. And yet—" He paused. "Let us hear this story you were going to tell."

"Once," said Roberts coolly, calculating how to mix the large quantities of fabrications in with the very slender whiff of truth, "there was a leader of a mighty power allied with a still mightier Empire. All that was needed to make the happiness of the leader complete was to possess Citizenship in the great Empire. But this Citizenship was hard to achieve, particularly since the leader was of a completely different race from that of the Empire. It could only be won by proof of valor and craft in a good cause, in service of the mighty Empire. Much time passed, and then the opportunity presented itself. Another power seized certain Citizens of the Empire, and held them against their will.

"The mighty leader selected two hardy friends, disguised his most dread warship as a liner of Earth, and disguised the liner of Earth as a ruined alien hulk . . ."

Ialwo sucked his breath in—suggesting that Interstellar Patrol camouflage was better than Crustaxan detectors.

" . . . And," Roberts went on, "journeyed to the space fortress where the Citizens were imprisoned. Once there, he was admitted by the crafty governor, and taken on board along with his friends, and a robot packed solid with *Ultrax* instantaneous fulminating-gas explosive, to a large audience chamber. Here, the governor menaced him, and the mighty leader set the robot to explode at the first sign of hot metal which the governor threatened to pour in. The pressure generated by the explosive would, of course, shove the hot metal back in its passages, and probably blow the roof off the audience chamber.

"Meanwhile, the warship in the spaceport of the fortress had taken note of the defenses, and was now prepared to raze the interior with its powerful guns. Outside, at a distance, a fleet of the leader's warships stood by, to inflict retribution if the leader should be harmed. Attacked inside and out, with the landing force already within its gates, the situation for the fortress commander did not suggest the likelihood of victory.

"That," concluded Roberts, "is the story. And now I suggest that you consider it carefully."

There was a faint tremor underfoot, and the governor murmured, "That *is* a warship. Well, well. Now I will tell *you* a story." He gave a low grinding popping noise that the suit tentatively translated as a laugh. "Once there was a young survivor of Crustaxan seas, who entered into adulthood with high promise, was chosen as the successor of a great leader of high position, and succeeded to command of a mighty fortress. His future seemed to glitter before him. Then Earthmen destroyed the great leader, brought him down in disaster. His successor was forced to abandon the name, covered with dishonor, and enter into a much lesser succession. Meanwhile, some captives being squeezed for information exuded a story about an Empire that no one knew to exist, and stuck to this impossible story until three equally impossible Earthmen disguised as monsters turned up at the space fortress, and were entrapped inside, along with a camouflaged warship, which floated in the spaceport under the far mightier camouflaged guns of the fortress. At this point, the impossible monsters, trapped in a heat-treatment room, repeated the same impossible Empire story, leading the governor of the fortress to see the connection between the two, and recognize the story as a clever posthypnotic sidetrack to mislead interrogators seeking admissions under torture. Very clever. But now the governor could see the way to great honors by capturing the warship of the Earthmen, regardless of the price, and the Earthmen themselves, dead or alive, because after what happened at Storehouse, *the leaders of Crustax will delight in such a victory over Earthmen.*

"How," Ialwo concluded gloatingly, "do you like *that* story?"

"Somewhat boring," said Roberts uneasily. The battle armor strained the uneasiness out of his voice, and added, "A clumsy warrior thrusts too soon, revealing to his opponent his weak point, whereupon he must pay the penalty."

"Meaning what?" said Ialwo sharply.

Since Roberts didn't know, he was relieved to hear the armor answer coolly:

"Meaning that what you cannot bear is further disgrace. *Personal* disgrace, Ialwo. Disgrace that you must *live* with indefinitely, or else destroy yourself."

"The possibility of such disgrace does not exist in this situation. Combat, yes! But that is honorable. Disgrace? *No!*"

Somewhere, there was an odd grating grinding noise, like a set of drills and scrapers busily at work.

Roberts still didn't see the outcome, but his voice was cheerfully insinuating:

"And suppose you are associated with a worse disaster than your former sponsor, Admiral Nade? What then?"

There was a final scrape-*grind* noise, and a small dully-glinting thing popped into view, and ran ratlike along the base of the wall to the far end. There it huddled in the corner and quivered and shook as new grating, grinding noises accompanied the accumulation of a pile of metal shavings.

Roberts looked on blankly.

There followed a sound as of a thick wad of metallic cloth shoved through a small opening, and a second thing just like the first popped into view, to scuttle along the base of the wall and join the first one.

Ialwo murmured, "What kind of thing—"

Roberts' brain sluggishly added up the facts: *He* had never seen anything like that. Ialwo had never seen anything like that. But who else was involved in this collision? Only the symbiotic computer. But the hole the thing made was too small to help. Wait, now. Suppose—

Roberts was still working it out as his voice said, "Watch it closely, Ialwo. Dozens of such things are loose in the fortress. As they reproduce quickly, soon there will be thousands—unless you can persuade *us* to take them with us when we leave."

"But what *are* they?"

"Just a development of a thing called a *rat,* which is a pest amongst the humans. This variety is a result of much development. It utilizes iron in its metabolism, in a form which makes it exceedingly tough, hard to kill, and capable of gnawing through almost any barrier. What it is after, of course, is your stores, reserves, food stocks, though it can live for some time, if need be, on spaceship fuel—such as doesn't leak out after it gnaws through the tanks. It is a very dirty creature, and—"

"Spaceship fuel," muttered Ialwo. "Stores, reserves, and food stocks!"

"At this moment, the things are eating and reproducing all over the fortress. All they do is eat and reproduce. Except, of course, to—"

"Hold your explosion!" roared Ialwo. "This is not aimed at you!"

A white-hot stream poured down from a hole high up, at the far end of the chamber. It landed away from the corner. The creatures there gnawed frantically. There was a second, much briefer dazzling spurt, with less pressure behind it. It fell too far out, but spattered the corner.

There was a desperate squeal, and one of the ratlike creatures tore around the floor, jumping into the air, twisting backwards, and biting at its glittering fur. The other, however, suddenly popped out of sight, leaving a single hole behind it. The first ran, humping itself desperately, along the base of the wall toward the place from which it had come in, then suddenly reversed itself and popped out—amidst streams of flowing metal—through the new hole.

Behind it, others began to come in through the original hole. These ran, humping and scuttling, with momentary unpredictable pauses, along the base of the wall and vanished out the fresh hole at the far end.

Ialwo cursed, and urgent spurts of flowing molten metal rained down, to miss them completely.

In the silence that followed, Roberts said, "They are not easy for a nonexpert to kill. Much skill and know-how is required."

Ialwo's voice sounded suddenly sober.

"How did these things get *in* here?"

"No problem in that," said Roberts' voice, matter-of-factly. "They are adept at concealing themselves. You have sent a number of your shuttles out to the ship. That's all it takes. They, for that matter, could easily throw themselves across the gap from ship to docks. One good shove, and they will drift the rest of the way."

Ialwo didn't say anything.

Roberts' voice was almost regretful.

"You can imagine how these things will spread, what damage thy will cause, and what honor will be heaped on whoever is considered responsible for letting them get started. You do understand who will get all the credit for the trouble these things will cause, don't you, *unless* you can persuade us to get rid of them for you? Bear in mind that they are reproducing while you think."

Ialwo's voice came out in a croak:

"What do you want?"

The camouflaged battle ship was well on its way back, with the rescued prisoners recuperating in deep sleep, when Hammell said wonderingly, "Who would have believed it? He was ready enough to fight a war—that didn't bother him—but *rats* were too much."

Roberts said thoughtfully, "The effect of a blow depends not only on how hard it hits, but on where it hits, and how unexpectedly. He was a fortress commander, and all set for a fight. But the rats hit him on the raw nerve ends, *unexpectedly*. He couldn't gather from questioning us that anything like that was coming, since we didn't know it ourselves. The symbiotic computer cooked that one up all on its own."

Morrissey smiled. "*There's* deception for you! The Crustaxans are pretty good at it. But how do they compete with that?"

"Two heads," agreed Roberts cheerfully, "are better than one. Even if one *is* a symbiotic computer."

THE UNKNOWN

Vaughan Nathan Roberts, at the patrol ship's viewscreen, studied the rotating close-up image that looked exactly like a patched-up Stellar Scout ship. He glanced at Hammell, who was watching from the aisle beside him.

Hammell nodded.

"If we have to fool them, that should do it. But they may not have noticed us."

Morrissey, coming up the aisle, ducked to avoid knocking himself out on the highly polished, practically invisible mirror-like cylinder that ran along the ship's axis at head height. He leaned over to take a look at the screen.

"Ouch, a Stellar Scout ship. Is that what we look like now?"

"Correct," said Roberts. "What's wrong with it?"

Hammell said, "It's accurate."

"Oh," said Morrissey, "I know that. But the Stellar Scouts are fanatics for new equipment. Won't it scare off these bloodsuckers if they see that ship?"

"The idea is to confuse them—and to provide ourselves with justification for whatever we choose to use. We want, if possible, to hit them without their knowing what happened. If they *did* detect us, *then* we want them to think they're up against pure amateurs, but dangerous amateurs. Amateurs with *teeth*."

"H'm. I think I see it."

Hammell explained. "If they see an Interstellar Patrol ship, *then* they'll clear out. A thief that starts into a house at night

63

and spots a lion waiting in there is going back out the window as fast as he can get through it. He'll rob some other place. But if—instead of a lion—he sees a friendly wolfhound lying there banging his tail on the floor . . . Well, the thief just might decide to stay there and clean out the place."

Morrissey considered it, and nodded.

"The lion would be sure to eat him up. The wolfhound has plenty of teeth, but maybe he can be fooled."

"Right," said Hammell.

Roberts added, "And we don't want to trail this crew around from place to place while they polish up their technique. We want to end them now."

Up the aisle toward the bow of the camouflaged Interstellar Patrol ship, Dan Bergen, at the spy screen, cleared his throat.

"Boy, this gang is *tricky*."

"What now?"

"Let me switch it to your screen."

"Go ahead."

The viewscreen at once showed, standing, a dazed-looking rough-hewn figure; and, seated behind a small table, hands spread in glowing good nature, a pink-cheeked clean-cut individual radiating honesty and friendly sincerity.

The big rough-hewn man was saying, "You don't know what this means to us, Dr. Fellows. This is a rich planet, but we've run into one thing after another. First the local life-forms. Then the winters. And now this. We've heard of the pox, of course. But we didn't think there was any cure. Your coming like this is like—like manna from heaven!"

"Dr. Fellows" smiled modestly. "My boy, the pleasure is mine."

"You've saved our lives!"

"What better reward could I ask than that?"

"Some day we'll be able to pay you back!"

"Don't think of it."

"We will. I mean it! This planet is rich. All we have to do is to get the ore out, and for that we only need our health and more time to work. We're used to work here. And you've saved our health."

"I know. But I don't ask any reward. Your good fortune is *my* reward."

The rough-hewn figure looked away a moment, overcome with emotion.

At the desk, "Dr. Fellows" sneaked a quick glance at his watch. A look of irritation flitted across his face, to vanish in smiling good nature.

The big man passed a corner of his leather sleeve across his eyes, took a deep breath, and said, "Nevertheless, we *will* repay you. And if there is ever anything you need, just call on us."

"My boy, doing good is all the reward I ask. I only hope that the work I've been privileged to do here will turn out well. You see, there was so little time to diagnose, and so *very* little time to synthesize the curative agent, that scientific objectivity compels me to ask you again: Are you *certain* that there have been no unpleasant reactions?"

"*None.* No, sir. And after a day or two in bed, our people get up *cured.*"

"Then I feel free to trust the cure, and shall stand ready in case the infection should reappear."

"You're going to stay around the planet, just in case it should break out somewhere else?"

"My boy, I consider it my duty."

The big man wrung the hand of the modestly beaming individual behind the desk, stood momentarily speechless with emotion, then went out.

The instant the door closed, the man at the desk let out his breath, slid out a panel above the desk drawers, and punched two of the panel's many buttons.

A few moments later, another door across the room opened up, and a small neat individual wearing a gray laboratory coat walked in, his expression solemn and serious. Piously, he glanced around.

Behind the desk, "Dr. Fellows" sat back.

"I'm alone, Vank."

The look of pious solemnity vanished from Vank's face. A look of rapacity that seemed more at home there settled on his features.

"Where's the dummy?"

"Just went out, swearing to repay us."

Vank laughed.

"You know, Fox, we ought to—"

The pink-cheeked individual sat up.

"Until we're out of here, *I'm Dr. Fellows!*"

Vank winced. "Sorry. I was going to say, we ought to work this play on Tiamaz. They *could* repay us. Quick."

"I have a little something in mind for Tiamaz—some day. This wouldn't work."

"Package it a little different—"

"No. There aren't enough dummies on Tiamaz. They'd see through the whole thing like a plate of glass. There's something about the fresh air on these colony planets that restores the suckers' faith in human nature. You could only *hit* Tiamaz. This place, you can *milk.*"

There was a rap on the same door Vank had come through, and "Dr. Fellows" called, "Come in!"

The door opened, to let in a tall worried-looking individual with a slip of paper in his hand.

Fellows leaned back, his face expressionless.

"Let's have it."

"The massometer reading checks. But strange to say, we have *nothing* on the detectors."

"What's that mean?"

"Trouble."

"In what size?"

"The ship itself is small. On that basis alone, it could be anything, and the odds favor some local spacefreight rig, a retired spacer sightseeing in one of these toothless yachts, a prospector nosing around, or something on that level."

"Then what are we worrying about?"

"The detectors didn't pick it out."

"So?"

"Only the massometer found it."

"I'm waiting. What of it?"

"The thing was *invisible.*"

Fellows sat up. "The detectors couldn't see it, or *we* couldn't see it?"

"If we could see it, the detectors could see it. Better to put that the other way around. If the detectors couldn't see it, *we* sure couldn't. Unless it was a pure illusion."

"And the massometer wouldn't have picked up an illusion."

"No, it sure wouldn't."

"You're saying there was visually nothing there?"

"Visually, optically, so far as radiation was concerned, the sky was empty. Nevertheless, a detectable mass passed overhead at moderate speed."

"How high?"

"As an estimate, three thousand feet."

"And moved on?"

"Correct."

Fellows sat back, frowning.

"This couldn't be some kind of freak warm-air mass—what do you call it? A—an inversion?"

The tall man smiled.

"It would have to be pretty heavy hot air. This was a material object."

"All right. You're the expert. Why should we worry about it?"

"Let me make a comparison. You open the door to your room. You walk in. You glance around the room. There's nothing to be concerned about. You toss your hat toward the table. Before the hat hits the table, it bounces back from nothing. There's a heavy crash as something—nothing you can see—lands at the base of the table and jars the room." He paused to look quizzically at Fellows. "What's there to be worried about?"

"H'm," said Fellows. "I see." He sat back and swung his chair lightly from side to side. "Not so good. Who could this be?"

"There's only one outfit I can think of. I just hope I'm wrong."

"What outfit is that?"

"The IP."

Fellows came halfway out of his chair, his hands making abortive grabs at the desk, as if reaching for controls that weren't there. He let fly a string of livid curses.

Beside him, Vank looked confused. "What's the IP?"

As, on the screen, Fellows explained this in words of few syllables, Roberts looked up from the screen, to glance at Morrissey.

"Now we've got to convince them we've got enough teeth so they better leave us alone, but not so many they have to be afraid of us."

Morrissey shook his head.

"If only we'd stayed low. Their massometer probably wouldn't have picked us out, if we'd been against some solid background."

Hammell, who had been piloting the ship at the time, said defensively, "Damn it, the screen didn't show anything!"

A familiar, maddeningly cool voice broke into the conversation.

"Incorrect. Their ship *did* show on the screen, but was not highlighted to call your attention to it. You overlooked it."

"But," said Hammell, "now we have this mess. The ship *should* have been highlighted!"

"Not at all. Members of the Interstellar Patrol are supposed to have some powers of observation. For a symbiotic computer, with its vast superiority, it is admittedly much easier to detect such objects; but, for the symbiotic computer to do *all* the work would lead to a further deterioration of the atrophied power of observation that the patrolmen *do* possess."

Hammell bared his teeth.

Morrissey murmured irritatedly, "Maybe *it* didn't see it, either."

Roberts called, "Bergen!"

"Sir?"

"You see the problem we've got?"

"Yes, sir."

"Can you fix yourself up to be a happy-go-lucky but tough prospector with a couple of pals, just drifting around watching for whatever turns up?"

"Sure!"

"Take over."

Twenty minutes later, the patrol ship, disguised as a Stellar Scout ship, and the whole thing invisible, drifted over a wooded hill, and descended toward a massive cruiser resting in the valley, partly hidden by big trees.

Roberts, at the spy screen, watched with Morrissey as Bergen went out on the hull, and called. "Ho! Hello, Space Force!" An instant later, he shouted in the hatchway, "They can't see us, Rick. Throw the switch!"

On the spy screen, Fellows was in the control room, glancing at the outside viewscreen. Bent over it beside him was the tall man who had warned him about the massometer. Fellows stared at the screen.

"Now we can see it. But who's the young kid on the ship? *That's* the IP?" He glanced around. "What kind of ship is it, Mape?"

The tall man straightened, scowling.

"The lines aren't right for the IP. But they're *tricky* . . . I don't place this rig."

"Whoever it is wants to talk to us. Does *that* fit the Patrol?"

"You can't tell. That's the trouble."

"Well, this isn't my line. You handle it."

Mape hit the outside speaker control. His voice boomed out. "Hello, Spacer."

Bergen, in ragged jeans and torn shirt, looking greasy and unshaven, grinned and called out, "Hello, Space Force!"

"We aren't Space Force—this is a surplus cruiser, private-owned. What are you?"

The ragged figure glanced over the big ship, and looked impressed.

"Private? Sorry, I thought you were living off the tax on my finder's fees."

"Prospector?"

"Right."

"What's here to interest you?"

"Oh, we're just free-lancing around. Never know when you might run into something somebody might want."

"This planet has the pox. We're a private medical research ship. We think we've got it licked, but it's too soon to be sure. How many more ships do you have? You could spread this without meaning to, and come down yourself, if you're not immune."

"There's just one of us. We don't want to fool around with the pox. But we'll look around, see what our instruments show. You know how it is. Is the place quarantined?"

"We aren't that official. You been over our way before? *Recently?*"

"Sure. Not long ago, at that."

"We didn't *see* you."

"You wouldn't," said the ragged grinning figure at the hatch of the smaller ship. "We're inconspicuous."

"Don't be too inconspicuous. You could get swatted by accident."

The grin moderated into a smile. It wasn't an unfriendly smile, but there was no sign of fear. Mape watched closely, eyes narrowed.

Bergen said, "Don't try to swat us, friend, accidentally or otherwise. We've got teeth at one end, and a sting at the other. You may get us, but you'll pay the price. You're big, but size isn't everything."

"I don't read your lines. What are you?"

"Salvaged Stellar Scout ship."

Mape gave an abortive reach for the controls, much as Fellows had done earlier. He gave a low mutter that the outside speaker duly transmitted. Then he had himself under control.

"Stellar Scout. *Are* you Stellar Scouts?"

"Not us. Just the ship. And you aren't Space Force, right?"

"Right,"

"Okay. I just wanted to be polite. We'll be around. I don't know how long. We don't know what there is on this planet."

"It's settled and claimed."

"Not every inch of it isn't."

Mape grunted, then said pleasantly. "Well, nice of you to let us know who it was went over. Set down here beside us, and we'll give you some first-class refreshments."

Bergen grinned. "Thanks, but we've got a schedule. See you."

Mape looked disappointed. "Good luck."

On the screen, Bergen waved, and the small ship moved off. Mape snapped off the outside speaker, and turned to Fellows.

Fellows said, "Well?"

"Well, what? There it is."

"What do you think?"

"As far as I can *tell*, they're all right. But that doesn't prove anything."

"Are they what they say they are?"

Mape shook his head. "Don't ask me that. Maybe so, maybe not. It sounded all right to me. Better yet, it *felt* all right. But that doesn't prove a thing."

"What's this Stellar Scout outfit? Are they as bad as the IP? I don't think I ever heard of the Stellar Scouts."

Mape watched the little ship move away on the screen.

"You've heard of PDA?"

"Planetary Development Authority? Sure."

"The Stellar Scouts are the advance men for PDA. They do the first investigations into new parts of space, the first mapping, make the first reports. Sometimes, of course, private outfits beat them to it. But they're the official advance men for PDA."

Fellows looked unconvinced.

"Listen, when he said he had a Stellar Scout ship, you almost threw us into orbit. Let's have the facts."

"I'm giving you the facts. The Stellar Scouts don't bother anyone, but they're fanatics for new equipment. They aren't fighters, but they're always *equipped*. A buddy of mine ran into a Scout in a bar one time, and I don't know whether to believe half of that stuff. But I tell you this: A Stellar Scout ship is poison. They're always loaded with experimental stuff, and no one knows *what* will happen when they fire it off at you. Maybe they'll blow themselves up. Or maybe they'll do things to you that you never dreamed could be done. We better just leave this one alone."

"Where does this leave us?"

"Don't ask me. You're the boss."

"Suppose that kid comes back and leans on us? Then what?"

"Then we fight. I'm not saying we have to fold up. I just say, leave him alone."

"But, for all we know, it *could* be the IP."

"Sure it could."

Fellows hesitated, eyes narrowed. Then he shook his head.

"I don't think so. It doesn't feel right for that. Okay, we'll go ahead. But we better keep our eyes open, and keep that massometer going."

Roberts turned from the screen to Bergen.

"Good work. You fooled them."

Bergen grinned.

"What next?"

"First we have to be sure we know the exact details of what's going on here. Morrissey?"

Morrissey, now working the spy screen, said, "We just got a view into another part of their ship. But it faded out again."

Hammell growled. "That's the trouble with these ultraminiature spy-circuits. They drift in like dust motes, but you have no control over *where* they drift. An air current, or a static charge, can completely foul up your arrangements."

Roberts said, "We still don't have any view into the aft section of that cruiser?"

"Nothing," said Morrissey. "Except— Here we go again. Mape is walking along the main fore-and-aft corridor, and the view goes along with him . . . *Agh*. There he goes out. All I can tell you is:

The ship is heavily stocked with *something;* there are only the three men on board as far as I've seen so far; and they aren't medical researchers, believe me."

"Well, we'll hope we get something in there." He turned to Hammell. "It was a good idea to drift those circuits when you realized we were going to pass overhead."

Hammell nodded. "Thanks. But the computer's right. I *should* have noticed it."

Bergen said, "Still, we know *enough.* Just from what they say, we know that they're planning to rob the colonists, and we know that they have the colonists fooled as to what's going on. You only need to listen to them for a few minutes, to know what the general idea is."

"Yes," said Roberts. "But we need more than that."

Morrissey called, "We've got a view into the aft end of the ship. Take a look at this."

Roberts glanced at the screen, to see "Dr. Fellows" and Vank looking at what appeared to be a large sleeping bird—perhaps a falcon. The peculiar part of it was that the falcon was not asleep on a perch, but was in a transparent case, roughly the size and shape of an artillery shell.

"M'm," said Fellows, "we want to be sure this destructs properly. We could take things a little easier except for these prospectors nosing around."

Vank said confidently, "It will destruct. Don't worry."

"How about the case?"

"When you fire it out, the seals puncture to start a timed reaction."

"The thing doesn't burst into flame?"

"Nothing like that. Right now that case is a tough but glassy substance. The timed reaction reverts it to the crystalline state. At the slightest touch, it will crumble into fragments, then into a fine dust. There's no evidence—nothing."

Fellows nodded. "And the bird?"

Vank gave a modest laugh.

"The bird is long dead, and seeded with encapsulated spores of a very special decay organism. Don't worry about the bird."

"Ah . . Is this decay organism likely to . . . cause trouble later? That's important to us, you know."

"Nothing that will bother us. The rot will sporulate, and

the spores will be destroyed by the radiation from the planet's sun."

"Er—"

"Don't worry about it. This is *my* specialty."

Fellows let his breath out slowly.

"And the—the special dose?"

"The powder will drift all over this part of the planet. This bird is a predator. It can glide for hours. When the shell passes the top of its trajectory and starts down, the cover will blow off the rear of the shell, the bird will be shoved out, and the flight-control systems will take over. With every tilt of its wings, a little powder will drop out of the hollowed out seeding canisters."

Fellows nodded approvingly.

Vank concluded, "With a little luck, the colonists will be down with the pseudopox inside a week or two. Enough of them should die this time to make us even more popular with the ones we save."

"The important thing," said Fellows, "is to *leave no trace.*"

Vank grinned.

"We want to leave them enough strength to work, too."

Fellows smiled in turn. "*Very* true."

Roberts glanced up from the screen, punched the button to the left of the glowing lens lettered "Smb Cmp," and asked, "What can you tell us about this harmless spore the dead bird will release on the planet in the process of rotting?"

There was a brief pause, then the symbiotic computer said, "Not to over-burden you with scientific details, the information given is inadequate to pinpoint the precise nature of the organism—"

"In other words, you don't know?"

"But," the symbiotic computer went on, "the most common organism which appears to fit this inadequate description is the *diabolus rot.* While the spores are unusually sensitive to ultraviolet radiation, other forms of the organism are not. In certain of its forms, *diabolus* resembles the slime molds, forming exceptionally large swarms known as the *diabolus horror.* Save for its appearance, it is harmless, and, except for the psychological reaction induced by its appearance, it is even believed to be edible and nutritious."

Roberts could feel his stomach turn over.

"It sounds nice. Now, what about 'pseudopox'?"

"There is less doubt regarding this. There is a bacterium capable of producing all the external manifestations of planetary pox. It, too, is fatal, and, like the true pox inflicts a heavier proportion of fatalities on girls and women. It is, however, comparatively simple to cure, and is a very rare disease."

"Can Dr. Fellows spread pseudopox by sprinkling powder over the planet?"

"Yes. The disease can be spread by inhalation or ingestion of the organisms, and is highly contagious."

Roberts sat back, frowning.

"Okay. Thanks."

The symbiotic computer added, "In case you're wondering, the larger moon will pass slowly above the ex-Space Force cruiser tonight, and will be high in the sky most of the night."

"Exactly what I was thinking about," said Roberts. "Now, I would like to know how good you are at manufacturing mobile imitation biological objects. Objects that can stand close examination."

The symbiotic computer's voice held a note of modest creative pride. "What did you have in mind?"

"This is going to be tricky, and difficult."

The symbiotic computer almost purred. "Let's have the details."

Roberts glanced up.

"Morrissey?"

"Sir?"

"When Hammell released the spy-circuits, some were drawn into the cruiser down there, and some went elsewhere. How is our general coverage on this part of the planet?"

"*Most* went elsewhere. We have a wealth of coverage where we don't want it. We've got an inside view of deserted parts of the forest, we're snooping in all the cabins we don't want to be in, we've even got a close-up view of a pot-hole at the bottom of a waterfall, with rocks and gravel grinding around inside; but we still don't have as much overlapping coverage as I'd like of that cruiser."

"How widespread is our coverage?"

"It takes in a lot of territory. The heaviest concentration of settlers is to the northeast of here, where the mines and separation apparatus are located. We have good coverage there."

"Good enough," said Roberts. "If I'm not mistaken, that is what they'll aim to hit."

Hammell said, "Excuse my curiosity, but what does the *position of the moon* have to do with this?"

The moon was high in the sky as the spy screen showed the gravitic launcher slowly rising from the blunt tower just aft of the converted cruiser's main forward turret. The launcher's snout swung slowly around to aim toward the settlement, near the mines. The launcher lifted. There was a sudden indistinctness at its mouth.

On Roberts' battle screen, a long wavy blur showed the track of the gravitor beam projected by the launcher. A dot traveled rapidly up this wavy blur. The blur abruptly vanished. The dot continued onward and upward.

Roberts' hands reached out to the control board. A second very faint wavy blur appeared.

The dot gently shifted its course. The new beam eased steadily ahead. Instead of falling, the dot held its speed, moved over the target still gently rising, and then gathered speed within the beam, to climb rapidly upward. As the beam continued to slightly shift its angle, the resulting course for the dot was a long curving gentle rise, followed by a steep climb.

Morrissey, watching the spy screen, said, "They're in the control room. Mape is watching on their screen."

"Good," said Roberts, watching his screen. "What do they have to say?"

"I'll turn this up."

The voice of "Dr. Fellows" carried clearly: "Fine. That's taken care of. Now, the bird will be released, the carrier case will crash and break up, and after spreading the—er—seeding, the bird will become harmlessly dematerialized?"

Vank's voice chuckled.

"Exactly."

There was a brief silence, and then Mape's voice gave a low growl.

"Just what in hell is *this?*"

Fellows said, "What is it, Mape?"

"Something took off straight *up,* beyond the settlement."

"No trouble, surely?"

"Maybe. I don't know. But what is it?"

"The prospectors, hopefully? We'd be glad to see them leave."

"It isn't that big. This is a little thing, about the size of the bird, and it's headed straight up, for the moon. Of course, the prospectors could be *behind* this."

"I don't follow, Mape. What possible connection could there be between this thing and our—ah—affairs?"

"This disappearing Stellar Scout ship of theirs won't show up on the massometer with the moon behind it."

"And you think—"

"They may have grabbed the bird, and be reeling it in on a gravitor beam."

Fellows' voice took on ugly overtones.

"Then, they would be in a position to—to *blackmail* us. We'd have to give *them* a cut?" Fellows said angrily, "I *despise* blackmailers. There's nothing lower. Dirty, rotten, sneaking, *underhanded—*"

"Incidentally, if we try to take off, they're in just the spot to knock us flat."

"After all the thought I've put into this, I *won't* be skimmed by a damned sneaking blackmailer! Is it too dangerous to use the guns? This *was* a Space Force cruiser!"

"The spot we're in," said Mape, "I'm all for using the guns. What have we got to lose?"

"*Hold it!*" said Vank. "You're just guessing. You don't know it's the bird!"

"No, I don't know it. But what else is it? I didn't *know* what was behind that massometer reading, but what could it have been but a ship? Things don't fly from a planet up toward its moon for *no* reason. If it isn't the bird, what is it?"

"But you said yourself it didn't start up right away. Why the lag?"

"To give them time to ease it on with gentle touches of the gravitor beam, to get it away from where we could follow it direct, so we wouldn't *know* what had happened."

"Yeah, that fits . . . What's the worst if we're wrong and take a crack at them?"

"If we're completely wrong, we'll make noise and wake the people sleeping around here. If they're up there doing something else, one or the other of us will get finished."

Vank hesitated, but Fellows said coldly, "The danger justifies the risk. Go ahead, Mape."

Mape reached for the controls.

On the spy-screen, the covers slid back in the moonlight from the cruiser's weapons.

A volcanic eruption escorted by squadrons of lightning bolts hurled itself toward the moon, and hurled itself again and again.

Roberts eyed his battle screen alertly.

"So far, so good. It's nice we're down here with a pressor beam instead of up there with a tractor beam. Now, did they do us the favor of finishing off the bird?"

The voice of the symbiotic computer replied, "The second salvo from the main fusion batteries destroyed the container and contents."

"Good. Did we lose any of it on the way up?"

"It was all held in the beam—assuming, of course, that the initial launching was efficient."

"Okay. Morrissey—"

"Right here," said Morrissey. "You want our replacement for the bird on your screen?"

"Yes."

"Here it is."

Roberts found himself looking around the interior of a darkened room on the screen, a room lit only by a little moonlight diffusing through a window high up.

A man's voice spoke in a whisper. "Did you hear that crash?"

There was a woman's murmur.

A little girl cried, "Mommy! Mommy! Something *bit* me!"

The woman screamed, "Jim! The window!"

At the small window, high up, a batlike form momentarily blotted out the moonlight.

Perhaps a tenth of a second later, flame spurted from the muzzle of an upraised gun, the crash echoed around the cabin, and there was a thin shriek and a rattling bumping noise as something fell down the cabin wall, followed by a thud as it hit ground.

The woman screamed. *"Be careful!"*

The door banged shut behind him.

"Mommy! sobbed the girl. *"It bit me!"*

"Don't move, Janey. *Stay where you are!"*

From outside came an oath, then a bellow.

"Look at this! Bill! Sam! Come out here!"

The scene shifted to the outside, where, amidst a bristle of guns, several men crouched in the moonlight, to straighten slowly and glance at one another.

"That thing isn't dead. Pierce its wing and tie a thong to the bone. Put it in a leather sack, and we'll take it with us. I'll get Peters and his crowd, we'll all be dressed in five minutes, and then we'll be right with you. See the women shutter those windows and keep the lamps dim. Leash the hounds on the poles, and we'll take two sticks of them."

Roberts straightened from the screen. "So far, so good. Now let's see how the kindly medical missionaries are making out in their private battleship."

Morrissey said, "I've got it on a split screen. It's very inspiring. Here it is."

Before Roberts, the scene changed, to show the cruiser's control room. Mape was shaking his head.

"No, no, there was nothing there. I *don't* explain it. *Unless—*"

Vank said, "A little more of this dung, buddy, is about all we're going to take. You *sure* you didn't imagine it in the first place?"

Mape looked at him. His voice became soft, courteous.

"Would you like to *say* I imagined it?"

Vank snarled, "I'm not in the mood to play games! Quick reflexes, with a pea for a brain! All I'd have to do is give you one squirt from a pressure-hype at breakfast, and you'd be dead with the cultured pus squirting out your ears by lunch. *You* are going to scare *me*, eh?"

Fellows said uneasily, "Vank, my boy—ah—we're all a little overstrained—let's not . . ."

Mape turned away, and worked small controls at the side of one of the cruiser's screens. The scene on the screen vanished, to be replaced by a black field marked with pale green outlines of the horizon as seen from the ship. A white dot disappeared over the horizon, and Mape said, "This is the recorded track of the bird. Watch it, and see what you think."

Vank frowned, but looked at the screen.

For a long moment, the screen showed nothing but the green outline of the horizon. Then, to the side, the white dot reappeared, climbed with increasing swiftness, to finally lift nearly straight up as the screen shifted its angle of view, to show the larger of the planet's moons, with a white dot climbing toward it.

Vank glanced swiftly at the controls Mape had just handled. "Do that again."

Mape worked the controls.

Dr. Fellows came over and watched.

"Mape," he said, "excuse me, but I wonder if you'd replay that for me? And Vank, I wonder if you'd step aft, and just check—"

Mape said politely, his voice soft, "Go right ahead, Dr. Fellows. But as for Vank and me, we have a little something to talk over. Here, I'll set it to replay for you."

Dr. Fellows stood irresolutely at the screen as Mape and Vank went out. Perspiration rolled down Fellows' forehead. He mopped it with his handkerchief, took one or two steps after them, then let out a deep shuddering breath, and came to a stop. He looked around uneasily. "It's going sour," he said. "It *was* perfect, but it's going *sour.*"

Roberts looked up from the screen.

"Fellows just might have enough intuition to get out of there. Do we have coverage of Mape and Vank?"

"No," said Morrissey. "Worse luck."

"Okay. If they decide to break for it, we're going to appreciate every hour of sleep we get tonight. It's going to take time for this to work itself out, and there isn't a great deal we can do until it takes shape. Let's set up watches."

Roberts was on watch as things came to a head, a little before dawn.

Inside the converted cruiser, everything was quiet. The action was taking place outside, though there was, in fact, not very much to see except eyes.

Roberts, at the spy screen, had some difficulty spotting the unmoving faces, smeared with resin and leaves, just back from the edge of the clearing, where the trees' many leaves, angled to catch the light, provided cover. By careful use of the spy screen, Roberts had uncovered eighteen of the hidden figures, some well back from the cruiser, some in the very trees that provided it with cover. They all were watching, but as the sun gradually began to light the clearing, they did little else. It was, however, possible to see the pupils of their eyes move, back and forth, the eyes narrowed into hard slits, as they followed the batlike forms that came to, and departed from, the upthrust snout of the gravitic launcher. For a time, in the earliest light of the dawn, the cruiser had the look of some kind of interplanetary hornet's nest, bats scuttling in and out the tilted launcher, flitting around the clearing as if to get their bearings before setting out. In the actual light of dawn, this traffic thinned out, let up entirely, and the cruiser sat there, the beaded dew shining on it, under the hard gaze of numerous watching eyes.

Now there appeared, from the direction of a path through thick forest, a man carrying a little boy in his arms. He approached the ship with a look of touching trust and confidence, paused at the edge of the clearing, and glanced up at the closed hatch at the head of the ramp.

"Ho, Doc!" he called.

He started up the ramp.

"Doc! You folks awake in there? Doc! Open up!"

The cruiser's alarm system, apparently programmed to ignore small animals and signal the arrival of humans, gave a warning buzz.

Suddenly the hatch swung open at the top of the ramp.

"Dr. Fellows" appeared, scrubbed, benevolent, but slightly bloodshot.

"Come in! Come in! Ah, here's a tragedy! Poor little fellow! What's this? Are there more? Has it broken out again, then? I'm certainly glad I'm still here!"

As the distressed parents—strangely all male, this time, thronged up the ramp, and as Dr. Fellows and his somewhat bandaged assistant readied the merciful hypodermic needles, a large bat flitted across the clearing, scuttled over the forward main turret of the cruiser, hopped up into the launcher, and vanished inside.

"Welcome, welcome, children," Dr. Fellows was saying. "We'll have this cleared up in a—ah—*What*—"

Half-a-dozen big hunting dogs, with teeth like cougars, shot up the ramp.

Roberts shifted views on the spy screen.

Vank was suddenly tied up, his arms behind his back. "Dr. Fellows," the look of surprise still on his face, was done up in leather thongs. Down in the bowels of the ship, Mape, by pre-arranged policy staying away from the other two in case there *should* be trouble, was backing away from a batlike thing that had apparently come in through the open launcher slide. Mape's bafflement and distaste were evident on his face. But he had now, by staying calm, succeeded in maneuvering around it, to open the safety door that led to the corridor.

Outside in the corridor, a big hound on a leash whimpered briefly, and two roughly dressed men stepped forward. One rammed the muzzle of his gun in Mape's side. The other judiciously kept the gun muzzle out of Mape's reach, while his grip eased a little tighter on the trigger. A third held the dog, and eyed the bat.

Mape said sharply, "What's this? While the Doctor heals your pox, you stick up his ship?"

The dog was staring into the room beyond. The bat scuttled across the floor. The man holding the leash said, "Ungrateful, aren't we?"

The bat took off, flitted around in large circles, then shot out through the door, to settle very lightly on Mape's shoulder. Once there, the hideous thing raised a wing, and began to clean itself.

Mape was saying, "It would serve you right if Doc left the lot of you to die after this!"

The dog eyed the bat, and its jaw quivered.

One of the men cautiously reached up. The bat hissed and bared its teeth, then snuggled closer on Mape's shoulder.

Mape heard the hiss, felt the movement, looked around in surprise, and saw what was cuddling close to him.

The colonists snorted.

"Don't act like you never saw it before! Look how it cuddles up to him. Okay, you, start up the corridor. *Move!*"

Mape, the horror nestled beside him, its scratchy bristles against his neck as it made little happy chittering noises, swallowed hard and did as he was told.

As Roberts shifted scenes, Fellows, thoroughly trussed up, appeared, his expression hurt, his tones earnest.

"But, my dear young man, pox is *not* spread by the bite of an animal. And, even if it were, what have we to do with it? Ours is a humanitarian mission!"

"How is it," said a tall hard-eyed colonist, "that you've had bats going in and out of that raised chute overhead since before it got light out there?"

"I'm sure I don't know, if it is indeed true, and not an optical illusion. Certainly *we* are not responsible if local life-forms choose to land on our ship."

"They were going *in and out* the chute."

"If there were any such things, we know nothing of it. We were asleep. Rather than be disturbed by every mouse or chipmunk that might set foot on the ship, we had adjusted the intruder alarm to register only *human* or larger intruders. And these, we expected to treat as *guests.*" His tone was injured, it rang with sincerity.

The colonist said, "You don't know anything about these bats?"

"Nothing. If there are any such things, we have had nothing to do with them."

Mape was prodded into the room, the bat nestling on his shoulder, cleaning the underside of its wing.

"Well," said the colonist spokesman, "tell us, how do you explain *that?*"

Fellows stared at Mape, who shrugged helplessly.

"Euh—" said Fellows, looking at the bat. "Mape, my boy—surely *you're* not implicated in this—this—"

The bat spotted Fellows, gave a little chirrup of delight, took off, and landed on Fellows' shoulder. Fellows sat frozen.

The colonists delivered themselves of pithy expletives of disgust.

"Why," said Fellows, "It—ah—it's friendly. Surely, no harm could come from this—this friendly little cuddly creature?"

The thing peered over its shoulder, hissed and rattled its teeth at the colonists, spotted Vank, staring and perspiring, and at once made a chortling noise and deserted Fellows for Vank, who let out a yell and rolled around as the bat hopped lightly over him, making happy chirruping sounds.

"M'm," said the colonist spokesman, "*it* loves *him,* but he doesn't want it anywhere near him. Why is he afraid of the friendly little cuddly creature? Jim—if you'd just bring that sack up here—"

A colonist holding a leather sack stepped forward, opened the sack, and a hissing ball of rat-colored fur, clicking its teeth together, rolled out on the end of a cord, flapped across the floor, stopped, hissed all around, then saw the perspiring "Dr. Fellows." The thing gave a pathetic bleat, scuttled over, and huddled close, shivering.

"Fellows" began to shiver, himself.

"Oh," said a burly colonist. "He never *saw* the thing before."

Fellows glanced at Mape, who looked back ironically. He turned to Vank. Vank was out cold, with the monstrosity perched on his head. For the first time, Fellows noticed the dull glint of steel around its mouth.

"What's this," he said. "Does it have artificial teeth of some kind?"

The spokesman for the colonists put on leather gloves, grabbed the injured bat, and held it up.

"Here, take a good look, Fellows. You see the little hollow needle in the left side of its jaw, and the recurved needle in the right side? Do you think we're such dolts we can't figure this out? The left needle feeds from the left sack in that harness, and *it* will inject into whatever the bat tries to bite. The right needle feeds from the right sack, and it will flow back into the bat's mouth. The teeth are trimmed blunt and a little short, so they only give the bat the *sensation* of biting. The thing flies out of here, spots some poor fool worn out after a hard day's work, lying there asleep after telling his wife how lucky we are Doc Fellows is here to take care of the pox, and then this bat sent out by Dr. Fellows sets down lightly beside the poor fool, nips him in the neck with this hypodermic, which I suppose has some kind of anesthetic in it among other things, and as the bat bites, this little plunger on the hypo is shoved back and forth, and the little pump attached pumps air into the bag on the right side as well as the left, and warm blood or whatever is in that bag flows into the bat's mouth. When he's satisfied, the bat lets go, takes off, and comes back and goes to sleep for the night, or gets refilled and roosts in the trees, or however you've got him trained. But never mind. The main thing is, *now the colonist has been infected with the pox.*"

Fellows was speechless.

The colonist spokesman waited grimly.

Fellows said, "But—you can search the ship—" He paused, and looked worried. "Look—what would be the advantage to us of a thing like that? Why, my dear man, we have *cured* you! It would be utterly senseless to infect you merely in order to cure you. Although if we did—simply for the sake of argument—what would be the harm? If, through some accident, you had become infected through our agency, and we corrected the situation, could you blame us? Why, our good will is evident on the face of it! Surely this is obvious. You are cured, and it is we who have cured you! Now, untie us. Enough of this nonsense!"

The spokesman for the colonists glanced around.

"Any suggestions?"

A burly colonist with large hands said, "Heat up some irons. If that don't work I know a good stunt with water. None of you boys don't want to watch this, but stick around near, where you can hear what they say, and give me a hand, in case they go out of their heads. Kind of a mess there toward the end sometimes . . . I used to be a guard on one of them prison satellites. Wasn't my job, but I had to help out. I never thought it would come in useful, but you never can tell, can you? Just get me them irons and a blowtorch and a bucket of cold water."

Several of the colonists went out of the room.

Fellows swallowed and looked around. The only friendly thing in sight was the bat.

Mape spoke up. "*You* tell them, Fellows, or I'll tell them."

"How—"

The same burly colonist said, "Get them separate. We can check them against each other." He grunted. "Work hard all day, and then these sons put poisoned *bats* on us at night."

Fellows said desperately, "We *didn't*."

"Split 'em up. You got to play 'em together sometimes, and sometimes apart. We'll harmonize them."

There was a murmur amongst the colonists, and while it was impossible to say for sure what it might mean, Fellows said urgently, "*Mape!*"

"Right here," said Mape grimly.

"I'm going to tell them the complete facts, with nothing held back. You understand? I want you to do the same. If we had a chance, it would be different, but I don't want to play *this* hand to the end. Answer anything and stick to the truth. That's the only way we can get our stories to match. Do you follow?"

"I follow."

"I'll tell Vank the same when he comes around. All right, don't say any more till we're separated."

The burly colonist smiled faintly, but said nothing. Mape was hustled out, then Vank was jarred awake, listened to Fellows, and was lugged off to some other place.

Fellows, perspiring, said, "All right. Anything you want to know."

The spokesman for the colonists, his eyes hard, watched Fellows intently. "What was the purpose?"

Fellows took a deep breath.

"The cure was drugged."

"What do you mean, drugged?"

"The—the disease was pseudopox. The same symptoms and effects as real pox—but we could cure this by a simple injection. Only, in the injection was an *impurity*."

"An *impurity*. It was there on purpose?"

"Yes. On purpose."

"What did the impurity do?"

"The name of it is ecstatin. We used a very small concentration. It's exceptional in that it stays in the blood for about five to six weeks."

"Then what?"

"Then the last of it is excreted."

"What's the effect?"

"It makes a person more—more cheerful. Used in strong concentrations, it's lethal."

"All right. Come to the point. You used it in a light concentration. What harm did it do?"

"In itself, none, yet. But—ah—after it's all excreted, everyone who's had it will feel *depressed*."

"*How* depressed?"

"Almost to the point of suicide. It's a severe depression."

"What's the cure?"

"More ecstatin."

The colonist considered it.

"Let's be sure I get this. *First* you infected us with pseudopox?"

"Right."

"Then you cured us of the pseudopox, but injected *ecstatin* into us."

"That's it."

"Why not hit us with ecstatin to start with."

"We needed the pox first to explain the ecstatin later."

"How—"

"After we cured you of what apparently was the pox, we would be heroes. Right?"

"Yes. Sure. You *were*."

"*Then* the results of the ecstatin would show up. We would be shocked, stunned. We would check our instruments, find a trace of it, and checking back, we would discover that a supplier of plasma had unwittingly supplied us with a batch contaminated with ecstatin. Such things happen. You couldn't blame *us*. The supplier could hardly be blamed if the plasma came from a planet where there's been no known trouble with ecstatin. The only thing is—*now* you'd have to have more ecstatin!"

The colonist smiled with his mouth only.

Fellows hurried on.

"Now, on some planets, ecstatin is legal. On others, possession is punished by death. As it happens, in *this* region of space, there is no planet where it is legally supplied."

"I still don't get it."

Fellows gave a little laugh.

"The thing is—it's not *illegal* for us to supply you. You don't have any law one way or the other about it. But now you'd have a *need*."

"And *you'd supply it?*"

"Yes. And, of course, you'd be willing to pay well, because it would cost us so much to drop everything and go way off to where it *is* legally supplied, to get a supply for you."

The colonist put his hand to his chin.

"Of course, we wouldn't blame *you* for this."

"How could you? After all, thanks to the pox ploy first, we'd saved your lives."

"*Pox ploy.* Yeah. But—wait a minute. How is it we don't notice the effects of this ecstatin?"

"First, it's in so low a concentration. Second, naturally you're relieved to get over the pox. That makes you happy, which masks the effect of the drug. That's one reason we timed it to get here in the spring. If it hit you in the winter, you might wonder."

"So, you'd supply us with this stuff, at great expense, and we'd pay you. Where's the gain?"

Fellows looked blank a moment, then shocked.

"There's no great expense involved. Not for *us*."

"You just said you'd have to make a long trip—"

Fellows snorted.

"That's only how it would be if we *hadn't* planned. But, naturally, we're loaded up with ecstatin. We would go away for a time, after supplying you with enough to get by on out of our emergency chest. Then, *later*, we'd bring in the load, which you'd pay very steep for. But, you see, we wouldn't have been able to get all you needed on that one trip. *Something* would have gone wrong. We'd have to go back again. That would cost more."

The colonist squinted across the room. He gave a kind of low growl, and then shook his head.

"Each of these trips would take a long time."

"Right."

"But, you wouldn't actually *make* the trips?"

"No. That's just what we'd tell *you*."

"Then will you kindly tell me—What did you intend to do, stand around and *wait* between trips?"

Fellows looked incredulous.

"Don't you get it? We'd hit *other* planets!"

The colonist stared at him.

Fellows said, "Why stop here? It's a good game. We'd hit every colony planet at your level in the whole region.

"*What? With the same thing?*"

"Why not? We figured out a regular circuit. We'd milk maybe a dozen of you, then be right in time back at the first one to tell what a rough trip we had making it in with the last half-load, and how they raised the price on us because they knew we were in a hurry. We'd do the same act on each planet, and it would be just as good on one as another. Meanwhile you'd be killing yourselves working to get enough export to pay for the ecstatin. When you got self-governing, you'd vote the ecstatin legal because you'd *have* to, and we could sell the circuit at a good price to a regular dealer and he'd maybe crack the whole region open."

The colonist, with an effort, unclenched his fists. He looked away for a moment.

"Fellows," no longer with any detectable trace of his previous lovable grandfatherly air, said, "I'm telling you the truth."

The colonist let his breath out. "That's the only reason I haven't touched you."

"We'd have made a fortune on this."

"All right. Now explain to us about the bats. Where do you keep them? How do you feed them? How does *that* work?"

Roberts turned, to call Hammell, Morrissey, and Bergen. But they were already right there behind him, watching the screen wide-eyed.

On the screen, Fellows perspired, and gave a little laugh. "The bats—"

"The bats," said the colonist. "Come on, let's hear about *that*, too."

Fellows looked around and licked his lips.

Morrissey murmured, "Quite an interesting problem to explain something you can't understand yourself."

"Especially," agreed Roberts, "when there's somebody in the next room who doesn't understand it, and *he* has to explain it, too."

"So that the stories have to check afterward. Yes, that adds an extra dimension."

On the screen, Fellows was earnestly explaining, and the spokesman for the colonists irritatedly brushed the explanation aside.

"Listen, *friend*," he snarled, "we're just a collection of plodders. Never in a hundred years would we have thought of a scheme like this one. If you hadn't had a streak of bad luck, we'd never have seen any of your bats at work, and we'd *never* have caught on. It would have worked just as you say. But—"

"But," screamed Fellows, "we *didn't use bats!*"

The colonists murmured. Their spokesman pointed to the form curled up against Fellows.

Fellows opened his mouth, stared at the bat, and shut his mouth.

"Now," said the colonists' spokesman, "we are not going to be safe until we get rid of those things. We've already got pox victims and ecstatin addicts among us for no fault of their own. But there's no reason why the bats couldn't hit us with instant poison as well. We want the end of these bats. Now, don't tell us you didn't use them. *Tell us the truth!*"

Hammell grinned. "Did you notice how this bird was contemptuous of the colonists a little bit ago? He doesn't look contemptuous now."

Roberts nodded. "For someone willing to put twelve colony planets in a trap, he doesn't enjoy being in one himself. —Although, he's lucky to be alive."

Morrissey watched the screen.

"So *far.*"

Hammell bared his teeth, eyes focused on the screen.

Bergen looked serious, and Roberts winced.

The bat flew off, to momentarily provide a distraction.

Some minutes later, the symbiotic computer spoke cheerfully.

"The last of the quasibiological artifacts have been recovered, and our job here is now finished. The damage to this planet has been minimized. 'Dr. Fellows,' Mape, and Vank are now serving the beginning of their sentence as visited on them informally by the colonists, and if they ever get away from this planet, they will think twice before hitting another colony planet. This is a creditable achievement. There are, however, more planets in the vicinity in this same vulnerable stage of development."

Roberts guided the Interstellar Patrol ship rapidly up from the planet.

Bergen said, "I have a question."

"Proceed," said Roberts cheerfully.

"The *standard* way to handle this would have been to imprison Fellows and the rest, and provide special medical care for the colonists. Our way gave me a lot more satisfaction, but—how come we didn't do it the standard way?"

Roberts smiled.

"I imagine Fellows could get a lawyer who knows his way around in court, don't you?"

"Probably so."

"And suppose this lawyer is smarter than the prosecutor?"

"Well, if the evidence is overwhelming—"

Roberts shook his head.

"Fellows had *already* defeated, in advance, all the ordinary methods of applying justice. The Space Police, Space Force, P.D.A.—he'd gotten around the lot, and for all you and I know, he'd have gotten around the courts, too. At that, if it hadn't been for the bats, he would have ended up a *hero* to the colonists themselves. The bats were the unfair blow that did it for him.

"Now," Roberts went on, "there's the 'rule of law' and the there's the 'rule of men,' but both tend to work down to standard procedures, standard views, standard prejudices, and all this can generally be manipulated by a clever crook. But exactly how does the clever crook manipulate *what he can't understand himself?*"

Bergen rubbed his chin.

"I think I get it. They can't reduce the Interstellar Patrol to rule, so they can't figure a way around it."

Roberts nodded.

"The criminals we have to contend with couldn't care less for law. *Men* they respect a little more.

"But," he said, "what really gives them pause is the Unknown.

"That's where we make *our* contribution to Justice."

THE THRONE AND THE USURPER

In the moonlit fog, the gentle swell of the sea rolled past toward the beach. Straight ahead, there was a faint pale flash, as of a white robe peeled off and tossed on the sand. Then there was the flat splash of a swimmer hitting the water in a flying dive.

Vaughan Roberts, watching intently, was up to his chin in cold salt water. He gripped in his hands a flat smooth rock heavy enough to overcome his buoyancy, and breathed steadily and deeply. At the sound of the splash, still breathing deeply, he began to count, and when he reached ten, he ducked underwater, and let the rock take him down to the soft sand at the bottom. Methodically, he kept on counting. As he counted, mental pictures of what was taking place at the surface, where someone had just dived in for a moonlight swim, were suggested to him by the numbers of the count:

Fourteen. Not far from the swimmer, a small buoy-like object bobbed to the surface.

Fifteen. A puff of vapor escaped from the buoy into the fog.

Seventeen. The swimmer, breathing vapor, went slack in the water.

Eighteen. Flipper-like hands slipped a mask over the swimmer's nose and mouth.

Twenty. Other hands gripped the lower part of the slack body, and slid the swimmer under the surface.

Twenty-one. The buoy-like object dipped out of sight.

Twenty-five. The fog, drifting past, carried away some remaining traces of the rapidly decomposing vapor.

As Roberts counted, toward the moment when he could surface, his thoughts traveled back, and in his mind he snapped the spool from the viewer, to turn exasperatedly to the lean sector chief of operations, Colonel Valentine Sanders.

"Can't the Space Force put a bullet through this murderer's head?"

The colonel sat back.

"If they kill Lieutenant Gafonel, what happens to the 'exotic gases' last known to be in the lieutenant's possession?"

"Since he escaped from the courier ship to this resort planet, Idyll, it follows that the exotic gases aren't far from Idyll."

The colonel nodded, and clasped his hands behind his head.

"Remember, the courier ship itself has disappeared without a trace."

"Then the courier ship is somewhere on Idyll. If not, the Space Force should have located it."

"To know the rough general whereabouts of the ship doesn't solve the problem. The Space Force has got to recover the actual vials of gases. Even in their shock-proof cases, these are small and readily transportable. Contents unknown, each vial could be sold for a fortune. Used by someone who understood their properties from the beginning, the trouble they could cause is impossible to predict. And the only key to their whereabouts is Lieutenant Gafonel. The Space Force would doubtless like to put a bullet through the lieutenant's head. Unfortunately, he is the only link to that shipment. And they can't reach him, because he has them legally blocked. They can't even prove his story false without the courier ship for evidence, the ship has disappeared, and deduction suggests the ship is hidden where they can't go in and search. Where does that leave them?"

"He's still a deserter. They can get him on that."

"In the medical and legal situation the lieutenant has constructed, even *that* isn't any too clear." The colonel added, "Of course, what *actually* happened is obvious enough. But how do they prove it?"

"All right, then. Let them kidnap him and put the screws to him."

The colonel shook his head.

"The Space Force isn't set up to carry out illegal operations. And this resort planet, Idyll, is a fortress of legalities. It's a resort—a playground—mainly for the rich and influential. They, for their own purposes, have come to a mutually satisfactory understanding with the native inhabitants—the descendants of the original settlers—so that the planetary government—"

Roberts could feel the sticky spider-strands of legal logic start to descend on him, and spoke impatiently.

"Yes, sir. I know. But—"

"But," said the colonel, "this is the problem. The actual control of the planet's government has been left in the hands of the native inhabitants, who legally select a king to be titular head of the government. The king isn't necessarily one of their own number. Usually, they choose a rich and influential vacation-time resident. He, in turn, gives a lavish present to the natives. The wealthy resort-dwellers thus have a benevolent government which routinely provides law and order, but doesn't interfere otherwise. The natives have congenial work at good pay, plus bonuses from grateful tycoons who are tickled at the thought of being kings. The arrangement is mutually beneficial, *and legal.*"

Roberts massaged his chin.

The colonel, leaning back, hands clasped behind his close-cropped head, smiled faintly.

"Consider, Roberts, what will take place if the Space Force stages a raid on this planet, populated by vacationing influential people, including the heads of various governments, of giant business organizations, of huge universities—including retired officers and generals still on the active list. Suppose the Space Force says 'Legality be damned,' nails Gafonel in their midst, shoves the populace into a corner, and searches the planet for the missing ship? Where will the officers in charge of this operation ultimately end up?"

Roberts nodded slowly, "On an outdated destroyer, cataloguing asteroids by hand—if they're lucky."

"Exactly. And the search for the courier ship and gas capsules may be stopped before there are any results. You see, they *cannot* use force."

Roberts, exasperated, considered the lieutenant's record. Born on a frontier world, Gafonel had enlisted in the Space Force with a mental test score slightly above average. In service school he made an impressive record and tried to apply for admission to the Space Academy. His commanding officer arbitrarily refused. Soon, a black-market operation was traced to the commanding officer, who was sacked, and Gafonel went on to the Space Academy, where his scholastic record was dazzling. On graduation he married the daughter of the commandant and the commandant's estranged but wealthy wife. Then peculiar things began to happen.

The day following the wedding, the little sports flier carrying the lieutenant's rich new mother-in-law went up in a blinding flash, the cause of which proved hard to discover, since there wasn't much of anything left to examine.

The mother-in-law's fortune was willed, not to her estranged husband, but to her daughter.

The daughter promptly took a fatal overdose of sedative.

The mother-in-law's fortune passed on to the daughter's new husband—the lieutenant.

The lieutenant had a nervous breakdown and went into the hospital, to come out a tragic figure, brilliant but apparently unlucky, and incidentally rich.

In view of his brilliant scholastic record, he was put on the staff of the general in charge of chemical warfare research and development, who sent him as assistant to the major in charge of a shipment of exotic war gases, to be delivered to a distant base, aboard the ultrafast Space Force courier ship *Whippet*. The last thing heard about the *Whippet* was that a meteor shower had hit the ship at enormous velocity, and the lieutenant, inside but still wearing a tank suit in which he had been inspecting the hull, had been the only survivor to escape alive, in the ship's tender. The *Whippet* itself vanished without a trace.

Roberts shook his head.

"That s.o.b. is too tricky for subtleties. One good grenade dropped on him without warning—"

"That leaves the exotic gases unaccounted for."

"Yes, sir. But it would end *him,* and that might be more important in the long run. His record up to this business is tricky enough when you think it over. But this explanation about the courier ship—"

The colonel smiled. "A little hard to swallow, isn't it? It's almost superfluous to find that he had already, before the trip, transferred his wife's money to a bank on the resort planet."

"Yes, and on top of that, to have set it up for himself to be proclaimed 'king'—so that now he is King Oumourou, Head of State—"

Roberts ran out of words.

The colonel added drily, "Don't forget the 'retroactive amnesia,' Roberts. There would be no point questioning him anyway, because the dreadful experience destroyed his memory of everything connected with the event, soon after he gave his report. We have copies of the medical affidavits from Idyll certifying to *that*."

"He being the king of the place."

"Naturally."

"Sir, with a record like that, so far, what comes *next*? He's promoted himself from nobody on a remote planet to riches and kingship, with a shambles of betrayal and dead bodies behind him. Where does he go *next*?"

"He seems to be enjoying himself. He has his private mansion, plus the local palace, and a little sixteen-room cottage at the beach, a bank account running to seven figures, his private harem, two seagoing yachts—what more would he want?"

"He might feel cramped on just one planet. Meanwhile, there's no telling what he may try with these gas capsules."

"*That's* the problem."

"Why not warp him into a cooperative viewpoint with the want-generator?"

"It's a densely populated planet, and most of the time he's out of sight. To keep an emotional-field generator focused on him is impossible in this situation."

Roberts thought it over. "Then, when he goes for this habitual nightly swim of his, seeing the Space Force is bashful, suppose we drop down there some dark night, grab him, put the screws to him, and find out about these gas capsules."

The colonel beamed.

"Fine, Roberts. Now, that's more sensible than blowing his head off, isn't it? But after we find out where he's got the gas capsules, then we have the problem of doing something about it. His disappearance, of course, will cause an alarm locally. Isn't it better, from our viewpoint, if he *doesn't* disappear? In order to avoid that, our man, thoroughly disguised by our—ah—make-up department, could be right there to take his place and so be in a position to get the capsules. Now, Roberts, there isn't much time to waste, so we'll follow your plan at once, and since it's *your* suggestion—"

✤   ✤   ✤

Lungs straining, the cold water swirling around him, Roberts let go the rock and came to the surface. He sucked in a deep breath, exhaled, breathed again deeply, and swam for shore. He staggered out of the water, his feet sinking deeply in the wet sand, and strode up onto the beach.

Just ahead was that lighter patch where the "king" had tossed his robe.

Roberts crouched, to feel carefully around the robe. If Gafonel had been wearing a swimsuit when he was captured, it was to have been tossed here by the crew that captured him.

Finding nothing, Roberts shrugged into the robe and walked along the beach. His mental time-table told him these evening swims and strolls usually lasted about twenty minutes. This left plenty of time for the other members of Roberts' party to check and be sure this *was* Gafonel. If by some accident they had the wrong man, the precisely repeated call of a sea bird was to warn Roberts. Hearing no call, Roberts kept walking. He reminded himself that Gafonel's swim was usually followed by a hot, spiced drink and possibly a midnight frolic with the companion or companions of his choice. Considering Gafonel's position, this offered a wide selection. As Oumourou, the "native" king, there were the native girls to choose from. As the rich Gafonel, there were the non-native daughters of wealthy families on the resort world. As the proprietor of a cache of advanced gases of enormous price, there was still further bargaining power.

Roberts felt again the urge to plant a bullet in Gafonel's brain. But then he felt something else—uneasiness.

Considering the craft of his opponent, could his capture have been so easy?

Frowning, Roberts strolled back along the beach, belted the robe more tightly around him, and headed for the faint glimmer of light that his mental diagram told him was the beach mansion's so-called cabana. The light, mounted above the roof, offered little enough illumination outside and left the interior of the open building unlit.

Roberts paused just outside, and as the fog drifted past silently, there was a sense of distance and a not-quite-there sensation that vanished when he stepped forward, felt the cold flagstones under his feet, and then stubbed his toe on a flagstone set slightly higher than the rest.

He sucked in his breath, and somewhere to his left, there was a soft feminine laugh.

"Ooh—is Oumourou so impatient? Who is Oumourou impatient for?"

Roberts instantly recognized trouble.

In the fast preparation for this job, it had been found out that Gafonel's two favorites were a local girl named Dianai, and the vacationing daughter of a wealthy exporter, named Janine. Each was violently jealous of the other.

Since these were the two people most likely to spot the substitution, their appearance and known histories were all but imprinted on Roberts' brain. *But he didn't know their voices.*

Somewhere, the girl giggled.

Roberts peered around in the gloom. Now—was this Dianai, Janine, or some other member of Gafonel's harem?

She called softly, playfully, "Are you now so bashful? Tell me, who is Oumourou impatient for?"

All Roberts had to do was to give the wrong name, and there would be a volcanic eruption. In a rough whisper, he called, "Come here, and I'll show you."

There was a giggle, followed by the soft patting of bare feet on flagstone.

Her voice spoke out close at hand, in a faintly mocking, teasing tone.

"Does Oumourou want his mintmig?"

Mintmig was the local hot, spiced drink. But they didn't serve it here. They drank it in front of the fireplace in the beach mansion.

Roberts realized he was now up against some kind of private joke. It was almost as good as running into a prearranged code word, since a wrong guess would give him away.

He murmured, "Come close." That, at least, seemed safe.

There was a soft brushing sound and a faint scent of perfume.

Roberts stretched out a hand, to touch cool petal-soft skin.

An explosion of sparks burst across the sky. Darkness opened up, and he fell into it headlong. The awareness came to him dimly that he had not been out of the water half an hour before Gafonel's defenses stopped him cold. And that meant—but then the thoughts trailed out in a long, long thread, and then he lost track of them entirely.

Somewhere, there was a sound of voices, and now and then a snatch of conversation began to come across:

"... sure? The net didn't show ..."

"... remarkable, I know, but ..."

"... not a trace ... There's no chance he was rung in earlier?"

"No. It had to be the beach. And that fits the girl's story."

Roberts came awake with a painfully throbbing head, felt a light blanket over him, and a firm support under him. He tried carefully to move one limb after the other and discovered a gentle but increasingly firm restraint that drew his limbs solidly back where they had been to start with. Meanwhile, the conversation went on:

"Hard to see how it was done." The voice was slightly the deeper of the two. "The whole beach was wired. His approach *should* have showed on the board."

"Out of my field. But it suggests very sophisticated equipment."

"Well—I suppose we don't need to worry about it. As Supergaf says, 'Control the human element, and you control all.' When should we—"

"He's coming awake now. And I'd watch that 'Supergaf' routine."

"Listen, I—"

"It's not just that the *walls* have ears, you know."

"Every time I think of—"

"The thing to *think* is, we're well paid for our trouble."

"I suppose. Well—he's conscious. Let's deliver him."

Roberts heard footsteps approach, felt a sense of motion, and heard the hiss of tires. He opened his eyes, to see a bright-yellow tiled wall slide past, and shiny metal cabinets with glass fronts. Overhead, the ceiling was softly aglow. The air held a faint trace of antiseptic. The wheeled stretcher he was lying on approached a wall.

From behind Roberts, the deeper voice growled, "Next, the corridor."

A pair of metal doors slid past.

Roberts caught a glimpse, through a window, of a beach outside.

"Where are you taking me?"

"To see Mr. Gafonel—himself."

There was a mocking emphasis on the "himself" that brought a warning hiss from the other attendant.

The stretcher rolled into an elevator, and the door slid shut. The elevator plunged, slowed, accelerated horizontally, dropped again, accelerated sidewise, and finally slowed to a stop.

The stretcher rolled out on a platform.

Roberts, looking up, was treated to the sight of a ceiling pattern apparently made up of the muzzles of selected guns packed together vertically so that snouts of various types and sizes looked down on him in a regular pattern until the cot rolled past an open metal door into a small metal cubicle. Another door opened to one side, and the cot was rolled out, around corners and along inclined ramps whose changing directions suggested the approach to an ancient castle. Eventually, they emerged into a wide, high-ceilinged hall facing two oversize bronze doors topped by an enormous gold G. To either side stood an armed guard dressed in black with a gold G on his tunic.

The stretcher stopped before the door, and the two attendants stood tensely silent.

Slowly, the bronze doors swung open, and the stretcher wheeled forward through a high-ceilinged anteroom to a second set of doors that reflected in a dazzling golden glitter the brilliant light from a chandelier overhead. These doors, in turn, swung slowly open, the stretcher rolled forward, and Roberts found himself looking at a solitary crowned figure in silver and gold robes, seated on a purple throne atop a dais raised six steps above the floor.

A voice boomed out, *"Kneel to the Presence!"*

Roberts took a hard look at the crowned figure. Obviously, this was Gafonel. But, if this was Gafonel, then *who had been picked up at the beach?* Since no warning signal had been given, it followed that *that* had been Gafonel.

Either Gafonel was twins, or the Gafonel picked up at the beach had been a double. That fit in with snatches of conversation Roberts had overheard earlier. But, in that case, the double must have been *bait*.

The two attendants, meanwhile, had dropped to their knees. There was a brief silence as Gafonel looked at Roberts, and Roberts looked intently back.

Gafonel's lips moved slightly. *"Unbind the prisoner!"*

As the command boomed and reverberated, Roberts glanced around. There were no visible guards in the room—only Gafonel and the two attendants. Roberts relaxed his muscles. All he asked was to be let loose for a few minutes.

The two attendants straightened, and one said hesitantly, "Sir, this is a strong and dangerous man—"

Gafonel's lips moved slightly, and there was a crash like thunder. *"Obey or die!"*

The guards made haste to obey.

The cover was pulled off Roberts, and the webwork of bonds that held him to the stretcher was released. Roberts was swung to his feet.

"Remove the stretcher!" roared the voice. *"Withdraw from the Presence!"*

Roberts let go the light grip he had taken on the nearer attendant's sleeve.

The attendants turned and rolled the cart out the huge doors. The doors swung shut behind them.

Roberts turned to face Gafonel, and suddenly the situation made no sense. After installing himself in massive underground defenses, with a double in view for the opposition, would Gafonel risk capture alone at close range? Somehow, this must fit in with *Gafonel's* plan.

Roberts glanced around for any hint of hidden devices, and saw nothing—which, of course, was exactly what he could expect to see.

Gafonel, on the throne, watched Roberts intently.

Roberts, trying to fit bits of information together, could not find a pattern. Somewhere, there was a piece he didn't have. Meanwhile, precious seconds ticked past.

Gafonel rose smoothly from the throne and began to descend the six steps to the marble floor.

Roberts wearied of trying to untangle it mentally.

As Gafonel descended, Roberts walked toward him, testing his muscles and estimating distances as he walked. Somewhere, there ought to be a weak joint in Gafonel's setup. All this business with the throne, the crown, and the amplified voice—on a planet where kingship was a legal formality for sale to the highest bidder—it all suggested a case of galloping megalomania. That was *bound* to produce weaknesses.

As Roberts thought this, Gafonel removed his jeweled crown and tossed it.

"Here—the amplifier control goes with it."

Roberts at that instant got a favorable response to his estimate of time, distance, and muscular readiness, and sprang for Gafonel.

Gafonel snapped a short-barreled weapon from his silver-and-gold robes, and there was a faint *buzz*.

Roberts' left leg from the knee down went numb. As he broke the fall with his hands, his lower right leg also went numb.

Gafonel, smiling, put away the gun.

"Excellent reflexes. Impressive muscular conditioning. You have, of course, been consistently out-thought, but that is to be expected. What counts is that you are inherently loyal and tenaciously obedient to orders. Very good. Now, let's see . . . you are . . . yes, Vaughan Nathan Roberts, of the Interstellar Patrol. Rank of captain. Formerly captain of the fast transport *Orion*. Before that, in the Space Force, let go in the economy drive; earlier, special training in the Tactical Combat Command Advanced Training Center. All excellent. Now, how did you come to enter the Patrol? Let's see . . . h'm . . . Duke of Tresimere—what the devil! Earl of Aurizont? *Prince-Contestant to the—*"

Just what Gafonel was doing, Roberts didn't know. But his tone of voice showed confusion, his expression was momentarily dazed, and he was standing not far from where Roberts had hit the floor.

Roberts could ask for nothing more.

With his lower legs numb, he couldn't run. But he could so brace his feet and legs as to lay the foundation for one attempted spring. While Gafonel had talked, Roberts had positioned himself almost unconsciously. And now Gafonel showed confusion.

For a brief instant, Space Force close combat clashed with Interstellar Patrol close combat.

Then Roberts had the gun. Gafonel was laid out senseless.

Roberts paralyzed Gafonel's hands and feet, then laboriously swapped clothes with him.

Now, so far as any uninitiated onlooker could tell, Roberts was the wealthy Gafonel, king of the planet, and Gafonel was the infiltrating impersonator, Roberts.

This was more like it. But it occurred to Roberts to wonder about the other double, picked up at the beach.

So far, counting himself, there were *three* Gafonel's. Could there be more? How could he be sure this was the *real* Gafonel?

There was a low moan, and the figure in the pajamas opened his eyes.

Roberts aimed the gun.

Gafonel's eyes glittered.

Roberts watched alertly.

Now, anger suggested a failure of plans. Perhaps, this *was* Gafonel.

"Excellent weaponry," said Roberts pleasantly. "Impressive fortifications. You have, of course, been consistently out-reflexed, but that is to be expected. Keep your voice low, or I'll give you a dose of this in the vocal cords."

Gafonel tried to grope at one of the wide blocks that formed the floor and discovered that his hands were numb. He looked at Roberts with a fairly sick expression.

Roberts, groping for the next move, ran into the fact he was still in an underground fortress. Before he could act with confidence, it would be necessary to get a little more information.

Before Roberts' eyes, Gafonel's sick expression evolved into a look of assurance.

Roberts glanced around. Save for the two of them, the room was still empty. What had caused this change of attitude? Considering that this was Gafonel's own place, paralyzing hands and feet might not be enough. It might be a good idea to—

Awkwardly, Gafonel sat up.

"It fires a cone, not a beam. You've already paralyzed my arms halfway to the elbow."

Roberts considered this reply to an unspoken thought.

Gafonel said, "What I can't understand, Roberts, is that you, with your want-generator, *could,* in all truth, have become the ruler of an empire. You *were* the ruler! And yet—you gave it up, stepped back—" He looked at Roberts intently. "*Why,* Roberts?"

Roberts stared at him.

Gafonel, his expression intent, hesitated a moment, then went on. "Yes, I see, you assumed the rank merely to do a job—to save the inhabitants from a serious difficulty. But you had the means, as you well knew, to expand the control you exercised—After all, with a device that controls *desires,* you could ultimately have gained control of the whole human system. Wherever you could put the device, there you could exercise control."

Without Roberts saying a word, Gafonel was following his thoughts.

Abruptly, Roberts had the missing piece, and everything else fit together.

In his mind's eye, Roberts could see Gafonel's record in a new light. The first ordinary mental test, the bright record among bright students in service school, the sacked commanding officer who had made the mistake of getting in Gafonel's way, the dazzling record among the elite at the Space Academy, the murdered mother-in-law, the murdered wife, the slaughtered crew of the courier ship—all steps in a staircase to power, built by an unscrupulous—

Gafonel interrupted. "You don't understand, Roberts. The jailing of that jackass commanding officer, the explosion of the sports flyer, that overdose of sleeping pills, and the premature departure of the crew of that courier ship—this was not murder and betrayal. When you kill a chicken, Roberts, that is not murder. When you select a watchdog, that is not friendship. Murder and friendship imply some equality of biological status. A man does not murder a weed, or a mosquito. He *swats* the mosquito, and *uproots* the weed. Similarly, the spanking of a child is not assault and battery. Again, there is no equality of biological status—only a potential equality. So you see, Roberts, you would not be justified in pulling that trigger. Quite the contrary. You—"

With a very faint tingle, the paralysis was gone from Roberts' legs, first the left one, then a moment later the right one.

It dawned on him that this flood of words was at least partly meant as a distraction.

"Right, Roberts," said Gafonel. A moment later, he added, "Yes, it was irrational for me to risk this situation. I did it because you are important to a plan I have in mind. And I suppose I overrated my special talent. But now you are underrating it. Remember, Roberts, there is not always so much difference between the man at the top and the man at the bottom. It takes only a very slight advantage, compounded again and again at every turn, to produce an ultimately very large difference in position. And this present position is a mere stepping stone, Roberts. What amazes me is that you have already had the opportunity that is now mine, and you set it aside. *Why?* This device your friend stumbled on—this want-generator—with that you could ultimately have ruled the universe. Even I, with my talent, would have become your loyal follower. Why *not,* Roberts?"

Roberts could feel an intense desire to end this conversation. Unfortunately, there was still the question of the chemical gases.

"Yes, Roberts," said Gafonel. "Well, I will gladly show you those gases—"

How many minutes had passed since Roberts paralyzed Gafonel's hands?

Roberts raised the gun.

Gafonel's hand, resting on an apparently blank block, suddenly moved.

The whole room seemed to explode in a dazzling flash.

Then, once again, Roberts was aware of the vague sound of a voice.

" . . . not necessary. Just . . . "

" . . . sir . . . "

Roberts lay still. He was flat on his back, apparently this time on a mat thrown on some hard flat surface. He opened his eyes, to see a row of vertical bars, extending from floor to ceiling.

"Right." Gafonel's now familiar voice spoke with satisfaction. "You are in a cell, Roberts. It will do you no good to lie there with your eyes half shut. I was aware of your thought the instant you came partly awake. It isn't necessary even for you to be fully conscious of the thought yourself. No, you cannot deceive me indefinitely by refusing to think. I repeat, I detect not only the thoughts you are actually thinking—consciously—but others that are somewhat below the surface. Ordinarily, I can follow certain mental paths, frequently used, with ease. In your case, there has been a very evident attempt to deceive me, by superimposing on your habitual thought patterns, another layer that is completely irrelevant. This is somewhat puzzling, but nevertheless, I can penetrate it."

Roberts started to speak, but changed his mind. The voice answered his unspoken thought.

"No, you are not aware of this special treatment. Of course not. If you had been aware of it, I would immediately have known the answer. As it is, I am somewhat slowed by the deception. There is no mental link in your mind to classify this other layer of latent thoughts as fantasy. It is a remarkable effect. But I accept the Interstellar Patrol as an opponent of merit. Think how much more effective the Patrol will be, Roberts, when *I* control it."

Roberts felt a wave of negation and disgust, that was impossible to conceal.

There was a brief silence, and then Gafonel spoke in a slower and more serious voice.

"My apologies, Roberts. I realize that it is inexcusable for me to toy with you. Let me restate what I have just said: The Patrol may operate more effectively under the guidance of my special talent, to our mutual advantage."

Roberts kept a careful grip on himself. It came to him that, among other things, he was now being used for a sounding board.

"Right, Roberts," said the voice.

Roberts sat up.

Gafonel said humorously, "Not a promising view, is it, Roberts?"

From ceiling to floor, a ring of vertical bars surrounded Roberts. He was on a folded white blanket on a pale-brown tile floor that stretched beyond the bars to another row of bright vertical bars. This second row reached straight across the room from one wall to the other. On the far side of the room, beyond the straight row of bars, stood Gafonel, wearing a close-fitting dark-purple garment, with a wide black belt and two holstered guns.

To get to the telepath, Roberts had to somehow get past two sets of bars, and when he got there, he would be unarmed, and Gafonel would have a gun in each hand—and would know in advance every move Roberts planned to make.

Gafonel chuckled.

Looking around at this setup and then back at the telepath, Roberts realized that everything in this place cost money. Enormous sums of money. Just how rich had the telepath's mother-in-law been? Or was he just one member—perhaps the tool—of a combine of extremely rich individuals seeking to infiltrate the Patrol for their own ends?

Gafonel said quietly, "No, not a member or a tool, Roberts. The leader. You see, you still don't appreciate the advantage conferred on me by my—special ability. What do you suppose it means, for instance, to be able to talk with an expert and to be able to follow, not only his words, but nearly *his complete process of thought?* The ultimate result of such experiences is a mental advantage, completely apart from telepathy as such. What does it mean to grapple with a close-combat expert and share his sense of balance and an awareness of the sequence of his moves? The result is a swift understanding of his purposes that would ordinarily take a long time to acquire. What does it mean to take a sum of money to a broker and to know his actual thoughts at the same time as his recommendations? What does it mean to go to a financier and follow his thought processes, his intuitions, his basic structure of general and specific observations about his own experiences and those of others. What does it mean to make a suggestion and know at once the true underlying reasons for the responses of others? Now, you see, these and other advantages, Roberts, result from the one basic talent. But the resulting mental and material advantages in time become so great that—even without the talent—these other advantages, taken by themselves, would still be formidable. After you learn enough from others, you have the knowledge yourself. No, the evidence of wealth you see around you is not derived from anyone else, though it is true that I need the *cooperation* of others—and pay well for their services. I am in a position to pay well. Consider that, Roberts."

Roberts, again wearing the cotton pajamas, came to his feet, aware of the cold tiles underfoot as he methodically tested the bars. Each one was solid.

Gafonel said thoughtfully, "There's no way out of there, Roberts. I am surprised to see a member of the Interstellar Patrol refuse to accept the self-evident."

Roberts didn't answer, and kept moving.

The tile floor also was solid.

Roberts swiftly climbed the bars and struck the ceiling with his fist. Flakes of paint fell off. Cracks shot out from the place he had struck. He struck it again. A chunk of plaster fell off, uncovering a flat metal box bearing short cylinders, one with a lens at the end. Roberts wrenched the box loose, saw a couple of dangling wires, and touched the ends.

There was a dazzling spark. The lights in the room went out.

Above Roberts was a square hole through which light shone dimly. Roberts shifted grips on the bars, reached up, caught an edge, and squeezed himself up through the hole.

Gafonel's voice reached Roberts from below.

"My guards are on the way, Roberts! Don't move!"

A quick glance showed Roberts that he was in an access space, completely unfinished, that provided room for cables, air ducts, pipes, and wires, which looped and crisscrossed around him. A heavy flanged metal plate the size of the hole Roberts had come through leaned against a brace nearby. The dim light in the access space came from an overhead luminous panel about five feet away. A walk, of rough boards, extended past the hole in the direction of another luminous panel some thirty feet away. Beyond that, other panels lit more distant spaces.

Roberts seized the heavy metal plate, pictured himself diving behind the plate toward the sound of Gafonel's voice, and heaved the plate. The heavy plate tore loose a chunk of ceiling, and narrow lines of light slashed up as Gafonel fired from below.

Roberts screamed, pictured himself clawing for support, and simultaneously jumped.

He plunged into darkness, and one arm brushed cloth. That was all he needed.

A few minutes later, the lights in the room came back on. The door to the corridor burst open.

Roberts glanced down at the battered figure in cotton pajamas, shook his head, and glanced around as two guards in black burst into the room, guns in hand.

Roberts raised one arm, clothed in dark-purple velvet, and pointed to the circle of bars across the room.

"He went up those bars, smashed through the ceiling, got into the access space, and dove through the ceiling here. Thanks to someone's carelessness, there might have been trouble."

One of the guards glanced at the heap on the floor, looked around at the hole in the ceiling, and swallowed.

"We don't—"

"I know. Go get medical help."

The guard stepped back, saluted, whirled, and ran out down the corridor. The other guard swallowed, stepped back, saluted, and shut the door, to stand on guard outside.

Roberts glanced around the room. He still had no idea where to find the exotic gases.

There was a sound of running feet, and the door opened again.

The two—attendants?—who had taken care of him at first stood nervously on the threshold.

Roberts adopted Gafonel's arbitrary manner and gestured to the one who had expressed criticism of "Supergaf."

"You, come in." He glanced at the other. "Close the door and wait outside."

The attendant came in warily. Roberts glanced at the motionless form on the floor.

"Examine him."

Frowning, the attendant knelt. After a few moments silence, he looked up.

"He's in pretty bad shape. However, he'll live. He should regain consciousness soon and be available for further questioning."

There was a faint hint of reproach in the voice, and Roberts wondered how well he could imitate the telepath. Coldly, he said, "Spare me your mental criticism."

The attendant stood up. He said tightly, "Is that all you want, sir?"

"No," Roberts said, "Your thoughts are *not* your own."

"Damn it! Keep out of my—"

Roberts stepped forward and clapped a hand over the attendant's mouth, turning him at the same moment so that he was off balance and ready to be thrown to the floor.

"No argument! If you want mental privacy, *do your job!* You haven't examined this man carefully. Now, do a *thorough* examination!"

The attendant, looking dazed, knelt again at the crumpled figure. He felt carefully of the limbs, caught his breath, and felt very thoroughly of the skull. After a moment's silence, he looked wide-eyed at Roberts, glanced around, and motioned toward a spot further from the door. He spoke in a whisper.

"How did you do it?"

"Where are the surveillance devices?"

"None in this end of the room. There was a combination bug-and-execution-box over the cell. There's nothing here."

"How can you be sure?"

"I helped put in the system. Gafonel didn't want things that could be used to spy on *him*. How did you get him?"

"Who designed that cage?"

"Not me. Why?"

"There was an opening in the ceiling to service this combination box you spoke of. The plate above that opening was left loose. That gave a clear path into the access space and down on his head."

"Good. I tried to tell the fool you were tough."

"What's your job here?"

"Electrical installation to start with. Now I mostly help with first aid. I took medic's training in the Space Force but got out because I wanted to be on my own. I never thought I'd end up in an outfit where there was no privacy even in your own head."

"Any other dissatisfied followers?"

"Those that aren't scared are dissatisfied."

"Why?"

"There's no team sense. We're trained animals. The boss is the next stage in evolution beyond the human. All that holds this outfit together is fear and money."

"What about his girls?"

"That I don't know. He has a unique advantage there, I guess. On the other hand—" He shook his head. "I don't know."

"Who is his most trusted collaborator?"

"Supergaf has no trusted collaborators. You only collaborate accidentally, when he picks your brains—or else purely for hire."

"How about his rich associates?"

"That's above my level. But I don't think they're associates. More likely customers or subordinates."

"And the guards?"

"They'll obey, if they recognize him. I guess they're as loyal as any you can buy."

Roberts considered the situation in silence and glanced at the crumpled heap at his feet.

"Will the other medic notice what you've noticed? And, if so, what will he do?"

"He's more likely to notice than I was. As for what he'll do—if there's money in it, and no danger, he'll do whatever he's told, as far as I can see."

"Anything Gafonel tells him?"

"Or whoever else pays his wages. As for myself, I'm fed up. I won't kill him. But if you want to finish it and take over, I'll just step outside, and keep my mouth shut. Then the outfit will be all yours."

Roberts nodded thoughtfully. The picture was clearer, but he still had no idea where to find the missing gases. He glanced at the attendant.

"How did the girl in the cabana know there'd been a substitution?"

"She's one of his guards. He's the only one who can touch a finger to his girls—and since he's a telepath, there's no cheating. None of the girls know at the time, when he goes on this walk and swim of his, whether it's Supergaf or, more likely, his double. But when he comes back, they challenge him and think of the answer they want him to give. Supergaf, being a telepath, can give it. The double can't. You didn't give the answer, so you weren't Supergaf. You did call the girl over and put a hand on her—which the double would have been afraid to do, knowing the telepath would find out. She therefore knew you were an intruder."

Roberts considered the explanation. As Gafonel had pointed out, there were more advantages to his particular skill than appeared on the surface.

"Are you familiar with any of Gafonel's recent operations?"

"No. There's no gossip. No rumors. He'd trace any leak back to the source and eliminate it. There was plenty of talk about this Space Force ship he was supposed to have hijacked, but that was at the beginning. It wasn't actually so long ago, but it's decades away in attitudes. All speculation ended once he put out the red-hot tongs and made an example. We don't even *think* about any of his possible operations. Personally, I just take it for granted he wants to take over the universe, and let it go at that. Why, is there something you need—some evidence—some stolen device from that Space Force ship?"

"Yes."

"Sorry, but I don't know anything about it. I don't think there's anyone who *would* know. There's another thing. Information flows from us to him. All that flows back is orders. And pay, I'll grant him that."

"Is there any safe room, any strong point, anything like a citadel in this fortress of his?"

"Yes, his own quarters."

"How do I get to them?"

"We aren't far away right now. Go out this door and turn left. At the end, the corridor turns right, then left again, and goes on to an elevator that's never used. It may be a dummy. When you turn right at that first corner, place your hand flat against the wall, anywhere just around that first corner. I'm not clear how it works but if you're as close a double as you seem, it *might* open for you."

"Worth a try. All right, get your helper—"

"I'm *his* helper. He'll wonder why you singled me out to talk to."

Roberts gestured to the ripped ceiling.

"About improving the surveillance system. I'm boiling mad about this incident. This double here, on the floor, has a distinct trace of telepathic talent, and to an extent, he can seize control of your faculties if you're in physical contact with him. He's dangerous and belongs to an organization that I—Gafonel—am in a tough fight with. We need to tighten up internal security, and I'll want to see you again to go into further detail. How does that sound?"

The attendant nodded approvingly.

"That should do it. Okay, we'll try to get this interloper tied down where he can't do any more damage."

The wall, when Roberts placed his right hand flat against it, at once opened up, the left-hand section rolling back to reveal a curving high-arched doorway.

Roberts looked at beveled foot-thick edges of exactly matching steel surfaces and thought of that access space above the bars. If he had seen what he thought he had seen, that access space extended above even this ultimate stronghold.

What was the point of a foot-thick wall, with a paper-thin ceiling above it?

Roberts, frowning, stepped into a small, luxuriously paneled foyer with Gafonel's initial, the letter G, in gold, inset in the center of each panel. Behind him, the corridor opening whispered shut. He pushed open the door leading into the apartment and found himself in a kind of living room paneled from waist height to ceiling with mirrors. Below the mirrors was a border of small interlinked G's. On the ceiling was a crowned golden G surrounded by shining rays of gold leaf. The door to the next room bore a full-length mirror under a crowned G. There were G's on the doorknobs, the cabinet handles, the rugs, bedspreads, sofa cushions, draperies, bathroom tiles, shower curtains, bath mats, and around the edge of the sunken oversize tub. There were G's in all styles, in silver and gold, in royal purple, jeweled, and bordered with pearls and diamonds. One often-repeated favorite was made of a black, glistening stone with a surface that shimmered and glinted so that from certain angles the G seemed to stand out from the wall and hang in space.

Where there were no G's, there were mirrors, and Roberts looked around, irritated at the multiplied reflections.

Where, in this palace of self-worship, was there any place where the canisters of exotic gases could be hidden?

He pulled open drawers, to find towels and blankets marked with G's. He opened closets, to find jackets with crowned G's, and robes bearing G's in wreaths. He knelt to glance under an oversize bed with G on the coverlet and found a pair of bedroom slippers ornamented with tiny gold G's running around the sides, to form a pattern of bouquets of flowers with a crowned G at the toe.

Roberts searched the whole place and found nothing resembling the Space Force's missing gases.

Then there came a sudden rending sound, and Gafonel's voice warned, *"Don't move!"*

This time, when Roberts came awake, he was simultaneously aware of the headache and of tight bands that gripped him despite the fact that he seemed to be spiraling over and around at the same time, as if lashed to a turning spit on a merry-go-round.

He opened his eyes a slit, and the whirling dizziness faded to an illusion of sidewise rotation that was mild by comparison.

The light was dim. Wherever he was, it was cold. He could see a wall of small glass doors, rotating slowly but steadily, and then his own rotation somehow synchronized with the rotation of these glass doors, and both were uneasily still.

Roberts came fully awake and realized that he was lashed to pipes in a gray, dimly lit, refrigerated room.

"So, Roberts—" Gafonel's voice had a grim quality—"you are conscious again."

Roberts carefully began to test his bonds.

Instantly, there was the sound of footsteps, followed by a *buzz-buzz.*

Roberts' right arm and leg went numb.

"This time, Roberts," said Gafonel, with a faint tone of regret, "the trip will be final. After this, I will have no further unbiased opinion from you. But it will all be for your own good."

Roberts continued testing his bonds with his left hand.

Gafonel stood studying him with a peculiar expression.

The paralysis time, Roberts was thinking, was about ten minutes. The glass in the little doors in that wall would break, to make cutting edges. If these pipes the rope was fastened to were thin enough, it might be possible to squeeze them together and get a little slack in the rope. Did the pipes run straight from ceiling to floor? If so, they would squeeze together more easily from a standing position. The pipe was wet with condensation. It was small diameter piping. That water would lubricate his wrists. What type of rope? This pipe had a rough spot. Would the rope chafe? Here was a pipe union with a projecting edge that felt sharp. What was the floor made out of? Suppose he stood up and heaved against the ropes? Would the pipes bend? It looked as if there were only two lights in the room. There was a switch box on the wall. Put the lights out, and then what? Was Gafonel's telepathy directional? Doubtful. What's behind those glass doors? Would Gafonel dare use anything but that paralysis weapon?

Aloud, Roberts was saying, "I suppose so. It looks like you've got me this time. How did you get away from the attendants?"

Gafonel, scowling, walked around to Roberts' left side, and raised the gun. *Buzz. Buzz-buzz.*

"Pardon me, Roberts. If you are a fair sample of the Interstellar Patrol, I can see the futility of trying to *persuade* the Patrol to cooperate with me."

Roberts looked around, to see that he was near a bend in the rear wall of the room. To his left was a partly open door, looking into the paneled foyer he had entered on going into Gafonel's apartment. The "foyer" must actually be—

"Correct, Roberts," said Gafonel. "It is an elevator. And you are paralyzed hand and foot, arm and leg. Whatever plan your mind may create, you cannot carry it out in *that* situation. I have to admit, my experiences with you have given me a respect for the power of determination and fast action, even with a blind mind—"

"A *what?*" said Roberts.

"A blind mind, Roberts. A mind imprisoned in a cage of bone, unable to reach out and share the thought of other minds."

"That's an inaccurate comparison. A *lone* mind is what you mean. And this *loneness* can be overcome in quite a number of ways."

"Who are you to—"

"Inaccurate comparisons," said Roberts, who had ten minutes to use up, "lead to inaccurate thinking. Inaccurate thinking leads to blundering. Blunderers aren't equipped to rule the universe simply because they have a useful special ability, the lack of which was already fairly well compensated for even before the rise of technology."

Gafonel said grimly, "Nevertheless, I *will* rule. Bear in mind that I am younger than you. I have time to learn. *You* have missed your chance."

"What chance?"

"Your chance to truly be king and emperor. King and emperor of the *universe*, Roberts!"

"And have chains of my own gold R's running around the mirrors in my palace?"

Gafonel stiffened.

Roberts said, "The justification for rank is superior insight and ability. For a person with rank to dwell on the glory of his rank warps his insight and saps his ability. It undermines the justification for his possession of the rank. For me to be a duke, on a backward planet, was justifiable. Only by assuming that rank could I have the authority to get the planet out of the mess it was in. To seize the same authority over equals and superiors, when there was no need, would have been unjustifiable. It would have ended up as a case of self-glorification, which is poison. When you tell me I missed my chance, what you say is that I had the opportunity to get drunk on poison, and passed up the chance. Well—I can't say I miss it."

Gafonel frowned. "This may hold for you, but I—"

"We were talking about me, remember?"

"Nevertheless, I *do* have superiority. I see your point, Roberts. It was well for you not to claim the kingship. *My* situation is different."

"When you feel the power running through your veins and start spending time thinking how impressed other people are with you, look out. Your special ability is limited, and you can't use it properly while meditating on your own glory. The fact that you glorify yourself demonstrates a lack of insight, regardless of your special ability."

Gafonel turned away. After a considerable silence, he opened two doors in his wall of small glass doors and took out two squat metal containers, each one a little smaller than a man's clenched fist. One of these containers was dark purple. The other was diagonally striped, black and silver. Gafonel walked over towards Roberts and set the two containers on the floor, well out of Roberts' reach.

"The Patrol, Roberts, is a shrewd and somewhat baffling opponent. I will admit, if I possessed *only* my special ability, I would be at a loss how to approach the Patrol, although it offers an ideal instrument for a ruler. But, as I have explained, a special ability such as mine is not just a thing in itself, merely *added* to other abilities, like a new pistol added to an arsenal of guns. That is not it. Such an ability *compounds at every turn my other abilities*. Mentally, socially, financially, I am far stronger than you imagine. The contest between us has been physical, so you do not appreciate this point. The self-glorification you sneer at induces an 'aura of power' that has a highly effective reaction on many people. When it does not work, I need merely switch it off, because *I instantly know the effect I am creating*. Now, to seize control of the Patrol, or of any segment of it, would be nearly impossible by my special skill alone. It would even be difficult with this skill plus my other abilities. But—this skill gives access to yet other resources. Do you follow me?"

"I see the point. The trouble is, a king can't judge the worth of an approach solely by how it impresses other people. As for this 'access to other resources'—you mean the 'exotic gases'?"

Gafonel glanced at the two roughly fist-sized containers on the floor.

"Among other things. The Patrol obviously has some interesting devices. But so does the rest of civilization. You realize that the usual aim of the Space Force, for instance, is maximum effect with minimum loss of life. This purple container, Roberts, contains a minute proportion of the gas that was in a storage vial from the *Whippet's* shipment. When this container is sprayed at you, you will become totally attentive. You will hear, and believe, whatever I say to you. It is the *command chemical*. From that time forward, if I so direct, you will be my obedient subordinate. Unlike the Space Force, I will not later release you from this obedient state, nor will I release the other members of the Patrol as I extend my control over *them.*"

There was a lengthy pause, in which Roberts kept a tight hold on his mental responses.

Gafonel went on.

"No, Roberts, the fact that the Patrol has a kind of partial computer control will not nullify the effect of human loyalty to me. Not at all. Because the computer will be eliminated, subject to its realignment in accordance with my own aims."

He raised the diagonally striped black-and-silver container.

"You see, the Space Force, too, faces the difficulty of computer-directed defense systems. A surprisingly small concentration of this gas in the atmosphere will find its way through any crevice or opening into no matter how effective a computer, to start a reaction—and that is all that is needed, just the *start* of that reaction. This is another 'tailored chemical,' Roberts. The computer's essential internal elements will suffer a change which will render them inoperative. The computer will break down. Then only the *human* component remains to be considered. The command chemical will decide that battle."

There was a silence as Roberts considered it.

"You have the problem of getting it there."

"True. And here I have a considerable advantage. You see, Roberts, I can instantly detect the difference between the deceptive product of advanced robotics and an actual human, while there is some delay before the Patrol can detect the same difference. When you came ashore, my 'double,' so-called, was captured. This 'double' was a highly specialized robotic product which sensed the alteration in the atmosphere, lay still, and sensed the arrival of the Patrolmen who sought to capture it.

"Your patrol ship, I admit, skillfully neutralized my warning system, but that didn't matter. My robotic bait, an outwardly exact replica of myself, with my own voice, appeared to regain consciousness, surfaced, and in the resulting violent and unexpected struggle, *released the command chemical and stated the basic requirements of obedience to me.* The three members of the Interstellar Patrol became my loyal subjects, just as you will, Roberts, before I am through. They made a slight delay, to report to me on the beach shortly after you were captured. They returned to your patrol ship with their 'prisoner' and their own stocks of the obedience chemical. I was flattered to learn from them that an Interstellar Patrol dreadnought was close at hand, especially to take care of me. This short distance made the return of the patrol ship to the dreadnought a brief trip. So, you see, Roberts, the plan has already been put into action."

Gafonel straightened and watched Roberts intently.

Roberts, as he had intended, had now forgotten everything but this conversation. Frowning, he tried to estimate the chances of the plan for succeeding, and at once ran head-on into the fact that the Patrol was very sparing with information. No one, for instance, had ever explained to Roberts the functioning of the dreadnought's air system. No one had mentioned the location of what must be a master computer of some kind. That there was a type of monitor system that watched activity throughout the ship, he knew, as he had used it—but how did it work? No one had tried to prevent him from learning these details. But no one had volunteered the information. If he wished to spend his free time delving into mountains of facts, that was his business.

He hadn't done it.

He therefore had no way to know if Gafonel's plan would work.

Gafonel watched him, frowning.

Roberts shook his head.

Gafonel said, "The commands on the dreadnought were to be given in the guise of a joke, Roberts. One of my men would approach one of the as-yet-unconvinced members of the Patrol, motion to him, and say, smiling, 'Have you heard the one about the Space Force general?' My man would then show a small star made of very thin silvery paper impregnated with the command chemical and having a faint minty fragrance. He would whisper the command in the ear of his 'recruit,' who, meanwhile, aware of the mint aroma, would sniff curiously and absorb the chemical. My man would give the new recruit a small stock of the impregnated stars, with instruction to pass some on to each person he tells the joke to. One of the whispered commands, by the way, instructs the new recruit to laugh uproariously at the conclusion of the whispered 'joke.' Would your symbiotic computer interfere with a private joke, Roberts?"

"I don't know." Roberts glanced at the wall across the room. "Is that filled up with all the exotic chemicals?"

"Yes. We are in a place where no one can reach them but myself."

Roberts said drily, "I suppose these two chemicals are just a sample?"

"That's right. The entire shipment is right here under my thumb, immune to any outside attack and a source of fantastically varied power, or—if I choose to trade it—wealth."

Roberts was only dimly aware of numbness going out of his right arm and leg, then a few moments later, out of his left arm and leg. His mind was still grappling with the problem as all the numbness evaporated, and his reflexes, like an alarm clock set beforehand, suddenly triggered his body into action.

The ropes slid as Roberts thrust himself upright, sucked in an enormous breath, braced arm and shoulder muscles against the rope—

Gafonel jerked the gun up.

Roberts' legs swung up from the waist, his outstretched feet jarring the gun barrel upward. There was a sudden yielding of the rope that held him, and Roberts dropped, catching himself awkwardly as his feet fell, his back still against the pipes.

Gafonel sprang back, well out of reach.

Roberts threw the tangle of suddenly loose ropes over his head and dove for the squat purple can.

There was a buzzing sound, and Roberts' right arm went numb.

There was another buzz. And another, and another.

Roberts sucked in a deep breath as if to hurl himself across the floor by sheer strength of will.

Gafonel, shaken, grasped at the purple can, aimed it at Roberts, and pressed the plunger. He shouted, "You will obey my orders! *I am the king!*

Roberts blanked his mind and lay motionless, unbreathing.

Gafonel, breathing hard, suddenly gasped.

Roberts raised his head, to see the triumph on Gafonel's face change to shock.

Roberts let out his hoarded breath:

"YOU WILL OBEY *MY* EVERY COMMAND! KNEEL NOW, SILENT AND MOTIONLESS, TILL I STATE MY WILL!"

Gafonel's face went blank. He dropped to one knee and, head bowed, waited like a statue.

Roberts sucked in a breath, aware of a faint scent and a sudden blank-minded eagerness to please. All that was necessary now was for someone, anyone, to state a command. Roberts would dutifully obey.

But no one else was there except Gafonel.

And Gafonel knelt, silent and motionless, as the air slowly cleared.

When the numbness passed, Roberts got to his feet.

A day and a half later, Roberts again faced the chief of O-Branch.

"Sir," said Roberts, "with all due respect, if I had some idea what was going on now and then, I think I could do a better job."

The colonel leaned back behind his desk, smiling. "Well, Roberts, we trust your power to improvise. Any *plan* you might have thought of could had been nullified by the telepath."

Roberts looked blank for a moment, then nodded.

"With his advantage, he should have had such a superiority that I'd have had no chance at all. But—there was that impregnable retreat with foot-thick walls and a tissue-paper ceiling. And that ring of bars with the loose plate at the top out of the way. At the end, when he tied me up, the knots didn't hold. And he was so sure of the effect of the obedience gas that he sprayed it at me—then breathed it himself. *Phew!* If that's telepathy, he can have it."

The colonel smiled. "Telepathy plus megalomania. You can't judge telepathy with *that* handicap. Great success without self-control is dangerous, and Gafonel had had enormous success. At some point, it dawned on this telepath that he had a 'seeing mind,' could look into all other minds, learn their processes of thought, their true reasons, their honest opinions, and hence outshine them all." The colonel shook his head. "There was a hole in his reasoning, but he never recognized it."

Roberts said, "He could look into other minds and learn their true reasons and honest *opinions*."

The colonel nodded. "Their *opinions*. He thought he was *omniscient*. Instead, he was *omniopinient*. If one expert worked on one part of his arrangement, and another worked on another part, he thought he need only scan their minds, to learn whether each one had done his job. But that only told him the answer *so far as they themselves knew.* If he got well-meant bad advice at some point, he had no way to analyze it on his own. This weakness didn't bother him in his investments, because on balance the advice was usually right. But when a man tries to make himself Emperor of the Universe overnight, little flaws in his arrangements have a tendency to magnify themselves."

Roberts nodded thoughtfully. "And yet, he certainly had a special advantage."

"Yes, and as often happens to people with a special advantage, he let it become a substitute for his own thought. If you look back at the past experience of humanity, you'll see that this or that specialty—strictly formal logic, religion, government, science—some one thing or viewpoint, has been expected to solve all the problems. But reality is too varied to be handled completely by one method. As soon as the one method is nicely codified, then the whole crushing burden comes to bear on one solitary support. It doesn't work, but once there's an official solution around, people tend to quit thinking."

Roberts said, "There ought to be some saying about this, for a warning."

"There is."

"What?"

"You tell me."

Roberts looked at the colonel with a familiar sense of exasperation. Then his thought processes jarred into action.

"No special skill," he said, "no standard attitude, no technology— no matter how valuable—can safely replace thought itself."

The colonel smiled. "You've omitted a common substitute."

Roberts frowned, then in surprise he saw one reason why the Interstellar Patrol provided so few ready-made answers to its members.

Roberts cleared his throat before he spoke.

"No special skill, no standard attitude, no technology, and no *organization*—no matter how valuable—can safely replace thought itself."

The colonel nodded.

"*Now* you've got it."

THE TROJAN HOSTAGE

The blow to the head came without warning, and knocked Roberts against the white-painted concrete-block wall of the spaceport washroom. A second blow followed so fast that he was unconscious before his body hit the pitted, urine-smelling floor.

Roberts' arms were jerked behind his back, steel cuffs clamped on his wrists and ankles, and a heavy padlock slid through the links to bind his hands close to his feet. He was lifted, carried through a door, and slid along a truck bed sheathed in iron. The door clanged shut behind him. With a jolt, the vehicle started forward. Roberts was unaware of any of it. The roar of the departing ferry rocket, that had brought him to this world less than an hour before, passed over him unheard, just as it passed over the sand, the rocks, and the weeds growing in the shellholes beside the road.

Roberts had been none too happy when the Chief of Operations had first suggested the plan. Seated before Colonel Sanders' desk in the Interstellar Patrol dreadnought that served as command ship, Roberts hadn't concealed his doubts:

"Sir, I can see it might not be right to just kill the lot of them. On the other hand, at least it would work. This—"

The Colonel shook his head. "Amongst other things, if we kill this lot of home-grown barbarians, just possibly we might kill our own people being used as shields. A little subtlety is called for."

"Subtlety may not work. But if we make an example of the worst of these macho bandits, the rest should be more cooperative."

"Unfortunately, they aren't stupid. Before you hit them, you have to find them. And we want our people back alive, if possible. In any case, we want to handle this in such a way that, afterwards, no one will be overeager to use us for shields, or for trades in an interstellar prisoner swap." The colonel handed Roberts a sheet of paper. "A little of this is plenty."

Roberts found himself looking over a copy of the news-sheet that had popped out of innumerable printers at breakfast. One of the articles was circled:

IP AT BAY
HARSH ULTIMATUM

The Interstellar Patrol, the shadowy quasi-military organization that for many people represents the ultimate human power in the universe, finds itself today at the mercy of a band of anarchists. FIAM, the Freedom in Anarchy Movement, founded by imprisoned planetary raider Ian Pulgor, today announced the capture of twenty-seven IP members in a raid carried out late last month on the planet Tiamaz.

In a terse ultimatum, FIAM warned: "... These prisoners, who have now been fully questioned, will be killed one by one until Colonel-General Ian Pulgor is released unharmed from the detention facility..."

The IP members had apparently been on leave on Tiamaz, the popular gaming and vacation planet, and were seized, the FIAM spokesman reported, without casualties to the Shock Troops of the Movement.

FIAM Shock Brigades VIII and XVI are reliably reported to have returned with their hostages to the bleak and desolate home planet of Anarchy...

Roberts skimmed the rest of the article, then looked up.

"You want me to *volunteer* to carry out 'a check of the physical condition of the prisoners'?"

"Correct, Roberts. The proofs the Pulgorites sent included photographs evidently taken on Tiamaz, details of build and age, fingerprints, a few sets of retinal patterns, and messages anyone could have fabricated. The total seems convincing, but all it really shows is the someone has investigated these men. That doesn't prove they've been captured. All these so-called hostages could actually have been killed in the raid on Tiamaz."

Roberts nodded. "If the reports are right, a good part of the casino district was blown to bits."

"And the main part of the resort our people were staying at was vaporized. The Tiamaz authorities think upwards of ten thousand visitors got killed in that blast alone. We could humbly do as we're told, then find that the killers had parleyed a witless slaughter into a victory through a faked kidnap. As a matter of fact, they may already have killed all of our men."

Roberts nodded. "They may have no hostages *now*. But they will have, if I go to check up on them."

The colonel nodded matter-of-factly. "That's true, Roberts. Namely, you."

"That's my point, sir."

"But you see, Roberts, we need to find out for certain whether they do have prisoners. However unlikely, we have to check that possibility."

"Sir, I'm prepared to risk my neck. But you are asking for a volunteer. I won't volunteer to be the one they boot around to soothe their egos, and then trade for the colonel general."

There was a little silence, during which Roberts saw no interpretable expression on Colonel Sanders' face, but nevertheless got the impression of a backwoodsman switching baits in his trap.

"Roberts, they have *guaranteed* the personal safety of any representative we might care to send, specifically the safety of Captain Vaughan N. Roberts, I.P."

"I'd as soon sleep with the crocodiles as trust that guarantee."

"Trust," growled the colonel, producing a uniquely unpleasant smile, "was not exactly what I had in mind. The odds are that they've killed no less than twenty-seven of us. We aren't handing you over to them as a free gift. I hope you don't think that."

"Sir, from what I've heard of this plan so far, suicide looks good by comparison. I suppose there's something you don't want to tell me, because if I don't know it, I can't reveal it. Well, maybe someone else will volunteer."

"Roberts, there is a very real risk for you. But if you should become their hostage, the risk to them will be worse."

Roberts felt the curiosity this statement naturally roused. And like a predator noting tasty bait in a deadfall, he moved on. "If I had some idea why that should be, it would be different. But why hand myself over as a prisoner to this bunch of murderous lunatics, for no reason I can understand".

"Well, the reasons are clear enough. First, we have to know whether our men are or are not prisoners. If they are, we aim to free them. If not, we will take care of whoever killed them. But before we do either, we have to find out what happened, and that is the second problem. Third, what *is* this 'freedom in anarchy' movement? There are possibly a hundred crackpot organizations, born of a combination of frustration and a lack of historical perspective, to each organization that makes sense. Which is this? We need information, and this outfit is cunning and secretive. We have drugs that would, amongst other things, induce them to talk freely, but first we have to make contact. They won't come to us. So—"

"Where's the connection between handing me over to them, and your getting the answers?" Roberts shook his head. "Are their so-called Shock Troops back on Anarchy?"

"That's the information they've leaked out."

"I'll volunteer for the first wave to hit the place."

The colonel shook his head. "If it were that simple, the Space Force would have wiped them out long since. It isn't a question of force. The problem is that they are *clever.*"

Roberts considered the peculiar expression on the colonel's face as he spoke the word "clever."

"There must be quite a few things I don't know."

The colonel looked at Roberts with exasperation, then sighed and nodded.

"These *are* very clever people. They are shrewd swindlers and cunning bush-whackers. But there's more than one way to use brainpower. For years, we've been doing research on jump-points—what R-Branch refers to as 'singularities in space.' These things are used regularly to cut travel distances and lower freight rates—you shoot the freight through jump-point Ceres, say, and it comes out on the other side for a total two-month trip instead of one that takes six years. In effect, two different locations in space are joined, and the join can be used as a shortcut."

Roberts felt the disorientation of the desert traveler, prepared to endure heat, glare, and blowing grit, who trudges over a sand dune to find blue ocean in front of him.

The colonel, outwardly unaware of the effect of this change of subject, was going on: "Now, how does this work? What are the principles behind it? Could the principles be used differently? Could we, perhaps, find a way to create this kind of effect ourselves?"

Roberts said warily, "As I've heard it explained, sir, there are at least two parts to the theory. One has to do with the curvature of space, and the other with the effects of unusually intense gravitic fields. In short, an extremely concentrated gravitic field may make a hole from one section of space to another. But what does this have to do with the Pulgorites?"

"Do you know of a theory that would enable you to *construct* a jump-point?"

Roberts looked blank.

The colonel said, "Without gigantic masses of collapsed matter, Roberts, or huge magnetic or gravitic fields—using tiny focused gravitic generators controlled by ultraminiaturized processors, the whole works small enough to fit in your pocket, and all perfectly safe and inoffensive when you put it there—that is, if you leave it turned off."

He reached into the top drawer of his desk, and tossed across a thing like a small mother-of-pearl spoon with no handle, about an inch and three-quarters long by an inch at the widest, with a smooth slick surface that felt faintly warm to the touch.

"That, Roberts, is a demonstration unit in the larger size. Put your thumb in the center where it's dished in, with the palm of your other hand on the opposite side, and press hard."

Roberts did as told.

Abruptly his hands were pushed aside, there was a six-inch hole in the air, and Roberts, his mind numb and hands pressed against a hard unseeable edge around the outside of nothing, was looking through the hole into some other room where there was a laboratory bench on which lay a hand slate and, beside the slate, a stick of white chalk.

The colonel said, "I can't see it from here, Roberts, but you should be looking into R-Branch's molecular physics lab. The usual connection is near a bench with something on it like a pencil, puzzle cube, or some other small object."

Roberts stared at the colonel, then leaned forward to look at the hole from the colonel's direction—and found he was looking through the space where the hole had been and it wasn't there any more. He sat back, feeling foolish, and there it was again, and, inside it, the top of the lab bench.

The colonel said, "Our original model was not only invisible from the back, and unstable, but had a rim like the edge of a razor blade. This is better, believe me. But it's still invisible from the back. It's almost as if you had a small hatchway, with one side in one location in space, and the other side of it in a different location."

"What happens if I try to reach through this hole?"

"Try it."

Roberts, expecting something like a closed window or porthole, cautiously put his hand in, met no resistance, reached through, picked up the chalk, and then the view shifted, his hand and half his arm disappeared, and the inner edge of the hole dropped free of his other hand to rest on his arm like a small, light, unseeable hoop. It dawned on Roberts that he had been trying to hold it with one hand and must not have gripped the edge tightly enough.

The colonel stepped out from behind his desk. "Don't move, Roberts. It won't hurt you, but we could have trouble finding it if it lands wrong side up. It's thin, and transparent from the back." He put his wide open hands on opposite sides of the outer edge of the hole, fingers spread, lifted it up, and Roberts withdrew his arm and opened his hand, the chalk resting on his palm.

Roberts felt the chalk, glanced up at the colonel patiently holding the device, then reached back through, returned the chalk, briefly weighed the hand slate, then pulled his arm and hand back out. He gave a low, fervent exclamation.

The colonel said, "Now, put your hands back on the outer edge, and press. Keep increasing the pressure."

Roberts put his hands on the outer edge of the hole, pressed lightly, and nothing happened. He pressed harder, and the circular rim resisted, then abruptly collapsed to an oval, then, by stages, to longer narrower openings, then the lab bench was gone, and he was holding the little rounded dished-in bit that looked like mother-of-pearl.

The colonel sat down behind his desk.

Roberts exhaled slowly. "You say this is the 'larger size'?"

"Correct. The smaller size would fit easily on the nail of your little finger."

"There are just two sizes?"

"There seem to be two *limiting* sizes. At best, they aren't easy to make. And when we try to use this method for one much larger or smaller, the border wavers, and sooner or later the connection breaks down. But we now have several sets of these space-connectors that are reliable."

"What's on the other end, in the lab?"

"A second unit, keyed to the demo unit you've got there. The second unit is ordinarily kept turned off, and mounted in a circular holder that fits tightly around its rim. Both units have to be turned on for the connection to function. When your unit is off, the other just looks like a short pedestal mount holding a rim that you can look through—like a mirror frame with no mirror in it. When your unit is turned on, you can see from the proper side a six-inch hole into the place your unit is in. In this case, someone in the lab could look—and could reach—into this room."

Roberts sat looking at the little curving piece like mother-of-pearl. "Suppose one place has a much heavier gravity than the other?"

"If you reach through, you might feel it. If there's a higher atmospheric pressure in one of the places, there will be a flow of gas from the higher pressure toward the lower. R-Branch says they've found no measurable effects due to relative velocity, or to a greater potential energy on one side of the connection."

"Meaning?"

"If one connector was to be put, say, in a fast-moving satellite, and the other were motionless on the ground below, you'd expect an object passed across from one side to the other to come through with high velocity. It doesn't. Any difference in velocity, or potential energy of the places joined, seems to be absorbed. R-Branch tells me there are theoretical difficulties, but it's as if places joined were motionless with respect to each other."

"Suppose something is thrown through from one side to the other?"

"It goes through as hard as you throw it."

Roberts thought it over, frowning. "How far apart can the places be that you connect?"

"We have yet to find the upper limit. Whatever it may be, the Pulgorite planet, Anarchy, is well within it." He added with no special emphasis. "The connection is made, Roberts, by having someone go the place with the device."

Roberts considered that for a while, then he smiled, and looked the colonel in the eye.

"Sir, I volunteer to check the physical condition of the hostages the Pulgorites claim to have taken."

Roberts became aware of voices, and of a muted throbbing somewhere in his head. He tried to move, and found that he couldn't. He managed to partly open his eyes, and a white light was glaring down from overhead. In the light, a short, very sharp knife glittered as a square competent hand held the knife out, and a more slender hand took it, and passed over a clamp, then another clamp, and another.

A male voice spoke quietly: "That's it."

A rougher male voice said, "Find anything more?"

"There are no artifacts actually inside the body itself, so far as we can determine."

The rough voice grated. "I asked you if you'd found anything more."

"No, sir. We did not."

"Just a minute, Surgeon. When I ask a question. I expect an answer in a certain form. And I will either get it, or you will find that those hands you're so proud of will break easily. Understand?"

"Yes, sir."

"All right. Now I'll ask you again: "Find anything more?"

"No, sir."

"What chance is there that something has been miniaturized, or that there is something there made to resemble body tissue?"

"I don't know, sir."

"But you don't see anything?"

"No, sir."

"Nor any sign that anything was inserted?"

"No, sir.

"Everything looks normal to you in the body cavities?"

"Yes, sir."

It dawned on Roberts suddenly that they were talking about him. It was him that was stretched out on this table.

The harsh voice said, "Does it mean anything to you, Surgeon, that that slab of meat you're working on represents victory for the Movement? *If* we can block every one of their dirty little tricks?"

"No, sir."

"No. You're not one of us. All right. Sew him up. And he'd better live long enough for us to wring the juice out of him."

"Yes, sir."

The rough voice grated. "Did I just ask you a question?"

"No, sir."

"Then shut up."

There was a silence, then another male voice spoke nervously, "Request to increase the anesthetic. The patient is regaining consciousness."

The rough voice answered. "We're short on anesthetic. To hell with him."

The surgeon said, "I can't promise the patient will survive if he becomes conscious in this situation."

"He's in the IP. They're tough."

"In this situation, no-one is tough."

There was a silence, and it penetrated to Roberts that he was lying on his back opened up on a table while an argument took place whether he could have anesthetic.

There was the sound of someone spitting. "All right," said the rough voice. "Give him some more gas. But you'd damned well better not waste it on him."

Roberts smelled something sweetish, and instantly passed out.

Somewhere nearby, a coldly sneering male voice was saying, " . . . don't know what's wrong with Guff and Petzky. They were OK when they brought the jerk, here, to the blockhouse. But now they've got chills, fever, and the shakes. I've put a ton of blankets on them in there. Guff is starting to hallucinate."

A feminine voice said, "Sounds like they've got the grakes."

"The what?"

"Grakes. In the settlement where I grew up, every spring at least half of us would come down with it."

"Never heard of it. What is it?"

"Chills, fever, and shaking. The worst is, you have vivid dreams. Well—vivid—nightmares."

"What causes it?"

"I don't know."

""How do you cure it?"

"We never found a cure. You just endure it."

"Great. Those two are worthless, then. For how long?"

"It usually took us about three or four days to get over the worst. By the end, we were worn out."

Roberts eased his eyes to narrow slits, to see the small passenger compartment of the tug that had brought him to the surface of Anarchy. Since this tug served as a kind of shuttle between the planet and the nearest space station, and had been about to leave the planet as Roberts had stepped into the spaceport washroom, it followed that the tug had taken off, returned later, and Roberts had again been put on board. Supposedly this would have had to take a good deal of time.

Up front, one of the cabin lights was shining on a metal trim-strip. Roberts head moved slightly, the strip glittered, and Roberts suddenly remembered the surgical knife, and realized where the time had gone. The realization was followed by urgent thought, and the memory of the colonel's voice:

"Needless to say, Roberts, there are limits to what we should tell you in advance. But you can expect to be very thoroughly searched on arrival. Naturally, we will be prepared, so don't worry about that." It occurred to Roberts to wonder just how thorough an examination the colonel had expected.

Beside him, now, the male voice was saying, "What are the odds on this sucker catching it?"

The feminine voice replied, "The grakes?"

"What are we talking about?"

"You tell me."

"Guff and Petzky were carrying him, and they've both down with it. Could he get it from them?

"I don't know why not. I'd think the odds were good."

"Does it kill?"

"Sometimes."

"So, after all we went through to catch the bastard, he could die on us before we've used him?"

"People in bad shape were the ones who usually ended up dying. The rest of us only felt like it."

"Well, he's already been sliced open, so that will weaken him.

And they're putting him through a full-suite psycho battery when we get him there."

The feminine voice said judiciously, "It *might* kill him. The hallucinations can be really hellish."

"I don't mind putting him through hell. I just don't want him to die on us before we're through with him."

Roberts opened his eyes.

Beside him, the male voice gave a low chuckle. "Well—the sleeper awakes. Give Prince Charming a kiss, Ginette."

The feminine voice spoke softly. "I'd love to."

There was a faint hissing sound, as of a spray can, then a feeling of cobwebs brushing Robert's face and shoulders, then a pain that blotted out the headache, and brought Roberts wide awake. For an instant he was on his feet, straining at a wide band that covered his chest and arms, and another band that bound his legs together. Then a particularly agonizing pain warned him that, just a little while before, he had been on an operating table. He felt a great weariness, and his eyes went shut. As he fell back into the seat, the soft feminine voice spoke from his left: "Sully? Again? There's still plenty in the can."

From his right came the sarcastic masculine voice: "Oh—not just yet. Keep it handy. We'll have a few questions, and if he acts too smart, we'll give him a squirt. After a while, you can make a hiss with your mouth, and he'll jump."

The girl giggled. "Fun."

Roberts gave an involuntary shuddering gasp, got his eyes open, and saw that he was wearing a kind of hospital robe partly pulled down over his bare shoulders, and that the passenger compartment was empty forward of his seat. To his left was a pretty woman of perhaps twenty-five, dark-haired, demure, pertly holding what looked like a can of insect repellent. To his right was a well-dressed man of about forty, wearing a dark business suit. Both of them looked highly respectable.

Roberts recovered from the mind-stopping pain, and his instinct for self-preservation prompted him to try to distract this pair. The best he could think of was to get them talking. He turned to the man. "The ship is grounded on Anarchy?"

A look of contempt lit up in the man's eyes, and then there was a very faint hiss. Roberts' muscles tightened of their own accord. He turned around toward the girl, who favored him with a sweet smile and suggestively raised the can. The hiss was still going on, but she wasn't causing it. It was a faint hiss that he could just hear in his right ear. As he turned back to face the man, the hiss suddenly stopped.

His well-dressed seatmate had a look of glazed puzzlement. He hesitated, appeared to be groping mentally, then shrugged. "We're in flight. The so-called home planet is well behind us."

Roberts alertly studied the glazed expression, then said, "I thought the prisoners were being held on Anarchy?"

"Why should we make a target you could hit? You know where Anarchy is. We said they were there, so they aren't."

"There was an announcement that the Shock troops who carried out the raid had returned to Anarchy."

"We make statements to mislead. Why give free information to our enemies?"

"The Interstellar Patrol is your enemy?"

"We killed twenty-nine of your people. Sure you're our enemy. We didn't intend it, but we might as well make the most of it."

"Twenty-nine?"

"At first we thought there were twenty-seven. But the records show a K-class IP ship was on the planet, along with the G-class ship we'd known of. The K-class ship had a crew of two."

Roberts kept his voice casual. "What records do you mean?"

"The Tiamaz internal security records. The planet has probably the best internal security of any planet not run by a dictator—and it beats some of *them*. We aimed to get the records. We did get them. That part, at least, worked."

The girl leaned across Roberts. "Sully, he's questioning *you?* Shouldn't we be questioning him?"

"Why do I want to ask questions? They've got a bunch of experts lined up for that."

"Yes, but—"

His tone was offended. "But what?"

"I thought—"

"Thought what?"

Listening to this exchange, and seeing the angry, defensive and still glazed look on Sully's face, while the girl looked incredulous and angry, Roberts remembered the faint hissing sound in his right ear. He felt a sensation as of chills and fever. He twisted around his seat—no small achievement considering the bonds, the aches and pains, and the girl's raising of the spray can—and said, while looking over the back of the seat, with his right side toward the girl. "Are we alone in here?"

She said, ignoring Roberts after one quick puzzled glance, "Sully, are you all right?"

There was no one in sight in the seats behind them. Again there was a faint distinct hiss, which went on for some time, to end only as he turned toward the front again. As he turned, Sully was saying resentfully, "I'm in charge here. You understand that, Ginette?"

Roberts automatically braced for her sharp response.

The girl said meekly, "I understand, Sully. I just wondered, that's all. I'm sorry."

Roberts sensation of chills and fever produced an actual shiver as he recognized the unlikelihood of this submissive reply. Like Sully's cooperativeness, it followed closeness to the right side of Roberts' face—more specifically, closeness to his right ear. More-over, there was a distinct unmistakable sense of coldness in his right ear. Not for the first time, he damned the colonel's reluctance to give information, and his own willingness to act without get-ting it. Thanks to that failing, though he now had an idea what was going on, he didn't actually know, and might make a slip anytime. He turned to Sully, and casually asked, "What was the point of the raid?"

Sully sighed, and settled back. "We intended to replace the internal security on Tiamaz with our own people. It didn't work. But we did get the records."

Roberts stared at him. "You were going to take over Tiamaz?"

"Just the internal security section."

"But you couldn't stop there. The planetary government wouldn't have put up with that."

"Why not? Tiamaz is run by a syndicate of financiers, gam-blers, and entertainers. Naturally, we weren't going to tell them we were taking over the planet for Colonel-General Pulgor. We were going to tell them we represented Intergalactic Security, a competitor of Transspace Security—the outfit they'd contracted with—and that we had spotted a hole in the Transspace security set-up, and pushed Transspace out of there. Then we'd offer to take on the security contract on the same terms, and do the job right. What do they care who does the work?"

Roberts, suffering from a severe headache, a number of pains and twinges, and a general feeling of weakness, asked himself if his own physical shape might be the reason for his difficulty in following this explanation. He cleared his throat.

"But there *is* an actual Intergalactic Security. What were they going to do when they heard about this?"

"Why should they complain? Tiamaz is a big contract. What do they care if Transspace gets a bloody nose? What Intergalactic would want is the money."

"Yes, but wouldn't they be surprised to find out they had a branch office they didn't know about?"

"Oh, sure, but we weren't going to tell *them* we were from Intergalactic. Hell, no. We'd tell them we were an independent outfit called Unicorn Investigations. We'd already set Unicorn up, so, if they checked, that was documented. We'd say we'd found holes in Transspace's set-up, penetrated it, and Transspace had resisted, and one thing had led to another, and we'd had to clean out the whole operation. Now we wanted to affiliate ourselves with a real professional security outfit, and would they take us on as part of Intergalactic. Then they'd ask who gets the payment, and we'd say they did, and they could pay us at their wage rate, and we figured they'd jump at it. Tiamaz is a gold mine."

Roberts remembered the peculiar expression on the colonel's face as he said, "They're *clever.*" He grappled with this explanation, and asked himself if this could have worked. With a sense of shock, it dawned on him that it appeared so tailored to the greed or ignorance of everyone involved that it just might have worked, at that.

To his left, the girl sighed, and settled back, and the girl's sigh seemed loud, while the man's voice seemed somewhat low, as if Roberts' right ear was partly plugged. Automatically, he tried yawning and swallowing to clear his ear, then realized that wasn't going to work, and said, "So, you'd finish off the team from Transspace, and try to join up with Intergalactic?"

"Correct."

"How about Transspace?"

"As soon as we'd wiped out their people, we'd send Transspace a message over their planet chief's name, saying we'd gotten a better offer from Modular Investigations, and had accepted it as a unit."

"This would be a message supposedly from Transspace's people on Tiamaz?"

"Right."

"The ones you'd just killed?"

"Sure. They couldn't deny it."

"What—"

"Transspace wouldn't know what to think. Because there *is* a Modular Investigations, but it's halfway around the universe. If Modular needed people to work in some place far from home, this is just what they might do."

"So Transspace might believe it."

"Might. They wouldn't know."

"Couldn't they check?"

"Sure." He chuckled. "They could ask Modular."

Roberts considered the chuckle. "Ah—"

"Naturally, Modular would deny it."

"The—"

"They'd deny it either way, whether they did it or not."

"But if Transspace believed they had a message from their own chief of planet, naming Modular, why would they doubt—"

"How do they know whether *he's* lying? He could have joined some other outfit, and named Modular to lay a false trail."

Roberts considered it in silence. "All right. Suppose Transspace got in touch with *you*?"

"Ah, we'd have loved that. We were Unicorn Investigations, and we'd done a small job for the Transspace outfit on Tiamaz, and their planet chief had got in touch with us, and asked how we'd like to fill in on Tiamaz for them, and we'd asked why, and he'd said he'd had an offer from Pilgrim Protective, but don't repeat it, and so we'd gone to Tiamaz, and the planet chief had eased us into the job, and then left with Transspace's people, and here we were, and he'd suggested we get in touch with Intergalactic, and we'd done it, and Intergalactic had asked no questions and just taken us on. Naturally, we wouldn't tell them this all at once. We'd let them dig it out, a piece at a time."

Roberts sat back. "There *is* a Pilgrim Protective?"

"You bet."

"So Transspace would—"

Sully chuckled. "Probably they'd just drop it. They'd have a sweet time checking it out."

Roberts exhaled carefully. On top of his pains and general sense of enfeeblement, he was suffering from a growing impression that he was mentally dull, and badly out of step with the latest progress in crime.

"Did you," he asked, "work this out yourself?"

His seat companion smiled with quiet pride. "Oh, we all had input. Where you have to be careful is getting rid of the bodies."

"How—"

"We left that to Marty. He's careful. It's better if not too many know just what happened."

"Yes, I guess it would be, at that."

Roberts sat back, and gathered his mental faculties together. He had the impression that he had to get out and push to get them to work. Stubbornly, he went through the explanation again, trying to pin down just what it was that seemed to be lacking. Let's see, he thought, the Movement kills Transspace's people on Tiamaz. They send a false message so Transspace will think their people have quit their jobs. The Movement tells Tiamaz that they work for Intergalactic. They tell Intergalactic they are a small outfit and want to join Intergalactic. They agree that, in exchange, Intergalactic can have the lavish payment from Tiamaz, while, for its part, Intergalactic will pay their wages. Roberts thought that over.

No matter how he examined it, it appeared to Roberts that, after a complicated string of lies, murder, and trickery, the payoff was that the Movement had got into a position where now it could work for Intergalactic.

"What," said Roberts, "would you get out of this?"

"Me, personally, or the Movement?"

"The Movement."

Sully smiled expansively.

"Think of all the important people who come to Tiamaz, how they can be set up while they're there, and the information you can get on them. There's a lot of angles there. Then there are the entertainers. Just for starters, we had a show on the colonel-general's life—a sympathetic show—and someone from Anarchy was going to take it around to the entertainers. If any one of them would it handle it right, we—internal security—would help that entertainer. There was a lot we'd be able to do to favor one of them over another after we'd been around a while."

"That was a public relations gimmick? To build up your leader's reputation?"

"Sure, why not? All these influential people pass though Tiamaz. If you're on Tiamaz, you've got a handle on them, not to mention the information you can use or sell."

It occurred to Roberts that being told all this would do nothing to improve his chances of getting home alive to repeat it. On the other hand, he was being told, and just possibly he was not the only one hearing it. He cleared his throat.

"What went wrong?"

"It never occurred to us there would be off-duty police or troops there. All we expected to run into was Transspace, and maybe the local police. But there was a platoon of Space Force combat infantry in civilian clothes taking their furlough there, and the two IP ships we didn't know about till later. Then there was something else—we don't know what it was—and the scam turned into a shambles."

"What happened?"

"The idea was to do away with Transspace's operatives—all of them—in about a three-hour period. The problem was to keep it quiet. We had their schedule, and one of our own people was their dispatcher on duty. We knew where everyone on duty was going to be, they didn't expect trouble, and the dispatcher could pull in the people off duty when it suited us. It should have gone like silk."

Roberts, soberly considering it, could see the point. "But it didn't?"

"What we didn't know was that two of the Transspace women operatives had made friends with a couple of Space Force sergeants. That is, we knew they had boyfriends, but it hadn't dawned on us that the boyfriends were combat troops with buddies all over the place. When we tried to get rid of these female operatives, all hell broke loose. To make it worse, some Space Force men had got friendly with the IP, taking their own vacation there, and they got in it, too, and damn it, no one is supposed to be armed on Tiamaz except the Tiamaz police and internal security—but several of these holier-than-thou IP bastards had guns."

Roberts murmured, "Oh, unfair."

"Well, if *they* don't obey the law, who *can* you trust?"

"What happened?"

"We cleaned out most of Transspace, but the two women caught on, warned the rest, and it was like a nature vacation where you go to shoot the tame rock hen for dinner, and waiting there for you is a giant constrictor. The Tiamaz police got in it along with the Space Force and the IP, and what was left of Transspace. We loaded up the Transspace files, blew up the internal security headquarters, and on the way off the planet a big IP ship came at us low and fast, we fired everything we could throw at it, accidentally hit some building on the edge of the casino district, and that went up like a torch with the IP ship right over it, and this building and the IP ship blew up. We don't know what happened. But we were far enough away to live though it, and it did so much damage we thought it would build up our reputation to claim the credit. After that blast, anyone who knew what was going on was probably dead, so we could claim anything. So we called it a raid."

"The hostages—?"

"The last thing we were thinking about was hostages. We wanted out of there with a whole skin. What we said afterward was just to look good. See, we're not scared of the Patrol. First we question them. Then we kill them, one at a time. How is anyone going to know what happened? Of course, now we *have* got a hostage. You."

Roberts noted that the glazed expression was wearing off, and Sully was now acquiring a faintly puzzled look—possibly as if he wondered just why he was telling Roberts all this. Roberts nodded moodily. "These—ah— Shock Troops—?"

"Same idea. Like the colonel-generals' rank. He's got followers enough in the Movement so he could claim to be, maybe, a lieutenant or even a captain. How's that sound—Lieutenant Pulgor, Supreme Commander? You can hear the press: 'In a dramatic development today, First-Lieutenant Pulgor announced that his troops, based on the home planet of Anarchy, will destroy any commercial traffic in the region.'—Kind of unconvincing. You don't dare do that unless you've actually got the power. So he reached into his imagination, and now he's a Colonel-General. We got the Shock Troops out of the same place."

It occurred to Roberts again that this frankness did not bode well for his longevity. He waited until a particularly vicious jolt of pain passed, and until the detestation he was beginning to feel for his seat companion died down a little, then he cleared his throat.

"So, obviously, there is no point to my checking the condition of prisoners."

As if the words were some kind of signal, the girl at once lifted the spray can, and aimed it at his face.

The man noted Robert's wince, and laughed. "Not yet, Ginette." He glanced at Roberts. "You see, we're pretty sure the IP isn't actually stupid. The Space Police—by and large, they're stupid. The Space Force? Well, it depends. They're one-sided. You get in the way of their specialty, and they're anything but stupid. But they just fight outsiders, so we don't have to worry about them. See what I mean?"

Roberts noted the complete disappearance of the glazed look, nodded, kept his mouth shut, and listened.

"Planetary Development? It's full of smart people, but the organization is bird-brained. But except when they take over a settled planet, that's no problem. Obviously, as the colonel-general says, we need to get rid of the Space Police. You can't have real individual freedom—Unrestricted Individual Freedom—Anarchy—with police around. And Planetary Development's regulations have to be changed so they can't interfere on a planet after it's settled. That's all. But the IP?" He looked at Roberts.

Roberts kept his mouth shut, and looked attentive. His seat companion nodded.

"We don't know. We don't truly know what it is. But now we've got a grip on a piece of it, and we aim to find out what the IP *is*. Maybe we can use it. Or maybe we have to eliminate it. For all we know, it's a secret government, the very opposite of anarchy. *You* may be part of anti-freedom. We have to find out."

Roberts observed the bright glow in his seat companion's eyes, looked around and saw the spray can aimed at him. He glanced back to the man, who was smiling. The silence began to stretch out uncomfortably.

"How," said Roberts, "do you find out?"

"Well, like I say, we're a small organization. But we have some shrewd people. As an organization, we're sharp. A lot sharper than the IP. You see, we trapped you because you couldn't be sure we didn't have some of your men as prisoners. You probably didn't really believe it, but you had to be sure. Right?"

"That's a fair statement."

"You bet it is. Now we've got you. The rest of the Patrol knows we've got you. When we send back a finger, they'll know it's your finger. When we send back an ear, they'll know it's your ear. We can stretch that out a long time. They won't be able to bear it. Sooner or later, they'll attack. That's when we'll get some more hostages. Because where are they going to attack? Why, Anarchy, of course. Everything will be datelined Anarchy. The press will have interviews there. It's established that we're there. But, of course, we're not. What is there is a few of us and a damned big booby trap. Ordinarily, I suppose the Patrol wouldn't make a land attack. They could just pull a warship into range and blast us from a distance. But we've got *you*. They'll *land*."

Roberts considered the words, "When we send back a finger, they'll know it's your finger," and reminded himself that if he got out of this in one piece, in the future to be a little more restrained when the next chance came along to volunteer. He said, as if uncertain. "You can't be sure they'll land."

His seatmate looked exceedingly shrewd. "Well, I think they'll land. You'll be surprised how we'll play them. And when they land, the odds are we'll get a few of them, anyway. They'll suffer heavy losses. And then they'll realize they don't know where we are. We'll find out just what the IP is like. And we'll get the colonel-general free in the process. It'll tear the IP to bits. And you're the start." He looked at his watch. "OK, Ginette, give him a dose."

There was a hiss, a sense of brushing into cobwebs, and an agonizing pain. The hissing kept up, and pain knocked the vague hopefulness Roberts had started to feel out of his mind, spread over his exposed head, neck and shoulders to turn into one livid blinding agony—and he was unconscious.

This time when he came to, Roberts had a distinct sense of the passage of time. His first clear conscious thought was—"Don't volunteer!" Then his eyes focused, he remembered the operating room and the space tug, and realized he was no longer on the space tug.

The room he was in was large, the plastered walls water-stained, and the ceiling high. The closed doors were paneled, dark, and set in massive frames. Here and there, plaster had fallen, to give the impression of a mansion in ruins. Roberts himself was lying on his back in a double bed with several woolen blankets on it. Watching from across the room by a high closed window was the girl who had wielded the spray can. She smiled and smoothed her brief playsuit.

Roberts winced and revised his estimate of the anarchists downward as she spoke:

"We don't have to be enemies," she said. "We could be a *lot* more friendly."

He tried to sit up, and discovered he was in a kind of straitjacket, though now his legs were free. He glanced at the girl.

"Now where are we?"

"Home. You've been examined by our experts, given nourishment, psychologically tested, and now the Veep is going to talk to you."

"Who—"

"The colonel-general's eldest son. He is in charge of the Movement in the absence of Colonel-General Pulgor himself. You see, the colonel-general is Presiding Officer of the Movement."

She rolled the titles reverently off her tongue as Roberts bit back sarcastic comments and noted that the feeling of weakness seemed to be gone, while his headache had died down to a hammering throb with occasional blinding sensations as if his head were being split open down the middle. This seemed, by comparison with what had gone before, almost good health, just as being in a straitjacket with his legs unbound seemed almost like freedom. Before he could congratulate himself on any of this, a massive paneled door swung open to let in a tall, bent individual who looked to be in his mid-thirties, and who spoke in a whining voice.

"Damn it, Marty. I never get a chance to do what I want. If the old man wants to run this damn show, let him run it. I don't give a good—"

"Now, Mr. Vice-President, you know that His Excellency is imprisoned. That's the whole point of all this. To get him out of prison. You know that."

"And then what? He'll yell at me! He'll tramp up and down the room and scream and holler and demand what I'm doing with my life and why I don't care two—"

"Sir, please—"

"He'll say I'm supposed to give my life for the Cause, and how he's devoted his all to the Movement, and, damn it, Marty, the damned Movement is supposed to make everybody free, but tell me, am I free? Heh? Am I? All those people got blown up, and now we've got the Space Force, and the Interstellar Patrol, and God knows what else after us—I mean, it's personal now! Don't you see what I mean?"

"Sir, permit me to introduce Lieutenant-General Vaughan Nathan Roberts of the Interstellar Patrol. General Roberts, you are in the presence of the son of His Excellency, Colonel-General Ian Pulgor, Presiding Officer of the Movement for the Creation of Universal Freedom In Anarchy. Gentlemen, time is limited. Permit me to urge that we waste no effort to arrive at a mutual understanding as soon as possible."

Roberts, gaining the impression he was among lunatics, while himself trying to loosen the straitjacket, now became aware of a faint hissing sound that intensified any time he turned so that the right side of his head was toward either the vice-president or his companion. Roberts glanced around, and said absently, "Just Captain Roberts. I'm not a general."

The tall vice-president of the Movement laughed. "It's all right. Nobody speaks the truth around here. We're all free to lie however we choose. Even our own names aren't true. They're picked to conceal our identity, not state it. That's just another part of anarchy. But the rest of what he said, aside from the lies, is true. We'd better get down to cases pretty fast. You're in trouble."

Roberts said seriously, "I'm listening."

"We've delivered an ultimatum, stating that the captives are being killed, one at a time. Each day, we 'kill' another, giving his name and a personal description. We get that from the internal security documents we captured on Tiamaz. The Transspace operatives had files on all kinds of things. It looks to us as if they had in mind the kind of scam we were planning ourselves."

Roberts noted the way this statement somehow slid from a threat to a delivery of information. He glanced around, to note the various expressions.

The "Veep" looked glazed, and faintly puzzled.

His companion, Marty, looked glazed and thoroughly confused.

Ginette was watching Roberts in puzzlement, and smiled as he looked at her.

Roberts, as he turned his head, was conscious of a succession of faint hissings, and a damp cold sensation in his right ear. He looked at the tall fretful Veep.

"What do you gain by claiming that you're killing men who have already died?"

"What do we get from it? Well, we get the direct personal enmity of the IP. I get nightmares. My buddies on the Governing Council get a sense of power. That doesn't help me any, but what can I do? I've got one vote on the Council, and I get outvoted every time. But never mind that. Now, we've got twenty-nine names to go through, and then we arrive at you. Your name is last on the list. I'm telling you, you'd better take that fact seriously. Just about every male member of this outfit except me is a homicidal maniac. They aren't stupid; they're vicious."

"What do you want me to do?"

"Cooperate. Tell Ginette here—that's not her real name, by the way—everything you know about the Patrol. Everything. All our members will be delighted if you and she really get along in a personal way, because they'll think it's a real joke to see a member of the IP on the film that will be made up from the hidden cameras around the room. But they won't insist on that. All they want is the information. Everything else is irrelevant, if you know what I mean. What counts is that you spit out your guts and tell everything—everything—everything that you know about the IP. Don't hold anything back. Your life depends on it. Believe me, there's a body blow to the prestige and image of the IP with every death announcement, but that's nothing compared to what's coming. What they're going to do to you. If I could stop it, I'd stop it. I'd just kill you, not do what they're going to do. But I've only got one vote. What they're going to do to you will scare everyone else into line, believe me. We're going to leave now, but Ginette will stay here. With you. You two will be all alone together here. You can do anything you want. But before we go, I just want to say one more thing. OK, Marty?"

Roberts glanced at the second man, who still looked as glazed as the vice-president, and who shook his head, then shrugged. "Go on. After all, you're the Veep."

"OK, it's my judgment. I believe in being honest. Why not tell him?"

Marty looked as if he were trying to think, but couldn't find the controls. "I said OK."

"All right."

"Then go ahead and *tell* him. Whatever."

The girl, looking at the same time puzzled and anxious, spoke up: "Marty—look—he's tensing and relaxing different muscles. I've been watching him. I think he's getting ready to try something."

"I noticed it. He can't do much in that jacket."

Roberts, who had been trying to calculate the odds if he did try something, said candidly, "What I'm trying to do is loosen the thing up a little. What were you going to say?"

The vice-president cleared his throat.

"I have to tell you, your lack of consciousness, both here and on the planet Anarchy, was not natural. We have some very capable medical people working for us. You have undergone a most thorough physical examination. We know the Interstellar Patrol is a scientifically formidable opponent, and we have been taking no chances. As a result of our examination, we have removed from the soles of your feet two closely adhering containers made of a fleshlike substance, containing picks to be used on locks. From the roof of your mouth, we have removed a similar substance in appropriate pink color, containing a small very thin sharp blade and a loop of fine wire. From your intestinal tract we have extracted a series of capsules containing light weapon components that might be assembled. Even your body cavities have been examined. Your clothing has of course been searched, and found to contain a really incredible number of deceptive arrangements and devices. The belt buckle, the wire woven in the trouser weave, the boots—everything has been checked, and just in case we've somehow missed something, we aren't returning anything to you."

Roberts nodded moodily. He thought he could survive the disappointment.

The vice-president continued. "Your equipment, clothing, and your body itself have all been thoroughly examined. We have left nothing to chance. It is obvious that you expected to be able to produce an arsenal at will. But there is nothing left." He looked at Roberts with a glint of satisfaction and said, "I'm sorry." He noted Roberts' expression, glanced at Ginette, and looked back at Roberts. "Your fate really is in the soft caring hands of that lovely girl there." He added earnestly, "I hope you can find it in you to show the courage to recognize facts, and I sincerely hope you reach a satisfactory accommodation. The two of you."

Roberts drew a breath to speak, and the vice-president, with an air of having just remembered something, said, "Oh, yes, there was something else. We also examined your teeth, removed the old-fashioned fillings in some of them, and replaced them afterward, having removed the miniaturized circuits embedded in the fillings. It would be nice to know just what *they* were. You can tell Ginette." He nodded and left. His companion studied Roberts' face, smiled like a shark, and went out, closing the door behind him.

Ginette looked at Roberts, and raised her eyebrows. She reached behind her, and held up the pressure can. Her voice was soft and pleasant:

"The Lady or the Tiger?"

Roberts winced at the sight of the can, and shook his head.

"Why bother to *ask* me to answer? The obvious thing is to put the questions under hypnotic drugs."

"As you well know, that's been done. Every answer was silly. At one point you said you were really a fusion bomb which would go off as soon as you reached a vulnerable spot in our arrangements. Another time you said that you were being shadowed by an IP dreadnought in kappa space, and that this dreadnought would materialize out of kappa space in seventeen point four seconds. Seventeen seconds later you laughed and said you hadn't started to count yet. This happened under a combination of hypnotic drugs that is supposed to make any lack of cooperation totally impossible." She looked at him uneasily, and shivered. "It really shook the experts. You didn't make any friends during the questioning, I'll tell you. You should have been a good boy."

"What did they do beside question me?"

"Oh, the doctors examined you, and said you'd had a course of immunization treatments they couldn't truly understand. You seemed to have been immunized against all kinds of sicknesses. There were things in your blood stream they didn't remotely begin to understand."

"Anything else?"

"Well, there were—ah—several interruptions, and it sort of threw things off schedule a little bit."

Roberts looked at her. "Interruptions?"

She said nervously, "The inspector-general of the Movement had just got back from Anarchy, and he wasn't in a very sweet mood. He and one of the doctors had sort of a little disagreement. After they'd got the inspector-general bandaged up, and gotten the bullet out of the doctor, they went back to work on you, only somehow there were a lot of tiny insects in the room—so small you could hardly see them—and every time the doctors would try to do anything, they would bite, and the doctors accused the nurses of leaving the windows open, and the nurses said some pretty bad things to the doctors, and the inspector-general threw such a fit that some of his stitches came out, and in the middle of this, the patient—that is, you—said in a loud voice that if anarchy was what we were aiming at, we'd achieved it, and how did we like it?—Don't you remember any of this?"

Roberts said regretfully, "I missed it. I suppose it was the drugs. Where did all this take place?"

"Right here in the Citadel—Well, not in this room, but in the interrogation room, upstairs."

"Are we at the headquarters of the Movement?"

"No, the colonel-general himself is the real Headquarters. But most of the rest of us are here now. This is our safest place—our citadel. I guess it can't do any harm to tell you now."

"What happened then?"

"The inspector-general said something like, 'Get that bastard out of here before I kill him,' and the doctors went through their checklist and decided they had done everything to you they had to do, so they brought you down here, put you in a straitjacket, and the Veep said, 'I told you it would be a mess to take on the IP. We've had more trouble since we caught him than we've had in the last five years,' and Marty said, 'But where did all these damned tiny bugs come from? Don't we have any bug killer?' and someone by accident picked up the pain spray and used it, and got Sully and the Veep with it, and when we'd recovered from that, Marty got me off in a corner and said, 'Look, Ginette, somehow this SOB is more trouble doped unconscious than the whole twenty-seven of them on Tiamaz. What's it going to be like when he comes to? You've got to make the ultimate sacrifice for the Movement and at least keep him distracted.' And the Veep overheard the last of this and he nodded and said to me that they'd used science and it hadn't worked worth a damn, so it was all up to me now—and we all went to sleep for what was left of the night, and you know the rest."

Roberts, who thought he finally understood what was going on, said, "If we're supposed to be friends, what's the point of the straitjacket?"

"I can let you out of it, but first I have to sure you're not going to make trouble. So far, I'm not sure."

"Were you there on Tiamaz?"

She hesitated, then nodded. "I don't know why I should tell you, but why not?"

"After all," said Roberts, "if we're friends—"

She looked at him with no great conviction, and shrugged. "Yes, I was there. It was awful."

Roberts said, "Shouldn't there have been at least some survivors?"

"IP survivors?"

"Yes."

She shook her head. "The only man in this outfit who doesn't hammer on his chest all the time is the Veep. He spends *his* time whining and complaining. The rest are all so macho it would make you sick. Sully—he's the one on the tug—it sounded as if he was being frank, but in fact he covered up just how awful it really was."

"He said it was a shambles. It was worse than that?"

She nodded. "The takeover from Transspace was going all right until we ran into the Space Force and the IP—that was just as he said. But the unarmed Space Force men more than held their own when they protected the two girl operatives, and then when the IP got in it, it was horrible. Sully made it sound as if he took a cold look at the situation and decided to salvage what he could. In fact, we were run off the planet, and the only thing that saved us was the explosion, and he doesn't have any idea what made that."

"You're saying—"

"I'm saying the IP ship was probably fully manned. There weren't any survivors spread around through the casinos and fun houses. When the IP man with the Space Force saw what was happening, he called for help. So did Sully. We had the internal security setup, but the IP got there faster. Our men were armed to the teeth. When Sully and his boys let loose, it sounded like the end of the universe. I don't know how many people got killed by accident with the shots that missed. But every time the IP shot, somebody on our side went down. The IP ship, held at the spaceport, blasted loose and got there before we could get away. If you ask me, the IP men got on their ship. That's where they belonged, so that's where they were. There were no IP survivors because when the ship went up, they all got caught in the explosion."

"And you don't have any idea what caused that?"

She shook her head. "Sully and the others think it was some kind of illegal explosives factory. But he doesn't know."

"You don't sound to me as if you hate the Interstellar Patrol."

She smiled wistfully. "A girl likes a man who can do things."

Roberts reminded himself how enthusiastically she had wielded the can of pain spray, then said, "It's a shame you're on the wrong side."

She shook her head. "No, you're on the wrong side. Your side will lose this one. Because, even though Sully got beat by the IP, and he'll get beat every time he comes out in the open and fights the IP, Sully isn't stupid. He's crafty. Every one of these macho swaggerers is an underhanded sneak, and the Patrol will never know what hit it. Even the Veep is crafty. And for pure slick cunning cleverness, no-one beats the colonel-general."

"He's in prison."

"Sure he's in prison. That's where he recruits."

Roberts looked at her.

She laughed. "You see, you don't know how to beat cleverness. What's wrong with the Movement is, it's macho. But after what the Patrol did to us on Tiamaz, it will be a long time before Sully and the boys come out in the open and fight again. They'll boast and brag and swagger, but when it comes right down to it, from now on, they'll stick to dirty tricks, clever ploys, lies, stabs in the back, bushwhacking—all the things they're good at."

"If the colonel-general is in prison to recruit, why can't he get out?"

She shook her head. "Of course he can get out."

"Then why does a captive have to be traded for him?"

"That's to embarrass the IP. We know they can't get him out without making a lot of trouble and losing their reputation. So that's why we demand it."

Roberts looked totally blank. She looked at his expression, and smiled. "You don't understand, do you? We make the demand that will make you go against your own standards, and that will turn you and the other authorities against each other. No matter how that turns out, we can't lose." She added, "You're cute when you're confused."

Roberts reminded himself that this was the same girl who had shown no hesitation to blast him with the pain spray. She, however, apparently interpreting his silence as embarrassment, came closer, watching his face and smiling. Roberts looked away, and jumped at a faint hissing sound before realizing it must be within his own ear.

"There, there," she said, smiling. "I won't bite you." She stood close beside him, bent, and gave him a kiss on the cheek.

Roberts remembered her aiming the pain spray and saying, "Another dose?" and he glanced around the room. "Are there really cameras all over in here?"

She nodded. "There are. And even if there weren't, the doors are handy to peep through. The Veep is good at telling you something that's true, and because you know he's a liar, you don't believe the truth he tells you." She looked at him, still smiling. "You're embarrassed, aren't you? Because of the cameras?"

"Well," he said, groping for a suitably embarrassed answer, "there's no privacy, no—"

"Here," she said, giggling, and suddenly undid the straps of the straitjacket that bound him, slid it free, and said, "I knew you liked me."

A tiny voice spoke in Roberts' right ear:

"Roberts, get the seductress into bed with you, and turn your head so this ear is against her nostrils. Don't waste any time. All hell is going to break loose shortly."

Roberts, of two minds on this idea, recognized the urgency in the voice, and did as he was told.

"Oh," she said, and abruptly lay still, the triumphant smile still on her face.

The voice spoke urgently in his ear. "Roberts, lie flat, face-down, turn your head to your left, and pull the covers over your head." An instant later, there was a brief sense of pressure and a scraping in his external ear canal, and something landed beside him. He found a thin tube, the cap off one end, a little ointment coming out.

The voice was tiny but clear. "Rub it over your face, neck, and shoulder, but not your ears. Stay under the covers. Rub it on her face, neck, and shoulders. And keep well under the covers while you do it.

Roberts busied himself with the ointment.

From the door of the room came a puzzled murmur.

The tiny voice in Roberts' ear said, "OK. Now listen closely. Arrange the covers to make a channel from the right side of your head to the room. Lie flat on your face. Whatever happens, don't move, even if you feel a severe pain."

Roberts did as he was told, and lay flat.

There was a rapid crawling sensation as of a half-dozen tiny clawed feet hastening through his ear, accompanied by a bristle brush that just fit the ear canal. Something landed lightly on the sheet beside him. There was a second sensation just like the first. Then there was a buzz, that diminished into the room. Then there was another of the same set of sensations, and another buzz. And another. And another.

Across the room, the door slammed back against the wall. A baffled angry voice shouted, "All right! On your feet!"

Roberts didn't move.

The air instantly filled with a menacing whining droning sound. The sensation of thrusting crawling dozens of hurrying claws in Roberts' ear continued, and he lay severely still as the yells and screams echoed around the room, then moved off into what must be a hallway outside, to dwindle into the distance and mingle with a volley of shots and new screams from other parts of the building.

The crawling sensations in his ear stopped. The buzzing droning sounds were gone.

The tiny voice said, "Move further away from the woman, Roberts. Very slowly . . . now, open your eyes slowly . . . Do you see any insects? Speak in a low voice and we can hear you."

"No," said Roberts.

"Good. Turn over carefully . . . Slowly . . . Any insects on the covers?"

"No."

"OK. Lie still, face up. Pull the covers over your face. Don't get impatient. Don't move."

Roberts pulled the covers over his face, and lay very still.

There was the feeling of a stiff hard wire forcing its way out his ear. It was a tight fit, and very stiff, and it felt for an instant as if it would tear his ear off from the sheer force of its passage. Then the pain died away.

There was a light small sound, as of a feather brushing the sheet beside him. Then the mattress was pressed down, as if a large heavy hand pushed down on it beside him. Something cold and hard scraped past him. There were metallic sliding clicking sounds, as of machined parts being fitted together to form a larger assemblage.

"Roberts, whatever happens next, don't move. One way or another, it should be over very fast."

Something heavy was in the bed, under the covers on the opposite side from the woman. The thing moved down next to his side, to his waist, and stopped. He could feel the mattress give under it as it moved. There was a faint hiss, a smell as of burnt wool, a flare of warmth against his side, a snap, a sizzle, a second sizzling noise, and a repetition so fast that for an instant the air seemed filled with hissing sizzling snapping noises, as if sparks and bolts of flame momentarily filled the space of the room.

From all sides came a crash of plaster, the thud, bang, and clatter of heavy mechanisms striking the floor. Something whistled past his head, there was a dull crash, and bits of plaster pattered on the covers.

The voice in his ear said, "OK, Roberts. Wait a minute." Whatever it was traveled further down in the bed, to pause by his calves and ankles. There was a fresh smell as of burnt wool, and silence.

The voice sounded pleased. "Now, the room you're in should be clear of ordinary surprises. But take a look on your right side. Move slowly."

Roberts, wearying of this, opened his eyes slowly, and at once growled, "Could you put a weapon through?"

The small voice said, "Stay right where you are."

Beside him was a neat precise six-inch round hole opening straight down for a clear drop of what looked like about eighty feet, to a gray deck where he could see figures moving around lathes, drills, and a flexible arm that swung precisely around a workpiece. Roberts' view was obstructed by a thick flexible black cable that was bent over the edge of the hole toward whatever was lying, heavy and cold, beside his right calf and ankle. From under the covers came a click and snap, and at nearly the same moment, a gauntleted hand appeared briefly down in the hole and hauled the cable, a metal connection at the end, down the hole and out of sight.

It occurred to Roberts that if he did what he was apparently expected to do, and stayed where he was, and if he survived whatever was coming next, he would need quite a lot of ingenuity to explain what he had done while the Patrol settled with the Pulgorites. He could hear the questions already, before he was even out of the place:

"Say. Captain, were you actually in the Pulgorite safehouse when the attack came through?"

"Well . . . yes."

"You were a prisoner?"

"That's right."

"A hostage?"

"Yeah."

"That must have been rough."

"Well—no complaint. I volunteered for it."

"Yeah? Gee. That took courage. Just where were you when the attack came in that got you out of there?"

"Ah—I was—well—you see—"

"Lieutenant Jones is telling everyone around that when *he* got there, you were in bed with one of the anarchists. Is that right?"

He could, of course, be suffering from some form of paranoia to even think that anyone might say this, and of course there were a number of ways this conversation might go; but there was no way it could go that Roberts wanted to actually experience. He cautiously tensed one muscle after another, and while there was soreness, and a cramped sensation, he found nothing that seemed touchy or severely painful. He carefully began to ease himself out of bed. The massive object under the covers near the foot of the bed was incidentally in his way. He tried to get a foot over it, and the thing made a quiet ticking noise as it moved its gun-like snout projecting through a burned hole in the covers. What the thing looked and acted like was a standard small-size turret, which suggested he shouldn't have an attack from FIAM to worry about from that direction, except that, for some reason, the turret's power cable had been disconnected.

"Roberts," said the tiny, very clear voice in his ear, "try to steady the rim."

Roberts carefully turned on his side, and put a hand on either side of the hole.

From somewhere down the hallway outside came a scream, then a volley of muffled yells:

"Kill the bastard!"

"Look out! There's another one!"

"Get the thing, damn it! Get it!"

"That's it! Come on!"

The small voice said, "Don't move, Roberts."

There was the sound of running feet approaching up the hallway. Roberts thought of the turret, and stayed still.

Through the hole, Roberts could see, as he carefully lowered his head to try to get a wider angle of vision, a railed work platform to his right, where a man in an informal pale blue-gray Interstellar Patrol uniform raised one of a set of checkered black-and-yellow paddles, gesturing with the raised paddle toward his own left. There was a thump, and he winced, gesturing downward with the other paddle. He then moved both paddles urgently back toward himself.

Roberts put his head closer to the hole, and could see to his left, a little K-class patrol ship, with a kind of slender periscope mounted vertically aft the turret belt. A second glance showed him that the periscope was vertical only because the ship was tilted, to avoid the main upper turret interfering with the slender metal cylinder.

Whoever was in charge of the ship apparently had the problem of getting the periscope up through the other half of the hole Roberts was looking down through.

The shouts, screams, and shots faded from Roberts' awareness as he considered the problem. No doubt if he could see the inside of the ship, he would have a better chance to understand what was wrong—but, no problem, he thought—and moved his part of the hole to try to see if he could center it over the periscope.

The scene stayed the same, moving as he moved the hole, and it dawned on him that it was the *other* half of the hole he would have to move if he was going to do it that way, and the other half of the hole was doubtless clamped solidly in place. There was another thump, and a string of curses came up through the connection as Roberts asked himself what imbecile was responsible for this set-up. All that should have been necessary was to leave the ship in its rack, and just slide the other half of the pair of space-connectors over the periscope. Exasperated as he watched the ship move backwards, forwards, and sideways without getting close enough, he reached down through the hole toward the periscope, and a voice instantly shouted, "Now I see it!" The ship at once came closer, and Roberts yanked his arm back, and moved his head aside.

From somewhere close by in the hall came a scream:

"Die, damn you!"

Roberts glanced toward the door of the room.

From beside Roberts' ankle came a brief low whine, then a sizzling snap, and the room lit up in a blinding white glare.

There was a brief humming twanging sound, followed by another blinding glare, and a crash like a lightning bolt striking thirty feet away.

At Roberts' elbow, a male voice said casually, "Here you go."

Roberts, temporarily blinded by the glare, tried to look around, saw nothing but afterimages, listened to the smash of falling plaster, smelled smoke, and banged his head on a steel-hard column that rose up out of the hole to tower above him like a periscope. As his vision recovered, he could vaguely make out grid-like geometric forms folding out of an opening in the side of the cylinder. An inverted cone swung slowly around, made a number of fine adjustments, then locked into place.

Somewhere amongst the crashes and yells, a voice seemed to be singing a song with the refrain, "Never ever volunteer," and Roberts didn't know if he was hearing the small voice inside his ear, someone on the other side of the space connection, one of the Pulgorites, or if it was all strictly in his imagination. Wherever it was, he agreed with it. He started to get up, and the clear tiny voice said sharply, "Stay where you are, Roberts! It's almost over!"

This comment bothered Roberts more than the mounting volume of sound, or the menacing whine that shot past his head from time to time.

From outside came a sound like thunder, that grew louder and louder, and then there was a fresh set of yells, from inside and, now, from outside.

Roberts' hand bumped something, he felt again at his side, and his fingers closed around the muzzle of a hand gun. At once, he remembered the words, "Here you go." The gun must have been pitched through just ahead of the periscope. He switched grips on the gun as someone yelled from the hallway.

He jumped out of bed, to hear the words, "The son of a bitch is still alive!" Able to at least see as if through a fog, Roberts fired at the doorway, fired again, the whole room lit up as the turret fired, and an instant later the window where Ginette had stood earlier smashed in, and three figures in camouflaged armor were in the room, and then more came pouring through behind them.

The colonel tossed across the latest issue of the news sheet. Roberts caught it, and read the circled item:

PUZZLE
MOVEMENT DISAPPEARS

The Freedom in Anarchy Movement, headed by jailed leader Colonel-General Ian Pulgor, seems to have vanished into thin air.

Reporters seeking information at the devastated news conference site on the planet called "Anarchy" left when no one showed after a wait lasting for five days. There have been no recent announcements from FIAM.

The Anarchy Movement achieved notoriety recently with its raid on the planet Tiamaz, and its capture and reported execution of many members of the Interstellar Patrol. The Patrol has refused to comment on the abrupt disappearance of FIAM.

The attempts of reporters to connect this disappearance with terrific explosions on the planet Anarchy, with an abortive FIAM victory announcement, and with reports of screams, armored troops, and heavy gunfire at a suspected safehouse of the Movement, have all been inconclusive to date.

In short, no one seems to know what has happened. Colonel-General Pulgor, due to be released on parole, had stated that FIAM has merely gone underground. But his voluntary confession yesterday to a crime carrying a five-year prison sentence, and his lawyer's insistence that he spend the sentence in prison, cast some doubt on the colonel-general's assertion.

What has really happened to the Freedom In Anarchy Movement? No one who knows is saying.

Roberts handed back the paper. "According to what Ginette said, the colonel-general recruits while in prison."

"We doubt his latest recruits will show much enthusiasm, as things have turned out."

"Eventually, he'll be out again."

"Oh, not necessarily, Roberts. We've looked into his history, and there are quite a few more crimes he can confess to, in order to not get out."

"Where's Ginette?"

"Back on her home planet. There are those who'd say that was a severe punishment, but she was happy. She was, by the way, the only one of that crew who hadn't yet committed a capital crime."

"If pain spray would kill—"

"Yes, she had a talent there that it was just as well not to develop."

"I have a few questions."

The colonel nodded. "I'm listening."

"Why didn't I have a better idea of what was going on?"

"At the beginning, we had no way to know how capable their doctors and interrogators might be. The less we told you, the less they could get out of you. Moreover, we knew you were resourceful, and would catch on by yourself, provided you lived long enough. One way to keep you alive was to not satisfy their curiosity."

"OK. Now, what happened? I was there. I saw part of it. I have theories. But, I'd like to *know*."

"You understand the working of the space-connector?"

"I saw what it does."

"Good enough. The smaller size was almost a custom fit for the external passage of your right ear. We pumped you full of counteractants for a variety of drugs, some of which we expected them to use, and some of which we planned to use ourselves, put together a holder for the other half of the connector pair, got a volunteer to have that connection fitted in his ear every time you were examined—"

"Why?"

"Because they very thoroughly examined you, and used a flexible explorer device to look up your nostrils, down your throat, and into your ears, amongst other places. If we hadn't had the other half of that connector in *someone's* ear, what would they have seen?"

"This explorer device would have come out in your lab?"

"It would have come out the other half of the pair of space-connectors, in our lab. It would have been as disastrous as for a couple of Greek soldiers to have stuck their heads prematurely out of the Trojan horse."

"I see. This way, they saw the inside of an ear, albeit a different ear."

"Exactly. Fortunately, they made the natural assumption that the inside belonged to the same person as the outside. When they weren't examining you, we felt free to put our half of the connector pair back in its mount, and spray hypnotic drugs or distractants, or pass through a particularly vicious type of tiny black fly, or bad tempered bees, or spray a kind of quasi-human pheromone, or push a tube of—"

Roberts looked blank. "Quasi what?"

The colonel looked faintly embarrassed. "We thought it prudent to moderate the girl's tendency to empty the can of pain spray into your face."

Roberts started to ask another question, then changed his mind.

The colonel went on, "Well, you know what happened. We sent a tube of special-purpose insect repellent through this little jump-point straight into their so-called citadel. We put through spy devices so small no one who doesn't know about them believes in the possibility of their existence. When the opportunity was offered, we could aim a hypodermic gun through, and inject the thugs who were carrying you with a particularly nasty variety of planetary flu."

" 'Grakes'?"

"Right. Of course, it was important that no one actually see these things as they happened. If, near the end, they had seen the oversized bees emerge in large numbers from your ear, anyone who happened to get away would have had something to talk about. For that same reason, you had to be under some kind of cover when we put through one of the larger size of space-connectors, squeezed into a narrow elliptical shape. The first thing we fed through that was a device to change the opening to a more usable circular shape, and the second thing was a kind of modular small-size mobile fusion turret that detected and blew the spy devices in the room to bits, and guaranteed problems for anyone on the other side who tried to get at you."

"Why disconnect the power cable? To make room for the periscope?"

"Partly. Mainly because we had a better connection, through a pair of space connectors. We wanted to be certain that worked before disconnecting the cable. Next, we ran the specially fabricated periscope through, after a trifling little contretemps that could have wrecked the whole operation if you hadn't seen what to do,"

"Getting the periscope through the hole."

"Right, Roberts."

"Why not slide the hole over the periscope?"

The colonel shook his head. "Well—I'm afraid my explanation of the nature of the device must have taken too much for granted. I warned that it couldn't be seen from the wrong side. The officer in charge concluded that it would be a lot safer if it were screwed down, and for some asinine reason he put the whole ship—well, you saw it. So then the captain of the ship had a shadowy hole in a grey rim to find against a grey background, and amongst the experimental junk on the ship, and the pipes overhead in the workshop, he almost didn't do it. Fortunately, you saw what to do."

Roberts, who had acted out of exasperation, on the thought of taking hold of the periscope to guide it to the opening—which overlooked the mass of the ship—kept his mouth shut, and the colonel went on, "Once the periscope had passed through into their stronghold, it, among other things, emitted a signal we picked up from outside, that enabled us to locate the place exactly. And that was that."

"Ginette was sure we were too dull to compete with their cunning minds. Sully was positive they were a lot sharper than we are."

"Which was all a big help to us." The colonel added innocently, "Of course, Roberts, they were judging our intelligence by their captive."

Roberts said ruefully, "A serious mistake on their part."

"It's hard to shine after you've been knocked over the head, put through surgery, and pumped full of two organizations' special drugs."

"Yes, but it was their framework of calculated lies that stunned me. Not a word of truth; but if they hadn't run into trouble, would anyone have known?"

Colonel Sanders nodded.

"They were clever, but on a basis not in line with the facts. When they spoke to you, their words came out in our laboratory. When they took you into their 'citadel', they opened it up to our selection of small pests, and ultimately to anything the parts of which we could get in through a six-inch hole, including a device that could locate their position exactly. Springing dirty tricks on the suckers seems a lot more clever than research. But research can change the conditions to such an extent that, for the time being, at least, the clever swindlers can't even recognize the game. And quite a lot can happen before they figure out what went wrong—if they're still around to figure."

Roberts said thoughtfully, "To those on the receiving end, that must seem like quite a clever trick from such a bunch of gullible innocents."

The colonel smiled.

"That's true, Roberts. To someone who has a racket nicely adapted to present circumstances, research that unexpectedly changes the circumstances is in the ultimate class of mind-stopping underhanded knockout blows—right along with older versions like the Trojan Horse."

WARLORD'S WORLD

I. The Appeal

Vaughan Nathan Roberts was on the fast curving upslide coming out of the Temple of Chance on Tiamaz when he saw the girl.

Roberts, just before that moment, was free of care, his mind cheerfully alternating between curiosity as to the slide's construction—it must be a sequence of gravitors, their fields so angled as to create a strong upward component against the slick, many-colored glowing surface of the slide—and the thought of the steaks awaiting him and his crew at the establishment known as "Chez Dragon."

Hammell and Morrissey, the two older members of his crew, were well ahead of him on the slide. Dan Bergen, considerably younger, was right beside Roberts, his expression showing his shifting feelings as they shot up toward the flight level.

"Weird effect," said Bergen.

Roberts himself felt as if he were shooting *down* the slide, until he glanced around at the elaborately curved ruby and emerald pillars that rose from the game floor below to the surface above. "Why?"

"Why," said Bergen. "It *feels* like we're going down. But I can *see* we're going up." Ahead, a second slide curved amongst the glinting pillars, to take patrons and sightseers down to the game floor. Just ahead, the two slides passed close together.

"Be glad," said Roberts, "that we're going *up*. On that one ahead, that goes down, the slide speeds up, and—" Roberts paused, the rest of the sentence forgotten. On the down slide ahead, curving toward him, coming so close that the two slides passed within six to eight feet of one another, Roberts was suddenly aware of one single individual amongst the crowd. It was a girl.

What took place next happened so fast that no thought seemed to be involved. At one instant Roberts saw the face, the honey-blonde hair, the dark-blue eyes looking straight into his—he felt the impact of a desperate silent appeal flashed between their locked glances as they stared at each other, were swept toward each other, then curved sharply away.

In that instant, Roberts was aware of the girl as if they were one person—as if he were in two places at once. Then she was past. The last thing that he saw was the look of desperate appeal on her face.

Roberts was near the flickering edge of the slide, by the waist-high silver rail. The up-slide he was riding was higher here by several feet than the down-slide the girl was on.

As the two slides began to diverge, Roberts gripped the silver rail, vaulted onto it, crouched and sprang, the whole action so fast as to seem all one motion, and so spontaneous that he did not realize what he was doing until the three-hundred foot drop to the floor was beneath him.

He sucked in his breath in silent prayer, the golden rail of the down-slide loomed in front of him, he dropped from the rail to a momentary clear space in the crowd, heard the indrawn gasp behind him, glanced up and saw the staring faces on the up-slide as he shot back through the closest approach of the two slides.

In that instant, he saw something else. On the up-slide, a figure in the multicolored silk clown-suit and silver and gold domino mask of a bar boy from the game floor was aiming toward Roberts a shiny chrome object with a round black hole in the center.

As Roberts dropped, the figure in the domino mask was twist-ing, and reached out to grip the silver rail as if to try for a better shot. Then the figure was past. Somewhere behind Roberts, there was a yell that faded almost as it began.

Ahead, the slide seemed to slope ever steeper, to almost dip into a vertical drop. The wind blew in Roberts' face. Around him, there was a gasp from the crowd. The gold rail beside him flickered and blurred. Ahead, the game floor enlarged visibly as they rushed toward it.

Roberts stood up. In front of him, the slide leveled out, seemed to press up under his feet, gave the illusion for an instant of climbing steeply—and then he glided out onto the floor, looking quickly around.

The white beam of an idly revolving spotlight paused for an instant, to shine on honey-blonde hair. Roberts thrust through the crowd, leaving behind him a trail of low curses, and his own murmured excuses and apologies.

Ahead of him, two broad-shouldered men in dark evening clothes, their movements brisk and athletic, stepped one to either side of the girl, who drew back, then paused defiantly.

They stepped close, to grip her by the arms, from either side. The taller of the two, to the right, slipped his hand in his pocket. As his hand came out of the pocket, there was the brief flash of a hypodermic.

Roberts had had no time to stop and think since that first glance going up the slide, and he spent no time in thought now. His left hand gripped the taller of the two men at the base of the neck. His right hand clamped the wrist above the other's hand that held the hypodermic. His left hand found the nerve he sought, and his opponent sucked in his breath. The hypodermic dropped to the floor and smashed.

"Let go of her," said Roberts, his voice low and reasonable, "or you will both be dead before seconds pass."

"Who in—"

Roberts' brain now had time to function, and in a brief instant deliver several unpleasant conclusions to him. For a start, it occurred to him suddenly that he was, in fact, all alone here. Hammell and Morrissey were, at this very moment, doubtless settling pleasantly into their seats, admiring the huge dragon of transparent red and gold glass that formed the central attraction around which the tables of "Chez Dragon" were grouped, and from which the pretty girls, their hair tied back, cheeks flushed from the heat, carried the steaks from the grills. Bergen, for his part, had had no warning, and would have been carried quickly out of reach by the slide.

That meant that Roberts had odds of two-to-one to deal with for a start, with the clown-suited bar boy doubtless approaching the top of the up-slide by now, and heading for the down-slide, which would very shortly land him at Roberts' back.

Then Roberts remembered the way the spotlight had lingered on the honey-blonde hair, and realized that very possibly he had worse to contend with than that. The management of the casino itself could be involved.

Roberts at once felt the need to fill in his lack of allies, and generate some confusion at the same time. This was made easier for him by the less tall of the two men, whose gaze flicked casually over Roberts. This glance had the bored quality of a technician in an automated packing plant looking over the incoming beef. As the first of the two sank to the polished floor, this second one spoke up.

"Don't move, poko. You're covered from all sides." Roberts could, in fact, sense the likely truth of the comment in his twinging flesh. He could feel the sights of guns centered on his back, neck, and both sides.

"Unfortunate," Roberts said, "but we have our orders."

There was a faint flicker of interest in the bored gaze resting on him. "Orders from *who?*"

Roberts' racing mind sought the vague, the unverifiable and yet alarming, at the same time that his hands sought nerve centers. He considered swiftly the patronage the casinos of Tiamaz received from various aristocrats, titans of trade, and planetary leaders, large and small. Which ones would they least care to antagonize?

"From the King," said Roberts, his thumb finding the spot he wanted. The girl was suddenly free, staring at him.

The second of the pair who had held the girl had let go and stepped back, staring at Roberts. The two men, Roberts and the girl, were now in the center of a cleared space roughly fifteen feet across. The customers of the casino, taking in the situation, were giving it a wide berth. Bar boys in clown suits and neatly dressed guards in evening clothes were congregated around the little scene, evidently awaiting instructions. Roberts became aware of a peculiar sensation, as if his words had rung in the air, and now echoed back.

"The King," murmured the less tall of the pair who had held the girl. He looked at Roberts uncertainly. Roberts seized the opportunity.

"Did you actually think," he said, "that you could get away with this?"

"I—"

Roberts no longer felt that sensation of guns aimed at him. The little circle surrounding him suddenly had a nervous look. Roberts gave the girl his left arm, and as she clung tightly to him he turned toward the surliest face in the circle before him, and walked directly forward. Behind Roberts, someone sucked in his breath.

"Not *likely*. Stop the—"

Dan Bergen's voice was low, but it carried. "Better not. *The King wouldn't like it.*"

There was a heavy thump, and the surly face before Roberts changed expression and suddenly there was room for him to pass. In front of Roberts, Hammell's powerful figure emerged from the crowd just leaving the down-slide. Behind Hammell came Morrissey, taller and more slender, but obviously fit. They glanced questioningly at Roberts.

Roberts, conscious of the recording instruments that might now be focused on him, murmured, *"Bergen?"*

Hammell's lips scarcely moved. "Coming now."

Roberts nodded, groped for a way to sow confusion, and kept his voice low. "None of the rest had to break cover. We'll leave them."

"Good," said Hammell, exactly as if he knew what Roberts was talking about. Morrissey nodded, and managed a thin smile.

"Where to?" murmured Hammell.

"Refreshments," said Roberts, acutely aware of the need to leave the planet as well as the casino, but also aware of the embarrassing non-availability of his ship. The patrol ship was at the spaceport, and was in the guise of a space yacht, since the arrival of Interstellar Patrol ships had a tendency to create more stir than the arrival of a Space Force dreadnought. Small as Roberts' ship was, its lines would be recognized on sight. And as in the case of a dainty perfume bottle filled with nitroglycerin, it wasn't the outward *appearance* of the thing that brought on the nervous perspiration, but the realization of what the thing could *do*.

Roberts could hardly wait to get back to his ship. But Tiamaz Quarantine, in addition to the standard tests for disease, periodically claimed to also run an "incubation test" which took a total of seventy-two hours. No one could leave the planet until the results of this test were in. Roberts had been on the planet a little over two and a half days. Until another twelve hours went by, the quarantine sticker would not be removed from Roberts' "space yacht". The guards would not admit Roberts to the space-port where the space yacht was kept, and the okay would not even go out to allow Roberts to enter the shuttle to travel *to* the spaceport.

Very conscious of the girl clinging tightly to his arm, and of the tendency of even the best bluff to evaporate with time, Roberts stepped off the top of the upslide. He stepped past the first of the fantastic gravcabs waiting nearby, and selected a pumpkin-shaped coach with the name "Cinderella" in an arc of imitation diamonds over the door.

Roberts opened the door, and helped the girl climb in. Once the five of them were all settled inside, the "coachman" turned on his seat to look in through a little grilled opening. Roberts pulled open the small glass window hinged beside the opening, and called loudly, "Palace of Fortune!"

The coachman nodded. "Palace it is!"

The coach began a rocking motion, to simulate the movement of a horse-drawn carriage. Outside the window flashed the golden spires, granite towers, silver minarets, and floating many-hued banners of Tiamaz. The glint of inlaid jewels, glitter of silver and gold, the green of the trees below, the deep violet of the tiled conical roofs—all were a treat for the eye of the spaceman—an explosion of color and form against a turquoise sky where a golden sun blazed down through pure white clouds.

The coachman called in, "Palace!"

Roberts glanced out the little grilled window. "Go to the front entrance, as if to let us out. Stop near that crowd. Then go around in back."

The coach rocked forward, stopped, then the coachman said, as if surprised, "Oops, sorry, sir. I thought you said the front, not the side." The rocking began again.

Beside Roberts, the girl still clung to his arm. Her head was bent against his shoulder, and she was trembling. Roberts was aware of a fierce possessive tenderness as he looked down at the honey-gold hair. Across from him Hammell and Morrissey, watching, glanced soberly at each other.

Roberts looked out the window, then spoke through the little grille.

"Don't stop. Keep going to '*Chez Dragon*'."

"Yes, sir."

Roberts shut the little window and glanced around uneasily. The need to plan was urgent. But the elaborately cushioned and decorated coach might have concealed a thousand pick-ups. In fact, on Tiamaz, where was the place that didn't?

The girl looked up at him. Her deep blue eyes were like the sky at dusk. Suddenly, she followed his glance of a moment before. Her lips parted in a sudden flashing smile. Her voice was soft, and faintly husky.

"My brother the King," she said, her tone quiet and conversational, "is more a warrior in his boyhood than these gamblers in their prime. They have lowered him by their clever debauchery, but—" a faint cold note entered into her voice—"we will show them that the steel of Festhold will cut much deeper than the gold of Tiamaz."

She tightly held Roberts' arm and said, "I know of your organization—and that the King is in touch with you—but if we are to save the throne and Festhold itself, we must free him from the grip of Tiamaz' advisors at home. His inherited power of decision in a crisis is still strong, but no constitution can endure forever the debasement in which they have entrapped him."

Roberts, filled with delight by the clear sweetness of her voice, realized with a sudden shock that she had just filled in the whole background of the situation—without revealing for an instant that there had been anything false about Roberts' bluff. If anyone were listening, the bluff had suddenly taken on solidity. Roberts, for his part, could now understand the look of nervous sweat on the faces of the guards in the casino.

To seize a blonde-haired girl was one thing. To seize a princess of the Kingdom of Festhold—provided the King was in the power of those who seized the princess—was still not too bad. A gambler might well risk it for high stakes.

But Festhold was one of the largest of the independent human allies of the Federation, and one of the very few that adhered to the ancient code of the warrior. Each male citizen bore arms from childhood, and took his personal sidearms into the flame which consumed his bodily remains at death. The population was made up of warriors, while the kings of Festhold were renowned strategists.

To seize a princess of Festhold, and to have fighting men at once appear on the King's order—there was a situation to chill the blood of the fondest gambler.

She said quietly, looking at Roberts with her deep blue eyes, "Call me Erena." She spoke the name as if it were spelled "Erayna," and added, "Knowing your purpose to free the King, I wish to join your organization. I swear that I have always been true to the Code."

Roberts felt a second shock. Which organization did she "wish to join"?—The mythical organization from Festhold which was pure bluff?—Or the Interstellar Patrol to which Roberts, Hammell, Morrissey, and Bergen belonged? Roberts, being the captain of a patrol ship, had the power to admit whoever he wished to the Patrol—though whoever was admitted must afterward pass through a training course and a series of tests that Roberts did not care to think of, even in retrospect. But Roberts' hesitation lasted less than a fraction of a second.

"I admit you, Erena," he said, "and although I do not need anyone else's agreement, I know that we are all agreed." He glanced at Hammell and Morrissey, then at Bergen, and the smiles that answered his glance also answered his question.

The coachman bent to the little grille. " 'Chez Dragon,' gentlemen."

Roberts stepped down, and helped Erena to descend. As the cab rocked away, they turned to climb the ramp of New Venusian teak with its rail of jade, toward the huge ivory tusks in the open jaws of the dragon's head. Beyond these jaws they could see the double doors of walnut with their broad hammered iron hinges. But they had not reached the nostrils from which flames billowed out above the walk when the whole scene became suddenly hazy. The girl gripped Roberts' arm more tightly.

Hammell growled, "Gas."

Roberts suddenly changed his estimate of the opposition, and with this changed estimate he suddenly cared nothing for the concealment he had tried to maintain. Bergen managed a yell of warning.

Out of the corner of his eye, Roberts could see Morrissey grappling with someone in white. Simultaneously, Roberts could feel himself falling, seeking to protect with his body the unconscious girl who had slumped to the dark wooden floor of the ramp.

Roberts' last conscious thought was an intensely focused command:

"Override! *Come!*"

II. IPS 6-107-J

The wind on the spaceport chilled the two men in coveralls who eyed the space yacht. Like a big gently curved ice-cream cone set upside-down, the space yacht was all curving smoothness, a harmless piece of ostentation and luxury which nevertheless had resisted the master signal box, and was now resisting a six-foot tool steel bar with its end in the lip of the hatch.

"Damned thick metal for a yacht," growled one of the workmen.

"Must be some off-standard job. Has kind of stubby lines when you look it over."

"Put your weight onto that bar. The sooner we get this finished, the sooner we get out of this wind."

"What do you think I'm doing?"

As they strained at the bar, several hundred miles away, Roberts was falling. The last thought that passed through Roberts' mind: "Override! *Come!*" triggered a tiny transceiver in his body. An all but imperceptible impulse flashed skyward, was detected by a tiny satellite, retransmitted—

The two workmen paused, exasperated. "Who owns this rig, anyway?"

"Just somebody the big boys want ended. We plant the stuff, and it finishes them after they're off-planet. No trouble. No sweat."

"Well, let's try a—"

The faint impulse flashed along its tight beam to the ship. Beneath the disguise of the elongated cone-shaped hull, the Interstellar Patrol ship very quietly clicked and murmured. As the signal reached it, the ship was checking its missiles, idling its turrets around to timed signals, and running test problems through the battle computer. A small part of its attention was devoted to the pair straining at the imitation spacelock. A combination of minute traces of gaseous drugs and pseudotelepathic signals was prying information from the pair, while the molecular emplacement of a directed flow of alloy steel further frustrated the struggle at the hatch.

The arrival of the override signal put a sudden end to this cozy house-keeping routine. The ship, unprepared for this signal, wasted a measurable fraction of a second in confusion, its attention and resources scattered—and then made up for it in a hurry.

BAM!

The external camouflage cover exploded in blazing fragments. For a brief instant, the patrol ship, with its two big fusion turrets, its number one snap-beam probe head looming above them, and its movable belt of smaller turrets circling its midsection, stood there unnaturally balanced on its tail amidst the burning fragments.

The two workmen, knocked flat on their mobile ramp by the explosion, stared in a daze at this transformation, and one of them suddenly recognized the letters on the side:

IPS

6

107

J

The workman's scream was lost in the sudden whine of the patrol ship's gravitors. The ship sprang skyward. An instant later, the reaction drive nozzles lit. The ship hurtled toward the capital city of Tiamaz.

On the ramp outside "Chez Dragon," the white-jacketed men pulled Roberts, Hammell, and the others to their feet. Behind them, a blue-uniformed figure displayed a badge to a crowd of patrons alighting from an imitation street car.

"Police business," said the figure in blue. "Just stay back here. Wait until the attendants have these escapees under restraint.—They're congenital defectives from Happy Hills Training Institute.—Ah, here we go. Just keep back, now. The chemical restraint doesn't hurt them. It just makes them harmless to normal people."

Roberts could see the ramp, the staring crowd, and the blue-uniformed figure. It all meant nothing to him. A voice spoke in his ear.

"Walk down the ramp." Roberts walked down the ramp.

"Now turn right." Roberts turned right.

Behind him, he could hear similar orders given to Hammell and Morrissey. It didn't mean a thing to Roberts.

Over the horizon to the northwest, a glittering streak hurtled through the midday sky toward the city. A police cruiser on routine patrol spotted it, spun, and flashed the news:

"Unidentified small spaceship leaving vicinity Parking Spaceport Eight on course Tiamaz Center extreme boost we are following request area alert . . ."

From the police cruiser came the warning: "You are sighted! Decelerate at once to zero! Stand by and open your hatches for boarding!"

From the patrol ship came the answer: "Interstellar Patrol Ship 6-107-J, on Official Patrol Business under Mandate Override Command Authority Paragraph 1064b, Subheading 44p through z, relevant Emergencies to Patrol Personnel On Active Duty, Enabling Authority Subsection J through Q . . . *THIS IS A RELEVANT EMERGENCY!* . . . Stand by to render assistance on request."

On the police cruiser, grim purpose dissolved into chaos.

"Holy—It's an I. P. ship!"

"Wait now! How do we *know* it's an I. P.? Just because they say—"

"—What's 'Mandate Override Command'? *I* never heard of 'Mandate Override Command.' Did anybody here ever hear of 'Mandate Override Command'?"

"They're outdistancing us!"

"Standard regs say we've got to stop *any* ship showing in the inner ring. It doesn't matter if it's the Space Force!"

"Look, what's a 'relevant emergency'? Did anybody here ever hear of a 'relevant emergency'?"

"I'm telling you, you don't mess with the I.P.!"

"But how do we know for sure it *is* the I.P.?"

"Pass the message to HQ and let *them* figure it out!"

At Tiamaz Central Police HQ, calm efficiency dissolved into confusion: "Cruiser 89 has a spook in the Inner Ring."

"Stop and search, or blow it out of the sky."

"Cruiser 89 reports stop and search order out."

"Pull the spook in to Central Detention. We'll want to go over this very carefully. Could be a—"

"Hold everything! This spook is an I.P. ship!"

"Cancel the Stop and Search!"

"Hold it! Hold it! How do we *know* it's I.P.? Anybody could say that! Stop it just the same!"

"If it *is* I.P., how do we stop it?"

"This is a General Order: Capital Squadron to maximum alert!"

"Sir—this I.P. ship reports it's on Official Business acting under Mandate Override Command Authority. It's an Emergency. They request us to stand by to render assistance!"

"Well—*that's* different."

"Wait a minute, Ed. *How* different? How do we *know*—"

"What *is* Mandate Override Command Authority?"

"Get out the space regs."

"Damn it! Who's got the authority under Mandate Override?"

"Let's see that message . . . H'm . . . This sounds right; they got the subheadings and all . . ."

"I can't find the space regs!"

"Well—either it's the I.P. or it isn't. If it is, we aren't going to stop them. They won't stop, period . . . But, if it *isn't*—"

"Send this reply: 'Tiamaz Central Police HQ to IPS 6-107-J. We are alerting the Capital Squadron, and standing by to render emergency assistance on request. We request further information regarding nature of this emergency. You are in a Closed Zone, due to sensitive native installations throughout the Capital Area. We are authorized to seize or destroy all ships of whatever nature in this area on sight.' Send that. That covers everything."

"We still don't know who's got the authority under Mandate Override!"

"Where's the damned space regs?"

Roberts entered the roofed-over walk that led to the slide entrance and exit in the Temple of Chance. A faintly amused voice said, "Head for the downslide."

Obediently, Roberts joined the crowd pressing forward at the out-curved head of the slide. The voice beside him murmured, "Halfway down, where the two slideways come closest together, there's a sheet of nonreflective glass that slopes off to the right. Understand?"

Roberts' mind seemed to split in half. "Nonreflective glass?"

"Right. It's sloped to the right. It's thick armorsheet nonreflective glass, curved in a big trough, and it leads off to the right, sloping downward. It's put there to protect anyone who would try to jump from one slideway to the other."

"Oh," said Roberts. He could understand that. The two separated halves of his mind seemed to come together again.

The voice went on: "This armorsheet nonreflective glass slopes off to the right, and takes you to the casino office. When we get to the halfway point, where the two slideways come close, jump down onto the nonreflective glass. You can't see it. Bend your knees a little to take the shock when you hit. You'll drop five to six feet, land on the glass, and slide to the right. Stay seated on the glass slide.—Understand?"

Roberts' mind again seemed divided, and one part was trying to tell his consciousness something, but it could not get through to the other part.

"Okay," said the voice, faintly amused. "Here we go now, onto the slide. When we reach the halfway point, vault over the rail and bend your knees. Understand?"

"Yes."

They stepped onto the smoothly downcurving slide, and Roberts glanced over the golden rail. Three hundred feet below, the figures were tiny on the game floor. Somewhere behind him, there was a crash as of heavy thunder.

The Interstellar Patrol ship had crossed the horizon like a meteor, ignoring the police cruisers forming into a circling pattern overhead. The sensitive receptors of the patrol ship were now picking up a faint signal which radiated from a crowd passing under a canted roof gleaming silver under gigantic golden letters reading, "The Temple of Chance."

The patrol ship dove toward the canted roof. Small doors slid back to uncover grilles inset in the ship's flanks. A siren wail split the air, its volume suggestive of a rocket engine being tested to destruction. Below, the crowd stared around, looked up, saw a dazzling red and yellow flash descending, and bolted to get out of the way.

The patrol ship braked with a whine from its gravitors, passed under the canted roof, retracted its probe heads into their wells, and followed the faint signal to the outward slanting entrance of a slide. Here the downward slanting roof overhead, and the protective wall at the edge of the walk, made the distance too small for the patrol ship to pass.

On the downslide, Roberts saw the slightly higher slide that rose from the game floor approaching. Beside him, the gold rail of the downslide flickered. As the two slides approached, Roberts braced himself.

From somewhere behind him came the wail of a siren, rising louder and louder. The two slides came close.

Beside Roberts, the voice said, "Jump!"

Inside of Roberts' mind, something clamored to speak to him. His mind seemed split in parts, one part unable to communicate with another.

"Jump!" said the voice in his ear.

Roberts gripped the golden rail, and vaulted over it. From behind him came an amused chuckle. Roberts bent his knees to take the shock.

Below him, the little figures were moving on the game floor. He dropped four feet. He braced for the impact. He dropped eight feet.

The tiny figures far below turned small faces upward, apparently attracted by the wail of the siren. Roberts dropped sixteen feet. He was tilting off-balance now. Where was the glass slide?

Below, small dark ovals appeared in the upturned faces—the mouths of the watchers seeing a little figure dropping toward them. Roberts fell thirty-two feet.

Roberts' heart pounded. His lungs sucked in air. The sudden increase in blood pressure and oxygen level seemed to burst the barriers that had split his mind. Abruptly he realized that there was no glass slide, that he had been tricked by casual drugged suggestion into committing suicide.

To either side of him, he could see the curving undersides of the slides, silver for the upslide, gold for the downslide. From the floor below, pillars of synthetic amethyst, ruby, and emerald, climbed toward the ceiling far above, and the silver and gold slides threaded their way between these pillars.

Now, tilting forward, the little figures below running to get out of his way, Roberts realized what had happened. But now, it was too late for him to do anything about it. Roberts fell sixty-four feet.

The patrol ship, its blunt nose over the high parapet, suddenly rotated, swinging the two main fusion turrets in an arc. A dazzling circle of glowing red appeared on the surface of the parapet.

The patrol ship slammed forward, shot down along the edge of the downslide, eased directly over it, moving in a blur—

Roberts, the game floor rushing up at him, his heart pounding, could feel the smash before it happened—could feel the bones break and the flesh smash into pulp—but, trained beyond the point of giving up, he drew his legs and arms in to speed the rotation of his body. He put out arms and legs in the attempt to land on all fours, arms and legs bent, muscles braced to take the terrific impact, then either roll, or land as flat as possible.

The floor rose beneath him like a swinging giant sledgehammer. Somewhere, someone screamed at the top of his lungs. The pattern of the game floor—tokens, coins, and bills interlocked and interwoven, was suddenly big in Roberts' face. He hit the floor. The impact was crushing. With every ounce of his strength, he struggled to push away the sledge-hammer that was smashing up below him.

For an instant, its bone-breaking power gripped him, crushing, squeezing, ready to burst him to a pulp—and then, somehow, everything swayed in the balance. Roberts' straining muscles held. Then the force against him began to ease.

Incredulous, Roberts glanced up. Over the gold of the downslide, flashed a length of curving metal—the patrol ship.

Behind Roberts, Hammell, his face red and strained, blood vessels standing out, crouched on the polished game floor. Behind Hammell, Morrissey balanced on one foot, and Bergen alighted gently on the shining floor.

The scream sounded again, and now Roberts could place it.—It came from the ramp. He took a step toward the ramp, then paused blankly.—There was something he wanted to do, but what?

His pulse, slowing now that his feet were firmly on the floor, and his breath, coming more easily now that the strain was over, seemed to be letting doors close between separate parts of Roberts' mind. A vague uncertainty was replacing the sense of urgency.

"Jump!" came the remembered order, spoken in his ear. But he *had* jumped.

Blankly, Roberts stood on the game floor, awaiting further

orders, as somewhere in the locked compartments of his mind, a memory clamored in vain for attention.

Overhead, siren screaming, red and yellow lights flashing in a blinding dazzle, IPS 6-107-J finished stuffing the last screaming white-coated figure into its materials intake, jammed in beside the rock drills and crusher jaws, and then the doors of the intake slid shut over them.

A voice boomed out, painfully magnified by an apparently defective speaker system:

"... ATTENTION! ... WARA ... COMPLIANCE BLIH SSSSSSTRUCTION IMMEDIATELY TO THE FULL EXTENT REQUIRED BY ... RRRTANNNACTIVATION! *THIS IS AN EMERGENCY!* ... ZZZZZBBBY IMMEDIATE COMPLIANCE OR FACE THE FULL AND PROMPT APPLICATION OF THE EXTREME PENALTY! ... YOUR ATTENTION! ... WARA ... COMPLIANCE ... SSSSSSSSTRUCTION *IMMEDIATELY!*"

This announcement, containing within itself an additional source of confusion from an overlapping repetition as if two speakers gave the same message at slightly different times, crossed the gap where below the sparkling pillars and curving slides the patrons stared up from the motionless wheels and the oblong and horseshoe-shaped tables. The announcement reached the sheer walls that bordered the game floor like the sides of a canyon, to echo and reecho in a chaos of overlapping, totally incomprehensible commands.

Under the cover of this deafening uproar, in a dazzle of blinding red and yellow flashes, with the siren starting up again in the background, Roberts suddenly found himself rising in the air, halfway up from the game floor, an emerald pillar glittering off to his right, the golden sheathing of the downslide curving through the air before him.

His perceptions were a chaos of overlapping sensations, his senses swamped by the brilliance of the flashes, the volume of the commands, and the nerve-jangling effect of the swelling siren:

> *FLASH!* (RED)
> "ATTENTION!"
> "*IMMEDIATELY!*"
> *FLASH!* (YELLOW)
> "REQUIRED BY THIS RRRTAN ..."
> *FLASH!* (RED)

FLASH! (YELLOW)

. . . rrrrrrRRRRAAAHHRRRRAA . . .

The curving hull of the patrol ship was just above him. The ramp seemed to move under the ship, and then Roberts was dropped, bathed in red and yellow light, reverberating commands, and vibrations that rattled his teeth. From the slanted setback just aft the amidships turret belt, there was a tiny glint of reflected light. Something struck Roberts' left forearm, and stung like a wasp. A wave of stinging fire went through Roberts, to leave him for an instant totally blank—and then suddenly his awareness returned.

Roberts glanced up at the tapering tail of the patrol ship, crouched, and sprang up to seize the Number One reaction-drive nozzle. He pulled himself up onto the massive fin on which the nozzle was mounted, stepped up atop the Number Two fin, found the entrance hatch forward of the fin solidly locked, snarled under his breath, walked up the setback with the turret belt's Number Three fusion turret looking him in the eye and walked by the turret with the sleek gray curve of the patrol ship like the back of a metal whale underfoot. Now he saw that the upper snap-beam projector head had been almost fully retracted into its well. Just behind the head was the motionless Number Three belt turret. Just before the head was the bulge of the main upper turret, which was slowly idling around, swinging around a fusion gun big enough for a man to put his arm in it up to the shoulder.

From somewhere aft came a grunt, and a faint clang, then another grunt and a low curse. Roberts sat down between the main upper fusion turret and the retracted probe head, and leaned around the turret to search the game floor below. All around him now was a weird singing sound, as from behind him came the low growl of Hammell's voice.

"Is that the garbler?"

"If it isn't," said Roberts, "I don't know what it is. Do you see her?"

"Nowhere. They separated her from us right after they hit us."

"Where did they take her?"

"I don't know."

Roberts craned back over his shoulder, to see Morrissey and Bergen standing on the massive horizontal fins, leaning inward against the upper fin, holding on to the upper reaction-drive nozzle.

Morrissey and Bergen looked back at him sadly, and shook their heads. Roberts damned himself, looked urgently around, then heard, through a volley of incomprehensible orders, a faint metallic scrape.

To his left, almost halfway down the curving hull, there slid out of a turret-like bulge in the hull a three-fingered hand on a thick flexible cable.

Roberts growled, "Hang on. Here comes the extrudible arm if you slip."

Hammell looked at the glinting metal fingers, and gripped the thick support of the detector head. The casino seemed to whirl around them. The upslide with its gold rail flashed past below. Directly ahead of them was a circular cut through the high parapet, at the top of the wall above the game floor.

Abruptly, the wall was behind them. The canted roof sheltering the walk and the gravcabs flashed past. They were in the open air. Roberts looked down over the curve of the hull.

The green of the trees, the deep violet of roofs, the flashing silver and gold spires looked up at him. How long ago had it been that Roberts, perfectly content, had been on the upslide coming out of the Temple of Chance?

Now, still in the same day, he felt mentally blackjacked and, far worse, had an aching sensation that some part of himself had been cut off.

Where was the girl? Who had her? What were they doing to her?

Roberts banged his fist on the hull. "Open up. We've got to go back there!" But IPS 6-107-J didn't answer, and didn't open the hatch. Instead, the wind whistled past ever louder, and the scene below shifted in a rapid flow, as to either side and above the big police cruisers sought to match the pace.

III. "Personal Considerations Are Not Important"

As Roberts and his crew clung to the hull, the tiny satellite that earlier had relayed Roberts' call to the patrol ship now relayed the patrol ship's report, sending it to a second tiny satellite, which flashed it on to a little sphere drifting outside the plane of the ecliptic in an orbit gradually drawing closer to the planet. From this little sphere, the message flashed straight to its destination, a region of space where nothing at all was visible, but where the usual standard massometer would have run its needle off the spaceship scale.

Somewhat off-center in this invisible mass, a spare athletic individual, with colonel's eagles and crew-cut hair, impatiently paced in a small neat room.

"Damn it," he said, "we don't get a reading like that on the emotional probe without good and sufficient cause. It *never* fails when it's that extreme."

The bulkhead which served as one wall of the room had a solid enough appearance by the cot, whose post came within a yard or so of touching the massive desk in the corner. But adjacent to the desk, the bulkhead seemed to have vanished, to show a strongly built man with piercing blue eyes sitting back, frowning, behind a desk similar to the colonel's.

"*If* there's something, we should find it."

"There's no 'if,'" said the colonel. "There's *got* to be something there."

"I have to admit, the e-probe suggests the *intent*, and with the amount of money that passes through that gamblers' paradise, there's bound to be the opportunity."

The colonel shook his head.

"It's worse than that. The emotional probe is no more perfect than any other instrument, but we don't get this reading from *intent* alone."

"Extreme intent—a strong lust for power—"

"No. As a matter of experience, we've found no degree of desire or determination that produces this reading. There has to be *belief in the imminent attainment of the objective.* That's for the *degree* of the reading. Next we have the bandwidth. That implies an *organization* of individuals all sharing this belief."

"H'm . . . well—we've had three crews in there—there's no indication of secret armaments—there's nothing to suggest that Tiamaz is any different than it ever was."

"Except," said the colonel, "a gradual steady rise in the probe reading."

"It's getting *worse?*"

"Correct."

Beside the colonel's desk, the lid of a pneumatic chute popped open, a shiny metallic cylinder popped partway out, opened, and ejected a message spool. A voice said, "Communications monitor. This is a message to Colonel Valentine Sanders, from J-Class ship 6-107. Please acknowledge receipt and read immediately."

The colonel frowned. "I acknowledge receipt." He reached for the message.

"And," said the voice meticulously, "you are the aforesaid Colonel Valentine Sanders?"

The colonel snarled, "I am the aforesaid Colonel Valentine Sanders." He unfolded the message and read aloud.

"IPS 6-107-J to Symcomp (copy). IPS 6-107-J to Colonel Valentine Sanders, Chief, Operations Section (message). Current Code 060479.

"Crew of this ship attacked with intent to kill, in or near Temple of Chance, in Planetary Capital of Tiamaz. Crew previously drugged. Code 66 suspected. Crew is now safe and three assassins are in protective custody, following memory simulation and deep mental examination. Summarized results of this examination are as follows:

"The three prisoners are professional killers, currently in the pay of one 'Marius Caesar,' who controls a gambling syndicate on Tiamaz. Marius Caesar has seized Erena, sister of the hereditary ruler of Festhold, and is apparently holding her as a means of coercing Festhold. For whatever reason, the three killers are all convinced that Marius Caesar, as he calls himself, aims to become the ruler of Festhold, as a means to seizing further power.

"The crew of this ship became involved in this situation as follows:

"1) Vaughan N. Roberts, Captain, saw the Festhold princess being taken under guard into the Temple of Chance. Roberts risked death by vaulting across a three hundred foot drop from one gravitic ramp to another, freed the girl from two thugs, found himself ringed by other thugs, and presented himself to them as an agent of the Festhold ruler. Roberts warned them that they faced instantaneous death, and taking the princess on his arm, walked through the ring.

"2) Dan Bergen, Crewman, seeing Roberts vault onto the opposite ramp, and seeing an assassin take aim at Roberts, overpowered the killer, knocked him unconscious, appropriated his weapons, secreted the unconscious assassin in a trash can, and went down the gravitic ramp into the Temple of Chance. He arrived just as Roberts bluffed the ring of hired killers, one of whom began to call Roberts' bluff. Bergen at once knocked this killer senseless.

"3) Crewmen Hammell and Morrissey, meanwhile, had been alerted by Crewman Bergen, and stepped off the descending ramp just as Roberts, with the princess, approached the ascending ramp.

"4) This whole sequence of events was viewed by the management of the Temple of Chance, which is owned by Marius Caesar. Three groups of four hired killers each were dispatched to overtake Roberts, his crew, and the girl, who meanwhile had left by gravcab. Roberts succeeded in leading two groups of the killers to the wrong places, but was caught by the third group on entering "Chez Dragon," a restaurant near the Temple of Chance. An airborne drug was administered to Roberts, his crew, and the girl. The girl was taken into the Temple of Chance by another entrance. Roberts and his crewmen were deceived into jumping from the gravitic ramps at a height of about three hundred feet above the floor of the gaming room.

"5) Apparently at the moment of the attack by gas, Captain Roberts sent the override command. IPS 6-107-J arrived barely in time to save Crewmen Hammell, Morrissey, and Bergen, by use of tractor beams. Captain Roberts was already striking the floor. A tractor beam was used, however, on the principle that everything should be done until it is proved impossible to save the crewman. For some reason that is not known, Roberts survived this fall, apparently without serious injury.

"6) Discussion between Roberts and Hammell following administration of antidote shows that Roberts has one thought—to free the girl. He had given orders that IPS 6-107-J admit him and his crew, in order to return to the planetary capital.

"7) In view of the fact that this may have been a Code 66 drug, IPS 6-107-J requests instructions whether to readmit the crew.

"8) IPS 6-107-J requests instructions as to the disposal of the captured assassins.

"IPS 6-107-J to Colonel V. Sanders, copy to Symcomp Current Code 060479. Message ends."

The colonel looked up. Behind the other desk, the strongly built figure with piercing blue eyes sat tilted back in his chair, thumb and forefinger to chin, frowning thoughtfully. Abruptly, he sat up.

"Someone's out of his head."

The colonel glanced back over the message, and nodded. "It must be that the killers have a false picture of what is actually taking place. To *them*, it seems that the princess—what's her name?—Erena—is being held hostage. But that doesn't fit."

"No. That play would work *some* places. But not with Festhold. You might as well grab a bear's cub, and then tell the bear to act right or you'll start chopping up the cub.—You'd never live long enough to get the threat completely formulated."

"And this J-class ship's symbiotic computer has that information.—It knows it as well as we do."

"Come to think of it, Val, there's a peculiar tone to the whole message. It's stilted."

The colonel scowled, pulled out his chair, sat down at his desk frowning, and reread the message. He shook his head. "There's something here I don't follow. But while we grapple with it, Roberts is apparently stuck outside hanging onto a fin." The colonel reached out to a dial on the wall, and quickly tapped out a call number and his own identification code. A brisk voice spoke: "Communications Monitor."

"Colonel Valentine Sanders to IPS 6-107-J."

"Do you wish this message to be sent as you speak, or to be held for rereading and correction?"

"Hold it for correction. Put the copy to Symcomp, current code, and so on, in the heading."

"One moment. That is done. You may proceed."

The colonel glanced at the sheet of message paper. "In reply to your message Current Code 060479, the situation you mention highly important, but suggest some data still missing. Admit Roberts and crew—Repeat, admit Roberts and crew—regardless Code 66 risk. I take responsibility for full restoration of command authority. Repeat—I take responsibility for full restoration of command authority."

The colonel glanced over the message. "Regarding disposal of the captured assassins, refer this question to Roberts."

The colonel glanced at the ceiling. "Monitor—Let's hear that."

He sat listening thoughtfully, then said, "Insert the name 'Roberts' before the words 'command authority.'—In both places where the words 'command authority' are used."

The Communications Monitor said primly, "The *possessive case* of the proper noun 'Roberts'?"

The colonel opened his mouth, repressed a snarl, and repeated, "Yes, the *possessive case* of the proper noun 'Roberts.'"

"Very well. Then that is the message?"

"It is. Put the usual close on it, and send it out right away."

"Very well." There was a *click*. The colonel's lips drew back from his teeth.

Across the two desks, which in the illusion of closeness created by the ship's communications system appeared to be in contact, the strongly built figure was leaning back, grinning.

"—Do you have the impression now and then that this whole symbiotic computer set-up is somehow female?"

"*Phew!*" The colonel sat up. "Possessive case of the proper noun, Roberts." He glanced across the desks, and suddenly looked startled, "'Female'?" He looked at the message from the patrol ship. Before him, the words stood out: "Discussion between Roberts and Hammell following administration of antidote show that Roberts has one thought—to free the girl."

The colonel bit his lip, looked back in the message, and read: "Roberts risked death by vaulting across a three hundred foot drop . . . freed the girl from two thugs, found himself ringed by other thugs . . . and taking the princess on one arm—" He looked up.

"You're right. That must be what we're up against. Roberts has fallen in love with this girl! Every time something like that happens, we have a weird response from any patrol ship involved.—You might almost say they get jealous!"

"What sort *is* Roberts? Is he going to want a quick whirl with this princess? Festhold is the Federation's main ally in this region, you know. And the Festholders have very stern views.—Or is he going to want to marry her? I'm assuming the girl might be willing. But, even so, do you know what is required of someone who wants to marry a princess of Festhold? It looks to me as if there's the possibility of quite a stew here . . . Say, Val—*You* took full responsibility for putting him back in charge of that J-ship, remember?"

⚜   ⚜   ⚜

Hammell, seated behind Roberts, clinging to the support of the detector head, said, "Hey, the hatch is opening up!"

Roberts craned around, watched Bergen and Morrissey come quickly and carefully up the thick slanting fins, and drop in through the hatch.

Roberts murmured, "After you."

Hammell twisted around, crouched, stepped down the slanting set-back just aft the turret belt, and dropped through the hatch.

Roberts took a quick look around at blue sky, drifting white clouds, and dark green forest below, then followed Hammell through the hatch, which immediately clanged shut behind him.

Roberts pulled the hatch lever down, spun the lockwheel clockwise, and shoved the clamp tight. He went down several steps out of the cramped aft section of ship, passed the bunks, ducked under the three-foot-thick shiny cylinder that ran the length of the ship, and slid into the control seat. A quick glance at the external screen showed drifting clouds above, green forest below, all gradually shifting left, which told him that the patrol ship was circling to the right.

On the battle screen, little symbols showed Roberts his own ship slowly circling above a wild section of the planet, while behind him an array of police cruisers blocked him off from the capital of Tiamaz, with its endless gambling houses and pleasure palaces.

Roberts, frowning, pressed a button to the left of the instrument panel, near a glowing lens lettered "Smb Cmp."

"What," he said, "is the make-up of the government of Festhold?"

The symbiotic computer replied, "Festhold is at present in the control of a regent, acting for The King, who will assume control on reaching his twenty-first birthday. The government of Festhold is a hereditary monarchy, and descends from father to son, always in the male line, provided the heir passes two tests.

"The first test is religious, or moral. The King must be able to withdraw a particular broadsword from a large dull crystalline rock situated near the altar in the Cathedral of Truth. It is assumed by foreigners that some device controlled by the priesthood decides whether or not the sword can be withdrawn from the crystal. This would enable the priesthood to pass on the fitness of the heir to the throne.

"The second test is political. The heir apparent must meet with the assembled nobility of the realm, address them, and receive the approval of at least two-thirds of the nobility.

"If the heir apparent fails either test, he is stripped of royal rank, and becomes the lowest nobleman of the realm. The tests are then repeated for those who stand next in line.

"If all the males of the ruling family should fail, the tests are repeated throughout the nobility in order of rank. Any nobleman may take the test, or decline. Each nobleman who fails becomes a commoner. The first man who passes both tests becomes King. The full title is 'Ruler and Warlord, King and Emperor of Festhold.' The King is a constitutional ruler in peacetime, and has dictatorial powers in wartime. He rules through a Council responsible to him, a Lords' Chamber responsible to the nobility, and an Assembly of the Commons responsible to the general population.

"The rulers have all come from the same family for the past hundred and sixty years. This family, by a series of fatal accidents, is now reduced to the heir apparent, Prince Harold William, and several princesses. The actual control of the country is in in the hands of the Regent, Duke Marius Romeigne, who is the highest member of the peerage.

"It is taken for granted by the population that Prince Harold William will pass both tests and become King, and he is referred to commonly as 'The King.' He is now four months short of twenty-one years old."

The symbiotic computer came to the end of its explanation. There was a silence. Hammell, Morrissey, and Bergen, grouped nearby, listening, glanced at Roberts.

Roberts said, "Name the princesses of the royal family."

"Erena, Catherine, Eloise."

"What rank or power do they have?"

"None save the title, 'Princess of Festhold,' an allowance, and a small personal retinue. Their husbands acquire no rank in marrying them, but their children, if of age, are considered members of the royal family and eligible to be tested for the throne if all members of the direct male line are wiped out."

"H'm."

The symbiotic computer added drily, "To marry a Princess of Festhold, the suitor must be able to withdraw the sword from the crystal."

Roberts looked up sharply. Morrissey winced. Hammell coughed. Bergen looked concerned.

"Suppose," said Roberts, his voice even, "that he fails?"

"He is banished without further sight of the princess. He is forbidden to return."

Roberts' fingers tightened on the arm of the control seat. He drew a deep careful breath, then with an effort of will relaxed one group of muscles after another. His voice sounded reasonably normal when he spoke.

"In the Temple of Chance, I met someone who called herself 'Erena.' She is a little taller than my shoulder, has blonde hair and deep-blue eyes. She has great presence of mind, and after Bergen and I got her out of the Temple of Chance with the help of Hammell and Morrissey, she said—" Roberts frowned.

"Let's see, she said—" Roberts cleared his throat, and repeated slowly:

" 'My brother The King is more a warrior in his boyhood than these gamblers in their prime. They have lowered him by their cunning debaucheries, but we will show them the steel of Festhold cuts deeper than the gold of Tiamaz.' "

There was a momentary silence, then the voice of the symbiotic computer spoke. Now, for some reason, the stiffness was gone, and this voice had more of its usual characteristic ring: "This is the exact wording, or a free rendering of the same?"

Roberts glanced at this crew. "I think it's close to exact—but I can't swear to it."

Morrissey said, "It sounds word-for-word to me."

Hammell shook his head. "It's close, but there's a slight difference somewhere."

Bergen said, "She put more emphasis on Festhold being stronger than Tiamaz. She said Festhold will cut much deeper than Tiamaz."

Roberts said, "I think that's right." The symbiotic computer was momentarily silent.

Roberts said, "It sounds to me as if this Regent aims to disqualify the King, and take over himself. No one so unprincipled is safe to have as King of a place like Festhold."

The symbiotic computer replied matter of factly, "That is correct."

"Before we do anything else," said Roberts, "we need to get Erena out of that casino."

"It is not known that she is in the casino."

"Then we have to find out."

"This is inaccurate. No *necessity* to do this exists."

Roberts said stubbornly, "I'm not *leaving* her there. I'll get her out of there or die trying."

The symbiotic computer said tonelessly, "This is not necessary. The princess should be in no immediate danger. The true problem is on Festhold, not here."

Hammell and Morrissey glanced uneasily at each other. Bergen shook out a handkerchief and mopped his brow.

Roberts said flatly, "There isn't any choice in the matter. We're going back."

The symbiotic computer did not sound convinced. "The need is unproven."

Roberts took hold of the drive controls. The controls resisted his pressure. The muscles of Roberts' arms stood out. The gravitor control yielded grudgingly to the strain. The outside viewscreen showed the increase in speed as the landscape slid back below the bow.

The gravitor control began to pull with increasing force against Roberts' grip. Roberts gripped the control harder. The ship continued to accelerate.

The battle screen began enlarging one after another of the police cruisers, as if to emphasize the danger. Roberts changed hands on the gravitor control, and reached for the firing controls. Hammell murmured fervently under his breath.

Roberts felt the resistance in the firing controls, and snarled, "Crew to battle stations! Prepare to fire by manual control!"

Hammell, Morrissey, and Bergen were gone in a flash. Hammell and Morrissey to the main fusion turrets, Bergen to the manual control station governing the missile bay and belt turrets. There remained a number of smaller turrets that, for sheer lack of hands, could not be brought under manual control.

The voice of the symbiotic spoke disapprovingly. "This is an attack on a legal planetary authority without justification. A patrol ship cannot be used for unauthorized personal ends. Moreover, this approach is stupid. Personal considerations are not important enough to justify illegal and stupid actions."

The gravitor control began to pull with compounding force against Roberts' grip. Grimly, he held the control in place. But, while he held it, it was becoming clear to Roberts just how ineffective a fight he could put up in a ship with the guns worked manually, and the flying controls fighting him every step of the way. This was, moreover, as Roberts knew, only the first hint of what the symbiotic computer could do. Already, there was a faint suggestion of a close stuffiness in the air. That would follow from shutdown of the air system. To partly compensate for that, the entrance hatch would have to be propped open. And since that hatch had an automatic open-and-shut control as well as the manual lock, merely keeping the hatch open was going to be no small problem in itself.

Roberts, with straining muscles, held the controls in place, and glanced at the battle screen. The police cruisers were swinging into position as if to block him. The communicator buzzed imperatively.

"Police Cruiser 187 to IPS 6-107-J. You are approaching the border of the Greater Capital City Metropolitan Area. We warn you that intrusion on this border is forbidden except in case of a justified emergency situation, and we order you to stop under penalty of arrest, fine, and punitive detention."

Roberts released the gravitor control, which went all the way to its centering stop with a sledgehammer thud. He spoke politely.

"IPS 6-107-J to Police Cruiser 187. We regret to inform you that this is a serious emergency situation. Five members of the crew of this ship were attacked, gassed, and detained in the vicinity of the Temple of Chance inside the Capital City Metropolitan Area. Four members of the crew have been recovered, but one remains a prisoner. We wish to recover our missing crewman."

"PC 187 to IPS 6-107-J. No ship of your designation has officially been admitted to any entry port on the planet."

"IPS 6-107-J to PC 187. We entered under the guise of a space yacht, the Gala IV."

Around Roberts, the stuffiness of the air was increasing. From time to time, the lighting system flickered.

The voice from the police cruiser burst out, "Well, what the devil do you claim happened? Did one of your crew give birth, or what? *Four* of you went in. *Four* of you came out. Where's the problem?"

Roberts said evenly, "While on the planet, we accepted a volunteer."

There was a further silence, then, "Are you authorized—"

"The captain of an Interstellar Patrol ship is fully authorized to accept and enlist volunteers. I did so accept and enlist one volunteer, who thus became a candidate member in good standing in the Interstellar Patrol. This crewman, after enlistment, was illegally attacked, illegally seized, and is now being illegally held captive on your planet. I want this crewman released."

"Well, I—can you identify this volunteer—this crewman?"

"Certainly. Princess Erena of Festhold. She has blonde hair, her eyes are blue, her height is approximately—"

"*Princess Erena of Festhold!* You can't enlist—"

Roberts' voice grated. "Can't I?"

There was a silence. Roberts hadn't been aware that the lights in the ship had gradually dimmed. He only realized it when abruptly they came back to full power. The stuffiness in the air was suddenly gone.

Abruptly Hammell reported, "Full power on this turret!"

Morrissey's voice repeated from a different station, "Full power on this turret."

Bergen's voice was eager. "*Missile bay and turret belt!* Full power on automatic control!"

Roberts checked the control board, found it worked easily, and said by routine, "Acknowledge. Stand by at battle stations." He spoke coldly into the communicator pick-up. "Are *you* deciding the enlistment policies of the Interstellar Patrol?"

"I—" Paralysis seemed to set in after the one word. It dawned on Roberts that the police officer on the other end of this hook-up had undoubtedly overheard Hammell, Morrissey, and Bergen, and Roberts' own order to, "Stand by at battle stations." Anyone on Police Cruiser 187 would find it logical to think the Interstellar Patrol ship was preparing to attack.

Roberts' voice was courteous but definite: "Princess Erena of Festhold voluntarily requested to join our organization. I am fully qualified to pass on the fitness of any volunteer, and I adjudged this volunteer to be qualified. I accepted her. She thereby became a candidate-member of the Interstellar Patrol. I have three witnesses here to back up my word. Now, are you, or are you not, going to recover this crewman for me?"

"But she's a subject of Festhold!—And a member of the ruling family! We can't—"

"That," said Roberts, "is a problem you will have to settle with the Warlord of Festhold. I am sure he will feel the same way about this abduction as I do. But what Festhold does to punish the crime and avenge the insult is entirely up to Festhold. *My* problem has to do with a missing crewman. Either I get this crewman back unharmed, or I will take the matter up with Sector Headquarters, and you can deal with them. Now, do I get my crewman back, or not?"

"I-I'll have to contact Tiamaz Central Police Headquarters—but I don't think we can—"

From a previously unused speaker to the left of the instrument panel came a harsh voice: "Office of the Sector Controller, C. D. Johnson speaking. Captain, I have a routine communications-monitor intercept keyed by the words 'abduction' and 'candidate-member.' Do I understand correctly that a member of the Interstellar Patrol has actually been *abducted* on a Federation planet?"

Roberts realized with a start that the patrol ship was now backing him up. He glanced at the coldly angry face on one of the small auxiliary screens to the right of the communications screen.

"Yes, sir," said Roberts. "We were hit with a gas attack in the planet's capital district, where we supposedly were under police protection, and were not supposed to carry arms. Only the intervention of my patrol ship saved me and three of my crew members from being killed. Our recruit was seized, and the local authorities seem very reluctant to do anything about it."

C. D. Johnson's voice was flat.

"What planet is this?"

"Tiamaz."

"Tiamaz, eh? All right, Captain. I'll handle this direct through the Planetary Manager's office. Stand by to serve as message-relay station, and to either pick up the patrolman or emplace the quarantine satellites."

Roberts, who had not the faintest idea what all this meant said promptly, "Yes, *sir.*"

A few minutes of total silence passed, each individual second of which seemed to take its own good time in passing, then two faces appeared before him on the divided communications screen. One face was that of "C. D. Johnson." The other was that of a lean, imperturbable-seeming man whose finely chiseled and aristocratic features expressed distaste.

"You understand," said Johnson, "this was a *member* of the Interstellar Patrol, Mr. Roman."

"This is an unproven allegation," said the aristocrat, one nostril twitching, as at an unpleasant odor. "The matter will be investigated in due course by the appropriate authorities. I certainly shall not interfere in any way to speed or slow the investigation. When the investigation is completed, *then* we will notify you of the result. Not before."

"You realize that *five members of the Interstellar Patrol* were attacked, that murder was attempted against four of them, and that one has been abducted—"

"I reject this entire fabrication of allegations out of hand. Such things don't happen here. Very likely your crewmen were drunk or under the influence of drugs. As for this so-called 'princess,' more likely she was some ordinary lady of light virtue your crewmen had engaged for the evening, and who left when she found their company boring. But the allegation, however transparently false, will be investigated in due course. I trust that is satisfactory. Now, I'm afraid I have rather a pressing engagement. Was there anything else?"

Johnson leaned forward. "Do you have any conception, Roman, of the people who take an interest in Tiamaz, but who hesitate to do anything because they know that the Space Police, the Space Force, and the Interstellar Patrol, are all backing up your local police?"

"I'm sure I couldn't care less. Good day, Policeman!" The aristocrat's half of the communications screen went blank.

A moment later, Johnson's half of the screen went blank, and his face appeared on one of the small auxiliary screens to the side.

"Roberts."

Roberts, who was beginning to wonder if "C.D. Johnson" was a bluff by the patrol ship, or might be real after all, said "Yes, sir?"

"Deploy three I. P. Planetary Quarantine satellites, and report to your Chief of Operations."

Roberts said, "I hesitate to leave a—a good recruit in their hands, sir."

"I fully agree with your sentiments, but we've done everything we can for the moment. Any overt attempt to free the recruit might boomerang."

Roberts nodded.

"I'll deploy the satellites."

"Good."

The small auxiliary screen went blank. Roberts pushed the button near the glowing amber lens lettered "Smb Cmp."

"Do we have three I.P. Planetary Quarantine Satellites on board?"

The voice of the symbiotic computer replied, "They are now being fabricated."

"What will they do?"

"These satellites warn approaching ships that the protection of the Interstellar Patrol has been withdrawn from the planet involved."

"What is to prevent the planet involved from knocking the satellites out of orbit?"

"Over the short run, the danger that such an attempt would involve. Over the long run, the fact that something unfortunate will have happened to the governing authorities of the quarantined planet. Satellites are never emplaced except at a planet governed by individuals seriously involved in underhanded manipulations."

"C. D. Johnson," said Roberts, "did not say it was necessary to report *in person* to the Chief of O-Section."

"That is correct."

"It might," said Roberts, "be a good idea to send in a brief report, and then go back down to Tiamaz, and try to find our—our missing crewman."

"It *might* be," said the symbiotic computer, "except that this planet is already heavily infiltrated in the attempt to determine the cause of an abnormally high emotional probe reading. Once the information from your conversation with the Princess Erena was forwarded, the cause for the e-probe reading was clear: A cabal has been formed for the purpose of seizing the government of Festhold, which is an important Federation ally. An immediate check was carried out to determine the location of the Princess Erena."

"*And?*" said Roberts.

"Immediately following her recapture, she was removed from the planet."

With an effort, Roberts forced himself to stay seated. "She was put on a ship—"

"Yes."

"Where is she?"

"We do not yet have this information. Tiamaz is located near the junction of important trade routes. Princess Erena was removed to the nearby Space Center. We have no definite information as yet regarding the flight she followed from this point."

Roberts exhaled slowly. "We're sure she's not on the planet?"

"This is certain."

"But she could be *brought back*."

"That is correct. But it appears unlikely. There is no perceptible gain for the opposition in that course of action."

"All right," said Roberts. "Let's get the satellites in place. Then I'll report to O-Section. There must be some way to straighten this out."

IV. THE INSIDE JOB

Roberts, his gaze intent, stood before the desk in the office of Colonel Valentine Sanders, Chief of Operations Branch. Colonel Sanders frowned as he finished reading the last page of a thin sheaf of papers, gave a low growl of irritation, tossed the papers on his desk, and looked up.

"Have a seat, Roberts."

Roberts pulled over a straight-backed chair from near the wall, and sat down.

The colonel said, "You know, Roberts, we have been going over Tiamaz with a fine-toothed comb, trying to find out just what caused the emotional probe on the planet to wrap its needle around the pin. And we had gotten nowhere. *You* walked in to enjoy a little diversion and some good food following a successful job elsewhere—and in well under seventy-two hours, you had the solution."

Roberts said, "Dumb luck, sir."

"Have you considered any alternative?"

"No, sir. There is exactly one thing in which I am interested. That is getting Erena free of that collection of crooks."

The colonel said thoughtfully, "'*Erena.*' You realize you are speaking of a Princess of Festhold, sister to the Heir Presumptive himself?"

Roberts said, "I know it, sir, but I'm thinking of the girl, not the title."

"If you end up with one hand on that sword hilt, you'll appreciate the significance of the title."

Roberts nodded. "I suppose if the local priests push a switch that turns on the electromagnets and keeps the sword stuck inside the crystal, I *will* feel pretty foolish."

The colonel watched him alertly, and then smiled.

"Well, I'm glad to see that your intentions are honorable. On Festhold, they have a high regard for honor. And don't be too sure they use electromagnets in that crystal.—We've had some peculiar reports on the subject." The colonel frowned. "But let's get back to the question of an alternative explanation for this incident.—Has it occurred to you that the whole scene could have been faked for our benefit?"

Roberts shook his head.

The colonel said, "Why not?"

"I don't say it couldn't have. I only say it hadn't occurred to me."

"What do you now think of the possibility?"

Roberts thought it over carefully. "It *is* peculiar that it worked out as it did—that I happened to be coming out of the Temple of Chance as Erena was going in, and that what she said to me answered a question you were working on that I didn't even know about. But as for its having been a put-up job—No, sir. I don't believe it."

"Why not?"

"In the first place, I don't think we were known to be on the planet. In the second place, I don't see how they could have timed it so that Erena and I would reach the spot where the upslide passes near the down slide. Next, they couldn't know that I'd be looking in her direction. Finally, they couldn't know in advance that I'd jump to the other slide—it was pure impulse. *If* they were using her to pass information to me, they gave a convincing imitation of being prepared to stop me until I happened to say the right words when I got Erena away from then. And they would still have stopped me, except that Bergen showed up just in time."

"They could merely have *sounded* rough."

"Yes, but now we come to the most convincing proof, at least to me. *After* Erena had passed her message to us, *then* they recaptured her, and came within a hair's breath of disposing of the rest of us."

"According to the patrol ship, you survived that fall on your own."

"No, sir."

"The ship should know."

"The fright from that fall temporarily cleared my head, and I was determined to survive if I could. I don't know if it was owing to the drug, or if it just followed from the situation, but time seemed to slow down. I did everything I could to break the force of the fall, and to distribute the impact, but I could tell that it was all going to work out the same way in the end—and then something happened to ease the pressure. The patrol ship had gotten there, and was using its gravitor beams. Now—it may be that if I hadn't tried, the ship couldn't have broken the fall. But if the ship hadn't gotten there, what I was able to do wouldn't have been enough either. I wouldn't have survived that fall."

The colonel nodded slowly. He cleared his throat. "It was either an *extremely* clever method of planting information; or else it was what it seemed to be—a stroke of pure luck for us."

Roberts nodded. "And I don't think it was cleverness."

The colonel said, "All right. I agree. Now, Roberts, we have a peculiar situation here. As you know, Festhold is not part of the Federation. Here and there, there are individual planets, and even star systems, which are independent. Festhold is one of the largest and most formidable of these. Strictly speaking, we have no right to intrude in Festhold's internal affairs."

Roberts said, "Neither does Tiamaz."

"Exactly. That's the other half of the dilemma. We have no *right* to intrude. But whether we have a *right* or not, we have to intrude. Festhold is too important to permit outsiders to intervene while we stand by with our thumb in our mouth. If a combine from Tiamaz, for instance, should get control of Festhold, we would have a combination of the financial power of Tiamaz with the military power of Festhold. Now—since Festhold is not a part of the Federation, Festhold is theoretically free to make alliances where it will. It has always, *so far,* been allied to the Federation of Humanity. But if it should choose to join with some alien outfit, it would be completely within its rights. But we couldn't afford that."

"Therefore, Festhold *must* be influenced?"

The colonel nodded, and picked up the report he had been reading when Roberts came in. "Festhold must be influenced. Yet, no proofs can remain that Festhold *has* been influenced. And Festhold is highly developed technologically. Crude interference would risk creating a serious reaction against us. Festhold is therefore subject only to occasional and very careful influence." The colonel looked Roberts directly in the eye. "Nearly always, Roberts, we are forced to rely on an *inside* job."

Roberts noted the colonel's emphasis, but looked blank. "I'm not familiar—"

"I know it. But when this job is over with, you *will* be, believe me."

Roberts straightened alertly. "Sir, I'm sorry, but—"

"Never mind that, Roberts. This—"

Roberts voice stayed polite and respectful, but took on an undertone of stubborn and unyielding determination. "Sir, excuse me, but I have to say this."

The colonel started to speak, but Roberts spoke first: "*I have to find Erena.*"

The colonel straightened in his chair as if drawn up by a hand at the back of his neck. He grinned suddenly, and raised his right hand, palm out.

"Are you prepared, Roberts, to risk your life for this girl?"

"Yes."

"You realize she is part of a royal family in a place where royalty commands respect?"

"Yes."

"Will you, if necessary, resign from the Patrol?"

"If I have to, to get freedom of action."

The colonel tossed across the desk the report he had been reading. Roberts glanced from the colonel to the report, and picked up the report, to read:

TIAMAZ REPORT—SUMMARY:

1. Routine emotional probe of this planet revealed (see sequence list for dates) presence of a group engaged in profoundly illegal and apparently dangerous cabal.

2. Repeated attempts to identify the individuals involved failed, although they were localized in the Tiamaz Capital District—the main gambling district as well as the administrative center of the planet.

3. An off-duty I. P. captain and crew, in a casino on the planet purely for pleasure, accidentally encountered the Princess Erena of Festhold, who in some still undetermined way appealed for their help. They responded at once, and spirited her out of the grip of the casino employees.

4. Princess Erena stated that a Tiamaz cabal had control of her brother, the heir-apparent of Festhold, and . . .

Roberts skimmed the description of what he already knew, flipped to the next page, and suddenly stopped.

7. Princess Erena, still drugged, was rushed to the nearby Space Station. Checks at further stops, boardings, and transelectronic surveillance, show that she was put aboard a fast liner bound for Festhold, with only two stops on the way. This liner is being shadowed by an I-class patrol ship,

8. A preliminary emotional probe of Festhold reveals two distinct spectra, one intense, and the other faint but detectable. The distinct spectrum has the usual characteristics of Festhold. The faint spectrum closely matched that found on Tiamaz.

9. The conclusion seems inescapable that the two are connected, and that a group based partly on Tiamaz is attempting to gain control of Festhold.

10. Owing to the seclusion of the crown prince of Festhold, it has so far proved difficult to . . .

Roberts looked up, and drew a deep breath. He handed the report to the colonel, and cleared his throat. "So, Erena is being taken back to Festhold?"

"Evidently." The colonel tossed the report in a wire basket at the corner of his desk.

Roberts said, "Sir, I would like to get her away from them."

The colonel briefly had the look of a farmer whose pet bull has just knocked the rails loose from the fence. The colonel's expression was alert, and extremely calculating. Then slowly, he sat back. His expression became frank and open.

"I don't blame you, Roberts. But the girl is, of course, bait."

Roberts looked startled. "Why do you say that, sir?"

"The *manner* in which Tiamaz refused our demand for the girl was provocative in the extreme. It was an invitation to us to take severe measures. And this princess was already on the way to Festhold by the fastest available transportation. Why to Festhold?" The colonel leaned forward. "Any seizure of the princess by outsiders from the Federation would raise feelings *against* the Federation."

Roberts winced. "And we're already on record—"

"Right. And bear in mind, if what we think is true, the cabal will want some excuse to pry Festhold loose from its traditional automatic alliance with the Federation."

Roberts sat back. The colonel said quietly, "I don't think an outright seizure of this princess would be a good idea."

Roberts nodded, then frowned. "But suppose this clique should *fake* a kidnapping, and blame us for it?"

The colonel smiled. "Exactly why we have our 'I'-class ship on the spot."

Roberts smiled, then thought it over a second time. "People," he said, thinking of the deep blue eyes and the honey-blonde hair, "might get hurt in the process."

The colonel said carefully, "I'm more worried, myself, about what might happen to her *after* she gets there. We can shadow the ship, but we can't provide protection once she's on the planet. Everything *there* is under control of the Realm of Festhold."

Roberts felt the overpowering urge to do something. The colonel sat back, frowning, and said carefully, "It will *have* to be an inside job. I had intended to offer this job to you, Roberts. Among other things, it would have put you where you could almost certainly keep an eye on Erena. But since you seem to feel that only direct intervention would work—"

Roberts had a vivid picture of a little pea disappearing under a walnut shell, which, being rapidly switched with another shell, and another, suddenly presented him with a blank row of shells, while the pea itself was now elsewhere.

Roberts looked at the expressionless face of the colonel. Roberts smiled. "I'd say it was under the center shell, sir—if, that is, you haven't palmed it."

The colonel looked blank. Roberts leaned forward, his voice quiet. "I want to see her again, and I want to see her unhurt. If this 'inside job' will help me do it, I'm interested. You don't have to bait the hook with fresh worms, or spin me around blindfolded half-a-dozen times to get me off-balance. What do you have in mind?"

The colonel grinned, and sat back. "Nevertheless, Roberts, it would be one hell of a spot for you, if you're in love with this princess."

"I'd be where I could see her?"

"Oh, yes."

"And block any attempt to hurt her?"

"Very possibly."

Roberts frowned. "I don't see the drawback."

The colonel said drily, "You would even be free to *love* her—"

Roberts looked at him sharply. The colonel smiled angelically, and finished the sentence: "—as a brother."

Roberts frowned, then felt the sudden chill as a hint came to him of just what an "inside job" might be.

He sat up straighter, and his voice came out in a growl. "Don't stop there. What *is* it?"

The colonel dropped all pretense, and began to explain.

V. REBORN

The high whine of the equipment, the white-swathed figures bending over him, the voice calling methodically in the background, all began to fade as the helmet was lowered carefully over his head. On the screen within the helmet, before his eyes, two faint dots merged into one, and the one expanded, faded, formed a tiny dim distant scene, as of a room seen through a pinhole, and then faded again. Then Roberts felt as if this room rushed toward him, and he toward it, and then painfully the motion ceased, and began again, and stopped. Then, after an indeterminate expanse of time, suddenly the scene began to come into focus, the universe seemed to flow past and through him in a rush, there was a sensation as of a faint *click* suggesting something locking in place, and Roberts, head aching, body as heavy as lead, looked dizzily around a room brightly lit by moonlight. One thought spun through his mind:

"Thank God! It's *over* with!" Exhausted, he fell asleep.

Somewhere, birds were singing. In the distance, a bugle call sounded sharply, and was methodically repeated. There was a faint murmur of voices.

There was a casual double rap on a door, a high-pitched exchange of laughter, and Roberts was jarred awake. He saw, first, a wide window made of many small panes of glass, beyond which moved a branch bearing many large light-purple flowers with yellow centers. Beyond the lightly moving branch was a pale blue sky with a few high distant clouds.

The branch was bathed in sunlight, which shone into the room on a far less pleasant scene. There was a pile of dirty clothes below the window. A stack of books leaned against the wall beside the window, and a second stack had fallen over onto the floor. In the corner, a steel clothes locker stood open, to show half-a-dozen uniforms on hangers. Against the side of the clothes locker leaned a businesslike sword. In a rack on the wall beside the locker were two well-oiled rifles and a handgun.

The room was a corner room, and the other wall had a second large window, through which bright daylight flooded a desk littered with crumpled papers, its finish marked with innumerable rings where glasses had been set down. Beside the desk was a large wastebasket filled to overflowing with empty bottles.

Beside the desk stood a girl of eighteen or nineteen, heavy, wearing a tight pink skirt and a tight flowered blouse, her light-brown hair carelessly pulled back. In her left hand she carried a silver tray bearing an assortment of dishes, glasses, flavorings, and a white linen napkin which stood up in a tentlike peak.

"Well, good morning, Charmer," she said irritably, looking around. "Where do you want this?"

Roberts tried to sit up, and lay back with a gasp. The girl looked at him, put the tray on the edge of the bed, set her hands on her hips, and burst out laughing.

"What a sight! Gahr, you really laid it on last night, didn't you! Well, there's the twist on the tray under the napkin. You *wanted* it, so there it is. You've tried everything else, so I suppose you might as well try that. But don't say I didn't warn you—the shape you're in, Charmie Boy, it will blow your brains right out your ears, Duke Marius will crack your knuckles again when you come around."

She turned to leave, paused, and said, "In case you're interested, the tutor will be here in an hour."

The door shut with a thud and a click, and Roberts lay with the room swimming around him, a blinding headache, and a sense of feverish unreality.

The colonel's words came back to Roberts, sharply emphasized by what had happened so far: "An 'inside job,'" the colonel had said, "is no bed of roses, Roberts. And tough as I know you are, I'm not so sure you won't find this to be a little more than you bargained for. But somebody has to do it, and you have a personal interest in what happens to Princess Erena. If you want to do it, I will be very happy to have this problem taken off my hands."

Roberts had said, "I still don't *know* what the job is."

"The information you gave us dovetails with other information that we hadn't added up. A series of accidents—each one perfectly understandable—eliminated all but one of the direct male line of the present royal family of Festhold. The Duke of Romeigne was chosen as Regent, and incidentally took over the guardianship of the heir, Prince Harold William. Our information is that the heir has acquired a reputation amongst the higher nobility as a ne'er-do-well. The Regent isn't blamed for this. But what you've been told suggests that the Regent may very well be responsible. It looks like a case of destroying the heir in order for the Regent to become King. The Regent is evidently part of the cabal we're trying to stop. If we can save the heir, we derail the whole cabal."

"I follow that," said Roberts. "But if I understand this correctly, the heir is tested when he reaches twenty-one."

"That's right."

"And he is now four months short of being twenty-one years old?"

The colonel nodded. Roberts said, "How long has this Duke of Romeigne been undermining the crown prince?"

"Since shortly after the death of King Charles William of Festhold, at the Battle of the Ring Nebula, when the prince was nearly eighteen years old."

Roberts thought it over. "Up to that time, the prince was considered to be all right?" The colonel nodded.

Roberts said, "In that case, I'd think conceivably it *could* be done—but four months is a short time to train someone who has been systematically *un*trained for about three years. The worst part of it is, how do we reach him?"

"Exactly why it has to be an inside job."

"We're back to that again."

"It's the only way we can find to handle this."

Roberts sat up exasperatedly. "What *is* it?"

The colonel glanced off at a distant corner of the room. "To explain the process is beyond me. But I can tell you what happens. You will go down the hall to M-Section, having bathed thoroughly, shaved, and received a haircut, and wearing a hospital gown, you will be wheeled on a stretcher into a totally aseptic room where a sort of helmet will be lowered over your head. You will see a scene indistinctly, and when this scene finally becomes clear to you—assuming it does—you will find yourself apparently transformed into Harold William, heir to the throne of Festhold."

Roberts say up straight. "You mean, *my* consciousness will somehow be translated into *his* body?"

"That's what I've been trying to avoid saying. But that is substantially it. Your consciousness will be operating his body—and from the information we have about the shape this prince is in, that will be no picnic."

"M'm. The idea is, to put someone already trained on the spot, to train the prince under the nose of the Regent?"

"Exactly. Or rather, that's *half* of it."

Roberts said, "And where is the prince's consciousness. Do the two egos share the same body, or—"

"The prince's consciousness will be here, Roberts. Try to think of the physical body as the old metaphysicists spoke of it, as a 'vehicle.' You will be operating the prince's vehicle. The prince—"

Roberts said flatly, "No."

The colonel smiled. "I see you now have the picture."

Roberts drew a deep breath, and let it out slowly. The colonel said, "You see why it is going to be no easy job to find a volunteer."

Roberts said, with feeling, "I see *that*."

The colonel nodded. "I suppose I will end up with the job. I can tell you, I don't relish it."

"Is there an actual transfer of—of soul or spirit—or is it a form of overriding signal by which one individual here, controls the other's physical mechanism there, and vice versa?"

The colonel shook his head. "There are two explanations, a scientific explanation, and a metaphysical explanation, and frankly I don't fully understand either of them. As far as *I'm* concerned, the process isn't actually understood. For convenience in thinking of it, I look on it as switching pilots from one ship to another, or drivers from one ground vehicle to another. But that's not all of it because, if one of the two bodies involved should be fatally injured, the 'driver' in the *other* one dies."

Roberts looked blank. "That is, the *original* ego—or the other?"

"The original."

"So if I should go along with this, and the prince falls out a window, that kills *me*?"

The colonel frowned. "Let's be sure we have this straight. To start with, there are Roberts and Harold William, the prince."

Roberts said drily, "I can follow it that far."

"All right, now by my simplified approach to this, we need to distinguish only two parts to each individual. The official explanations are a lot more complicated, believe me; but as far as I'm concerned, two parts are enough. Call them 'vehicle' and 'driver.' "

"All right."

"Now, suppose we abbreviate 'Roberts' as 'R', and 'Harold William as 'HW'. And abbreviate 'driver' as 'D' and 'vehicle' as 'V'. We then have four parts, RD, RV, HWD. and HWV. Now, regardless of which driver is in control of which vehicle, if RV is fatally injured, that finishes RD. If HWV is fatally injured, *that* finishes HWD. Don't ask me why."

"That," said Roberts, "gives me a profound desire to keep RD in charge of RV."

Colonel Valentine Sanders nodded glumly. "I have the same urge to keep VSD running VSV. But I'm afraid it isn't going to work out."

"What happens when this spoiled prince takes over the 'vehicle' of whoever volunteers for this? Is this ne'er-do-well free to amuse himself as he wishes?"

The colonel looked shocked. "That way, we would throw away half of our advantage.—No, he will be put through a rigorous course of training, and watched every second."

Roberts thought it over. "I still don't like it."

"Who would?"

"Suppose the ne'er-do-well declines to cooperate?"

The colonel smiled. "Believe me, Roberts, we can *guarantee* cooperation. But I don't think that difficulty is likely. The prince comes from a long line of able warriors, and in my opinion he will respond to the right impulses. He's just been kept carefully isolated *from* the right impulses."

Roberts was thinking of Erena, completely under the control of the members of the cabal, and being sent back to a place where she had no one to protect her except a brother kept carefully incapable of protecting anyone. Once again he saw, and felt, her look of appeal.

Roberts said, "I'll do it."

And now, with the click of the door in his ear, the headache throbbing in time with his pulse, and the room swimming around him, Roberts' right hand—or rather Prince Harold William's right hand—reached out, pushed aside the napkin on the tray, and picked up the twisted bit of paper.

VI. "Indisposed?"

Roberts, startled, watched the hand, faintly trembling, open the paper, and shake the contents into a tall glass of water on the tray. The hand then picked up the glass of water, and approached the Prince's lips.

Roberts clamped his—Harold William's—jaws and lips tightly shut, and stopped the hand partway from the tray.

" . . . drink . . ." said a small voice clearly in his ear.

The hand began to approach with the glass. The small voice spoke again clearly in his ear.

" . . . You will drink . . . your hand will shake the powder into the glass . . ." said the small voice . . . "and then the hand will carry the glass to your mouth, your lips will open, and you will swallow, again and again ... "you will drink the draught ..." said the small voice ... "you will drink it to the end ..."

Roberts' lips trembled. The hand approached with the drink. Roberts glanced around. No one was in the room with him. The voice had spoken *in his ear*—almost as if it were inside his head. Roberts stopped the approaching hand.

" ... You *will* drink ..." said the small voice ... "your lips will open and you will drink ... The hand will carry the glass to your mouth, your lips will open, and ..."

Roberts concentrated on the hand, moving it further away. He tipped the glass and deliberately emptied it onto the scratched hardwood floor. When the glass was empty, he turned it upside down, and put it on the tray. The voice was abruptly silent. The headache was gone.

Roberts carefully swung his—that is, the prince's—feet to the floor. He got up, and became conscious of a profound weakness. Roberts seemed to be operating an ungainly piece of apparatus, rather than merely walking across the room.

Around the corner of the room was a door to a small bathroom. Roberts got a towel, and mopped up the pool on the floor, being careful to get none of it on his hands. What the active ingredient of "twist" might be, Roberts didn't know, and he wasn't certain whether it might leave a tell-tale, incriminating stain on his hands. He put the sodden towel in the flush toilet, held on to the dry end, and pressed the button that worked the toilet.

The outside door of the bedroom came open, and the same female voice called in, the words faintly sarcastic, "Tutor in half-an-hour, Charm."

Roberts, frowning, released the button, went out to the door of the room and looked it over. The door was held by three hinges on the left, and had no lock, keyhole, chain, or other device on the right to keep it shut, except a knob. The knob was placed unusually high. Roberts, still with the sensation that he must force each ungainly motion, brought the chair over from the paper-cluttered desk, and set it by the door. The chair back was eight inches below the knob. Roberts put the chair back by the desk, went into the bathroom, finished with the towel, washed, came out and looked over the breakfast on the tray.

Methodically, tasting each bite cautiously, he ate two slices of toast, a small container of a kind of dark-purple jam, and drank a small glass of clear pinkish juice that was sweet and faintly astringent. He reached for the milk on the tray, in its tall dark-brown glass, and then hesitated.

He took the small clear empty glass that had held the juice, rinsed it, considered the milk for a moment, then poured part of it slowly into the juice glass.

The milk poured out with a peculiar suggestion of foam—yet there was no foam. Roberts, frowning, emptied the small glass carefully into the sink, caught his breath, and put a finger in the milk.

There was a faintly gritty feel, as of countless very tiny grains or capsules, that crushed between his fingers to form a faintly sticky slime. Roberts emptied most of the milk from the glass, put the glass back on the tray, and rinsed the sink.

There was brisk knock on the door. A voice, high-pitched, with a peculiar catch, called out, "Lessons, Your Ex!"

Roberts stood up slowly, and looked at the door. He spoke carefully, and the prince's voice came out, deep, with a pleasant timbre.

"Come in."

The door opened. A short, plump, red-faced, perspiring man of about thirty, his head completely shaven, stepped in and cast a quick perceptive glance at the tray, and then at the figure of Prince Harold William, standing silently before him.

The tutor shut the door and snickered. "How is it, Ex?"

Roberts was unconsciously adding up the maid's dress and manner, the small voice in his ear, the "twist", the tiny capsules in the milk, and now the tutor's appearance and way of speaking. The tutor giggled again.

"Can't move, eh? Oh, but Duke Marius will be displeased!" The tutor waggled his forefinger. His grin widened. "Naughty, naughty, fellow! Well—what shall we learn today?" He came closer, grinning widely, his teeth shining, his expression archly mischievous.

Roberts, groping amongst the unpromising bits and pieces of what he had experienced so far, felt a profound desire to deal out a few blows for a change.

"Strange," said Roberts, casting the prince's expressive voice in a slightly lower pitch.

The tutor paused, glanced at the tray, and giggled. "Yes—that's the only drawback—it's unpredictable. But such *wonderful* visions, sometimes. Mystic experiences, actually. What are you seeing?"

"A throne," said Roberts carefully, "a throne, and someone is seated upon it."

The tutor's brows arched upward. His eyes blinked rapidly. "Who, Your Ex?"

"I know the face," said Roberts, keeping his voice low, and gazing across the room as if he actually saw something there beside the closed door.

"*Whose* face?" demanded the tutor curiously.

"He is speaking," said Roberts slowly. "Why—it is the *King!*"

The tutor blinked. His eyes blazed. "*What* king? *Duke Marius?*"

Roberts spoke carefully. The trance-like tone he was trying for came out naturally, helped by what was apparently the natural lassitude of the prince.

"Yes," said Roberts slowly, looking at the door, "but I thought—I thought it was an accident . . . then, that is *treason* . . . I did not know . . ."

The tutor whirled, stared at the door. Robert went on, "Then they are murderers, and we must have vengeance . . . I will block the traitor's way to the throne at all cost . . ."

The tutor spoke nervously. "Here—here now, Ex—I mean, Your—Your Excellency—you've having a bit of a bad time, that's all. This vision will go away, and you will have another—*God! Who would have thought it!*—take it easy, now—you'll be all right!"

Roberts turned, and walked carefully across the room to the locker. He picked up the sword, still sheathed, and turned. The tutor blinked, then backed toward the door. There was a harsh rap on the door. The tutor gasped. The door opened.

A tall dark-haired figure stepped in, wearing a jacket of black velvet with a gold chain around his neck supporting a gold eagle emblem, and also wearing blue trousers with vertical gold stripes at the sides. Directly behind him were two officers in dark green uniforms, one carrying a slender gold baton decorated with eagles and oak leaves.

The tall man looked ironically at the prince and bowed with flawless grace. His voice was gravely deferent.

"Your Excellency, as you mount the throne in less than four months, I deemed it urgent that you make the acquaintance of

Field Marshal du Beck, and of General Hugens, our Chief of the General Staff. I—" He paused, and his voice became smoothly considerate. "I assume you are not—not *indisposed*."

The tutor began urgently, "Your Grace, he—"

Roberts was finding considerable difficulty in operating the prince's vocal organs. But, once started, the resonant voice silenced the tutor in mid-sentence.

"I am delighted," said Roberts, and the voice came out grave and majestic, and seemed to fill the room. "I am delighted and honored to meet two such distinguished soldiers."

Roberts set the sheathed sword carefully against the locker, and turned toward the three in the doorway. Duke Marius was looking blankly at the tutor. The tutor, perspiring heavily, had his mouth open, but no words were coming out.

Field Marshal du Beck had been looking over the pile of papers on the desk, and the stack of bottles bulging out of the waste basket, while General Hugens' gaze was fixed on the oiled guns in the rack. At the prince's voice, the expressions of both officers cleared. They smiled, reddened slightly, and bowed.

"I appreciate your concern, Marius," the prince's voice went on, filling the room with its tones of majesty and power, "but I could never be too indisposed to see Field Marshal du Beck and General Hugens. I particularly wish to see them today. I want their advice on two subjects. Pray come in, gentlemen."

Field Marshal du Beck, and General Hugens, clearly pleased and flattered, stepped in,

Duke Marius took the tutor urgently by the arm. Roberts, aware that for the moment he had the initiative, did not hesitate to wring the last ounce from it. The prince's voice took on a hint of displeasure. "*Marius.*"

The Duke looked up in surprise and perplexity. The faces of Field Marshal du Beck and General Hugens expressed a quiet contentment, which suggested to Roberts that the two officers were not part of the cabal, and were not overly fond of the regent.

The tutor sucked in his breath, and burst out, "He's *drugged*, Your Grace!"

The prince's voice filled the room with quiet majesty as Roberts faced the startled officers. "That is the first point, gentlemen, on which I require your assistance. But first—" Roberts glanced at the duke, whose composure had returned. The prince's voice now held an audible undertone of disapproval.

"Have you finished whispering with the tutor, Marius?"

The duke had plainly recovered from his surprise. His eyes glinted. His voice was pitying. "I am concerned about your progress, Harold."

The prince's voice filled the room majestically. "That concern, Marius, is one which I share. I again ask if you are finished with this tutor. If so, he is dismissed."

The duke put his hand on the tutor's arm. The tutor looked as if he wished he could vanish. The duke looked gravely at the prince.

"The charge," said the duke silkily, "is most serious, Harold. Perhaps you should answer it."

"If Field Marshal du Back or General Hugens would pour that milk from its glass into the smaller glass on that tray," said the resonant voice, "and observe if there is something unusual about it, that will help me to determine whether I *have* been drugged."

Field Marshal du Beck cast an intent glance at Duke Marius and the tutor, then looked at the overflowing wastebasket, and hesitated. General Hugens glanced at the oiled weapons in their rack, and looked the prince in the eye.

The prince said, "Pour it slowly, General, and observe if there is what *appears* to be a foam."

The general set his gloves by the tray, and poured slowly.

Duke Marius said, "Foam is not unusual on milk."

Roberts didn't answer. He was wondering if the grit or tiny capsules might by now have dissolved in the milk. The tutor edged toward the door.

General Hugens said, in a low voice, "Look here."

Field Marshal du Beck put his gloves by the tray, and bent over. "H'm. It is like a very fine sand."

Roberts, relieved, glanced at the tutor, who was now at the door. The prince's majestic voice again filled the room.

"You will remain here, tutor, unless—" Roberts glanced at the duke—"unless, Marius, for some reason you now have changed your mind and *wish* him to leave."

Before the duke could reply, Roberts spoke to the two officers. "It was my experience that whatever is in that milk has a mildly gritty feel to the fingers and, when crushed, has the feeling of a glue or sticky paste."

General Hugens at once put his thumb and forefinger into the milk, rubbed thumb and forefinger together, eyed the ceiling thoughtfully, and handed the glass to the field marshal, who repeated the experiment. Duke Marius glanced uneasily at the generals with their fingers in the milk.

"Gentlemen, this situation is becoming ridiculous."

Roberts said at once, "It was *your* idea, Marius."

The duke turned angrily. His voice was like the crack of a whip. "Henceforth *you* will speak respectfully! Your tutor has something to say which is very serious, Harold."

Prince Harold William's magnificent voice created a contrast in tone which made the duke sound peevish. To Roberts' delight, the sarcasm of his own words was translated by the prince's voice into a crushing rebuke:

"'Henceforth' is a very long time, Marius. Does your authority extend beyond four months?"

Duke Marius stiffened, paled, swallowed, then smiled and relaxed. He glanced at the tutor. "Twist *is* unpredictable. It's said, you know, that our ancestors called it 'courage in a pipe.'"

The tutor said nervously to the duke, "May I go now?"

Roberts said to the two officers, "Gentlemen, have you any opinion to offer on that substance."

Duke Marius crossed the room before they could answer, picked up the water glass on the tray, and sniffed sharply. "There you are, gentlemen. The odor is faint but distinctive. *Twist.* Here. Smell it for yourself."

The general and the field marshal each sniffed sharply, and looked troubled.

Roberts ignored the duke, and said, "*Is* it twist?" The prince's voice sounded concerned and curious, but nothing more. The field marshal's frown vanished.

"I should say so, Your Majesty. As for this other substance, I suspect a sedative of some kind. You see, these innumerable tiny capsules have walls of different thicknesses, which successively dissolve away over a period of time. It is even possible, using drugs of different types in capsules of different wall thickness, to have roughly timed drug effects. We have used this in prisoner interrogation. The prisoner, not realizing that his body is being subjected to drugs of carefully selected types, believes that *he himself* is, for example, losing his nerve—it is quite possible to cause him to tremble involuntarily, for instance."

Roberts said, "Could this be used to create a feeling of fatigue?"

"Yes, Sir. The sensations of the prisoner subjected to this can be manipulated almost at will."

Duke Marius motioned the perspiring tutor to leave the room. As the door closed behind him, Roberts said, "The most important duties of a ruler, if his realm is well organized, are military. Whatever else he may know, he *must* understand the art of war, or he is unfit to lead."

The field marshal nodded and smiled. The general said approvingly, "That is true, Your Majesty."

Duke Marius said in irritation, "Let me point out, he is not yet king. Do not address him as 'Your Majesty.' If he fails—"

Roberts said coldly, "But he won't."

The effect of these three simple words, in Prince Harold William's majestic voice, momentarily gave even Roberts pause. The words seemed to ring in the air, an inviolate statement that could not even be questioned.

Duke Marius' mouth came open. A fine perspiration appeared on his brow. He turned as if to answer, but his voice failed to function, and his gaze fell as if his lids had grown heavy.

Roberts suppressed a sudden elation, and said gravely, "Gentlemen, I regret to have to say this, but facts are facts. That milk is apparently drugged. Evidently there was twist in the water glass. These are by no means the only peculiar manifestations I have noticed recently, but these things we have physically before us. I think you will understand when I say that I want a complete change of staff here, at once, and that I want a military guard unit I can call upon at any time. Other male members of my family have died in the comparatively recent past. *Apparently*, their deaths were accidental. But if an attempt is being made to tamper with the throne—" Roberts looked directly at Duke Marius—"I intend to unmask the traitors and kill them."

Field Marshal du Beck, watching intently, was the first to regain his voice. "Argent Company of the Royal Guard will be sent here at once, Your Majesty, with a mess unit to cook your meals. The Royal Guard is of course directly under your personal command. You are the colonel of the regiment, and have been, by direct line of inheritance, since the death of the King, your father."

Roberts had vainly been trying to unlock certain memories that must be available to Prince Harold William himself, but having had no practice with the technique, Roberts had had no success. He cleared his throat, and spoke carefully. "Excellent. There is another point—"

"Yes, Your Majesty?

Duke Marius looked up, but managed only an incredulous stare at the two officers, who paid no attention.

Roberts said, "It seems to me that by accident or design, my military education has been neglected. I want to repair this neglect. Can you find someone capable of acting as a teacher—"

Field Marshal du Beck beamed. "I would myself accept the great honor, but the military situation at the moment requires my full attention. Our Stath opponents are much encouraged by the recent cuts in our fleet strength. But General Hugens has an excellent deputy, who—"

General Hugens looked indignant. Field Marshal du Beck concluded— "who can take over for the general to permit him personally to act as your tutor. General Hugens is, in fact, an excellent teacher, twice assigned to the War College." General Hugens beamed.

Roberts—with troops of the Royal Guard at his command, with the Chief of the General Staff to act as his personal tutor, and incidentally as a direct link with the top command of Festhold's armed forces—Roberts, too, beamed cheerfully. "Wonderful," he said. "I could ask for nothing better."

It seemed to Roberts that—barely at the beginning of his assignment—he had already won. But, as they shook hands and exchanged pleasantries at the door, Roberts noted a vicious little smile on Duke Marius' face.

The duke's gaze slid away as Roberts looked directly at him—but the little smile stayed there. It appeared to be a smile of *anticipation.*

VII. CLEANING HOUSE

As the door shut behind them, Roberts asked himself what would justify that smile. Either Marius had already compromised the prince before Roberts had gotten here, or else Marius planned to do something before the troops took over from the present staff.

Roberts walked over to the locker, and discovered that he could move more easily. The leaden heaviness seemed to be very slowly passing away. Leaning against the locker was the plain businesslike sword, and Roberts now slid it from its sheath. The sword came out easily, the blade surprisingly light, the hilt so shaped that it seemed almost a part of his hand.

Roberts reached left-handedly for the handgun on the rack. He had scarcely closed his hand around it when the unlockable door across the room came open. Two burly men, wearing close black garments that fitted like a second skin, walked in, ignored the threat of the two weapons, and strode purposefully toward the prince.

Roberts felt a sense of paralysis—an unspoken warning as to what would happen if he should defend himself. By an effort of will, he raised the handgun and pointed it. The burly pair didn't hesitate. Roberts squeezed the trigger. The gun clicked. Roberts changed position, his right side forward, the swordpoint raised. The first of the two black-clothed figures reached up and closed his hand on the blade. The second stepped to the side, reached out to grip the prince—

Roberts reacted automatically, jerked back the sword, thrust at the closer of the two, backed the slight remaining distance to the wall, turned slightly, and thrust at his other assailant.

The sword moved like a weightless extension of his arm. The blade flashed. The black cloth reddened at the right shoulder of each man. The right hand of the first assailant dripped blood.

Roberts, crowded into the narrow space between the wall and the front of the locker, waited, the sword point raised. The two black-clothed figures stood motionless. The first glanced at his hand, red with blood where he had gripped the sword. The second made a hesitant gesture as if to bend forward and lunge ... The swordpoint moved. Roberts held it directly before the eyes of his assailant.

Outdoors, approaching, came the quiet rap of a drum. There was the tramp of feet, a called command—"Platoon *Halt!*"

The swordpoint with great delicacy and precision, was cutting the black fabric in a straight line across the chest of one of his assailants as Roberts sought to cut the cloth but not the flesh. The prince's two assailants began to edge backward.

From the door came an impatient voice. "Come on in there, hurry it up! They're out here already!"

A third black-clad figure appeared in the doorway. His eyes widened. Roberts aimed the gun.

"Don't move."

The black-clad figure dove headlong out of the room. There was a hasty scramble, then the sound of running feet echoed in the hall. The two black-clad assailants in front of Roberts backed and whirled to run. The sword flashed as Roberts struck carefully at the backs of their legs. They gasped, staggered, and fell.

From the corridor came a yell, a thud, and the sound of many running feet. Roberts watched the door, the sword at his side, but ready. The doorway filled suddenly with a huge, white-haired giant in dark-green uniform, with sergeant's stripes and a loop of silver braid at the shoulder. "First Squad A to me! *First Squad A to me*! Here's the King and two stranglers!" The building shook.

The doorway was suddenly jammed with armed men, and Roberts noted with surprise that each was white-haired, rough, athletic; their faces were grim as they stared at the pair on the floor.

In the doorway, the sergeant came to attention, and the men followed his example.

"At ease, men," said Roberts, and the prince's majestic voice projected the cheer Roberts felt on seeing these veterans. "If you will remove these uninvited guests, to be held for questioning. But take care. Each of them is unarmed, hamstrung in the left leg and cut in the right shoulder. But they may bite for all I know."

The sergeant stared at him, then grinned and said, "Lord bless you, Sir, these are vowed assassins. They kill with their victim's fear and their own hands, and they will *never* talk." After a moment he added, "But we *can* try." He glanced around, gave quick orders, and suddenly the room was empty. A powerfully built officer of perhaps sixty-five then looked into the room, snapped to attention, and brought his hand up in salute.

Roberts, without thinking, returned the salute with the sword, and at once wondered if the Festholders saluted with a sword, if their sword salute was the same as he had learned long ago. If not, what would the officer across the room think? But the officer appeared to notice nothing unusual.

"Lieutenant-Colonel Stran du Morgan, Your Majesty. I am your second-in-command, and will handle all the routine of the Regiment, unless you wish otherwise. Argent Company is in the building, Company Or is digging in on the hall, and Cuivre Company is settling down amongst the bushes and trees outside. General Hugens said that you wanted real security, and be damned with appearances."

Roberts himself had not the faintest idea of the significance of the terms "Cuivre Company", "Company Or," or "Argent Company," but he detected a faint flicker of meaning that he was unable to grasp. This must be knowledge that Prince Harold William possessed—but again, Roberts could not acquire it.

"Fine," he said, in the prince's magnificent voice. "Colonel, there is another matter which concerns me."

"Yes, Your Majesty?"

"The Princess Erena. There have been many untoward accidents in my family in recent years, and I no longer believe they were accidental. Have you any knowledge of the location of the Princess?"

Colonel du Morgan's eyes narrowed slightly. "It is strange, sir, that you should ask. The Princess returned only last night, amidst rumors that her ship had been shadowed by some unknown vessel, possibly Stath."

"She returned from where?"

"A visit to Tiamaz."

"And she is now?"

"In an apartment adjoining that of the Regent, Duke Marius. He is her guardian, and—"

"I do not trust Duke Marius."

The colonel blinked. "Does Your Majesty really think—"

"Drugged food preceded Duke Marius' visit to me, poisoned insinuations accompanied it, and two assassins followed it. I do not trust the Duke. How is the Princess guarded?"

"The Duke's own men guard the apartment."

"How numerous are they? And how well armed?"

"There are, I should think, possibly fifty of them. Ordinarily, a dozen are sufficient. But, for some reason, the Duke recently brought in more men. As for weapons—" The colonel frowned—"I would say they are about as well armed as most regular troops."

Prince Harold William's memory for the first time provided Roberts with a few bits of information. The Royal Guard was made of men selected from the armed forces of all Festhold, and grouped by age into three companies. The youngest went into Cuivre Company, and those in their prime into Company Or. Argent Company was made up of picked veterans of long service. Each company was maintained overstrength. The normal Festhold infantry company was made up of three platoons, each of which contained three sections of three squads each. But the Companies of the Royal Guard were made up of four platoons, each of which contained four sections of four squads apiece. As the standard peacetime squad contained twelve men, this meant that one platoon of the Royal Guard contained about two hundred men.

Then one more bit of information came to Roberts. There should be one more company, Company Fer, equipped with heavy weapons. Roberts glanced at Colonel du Morgan.

"Where is Company Fer?"

Du Morgan hesitated. "The Regent requested that it be used as a demonstration unit—"

"And it is now far from here?"

"It entrained this morning for the run to Schnyvasserport, to go from there by water to the training camp outside Haraldsburg."

"Can Company Fer be brought back?"

"Yes, sir. If you so command, I will send the orders at once."

"Good. Bring them back. And as soon as those orders are sent—"

"Yes, sir?"

"I will want to visit Princess Erena."

VIII. Just a Friendly Visit

The gate at the entrance of the Duke's apartments was of iron, tipped with imitation spear points at a height of eight feet. Behind this hinged grille was a closed door of polished glass. Before the iron gate stood two armed guards, one of whom returned a little handset to its small roofed box atop a vertical black pipe to the right of the gate.

"Sorry, sir," said the guard. "No one is to see Princess Erena. Her Highness is indisposed."

Roberts looked the guard over carefully. The second guard looked on indifferently, cradling a short-barreled large-bored fusion gun.

Roberts spoke quietly, and Prince Harold William's voice rendered what he said as a quiet but unmistakable threat.

"Guard."

The guard looked momentarily blank. "Sir?"

"I did not ask *permission* to see my sister."

"I'm afraid I don't—"

"I said, '*I am here to see my sister*'."

"Sorry, sir," said the guard promptly. "No one gets in without a special clearance in advance.—Duke's orders."

"I see," said Roberts.

The guard said, "No one's allowed in. And no one's allowed to loiter at the gate. Sorry, sir." He gave a jerk of his head, signifying that the Prince should leave.

The Prince's right hand, moving of its own accord, flashed to the sword at his left side, and closed on the hilt. The sword hissed from its sheath, flashed in the sunlight, and the point dropped to the guard's throat.

Roberts barely had control of the sword hand as the point drew a drop of blood from the suddenly pale guard. The Prince's voice was clear and carrying: "When you address a fighting man of Festhold, speak politely, Gambler."

The second guard swung up his fusion gun.

Crack!

The line of light seemed to hang in the air for an instant, leading from the center of the guard's forehead back to one of the clumps of brush that dotted the rolling, neatly clipped grasslands that gave seclusion to the elegant apartments. The guard dropped. The fusion gun clattered on the flagstoned walk.

Roberts said, and the Prince's voice was courteous, "Guard, I am here to see my sister."

"The Duke—"

Very slightly, the sword point quivered. The guard stood perfectly still.

"The Duke's authority," said Roberts carefully, "does not extend to controlling arbitrarily the movements of the Royal Family—or, in fact, the movements of any private citizen whatever. Even the King," said Roberts pointedly, "cannot do that in peacetime. If the Duke is holding my sister prisoner, it will be cause for his dismissal from office. As the Duke, therefore, has no authority to *give* the order, you have no authority to carry it out.—*Open the gate!*"

The guard, his expression dazed, took out a set of keys, unlocked the gate using two separate keys in the gate's two locks, and stepped back to let Roberts enter. Roberts stayed where he was. From the road leading to the apartments, came the sound of bootheels.

Roberts said, "Open the inner door."

The guard hesitated, looking toward the road. "Who—"

Roberts said quietly, "*Open the inner door.*"

A magnificently uniformed captain, tall and powerfully built, wearing sword and pistol, appeared around the tall hedge that bordered the road to the left, and started up the walk to the apartments. Following the captain came an equally handsome and powerfully built lieutenant, and three sergeants in battle dress, armed to the teeth. Despite their size, they all moved lightly, with an athletic spring to their step. The guard, perspiring, opened the inner door.

Roberts said to the guard, "You will kindly lead me to the apartment of the Princess."

"I must stay at the gate!"

"No necessity at all. My men will guard it."

Behind the three sergeants came three open columns of men in camouflage battle dress, heavily armed, weapons at the ready.

The guard swallowed, and turned. "This way."

Roberts' sword was still in his hand. He brought it up carefully so that the flat of the blade rested lightly against his shoulder. The Captain and the Lieutenant, observing that their Prince had his sword in hand, each drew their own swords. The three sergeants glanced around alertly.

The Duke's guard, sweating profusely, opened the door of an elevator, and bowed slightly, for Roberts to enter.

Roberts said, "On what floor is the Princess' apartment?"

"The sixth floor, Your—er—Your Highness."

"Are there stairs?"

"It would be much quicker—"

Beside Roberts, the Captain said shortly, *"His Majesty asked you a question."*

The guard stiffened. "There are two sets of stairs. One in the front of the building and one in the back."

"Where," said Roberts, "are the entrances to these stairs?" The guard pointed out two corridors leading in opposite directions.

The Captain turned and raised his voice. "A Squad and follow-up, down that corridor to the north steps. Three men in at a time, watch for grenades, and secure each floor both up and down to the first cross-corridor. B Squad and follow-up, down *that* corridor to the south steps. Same procedure. When all floors are secure to the first cross-corridor, report in by handset. Let's go!"

Roberts turned to the guard. "Is there also a set of service stairs?"

The guard stared at the door, where more men were coming in. He gave his head a little shake, and relaxed. "Duke Marius isn't going to like this."

Roberts said politely, "He should have obeyed the law. To hold a Princess of Festhold prisoner is a serious offense."

The Captain spoke sharply. "His Majesty asked you a question! One more delay, and I won't answer for your life!"

For emphasis he reached out, gripped the guard by the front of his jacket, lifted him bodily off the floor, and smashed him back against the wall.

"Is there a set of service stairs?"

"Y-Yes. You get into them from the basement."

Roberts said, "Why not this floor?"

"It's—quicker—the other way."

"Where's the guardroom?"

The guard swallowed. The Captain glanced at Roberts.

Roberts said, "Of course, we want in no way to cause any difficulty here. But in the event all the Duke's guards should be as uncooperative as this one, we may have to protect ourselves. Have C Squad secure those service stairs from *this* floor, then we'll go up."

"Sir, I don't trust this elevator."

"Neither do I." Roberts glanced at the guard. "There's no grav-shaft?"

"No. The Duke likes his visitors a few at a time."

Roberts glanced at the Captain. "I'm going to use it, because seconds may count." He nodded to the Lieutenant. "If you will accompany me—"

The lieutenant nodded obediently, and gestured to the guard. "Step in. And at the first sign of anything wrong, you will be forever beyond the Duke's power to reward you."

The guard stepped in, and gripped the controls. The elevator lifted, rose smoothly, and slowed to a stop. A sharp voice spoke from a grille at the center of the ceiling. "No visitors on this floor.—That's Duke's orders." The guard perspired.

"This is Prince Harold William himself." The guard's voice took on a peculiar inflection. "I thought the Duke would *want* to see him." There was a little pause.

"All right. Send him in."

IX. Dear Brother

The elevator slid open, and Roberts found himself looking at two tough uniformed armed guards and a faintly smiling sergeant, standing in a small, thickly carpeted, elegantly appointed room with hanging gold-colored drapes to either side of the elevator. The guard in the elevator with Roberts sucked in his breath.

"*Quick!* They—"

There was a sudden brief indrawing of breath, a sound as of a loose armload of firewood dumped on the floor, and then the lieutenant was beside Roberts, absently wiping his sword on the gold-colored drapes.

The two guards, at the door across the room, stood momentarily paralyzed. The sergeant's eyes widened and his face paled. Whatever scene had taken place behind Roberts had temporarily immobilized all three of the guards, and it was entirely possible that if Roberts had seen it, he would be immobilized himself.

The lieutenant said shortly, "The Warlord of Festhold demands admittance to the chambers of his sister. Will you stand aside, or will you join your fellow in hell?"

Roberts spoke flatly, and Prince Harold William's voice translated the ordinary words into an iron command which rang in the air like a sentence of doom: "*Open that door.*"

The tip of the lieutenant's sword flicked out, and lightly

pressed the sergeant's tunic. The guards stared at the sergeant for instructions. The sergeant, brow beaded with sweat, nodded ever so slightly.

The guards flung open the door, and stood at attention. One of them, lance-corporal's insignia on his sleeve, sucked in his breath and announced: "The Warlord of Festhold!"

Behind Roberts, there was a solid *thud*, and another sound as of a load dropping to the floor. The lieutenant spoke in a low voice to the guards: "When he comes to, remind him that a bump on the head is only temporary. If any of you intrude, you will have more permanent difficulties."

The door shut. Roberts looked around. Directly in front of him was a long white-carpeted corridor, the woodwork painted gold and ivory, with a rich light-colored wallpaper depicting a hunting scene done in tones of silver and gray. A door to Roberts' right was marked with a golden ducal coronet. There was no sound from behind this door. From the distance, down the hall, came a faint brief high-pitched sound which instantly faded.

Roberts started down the corridor. The lieutenant strode fast, and caught up as they rounded a corner to the right. Directly in front of them, back to the door, stood a tough-looking guard, a faint grin on his face. The lieutenant spoke.

"Open for the Warlord of Festhold!"

The guard blinked. Roberts tried the doorknob. The door was solidly locked.

From the other side, Erena screamed, a cry of defiance mingled with dread. The lieutenant said sharply, "Guard! *Can you open this?*"

"It—it's locked from inside."

Roberts, half-crouched, raised and bent his right leg, and kicked hard with the flat of his boot at about six inches above the doorknob. The door shook in its frame. Roberts kicked again. There was a loud *crack!* With the third blow, the door flew open.

Duke Marius, his face totally blank, stared at them from a shambles of a room, where the furniture was overturned, the drapes half-torn from the windows, the mattress thrown from the bed onto the floor—and Princess Erena, her face and bare arms bruised, stood gripping a slender leg apparently broken from some overturned piece of furniture. Behind Roberts, there was a thud and a ripping of cloth.

Erena stared at her brother, and cried out, "Oh, thank God!"

Duke Marius made an abortive gesture, as if to draw some hidden weapon. Prince Harold William's left hand went to his holster, withdrew the pistol, and had it aimed before the regent could complete whatever he intended to do.

"So," said Prince Harold William's iron voice, "this is how the Regent of Festhold carries out his trust?"

The gun spoke once, twice, three times, four times—Duke Marius jerked like a marionette, and fell to the floor.

X. A Hitch Has Developed In Our Plans

Prince Harold William was asleep, his lungs drawing in the deep calm breaths of the righteous and the just.

Vaughan Nathan Roberts was awake, trying despite a bad case of nerves to hold his attention on a tiny, barely audible tone that he seemed to hear, then lose, then hear again. It was a varying tone that almost sounded, now and then, like words, occasionally the whistle of steam from a tea kettle, or the brief scrape of branches against the wall outside the Prince's room. Roberts listened closely, clinging mentally to this varying tone as the murmur became clearer, and then out of the murmur came the voice of Colonel Valentine Sanders, and Roberts' chief in the Interstellar Patrol was saying methodically:

"Roberts—do you hear me?—Come in, Roberts . . . We have your—"

"Right here," murmured Roberts, pronouncing the words mentally, but not operating the Prince's vocal cords.

"Roberts?"

"Right here."

"Good. Can you hear me clearly?"

"Yes."

"Roberts—ah—how are things going?"

"The Prince is asleep. *I'm* lying here in a cold sweat. Is that possible?"

"If you're doing it, it's possible." The colonel cleared his throat, and the sound came across with a peculiar self-conscious emphasis. "Ah—*Roberts—?*"

"Sir?"

"How—ah—how—?"

Roberts decided that he would have to speak frankly. "Sir, this situation is fairly confused. And if you don't mind, I want to ask a few questions."

"Go ahead."

"Do you have Prince Harold William on your end."

There was a brief pause. "I mean," said Roberts, "his mind—his consciousness?"

"No," said the colonel.

"I see. All right, what *do* you have on your end?"

"Your body, Roberts, is lying here in some sort of stasis. This is the first time we've ever had anything like this. The only thing I can think of is that the Prince has been reduced to a vegetable, and there was no—ah—no mental function—no *personality* to come through. Wait a minute. What I'm trying to say is the complex electromagnetic function the technicians speak of has put in no appearance on this end; we therefore assume that it must have been destroyed, or reduced to so low a level that we can't detect it."

"I see," said Roberts tightly.

"How are things on your end, Roberts?"

"Prince Harold William this afternoon shot the regent in both shoulders and both knees; and if I hadn't—"

"Wait a minute, Roberts, keep the description clear. You mean, *you,* controlling the Prince's actions, shot the regent—"

"No," said Roberts. "I mean what I said. This degenerate, drugged hulk of a royal playboy has reflexes like chain lightning, and put four bullets into Duke Marius before I had time to think. The next two bullets were for the duke's right and left eyes, but I managed to override that."

There was a silence. Roberts became vaguely aware of the Prince's calm peaceful breathing, and went on. "Listen, when this technique is used on someone heavily sedated against his will, what happens?"

"I think this is the first time we've ever run into it."

"Well, if the Prince hasn't shown up on your end, I think I know why. He's still *here.*"

There was another little pause. "I see," said the colonel.

"The impression I have," said Roberts, "is that most of the time, I'm running things, but every now and then, things happen so fast I don't know what's taking place. Moreover, I am not getting much cooperation from Harold William's memory."

"*What?*"

"The Prince's memory isn't open to me. Occasionally, a few items of information come across, but not very often."

"That's not normal. The usual case is that the impressed personality becomes immersed in the memory and details of the subject's life."

"Then this isn't the usual case."

Another silence developed, and Roberts broke it by saying, "This is quite a handicap, if you see what I mean. I can control the Prince's *actions,* unless he suddenly decides to take over. But unfortunately, since I'm not in touch with his memory, I don't know what I'm doing. And there's another question. What about the Prince himself? His consciousness evidently is still here, on the spot. How does all this strike *him?*"

"I don't know. I'll have to take this up with the experts."

"There's another point. Are these Festholders particularly bloodthirsty?"

"No—Wait a minute. You have to remember, Roberts, that they're in a very exposed position, and have been fighting the Stath for a long time. The Stath are not nice adversaries."

"I see."

"The Festholders loathe traitors, and are merciless with them. Whoever breaks his word on Festhold gets very short shrift."

Roberts considered the events of the day, and said, "Well, that fits. All right, I'll tell you what happened." Carefully, he described what had taken place, in minute detail. At the end, the colonel said, "Roberts—were *you* in charge most of the time, or—"

"I was. Why?"

"It seems to me things have moved pretty fast."

"The regent was closing in to finally discredit the Prince."

"H'm. Yes, that's true."

"There wasn't much *choice.*"

"All right. Where is the regent now?"

"On a cot, done up in bandages, in a dressing station run by the Royal Guard."

"And Princess Erena?"

"With her two sisters, Catherine and Eloise. She's in an apartment in this building, heavily guarded."

"Good. Now, about Erena—you have to be careful—"

"The Prince," said Roberts drily, "is a lot more protective of the two younger sisters. Erena was his older sister, and when they're face-to-face, they get along like cats and dogs."

"Well, that's good. That—"

"Isn't it? said Roberts drily. "Now, sir—what are we going to do about this mess? I have the impression that as the drug they've been using on the Prince wears off, I'm going to have more and more trouble."

"Roberts, we *could* break contact, and then try again. But I hesitate to suggest it, because the second try might fail entirely. You've done all right, so far—"

"The situation is getting more complicated by the minute."

"Just do your best, and we'll move up reinforcements, just in case. Now, we don't claim to understand it, but you're going to need sleep, or your control will suffer."

"Okay," said Roberts. "As long as you see the situation here."

"I see it," said the colonel. "It represents an unexpected hitch in the plans, but I think we can get around it."

The colonel's voice faded, and there was only a varying tone that itself dwindled. Then there was the scrape of branches against the wall, and Roberts knocked the pillow into a more comfortable shape, and fell asleep.

He seemed scarcely to have rested his head against the pillow when the room was suddenly filled with light, and an urgent voice was speaking: "You Majesty—Duke Marius has escaped!"

XI. How To Kill Kings With Pictures

Roberts sat up, noting the early morning sun that lit the silvery dew on the lawn outside. For the first time, he had a sense of bodily well being. The drugged sense of having to force each motion was gone.

"Impossible," said Roberts, "because the Regent was not a prisoner here. Ask Colonel du Morgan to come to me as soon as is convenient for him."

Roberts got up, showered briskly, and briefly studied the Prince's physique in the bathroom mirror. The Festhold heir presented an odd effect of well-developed muscles under a pasty complexion and a thin layer of fat. His face presented the same peculiar effect of strong bone structure and formidable character—coupled with the suggestion of a sallow dissolute look. If the Prince' faint look of dissipation resulted from prolonged sabotage by Duke Marius, there obviously had been some force resisting this dissipation.

Roberts toweled briskly, dressed, and noted with approval the new lock on the room's hall door. He was just clasping the leather belt that held the sword when there was a knock at the door. Roberts opened the door.

"Ah, come in, Colonel!"

Colonel du Morgan, his face grave, his air faintly embarrassed, stepped inside. "I am afraid the Regent left us during the night."

The Prince's voice said, "I regret that I didn't kill him."

The colonel looked surprised, but nodded. "You would have been fully justified."

Roberts, who was more surprised than the colonel to hear the Prince's comment, said carefully, "To have killed him would have been justified, but we may better bring his whole treasonous plan, and his accomplices, into the open with the Regent alive but crippled."

The colonel nodded grimly. "He is, at least, crippled. Your Majesty is a deadly and extremely fast shot."

The Prince's voice replied on its own, "Long practice, Colonel. Since I was old enough to think, I have aimed to be a fighting man and a leader of fighting men, and have trained to acquire their skills."

The Colonel again looked surprised, and an expression of wonder crossed his face. The Prince spoke again, and Roberts listened, seeing no point in trying to intervene.

"Duke Marius," said the Prince, "has well deserved to be crippled. With deep cunning, while in the guise of my guardian, *he* tried to cripple *me*."

The words seemed to smolder in the air after they were spoken, and the Colonel nodded and sighed. "I am afraid, Your Majesty, that he has finally succeeded."

"What do you mean?"

Colonel du Morgan held out, face down, a small packet of photographs. The Prince reached out, took them, and turned them over. The sense of pain was instantaneous, as severe as the sudden pain of a sensitive tooth exposed to heat or cold.

The top picture was damming, a pose of the Prince, the tutor, and the maid who had brought the drugged food. The room seemed to spin around Roberts, who immediately sucked in a sharp breath, and as the grip of the Prince's hand loosened, Roberts tightened it again.

"Well, well," said Roberts, and the Prince's voice translated the words into a sound of grim satisfaction. "So, we have forced him to reveal his hand at last!"

The colonel looked blank. "Sir?"

Roberts looked the Colonel in the eye. "Can you conceive, Colonel, of the damage these would have done if released just before the Lords' Chamber? Would they grant the crown to any-one so debased as this?"

The Colonel looked totally blank. "I—No. But—"

Roberts forced the fingers of the Prince to steadily and care-fully leaf through the damning photographs one-by-one. Roberts had thought the first one might be the worst, but the Colonel had apparently tried to spare his feelings. What followed was indescribable. Roberts looked up, with a sensation of having wallowed in garbage.

"What you have been trying to tell me, Colonel, is that Duke Marius *was freed by my own men?*"

The colonel was watching him with a look of wonder. With a start, he answered. "Yes, Sir."

"Assemble the officers and non-commissioned officers in the courtyard.—Those who can be spared from guard duty. There must be no laxness at all, despite this very clever move. Where is Company Fer?"

"At this moment, they are detraining for the march here."

"Nothing must happen to prevent their reaching here. Check on them, and have those officers and non-coms in the courtyard as soon as possible. Let me know when they are there."

The colonel straightened. "Yes, Sir."

The ranks were stiff, and the faces expressionless as Roberts strode with slow and careful step past them, his tread echoing from the walls that surrounded the courtyard with its fountain and its banks of flowers. Roberts halted near the fountain, turned, looked at the hard faces briefly, and spoke. The Prince's voice, calm and cool, said the words.

"At ease, men."

In front of him, their faces expressionless, the officers and the non-commissioned officers of the Royal Guard relaxed, but their faces remained cold.

"A few minutes ago," said Roberts, and the Prince's magnificent voice spoke with grim satisfaction, "Colonel du Morgan gave me the most pleasant news I have had in some years.

"Colonel du Morgan told me that the Duke Marius had been aided to escape by my own men—" There was a low angry murmur, which Roberts ignored—"and that by some coincidence, damning photographs, supposedly of the future Warlord of Festhold, had been circulated amongst the Royal Guard. Pictures," said Roberts, and the Prince's voice translated his scorn, "like these which Colonel du Morgan gave to me."

Roberts looked directly at the ranked officers and non-commissioned officers, and saw their puzzled but stubborn look. He spoke with careful emphasis.

"Gentlemen, I will not waste our time by loudly denying what is set forth in these pictures. That they may be clever fakes is obvious. But it was only yesterday morning that General Hugens and Field Marshal du Beck confirmed for me that there were minute capsules—apparently of drugs—in a glass of milk brought to me by the servants of this same Duke Marius. Who knows what depravity may be arranged for a man under the influence of secretly administered drugs? But is the man then guilty? Or is he guilty who administered the drugs?

"I know this: I have no memory of any such incidents as shown on these photographs. But I wonder not only at these scenes, but at the mind and aims of the person who would *record* them. Is there any of us so free of blame that he could afford to have all the incidents of his life freely revealed? But fortunately, there is no one hiding there to record the incidents. When there is someone hiding there, *why* is he hiding there?"

Across from Roberts, the Guards officers and noncoms were frowning in thought. But, Roberts noticed, one or two of them glanced covertly at something held in their hands, and their expressions hardened.

Roberts could talk, but the thought was clear in his mind that the same man cannot be the object of deep contempt and be the King, both at the same time. Again, Roberts could feel the pain of the Prince. But Roberts paid no attention.

"So," he said, "while I remember no such incidents, and while all this trash may be completely faked, nevertheless I wonder at the aims of whoever distributed it. And it was this, gentlemen, which gave me great pleasure."

He had their attention now. He could see it in the alert faces, in the eyes turned toward him or staring judiciously at the wall opposite. Roberts lowered his voice, and the words came out with great intensity.

"How many of my line have died of strange 'accidents'? Where is my father, the King? Where are my brothers? Why am I the last of the line? *And why am I, the last of the line, to be branded with this depravity?*

"He who would destroy a royal family, root and branch, and take the throne for himself, must not only kill its members, but must turn its followers against it. How better to do that than by taking the last surviving heir, when supposedly too young to defend himself, and either sinking him in the foulest sin, or *creating that appearance?*

"What the Duke did not know was that his drugs would be found, at that worst of all times when Field Marshal du Beck could confirm it for himself, and carry out my request to replace the Duke's guards with my own men.

"Yet this Regent did not stop there. Very plausibly, Company Fer was detached from the Royal Guard. Quickly, two assassins turned up here. Next, an attempt was made against Princess Erena, by this selfsame Duke Marius."

From the group of officers, the Lieutenant of the day before spoke in a clear level voice: "I saw that. And the King instantly drew left-handed, and shot him four times cleanly while the Duke grabbed for his hidden gun."

There was a murmur. The murmur went on, and suddenly there was a laugh, and Roberts could feel the change in the atmosphere. To these warriors, Duke Marius was suddenly absurd.

Roberts spoke, and the Prince's voice contained a trace of grim humor: "So, after the drugs, the assassins, the detachment of Company Fer, and the attempt against a Princess of Festhold by this Regent, I could not help but wonder, 'What next?' He was helpless, shot in both shoulders and knees, but might have new and undreamed-of treacheries already in motion. It was then that Colonel du Morgan showed me this little handful of pictures, and that much was clear.

"Marius could gain the kingdom only by stopping me first. I must, therefore, fail either to draw the sword from the crystal, or to gain the support of the nobles. Either one would do the job. Prudence would suggest that he try to do *both*. Whether he has found some way to influence the crystal—or to somehow counterfeit the result—I cannot claim to know. *But he has been forced to reveal too soon his plan to influence the nobles.*

"This little pack of pictures, gentlemen, was not meant for you. He couldn't even know you would be here. These pictures originally had another purpose: To so shock and antagonize the nobility that the last male member of the royal family would become the lowest and most despised of all the nobles, *while the next choice necessarily fell to Marius.*"

The silence in the courtyard when Roberts stopped speaking was broken by the sudden sound of ripping pictures. The leaders of the Royal Guard were methodically tearing the damning photographs to bits. As Roberts watched, they passed the bits from hand to hand, and the officers at the head of the ranks made a little pile, and struck a light to it.

In the quiet, the faint tramp of feet could heard, and for an instant Roberts thought of Company Fer. But it was too soon for that.

"*Open,*" said a voice, small but clearly audible, "*in the name of the Regent!*"

"The traitor's troops," said Roberts. "Quick! Back to your men!"

The courtyard emptied in a flash. There was a blast of whistles, the shout of commands. On the flagstones, the flame flickered, consuming the torn photographs as Roberts ran past into the building.

XII. The Guard Does Not Surrender

Colonel du Morgan blocked the entrance, shouting to Roberts, "Back, Your Majesty! *They're inside the gate!*"

The sword was in the Prince's hand before Roberts could decide what to do. The Prince was past du Morgan, and threw open the front doors of the building. One quick glance showed the Royal Guard in disarray, officers, and noncoms shouting at sullen men. On the walk regular Festhold infantry, glancing uneasily around, backed up an officer in general's uniform arguing vehemently with the Lieutenant who had accompanied Roberts the day before. Their voices were plainly to be heard.

The general shouted, "It is the Regent's order! This has the force of Royal Command!"

"The Regent," snarled the Lieutenant, "is a traitor and a murderer! With my own eyes I saw this famous Regent attack Princess Erena! I saw this Regent turn in the presence of the King, and grab for a concealed weapon! I saw the King draw and strike this same Regent to the earth with four blows before this imitation warlord could get his hand on a weapon. Now *you* tell *me* that the Royal Guard will stand aside and hand the true Warlord of Festhold over to this toothless wonder, this lying poisonous murdering hypocritical simulacrum of a Regent built up out of moldy dung? I say you are badly mistaken, general! I say you had better get your troops out of here before we *throw* them out!"

The general said shortly, "I have my orders! You will obey, Lieutenant, or face the consequences!"

"Be damned with the consequences!"

The Lieutenant whipped out his sword. The General clamped a whistle between his teeth. Prince Harold William, obviously ready for a fight, evidently could find nothing to say in this impasse. Roberts at once raised the Prince's voice.

"One moment, gentlemen!"

The General shouted, "There he is! *You are under arrest for attempted regicide!*"

"By whose order?"

"By command of Duke Marius Romeigne, Regent of Festhold, who stands in the place of the Ruler and Warlord, King and Emperor of Festhold! By that authority, and in that name, the Regent hereby places you, Harold William, *under arrest!* Throw down your arms, and go humbly to judgment!"

Roberts spoke politely. "Are we at war?"

"WHAT?"

"Is the Kingdom of Festhold at war?"

The General for an instant looked blank. Then his face suffused with rage. *"Drag that dog to me in chains!"*

The Lieutenant pivoted on his right heel. His left fist smashed the General in the face, throwing him back into the arms of the men behind him. Blood welled from the General's nose and mouth.

Roberts spoke, and the Prince's voice was clear, calm, and carrying: "In time of peace, no one, neither King nor Regent, can arbitrarily arrest another. The Regent has no right to order anyone to arrest me. But I have every right to defend myself from unlawful arrest. *And I will do it."*

This was all Roberts had intended to say. The General dizzily staring at him, seemed to have comprehended the point. The Lieutenant, sword in one hand and gun in the other, was a visible demonstration that the Prince would not fight alone.

But now, from well back in the ranks before them came a loud voice, freely speaking unspeakable slurs, damning Harold William by all the names that could be applied to anyone about whom such pictures could be circulated as had been made of the Prince.

And suddenly the Prince's voice was answering, the pain evident in his voice, but something else evident under the pain: "Then Marius has won, and I may never be King! But you will learn now who is the Warlord of Festhold! Get *back* beyond that gate!"

The regular troops, confused, simply stared as Harold William advanced. The Royal Guard, seeing their leader advance alone and single-handed against such numbers, abruptly comprehended what their officers had been trying to tell them—the pictures could *not* sum up the Prince! And in that case, it was a moral certainty that the *Regent* was a traitor.

Roberts heard the shout, but could no more influence the actions of Harold William than he could have as a spectator. The Prince's sword flashed out, the flat of the blade striking the side of the General's head.

"Get these men out of here before I kill them, *and you with them!"*

From somewhere in the rear of the Regent's troops came a shout: "Forward! In the name of the Regent. *Forward!"*

A fusillade of shots smashed windows and powdered brickwork across the face of the building. A fusion beam lanced out and struck the building. There was a shower of white-hot glass and exploding brickwork.

Someone yelled, "Show the Prince what blood looks like!" A grenade arched forward and blew up over the heads of the Royal Guard. From well behind the troops of the Regent came another shout: "Death to the Royal Coward!"

The General, staring at the Prince's expression, suddenly reached for his gun. Harold William went berserk.

Roberts, like a passive spectator at a horror show, could only watch as the Prince waded into a chaos of guns, flashes, spurting blood and shattered bone. Explosions deafened him, and a flaming bar of white heat seared his left side. An eruption of flame burst in his face. Time passed in heavy shocks and boiling smoke. The ground jumped underfoot. Pain incarnate knit through the lower left side of his chest. Then clever staring faces briefly appeared before him, hands were flung up, and the faces dissolved into the bloody chaos that ringed the Prince of Festhold.

A familiar voice shouted urgently. The Prince, dragging in great breaths of reeking air, turned to see Colonel du Morgan.

"Take cover, Sir! We've cleared them back—but they're sending tanks! The Prince turned, and Roberts was presented with the sight of a hideous shambles of broken weapons and shattered bodies.

From the distance came a clank and roar of tanks, and the Prince turned to face the tanks, wide and low, looming through the smoke. The Prince's thought was plain to Roberts: "I will never back nor bow to any of these dogs."

With a violent effort, Roberts got momentary control of the Prince's limbs, and dove head-first into a nearby crater.

Roberts hit the stony dirt in an explosion of pain from his left side. Now that the Prince was no longer concentrating on killing enemies, Roberts became aware that his whole left side seemed to be on fire, and his chest felt as though iron hooks were imbedded in it. A wave of weakness and weariness swept over him. He pressed his head into the damp stony dirt.

There was a heavy blast that jarred the earth under him. Then there was a clank that sounded almost over his head. The blast and roar died away. Roberts opened his eyes to see nothing but blackness, then a brilliant white light that faded away. It came to Roberts that he had passed out—must, in fact, have slept, and now it was night.

A loudspeaker roared: "Guard!"

There was an answering, more distant voice, and Roberts recognized Colonel du Morgan: "We're listening, Traitor."

"Yield!"

"Never. *God save King Harold!*"

"The Coward Prince is dead!"

Colonel du Morgan laughed. "The Warlord may be dead or alive, but if he was a coward, you are less than rotten wood."

"Yield! Your leader, whatever you call him, is dead! *And you can't withstand our armor forever!*"

"The Guard may die, Traitor. But only Harold William may command us to lay down our arms!"

Roberts, lying motionless in the crater, sensed that the Prince was conscious. Roberts could detect the Prince's wonder at Colonel du Morgan's words. It dawned on Roberts that the Prince had expected no such support. Roberts became aware that the heir to Festhold's throne was now dominated by some powerful emotion. Roberts could feel the quicker respiration, could sense the increased blood pressure—but he did not know what the emotion was.

Just above, the loudspeaker roared again: "We attack in four hours! You will never outlast it! Surrender, or—"

Roberts' whole left side burst into one fiery agony. His chest felt as if stitched together with huge and rusty staples. The Prince rushed up the bank in the darkness, swung the sword like an axe.

The loudspeaker was roaring: "—we will pound you into—"

The sword struck with a jar that traveled up his arm. Roberts was standing upright on some sort of slanting plate that apparently covered one of the tank's tracks. The abrupt silence told him that the Prince must have just cut the wire to the loudspeaker.

Roberts, unable to see a thing, wondered that the Prince stood motionless, waiting. Then from far away, a sound reached his ear, a low distant whine. Through the pain of burns and untreated wounds, Roberts could sense the Prince intently listening. Suddenly, a thought came through to Roberts: "That whine is an antigrav transport unit, such as Fer Company uses for the automatic artillery. *Could it be?*"

Roberts, inescapably aware of the Prince's wounds, wondered at this continuing concentration on the fight. Was Harold William *that* tough?

"Ah, the *hatch*."

The faint grating noise came through to Roberts a moment later, followed by a murmur: "Put that light out! You want to be blown to hell? Now—careful—wire feels all right, so far."

"Maybe the whole damn speaker fell off. There was some kind of thud."

"*I* didn't feel any thud."

"Well, I did."

A third voice murmured, "Keep your voices down. *Hst!* What's that?"

Across the cratered and invisible landscape came the sound of a signal whistle.

"Funny. That's practically right on top of the Guards!"

"They aren't firing."

"No."

"Listen!"

A brief alternation of silvery liquid notes on some sort of trumpet reached across the field, to be answered instantly by another, from a slightly different direction.

"That's the royalhorn!"

"*Both* of them were royalhorns!"

"What the *hell!* It's reinforcements, then!"

"Back this thing up! We've got to get out of here."

The prince spoke, his voice silky and menacing. "One moment, gentlemen. I am the Warlord. And if you move a finger, you are dead."

There was a tense silence, broken only by the faint but steadily approaching whine from the distance. The Prince's voice was calm. "I do not ask that you *yield*. I command that you return this instant to your true allegiance." Roberts could hear a ragged indrawn breath.

"If," said the Prince, "you wish to live and obey me, *say so now!*"

"Yes," came a shaking voice. Two other voices trod on the heels of the first. "Yes!" "Yes, *Sir!*"

"How many of you are there here? This is an XS12 with a normal crew of five. Are the others inside?"

"No, Sir. We're all there is. We're running with a bare crew."

"Why?"

"To get maximum force on the line, the Regent put in the spares at the beginning."

"I see. All right, fix that loudspeaker."

"Ah—Sir, every minute here is dangerous. They're probably—"

The Prince's voice was flat. "I said, *fix that wire.*" There was a brief pause. His tone became humorous. "We might as well die now, as some other time, eh?" For some reason, the men all laughed.

"Here," said one of them. "The wire's all right to here. And—wait!—*Here* we are. We'll have to splice." There was a tense silence, and the blast of a whistle from the distance.

"All right," said one of the men.

The Prince said, "Can you hand up the microphone to me?"

"Yes, Sir."

"All of you, get inside, and hand it up."

There was a scrape of boots slipping on metal, then the Prince reached out his hand, and Roberts felt the fingers close on something round and ridged—a handle of some kind. The Prince raised it to his lips. His voice boomed out in the quiet.

"Colonel du Morgan!"

There was a bare moment's hesitation. "*Sir?*" The voice expressed shock.

"I am bringing in an XS12. One only."

"Y-*Yes, Sir!*"

There was a click. The Prince leaned into the hatch. "We are on the lip of a crater. Back. Go left around it, then straight ahead. Speed twelve—"

"Hadn't you better get inside, Sir?"

"I like the air out here. 'Tis cooler."

There was a second round of subdued but delighted laughter. The Prince, Roberts thought drily, seemed to have just the right sense of humor for this planet.

Conscious of his own total lack of protection, with the XS12 tilting underfoot, with his side on fire and each breath agony, Roberts felt more than saw the position of the landscape shift around him. The Prince sat, legs dangling, atop the big turret in the darkness. Ahead, finally, there was a faint blue light that flashed and disappeared.

The Prince turned and called in a low clear voice, "Speed Three." They at once slowed to a crawl. Straight ahead, the blue light flashed again.

The Prince called, "Du Morgan?"

"Here, Sir!"

The Prince turned. "*Stop!* Engines off!" They stopped. A moment later, the throb died away.

The Prince turned to look into the darkness. "The three men in this tank have returned to their true allegiance. See that they get food and a place to sleep as soon as their machine is under cover."

Du Morgan gave brief orders to someone nearby. The Prince slid over the side, and dropped to the ground. The pain was breathtaking, but his voice didn't waver.

"Company Fer is here?"

"Yes, Sir. They're just setting up."

"Is there an aid station nearby?"

"Yes—you're wounded?"

The Prince's voice was dry. "Slightly."

"M'm. Right over here, Sir. Squint your eyes when we go in . . . Careful as we go down, here . . . Now, through two doors, and this light is bright, now . . . My God!"

Directly in front of Roberts in the dazzling light was a sort of high cot with a clean white sheet over it; a man in a white uniform, eyes wide and jaw clenched, and a nurse in white, her hand to her mouth. An orderly, his back turned, was just carrying out a mop and a bucket.

The Prince said quietly, "The burn is from a flame gun—I suppose a Mark X. Then I think I ran into two or three solid shots from an explosive whip. I think they went through, but I'm not sure. The pain of the burn is intense, and continuous. The shot is particularly bad when I breathe."

The doctor said, "Nurse, a syringe—"

The Prince interrupted, and his voice was irritable. "No anesthetic. I am telling you this simply to explain what happened." He glanced at du Morgan. "Colonel."

Colonel du Morgan stiffened. "Yes, Sir?"

"There is to be no amputation. Not so much as a finger or a toe. If I die of this, that is unfortunate; but it is honorable, and I will take the risk. If there should *be* an amputation, contrary to my will, I will have the head of the doctor who carried it out. See that this is clearly understood. Now, while the doctor carries out his examination, get me a position map."

"Yes, sir." The Colonel turned and went out.

The Prince looked at the doctor. "How bad does this seem? Be truthful."

The doctor said, "I don't see how—" He paused and began again. "It is very unusual to see anyone in such condition on his feet."

"Since I have not yet killed the traitor, I must remain on my feet. Is there anything you can do to keep down infection?"

The doctor approached, and very cautiously examined the Prince's left side. Next, he studied the Prince's chest, gingerly lifting away layers of clothing. "Fortunately, the slugs went clean through. But—in all honesty—you should be in the restitution baths."

The door opened, and the Colonel came in with a captain and two sergeants, carrying a large map on a stand. The map bore little symbols in red and green.

"Ah," said the Prince. "Good." He walked over. "How accurate is this?"

"As of now," said the Colonel, "I believe it is substantially correct. We sent up drones at dusk, and have heard little movement from them since then."

The Prince touched his finger to a small purple oval well back on the map. "Are we sure the Traitor is here?"

"He was seen there yesterday afternoon. A special medical unit is attached to him."

"Curious that he is here, where he could conceivably be wounded."

"What regular leader of troops can he trust with such a task as this? He *has* to be here."

The Prince nodded, and leaned forward. On the map, the positions of the little symbols resembled a circle within a larger semicircle of enemy troops, with a still larger oblong coming down the road from the north, and the little purple oval on the far side of the semicircle from the circle that showed the position of the Royal Guard. The road came down from the top of the map, passed through the semicircle to the north, passed through the circle representing the Guard, and bent off toward the southeast. The Prince straightened.

"It is true that they are not yet across the road to the southeast?"

"They were, but Company Fer passed that way."

"And this juggernaut coming down the road from the north?"

"The regent's reinforcements. Once they get here, we will be in a bad way."

The Prince glanced at the measure showing the scale of the map. He looked at the road, then back at the purple oval on the far side of the semicircle and distinctly to the east of the reinforcements on the road.

"To wait for the reinforcements to arrive," said the Prince, "would be mere suicide. To move cross-country to the southwest would be to flee, with no hope of victory. We might attack the center of this half-ring of disloyal troops, but that would warn the Traitor, and his reinforcements are nearby on the road.—What hour is it?"

"A little before one, Sir."

The Prince considered the map. "Suppose we move out, very quietly, along the road to the southeast? At best, they may not know we are gone. At worst, they will overhear us. But if they overhear us, what will they think?"

"That we are in retreat."

"The troops at the end of this semicircle were roughly handled?"

The Colonel smiled. "Company Fer was not gentle with them."

"Then they should be tired, and not eager to intervene. If we are in retreat, what will they care?"

"It is impossible to be sure," said the colonel, "but I would expect them to do nothing."

"Now, suppose that we move southeast along the road until we are well past the end of their line, and then swing north, across country. By dawn, the Traitor, if he is still where this map shows him to be, will have his half-ring of besieging troops to the southwest, his host of reinforcements to the west—*and us to the east.*"

The Prince traced the movement on the map with his forefinger, and there was a low involuntary murmur from the captain and the two sergeants.

The Colonel said, "If we could get there by dawn—"

The Prince nodded. "Then we could attack with the sun behind us, shining in their eyes. And if the reinforcements should be called in, they will be equally blinded."

"We will do it! But Your Majesty must remain here, to be treated—"

"No treatment will do me any good until we end this traitor. Let us waste no time. We have to be there before this situation changes."

XIII. The Regent's Unlucky Day

Roberts, aware of a ceaseless searing agony, and a sense that to breathe was to drag massive hooks through his chest, saw the dawn through eyes that swam with fatigue and poisons pumped through his system from the wounds and burns. The Prince, who must be aware of the same endless pain and fatigue, merely murmured, "There—a little to the south—"

Roberts caught the brief flash in the almost level rays of the sun, that lit brightly the flat green ground with its occasional clumps of trees.

Colonel du Morgan said, "Yes, I believe—it is! That is the window of a headquarters trailer!" The Colonel handed him the field glasses. A few moments of careful examination showed a small complex of low sand-colored buildings, with a flagpole in the center.

"We *may* be mistaken." said the Prince. "However, turn the column by platoons, and we will see what we catch in the net."

The Colonel passed his orders back, and the men spread out, and then the Royal Guard was a thin scattering of men in camouflage suits who blended into the scenery. A low whine from the rear told of Fer Company's transportation.

Ahead of them, a little speck rose jerkily above one the low brown shapes. The Prince raised the binoculars. It was a flag, going up the pole in the center of the little cluster of temporary buildings. The flag was of dark-blue edged in purple, with a golden circlet in the center. For an instant, the flag stood out almost straight, and Roberts could see that the circlet was a coronet.

"Duke Marius' own flag," growled the Prince, "with a royal edging. Ah, if only he is there!"

The low buildings very gradually loomed larger. The sides of trees and shrubs toward them were lit brightly in the rising sun. Ahead, a voice shouted warningly: "Who goes! *Halt!* By command of the Regent!"

A nearer, louder voice answered, "Isn't this General du Fenn's headquarters?"

"It is the Headquarters of the Regent himself!"

"What. The *Regent?* Is he there?"

"He is!"

The Prince growled, "Sound the attack."

The Colonel turned, and a moment later a silvery note sounded, rose abruptly higher, and repeated again and again. The Prince sprang atop the captured tank as it trundled up from the rear. To either side, men were running forward in long, well spread-out lines. Behind them, the low whine rose to a howl.

The sand-colored buildings were close now. The guards stared, saw the courtyard suddenly thick with enemies, and threw down their weapons. The Prince dropped from the back of the tank, walked toward the largest of the buildings, as his men appeared everywhere, and threw open the door.

A white-coated officer spoke angrily. "Out! You can't come in here!"

The Prince stepped in, sword in one hand, gun in the other. "Where is Marius?"

The officer looked blank. "I—Who—?"

The Prince's voice had its usual effect. "I am the Warlord. Where is the Regent?"

"I—he—through that door, Sir."

"Lead the way."

The terrified officer pushed open the door, and voices were heard in calm discussion. "Toward noon?" said the Regent's voice.

"Yes, Sir. The reinforcements will be in position then. The rebels will be wiped out."

"Excellent . . . yes, Doctor?"

The trembling doctor stepped aside, and the Prince walked in, closely followed by armed men. The Regent, heavily bandaged, was sitting up in bed. His eyes widened. The Prince's voice was quiet, but it spread out through the room, and left no doubt that what it said was final.

"You may surrender, Marius, in which case you may live, for the time. Or you may choose to *not* surrender, and I will shoot you through the head."

The Regent averted his eyes, and drew a slow breath. He said bitterly, "So I am surrounded? By *what?*"

The Prince, watching closely, didn't answer, and Colonel du Morgan said, "By the Royal Guard."

"By an element—what, a section?—of the Royal Guards."

Beside the Regent's bed, the officer in general's uniform who had been talking to the Regent spoke sharply, "It could hardly be even that. More likely a squad. Nothing more could slip through the lines.—*Guard!*"

Several more of the Prince's soldiers answered this invitation, and came in. More followed. The room grew crowded. The general stared, and abruptly turned away.

The Prince said quietly, "What have you decided, Marius?"

The Regent slowly shut his eyes. "I surrender."

XIV A Job Well Done

The agony of being lowered into the tank was as nothing compared with the slow, cautious removal of the charred cloth. But this was part of the Festhold process of treating severe burns, and there was nothing Roberts could do to escape it.—Nothing, that is, until the Prince, exhausted, passed out, and Roberts instantly did the same.

Roberts could feel himself spin into blackness, but much too soon he could feel himself again returning to consciousness. He fought to prevent it, failed, and became aware that he was lying between clean sheets.

He waited for the pain, but felt only a sense of calm rested well-being. Puzzled, he opened his eyes. He found himself looking at a white ceiling, in a dimly lit room with blank white walls.

Roberts sat up, felt his side, and then noticed *something*. There was a different bodily tone, a different feel, a something different—familiar yet strange. Roberts got out of bed, jerked open a door thinking it would lead into a corridor, and found himself in a small bathroom. A glance in a mirror showed him himself—not Prince Harold William.

Roberts stood frowning for an instant, uncertain whether he was dreaming now, had been dreaming before, was out of his head, or was wide-awake and in his right senses. Back in the small room he had come from, there was the brief crackle of a wall communicator. The voice of Colonel Valentine Sanders reached him.

"Roberts?"

Roberts made the mental adjustment from Prince to captain in the Interstellar Patrol.

"Here, sir."

"When did you get back?"

"A few minutes ago. Is *this* how it usually works?"

"No. How do you feel?"

"Unnatural. In a dream."

"Stay right there. Turn on all the lights, and move around. I'll be right with you."

Roberts wandered around the two small rooms, and snapped on all the lights. This helped some, but he still seemed to be moving in a dream. The door from the corridor opened, and Colonel Valentine Sanders, lean and tough, his hair close-cropped, stepped in. His voice sounded relieved.

"How do you feel now?"

"Unreal."

"M'm." The colonel glanced around the bare room with its blank walls and white cot. "I feel a little unnatural in here myself." His voice echoed faintly. "Can you walk all right?"

"I've been able to so far."

"Let's go down the hall to my office. I never did care for inside jobs, and this one is even more peculiar than the usual."

The colonel opened the door, and led the way down the corridor. Roberts followed, still with the impression that he was dreaming. The colonel opened a door marked, "Chief, O-Branch," and stepped back to let Roberts precede him. The colonel shut the door, pulled out a chair for Roberts, went around behind the desk, and sat back.

"What happened since the last time you reported in?"

Roberts, in careful detail, described everything that had

happened since he had been awakened with the words, "Your Majesty, Duke Marius has escaped." He told of the pictures, the attempt to arrest him, the battle, and the surrender of the Regent.

The colonel, increasingly wide-eyed, listened intently. At the end, he sat up, frowned, and very carefully sat back again.

"Where the devil does this leave us?"

Roberts shook his head. "I haven't the faintest idea."

The colonel frowned, and sat unmoving. Finally, he cleared his throat.

"What is your reaction to this prince?"

"Harold William?"

"Yes."

"Every time he was attacked morally, he folded up and I had to take over. Then they attacked him physically, and there was no stopping him."

The colonel sounded exasperated. "But what does *that* mean?"

Roberts thought it over. "It seems to me that he has been very cleverly drugged, in such a way as to make him detest his own reactions. He has no confidence in himself—he is ashamed of himself—morally."

"That doesn't fit with the rest of his actions."

"When I first got there, his room was a shambles, he was almost out on his feet, his servants or subordinates treated him with an insulting familiarity, the Regent dealt with him as if he were a nonentity—but in the midst of this ruin, there was a rack of well-oiled weapons. Even when he is to all intents and purposes unconscious, his reflexes are such that the weapons are like extensions of his limbs. When he decides to *do* something, his motions with weapons are like lightning. It seems to me that can only follow from hereditary aptitude and long training. In fact, he said to the officer who is second-in-command of the Royal Guard, that since he was old enough to think he had 'aimed to be a fighting man,' and had trained to acquire the necessary skills."

The colonel sat back, frowning. "The weapons you speak of were right there, in his room?"

"Yes."

"How fast did he seem to recover from the drugs?"

"Very fast."

"By your description of his actions, he sounds almost super-human."

"Either that, or he had almost superhuman motivation—to nail the Regent."

"All right, now let's think this thing through. Suppose *you* hadn't been there. Would he have done as well?"

Roberts considered the question. "He would have folded up any number of times. First, he would have used this drug, 'Twist'—whatever that is. I don't know just what would have taken place with the tutor. Next, the Regent burst in unan-nounced with two members of Festhold's high command. The Regent's manner was full of slurs and insinuations. When the Regent went out, two assassins came in, and the Prince made no voluntary motion to defend himself. I doubt that he would have gotten through the situation on his own. The next day, he wilted when the photographs were sprung on him—I could *feel* the pain it caused him—and I think he would simply have turned his back on the whole situation. What would have hap-pened when they came to take him prisoner, I don't know. If he had still been under the influence of the drugs, I suppose he wouldn't have resisted then, either."

"How was his judgment in battle?"

"Good. But since I could only occasionally catch his thoughts, I can only judge by results. He outfought and outmaneuvered the Regent as if the Regent had been asleep. But the Regent had already been shot through both arms and legs, so he couldn't have been in good shape. Still—"

"What's your overall conclusion, Roberts?"

"I think Prince Harold William is exactly what he claims to be, and what he wanted to be. He hasn't been proclaimed *King*—but by his own actions, I think he has won the right to the title of 'Warlord of Festhold.' And on a planet that reveres fighting abil-ity, that should count for a lot."

"Yes, but what about this sense of guilt?" The colonel frowned in thought. "Of course, he may, having fought, and having been badly wounded—"

Roberts nodded. The colonel said, "This brings us back to where we started. What the deuce *is* the situation there now?"

"You mean, legally?"

"Practically. Let's see now. The Prince, who is heir to the throne, but not yet of age—"

"Supposedly heir to the throne."

"Yes," said the colonel, "there's that. Well, the Prince, supposedly heir to the throne, discovers the Regent, who stands in the place of the King, dishonorably occupied with the Prince's sister—"

"Who," said Roberts, "was the Regent's ward."

"M'm. Yes. And the Prince shoots the Regent—"

Roberts said, "In self-defense as much as anger. The Regent was reaching for his own weapon, at the time."

"I see. Then the Prince takes the Regent prisoner—"

"Not exactly. He took him to his own aid station for treatment. He gave no orders that the Regent was to be held prisoner."

"Roberts," said the colonel exasperatedly, "I admit, you were there, you saw it, so this is how it actually happened. But consider how it is going to *look*. The Prince, backed by a small army, forces an entrance to the Regent's apartment, catches the Regent with the Princess, shoots him, drags him out, and that night the Regent escapes. The Regent comes back with troops, a battle erupts, the Prince beats the Regent in battle, *and the Regent,*—who stands in the place of the king—*surrenders to the Prince.*—What is that? Has the government changed hands? Is the Prince guilty of rebellion? What *is* the situation?"

Roberts shook his head. "I don't know."

"Well," said the colonel drily, "all I have to say, Roberts, is that this is an extremely inconvenient time for you to lose contact with the situation."

"Sorry, sir," said Roberts, "but as I think of the Prince in that 'restitution bath'—it strikes me that this is a pretty good time to be here. And just incidentally, there *is* something we have yet to clear up."

"What's that?"

"Erena."

"Roberts," said the colonel exasperatedly, "for all you know, the girl doesn't care for you. After all, you appeared as her rescuer, at an appropriate time—naturally, she—"

The colonel paused, frowning. He leaned forward. "Let's hear that again, Roberts.—How did you know she needed help?"

"She was on the downslide, sir, going into the casino. I was on the upslide."

"And?"

"Sir?"

"What *happened?*"

Roberts frowned. "I don't know. I looked at her. There was a—it was as if she made an *appeal.*"

"Did she *say* anything?"

"No, sir."

"This all passed in a *look?*"

"Yes, sir. It was obvious."

"And suppose I say you are to keep away from this princess, and forget the incident—?"

Roberts looked at the colonel, and smiled very slightly.

The colonel grinned. "The question was rhetorical, Roberts. No need to slice my head off." The colonel thought intently, then smiled. "Roberts, *if* the Warlord of Festhold wins his crown, and *if* Festhold remains firmly allied to the Federation, *then* it strikes me that if your name appears before the Warlord, in a request for permission to see the Princess, then you having influence at court, might be able to move the Warlord to say 'Yes.'—After that, you're on your own."

XV. The Baths of the Damned

Roberts put in a day of increasingly strenuous exercise, and ended up feeling almost like himself. He slept soundly, to wake up with a helmet on his head, and on the screen within the helmet, before his eyes, two faint dots that merged into one, and the one expanded, faded, formed a tiny distant scene, as of an underwater view which began to expand, and grow definite, then fade again, and then again to expand. The scene was suddenly in focus, clear, wavering before and around him, and he was conscious of one inescapable sensation.

Cold. Around him was a fluid, tinged very faintly pink, in which tiny crystals moved. Above him, a brilliant light shone down, its heat lost in the cold fluid that bathed him. The cold did not end at his skin, but moved slowly through his veins—an icy chill that seemed to reach the core of his being, to immerse him completely, inside and out, in bone-chilling cold.

To his left, something moved, and now he could see the monstrous half-men's head, shoulders, and arms alone—appearing at his left side, their eyes intent behind the lenses that formed the eyes of their grotesque white-plastic heads. Carefully, they examined Roberts' left side—and it slowly came to him that this must be the 'restitution baths' the doctor had spoken of earlier.

The Prince, surely, must be unconscious. But the Prince's eyes were partly open, and Roberts was treated to the sight of the surgeons working in this hydraulic womb to correct the damage done in battle.

Roberts tried to disconnect himself from the Prince—and couldn't do it. Time crept past. Despite the chill, Roberts could faintly feel the surgeons at work. The tone of the Prince's body—or rather the lack of it—began to impress itself on him.

Gradually, he became aware of the burn—somehow muted by the chill—that covered the left side of his body. It occurred to Roberts that he was, for practical purposes, in a form of purgatory. Why had they had to send him back *now?*

Then he recognized the symptoms of gathering hysteria, knew from experience there was no relief in that direction, and settled down grimly to endure what was inescapable. It seemed to go on for a long, long time.

Somewhere, in the distance, birds were singing. A quiet male voice said, "He is in here, Your Excellencies, but he regains consciousness only at long intervals."

A voice replied with a note like a mosquito, "The just reward of sin."

The first voice said, "The process of recovery is still in some doubt. Physically, most of the gross damage has been overcome. But there is a severe psychic drain with such wounds as these."

"We want to see how the prisoner has been marked."

Light blinded him as the eyelids opened. The dazzle faded away, as the eyes nearly shut, and through the slit Roberts could see a severely plain white room, with slightly open window looking out across the tops of trees to a brick building several hundred feet away.

Back over his right shoulder, the mosquito-voice was disappointed: "I understood the flesh was burned away on the left side of his face."

A second and similar voice put in: "The left side of the *body* is completely burned to the bone, is it not?"

Two men perhaps in their late sixties, robed in dark crimson with dark-blue cowls, stood beside the bed, their probing gaze hungrily searching the face and the form under the thin blanket.

An embarrassed doctor said, "The wounds were severe, Your Excellencies. Of course, the tank breakage caused trouble, but—"

The first turned to him. "Draw back the covers. This is Holy Business."

The doctor hesitated.

The Prince's voice, low but clear, suddenly dominated the room. "Take these vultures out of here, Doctor."

The robed figures jerked back. The doctor looked startled.

The Prince drew a deep breath, and let it out slowly. Roberts could feel the two legs flex, the right arm bend and extend, the left bend and extend. The was no sense of pain, but a faint stiffness. The first of the robed visitors raised a hand, palm out, and began to gesture in the air, as if warding off evil spirits.

The doctor said uneasily, "Perhaps, Your Excellencies, it would be better if—"

The wounds in the chest were scars—mere dimples to be felt with the fingertips. The Prince's voice was suddenly jovial.

"On second thought, Doctor, let them stay. These are, I'm sure, the Regent's *tame* theologians?" The robed figures drew themselves erect. Their eyes glittered.

"You blaspheme!"

Roberts, trying to quiet the Prince, found himself a mere spectator. The Prince sat up.

"To blaspheme is to claim godhood, or to be irreverent toward holy things. I claim no godhood. I am merely the Warlord!"

"You lie!"

The second robed figure made a sweeping gesture of the outstretched hand. "In the name of the Holy Crystal, curse your blasphemies! You are sworn condemned! In the Crystal Light, you are a sinner and less!"

The doctor wrung his hands. "Your Excellencies, the patient—"

The eyes of the two cowled figures glinted. Their hands traced figures in the air. Their lips murmured. Their fingers pointed to the Prince's eyes and teeth, to his arms and legs. An air of smoking witchcraft emanated from the pair. Occasionally recognizable words could be heard.

" . . . wither and shrink . . . eyes water and vision fade . . . teeth do ache and pain . . . trembling palsied hands . . . uncertain gait . . ."

Roberts could feel the shock. The room seemed to swim before him. With an effort of will, Roberts drew in a deep breath, exhaled forcibly. The room steadied around him.

Before him, an unholy glee lit the two faces, their teeth bared, fingers pointed successively at his eyes, his mouth, his arms, his legs—

Roberts drew another breath. The Prince's voice was august, said: "Doctor—"

The doctor, trembling, his face pale, eyes blinking, swallowed and turned. Roberts spoke carefully, "Close and lock that door."

The tone of the order left no possibility of disobedience. The doctor obeyed. Roberts drew another careful breath, and stood up. The faces of the gesticulating pair before him contorted with rage. Their gestures grew more emphatic, their murmurings more incisive. Roberts spoke carefully, and the Prince's voice was an iron and unbreakable command: *Be still.*"

The two voices ceased to function. Roberts spoke carefully: "Remove your cloaks."

The words seemed to echo in the room, filled with a restrained but terrible power. Uncertainly, faces showing evidence of struggle, they removed the cloaks, and stood holding them. Suddenly, they were plainly gripped by fear.

Roberts spoke carefully: "Bow once to the Warlord."

Teeth clicking together, the two figures trembled and bowed. Roberts turned slightly toward the door.

"Unlock that door, Doctor, and open it wide."

There was a click, and the faint squeal of a hinge. Roberts turned to the two figures shaking uncontrollably before him.

"Leave this room, and thank the Almighty Power that you still live."

Shaking, they backed to the door, turned, and the sounds of running feet dwindled down the corridor. Roberts breathed carefully.

"Close that door, Doctor." The door clicked shut.

"Come here."

The doctor, jaw clamped shut, eyes wide, obediently approached.

Roberts could feel a knot of cold terror within him slowly relax. Roberts sat on the edge of the bed, and spoke more easily.

"Now that the hirelings of the Regent are gone, we can speak less formally. The forces of the Traitor have now been defeated in personal combat, defeated on the field of battle, and defeated by spiritual power. What is the *legal* situation?"

The doctor hesitated. "I—until a few minutes ago, I had no doubts—" He swallowed. "I understand simply that the Regent had been ambushed, that there had been a local uprising, and the—the degenerate youngest son of the royal family had been captured, badly wounded, when the Regent put down the uprising."

Briefly, Roberts thought back. "And have there been no rumors?"

"Oh, there have been fantastic rumors! The Prince and the Regent have fought a duel. The Prince has declared himself Warlord. The Regent and the Prince have fought a pitched battle. It was only when the Regent gave a personal address and released the official report that the rumors died down."

"And the troops on the field of battle?"

The doctor looked blank.

Roberts said carefully, "What you have heard, Doctor, has been a carefully made lie. In this case, the rumors were much closer to the truth. The rumors could never have died down, or the lie been accepted—*if the troops who knew the truth first-hand could tell it.*"

The doctor blinked. "But—oh, I see." He turned, to look directly at Roberts. "But the troops were off-lifted because of the Emergency!"

"And what pretext was there for an Emergency?"

"There was the rumor of a Stath invasion fleet."

Not for the first time, Roberts was regretting that he had not let the Prince finish off the Regent when he had the chance.

"Has *this* rumor proved true?"

"No, but the Regent has warned that every precaution must be taken until we can be certain of Stath good-will."

"Ah," said Roberts. "And has any misfortune to any of the troops been reported?"

"I—not that I know of."

"The obvious thing would be to kill the witnesses. But in this case, the witnesses are armed and no doubt suspicious.—How long have I been under treatment?"

"Here? Or before the accident?"

Roberts looked at the doctor. "What accident are you speaking of?"

"When the restitution tank broke."

"How long ago was that?"

"Oh, that was—months ago. We had to start all over again."

"I suppose healing was almost complete, when the tank accidentally broke?"

"Well, not complete, but coming right along. You'd been several weeks in the tank."

"I see." Roberts thought it over. If he remembered correctly, the Prince was to be tested for his fitness to rule in *four months*. That had been back before the battle with the Regent. Thanks to the 'accident' with the tank, the time had been disposed of nicely. The Regent had meanwhile established his own story of what had happened. That was bound to be ruinous for the Prince. Roberts cleared his throat.

"Where are we?"

"This is Capital General Hospital. I am Doctor du Beck, and I've been in charge of the case since the accident."

Roberts said carefully, "You're no relation of Field Marshal du Beck, I suppose?"

The doctor looked tense. "Yes, sir. He is my cousin. But I assure you, I am in no way implicated—After all, that involved only the military."

Roberts said carefully, "Remember, I have been unconscious—or only occasionally conscious—for quite a while. Field Marshal du Beck was in good repute the last I knew."

"Yes—yes, that's true. But *that* was before the Emergency was declared! Field Marshal du Beck and several members of the General Staff were found to be in secret contact with the Stath."

Roberts nodded. "I see. Now, who guards this building?"

"The Regent's own Household Guard."

"And what is that building over there?"

"The City Palace—I believe, strictly speaking, it's the Capital City Administration Building, but everyone calls it the City Palace."

"The Regent's headquarters?"

"Yes."

"Now, is the Regent to be notified as soon as I come to?"

"Why, yes, that's correct."

"All right. Now, doctor, is your cousin's—disgrace—a burden on your mind?"

"It is a—the name—" The doctor couldn't go on.

Roberts nodded. "It was, of course, basically your cousin's word against the Regent's."

The doctor blinked.

Roberts said, "You have already seen what the Regent's *spiritual* advisors are like."

The doctor swallowed.

Roberts went on, "In every contest so far between Duke Marius and me, Duke Marius has been defeated. Unfortunately, the Regent still has the power of the state at his disposal. But the time remaining to him as Regent is now short. Field Marshal du Beck is a witness, as was General Hugens—"

"Hugens!" said the doctor. "He was the go-between!"

Roberts said patiently, "The guilt of your cousin and General Hugens consists in their being witnesses that I was drugged while under the care of the Regent.—Now, would you like to have your name freed of this suggestion of treason?"

The doctor's eyes suddenly filled with tears. With an effort, he looked away. He stood up, and after a moment, turned to face the Prince. "What can I do?"

XVI. EVERYONE HAS HIS REASONS

The voice of the guard said, "But we have no order to let you in!"

"I repeat," said Dr. du Beck, "the Regent *told me personally* that he wished to see this patient *as soon as possible* after he awakened—That was the Regent's *order.*"

"Yes, sir—"

Roberts looked around from the stretcher. From this angle, he had a view of a long, wide, high-ceilinged and immaculate hall with high double doors that opened off to either side. At the head and the foot of the stretcher bored burly orderlies held the grips, and waited. "My dear sir," said Doctor du Back, "if *you* wish to block the orders of the Regent—"

"Wait right here," said the guard. He turned and ran with a clink of metal and rap of heels down the corridor to the door at the far end.

Dr. du Beck glanced at Roberts. Roberts nodded toward the far end of the hall.

Dr. du Beck growled, "Damn these military, anyway! One says one thing, then another says something else, and—why do we have to wait *here* all day? The Regent outranks the guard, doesn't he?—Let's go!"

Both orderlies gave approving grunts, and followed the doctor down the long hall. As they approached the far end, they could hear the guard's trembling explanation, and the angry voice of the Regent.

"No," said the Regent flatly. *"Get out of here."* The guard backed out the door.

Dr. du Beck knocked both doors open wide, and said loudly, "Your excellency, I have obeyed your command precisely."

The guard sucked in his breath. The orderlies shoved their way past.

Ahead of them, beside a door at the end of a short entry hall, the Regent opened his mouth speechlessly. The doctor, the orderlies, and the pale immobile figure on the stretcher—all were now inside the Regent's office.

Across the room, bound tightly to a high-backed chair, sat the Princess Erena. The doctor paused, speechless. The orderlies blinked and looked again.

The Regent said shortly, "You are intruding in a matter of high State policy! *Who ordered you—*"

Dr. du Beck said, "You wished to see the prisoner as soon as he regained consciousness. Here he is."

The Regent looked at the Prince, and Roberts allowed his eyelids to shut, then raised them again.

"H'm," said the Regent. "Very well, Doctor. This is inconvenient in its way, but possibly some use can be made of it, after all. Leave the patient with me. I will have my—personal doctors—care for him."

Dr. du Beck bowed stiffly. "Set the stretcher down, orderlies, and come with me." The two orderlies eyed the beautiful woman tied to the chair, and hesitated.

Princess Erena smiled. "Don't try to help me. He has a guard outside, two more in the hall, half-a-dozen at the desk downstairs, and the rest of a fifty-man section of guards in quarters on the top floor. In any case, I am not worried now that my brother is here."

The orderlies glanced at the pale figure motionless on the stretcher. They looked at each other embarrassedly, and glanced at the doctor, who jerked his head toward the outside. The inner door closed behind them. A moment later, the outer doors banged shut. There was a sound of footsteps going down the hall.

The Regent exhaled, and sat on a corner of the desk. "So, Harold, even your vitality has its limits."

Roberts forced the eyelids open, then let them drop. The Regent sighed.

"Life is a curious thing. We act—for what reason?—and the act binds us. A motive is assumed. And if we cannot prove a different motive, we are bound by that one. We acquire a reputation, and our actions are interpreted in accordance with that reputation, and motives assigned to us that match the reputation. One man runs and he is a coward. Another runs, and he is going to get reinforcements. It is unfair, and yet it is often true. We shape the mold by our actions, and the mold we have made then shapes our actions. And it is a strong man who can break that mold, once it is formed."

Roberts sighed, but said nothing.

The Regent said, "*Why* should your family have such vitality? *Why* should they command and others obey? Why should I feel pain to see you lying there? Why, moreover, should I waste my effort with this sister of yours, seeking to gain approval when approval from her is forever denied me? Fool that I am, I would marry her if she would have me, and rear new little Harold Williams of the same breed, and then nothing at all would be changed."

Erena said quietly, "Duke Marius believes that our family is bad for Festhold." She glanced at the Regent. "But the kings of our line have been good rulers."

The Regent said, "I don't know why I should want to convince you. It is, of course, impossible. *Certainly* the kings have been good—as *kings*. If they had been bad, I would not have to end the line. The trouble is that they *have* been good. They have given validity to a form of government which otherwise would be invalid. My difficulty is that I must *prove* its invalidity. Yet—after three years of the most painstaking psychological sabotage—your brother—one of this abnormal line—at the very moment towards which all the preparation has been aimed—at this precise moment, your brother reverts to type. He regains his strength, outwits me, convinces the High Command itself, stands suddenly surrounded and protected by his own Guard, destroys the effect of a plan worked out over a period of years, and all at once to put him down is a matter that requires armed force. *Then* he becomes in actual fact the Warlord of Festhold, leads an attack straight into the teeth of an overpowering force, scatters it, captures a tank single-handed, goes back as much dead as alive, removes his troops from the trap I am preparing, and outflanks and captures *me*. Such a person may not be allowed to live!"

Princess Erena said exasperatedly, "*Why?* That is exactly how the King of Festhold is *supposed* to act!"

"Because," the Regent burst out, "it is *unfair!* The top should be open to *anyone!* Why should I, the second greatest in the realm, be barred off from the top by this—this barrier of royalty?" He whirled suddenly, and bent by the stretcher.

"How are you, Harold?"

Roberts murmured, "Harold?"

The Regent carefully drew down the blankets. "Agh! What a burn that was! The mind connected to the nerve-endings that felt that burn must have gone through hell! And here—" He drew aside the hospital gown. "—Yes, three such wounds as those—*plus* the burn—were you conscious when the restitution tank broke?"

"Broke?" murmured Roberts.

Across the room, Princess Erena began to cry. The Regent pulled back the hospital gown, and drew the covers up into place. He straightened.

Roberts, the surgical scalpel in his right hand, close to his side, lay still, but forced his eyes open. He looked blankly at Duke Marius. The Regent nodded slowly.

"It may turn out, after all. The rumors, of course, may never die completely. But it is the official history that counts, and I will control that." He nodded, and turned to the quietly sobbing Erena.

"Very well, my dear. He may have his public Trial, as the law requires. And afterward,—" The Regent hesitated, then spoke generously, "you may even go to visit him. Do not complain. You have lost. But you have not lost everything.—And it will be best for the country, too. You will see."

The Regent hesitated, then added, "*Actually,* that is why I am doing this."

XVII. THE TRIAL

The roll of drums and blast of trumpets, the snap of smartly handled weapons, the ground-shaking tramp of boot heels striking in unison—all were silenced at last as the procession halted in the high open-sided "Cathedral of Truth." The tall doors along the sides folded back between the massive pillars to allow a view of the proceedings to the ranked array outside, on the gently sloping rise of ground.

In front of Roberts loomed a plain altar. To the right of the altar, overhead lights came on, to illuminate a massive black square-edged opaque block lying tilted up at a slight angle on a strong wooden frame.

Before the altar, a dark-haired, dark-bearded man in dark crimson robe with dark-blue cowl thrown back, spoke quietly. "Our prayers for true guidance, and for a true sign, have been made, and the time is now come for the trial. Step forward, Harold William, and halt before the stone."

Roberts, who had expected to see a large quartzlike crystal, with the sword projecting upright, found himself instead before a sort of flat slate block with a hemispherical recess a foot across in the end of the block facing him. Inside this hemispherical recess, the hilt of a plain business-like sword could be seen.

The figure before the altar spoke again: "That all may know the outcome of this trial, let the Speaker step forward, and give true and just account."

A massive figure in dark crimson robe and dark-blue cowl

approached with stately tread from Roberts' right and halted oppressively close to him.

The figure before the altar said, "Let the heir seek to draw the blade from the rock."

Roberts, puzzled at the utilitarian look of the block and the sword, leaned slightly forward, and found the "speaker" slightly blocking him.

At the same moment, three things happened. Roberts, in leaning forward, was struck by the reflection from the end face of the block, which showed him a narrow horizontal line reaching out from either side of the hemispherical hollow. The line suggested a cleavage in the block, which would enable it to be opened up along the plane of the cavity in which the sword must lie.

As Roberts leaned slightly forward, the speaker beside him intoned, "The heir is trembling. *He falls!*"

At the same instant, Roberts felt a piercing sensation in his right arm—a sensation like the sting of a wasp. The cathedral spun around him, turned end-for-end . . . The speaker's voice was the last thing he heard.

"The rock has spoken—'*I reject him!*' "

Roberts felt the impact of the hard stones of the cathedral floor, and then nothing.

XVIII. The Lowest Nobleman of the Realm

There was a singing in his ears. At last, the singing died away to be replaced by a voice, and the voice faded into a desolate sobbing. He opened his eyes.

Erena, head bent, hands over her eyes, cried as if the world could never be right again. He sat up dizzily, and there was a rustle and crackle, and the faint stiffness of the cloth on his chest.

Puzzled, he felt his chest, found a piece of stiff paper, and tried vainly to remove it. Erena saw his movement, swallowed, and said, "Lie back, William. You—You're faint, still."

He saw her, and he heard her voice, but as if coming from a distance. His fingers found the head of a large pin, and he drew it out.

The paper—or card—fell loose, and lay face-up on the ground:

Patent of Nobility
*Know all men by this document that we, the Lords Spiritual
of the Holy Temple of Festhold, do hereby warrant that
Harold William (formerly of the Royal Family of Festhold)
is, of a right, and by ancient usage, secured, he and his
heirs and assigns forever, full title to the Baronage of
Scrattel and is to be known in future in the style of the
Baron of Scrattel, which rank and privilege is and shall
rank behind, beneath, and below, the rank and privilege
of each and every other Festhold title of nobility at present
existing, including but not limited to the former lowest
rank of nobility, the Baronage of Foulmarsh.
Done this day, by accord with ancient usage.*

From the bowl-shaped hollow surrounding the Cathedral of
Truth came a quiet shout—and then a curious sound, like a
drawn-out moan. Roberts, heart beating fast, looked up dizzily
from the paper. He was aware that, as he looked up, Erena looked
up too, at a crimson-robed dark blue-cowled figure which laid a
hand on her shoulder.

"The Regent commands your presence, Erena. It is not proper
that one of your rank should consort with the lower ranks of
lesser nobles."

Roberts, feeling urgently at his belt, discovered that the sword
he had worn to the ceremony was there—the same sword, apparently, with which he—or rather, the Prince—had fought several
months before.

A voice was intoning from the Cathedral: "The sword moves!
But now—something seems to draw it back—now the Regent
strengthens his grasp—the cloth tightens at his arm—"

Roberts glanced at the watchful crimson-robed figure, listened
to the voice, and suddenly laughed. He bowed slightly. "By your
permission, Your Worship."

He glanced at Princess Erena. "If Your Highness will for a
moment condescend to the lowest of the nobles—"

He took off robe and shirt. The crimson-robed watcher sucked
in his breath. "It is forbidden for a male to disrobe before a
Royal Princess!"

Princess Erena's eyes flashed, and her lips tightened. "What is it, William?"

"I am curious about the 'wasp' which stung me when the 'speaker' in there brushed my arm. Is there a swelling?—In the right arm."

The crimson-robed figure stepped forward authoritatively, blocked the princess with his arm—Erena's mouth came open. She gasped—and then crumpled to the ground.

The priest snarled, "You have shocked her! *Go!*" He raised his arm and pointed.

From the Cathedral of Truth, the voice of the speaker intoned: "Now—*now* it begins to draw out—but no—some malign force draws it back . . . The Regent, his great muscles distended—"

Roberts decided that the sword in the stone was at least the equal of Duke Marius, even if it had been slit open and half-a-dozen electromagnets planted in it by the temple priests. That left Roberts time for a more pressing question. He stepped forward, hit the crimson-robed figure across the face, jerked off the robe, and spotted the wrist strap with the round disk, a pointed needle protruding from its center.

"Now, by the Almighty Power—" said a familiar voice, and suddenly Roberts recognized the voice.

Prince Harold William, now the Baron of Scrattel, had the proof plainly before him of what must have happened. Too late, it dawned on Roberts that the Prince would have been far more overawed, and hence less capable of realizing what had been done to him, inside the Cathedral of Truth. But he knew now.

As the "speaker" intoned from within, describing further struggle between Duke Marius and the recalcitrant Sword, and as a low moan and a stamping of feet seized the assembled crowd, the Prince drew his own sword from its sheath, and spoke flatly: "One act of disobedience and your life ends here. Put on your cloak."

The Prince's sword reached out and lightly touched the strap on the temple priest's wrist. The strap parted, and the device fell to the ground.

The priest hesitated, looking at the very light line of blood droplets forming where the sword had touched him. Suddenly he began to tremble, and put on the crimson robe.

The Prince spoke coldly, and the words were an iron command: "Lift and carry the Princess."

The scarlet robed figure obeyed.

"Walk straight to the main door of the Cathedral." The Prince, sword drawn, followed close behind. Ahead of them, the tall doors stood open.

XIX. THE WARLORD'S CHALLENGE

The standing space of wide high-vaulted interior was filled, and the aisles clogged with armed noblemen straining to see better what was taking place up front.

The "speaker" was intoning: " ... Now ... now! ... *Now!* Now the stone yields! The sword begins to draw forth ... Hold! ... Something draws it back! ..."

The impatience of the crowd was evident in the murmurings, jostlings, and occasional tramping of feet that started up from one or another quarter of the crowd. The temple priest halted.

"We can't get through."

The Prince drew in his breath. His voice suddenly dominated the gathering, silencing the "speaker", stopping the disorder of the crowd, turning faces all over the cathedral. The command, loud, clear and carrying, seemed to remain, somehow echoing in the silence, after the words had been spoken: "MAKE WAY FOR THE WARLORD!"

As the crowd craned, the Prince spoke more quietly, but his voice still carried: "Step aside, gentlemen. We will end this farce, now and forever!"

Preceded by the temple priest carrying the unconscious girl, the Prince paced slowly up the aisle, the bare sword in his hand, as the curious nobles moved out of the way. At the front of the cathedral, there was silence as the temple priests and the Regent looked on, as much at a loss as everyone else.

Suddenly one of the temple priests smiled. His voice, amused and contemptuous rang out: "Why look! It is the Baron of Scrattel!"

Roberts could feel the sudden pain of the Prince, and realized that this insignificant blow had found the joint in the Prince's armor. Roberts didn't wait for the Prince to recover. He spoke carefully, and the magnificent voice rose over the crowd:

"IT IS THE WARLORD."

The statement rang in the air, flat, final, and definite.

Roberts suddenly could feel the change in the atmosphere. A murmur passed through the crowd, followed by intense silence. Ahead of him, the aisle opened up.

At the front of the Cathedral of Truth, the temple priests stood staring. The Regent, slightly bent over, drenched in sweat, one hand in the hemisphere of the crystal, looked on with a ludicrous expression of disbelief.

The scarlet-robed figure carrying the Princess now reached the head of the aisle. The Prince said, "Turn and face the assembly." His voice carried. The temple priest turned around, holding the Princess.

"My lords and gentlemen," said the Prince, facing still toward the head of the aisle, "I trust you will forgive my speaking with my back to you, but it is unsafe to take one's eyes from these clever hirelings who masquerade in the cloth of our Church, though they are in reality servants of this false and regicide regent.—The same who is still struggling here to draw the sword!"

Well above the level of the aisle, a white-haired, white-bearded figure in faded scarlet robes looked down from a little balcony, and a grim smile crossed his face. The Regent straightened, let go of the hilt of the sword still in the crystal, and began to speak.

The Prince abruptly stepped forward, his voice cut the Regent short. "Observe, my lords and gentlemen!"

With two quick strokes, he slit the back and then the arm of the 'speaker's' crimson cloak, reached out with his free hand, and tore the rest of the sleeve loose. Under the cloth was the same round device the other temple priest had worn.

"*Raise*," said the Prince—and the sting of a wasp burst at his chest into spreading waves of agony. For the second time the cathedral spun around him. White-hot fire seemed to bathe his body.

The Prince fought off the pain, and sucked in a deep breath. His voice rose over the assemblage:

"KILL ME THESE SCARLET HIRELINGS—AND THIS REGI-CIDE TRAITOR!"

Then the drug was swept on to his brain, and the last thing he heard was the shout of the crowd.

XX. The Regent's Reply

Somewhere, once again, birds were singing.

"Well, well," said a coarse feminine voice, "I see you're coming around, Charmer. Too bad your little dream didn't work out. But you've still got us."

The Prince's eyes opened. Beside the head of the bed stood a girl of nineteen or so, heavy, wearing a tight black skirt and a tight pink blouse. Near the foot of the bed, lips warped up in a smile that bared a lot of teeth, stood the short plump red-faced tutor.

"Well, Ex—about that twist—you always wanted—"

Roberts braced himself, heard the girl say insinuatingly, "After all, you're just the Baron of Scrattel now. You might as well enjoy yourself—"

The tutor added, faintly smiling, "—while His Majesty wins the hand of fair Erena—No relation to you any more, of course—"

The Prince tried to get up. The ropes held him where he was. The tutor glanced at the girl, and bared his teeth in a smile.

The Prince sucked in a deep breath. He wrenched, twisted. The blood pounded in his ears. The girl screamed. The tutor shouted, *"Get the hypo!"* The ropes broke.

The tutor jumped back, eyes staring, jerked out a knife—The Prince reached out, gripped an unlit lamp on a table, threw it hard—The lamp hit the tutor squarely in the chest, knocked him against the wall. He banged his head, fell to the floor—

The girl rushed in carrying the hypodermic. The Prince's voice was an iron command; *"Inject the tutor."*

The girl swallowed, tried to speak, looked blank, turned, knelt by the tutor, and pulled back his sleeve. She pushed the hypodermic into the flesh, and slowly pressed the plunger. She withdrew the hypodermic, stood up trembling, wiped her upper lip and then her forehead, dropped the hypodermic, turned, and suddenly left the room.

The Prince knelt by the tutor, and pried the knife from his fingers. He went out the door, and found himself in a rough room about twelve feet square, with a table in the center, an oil lamp with badly trimmed wick smoking on the table. Beside the lamp was the Patent of Nobility guaranteeing to Harold William the Baronage of Scrattel.

The Prince glanced briefly at the paper, then walked to what appeared to be the outer door of the room. Holding the knife by his side, the blade turned back out of sight, he pulled the door open with his left hand.

A burly guard, carrying a rifle in his right hand, turned around. His heavy brows came together to form a flat line over clear and startled eyes.

"Say, now—where do you think *you're* going?"

He planted his big left hand flat on the Prince's chest, and shoved. The Prince pressed his own left hand hard over the hand on his chest, pinning it there, and bowed, bending the hand sharply back on the wrist. The guard sucked in his breath, and went to his knees. The gun crashed on the floor.

"A slight motion," said the Prince gently, pinning the captive hand, bowing just a bit more, and showing the knife, "and your life's blood flows out on this dirt."

"No—"

"Who do you serve?"

"The Regent."

"Serve now Harold William, Lord Scrattel, Warlord of Festhold, or—"

"Your lordship is not as the Regent described. I transfer my allegiance. The Regent lied."

The Prince straightened. "And what did the Regent say?"

"He said you were a debauchee given to fits of fainting, living only for dope and depravity." The guard massaged his wrist. "No self-respecting freeman could willingly serve such a person, even were he the Lord of Scrattel himself. The Regent said it was not for long, and I would get two minims a week for each report."

"No reason why not," said the Prince, studying the guard's face. "Come to me, and we will work the reports out together. I must fail rapidly in these reports—but not so that I do not have time to deal with this Regent."

"But how will your lordship do that?"

"Surely the Baronage of Scrattel, though it is not the greatest on the planet, has weapons for the service of its lord?"

"Aye—There's Salver, the great sword of the Third Lord, and

there's the Gun in the Great House, where it is always kept. But—"

"But what?"

"How will my lord *reach* the Regent?"

"If you can send reports to him, I can reach him by the same road as the messenger who bears the reports."

The guard shook his head. "If your lordship has the time—I might show the nature of the difficulty."

The Prince nodded. "Good. But first, is there some weapon here? If the Regent has other guards—"

"No—or rather, I am in charge of such others as there are. The Regent wished to leave some of his own men on guard, but they swore that they would die out of his presence, and he finally decided that I could do it, with such freemen of Scrattel as I could muster. To watch such as he described—" The guard shrugged.

"Still, I would like a weapon."

"In the cupboard behind the door, there should be a hogsticker. One moment, my lord, I'll go look."

The guard led the way in, turned the lamp way down, growled, "What a fearful waste of oil," went into the darkest corner of the room, wrenched and twisted at what appeared to be the wall itself—then something gave a loud squeak, and the guard staggered back, grunted in satisfaction, then swore.

"Ah, well—here we are."

Prince Harold William stepped back as a large rat bolted past him for the open door. Then the guard appeared, carrying a short heavy spear.

"For such as we are likely to run into, this should be enough."

The Prince took the spear. "Do you have trouble with the rats here?"

"The cats are afraid of 'em, my lord. We can't seem to put them down. But the wild hogs are worse."

"M'm.—Well, lead the way."

The guard swung his gun so as to have it ready, and led the way down a path that led through heavy brush into a field high with hay. He pointed as he walked. "Yon's the Great House."

The Prince glanced at a sort of low stone barn covered with moss, and combined with a square tower at one corner. Roberts, seeing the same things that the Prince was seeing, asked himself what the history of Festhold must be for it to have such a place in it as the Baronage of Scrattel. Roberts had the sensation of being in a backwater of time itself.

The Prince growled, "Only show me the road out of here—"

The guard put his hand on the Prince's arm. "Careful, my lord. Every few years, we lose a child this way."

He pushed aside a dense growth of brush, and the Prince pressed forward, then abruptly stopped. The woods ended in empty air. He looked down to see the edge of a cliff. He leaned slightly forward. Hundreds of feet below, blue water sparkled.

As he pressed back the brush to see more clearly, his gaze followed the blue water, out and out—to the horizon.

XXI. Restlessness In Festhold

Colonel Valentine Sanders sat back, and ran a hand through his close-cropped iron-gray hair. "I have to admit, Roberts, I owe you a debt of gratitude for taking on this job. If there is anything I hate, it's an inside job—and this one tops the average by a long distance."

Roberts said exasperatedly, "No matter what I do, or what the Prince decides to do, Duke Marius had already worked out some low blow or dirty trick to nullify it."

The colonel's eyes narrowed. "Nevertheless, it has gained time for us—four months of unexpected surprises for the Festhold Regent."

"Who," asked Roberts. "is now king?"

"According to the Lords Spiritual of the Holy Temple of Festhold . . ."

"What about the nobility?"

"According to these same Lords Spiritual, the Regent was tacitly approved by a two-thirds majority of the nobility at the ceremony in which the Regent drew the sword from the stone."

" 'Tacitly'?—Isn't there supposed to be a formal vote?"

"Their constitution doesn't lay it down definitely."

"He *did* finally draw the sword?"

The colonel smiled. "By now, Roberts, we have crucial spots on the planet well saturated with parasite circuits. The technology of Festhold is highly developed, but one of the things they aren't familiar with is a spy-device that amounts to little more than a charged dust-particle. I doubt that it occurs to them that such a thing could be possible. We already had the parasite circuits there, and the micro-relays sowed, when the Prince went to draw the sword from the stone. We were watching when the "speaker" bumped the Prince with his arm. We were unseen observers when Duke Marius got a grip on the sword and tried to draw it from the rock, and when the Prince, preceded by the temple priest carrying Princess Erena, came back into the Cathedral of Truth. As for whether the Regent finally managed to draw the sword—well, he drew a sword, Roberts, and brandished it over his head."

"What sword was this?"

The colonel swiveled his chair, picked up a little pamphlet, and tossed it on his desk. Roberts found himself looking at a nicely printed booklet with the title in large red letters:

THE TRUTH ABOUT THE TRIAL

Roberts opened the booklet, to look at a remarkably well drawn sketch showing the Prince standing before the stone, with the "speaker" approaching from the side. Beneath the sketch was a single sentence: "Never before has a 'speaker' joined in a Trial."

Roberts turned the page, to read:

WHY WAS THE SPEAKER THERE?

On the opposite page, a sketch showed the Prince beginning to reach out to the stone, and also showed the "speaker" bumping the Prince.

Roberts turned the page, to see the Prince falling to the floor over the caption, "The heir is trembling. *He falls!*"

The next sketch showed the speaker's arm enlarged, his cloak cut away as if by a pair of scissors. Strapped to his arm was a round device with a sharp needle in the center. Roberts turned the page, to see the speaker faintly smiling as the Prince was carried out.

On the next page, the Regent, faintly smiling, reached out to grip the hilt of the sword in the stone. The next four pages, in realistic detail, were devoted to a progressively more disheveled and desperate Regent straining to draw the sword from the stone, as a progressively less confident "speaker" intoned:

"The sword moves!"

"The Regent strengthens his grasp..."

"Some malign force draws it back..."

"The Regent, his great muscles distended—"

The following two pages showed the Regent, the speaker, and the temple priests drawn back in horror, as the Prince, sword drawn, advanced up the aisle, preceded by a temple priest carrying Princess Erena.

Next came a view of a different temple priest crouched on a balcony aiming a long gun with large sights, and then a scene showing the Prince falling.

Following that, a crowd of temple priests stood around the fallen Prince, blocking the view, as other temple priests rushed up in a body to further block the view of the stone. Yet another, carrying something under his cloak, hurried toward the stone itself.

The next scene, magnificently detailed, showed the Regent, his expression relieved, drawing out a sword, the scabbard of which was held close underneath the rock by a crouching temple priest. When the Regent triumphantly waved the drawn sword overhead in the following scene, the sword had apparently been drawn from the stone itself.

Beneath the sketch were the words: "*Thus* he drew the sword."

The final sketch showed the Regent, still waving the sword, shouting at the blank-faced and confused nobles. The caption beneath read: "Thus he was approved by the nobles."

The last page bore the words:

IS DUKE MARIUS KING??

Roberts leafed carefully through the booklet once again, smiled, and handed it back to the colonel.

The colonel said, "A print shop set up very quietly on the planet, a few years back, turned this pamphlet out by the hundreds of thousands of copies. I think it's fair to say that there is now a certain amount of restlessness in the Kingdom of Festhold."

"Where is Erena?"

"She's the Regent's guest in his City Palace."

"How far are we from Festhold right now?"

The colonel smiled. "Just outside massometer detection range of the nearest Festhold warship."

"And where is the Festhold Royal Guard?"

"Loaded into transports and being shuttled from one destination to another."

"I see."

"What do you have in mind, Roberts?"

"I think we've gone about as far as an 'inside job' is likely to take us—unless *someone* wants to do an inside job on Duke Marius—"

The colonel shook his head. "Theoretically, there seems to be no reason why not. But in practice, something goes wrong—assuming we find a volunteer willing to let someone like Duke Marius—ah—'drive' the volunteer's 'vehicle' during his own absence."

Roberts said, "How many such volunteers are there?"

"For that assignment, we'd be doing well to locate anyone who would listen past the first three sentences. In all ways, it seems to work best if there is at least *some* compatibility in character."

"So that approach is out?"

The colonel said irritably, "Roberts, *I* am not volunteering. Are *you?*"

"No, sir," said Roberts flatly.

"Then," said the colonel, "I think we can safely say that approach *is* out."

"All right, then we had better approach this from the outside."

The colonel frowned, "The natural result will be a head-on clash between Duke Marius' supporters and whoever will rally to Harold William. This could result in a lot of casualties—and incidentally lose us Harold William."

Roberts said, "I think I see a way to avoid that."

The colonel looked interested. "What do you have in mind, Roberts?"

"Of course, it's only the beginning of an idea—"

The colonel leaned forward. "Never mind that. Possibly we can develop it.—Let's hear it."

XXII. The Outside Job

Roberts carefully looked over the filled-in message blank, sat back
in the patrol ship's control seat, and read intently:

MESSAGE BEGINS
H M FORCES CONTROL
FESTHOLD CAPITOL

TO COMMANDING OFFICER
OUTER DEFENSE COMMAND
SECTOR U3R

URGENT
ULTIMATE SECRET
TOP PRIORITY

EMBARK ROYAL GUARD REGIMENT AT ONCE
DESTINATION FESTHOLD CAPITOL
BY COMMAND THE REGENT

TOP PRIORITY
ULTIMATE SECRET
URGENT

MESSAGE ENDS

Roberts pressed a button to the left of the instrument panel,
near a glowing amber lens lettered "Sym Cmp."

Roberts said, "This order to the Commanding Officer of Festhold's
outer Defense Command will be sent by S-Wave?"

"That is correct," said the blank voice of the symbiotic computer. "A communications probe will enter and transmit from the
nearby Festhold communications node."

Roberts said uneasily, "Is this in the usual style of Festhold
military commands? For instance, there's no *name* for this commanding officer."

"Owing to the rapid depletion of manpower in Sector U3R," said
the symbiotic computer, "this is customary. Festhold commanders

usually lead their troops in person. In Sector U3R, which is in close contact with the Stath, the life expectancy of a Festhold military commander is low."

"Even at the top?"

"Average life expectancy of commanding officers in this sector is 4.9 weeks during active combat. Combat is now exceptionally severe."

"I thought the Stath were secretly negotiating with the Regent."

"This is the Stath manner of negotiating."

Roberts frowned, and glanced again at the message. "This is classified 'Ultimate Secret,' yet we're going to send it by S-Wave from a communications probe?"

The symbiotic computer sounded noticeably smug. "A Festhold encoder was covertly removed by one of our I-Class ships from a ruined Festhold command center following a recent heavy Stath raid. We have the encoder and the code-of-the-day signal."

"So this command will go out in code, by the usual military channel?"

"That is correct."

"It's sent on the authority of 'The Regent.' Hasn't he claimed to be king?"

"A peculiar situation exists. To the Festhold Armed Forces, 'the King' still means Harold William. To avoid confusion, Duke Marius is still using his title of Regent in military communications."

Roberts nodded, and looked at the second message:

MESSAGE BEGINS
H M FORCES CONTROL
FESTHOLD CAPITOL

TO SECOND-IN-COMMAND
ROYAL GUARD REGIMENT
URGENT
ULTIMATE SECRET
TOP PRIORITY
PERSONAL TO SC RGR
CHANGE IN CODE

SITUATION HERE REQUIRES TOTAL DEVOTION

TO THE REALM
YOU MUST BE PREPARED FOR DIRECT ORDER
TO CARRY OUT
TASK OF EXTREME DIFFICULTY AND DANGER
I COUNT ON YOU AND ON EACH GUARDSMAN
PERSONALLY
BY COMMAND
HAROLD WILLIAM
CO RGR
WARLORD OF FESTHOLD

CHANGE IN CODE
PERSONAL TO SC RGR
TOP PRIORITY
ULTIMATE SECRET
URGENT

MESSAGE ENDS

Roberts said, "This 'change in code'—"

The symbiotic computer's voice used the tone of a teacher explaining the alphabet. "Each Festhold soldier has a personal code. This is in order that personal information may be sent to him in privacy. When the message reaches its destination and is deciphered, and then decoded, that portion of the message between the words 'change in code' is left untouched. Any routine code-machine's attempt to interpret the personal message will produce gibberish, or occasionally, a completely false message. A—ah—'inside job'—has now been completed within the Festhold Inner Message Center, and the personal code-setting of Lieutenant-Colonel Stran du Morgan is now known to us. This code-setting is an instruction to be given to the code-machine, the so-called 'Festhold encoder.' The code-machine will then reduce the personal section of the message to the same form as the remainder of the message. The further application of the code-of-the-day setting will then decode the personal message. But this can only be done by someone knowing the personal code of the second-in-command of the Royal Guard Regiment."

"And if meanwhile he's been killed?"

"In that event, the message could not be decoded."

Roberts said exasperatedly, "The message isn't addressed to Colonel du Morgan. It's addressed to the 'second-in-command.'"

"Colonel du Morgan *is* the second-in-command."

"Yes, but if the casualty rate is so high—"

"The Festhold Royal Guard will reach this sector only shortly after the message reaches it. Because of a subspace anomaly, it is possible to reach the Outer Defense Command quickly from Festhold. The clique of Duke Marius now controls the High Command of Festhold. This clique has been keeping the Royal Guard in motion, to prevent the Guardsmen from fraternizing with other military units. By doing so, they would spread the truth about the battle against Duke Marius."

"It would seem to me," said Roberts, "that the place for the Regent to have put them, from the first, would have been where the fighting was so heavy that they would been quickly killed off."

"This is correct."

"Then—"

"The clique of Duke Marius, the Regent, was nervous and unhinged following the battle, and later the confrontation at the Cathedral of Truth. They have only by stages recovered sufficiently to dare to do this."

Roberts, having seen things only from the viewpoint of Harold William, said, "It seemed to me that they came out on top without much trouble.—No matter *what* the Prince did."

The voice of the symbiotic computer held a kind of grim satisfaction. "They expected *no* trouble from the Prince. They did *not* win easily. At each unexpected clash, they only won by a narrow margin. At the Cathedral of Truth, for instance, there were actually nobles who drew their weapons and started forward to obey the Prince's command."

After an instant's silence, the symbiotic computer added, "The aim of the Regent was to convince everyone that the Prince was unfit. Instead, there are now contrary rumors of all kinds. There is persistent unrest, and there are many actual witnesses that the Regent's claim to the throne is false."

Roberts smiled and nodded. "Okay. Send the messages. Then we have to find out what's taking place with the Prince."

XXIII. The Sailors

Harold William, Baron of Scrattel, glanced from the compass to the horizon, then once again looked at the chart in the old encyclopedia. The deck, if he could call it that, was moving around continuously underfoot, there was a ceaseless sloshing of water against the hull, and an endlessly repeated splash as buckets of water were poured overboard. The sails flapped occasionally, but the noise was apparently due to the motion of the boat, not the wind. The wind had given out shortly after they left the island-barony of Scrattel, and they had had to use the engine alone. The engine had failed shortly after taking them out of sight of Scrattel. As Harold William was aware, the next thing to give out would probably be the drinking water.

There was a clearing of the throat, and the former guard, who had turned out to be named Bor, was standing oppressively close in the still, humid air.

Harold William kept his voice level and his tone courteous. "What is it, Bor?"

"It's the men, Your Lordship."

There was another splash of water from up forward as another bucket of water was dumped over. "What about them?"

"They want to go back, begging your pardon, my lord."

Harold William glanced back, squinting his eyes against the glare of the sun on the slight roll of the sea.

"H'm." He tapped the compass repeatedly and the needle swung around fifteen degrees by small stages.

"Perhaps your eyes are better than mine, Bor. Can you see Scrattel?"

"No, sir. And I haint since yesterday."

Harold William looked up forward, where Rig Strun and Mak Stran bailed methodically. By the engine, Dar Strun patiently screwed the single spark plug back in, stood up, and put his foot on the starting lever. He straightened his leg with an effort.

Er-er-er-er-er

The engine didn't catch. The water sloshed and splashed against the hull. The sun beat down. *Splash*—another bucket of water went over the side.

Bor was apologetic, "The men, m'lord—they want to go home."

Harold William left the diluted glare where the worn strip of canvas partly covered the cockpit in which the warped engine cover had been lifted aside, and stepped out in the full sun.

Up ahead, Rig Strun, gnarled and aged, raised up and shouted, "*Bek!* Canna gun! Nae gut!"

After two days of this, Harold William could laboriously translate the words: "*Back!* Can't go on! No good!"

But after two days of it, he waited until he reached partial shade cast by the big—and motionless—sail further aft. Then he crouched, and spoke slowly and carefully: "Canna gae bed. Need's rae gut t'find."

This sounded to Harold William like a clear rendering of "Can't go back. Needle" the local word for compass "is no good to find."

But Rig Strun—and also his brawny grandson, Mak, who had paused to listen—took several minutes for a rapid-fire and incomprehensible exchange of dialect before Rig Strun turned to Harold William, and pointed ahead.

"*Nae* thin." He pointed back, roughly in the direction of the island.

"Smeh. Gae clash, us smeh the Oyl."

Harold William laboriously translated the first comment into ordinary speech: "No thing." Rig argued that there was no land ahead.

So much for that. Now, what might "smeh" mean? After a long silent struggle in which both Struns resumed bailing, Harold William found a combination that seemed to make sense: "Smell. Go close, us smell the Isle."

Harold William was laboriously composing a reply when a loud noise made him jump. BANG!

Back by the engine, Dar Strun waved his arms excitedly. BANG!

Bor, at the tiller, shouted to Harold William. "T'needle, m'lord!" BANG!

There was a cool breeze as the boat gathered speed. BANG!

Harold William tapped the needle, and found it was reading true. BANG!

With that vibration, there was no need to tap the needle. BANG!

The boat nearly cleaved the calm water. A wake showed up behind it. BANG!

Harold William pointed slightly to the north. Bor turned the tiller a fraction. The boat heeled slightly, swung a little northward.

Behind them, the wake stretched out. Dar Strun, listening anxiously to the deafening bang, nodded enthusiastically, and took hold of the warped cover. BANG!

Bor shouted, "Tiller, m'lord. I'll help Dar!" Harold William held the tiller steady. Bor sprang forward to help with the engine cover. BANG!

The wake seemed now to stretch out to the horizon. Rig and Mak Strun began to take in the useless sails. BANG!

Bor and Dar lowered the engine cover. Rig pulled back a small lever that started the bilge pump. BAM!

Faintly muffled by the engine cover, the noise was still an assault on the ears and a delight at the same time. BAM!

Harold William, expecting some argument in favor of going back, saw with astonishment Rig, Mak, and Dar go forward to the bow, and stand there beaming. Rig and Mak enthusiastically banged Dar on the back. BAM!

Harold William turned in bafflement to Bor, who grinned, and shouted: "The world is different when your engine works!"

Harold William nodded, beamed, looked ahead, and then checked the compass. Suddenly he looked up again, and peered intently forward. Dimly, on the horizon, he could see a low dark line.

XXIV. The Rivals

Vaughan Roberts, keeping his muscles relaxed with an effort, watched the spy screen that was set up in the forward part of the patrol ship, on the upward-warped deck over the missile bay. On the screen, Duke Marius smiled at Princess Erena, and the Regent's smile had improved of late. It had less of a sickly cast, and was much more a smile than a grimace. Roberts intently disliked this smile.

"You must understand, Erena," said the Regent, "that what I have done, I have done for our country."

Erena looked away, and said nothing. Roberts breathed a little more easily.

"I have," said the Regent, "become King to free Festhold of outworn superstition, and to bring the dawn of a new age to this outmoded land."

Princess Erena said quietly, "Superstition is undesirable because it is false, not because it is outmoded. Truth is never outmoded."

The Regent frowned, then suddenly laughed.

"Erena?"

She looked at him.

He said, "It is a proved scientific fact that 'acquired characteristics cannot be inherited.' Were you aware of that?"

She frowned. "I leave such things to men. All I know of science is that it is useful, and it is dangerous."

He nodded, still watching her with a smile. It was a smile that transformed his face, and Roberts growled, "Where's the Prince?"

Morrissey said, "His boat landed about two hours ago."

"Where is he *now?*"

"We've got a poor view through that forest. The last we saw, he was on a dirt road headed west." Roberts growled exasperatedly.

On the screen, the Regent was saying, "Since acquired traits cannot be inherited, your family must have experienced a mutation of the logical faculty in the past. In your father and your brothers, it had a terrible effect. In you, this logical insight is"—he smiled—"charming. There is not one woman in twenty thousand who has it."

Erena said stiffly, "Thank you for reminding me of my father and brothers."

"Erena," he said earnestly, "I faithfully served your father, and was as stunned by the misfortunes of your brothers as anyone could have been. The error of your logical faculty is that it jumps too soon to the belief in cause and effect. Yes, by your family's ill-fortune, I have profited. But I profit only for the benefit of the nation itself. The universe is ruled as much by pure chance as by this cause and effect you assume. You unfairly slander me by believing that where I profit, it is because I have sought profit. Have you seen, *yourself,* that what I say is false?"

She hesitated.

Roberts straightened, and banged his head on the three-foot-thick mirror-like cylinder than ran down the axis of the ship.

On the screen, the Regent said earnestly, "I could not love you if I did not love all your family, Erena. The woman has the same genes, the same chromosomes—is the same *thing*—with but a slight change, an insignificant alteration on one chromosome. But in you—"

Roberts snarled, "Bergen!"

Dan Bergen, further aft, in the control seat, said, "*Sir?*"

"Find out from the symbiotic computer if we can continue to avoid detection while we camouflage the ship's hull.—Or will the camouflage interfere, and make us visible to their detectors?"

There followed a low exchange between Bergen and the symbiotic computer, drowned out for Roberts by the Regent's impassioned plea to Erena, for understanding. Behind Roberts, Hammell said absently, "You know, the guy's sort of convincing, at that."

Roberts bit off the reply that came to him, and then Bergen called, "We can do it, but *why?*"

On the screen, the Regent took Erena's hand. Erena withdrew her hand, but slowly, her expression thoughtful. The Regent's eyes flashed, and his smile broadened.

Roberts turned and banged Hammell accidentally. He snarled, "Excuse me," and went back to the control seat. Bergen started to get up, but Roberts put a hand on his shoulder.

The voice of the symbiotic computer spoke from a little grille to the left of the external viewscreen. "Effective non-detectability may be maintained during and after normal alteration of the ship's appearance. Why should we do this, however?"

"The Regent of Festhold—"

"Correction, this is now Duke Marius. The Regent of Festhold has broken numerous laws, and betrayed his trust. His regency officially ended with the first betrayal of his trust."

"As far as the population of Festhold knows, he is now not only Regent but King!"

"The population is not informed."

"All right. The Re—"

"Duke Marius."

Roberts waited a moment, until his head cleared, then said carefully, "Duke Marius is trying to win Princess Erena over to him. If he can do that, and if she marries him, *then* to a large part of the population his position will be legitimized. The followers of Harold William's family will be split."

There was a brief silence. The voice of the symbiotic computer said, "This is at least partly correct."

"Moreover, such a marriage might badly damage Harold William's confidence. He could see it as meaning that his own sister had betrayed him."

"This appears to be true." The symbiotic computer hesitated, "This probability that the Princess will mate with Duke Marius is what?"

Roberts said carefully, "I don't know. And the word isn't 'mate', but 'marry.'"

"Another opinion on this subject might be advisable."

Roberts snarled, "Hammell!"

Hammell jumped. "Sir?"

"The symbiotic computer wants your opinion."

"What's the question?"

The voice was louder, and now came from somewhere overhead, about half-way between Roberts and Hammell. "The probability that the Princess Erena will marry with the Duke Marius is, namely: —*What?*" Hammell looked blank, then grinned. "No man could answer that question. With women, how can you tell?"

"This is prejudice."

"No," said Hammell, "that's not it. Men often marry women that *other* women regard as unworthy, and the same holds for women marrying men that other men dislike. These marriages are influenced by—ah—how do I explain—the *attraction* between men and women. And a man, not *being* a woman, can't judge the strength of the attraction another man has on a woman. So I can't tell you *what* chance there is that Erena will marry him."

The symbiotic computer was silent. Roberts, frowning in thought, decided to try a new tack. "The Patrol is low on personnel."

"This is correct. However, what connection—?"

"Princess Erena is a candidate-member of the Interstellar Patrol. If she marries Duke Marius, who has broken his trust, won't that disqualify her?"

There was another brief silence. "That is also correct."

"So there are several reasons to prevent the marriage."

"How do you intend to do this?"

"On Tiamaz, Princess Erena appeared to—that is, to some extent, she seemed—" Roberts hesitated.

The symbiotic computer prompted him: "She seemed to wish to mate with you instead of with Duke Marius?"

Hammell grinned. Bergen beat his head, and shook silently. From overhead, Morrissey, holding a wrench, leaned down grinning to look at Roberts' expression. Roberts drew a breath of air, and said carefully, "There seemed to be some attraction."

"Then," said the symbiotic computer, "if you were closer, *this* attraction might draw the Princess away from Duke Marius? This seems logical."

Roberts said exasperatedly, "Now that we've got that out of the way—"

The symbiotic computer cut him off. "The plan is specifically what?"

"To put a strain on Duke Marius' arrangements, take up his time, try to keep him from making headway with Princess Erena—and allow some time to get the Prince and the Royal Guard here."

"How is this to be done?"

"Duke Marius is now formally the Chief of State of Festhold?"

"That is correct."

"And the Chief of State *has* to welcome exalted visitors or give offense. Isn't that right?"

"It is, if the visitors are sufficiently exalted."

"In the past, Hammell, Morrissey, and I have played the parts of some very exalted—ah—visitors. If we drop in on Duke Marius now, we *ought* to be able to tie him in knots."

The symbiotic computer suddenly sounded almost friendly. "This is an excellent idea. The camouflage will be emplaced at once."

XXV. The Sovereigns' League

Marius, Duke of Rennel, Earl of Estmaertz, known to some as His Highness the Regent, to others as His Majesty the King, and to still others by shorter and less courteous titles—Marius turned from Princess Erena to the door. "*Who is it?*"

Princess Erena stood up and faced the door.

"Colonel du Berrin, Your Highness."

"Come in, Colonel." The Regent turned to Princess Erena. "Pardon me, my dear."

Princess Erena inclined her head, and stayed where she was.

The door opened, to admit a well built noblemen in the uniform of a colonel of mountain troops, who bowed to Princess Erena, then turned to the Regent.

"Your Highness, we have an exasperating little contretemps to contend with."

The Regent frowned. "What has happened?"

"The Baron of Scrattel has landed on the mainland."

The Princess straightened, her eyes glanced quickly at the Regent, then she clasped her hands and stood intently silent. The Regent stiffened.

"Impossible. That backwater had no way out. Moreover, he was left guarded, and, in fact—" The Regent suddenly glanced at Erena, and stopped in mid-sentence. "Even the reports," he began again, "on his welfare and progress were to be picked up periodically by armed courier-boats. He could *not* escape."

Colonel du Berrin said apologetically, "Nevertheless, Sir, we have the report. It seems that he came ashore in an antiquated boat used for local fishing by the goodfolk of Scrattel. He landed with several followers, and set out on the ring road, which in this locality is unimproved. On the way, they met a regiment of the Imperial Division, headed east to embark for the Outer Defense Command."

"What happened?"

"The Baron drew his sword, and saluted the regimental standard. The regimental commander apparently noticed the way the baron handled his steel, and called out to learn his name."

"And—"

"The Baron replied, 'Baron of Scrattel.'"

"Then what?"

"The regiment cheered, the standard-bearer dipped the standard, and the regimental commander saluted."

"The standard can only be dipped to the sovereign."

"I know it, Sir. I only repeat what was reported to us by the local Chief of Constabulary, who had it from one of his men."

"These people are reliable?"

"The Chief of Constabulary is. I can't vouch for his men, but apparently he does."

"And what did the Baron of Scrattel do?"

"Waved, and went on his way."

The Regent slowly relaxed. Colonel du Berrin said hesitantly, "Your Highness knows that the Imperial Division was second only to the Royal Guard in its devotion to the Royal Family."

"I am aware of it. Where is the rest of this division?"

"Strung out along the ring road on the way to the embarcation point."

"On *foot?*"

"Yes, Sir. Due to the—the unrest—they hadn't had time for their monthly training march, and are taking it *en route.*"

"So there are *other* regiments of this division coming along on this road?"

"Yes, Sir."

"The Baron of Scrattel will meet them one-by-one?"

"Under normal circumstances, Sir—yes, he will."

"What have you done about this?"

"Reported it to you at once, Sir."

The Regent frowned, glanced briefly at Erena standing straight and silent. Then his brows came together in a straight black line, he put his hand on the colonel's arm, as if to guide him outside. There was a harsh rap at the door.

The Regent called, "Who is it?"

"Captain Stang, Sir. Urgent message for Colonel du Berrin."

"Come in!"

A burly young captain came in, went straight to Colonel du Berrin, clicked his heels, saluted, and held out a long strip of yellow message paper unevenly torn at the top. The colonel took the paper, stared at it, then at the captain, and a fast low-voiced exchange followed. The colonel delivered himself of a choice epithet, turned to the Regent, saw Princess Erena, apologized, and again faced the Regent.

"Sir, I regret—"

"*Now* what? Has Baron Scrattel—"

"No, Sir. This has to do with—to begin—His Royal and Imperial Majesty, Vaughan the First, surnamed The Terrible—" The colonel glanced at the message paper— "Also, with His Royal Excellence, Rasgarrd Seraak. Adjunct-Coordinate to the Empire, Galactic

East. Next, Prince Gdazzrik of the March, Imperial Hoheit of the Imperium of Schnarzz."

"Who the devil—" began the Regent, then paused, turned to Erena, and bowed. "I beg your pardon, my dear."

Colonel du Berrin went on, "Last we have His Imperial Majesty, Sarkonnian the Second, Lord Auxiliary of the Realm to the West."

"Well, what has all this—"

"These—"

"I never heard of *any* of them!"

Colonel du Berrin turned to the captain. "Have you identified these individuals?"

"The first—yes, sir."

The Regent said, "Which one was that?"

"His Royal and Imperial Majesty, Vaughan the First." The captain hesitated and felt his pockets.

"Well," said Colonel du Berrin impatiently. "Let's have it."

"I took the liberty of running the reference through the duplicator—ah, *here* we are!"

The captain took from a pocket of his tunic a large sheet of paper, which he methodically unfolded. He cleared his throat.

"'Eminent Personages,' latest edition—let's see—here it is: 'Vaughan the First, also known as Duke of Trasimere; the Duke Vaughan. Full title: Vaughan the First, King and Emperor, Duke of Trasimere, Earl of Aurizont; surnamed: The Terrible. For associates, see: Personages of Paradise. Also: H.I.H. Ewald, Duke of Greme; H.I.H., Percy, Duke of Malafont; also: Oggbad, Prince of the Empire, Premier Peer of the Kingdom, High Master of the Unseen Realms. See also: The Empire; Earldom-designate of Paradise, Imperial Trasimere; Paradise; Boschock III; Flanders Foundation . . .'"

The Regent said, "Seems well documented. This was in 'Eminent personages?'"

"Yes, sir."

Colonel du Berrin said, "Cut out the nonessentials and let's have the meat of this."

"Yes, sir. Here we are: 'By force, Duke Vaughan then seized the Chief of Planet (see Glinderen, Philip W.), personally executed a Mr. Peen and one unnamed associate (see Krojac, Nels), and . . .'"

Colonel du Barren said exasperatedly, "Let's have that." He

took the sheet of paper, scanned it thoughtfully, then slowly read: "Vaughan the First, Full title, King and Emperor, Duke of Trasimere, Earl of Aurizont; surnamed The Terrible.

"Vaughan's claim to be the Sovereign of a large and formidable interstellar empire is backed by the now-known facts that:

"1) This personage appeared off the planet Boschock III, commonly and ironically called—because of the conditions on the planet—'Paradise,' and seized control of the Planetary government. He then organized the defense of Paradise City against an attack by an entity named Oggbad. After defeating Oggbad, word reached Vaughan that he had been chosen ruler of The Empire.

"2) On Vaughan's departure, this planet, which was then a member of the Federation of Humanity, was placed by the Federation under the administrative control of P. W. Glinderen as Chief of Planet. Glinderen attempted to arrest Vaughan upon Vaughan's return. When Vaughan instead arrested Glinderen, Glinderen sent for the Space Force. Vaughan nevertheless dismissed Glinderen, and reestablished personal rule over the planet.

"3) A large force of planetary raiders, believed to be under the leadership of Maury (q.v.) attacked the planet, and were severely mauled by Vaughan's warship and the reinforced Planetary defenses. The raiders withdrew on the approach of the Space Force fleet sent for by P. W. Glinderen, Chief of Planet.

"4) Vaughan's own space fleet now began to arrive, backed up by a sizable force containing at least one warship corresponding to the Superdreadnought class. Vaughan faced the approaching Space Force fleet, and compelled it to withdraw.

"5) Although Vaughan is not known to have returned to Paradise, the planet is governed strictly in accordance with his regulations, by duly appointed nobles previously chosen by him personally. This planet has become a formidable power in its section of space.

"The conclusion appears inescapable that Vaughan is the ruler of a large, formidable, but distant empire. Rumor holds that special navigating devices are required to reach these remote regions.

"Alternative theories for Vaughan's actions and evident powers have been advanced, including the thesis that this was an operation carried out by the semi-clandestine Interstellar Patrol; but this is believed to be merely a cover to explain away the backing down of the Federation Space Force before the Imperial Fleet.

"Vaughan's rank is provisionally rated as being formally equal to that of—say—the President of the Elective Council of the Federation of Humanity. In reality, Vaughan appears to exercise personal control over a powerful Empire whose actual size, however, we cannot accurately estimate. We can only rate him as a Chief of State of the first rank." The colonel lowered the paper.

"H'm," said the Regent. "What about these others—there was a—ah—Adjunct Coordinator, or some such thing—"

"Yes, sir. I didn't take time to look them up."

"Well?" said the Regent. "Now we know who one of them is, at any rate. But what is it all about?"

The colonel glanced at the captain. The captain said uneasily, "Sir, they're coming for a visit."

"What—*now?*"

"Yes, sir."

"*When?*"

"This afternoon."

The colonel swore. The Regent delivered himself of a sizzling oath. The colonel and the Regent then both turned and apologized to Erena. Erena, smiling faintly, accepted the apologies.

"This is," said the colonel, "a highly inconvenient time. We've got the coronation coming up shortly. The Baron of Scrattel is loose on the coast. The—"

"What?" said the captain. He glanced quickly at the Regent. "The Baron of—"

"*Scrattel,*" snarled the colonel. "And the whole damned Imperial Division—Pardon me, Princess—is on the same road. On top of that, the Royal Guard has disappeared from the plot somewhere out at the rim, and we think the damned—I beg your Pardon, Your Highness—Stath have got away with an encoder. Everything is up in the air. The last thing we need is this collection of potentates—"

"Begging your pardon, sir," said the captain stubbornly, "they didn't offer us a great deal of choice." He read aloud from the message form:

" . . . PURSUANT TO OUR MESSAGES NUMBER 106 AND 107: WE THE EXECUTIVE COUNCIL OF THE LEAGUE OF SOVEREIGN STATES AGAIN OUR ROYAL WILL TO END THIS PLAGUE IF NEEDS WE MUST BY BLOOD AND STEEL . . ."

The Regent said angrily, "*What* Messages 106 and 107?"

The captain shrugged. "We never got them, Sir. But *they* don't know that. Then there's this passage:

" . . . THE COMBINED IMPERIAL FLEETS OF THE LEAGUE WILL IF WE SO COMMAND LEND FORCE TO OUR PREVI- OUS MILD REQUEST . . ."

The colonel swallowed and looked at the ceiling. "This is a poor time for it. We've already got the Stath stuck crossways of our jaws. The last cut in fleet strength—"

"*Silence!*" snapped the Regent. "Let's see that message!" He read the message intently, then looked up.

"Have you replied to this?"

"No, Sir," said the captain. "I didn't even know who they were. I just looked up King Vaughan, and then got up here fast."

"All right. Send: 'I shall be delighted to welcome Vaughan, Ras- garrd, Gdazzrik, and Sarkonnian to the Kingdom of Festhold. But I must warn that my forces, now partly engaged in combat with the Stath Confederacy, may be even more heavily engaged in the near future. If peace cannot be arranged with this opponent, I will have little to spare for joint ventures with my fellow sovereigns. If, however, you will send copies of your messages number 106 and 107. which have not reached us, we will examine them at once.' Sign it 'Marius,' and send it out."

"Yes, sir."

As the captain turned to go, there was another pounding of fists on the door. "*Who is it now?*" roared the Regent.

"Lieutenant Ritts, Sir. To see Captain Stang!"

"Come in!"

Stang said urgently, "What is it, Ritts?"

"The League ship, sir! They're small, and even closer than we thought.—Covered with gold and platinum, sir, and they bristle with fusion guns. There's a fleet of prelaunched missiles apparently fed off beamed power from the ship. I hope I did right to give them landing permission, sir. They were pretty short about it."

"What?—you talked to them direct? What language—"

"Standard Terran, sir. It was all clear enough, but they've got a different way of putting things, and—"

"And you told them to land?"

"It was either that or war!"

The captain stepped back and turned to the colonel. The colonel let his breath out and looked at the Regent. The Regent put his hand to his head, then nodded. "All right, get an honor guard out—"

"Sir, they came down at the Old Palace field—Western Imperial Space Facility."

"*What?*"

The colonel snarled, "For God's sake! We haven't used that in—" His face blanked, and he bowed to Erena. "I beg your pardon, Your Highness." He glanced back at the lieutenant, and his face grew congested. "Listen, did you—"

"I tried to get them into a temporary holding pattern, sir. We've got military traffic over Capital Spaceport six deep. Before I could get through to the Slot Controller at Capital, one of these monsters got impatient—"

The Regent said, *"Monsters?"*

"They were transmitting with vision, sir. One of these creatures looks like a—some kind of shark—crossed with a giant squid. That doesn't cover it, but it gives you an idea. And he said something like, 'Durst these poltroons treat us to another delay?' and the one that looked human said, 'Let it not disturb us. There is a suitable field.' That's when they headed for Old Palace."

"You had already given landing permission?"

"Yes, sir. But I had requested that they hold off until we could fit them in."

The Regent said abruptly. "Colonel du Berrin, I trust you to see to it that the Baron of Scrattel is transported back to his island—unhurt, if possible. I will take care of these foreign guests, myself. *Captain!*"

"Sir?"

"Call out a regiment of the Parashock Division to serve as honor guard."

The colonel said, "Pardon, sir. The Parashock Division had that little disturbance when their officers got back from the ceremony at the Cathedral of Truth. Following your standing order, General Mertz sent them to the Stath front as soon as the shipping schedule permitted, and the last units left the day before yesterday."

"Then send a regiment of the Capital Division."

"Yes, sir."

There was a hammering at the door. The Regent, the colonel, the captain, and the lieutenant turned to look.

The Regent snarled, "Now what?" He raised his voice. "*Who is it?*"

"Sergeant Ayns, Sir! For Lieutenant Ritts!"

"Come in!"

The sergeant thrust inside, stared at the officers, saluted, and at once spoke to the lieutenant. The sergeant's voice carried. "They haven't landed at the Old Palace after all, sir."

"No?" said the lieutenant, his voice alarmed.

"No, sir."

"Well, don't stand there hoarding trouble! Let's have it! Are they down?"

"Oh—Aye, sir, they're down, all right."

"*Where?*"

"They didn't like the look of the Old Palace when they got close, sir. Too broke up. Place was all deserted. The one with all the teeth said he'd as soon land in a salt marsh as there. The human-looking one tried to calm them down. You know, sir, one of them things is in a kind of armored tank with—"

The lieutenant said impatiently, "Will you come to the *point*? They *are* down, are they?"

"Oh, yes, sir. They're down, all right."

"Where?"

"Well, they looked at this, and they looked at that, and for one reason this wouldn't do, and for another that was no good, and they finally set down on the ring road—"

The colonel said, "The ring road!—*Where* on the ring road?"

"Just about sixty-five and one-half feet from the Baron of Scrattel, sir, according to the escort boat following them down."

The Regent shut his eyes, the colonel swallowed hard, and the captain barked, "Well, don't stop there! *Then* what? What happened *then*?"

The sergeant said blandly, "Why, I dunno, sir. I left just then, sir. I figured you'd want to hear about it, sir."

XXVI. The Warlord's Army

Roberts was first out of the ship, wearing battle armor that blazed in silver and gold, the peak of his helmet adorned with a tapering spire, a coat of arms flashing on his breastplate.

Harold William, Baron of Scrattel, put out a hand to hold back his two rough companions, and advanced over the dirt. A little dust still drifted past from the feet of the regiment that had just marched by.

Roberts spoke, and his voice was amplified by the armor: "Is this, then, the Kingdom of Festhold?"

Harold William, whose voice needed no amplifier, spoke in the carrying tone of finality Roberts was so used to hearing: "This is Festhold. Who are you?"

Up the road, the regiment was becoming aware that something was taking place behind it. The shouts of officers and the shrill blasts of signal whistles split the air.

Roberts said, his voice carrying, "In this region of space, I am nothing but a visitor. Elsewhere, there are those who call me king. My name is Vaughan.—And who might you be?"

Harold William laughed, "Here, there are those who call *me* king, and others who say I am the lowest noble in the realm. We are, it seems, well matched. My name is Harold."

Roberts advanced, his armored hand outstretched.

"Welcome, Harold to the League of Sovereigns! Fear not the grip of this iron fist—I'll leave my hand relaxed—I am here with some friends seeking wrongs to right—a royal diversion—and the white-livered poltroons of yon city durst ignore my first two messages. Bedamned with them! The plague of unchallenged evil is spreading over this whole realm of space. Are we of the Empire to let it creep slowly upon us unchallenged? Or should we seek it out, smash its skull and rip its limbs apart 'ere it breeds fresh troubles? What think you, Harold?"

Roberts' voice, carrying, was reaching the wide-eyed troops who had halted and faced about, and their officers who were now hurrying to the head of the column.

Harold William's voice was enthusiastic, but faintly tinged with sadness: "I agree with you, Vaughan! I would that I were a king. But I have found that evil, well established, has many strings to its bow. I can claim one title only, but that title I *do* claim: *I am the Warlord of Festhold.*"

Harold William's voice rang in the air, and suddenly the closest of the troops shouted. Those further back joined in. Then the whole regiment was cheering.

Roberts' voice, amplified, carried loud and clear: "Well said,

Warlord of Festhold! Then let us all of good will unite, and meet the might of evil head-on, smash their bones and break their skulls, and hurl the false tyrants from their thrones!"

Roberts had been trying to frame his reply to suit the taste of the warlike subjects of Festhold. But what came out sounded considerably stronger than he'd intended. The troops, however, gave a roaring cheer, the officers drew their swords and waved them overhead, then the cheering settled into a thunderous chant:

"Harold to the throne! . . . *Harold to the throne!* . . . Long live King Harold!"

Up the road, a body of troops tramping on in clouds of dust heard the cheer, caught the words, and broke into enthusiastic shouts. The words echoed back from the distance: "Long live King Harold!" Harold William glanced intently all around, stepped forward, caught hold of Roberts' arm and pointed. "It is at such times as this, when I appear to have a chance to win, that some unfortunate thing takes place—and next I wake up helpless in a medical vat or marooned on an island. Do you see that speck on the horizon, Vaughan?"

"I see it."

"Do you notice also that dot in the sky overhead?"

"I see that, too."

"The dot is a patrol ship of some kind, which is undoubtedly relaying word of everything which takes place here. The speck, you notice, is growing larger, and dividing into several smaller individual parts. That will be air-borne troops. These troops here are the Imperial Division. They are among the toughest fighters in the Realm of Festhold—but they are unprepared, strung out on a training march, and in no shape to put up a fight. We are far from the Capital. My enemy is right there at the center of power, and manipulates the levers of control at his will. There is only one way to beat him, and that is not to strike at his hand or his armored glove, but at the nerve center of the whole conspiracy, Duke Marius himself. Is your ship fast?"

"It is."

"Then leave me here to head these troops. *You* go straight to the Capital! As you are head of a foreign power, you can demand to see Duke Marius. Only keep him away from controlling the levers of power for an hour or so, and I will turn this world upside down and dump him out of it!"

Roberts said, "I can give you armor—"

"Thank you, Vaughan, but keep the armor. The troops have to recognize me. I could kill them by the hundreds and never win. But let me talk to any true warrior of Festhold for one minute, and I will end the hold of this false Duke who serves as Regent—only just keep the Regent occupied! He can't fight, but he is a genius at trickery!"

Roberts growled, "I'll do my best." He raised his voice. "Then I'll do as you suggest, Warlord! Good luck!"

The troops, meanwhile, had followed the gesture of Harold William, seen the coming transports, and the officers had exchanged a few words. Now, the blast of signal whistles cut through the din of the approaching aircraft.

As Roberts waved briefly to Harold William before dropping into the ship, the troops spread out. The standard bearer ran up to plant the regimental standard beside Harold William. The regimental commander spoke into a handset, then stood, hands clasped, directly behind the Prince. Out of the center of the column of fast-dispersing troops glided a monster fusion cannon, apparently moving on antigravs, which settled down beside the standard, elevated its blunt muzzle, and with short sharp motions shifted from target to target amongst the approaching boxy aircraft. Along the road, in either direction, low clouds of dust spread out, and indistinct blobs began to resolve themselves into fast-moving tanks and gun-carriers.

Roberts settled into the control seat, carefully took the controls with his armored hand, slowly lifted the ship, and aimed its prow directly at the airborne troop carriers. Moving slowly, he headed directly amongst them, and watched on the outside viewscreen.

The screen presented him with a view taken from one of the prelaunched missiles that floated apart from the patrol ship, and that added a special flavor to the experience of the troops in the transports; the missiles, most of them being slim, and suggestive of the gigantic power let loose in interstellar wars, floated over, under, and through the formations of lightly armored transports. One of them, as if giving a pointed hint, lingered behind the rest, floated protectively above Harold William, then slowly passed directly through the formation of transports filled with nervously sweating troops. The patrol ship itself, flashing in accents of gold, silver, and platinum, emblazoned with dazzling coats of arms, moved daintily in the center of this armada of destruction. The eyes of the troops, nervously squinted against the dull glint of the slowly drifting missiles, turned their heads to be blinded by the blazing flash of silver and gold.

Meanwhile, the officers of the airlifted regiment, glancing alternately at the fusion cannon beside Harold William, his obviously loyal troops already spread out and under cover, the clouds of dust from reinforcements fast approaching from up and down the road, the standard beside him glittering with battle stars, and then—glancing up backwards over their shoulders at a drifting interstellar missile suggestively lingering on the scene—these officers were not in the best frame of mind to carry out the order they had just been given:

"Seize by force the false pretender incorrectly known as Harold William, Prince of Festhold—who is actually the insane Baron of Scrattel—and return this lunatic baron to the island of Scrattel, unhurt if conditions permit."

While the men sweated and the officers uneasily glanced at each other,—a clear compelling voice rose to greet them. It was a voice that carried, and that seemed to ring in the air: "Soldiers of the Capital Division! We see and recognize your emblem! We see it ringed with stars for battles you have fought for king and country! Will you still fight for the Realm? Do your swords and guns still belong to the Rulers and Warlords who have led you in a hundred battles for Right and Justice? Will you still rally to the Warlord of Festhold when his voice calls to you?

"Or are you held in chains by the false regicide who calls himself the 'Regent' of Festhold?—He who has killed your King—who has arranged 'accidents' for your King's sons, he who tries now to disinherit the last of the line of Festhold!

"Men of the Capital Division! I have defeated this false traitor in combat man-to-man! I have defeated him in fair and open war against the odds of heavy numbers! I have demanded the surrender of this so-called Regent at the point of sword and gun, and received it! Twice I have spared his life! And twice he has paid his debt with treachery!

"No regicide, no traitor, no liar, however clever, can rule over Festhold! Such a creature has no power to command any warrior of Festhold! You have no duty to this lying murderous tyrant! Your duty is to the Warlord of Festhold! I am now going to throw this dog from the throne! Warriors of the Capital Division! *Are you with me?*"

Roberts, watching the outside viewscreen, could see the soldiers in the hovering transports seem to go crazy. They yelled, banged each other the back, waved their weapons in the air, and shouted: "Long live the Warlord of Festhold!"

The regimental officers were beaming, and the commander turned to give his orders. His transport separated from the others, and sank to the ground. The commander stepped out, approached the Warlord of Festhold, and saluted.

Watching the screen, Roberts relaxed. "Now he's got an army . . . Morrissey!"

Toward the bow of the patrol boat, where the deck warped up over the missile bay, a thing turned that looked like a muscular sea horse in an armored tank.

"Sir?" said Morrissey's voice.

"Does the spy-screen show us anything about the Regent?"

"Yes, sir. He's just entering his Command Center with a colonel, a captain, a lieutenant, a sergeant, and a corporal."

"Fine. We've been neglecting the Regent. Now's the time to send a message."

XXVII. A Rough Day at the Com Center

"Yes, sir," Lance Corporal Zarn reported, "the command went out exactly as you called it in, sir. Third Regiment of the Capital Division went right out to nail the boozer to the wall, sir."

"Good," said Captain Stang.

Colonel du Berrin snarled, "I'll thank you, Lance Corporal, not to refer to a nobleman, however low, as 'the boozer.' This is the kind of practice that promotes confusion. Refer to him by name or title."

"The Baron of Scrattel, sir."

"That's better. All right, what reports have we on it?"

"Sir, I've been doing three men's work here, and there's some kind of confusion, because we've got a message from a General Harmer, to the effect that he will comply with the Regent's order concerning the Royal Guard."

The Regent said, "What about that ship of the Sovereign's League?"

"Private Beckel has been following that, sir."

A worn-looking individual, rushing nervously from one message-machine to another, said, "They took off, sir."

"With or without the Baron of Scrattel?"

"Without, Sir."

"Scrattel stayed on the ground?"

"Yes, Sir."

"Has the Capital Division gotten there?"

"Yes, sir. Regiment 3 CD got there just as the Sovereign League ship took of."

"Good, good. What does the Regiment report?"

"Nothing direct as yet, sir. We had a report from a boat that trailed them out from the spaceport. Just as it started back, sir, it reported that the regimental commander was approaching Baron Scrattel."

Colonel du Berrin looked approving. The Regent nodded. "All right. Then that's under control."

Lance Corporal Zarn spoke up stubbornly, "Begging your pardon, Sir. There's some confusion somewhere in this message from General Harmer, sir." The Regent frowned at the lance corporal as if he were a form of peculiar insect.

Colonel du Berrin said drily, "Pray enlighten us, Lance Corporal."

"Yes, sir. General Harmer only took over this morning. We just got the death notice on General du Streck."

Private Beckel spoke up knowledgeably, "Head blowed off by an air-drop drifter mine.—Begging your pardons, sirs."

Colonel du Berrins' brows came together. He and Captain Strang turned at the same time toward the private; but at the apologetic ending of the private's remarks, they turned away again.

Lance Corporal Zarn said, "General du Streck already acknowledged the order about the Royal Guard, sir. Yesterday."

Colonel du Berrin frowned. "It *is* odd that Harmer should acknowledge it."

Colonel du Berrin thought a moment, and shook his head. "Du Streck's acknowledgment would have been clamped to the original message, and our coded 'Ack Received' response would have been clipped to the back of the acknowledgement itself."

The Regent said, "I still don't see what harm the extra acknowledgement does."

The Lance Corporal glanced at Colonel du Berrin. The colonel uneasily cleared his throat. "I think, sir, that what we have here is the possibility of a *second* order to the Royal Guard. General du Streck acknowledged the first order—the order we *know* about, because we sent it. Now General Harmer acknowledges a *second* order."

The Regent looked sharply at Colonel du Berrin, then glanced intently at the Lance Corporal, who nodded. "Yes, sir. Because with standard MR routine, Sir, they wouldn't acknowledge *twice*—unless they'd been shot up, Sir, and we've got no word about that. This acknowledgement just fit right in, Sir, so it looks like—"

Private Beckel was still rushing from machine to machine as the various officers and noncoms delayed returning to their machines in order the better to hear what was going on. Private Beckel suddenly paused. There was the twice repeated sound of ripping paper.

"From the Sovereign's League, Sir! And here's one from the watch ship, sir! Watch ship reports the Sovereign's League ship headed for Capital at low elevation and high speed. The Sovereign's League says—I guess you'll want to read that for yourself, Sir."

The Regent took the paper from Private Backel, to skip the heading, and read:

WE VAUGHAN RASGAARD GDAZZRIK AND SARKONNIIAN ACCEPT WHOLEHEARTEDLY YOUR GRACIOUS WELCOME TO THE KINGDOM OF FESTHOLD.

SUBSTANCE OF OUR MESSAGES 106 AND 107 HEREWITH BEGINS 106

WE THE COMBINED RULERS OF THE LEAGUE OF SOVEREIGNS BEING DETERMINED TO STAMP OUT THE LICENTIOUS WAYS OF ILL ORDERED OUTSPACE REALMS ERE BY THEIR EXAMPLE THEY CONTAMINATE OUR OWN KINGDOMS

WE HEREBY CALL UPON THE RIGHTFUL SOVEREIGN OF FESTHOLD TO JOIN WITH US IN CRUSHING THIS FOUL EVIL

106 ENDS

107 BEGINS

WE HAVE RECEIVED NO REPLY TO OUR MESSAGE 106

WE REPEAT OUR CALL TO YOU TO JOIN US

DO NOT FEAR TO JOIN WITH US

WE ARE TRAVELING AS BEFITS LEADERS IN ADVANCE OF OUR MAIN FORCES IN HOPE TO TEMPT SOME FOUL PIRATE OR OTHER DOG TO ATTACK US BUT OUR GUARD FORCE COMES CLOSE BEHIND TO SHARE IN THE KILL AS WE REND THESE VERMIN AND BEHIND THE GUARD FORCE COMES THE COMBINED FLEETS OF THE IMPERIAL VENGEANCE FORCE IN HOPES WE CAN SCARE THESE WHELPS INTO JOINING TOGETHER—AND KILL THE LOT

WE DO NOT OUT OF WEAKNESS CALL TO YOU FOR AID OR SUPPORT

WE ASK INSTEAD THAT YOU JOIN IN CLEARING OUT THESE RATS AS FARMERS RIP UP SPREADING WEEDS FROM THEIR ADJOINING FIELDS

JOIN WITH US NOW THAT WE MAY KNOW YOU ARE FOR AND NOT AGAINST US

107 ENDS

KNOW NOW THAT HIS ROYAL AND IMPERIAL MAJESTY HAS HIMSELF BEEN ATTACKED BY THESE PIRATES AND HIS SUBJECTS HAVE BEEN CAPTURED BY THEM

KNOW THAT HIS ROYAL EXCELLENCE HIS IMPERIAL HIGHNESS AND HIS IMPERIAL HOHEIT HAVE BEEN TEMPORARILY CAPTURED BY ALIEN ENTITIES WHO INFEST THE OUTSPACE REGIONS

WE KNOW WELL HOW TO DEAL WITH SUCH AS THESE AND WE NOW AGAIN CALL UPON YOU TO JOIN US

The Regent handed the message to Colonel du Berrin, who read rapidly, looked up, and nodded. "It's these damned commerce raiders, Sir. The Federation is thick with them, and we aren't perfect ourselves."

"What's this about 'alien entities?'"

"No doubt the Stath—or possibly some Crustaxans. If these kings ran into them across the Federation boundary.—Which bunch is worse, I don't know."

"Have we actually *seen* any of these other warships?"

"No, sir. But evidently they're relying on concealment to trap the commerce raiders."

"Then," said the Regent, "these monarchs are completely *alone* now? Do I understand that?"

Colonel du Berrin looked puzzled. "Yes, sir. They're alone, as I understand it—running ahead of the main forces."

The Regent nodded. "Send another message of welcome. And since their ship is small, bring them down in the Royal Park. Have another regiment of the Capital Division there to welcome them."

"Sir, as I read these messages, only you can welcome them, without danger of giving offense. And let me respectfully point out, successful camouflage in space is evidence of high technological capability. I make no claim to understand the situation, but it is plainly filled with uncertainties and dangers."

Lance Corporal Zarn said respectfully, "General Harmer's acknowledgement—"

Private Beckel tore off another sheet of paper. "Sir, they're coming down in the terrace of the City Palace."

Colonel du Berrin glanced around, and suddenly roared, "What the devil are you all standing around for? Do you want the private to do all the work here? *Get back to your posts!*" The corporal, the sergeant, the lieutenant, and the captain sprang to their separate machines. Private Beckel said, "Another message here, sir. From the Inner Defense Sphere commander. He says 'IDS drone massometer probes indicate presence of masses unaccounted for by any charted natural objects or known derelicts, or otherwise-detectable ships.'"

"Sir," said Captain Stang in an odd voice, "we have here a routine duplicate of a communications order—Divisional airborne transport to report to Positions XK9-.2 on the ring road, to pick up the Imperial Division."

"Well," said Colonel du Berrin, "that's unusual, but—"

"Sir,—it's signed 'By authority of Harold William, Warlord of Festhold!'" The Regent, turning to leave, spun on his heel.

Lance Corporal Zarn's machine chattered, and he said, "I *knew* it! There's been a slip-up somewhere! Sir, here's a message from Lieutenant-Colonel Stran du Morgan, Second-In-Command, the Royal guard! He's skipping the landing pattern entirely, and coming down in the Royal Park!—I don't understand this, sir. At the end of the message, it says: 'Death to traitors! Long live the Warlord!'" Colonel du Berrin stood motionless.

The Regent said, "Alert the Parashock Division!"

"Sir," said Colonel du Berrin, "the Parashock Division is in the Outer Defense Command. They were unreliable."

Sergeant Ayn, his voice toneless, dry, noncommittal, said aloud:

"'General Order Number One. By Authority of Harold William, Warlord of Festhold. To all Units Festhold Armed Forces.

"'1) As of the time of receipt of this General Order, the governing authority of the former Regent, Marius, Duke of Rennel, is summarily ended, by command of the Warlord.

"'2) All lawful governing authority within the Realm of Festhold will henceforth emanate directly from Harold William, Warlord of Festhold, and from the duly constituted organs of government.'

"'3) The said Marius, Duke of Rennel, is hereby stripped of all command power over any and all men and officers, commissioned and noncommissioned, of whatever rank, unit, or duty, wherever situated, either within the Realm of Festhold, or in its conquered or occupied districts.

"'4) The said Marius is believed to be allied to alien forces opposed to the well-being of our Realm.

"'5) Whosoever obeys the orders of the aforesaid Marius does so in defiance of the direct command of the Warlord, and at the peril of his life.

"'By authority of

"'Harold William

"'Warlord of Festhold'"

Duke Marius stood as if paralyzed, then glanced at Colonel du Berrin, as if to see his reaction. Colonel du Berrin, without meeting this questioning gaze, moved a little away from Duke Marius. Duke Marius instantly noted the colonel's reaction, relaxed with an effort, and laughed.

"The Baron of Scrattel is as insane as I thought. My authority derives from passing the two tests required of any Ruler of Festhold—drawing the sword from the stone, and meeting the approval of the nobles. The weak-willed Harold passed out on the floor. *I* kept at it till I won! *I* am the Warlord of Festhold!"

The Sergeant eyed the dog-eared corner of a little pamphlet sticking out from under his communications machine, and said nothing. The colonel frowned, and stepped over to the sergeant's machine to read the message himself. From outside came the blast of signal whistles and the heavy tramp of feet. Duke Marius suddenly whirled and left the room.

XXVIII. The Guests

As seen in the spy screens in Interstellar Patrol Ship 6-107-J, the Capital Division controlled the spaceport and communications centers. The Imperial Division was camped in the Royal Park with more and more units being lifted in. The Royal Guard, under command of the Warlord, had the City Palace surrounded, and also controlled everything in it from the subbasement up to and including the fifteenth floor. The populace was in the streets, eagerly awaiting the latest news.

On the sixteenth floor of the City Palace, an uneasy truce held between the armed guards of Duke Marius and the Royal Guard, facing each other halfway down a gorgeously decorated hall, at the end of which a gilded elevator led to the seventeenth and eighteenth floors of the building.

"Just stay right there," warned the commander of the guards. "Otherwise the Duke kills the Princess. You don't want that, do you?"

Roberts, still in his armor, glanced from one screen to another, and growled, "We'll take care of that."

Morrissey, who appeared to be a kind of armored muscular sea horse looking out of an armored tank, said, "And what if that's the thing that sets off this maniac?"

"How could it?" said Roberts. "We're his only hope."

Hammell, in the guise of a giant armored python, gave a

little laugh, but said nothing. Overhead, in the space devoted to the big upper fusion turrets, a tangle of glittering armored tentacles showed where Bergen was also saying nothing, but waiting patiently.

Roberts slid into the control seat, snapped on the gravitors, and rose steadily up the side of the Duke's "City Palace."

Morrissey, watching the spy screen, said, "He's glancing around out the window—looking for some unit loyal to him, I suppose. There—he sees the ship."

Roberts slowed the climb of the patrol ship, and spoke through the outside speaker: "I am Vaughan. Are you the Ruler of Festhold?"

Duke Marius' eyes glittered. "Yes, but some disloyal local troops have me temporarily besieged here."

"We cannot intrude in the fight—but if you seek transportation—"

"Yes!—For myself and my fiancée!"

"We are always glad to help a fellow sovereign.—Would that we could fight in this conflict, but we may not do it."

"If you will just bring your ship closer—"

Roberts raised the ship, and swung it close to the building. Duke Marius turned toward the inside, and gestured. Two guards appeared with the struggling Erena, who looked grimly at the ship, then glanced far down at the ground below.

Roberts spoke, his voice carefully expressionless. "You will be safe aboard this ship, Princess."

Erena stood still, listening, glanced wonderingly at the ship, and suddenly reached out. She steadied herself against the curving flank of the ship as she stepped onto the gently sloping fin. Carefully, she climbed the fin toward the hatch. Duke Marius followed, and though his weight, in comparison to that of the ship, was not greatly more than that of Princess Erena, the ship seemed to dip noticeably beneath him as he stepped on the fin. The surface of the fin, apparently slightly rough beneath Princess Erena's feet—and hence offering a safe grip—seemed somehow slick under Duke Marius.

The Duke, teetering dangerously, reached out to steady himself against the flank of the ship. The flank of the ship delivered a blue-white spark about a quarter of an inch long. In the control seat, Roberts shut off the outside speaker, and punched the button near an amber glowing lens.

"We can't get the answers from this Duke if we drop him sixteen stories into the courtyard."

The symbiotic computer said regretfully, "That is correct."

Roberts glanced at the viewscreen, and noted that Duke Marius, perspiring freely, was now able to pick his way warily along the fin. Princess Erena had almost reached the hatch. Carefully she climbed up.

Roberts left the control seat, ducked under the three-foot thick mirrorlike cylinder that ran down the axis of the ship, and then paused. Back toward the drive units, Princess Erena stood just beneath the hatchway, her clear blue eyes wide, one hand raised to brush back her honey-blonde hair.

Roberts, paralyzed for an instant, recovered control of himself, and spoke quietly. "My colleagues may at first seem somewhat strange to you, Princess—but though they may appear alien, their hearts are true. Do not let the illusion of their outward form alarm you."

Roberts held out his hand, and the armor flashed in the overhead light. Erena stepped forward, carefully took his hand, smiled, and let him lead her further into the ship. For an instant, she paused, gripping the armor.

Hammell, in the guise of an armored snake of formidable proportions, graciously bowed with the upper—or uncoiled—portion of his body.

"Delighted to meet you, Princess. I am Prince Gdazzrik of the March."

The monster sea horse behind Hammell bowed suavely, and spoke in Morrissey's voice, "Sarkonnian the Second."

As Princess Erena's grip on Roberts' arm tightened, there came a flexing of tentacles from overhead, and the voice of Dan Bergen said politely, "Rasgaard Seraak, Adjunct-Coordinate to the Empire, Galactic East."

There was a heavy thud from aft in the ship, then the *clang!* as the hatch slammed shut. Duke Marius wiped his forehead. "Vaughan, I am truly indebted to you and your colleagues. If you will merely take me to System Command Center One, which I can locate for you very quickly, we will end this nonsense."

Just then, the Duke caught sight of Hammell, and suddenly stopped talking.

Princess Erena said earnestly, "I appeal to you Vaughan, on

behalf of my brother, the true ruler of Festhold. This man is a traitor. He is clever. He is foresighted. But he is a traitor!"

Duke Marius straightened and smiled. "Come, come, my dear, you are overtired. King Vaughan knows a revolt when he sees it!"

Roberts said, "Princess, you have my pledged word that you will be safe aboard this ship. Do you feel unsafe in the presence of this man?"

"Yes!"

Roberts at once came between Duke Marius and the girl. There was a faint hiss of metallic scales as Prince Gdazzrik of the March uncoiled ten or twelve feet of length and appeared at Roberts' side. Sarkonnian the Second added to the congestion in the already confined space by rolling up on caterpillar treads and resting a tree-trunk arm on Roberts' shoulder.

"*Is* it revolt?—Or an uprising against false tyranny?"

From up in the forward fusion turret, a number of armored tentacles reached down and visibly flexed. Bergen's voice was cheerful: "'Twould not be meet that the Princess observe the means by which 'tis done—but I'll warrant to have the truth out of this fellow in the blink of an eye."

As Duke Marius glanced back at the hatch, Roberts said soothingly, "I fear we sovereigns are a suspicious lot. You know—The thought of treachery is the common nightmare of kings. You have but to clear up the matter for us. We wish merely to be certain we are on the right side. Once we are sure—"

Duke Marius whirled, and tried to get out the hatch.

XXIX STEEL AND GOLD

Roberts stood before the desk of Colonel Valentine Sanders, who sat back, his hands clasped behind his head, listening closely.

"So," said Roberts, "to sum up the cause of the trouble, Festhold has a royal family, and a series of noble families. Two generations ago the head of the wealthy number-one noble family decided to take over the throne. The eldest son—Duke Marius—stayed home. The second son emigrated to Tiamaz. The third son joined the temple priesthood.

"Because of their wealth, rank, and their native ability, they each soon had a group of followers, all working toward the same end—the elimination of the royal family and the substitution of their own family in its place. At home, they carefully arranged accidents. On Tiamaz they raised money, in return for the promise of Festhold protection once the Regent became King.—At that point, the other brothers would have become members of the new royal family, which would rule Festhold, run Tiamaz, and also control the temple priesthood.

"As Regent, meanwhile, Duke Marius had made a carefully timed deal with Festhold's Stath enemies. Provided they would agree to settle down, he would cut the appropriation for the Festhold fleet, so that they, in turn, could afford to relax. He was sure that they would doublecross him, which would provide a crisis just when he was ready to take over the government. The crisis would unite the country behind him, and incidentally give him an excuse to get rid of any stubborn military units that showed support for the Prince.—They would be sent into the worst of the battle, and be ground up fighting the Stath."

The colonel shook his head.

"All the details were nicely worked out. What was the Command Center One the Regent wanted to go to when you 'rescued' him?"

"He had arranged that any commands to distant military units must pass through Command Center One. Command Center One was staffed with his own people, and was to act as a filter. Most orders got only a casual glance and then were relayed. But when Harold William gave his order commanding the Festhold Armed Forces to rally to him, Command Center One filtered out that order. It got no further. The normal arrangements for relaying such communications all fed through Command Center One."

"So that—"

"So that Harold William gained the support of the troops on Festhold—a total of some five or six divisions—while the enormous majority of the other troops, plus the bulk of the Festhold fleet, knew nothing at all of what had happened. From Command Center One, Duke Marius could then send out a false account of what had happened, bring down the fleet, and blast Harold to bits before he knew what had happened. Also, once at Command Center One, Duke Marius could fake messages of loyalty from the fleet to Harold William, so that Harold William would be unprepared for what would happen when the Fleet actually came down."

The colonel glanced at the ceiling, then shook his head. "I happen to have an idea that Maury and his commerce raiders are about to hit Tiamaz. I was thinking that it might be a nice idea to let Marius 'escape' to Tiamaz just before the raid."

Roberts shook his head. "They want him on Festhold."

"Yes—and besides, what if Maury captured him? He'd be Maury's idea-man in no time. No, Maury is tough enough as it is. We'll leave the problem of Duke Marius to Festhold."

Roberts said quietly, "I think they can solve it."

The colonel nodded, then smiled. "And what about you, Roberts? You seem to have formed the habit of associating with royalty. What about this Princess?"

Roberts looked at him blandly. "Princess?"

The colonel frowned. "Princess Erena."

"Ah, Private Erena, my probationary crewman."

The colonel sat up. "Listen, Roberts—what in—"

Roberts smiled and said, "You didn't expect me to propose on the spot, then go to the Cathedral of Truth with Harold William and take a second crack at drawing the sword all on my own?"

"No, I admit, that would have been rushing things, but I assumed—"

"Erena *recognized my voice.* She knew whoever had gotten her out of the Temple of Chance on Tiamaz had reappeared on Festhold in the guise of His Royal and Imperial Majesty, Vaughan the First."

"Well," said the colonel, smiling, "that must have made you an eminently eligible suitor."

Roberts said drily, "And then afterward?"

The colonel innocently spread his hands. "For better or for worse—"

"Well," said Roberts, smiling, "the first chance I had, I explained the situation."

"What did she—"

"She said that, in her opinion, if I wanted to I could claim royal rank by virtue of the situation on Paradise—but that she thought it would simplify everything if instead she was in the Patrol."

The colonel's brows came together. "Listen, Roberts, it may simplify things for *her*—and for *you*—but—"

"And, sir, the Patrol is on record with Tiamaz—accepting Princess Erena as a candidate-member of the Interstellar Patrol—and incidentally as a member of my crew."

"I have the feeling, Roberts, that the records of that call have mysteriously vanished from Tiamaz' files."

Roberts smiled. "But not from *our* files."

The colonel said grudgingly, "That's true." He frowned. "But look, Roberts, do you have the faintest idea what this—ah—pampered princess would have to go through to achieve full membership. The requirements for women are as tough, proportionately, as they are for men. And women recruits *invariably* make problems! Marry this princess if you've got to, but, for the love of—" He cut himself off, studying Roberts' expression. His own face showed a rapid succession of emotions. Abruptly he smiled, stood up, and thrust out his hand.

"Well done, Roberts—whatever happens—and good luck!"

Roberts shook hands, took one step back, saluted, turned, and went out. Ordinary prudence told him to leave before the colonel assigned him to some other little problem. The oversight would not be forgotten for long, if it was an oversight.

He stepped out into the corridor to see Erena, the neat uniform of the Patrol at once modest and perfectly suited to her blue eyes and honey-blonde hair. With her in the hall stood a captain, two lieutenants, and a major, all trying to elbow each other aside as they smiled charmingly at Erena. None of them were pleased at the approach of Roberts, all murmuring politely as she said good-bye and took Roberts' arm—and all looking after him with a "What's he got?" expression plain on their faces.

At the desk inside the office, Colonel Valentine Sanders finished punching the call number, waited frowning for the response, then turned at the sudden transparency of the bulkhead nearby. The wall screen showed a strongly built man with piercing blue eyes, who frowned now in faint puzzlement.

"Yes, Val? What is it? We've finally got this business with Festhold all wrapped up, correct?"

The colonel glanced at the door by which Roberts had just gone out. On the wall screen, the piercing gaze sharpened.

"Festhold *is* all clear, isn't it?"

"The last word," said the colonel, "is that the Warlord has drawn the sword from the stone, met with the nobles, spoken to them, and been thunderously acclaimed. Duke Marius is still imprisoned. Maury's commerce raiders are approaching Tiamaz, and we've withdrawn our teams from Tiamaz. Roberts has just reported from Festhold. His ship and crew are back."

"Ah—good. Then—" The piercing gaze sharpened again. "It's all cleared up, then?"

The left side of the colonel's lean face bent up in a brief smile. The right side stayed somber. "There's the question of Roberts and Princess Erena."

The figure on the wall screen briefly studied the colonel's expression. "M'm. Yes, that's right. Well—" The strongly built figure was momentarily silent, motionless. Then one of the hands resting palm-down on the desktop came up, turned—

"Well, Val, what can we do about it? Our man's overmatched, that's all. He shouldn't go around falling in love with princesses. Obviously, *someone* was going to get hurt. He'll get over it."

"That isn't what I—"

"At least, we haven't lost him."

"No, but—"

"Try to look at it this way. If he'd stayed there, she'd have come to see him not as her rescuer but as a nameless untitled figure—with a certain heroic aspect, yes, but heroes are commonplace on Festhold. And he would never reveal what he had done unless and until they'd married. But before that, he has to win her. So, he'd either have acted dishonorably by Festhold standards—and the consequences of that aren't worth thinking about—or, more likely, he'd have tried to draw this sword from the stone, if he ever got that far. And the odds are, he couldn't do it. And afterwards, what? He emigrates to Festhold? Or he goes renegade, and kidnaps the Warlord's sister? And *we* get stuck with the blame?"

The sharp eyes looked suddenly thoughtful. "And that isn't the worst, Val. *Theoretically,* you recall, this princess is a candidate-member of the Patrol. Now, if you want to try to visualize some real diplomatic and personnel problems, just imagine what *could* have happened."

The colonel's haunted expression showed that that was exactly

what he *was* imagining. The figure on the screen smiled benevolently.

"So—we'd better leave well enough alone. Right, Val?"

The colonel drew a deep breath, and came to his feet. He
crossed the office, and came back again. He spoke quietly and
respectfully. "Sir?"

A look of alarm flashed across the strong-featured face on the
screen. It was the look of the superior who knows that orders go
down, but problems come *up.* Then the face quickly composed
itself. The eyes were faintly narrowed and sharply focused. The
chin jutted. The voice was quiet and considerate.

"Yes?"

"There are certain problems I am not cleared to handle."

"Such as?"

"O-Branch merely handles *operations.* Entanglements with
foreign powers that are not members of the Federation, dealings
with outraged emperors, matters of high protocol—these are all
outside my range of action."

"Yes, but what—"

"Selection of personnel, advice to the lovelorn, disentanglement
of sixteen fire-breathing Interstellar Patrolmen all interested in
the same girl, explanations of the fine points of the situation to
naive computers, ship and job assignments complicated by personal attachments as airy as thistledown and as strong as steel
cables. Last but not least, marriage counseling—all this, too, sir,
is out of my line."

"Yeah—Listen, you don't mean—"

"That is exactly what I *do* mean.

"Oh."

In the office, the Interstellar Patrol thought deeply.

In the corridor outside, Roberts looked down at the honey-
gold hair of the girl walking close beside him, and he squeezed
her hand more tightly.

Erena looked up, and smiled.

AND OTHERS...

SOLDIERS AND SCHOLARS

GOLIATH AND THE BEANSTALK

Cord was lying on the bunk reading over his orders when he felt the rough foreign weave of the fabric at his back pull tight, and then grow loose again. He glanced up.

"Another correction?"

From the bunk overhead, Dave growled, "Yeah. They're rotten navigators. And I think that locker, for the five thousandth time . . ."

Cord glanced around to see the loose-hinged door of the weapons locker swaying back and forth. He got up and slammed it shut again.

The fabric of the upper bunk creaked as Dave craned around. "One of them got out again."

"Where?"

"In the corner, there." He pointed with a bandaged hand. "I hope it isn't armed."

Cord ducked under a suit of battle armor slung on a cable, its arms and legs pulled out tight by wires stretched from deck and bulkheads. In the corner lay a thing like a gray baseball studded with spikes. Cord rolled it carefully into his hands, and carried it back to the weapons locker.

Dave looked in the other direction.

Cord opened the locker door and put the spike-studded ball back in the grenade hopper. He glanced down at the rack of oddly-shaped guns, grenade-throwers, rocket-projectors, and close-quarter weapons.

One of these close-quarter weapons held his attention. It was about the length of a man's arm, and had a hilt like a sword. Five inches back from the point, the double-edged blade branched to form a circle of steel, sharpened inside and out. Sharp-edged teeth jutted from the flat sides of the circle, their points angled back toward the hilt. Where the blade ran back from the circle to join the hilt, there was a guard formed like a basket of knives.

Dave growled, "Shut the door on that thing, will you? Every time I look at it, it makes me mad."

Cord shut the door. "I have to admit it," he said, "it's a heck of a thing to run into in the dark."

Dave growled out a string of white-hot adjectives and lay back.

Cord sat down with his orders and again began to read.

There was a harsh knock at the door.

"Come in," said Cord absently. He realized he'd spoken Terran, and hastily called to mind the Stath equivalent. He called out, "I won't shoot."

There came a rapid snapping of choppy syllables. "My hands are empty. I have a message. You can trust me."

"Enter safely," said Cord, "and leave unhurt."

The door opened. A lithe slender creature about six-and-a-half feet tall, with a head like a weasel, came in and looked at Cord with bright eyes. "We approach the alien planet, Observers. The attack can be watched from the bridge. A good view. The Van Chief invites you."

"Thank him for us. We will come with empty hands."

"You can trust us. Fear not for your backs." The Stath hesitated, his sharp eyes focused over Cord's head. "You feud?"

Dave growled, "An accident."

"No offense meant. Can I help?"

"No offense. I have only curiosity on my part."

"Curiosity is the sword of the mind. You have but to ask. I will not betray you."

"What," said Dave, "is that sword with the sharp circle in the blade?"

"Pardon? No offense. I only do not understand."

"There is a weapon in the locker there. It has a guard like a handful of daggers. What's it for?" He dropped off the bunk and opened the locker.

"Oh," said the Stath, "that. I plan no treachery. Let me show you."

"We trust you. Go ahead."

The Stath jerked the weapon out of the locker. With one hand back, he held it in the other like a fencer's foil. He jabbed it rapidly back and forth. "Stab," he said. He turned it edgewise. "Split. Chop." He reached out and yanked back. "Teeth catch. Rip. Tear." He raised the blade. "Drop circle over head." His arm made a vicious jerking motion back and forth. "Behead." He returned it to the locker, and grinned like a shark. "You wish to use?"

Cord said hastily, "Many thanks. Regulations forbid it. Besides, we have our own weapons. No offense meant."

"No offense. The beheader is good only for practice to strengthen the wrist. Too clumsy in battle." He bowed and backed toward the door. "We await you at the bridge. Much blood."

"Much blood," said Cord mechanically.

The door closed behind the Stath.

Dave groaned. "Why I ever joined the Reserves, I don't know. Read me the orders again, will you?"

Cord got out the orders and read:

"To Captain, T. S. M. *Terra*. Effective immediately release following for active duty:

"1. Cordell T. Howard, 166-0-8473, 1st Lieutenant, TSNR;

"2. David R. Bancroff, 167-0-1062, 2nd Lieutenant, TSNR.

"These officers are to report immediately by dispatch spacer to Van Chief Stath Invasion Fleet now approaching 61J14, otherwise known as 'Planet of Peace.' They will act as Official Terran Observers. They are to undergo hypnotic foretreatment on board dispatch spacer, and hypnotic aftertreatment upon return. The following additional information is appended:

"61J14 is a system settled several generations ago by Terran humans. In accord with the religio-scientific precepts of the original founders, 61J14 refuses Federation membership, obligations, or protection. 61J14 rebuffs all offers of arms or assistance from us, and states that its policy is 'brotherhood with all races.' The military strength of 61J14 is regarded as negligible. Its sole exports are foodstuffs and botanical novelties. Its sole scientific personnel are apparently biologists and plant specialists.

"The Stath Confederacy is joined with us as signatory to the Triracial Mutual Nonaggression Pact. They have honored this pact rigidly. They would, therefore, probably refrain from attacking 61J14 if, even at this date, it would unite with us. As 61J14 refuses to do this, we must avoid hostilities, or ourselves violate the Nonaggression Pact.

"You are warned to avoid giving aid or comfort to the inhabitants of 61J14, regardless of your natural sympathies. Your sole function is that of observers."

Cord frowned and shrugged into his jacket. He helped Dave into his jacket. They buckled on the heavy gun belts that made the Stath feel more comfortable around them. Then they made their way to the bridge.

The Stath Van Chief was briskly giving last minute orders and general advice to his subordinates.

"Remember now," he said, "these people are not truly enemies, but more like draft animals to be caught, tamed, and set to use. Keep your men in hand. No blood baths without provocation. The thing to remember is, with these people safely under our control, our food worries are over. See to it that no one gets jittery and starts letting off kapa-bombs right and left. The human appearance of these people is not a sign of danger, as they are not armed. A snapperjaw is not dangerous with its teeth pulled out.

"To summarize: There will be no off-planet bombardment. Initial landings will be made at Points 1, 2, 4, and 7. From these points, attack parties will start out to seize communications centers, power plants and the like. The rest of the planet is not sufficiently developed to be worth the trouble. Once total control is established in these regions, we will arrange for permanent administrative personnel to take over.

"Bear in mind—again, please—these people look like humans, but their leaders are religionists and plant-farmers. No overexcitement. Each one captured means better food in the future. Each one killed is one that can't raise anything for us.

"That's all, gentlemen. Much blood."

The Stath officers all saluted. The Van Chief turned around and saw Cord and Dave. "Ah," he said, brightening, "my hands are empty. It is good to see you."

"You can trust us," said Cord, adhering strictly to ritual. "We thank you for the invitation."

"Your backs are safe here," said the Van Chief, in cordial tones.

"We're about to go down. I'm afraid it's a dry bone we have to offer you, though. This planet shows no sign of fight."

"Still, we appreciate the honor of being here. We hope we won't be in the way."

"Ah, never, Terrans. We are bound loyally as allies by treaty. Let your knives and ours ever be stuck in the same enemy. Besides, I've given out all the orders, the rest ought to be just routine."

Cord was momentarily at a loss for something to say. He was grateful to see a Stath subordinate approach the Van Chief.

"Sir, the local Chief is on the visor again. The reception's awful, as usual. I don't know what they're using for a transmitter."

"Hm-m-m. Your pardon, Terrans. I leave pleasure for duty. No offense meant."

"No offense," said Cord mechanically. He watched the Van Chief go to a big screen covered with a flickering jumble of murky blurrings.

A voice spoke clearly. "Heretic, are you there?"

The Stath colored slightly. "Control your tongue, toothless one. You lie before us like penned cattle in fear of slaughter. Cause overmuch trouble and your only value to us is lost. There is nothing left to you then but death."

Vaguely, Cord seemed to make out a face on the jumbled screen. The foggy vision of lips parted.

"Few are those who do not die, sooner or later, Heretic."

The Stath scowled, then looked intent. He remarked, "The purpose of life is to live long, otherwise why should there be fear of death? And you shorten your life gravely if you anger me."

"The length of a vine is not important. It is the fruit that counts. Bear in mind: though the days of a long life are many, they are numbered."

"Can a vine shortened by the sword bear much fruit? Why number your days meaninglessly?"

"A good point, Heretic, a good point. There is meaning. We attack no one. We are friendly to all. We devote ourselves to the cultivation of our planet and of ourselves. We have no antagonism toward you. Therefore you must have none toward us."

"We have no antagonism. Nevertheless, you are going to become part of the Stath Confederacy."

"We thank you. But we decline to join."

"This is not something you have anything to say about."

"But it is. Otherwise, you seek to enslave us."

"Put whatever words to it you want. We need food."

"We will trade with you—"

"Bah! Why bargain for the egg when we can have the bird that makes the eggs?"

"We will give you *teaching*. We can show you how to raise—"

"Enough of this chatter. I have heard this all before. My ears ache. If you have anything new to add, say it. Otherwise, you can tell the overseer when you report for work tomorrow."

"I have something new to say. I will say it only once. Listen carefully."

"My ears are up."

"Our beliefs are based on what we believe to be correct metaphysical teachings and precise scientific observations. It is one of our beliefs that a person who sets out to do evil causes himself, as a result, great trouble and hurt. This may take a short time or a long time to appear. Cause-and-effect may be plain or obscure. But once the grinding wheels are set in motion, it takes much to avoid them. We hold no evil intent toward you. We are very sorry that you will, if you land here, bring the punishment upon you. But we will not be slaves. Bombard us from space and kill us if you will. We are not afraid. Perhaps we have that coming to us for past sins. But do not land here."

"Is that it?"

"Yes, that's it. There are some here so benighted that they'd let you come down with no warning. But I adhere to the teachings. You are warned."

The fuzzy image vanished from the screen. The Van Chief turned away with a shake of his head.

"Sir," said an officer urgently, "no offense, but it's time to strap in."

Cord and Dave watched the landings on a huge multiple screen, then went with their host to a prefabricated headquarters building that had been rapidly slapped together.

"On most planets," said the Van Chief, "I would stay with the ship till the enemy was clearly hamstrung and helpless. On this planet, they're helpless to start with. I want to get the administrative machinery set up so we can pull most of the troops out as fast as possible. Cattle fatten best when they're left peacefully in pasture." He looked quizzically at Cord. "It is amazing that these people are—no offense—Terrans like you. Tell me, what would happen if we landed like this on Terra?"

"The chances," said Cord, "are that you would have been—no offense—blown to bits before you got within light-years of Terra."

Dave said nervously, "Isn't the air fresh on this planet?"

Cord looked around. He sniffed the air, then drew a deep breath. The air smelled unusually fresh and clean. The sky overhead was a clear, earth-like blue. The ground, as seen from overhead, was divided into large lush squares, with occasional groups of low buildings interspersed at great intervals. The roads through this flat country ran as straight as if drawn with a ruler. The Stath ships came down near major crossroads. The Stath ground-cars were spreading out on these roads in all directions. Light aircraft were being hoisted out of the holds of Stath ships, assembled while woven metal landing strips were staked down, then rolled onto the strips to take off on reconnaissance missions.

The Van Chief was soon surrounded by hurrying officers and message bearers. Cord and Dave had to stand aside, and soon began to feel like surplus baggage. Moreover, they began to realize that they were not really observing anything except hurrying Stath.

The attitude of these Stath subtly began to change. Cord became conscious of furtive measuring glances from some who had formerly been elaborately respectful. Spoken to directly, the Stath were still courteous, but their manner had something tentative about it.

Small numbers of human prisoners were now being brought into camp. The guards prodded them with their guns to hurry them along.

Cord and Dave watched soberly.

When the first of the prisoners were brought in, Cord overheard the remark, "Odd to see a human jump."

Later in the afternoon, a messenger hurried past Cord, stopped, stared, and went on by. Cord heard him say, "It stopped me for a minute to see one wearing guns."

As human prisoners were herded into the camp like cattle, Cord and Dave began to be treated with a courtesy that was over-elaborate. As often as not, the respectful phrases were spoken with a smile and slightly lowered lids.

Toward evening, a pair of husky Stath soldiers, carrying guns and smiling dreamily, strolled up to Cord and Dave. They glanced at each other, then looked at Cord and Dave.

"Take off the guns, and get outside with the rest."

Cord glanced at the Van Chief and the group of silent officers around him. Some of these officers were watching openly. Some pretended to be busy. The Van Chief gave no sign of knowing what was going on.

The soldier near Cord reached out to put one hand behind Cord's neck and jerk him forward. The soldier in front of Dave grabbed Dave by the sleeve.

Cord ducked and stepped back.

Dave whipped his arm up and around, breaking the grip on his arm.

The soldiers raised their guns.

There was an echoing double explosion.

The soldier in front of Cord was sprawled on his back. The other soldier had one hand pressed to his shoulder and a look of disbelief on his face.

Dave shot him right through the head.

Cord turned to face the group of Stath officers. The smoking gun in Cord's hand turned with him.

Most of the officers stood perfectly motionless. One made aimless pawing motions with his hands. The Van Chief pretended not to have heard the two deafening explosions, and went on with his work.

Cord broke the archaic gun open, kept his eyes on the Stath, tossed out the hot empty shell and replaced it with a bullet from his belt. He snapped the gun shut. The click was clearly audible throughout the room. Dave did the same, and still the Stath did not move. The Van Chief continued to be very busy.

Cord smiled and turned to Dave, the gun still pointed in the direction of the Stath.

Cord said, "You know, Dave, I believe those soldiers must have taken us for local inhabitants."

"Probably no offense was meant," said Dave, his gun aimed at the Van Chief's busy profile.

"In that case," said Cord slowly, "I suppose we shouldn't take offense, either."

"No," said Dave reluctantly. "No, I suppose not."

"Well," said Cord, "that does it, then." He shoved the gun back in its holster.

"Yes," said Dave, a little fretfully, "I guess that's all." He hesitated, jammed his gun into the holster, then thoughtfully loosened it a little.

They stood watching the Stath a moment, then turned away together.

A ragged sigh behind them broke the silence in the room.

Until that moment, Cord had acted without being aware of any thought or hesitation at all. Now, between one step and the next, he became conscious of what had just happened. He half-turned, to see the Stath soldier who had reached out for him stretched on his back with his head in a red pool. Cord looked at the base of the soldier's neck, and turned away.

There was a sudden rush of chatter in the room.

Dave said in a low voice, "Did we get that in the hypnotic foretreatment?"

"I don't know. If so, I see why there's an aftertreatment."

The room abruptly fell silent again.

Cord turned around to see a group of strongly-built elderly humans wearing long white cloaks, white trousers, and white sandals, and carrying in their raised right hands highly-polished black staffs about two-and-a-half feet long.

The Van Chief said angrily, "Throw those humans out of here. A subchief can talk to them tomorrow morning."

A crowd of soldiers, bristling with guns, was packed in the doorway. At the words, "Throw those humans out," a number of these soldiers started for Cord and Dave, whose guns instantaneously appeared in their hands. As if by magic, there was a cluster of yelling Stath officers between the two Terran observers and the rushing soldiers. These officers were dancing up and down, shouting, "No, no! Not these! The *tame* humans!"

The "tame humans" were reaching out with their black staffs, smashing soldiers alongside the neck, in the belly, and in upthrusting jabs to the chin. The wave of rushing soldiers reeled back and broke apart into howling individuals, clutching their heads, stomachs, knees, and groins.

Above the tumult was the regretful voice of one of the elders, saying, "Well, well, it's too late now. We tried to warn them, but they wouldn't listen. So be it. *Break the sticks!*"

The second wave of soldiers had the black staffs broken over their heads.

There was a puff from one of the staffs like a cloud of spores from a punctured puffball. Clarity of vision vanished in a murky gloom. In an instant of silence, there was a noise like a stream of marbles hitting the floor. Then a sound like a strewn handful of sand.

A choking yellow vapor spread over the room.

The Van Chief's voice, loud and carrying, commanded, "Kill the lot of them!"

There was a reverberating roar and the whistle of flying projectiles. Bright flashes lit up here and there in the darkness.

Cord dove for the floor, crawled to the wall, worked his way along it to the edge of a door frame and pulled himself out and down the steps.

Around him, there was shouting and confusion. A powerful voice roared out over the din:

"CAST THE SEED!"

There was a sort of low, continuous, sprinkling sound, then several voices shouted, "Run for it!"

Cord realized suddenly that all this had been in Terran.

Dave's voice said at his elbow, "Now what the devil do we do?"

"I think we'd better get out of here."

They started inching their way forward.

A thing like a delicate thread looped around Cord's foot. He jerked his foot loose. A slender cord coiled around his ankle. He stumbled forward, caught his balance, yanked his foot free, and strode ahead.

A length of stiff wire caught his foot and threw him headlong onto the ground. He jerked loose, got his legs under him and ran as fast as he could.

He tripped over a cable stretched along the ground, got to his feet, and heard Dave shout, "Cord, *look out!*"

There was a tearing sound. Something spiraled up his leg.

A vague human form went past Cord like a rocket out of its launcher.

The something around Cord's leg thickened from a hair to a thread to a wire to—

He let out a yell, jerked his leg with all his strength, threw himself forward—

There was a springy yielding of the thing that held him. It thickened and began to tighten. Something looped around his waist.

He sucked in his breath. He jerked, twisted, and strained till the blood pounded in his head and roared in his ears. There was a ripping noise and he staggered backwards. He was free.

He dragged in a breath of air and bolted through the gloom, jerking free of the fine tendrils as they looped around him, stumbling to his feet after every fall over the thick ropy trunks that sprawled along the ground.

At last he became aware that there was plowed ground under his feet. He stood still, breathing hard. There was a faint sound nearby. A hand ran over his face.

A voice said in Terran, "Human. O.K. This way."

Cord walked a little distance, then sank down on the yielding earth. He thought it was the softest bed he'd ever slept on.

He came to to see stars fading overhead.

He felt cold, cramped, and stiff. A stone was digging into his side. He got to his feet.

Dim forms were moving here and there around him.

Cord felt like a mass of bruises from head to foot.

In the distance, a fire was blazing bright. Cord went to it, found it surrounded by men stretched out with their feet to the fire. He warmed himself, got sleepy, lay down, and was shaken awake again in full daylight.

Dave's bruised face confronted him.

"Sorry," said Cord. He eased himself gingerly to his feet. The horizon tipped and swayed around him. "Merciful God," he said.

Dave gripped his arm. The world steadied, and Dave's voice came to him. "You'd better take a look at it, Cord. Words won't do it justice."

Cord took a deep breath and followed Dave.

They came to a sort of green mountain rising abruptly out of the earth. Knots of people were standing around looking at it. Dave and Cord stopped near several men in white.

Cord poked at this "mountain" carefully, glanced around and saw with a start that a wide road ran directly into it and disappeared.

He looked around. He could see in the distance another road approaching it, and another.

"Get it?" said Dave. "Remember this spot?"

Cord looked up at the greenery. A morning breeze ruffled the big leaves. Here was a glint of metal, wrapped in massive twining trunks. There was a fist of coiled vines about six feet long, with feet sticking out one end and a weasel-like head sticking out the other.

One of the white-cloaked men nearby remarked, "Well, we've got this to go through again."

"It's a fearful drain on the soil."

"Can't be helped. One thing just leads to another and—"

"Well, that's life. It's a judgment."

"Amen."

"Amen."

"Time to get back to work. We can't stand around all day doing nothing but talk."

Cord and Dave looked at each other. They looked around at the green inviting world. Everything was neat and tidy. There wasn't a menace in it anywhere. The little knots of men were moving away.

Cord and Dave looked at the mountain.

Cord cleared his throat and spoke gently.

"No offense," he said.

FACTS TO FIT THE THEORY

From: G. L. Park, 1st Lt., TSFR
To: Myron Baker, Capt., TSF
Subject: Operation Persuasion
Sir:

It is my duty to report that we have had no success whatever persuading the human colonists on Cyrene IV to join the Federation. We've told them what will happen if the Ursoids land on their planet. So far as it's possible to put it into words, we've told them what will happen if the Stath land on their planet. We've warned them that an unidentified scout ship of suspected Stath origin has been detected and backtracked to their solar system, and that the logical next step is a Stath occupation force, which can be thwarted if the colonists join the Federation. We've explained all about the Triracial Mutual Non-aggression Pact. The colonists, however, talk mystic gibberish about mind-states and self-control, and refuse to sign the treaty.

From: Myron Baker, Capt., TSF
To: G L. Park, 1st Lt., TSFR
Subject: Extreme Persuasion
Sir:

In view of the glaring realities of the situation, the colonists

323

must be brought, by whatever means are necessary, to join the Federation.

I hereby specifically authorize you to use force to compel the signing of the Treaty. An agreement made under duress will be held perfectly valid by either the Stath or the Ursoids, who use force whenever it appears profitable.

Any disciplinary action resulting from this will fall, not upon you, but upon me. I take entire responsibility.

By "force" I specifically refer to any and all methods of compulsion, including the taking of hostages, torture, and summary infliction of the death penalty.

These actions, however brutal, are precisely what the inhabitants of Cyrene IV will experience daily if the Stath take over their planet.

The need for speed is urgent.

A force of twenty-eight Stath ships, including transports, passed our watch-ship at Breakpoint Secoy at 0811 yesterday, and is expected in the vicinity of Cyrene IV sometime tomorrow.

From: G. L. Park, 1st Lt., TSFR
To: All Unit Leaders
Subject: Operation Persuasion
Sirs:

Because all methods of ordinary persuasion have failed to induce the colonists to join the Federation, and because a Stath invasion force is now en route, the signing of the treaty will be carried out by compulsion.

Seize immediately the elders of each community, and compel them to straightway sign the document of agreement.

Avoid unnecessary brutality. But where force is necessary, you must use it.

The Stath are expected tomorrow.

From: Sam Smith, 2nd Lt., TSFR
To: G. L. Park, 1st Lt., TSFR
Subject: Difficulties
Sir:

I am prepared to use whatever force is necessary to prevent

the Stath getting control of this planet, but unfortunately all the elders in my district have vanished.

From: G. L. Park, 1st Lt., TSFR
To: Sam Smith, 2nd Lt., TSFR
Subject: Signing of Treaty
Sir:

If you can't get the elders, seize anyone available, appoint him assistant elder, knock him over the head if necessary, and guide his hand across the page. The important thing is to get the papers signed.

From: Sol Abel, S/Sgt., TSFR
To: G. L. Park, 1st Lt., TSFR
Subject: Operation Persuasion
Sir:

Following your orders, I had four of the elders in my district seized for the purpose of signing the treaty. The elders, however, explained why they could not sign, and at the time it somehow seemed reasonable. We could not bring ourselves to force them, and they walked out. The papers are not signed. I request to be relieved of command of this unit.

From: G. L. Park, 1st Lt., TSFR
To: Sol Abel, S/Sgt., TSFR
Subject: Difficulty with Elders
Sir:

Forge the names of the elders on the proper lines of the documents. I will take responsibility. Have four different men sign so there is no unusual similarity of handwriting. Your request to be relieved of command is refused.

From: J. Hunt Rollo, 2nd Lt., TSFR
To: G. L. Park, 1st Lt., TSFR
Subject: Illegal Orders
Sir:

Operation Persuasion is an improvisation. The procedures, down to the smallest details, are irregular. Your latest order is completely unacceptable.

The Procedure of Federation, Section 21, Paragraph G, states: "No compulsion or extraordinary methods of persuasion shall be used."

It is my duty as an officer to uphold the honor of the Service.

I hereby notify you of my intent to report this infraction to H. James Rollo, the Inspector General of the Space Force, if you do not immediately rescind it.

From: G. L. Park, 1st Lt., TSFR
To: J. Hunt Rollo, 2nd Lt., TSFR
Subject: Disobedience to Orders
Sir:

You are hereby removed from command of Unit I.

You are under arrest.

You are ordered to report to the command ship by 1400 TST, or you will be considered AWOL.

Any attempt to use any communicator or other means to send any message off this planet, directly or indirectly, will be construed as insubordination, and dealt with accordingly.

From: G. L. Park, 1st Lt., TSFR
To: Myron Baker, Capt., TSF
Subject: Difficulties
Sir:

I transmit herewith communications relevant to incorporation of Cyrene IV into the Federation. Any suggestions will be deeply appreciated.

From: Myron Baker, Capt., TSF
To: G. L. Park, 1st Lt., TSFR
Subject: Suggestions
Sir:

H. James Rollo, I seem to remember, has an only son named

J. Hunt Rollo. The family is rich and influential. I think you are within your rights, but what will happen if Rollo's family goes to work on you, I do not know. They are what is known as an "Old Service Family." My advice is to show young Rollo my original order, do everything you can to conciliate him, give him a job as your special assistant, or whatever else he wants, within reason. As long as it doesn't interfere with your mission, handle the young heir with kid gloves whenever you can.

From: G. L. Park, 1st Lt., TSFR
To: Myron Baker, Capt., TSF
Subject: Progress So Far
Sir:

I am happy to report that we have now, by various methods that it is not necessary to go into here, got quite a few signatures on the Treaty. The papers are made up in proper legal form with necessary seals, signatures of witnesses, et cetera, all duly affixed. I am sending copies of the photostats to you by facsimile. These you can show to the Stath commander, so I guess that takes care of the problem of Cyrene IV.

As for Lieutenant Rollo, I have tried the things you suggested, without success. He insists that I rescind the order, destroy the treaty papers, and, if necessary, turn the planet over to the wringnecks when they get here.

He gives me one hour to comply with his demands.

Left to my own devices, I know what I would do.

From: Myron Baker, Capt., TSF
To: G. L. Park, 1st Lt., TSFR
Subject: Insubordination
Sir:

2nd Lt. J. Hunt Rollo is to be shackled and placed in the smallest compartment aboard your ship to await trial. He is to be fed, given water, and allowed the use of sanitary facilities. He may not communicate.

Two blasted careers are a small price to save a planet.

Have your communications technician check your facsimile machine. All we get up here are lines of segregated large and small letters, bits of what appears to be handwriting broken into its component parts, lines of dots, and other gibberish.

From: G. L. Park 1st Lt., TSFR
To: Myron Baker, Capt., TSF
Subject: Facsimile Error
Sir:

The communications technicians tell me there is nothing wrong on our end, and say the effect you describe would be possible only if the electromagnetic wave-trains were somehow altered en route, so as to arrive at your machine in a different sequence from that in which they left ours. This, the technicians say, is impossible in the circumstances.

Incidentally, I am unable to comply immediately with your order concerning Lt. Rollo. Your message reached me after the expiration of the hour's grace allowed by the lieutenant, who immediately went to the long-range communicator in my command room. The communicator just happened to be under repair at the moment, and a heavy electrical charge was delivered to the lieutenant as he switched it on.

He is now in sick bay.

From: Myron Baker, Capt., TSF
To: G. L. Park, 1st Lt., TSFR
Subject: Transmission Trouble
Sir:

We are still getting a mishmash on the fax. My technicians assure me there is nothing wrong on this end. I must have the necessary papers here when the Stath fleet shows up, so kindly get this matter straightened out.

From: G. L. Park, 1st Lt., TSFR
To: Myron Baker, Capt., TSF
Subject: Psychic Sabotage
Sir:

We have checked everything we can think of, and have run test transmissions using pages of regulations, maps, handwriting, and photos of pin-up girls. Everything goes through but the treaty. Your people transmitted to us the faulty copy you've been receiving. We received it, however, as perfect reproductions of the photostats.

One of the colonists told T/3 Berensen that the treaty cannot be transmitted, because we are trying to manipulate the colony against its will, and the elders are, therefore, psychically jamming the transmission.

That is as good an explanation as I have heard yet.

All I can suggest is that I call you on the communicator, and hold the treaty up to the screen while your men take photographs of it.

From: Myron Baker, Capt., TSF
To: G. L. Park, 1st Lt., TSFR
Subject: Communicator Trouble
Sir:

Something out of the ordinary is going on here.

All we could see on the screen was the same gibberish we get on the fax. Everything else on the screen came through, but not the treaty.

I would have my men run up a completely fake treaty, save for one thing: The Stath have a perfect right to send a ship down and demand to see the original. If you have the copy, and I have the original, it is going to look peculiar. A little heavy persuasion to get the treaty signed will never bother the Stath, since they would do the same themselves. But a completely *fake* treaty is something else again. To the Stath, only weaklings use fakery, and they despise weaklings. They would split this end of the universe wide open if they spot us at that.

I want to have a copy of some kind to give them when they show up. Read the treaty aloud over the communicator, and we will record it at this end. I will then give a copy of the record spool to the Stath, explaining that my facsimile machine is out of order.

From: G. L. Park, 1st Lt., TSFR
To: Myron Baker, Capt., TSF

Subject: Voice Recording
Sir:

T/3 Berensen *was* reading the treaty as written. Every one of us in the room heard him, and when I took the paper and read it, the others heard me. Moreover, when the recordings you took were played back, we all heard them clearly as first Berensen's voice, then mine. It was all perfectly intelligible to us.

From: Myron Baker, Capt., TSF
To: G. L. Park, 1st Lt., TSFR
Subject: Bad Transmission
Sir:

All we got on this end was gobble. I don't know who is bewitched, or where the trouble takes place. But I am not going to give this spool of gibberish to the Stath.

Instead, I will tell them that the treaty has been signed, but owing to freak communications troubles, I have no copy.

The trouble with this is, my say-so is not enough to keep them off the planet. Their whole landing force will probably go down, and there is no predicting what will happen.

Their landing force will outnumber you by at least ten-to-one, so you had better call in your outlying units, take over the most formidable piece of terrain you can find, sink your command and scout ships in mutually-supporting positions, arm yourselves to the teeth, and then act punctiliously correct when their high officers show up to inspect the treaty.

From: G. L. Park, 1st Lt., TSFR
To: Myron Baker, Capt., TSF
Subject: Change in Plans
Sir:

I am now fortifying myself in exceptionally rugged country, and expect no trouble from the Stath.

But as for showing them the treaty, a hitch has now developed. The safe in which the treaty was put is stuck shut.

We had half-a-dozen copies around, that might do temporarily in a pinch. The one on the fax, however, adhered to a part of the machine in a way I have never seen or heard of before, and peeled off in a long narrow strip with fuzzy edges, out of which it is impossible to reconstruct anything. The copy we tried to send you by communicator was inside the procedures manual we used as transmission check, and when we opened up the manual to take out the copy, the pages on either side stuck to it, so we had to use a knife to open them up. We then found that the paper had split down the middle edgewise so that there was nothing to be seen but two blank pages.

Another of the treaty copies was in the control room, but the cook accidentally set a tray of hot coffee on the treaty, and when he went out the treaty clung to the bottom of the tray. The cook then rammed the tray into the washer, and after the high-pressure steam nozzles got through with it, that copy wasn't worth thinking about, either. There were two copies together atop the safe, but after we landed here, an animal like a beaver ambled up the ramp into the command ship, walked down the corridor, went through the doorway as someone stepped out, and at this moment both copies blew off the top of the safe onto the floor. The beaver ate them.

We had six copies. This accounts for five of them. As you know, we were never able to get the jumbled versions you tried to transmit to us, because they came in as perfectly legible copies. Nevertheless, I have one of these copies on my desk. This copy now starts off as follows:

"AAAAaaaaaaaBBBBbbbbCCCC CccccccDDDDddddddddEEEEEe eeeeeeeeeeeeee"

Even assuming we get the safe open, which I doubt, it seems to me just as well not to show this treaty to the Stath. I hope you will agree with me that whatever we are up against here, what has happened so far does not auger well for getting rid of the Stath with this treaty.

From: Myron Baker, Capt., TSF
To: G. L. Park, 1st Lt., TSFR
Subject: Transmission Trouble
Sir:

Put the garbled copy on your facsimile machine at once. In your last message, the quotation from the beginning of the treaty was for the first time readable. It begins with the perfectly clear paragraph:

"AAAAaaaaaaBBBbbbbCCCC CccccDDDDddddddd EEEEEeeeeeeeeeeeeee

From: G. L. Park, 1st Lt., TSFR
To: Myron Baker, Capt., TSF
Subject: Garbling of Treaty
Sir:

I have now sent the garbled copy. But I hope you will change your mind, as we have finally got the safe open, and we find that the treaty itself is garbled.

From: Myron Baker, Capt., TSF
To: G. L. Park, 1ˢᵗ Lt., TSFR
Subject: Change of Plan
Sir:

The Stath invasion force is now in normal space approaching Cyrene IV.

I hereby agree to your request for a change of plan.

The copy of the treaty you sent by facsimile was received here in perfectly legible condition. Unfortunately, there appeared in large skeleton letters in the background, diagonally across the page from upper left to lower right, the word: INVALID.

I suggest you confine your future activities on the planet to observation.

Kindly send me immediately your impression of the technological level of the colonists of Cyrene IV.

From: G. L. Park, 1st Lt., TSFR
To: Myron Baker, Capt., TSF
Subject: Technology of Cyrene IV
Sir:

So far as we have been able to determine, the technology of the colonists is restricted to the working of wood, rock, et cetera, with minor production of copper, iron, silver, and a variety of precious stones. Their main activity seems to be a sort of mental discipline that they call simply "self-control." They claim to be able to control their "internal mental state" with great accuracy.

Their argument against joining the Federation was that by voluntarily agreeing to take up our system of technological development—a standard provision of the treaty—they would open themselves to mental distractions. This, they said, appeared more serious than a Stath invasion, which would involve no moral obligation.

Any attempt to get across various unpleasant aspects of Stath occupation was met by the comment:

"Do you fear it will cause us to lose our self-control?"

This seemed pathetic. But after this business with the treaty. we keep thinking of a comment of the elders, which I quote as nearly as I can remember it:

"Self-control is a tool which may be used within as well as without. When the emotions are stilled, and consciousness focused, and all the powers of a man leashed at his command, do you think this man is less for his diligence and effort within than if he had spent the same diligence and effort without? If ten thousand years of the combined labors of men suffice to disclose in the outer world such things as electricity, do you suppose that ten thousand years of inner search will disclose nothing?"

I think this answers your question. The chief industry of Cyrene IV appears to be the development of a philosophy of self-control.

I just remembered another of their comments: "Are man's external means to become ever greater and more dangerous without, and man himself to become no greater and more self-controlled within?"

From: Myron Baker, Capt., TSF
To: G. L. Park, 1st Lt., TSFR
Subject: Stath Occupation
Sir:

The Stath are, of course, now in effective command of the planet. I have obtained for you and your force permission to remain on the planet for the time being.

Let me know how the Stath occupation is proceeding.

✤　　✤　　✤

From: G. L. Park, 1st Lt., TSFR
To: Myron Baker, Capt., TSF
Subject: Atrocities
Sir:

The Stath occupation is proceeding just as you might expect.

We put camouflaged receptors in various places when we pulled back, and we now have a better view than we like.

The first attack was met by a concerted outpouring of smiling women and children who put wreaths of flowers around the necks of the dumbfounded soldiers. Before the soldiers could recover, the colonist men came out beaming and carrying big platters of food. The Stath, of course, are always hungry, and this broke up the invasion.

The Stath Invasion Force Commander, a long thin weasel with sharp teeth and shrewd eyes, immediately got in touch with us on the screen, and in the name of the Triracial Mutual Nonaggression Pact demanded to know what the colonists were up to. I tried to explain that the colonists were religious and probably were just giving the feast out of good fellowship. The Stath said, "In that case, we'll settle it soon enough."

About ten minutes later, fresh Stath troops marched up, fired into the colonists and feasting soldiers, and the invasion got back into the usual swing of things.

I am sending up some representative viewer reels by simultran.

From: Myron Baker, Capt., TSF
To: G. L. Park, 1st Lt., TSFR
Subject: Atrocities
Sir:

This is horrible.

Keep your defenses strong.

There is a peculiar phenomenon on this Reel #2 you sent up. In the sequence at the beach where the soldiers are charging the women with bayonets, the colonist men are in the background standing close together, faces blank and grim, and a dust devil sweeps across the beach to develop into a sandstorm and obscure nearly everything in sight. The way this happened is odd. Was this an actual sandstorm, or is there some defect in the film?

    ❧   ❧   ❧

From: G. L. Park, 1st Lt., TSFR
To: Myron Baker, Capt., TSF
Subject: Strange Phenomena
Sir:

The sandstorm was, so far as we can tell, perfectly real. The buffeting of the grains of blown sand and grit was so severe that it ground the lens and clouded reception from that receptor in subsequent transmissions.

This was by no means the only unusual phenomenon.

I am sending up several more reels, one of which, you will notice, gives a view of a very large waterspout, which disrupted a boatload of Stath soldiers on their way out to ransack a village on an island.

One thing worth mentioning is that we have seen none of these striking phenomena when an elder has been around. You will note on Reel #10, the Stath soldiers who somehow wound up on a tiny ledge about fifty feet up the side of a cliff. There was no elder around at the time, but only some of the younger colonists. How the Stath got up there is a good question.

One of the elders stopped by here a little while ago. He looked very self-contained, as usual. He said that the basic cause of the trouble is the Stath philosophy, which divides all things into *krang* and *blogl, krang* being those things that can protect themselves, and *blogl* those things which cannot protect themselves, and the Stath's basic law of nature being that anything which *can* protect itself *will* protect itself. The catch in this, said the elder, is that there are various ways of protecting oneself, and various motives apart from attack and defense. Earth's apparently most helpless and naturally unarmed creature is man, actually the planet's deadliest predator. Moreover, attack and defense are not man's chief motive; man's chief motive is, roughly, *control of self and environment.* But this motive makes man very dangerous when provoked.

We said there would be provocation enough now. The elder said, yes, and now we would see how much control the self-satisfied younger colonists really have.

If it were not for whatever slight comfort our presence may give the colonists, I'd want to leave now. To watch this idly is almost too much to bear. And in a few days, the Stath overlordship ceremony of *kranolol* takes place, in which choice young specimens of the conquered race are publicly cooked and eaten, as symbolic of absorption of the planet into the Stath Confederacy.

Do we have to stay for this?

From: Myron Baker, Capt., TSF
To: G. L. Park, 1st Lt., TSFR
Subject: Your Presence on Cyrene IV
Sir:

Stay, but don't watch the viewers. Before it starts, knock off watching the viewers for six hours or so, then take it up again, viewing only from the recorders. When you get to the start of this hideous ceremony, skip it and return to the viewers. I think this period would be a good time to keep the men busy with the ship's defenses, and preparing for take-off.

You ought to stay during this ceremony, because if anyone comes seeking sanctuary, he will be likely to need it more at this time than at any other. Afterwards, the colonists will be stunned, just so many vegetables. Then will be the time to leave. It won't matter then.

This is a horrible thing, but remember, we tried to save them. We did everything we could. I don't think we ought to start an interstellar war over this now when all they'd have had to do a few days ago was to sign a paper we were begging them to sign, and then just let us show it to the Stath.

From: G. L. Park, 1st Lt., TSFR
To: Myron Baker, Capt., TSF
Subject: Departure
Sir:

We are now entering the period when the ceremony of *kranolol* is to be celebrated. There is a peculiar feeling in the atmosphere, as if everything were a little bit smaller and brighter than usual. The air is very still. There is enough breeze to move the leaves, but looking out at them directly, it still seems as if we are seeing them on a screen with the sound shut off.

I am following your suggestions for viewing, and have the men busy on details of departure.

Lt. Rollo, who was going to report us to the Inspector General for illegality in trying to keep the Stath off the planet, escaped from sick bay a little while ago, and tried to get at the communicator. Several of the men grabbed him, and he is now the only man on the ship who will have the opportunity to watch *kranolol* as it takes place.

From: Myron Baker, Capt., TSF
To: G. L. Park, 1st Lt., TSFR
Subject: Ceremony
Sir:

For the benefit of our records, and of the next arms appropriation bill, I hope you are getting as much of the ceremony on film as possible; and for reference purposes, I hope all the films are synchrotimed as they come in.

From: G. L. Park, 1st Lt., TSFR
To: Myron Baker, Capt., TSF
Subject: Films
Sir:

We are getting everything we can on film. It is all being synchrotimed.

The ceremony started about ten minutes ago.

Lt. Rollo got loose from the viewer and went around like a madman, shouting for volunteers to go out with him and kill Stath. I was afraid the whole crew might volunteer, so I laid him out with a wrench that happened to be handy, and he is now back in sick bay.

The weather has been getting rapidly worse. In ten minutes it has deteriorated from a cloudy day to a whole gale.

From: Myron Baker, Capt., TSF
To: G. L. Park, 1st Lt., TSFR
Subject: Seismic Activity
Sir:

Volcanic activity has broken out on the far side of Cyrene IV from your base.

Be prepared to leave the planet at once.

✤   ✤   ✤

From: G. L. Park, 1st Lt., TSFR
To: Myron Baker, Capt.. TSFR
Subject: Seismic Activity
Sir:

Heavy earthquakes and volcanic eruptions are in progress in our section of the planet.

The winds here were clocked at a hundred and fifty miles an hour till the anemometer blew away.

We can't take off in these winds. We would be smashed to bits before we could gain altitude.

From: Myron Baker, Capt., TSF
To: G. L. Park, 1st Lt., TSFR
Subject: Survival
Sir:

I am still trying to reach you by every possible means of communication.

Reply when able.

From: G. L. Park, 1st Lt., TSFR
To: Myron Baker, Capt., TSF
Subject: Survival
Sir:

We are getting things put back together again.

We are all present and accounted for except Lt. Rollo, who came to in the middle of the hurricane and charged out to kill Stath.

In going out, he opened up the main hatch, and as he was blown away in no time, he was unable to shut it. Naturally, he had not set it on automatic-close, and he did not remember to shut the inner air-lock door, either.

The ship, of course, is airtight, and we had not opened it up since the rapid drop in atmospheric pressure began. It also happened that the hurricane was blowing crosswise of the hatch opening, which treated us to a Venturi effect. The result is that we are now suffering from a number of popped eardrums, burst containers, sprung bulkheads and jammed hatches.

I hope you will check and let me know definitely whether Lt.

Rollo is really a member of an "Old Service Family," as I am getting tired of handling him with kid gloves.

As soon as we have things straightened out here, we will go out and do whatever we possibly can for the colonists.

From: Myron Baker, Capt., TSF
To: G. L. Park, 1st Lt., TSFR
Subject: Aid to Colonists
Sir:

By all means do what you can for the colonists.

I have checked on Rollo and he is, unfortunately, actually a member of an Old Service Family. I didn't mean to imply that he can, therefore, get away with anything. You will find, however, if you incur the family's enmity, that funny little things will happen from time to time, and they will always be to your disadvantage.

I will see what backing we can get on this from higher up.

From: Myron Baker, Capt., TSF
To: T. Moley Lammer, Major, TSF
Subject: Personal and Private
Sir:

I am sending correspondence on a matter concerning which I would value your advice.

From: T. Moley Lammer, Major, TSF
To: Myron Baker, Capt., TSF
Subject: Personal and Private
Sir:

Good God, do you have any idea what you're doing? That is you-know-who's son. Don't try to drag me into this.

From: Myron Baker, Capt., TSF
To: G. L. Park, 1st Lt., TSFR
Subject: Disciplinary Action
Sir:

I'm afraid we will have to go it alone on this. But somebody simply has to stick his neck out occasionally.

How are your rescue operations coming?

From: G. L. Park, 1st Lt., TSFR
To: Myron Baker, Capt., TSF
Subject: Rescue Operations
Sir:

We found Lt. Rollo wrapped around a tree at the bottom of a nearby gully. He is now back in sick bay mouthing threats. If this is what Old Service Families come to after a few generations, it's a sorry commentary.

We are now over the site of the former Stath main headquarters base. As you see from the view tapes we are sending up, the base is completely demolished, the ships strewn in all directions.

You will note in the close view a mass of seaweed, a number of giant crabs, and an enormous squid with half-a-dozen arms wrapped around the Stath ships. These sea creatures came in on a tidal wave. You can probably hear on the audio the grinding, popping noises, and the Stath screams. When we get through rescuing colonists, we will come back here and see what we can do.

From: Myron Baker, Capt., TSF
To: G. L. Park, 1st Lt., TSFR
Subject: Rescue of Stath
Sir:

Don't burn out any bearings in the rush.

From: G. L. Park, 1st Lt., TSFR
To: Myron Baker, Capt., TSF
Subject: Cleaning-Up Operations
Sir:

Lt. Rollo, all of whose ravings I have gotten down in quintuplicate, on tape, has suddenly decided to forget about his various charges. In view of the fact that he has been almost electrocuted, hit over the head with a wrench, blown away in a hurricane, and this morning—while trying to get to a communicator—got himself wound up in a bandage-fabricating machine, I am inclined to let it go at that.

The Stath are just about wiped out. One small scout ship of theirs streaked out of here at a flat angle with its tubes white and the whole nose section cherry red. The remaining Stath survivors are hysterical. The mere sight of a colonist throws them into terror.

The colonists, meanwhile, are having a disagreement. I am sending you spools of what is going on between the elders and the other male colonists. The elders point to the huge heaps of seaweed, mud, tangles of uprooted trees, smashed houses, strewn wreckage from spaceships, tongues of lava thrust out into the steaming ocean, dead fish, feeding giant crabs, dead Stath, and demand, "Do you call this self-control?"

The colonists insist that the elders remember what the Stath were doing at the time. The elders say, "We don't approve of their depravity. But what did *you* do?"

The colonists hang their heads and mumble. The elders say, "Did you have to use a sledgehammer to squash a gnat? Don't you know what you can do with small measures rightly timed? How long do you think it's going to take to straighten out this mess? Where was all this vaunted self-control we've heard about?"

In accordance with standard procedure, I have sent in my final signed report on this situation by facsimile, one copy to you, and four copies to Major T. Moley Lammer for transmittal through channels to Sector HQ, Colonization Council, et cetera. The report was strictly factual, but I have already gotten a long reply from which I quote the following:

Without definitely saying so, this report raises the clear implication that the natural disturbances on Cyrene IV were somehow caused by the colonists and their odd religious cult. I cannot initial this report as it stands. My communications technicians assure me that the phenomena connected with the attempted treaty transmission are not possible in the present state of the art. I will excuse this first report because of the extreme nervous strain you have experienced in the last few days. But, if you insist upon these hallucinations, I will find it my duty to report you for rest, rehabilitation, and, of course, psychiatric examination—

All I have done is to factually report what happened. I have the proofs here in front of me, and they support every statement. Lammer knows nothing about it, has not been here, has seen nothing, but does not hesitate to state that it is all a hallucination. Now what? Am I supposed to lie to please him, and thereby misinform higher authority?

From: Myron Baker, Capt., TSF
To: G. L. Park, 1st Lt., TSFR
Subject: Report
Sir:

Congratulations that the Rollo mess is out of the way.

As for your report, I am afraid there is a little gimmick you will have to become acquainted with. It is known as "Occam's Razor." It is expressed as follows: *"Essentia non sunt multiplicanda praeter necessitatem,"* which means, roughly, "Root causes should not be multiplied without necessity." As usually applied, it really means, "without *dire* necessity."

In other words, you are to be extremely careful about introducing new basic concepts into any discussion of physical facts. Occam's Razor is necessary to save us from getting overwhelmed with Vital Essences, Natural Tendencies, Mutual Affinities, and so on, to the point where they clog the mental machinery.

Now, Occam's Razor has one disadvantage. Rather than change any basic concept, we tend to introduce a host of corrections and refinements to existing concepts. The resulting mental picture of reality is like the Ptolemaic picture of the universe. The picture becomes extremely complex, for want of changing a basic concept.

The Copernican picture, by contrast, is comparatively simple and easy to understand, because a change was made in the basic concept. But note that Copernicus did not publish his system till just before he died. The authorities, except in rare cases, are wholeheartedly in favor of Occam's Razor.

In fact, they often carry it further, knock off the last couple of words, and change it to Occam's Procrustian Bed: "Root causes should not be multiplied." Any fact or occurrence that does not fit present theories either gets stretched out or chopped off, to make it fit.

Your report introduces the concept that it is possible to affect the physical universe by some other process than the familiar "desire-intent-muscular contraction" process. This is a basic change of concept.

It seems to me, you will have to somehow make your report fit the present accepted concepts, in order to even get it into the records.

Be careful you don't change the facts. But do your best to dredge up some interpretation that appears to fit accepted concepts.

From: T. Moley Lammer, Major, TSF
To: G. L. Park, 1st Lt., TSFR
Subject: Report
Sir:

I am being pressed by higher authority for your report and full supporting documents on the Cyrene IV situation. Kindly send these as soon as possible.

Let me again warn you that an incoherent, fantastic, or unscientific report will be considered evidence of the necessity for your immediate removal from command responsibility.

Send me at once a brief précis of the situation, *in comprehensible form,* that I may forward in reply to urgent queries.

From: G. L. Park, 1st Lt., TSFR
To: Myron Baker, Capt., TSF
Subject: Further developments
Sir:

From recent conversations with these elders, it appears to me that they are well aware of having us in a bind. We disbelieve their theories, but, somehow or other, we now have to explain what happened. How can we possibly do that without getting some enlightenment jammed into our skulls whether we like it or not?

It appears to me that the elders have worked things so that we, the Stath, and their own overconfident younger colonists, have all gotten a stiff jolt to the midsection out of this. Maybe this self-control stuff has something to it after all.

Anyway, I hope your advice about the report is right, as I have just received an urgent demand from the major.

Wish me luck. I see I have got to fabricate a *scientific* explanation for what happened here.

From: G. L. Park, 1st Lt., TSFR
To: T. Moley Lammer, Major, TSF
Subject: Report
Sir:

Permit me to express my gratitude for your understanding and consideration.

Pursuant to your request for a précis covering developments in the situation, I enclose the following:

"On March 2, 2416, at 0817 hrs., TGT, Temporary Scouting and Reconnaissance Detachment 4662, consisting of four T6J scout ships, five T7 scout ships, and one T7A scout ship converted to command ship, carrying a total force of one hundred eighty-three men and four commissioned officers, 1st Lt. Gene L. Park, TSFR, Cmdg., landed on the day side of the planet Cyrene IV. Our mission was to: 1) warn the colonists of the imminent possibility of Stath or Ursoid occupation; and 2) if possible, persuade the colonists to join the Federation of Humanity.

"Due to the theological resistance of the colonists to Federation, the signing of the treaty was delayed until word of the imminent arrival of a Stath Invasion Fleet, consisting of twenty-eight ships, including transports. The completed treaty was obtained only at the last moment, and by dint of very strong and insistent urging.

"There now occurred an additional delay, which may be satisfactorily explained only in the light of subsequent developments. Transmission of the completed treaty to the watch ship overhead was garbled repeatedly. Thus when the Stath Invasion Fleet arrived it proved impossible to present them with the required certified copy of the treaty. We were now also notified by a representative of the colonists that the latter wished us not to transmit the treaty to the watch ship, as they considered it to be invalid, owing to their aforementioned religious scruples.

"The Stath Invasion Fleet then landed on the planet. The colonists attempted to welcome them with feasts and flowers, but violence broke out almost immediately.

"The colonists having destroyed our case by repudiating the treaty, the Stath immediately invoked the Triracial Mutual Nonaggression

Pact to assure our noninterference in the affairs of the occupation, but granted us permission, for the time being, to remain on the planet.

"The Stath occupation proceeded with its customary violence and brutality, until celebration of the Stath ceremony of *kranolol* was begun on March 26, 2416, at 0916 TGT.

"Prior to this time, there had occurred a number of minor but unusual meteorological disturbances, including severe winds, sandstorms, waterspouts, and local storms of unusual character.

"There now occurred a major seismological disturbance, culminating in near worldwide volcanic activity. Storms of hurricane force, coupled with earthquakes, tidal waves, and an uprising of the enslaved colonists, terminated the Stath occupation in a wave of catastrophe and bloodshed from which only one Stath ship is known to have escaped. No casualties to Temp. S. and R. Det. 4662 resulted from this storm.

"The colonists attribute their deliverance to a form of divine intervention.

"The failure of transmission, carefully investigated without satisfactory result at the time, may now be attributed to high-level electromagnetic disturbances in the atmosphere, contingent upon the extraordinary meteorological conditions obtaining at the time.

"Following relief and rescue operations on the planet Cyrene IV, Temporary Scout and Reconnaissance Detachment 4662 is continuing its efforts to persuade the colonists to join the Federation of Humanity."

From: T. Moley Lammer, Major, TSF
To: G. L. Park, 1st Lt., TSFR
Subject: Report
Sir:

I am forwarding your brief report immediately.

Let me congratulate you on the clarity, brevity, and soundness of this new communication. In contrast to your previous message, this explanation of the difficulties on Cyrene IV is truly scientific.

Kindly hasten your full report concerning the situation on Cyrene IV.

CANTOR'S WAR

Major-General A. C. Hewell stood in the dimly lit, glassed in balcony that overlooked the glowing white wall that illumined the rows of Space Force men and women down below at their computerized control centers.

Beside General Hewell stood a young colonel wearing a compact headset, who now said, "Density seventeen, sir. Plus one."

Hewell nodded, and one of the other two men in the room, a well-built expensively-dressed civilian, said, "Pardon me, General. That means—"

"Seventeen enemy warships per standard Tau-space unit, Senator."

"Which is an increase of one since the last reading," Hewell added.

"And the attacks usually come through—" The Senator looked a question.

"When the density is twenty-four or above."

"I see. Now, this large glowing wall-size screen before us—"

"Shows a schematic representation of Tau-space. It's impossible, of course, for a three-dimensional screen to represent Tau-space accurately. Roughly, this screen represents a cross-section. The center stands for an arbitrary fixed point in Tau-space. The scale changes as you move from the center toward the edge of the screen. The edge represents a space immeasurably far from the center. Enemy ships we show by silver dots. There are always enemy ships present."

The general turned to speak to the young colonel, and a moment later the contrast of the screen changed so that a multitude of silvery dots could be seen, like tiny darting minnows, in the central portion of the screen. These dots grew rapidly smaller as the eye glanced out toward the edge, to blend into a silvery background that merged at last into a silver rim around the edge of the screen.

"And," said the Senator, with a note of profound curiosity, "with a density of seventeen per standard unit—of *volume?*—I suppose—"

"That's right. Tau-space volume."

"—in this Tau space," the senator went on, "with a *density* of seventeen per unit, what's their *total strength* in there?"

"Infinite," said the general immediately.

The fourth man, possibly thirty years old, tall, and intellectual-appearing, spoke for the first time, his voice sharp. *"Infinite?"*

The sharp questioning tone caused the general to turn, and the colonel to look up momentarily.

"That's right," said the general.

"I would question that," said the fourth man, his voice sharp and critical, "unless you use the word merely in the lay sense of 'large beyond our ability to measure.'"

The general frowned, trying to place the peculiar quality of this voice. He glanced around. "You haven't introduced your friend, Senator."

The senator apologized. "This is Dr. T. Binding Phipps, General. Dr. Phipps, General Hewell. Dr. Phipps is a mathematician and a former classmate of my son Alex. Dr. Phipps happened to be with the committee when your report on this situation was circulated; his comments on it were so pointed and so interesting that I thought I'd bring him along. Dr. Phipps and my daughter—" The senator cleared his throat, let the sentence trail out unfinished so that the general groped for a moment after the precise nature of the relationship implied, then shrugged.

"Glad to have you with us, Dr. Phipps," he said.

Dr. Phipps inclined his head in bare acknowledgment.

The colonel said. "Density eighteen, sir. Plus one."

The general nodded.

"Might I ask," said the senator's companion abruptly, "how you determine the size of this presumed unit of volume?"

The general glanced at the senator, who looked benevolent and noncommittal.

"I think, Dr. Phipps," said the general with careful courtesy, "that Colonel Smith can answer your question better than I."

The colonel glanced around. "What was the question again, Dr. Phipps?"

"Precisely how do you determine the size of this presumed unit of volume?"

The question came over with a snap suggestive of the crack of a whip, but the colonel, after a pause, answered evenly.

"We don't *determine* it. It's a question of a repeated elementary volume that goes to make up the so-called 'Tau-space.' Another name for Tau-space is 'multiple space.' It's a space that's repeated, over and over."

"That evades my question rather neatly," said Dr. Phipps, a drill-like note evident in his voice, "rather than answering it. This inconsistency was sufficiently obvious in the report."

The colonel blinked; the general frowned. The senator looked on blandly.

"Perhaps," said the general, "we're working at cross-purposes here. There's no question about the facts."

The colonel, noting the sharpness in the general's voice and the perceptibly reddening face, said quickly, "Dr. Phipps, possibly I misunderstood your question. You asked, didn't you, how we determined the size—that is, volume—of this elementary unit when we say, for instance, that the density of enemy ships in Tau-space is seventeen or eighteen?"

"That is essentially correct." The drill-like tone gave the sensation of biting through into a nerve. "And your answer manifestly evaded the issue."

The general stiffened, and glanced sharply at the senator. The senator said nothing, continued to look on benevolently.

The colonel said carefully, "That depends on your meaning when you say 'determine,' Dr. Phipps. We don't *determine* volume in the sense that we might determine a volume of ordinary space."

"Why not, if I might ask?"

"For one thing, we can't enter Tau-space. If we send a human observer through, he comes back spread all over the inside of the ship—if we're lucky enough to get the ship back at all, that is. Then, too, we can't readily measure the volume in terms of normal space because of certain anomalous features of Tau-space."

"Then, in short, you don't have a unit volume."

"In terms of *normal* space, no. I can't say the unit volume in Tau-space is so-many cubic light-years, for instance, without creating a false mental picture. But for our purposes, we have a unit volume. It is simply the *volume of unit reception.* I'll be happy to explain what I mean by that if you're interested."

Dr. Phipps frowned as if uncertain whether it was worth bothering, but the senator said, "If you would, Colonel, we'd very much appreciate it."

The colonel said, "It's been an unusual experience for us, sir, and it's a little hard to grasp, even yet. You see, these raiders burst out to attack our local Space Center, rip up nearby cargo routes, then vanished back into what was apparently subspace. Our natural reaction was to follow them in, track them through, and find out where they came out. With manned ships, as I've mentioned, this proved disastrous. So we tried unmanned ships. Each unmanned ship we sent in had an ident-device whose function was simply to create a signal that would locate the ship. As soon as each of our ships went into what we supposed to be subspace the ident-display went insane. It was as if you tossed a glowing light-tube into a hall of mirrors, and got back images of an infinite number of images."

"You mean," Dr. Phipps interrupted patronizingly, "an indeterminate number of light-tubes."

The general drew his breath in slowly, as if timing it.

The colonel waited till the roaring went out of his ears, then said politely, "In this case, the ident-signal, which ordinarily measures Tau-distances by turning a needle over a precise distance on a dial, sent the needle spinning endlessly, as the same signal came in simultaneously from an infinite number of positions. When I say infinite, that is what I mean."

"I doubt," said Dr. Phipps, "that you are professionally qualified to appreciate the meaning of 'infinite.'"

There was a lengthy silence in which the senator, after first looking benignly at the colonel and the general, took out a cigar, lit it, continued to gaze benignly through a cloud of smoke. Meanwhile, the colonel struggled successfully not to do or say any of the things that it occurred to him to do or say, and finally was able to swallow and breathe in a more-or-less normal rhythm. But a certain light-headedness warned him to stand still and keep his mouth shut.

The senator, apparently to get the ball rolling again, said, "That's interesting, Colonel. I begin to get a picture the report didn't give. Now—"

Dr. Phipps said, "It presents nothing new whatever. The picture this presents is so—"

"Now, Binding," said the senator chidingly, "you're a Ph.D. and this is all in your field—but we laymen here have to potter and bumble around trying to find some handle on the thing so we can get a grip on it. Try to unjack yourself down onto our level. How are *you* going to understand how a layman sees these things, eh? No, when Colonel Smith was explaining that about the ident-signal, I began to get his point."

"There is no point. It would be preposterous to assume—"

"Tut, tut, Binding. *Are you professionally qualified to understand a layman?*"

Dr. Phipps opened his mouth, shut it in evident confusion.

The colonel's ears seemed to pop, and now he had the impression of being his normal self again. He said, "Senator, this is hard to explain. For one thing, we frankly don't pretend to know what's going on here. The *effect* is as if when we send a single ship through, it is reproduced an infinite number of times and so we detect it at an infinite number of positions. However, each ship is separately present in its own finite volume of space, which apparently remains constant—this is the 'volume of unit reception,' I was referring to. If we send six or seven ships through the entire group appears in each unit of volume."

Dr. Phipps made as if to object, then hesitated in perplexity—apparently hamstrung by the thought that he might not really have any idea what thoughts were being conveyed in laymen language.

The senator said, "And it's an optical-illusion kind of thing?"

"Well," said the colonel. "we thought so at first, but we've discovered that by a development of our remote-control technique we can concentrate two or more of these identical 'ships' in the same region—which would seem impossible if they were mere reflections of some one basic ship. By repeating a sort of subspace jump within Tau-space, we've concentrated up to several thousand ships within one given unit of Tau-space."

"When," asked the senator, "you'd only sent a few ships in there to start with?"

"Yes, sir. Unbelievable as it may seem."

"And when you come to get them out—then what?"

The colonel hesitated, and the general said, "Once we've gone through this hocus-pocus of concentrating a number of ships in one region, we don't *get* the ship out again."

"*No* ship?"

"No, sir. The ships, or 'quasi-images' of ships, or whatever they are, apparently have to be distributed, one to each and every unit of Tau-space—and positioned properly in the given units—in order for us to get back the original ship. Otherwise nothing happens; the ship stays in there."

"What happens to the ones that don't come back?"

"Well, it's hard to say what would happen if we could experiment at our leisure in there. But that isn't possible. There are always enemy ships in there, in infinite numbers just as ours are, and we're generally heavily outnumbered, so—"

"*No!*" Dr. Phipps put in sharply.

The colonel shut his eyes. The general looked around and said courteously, "Did you say something, Dr. Phipps?"

"Yes." Dr. Phipps seemed to be struggling with some awkward and unwieldy problem—possibly that of projecting his meaning down to the lay level. "Excuse me. But you said that you were *outnumbered.* You said that your ships were there in infinite numbers, just as theirs were, yet you were *outnumbered.*"

"Correct. We may be outnumbered twenty to one, or momentarily, it may be as close as sixteen to twelve. The point is, we usually go in there to try and find a way through. We don't stick around if it doesn't work—and it hasn't yet—because in a very short time they close in on us and we get eliminated. The difficulty is that we don't have enough remote-controlled ships to overpower them. They outnumber us. If we could put manned ships in there ..."

"Oh," said Dr. Phipps, "this is—this is simply—" He cleared his throat. "That is not, of course, my special field, but surely Cantor's Theorem covers this problem adequately."

The senator said, "Remember, Binding—we're just laymen. Whose theorem?"

"Cantor's." He cleared his throat. "Let me express it this way.

If we have two infinite series—say the series of integers: 1, 2, 3, 4, 5, 6, etc., and the series of *even* integers: 2, 4, 6, etc., and if these two series can be placed in one-to-one correspondence with each other, thusly—" He pulled out a piece of paper, to write:

1 2 3 4 5 6 7 8 . . .
2 4 6 8 10 12 14 16 . . .

"Then," he added, "it follows that the two series are *equally* numerous, since each series can be continued indefinitely—forever. Your problem is precisely analogous."

There was a brief silence, then the colonel said, "This is Cantor's Theorem?"

"Well, certainly it's a very elementary example—"

"But this theorem *does* say there are just as many *even* integers as there are odd *and* even integers together?"

"That is correct."

The colonel took the paper, and wrote:

1 2 3 4 5 6 7 8 9 10 . . .
2 4 6 8 10 . . .

"This," he said, "matches about the most favorable situation we're usually ever in. I'd say we were outnumbered two-to-one, wouldn't you?"

"Not at all."

"We *aren't?*"

"Certainly not. Any class the elements of which may be placed in one-to-one correspondence with the elements of another class is equal in cardinality—that is, in numerousness—with the other class. *That* is Cantor's Theorem."

The general said, "Let's see that paper."

There was a long silence. Then the general looked up.

"I've got to admit, I don't quite understand what we're up against here. Not if this theorem is true."

"There's no question at all of that," said Dr. Phipps. "Cantor's Theorem is completely accepted."

"Well, then—that gives us a way out of this hole."

The colonel said, "Sir. If we're outnumbered two-to-one in each and every one of an *infinite number* of finite regions, which is the situation we're up against here, I don't see how it's going to equalize matters for us if we juggle ships around from one region to another."

Dr. Phipps said, "Your error lies in assuming that you are outnumbered."

"We *are* outnumbered."

"You are not."

The colonel said exasperatedly, "Suppose there are thirty-six of their ships in each unit of space, to only one of our ships? Surely *then* we're outnumbered!"

"Not at all. What you seek is to compare the series of integers with the series comprising every thirty-sixth integer. Now, from any denumerable class, there may be removed a denumerable infinite number of denumerable infinite classes, without affecting the cardinality of the class. Therefore—"

"I can't follow that," said the colonel exasperatedly.

"The lay mentality," said Dr. Phipps, "has some difficulty in handling the infinite and its paradoxes. Naturally, a certain degree of professional education and training is a prerequisite."

The colonel swallowed hard, said nothing.

The general said, "If they have a density of thirty-six ships per each unit of space throughout the region to our density of one, then we have as many ships as they have?"

"Certainly." Dr. Phipps wrote:

    1 2 3 4 5 6...
    36 72 108 144 180 216...

He held out the paper and said, "Since you can match the series of integers one-for-one with the series of every thirty-sixth integer, it follows that the two series are equal in respect to numerosity."

The general looked at the paper. "Cantor's Theorem supports this?"

"It does."

"And Cantor's Theorem is accepted as valid?"

"Certainly."

"Well— That's *fine*. What we run up against, you see, is that if our ship-density starts to approach theirs, they increase theirs faster than we can increase ours. Now if actually they *don't outnumber us,* we can get control in there because our Class I ships are individually superior to the enemy type of ship. Now, excuse me, doctor, for asking this next question, but a good deal of expensive equipment can be lost if we make a wrong move. Are you really qualified to give opinions on the infinite as you've just been doing?"

"Certainly. While this is not my particular special field of study, this has all been quite elementary."

"All right, I'll take your word for it. We'll try it. *Colonel!*"

"Sir?"

"Order one Class I Tau-ship set up to make the jump."

"Yes, sir."

The general turned to the senator. "You'll get a chance to see, Senator, just how the command-center here functions. And if this works we won't be screaming for another big appropriation on this for quite a while."

Dr. Phipps finished giving his instructions for "matching" the two fleets, ship-for-ship; the general gazed off at the huge screen thoughtfully; and the senator walked over to the colonel, and said in a low voice, "Do you think this is going to work, Colonel?"

The colonel shrugged. "I couldn't guess. The way he's had us set that up, we've got ships coming on the flying jump from all over the place, in order to match up with the enemy ships at the head of that complex curve that he starts in the 'center' of Tau-space, and then twists out from there to finally include everything else. He says we can match them ship-for-ship, because we can *always* draw in more ships; so it's bound to come out even—I don't know."

The senator nodded, and drew on his cigar. "Well, either way, we win."

"How do you figure?"

"If he's right, we win in Tau-space; one of our Class I ships will beat an enemy ship, won't it?"

"Yes, but if it doesn't work out, and we're outnumbered, then we lose the ship. How do we win?"

"There are no men in this ship?"

"No, sir. It's unmanned."

"Well," said the senator, lowering his voice, "if we *lose,* then T.

Binder Phipps, Ph.D., falls flat on his face, and there is nothing I would more dearly love to see."

The now familiar dental-drill tone bit into their conversation. "General, I have checked the procedures. The matching process is entirely to my satisfaction. You may proceed at any time."

The senator growled, "How would you like to have *that* for a prospective son-in-law?"

The colonel shivered.

"In his natural state," said the senator, "he would be bad enough. But the refulgent rays of glory from his Ph.D. are forever poking me in the eye, or getting stuck crosswise halfway down my throat."

The colonel glanced at the senator. "But suppose that Cantor himself was wrong."

The senator grinned. "That's better yet. Then Binder gets to explain how a Recognized Authority In The Field could make a mistake."

"Is that so impossible?"

"For Binder it is. Binder is solid for Authority. Put him back in the Middle Ages and he'd chop Galileo's head off in a minute for arguing that a heavy weight and a light weight fall at the same speed when Aristotle said otherwise. How you can have a Believer In Sacred Authority in either mathematics or science beats me, but the bigger a field gets, the more of them migrate in and set up shop."

The general's voice said, "Density, Colonel?"

"Eighteen, sir. No change."

"Proceed."

The colonel spoke briefly into his microphone.

The big screen on the opposite wall was abruptly tinged pale-blue.

The senator said, "That bluish color—"

The general said, "One of their ships creates a silvery-white appearance on the screen. One of ours, a blue appearance. Since we're heavily outnumbered, the screen remains white, tinged with blue." He paused. "Ah—here we go."

In center of the screen, a bright blue dot had appeared, then put forth spiral arms, which, bright-blue in color, began to grow, then to curve in and out in a complex geometrical pattern that grew to fill up a small region at the center of the screen, then bend outward again—

"Minus twenty," said the colonel.

The general said, "With a concentration such as they have in there right now, we can only count on about twenty seconds, our time out here, till the enemy makes contact and starts to hit us."

Dr. Phipps said, "As you may observe, the region of one-to-one correspondence is expanding steadily."

It was true. In the huge, wall-size screen, the dark-blue area had now attained the proportions of a garbage-can lid.

"Yes," said the senator, "but it looks to me like it's expanding slower."

"Possibly, but only proportionately so. No limiting volume is involved. Of course, we must progressively obtain matching ships from further and further away. Since the supply is infinite, this is irrelevant."

The colonel said, "Minus fifteen."

The dark-blue disk now had an intense white ring around it, shading off gradually to pale-blue toward the edge of the screen.

The senator asked, "Why that intense white color?"

The general, evidently concerned, said, "Those must be the regions our ships were moved in *from,* in order to make a match in the center. Dr. Phipps, I thought you said—"

Dr. Phipps said impatiently, "It isn't important, general. We are dealing with *infinities.* All this has been taken into account."

The intense white ring faded out in a series of pulses to pale-blue around the growing dark-blue disk. But as the white faded to blue around the disk, the blue all around the rim of the screen paled noticeably at the inside edge. The disk added another few inches of diameter, the pale-blue around it bleached out to white again, and there glowed a glaring white ring several times larger than before.

The colonel said, "Minus ten."

"M'm," said the general, eyeing the dazzling-white ring around the blue disk. With a series of pulses, the inner part of this ring, next to the disk, faded to pale-blue, and, in due course, the disk built up again, as elsewhere on the screen the pale-blue leached out everywhere except at and near the very edge of the screen, and then there was a huge glaring region of dazzling white that made the disk in the center look smaller instead of bigger.

"Of course," said the general, "this screen gives us just a schematic representation, but—"

Dr. Phipps said, "Everything is proceeding quite satisfactorily, General."

The colonel said, "Minus five."

The general cleared his throat. "Contact will almost certainly be established in five seconds, and firing will begin automatically. Destruction of one element of the enemy's force will create a yellow flash on the screen. A red flash will signify the destruction of one of our force."

The blue disk expanded. Around it, the white ring expanded further.

"Zero," said the colonel.

All around the extreme rim of the screen was a brief pinkish light as the as yet unmatched human ships were destroyed. In the center, the blue lit with a mingling of yellow and red that faded out to a paler blue, as the individually-stronger human ships won out. Then the untouched ring of dazzling white squeezed in with a reddish glare that ate straight to the center of the blue disk, then faded out to leave one solid bright silvery-whiteness on the screen from end to end.

The general turned around and looked at Dr. Phipps.

The senator shook his head. "Well, General, I see *that* method won't beat them. I'll relate this incident to the committee when we get back."

Dr. Phipps said, "I—I don't—" The others waited for him to go on, but he only stared at the blank white screen, from which the blue had been wiped off with ridiculous ease.

The colonel turned and glanced at the general. "If I might ask Dr. Phipps a few questions, sir."

"Go right ahead."

"Dr. Phipps," said the colonel, "In this matching procedure you take a unit in one series, move it up to match it to one in the other series, and when you have a method by which you can match them one for one, you say they're equal, right?"

Phipps drew in a long ragged breath.

"That is correct."

"But at any given time, the *matched* parts of the two series are *finite,* aren't they? The parts of the series of digits, and the series of *even* digits, for instance, that you used as an example. Even after you've matched a million, a billion, or a quintillion terms, still, the part that's matched is *finite*, isn't it?"

"I—this is not— Well, I suppose that *is* correct."

"Then you're determining the comparative sizes of two infinite series by taking a finite end of each?"

"Ah—"

"And then, since the finite ends of each—which are always insignificant compared to the rest of the series—since these finite *ends* match, then you say the infinite remainders, which you *haven't* compared, but have only drawn numbers from—you say therefore *they* must be the same size, too? Is that right?"

Phipps mopped his forehead. "Ah—I'm afraid the difficulty is that the matching process must run on infinitely—then each of the two matched ends is infinite in length."

"Nevertheless, there remains the other end, that *isn't matched*, from which you're still drawing numbers for the matched end of the series. The procedure you use to match the series *only matches one end*, doesn't it?"

Dr. Phipps grappled with this problem, and a lengthy silence followed.

The colonel said, "Now, Dr. Phipps, just to clear the thing up, I'd like to ask you if this same matching method could be used, for example, to compare an infinite number of spaceships with an infinite number of pilots, assuming that exactly one-half of all the ships have a pilot, and the other half of the ships have no pilot. Could we use Cantor's method to find out *whether there are more pilots or spaceships?*"

"Yes. Yes, we could. Very easily."

"All right. Every alternate ship has a pilot locked inside. How do we use the method?"

"Well, we—ah—we line up the ships, and then we line the pilots up right beside them, one-for-one, which shows that there are an equal number of ships and pilots."

"Only every other ship has a pilot, but when we use this method, they come out even?"

"That is correct. There is a one-to-one correspondence."

"In other words, we match pilots to ships, by putting a pilot in the second ship in the line, for instance, using a pilot we took from further back somewhere?"

"Yes. We put pilots in the second, fourth, sixth, and eighth ships, and so on, to get a one-to-one correspondence between ships and pilots."

"All right. Let's go back to this first pilot that you put on the number two ship. *Where did you get him?* Remember, one-half of the ships have pilots, locked inside, one-half have no pilots at all. There are no loose pilots lying around. You had to get the pilot somewhere."

"Yes. I see."

"Now, when you put a pilot in ship number two, to start this one-to-one correspondence, *where do you get him from?*"

"I—ah—I took him from some ship somewhere else."

"So you take the pilot out of a piloted ship?"

"Yes."

"And you use that pilot to pilot ship number 2?"

"Yes. Exactly."

"Then, all you do is move the pilot around. Obviously, no matter how you switch the pilots around, if every time you put one pilot into a ship, here, you have to get him by taking one pilot *out* of a ship there, then there's no change in the overall ratio of piloted to unpiloted ships."

Phipps blinked. "Let's see now . . . That would seem to be correct . . . Yes. That is correct. Obviously, no matter *how* the pilots are transferred, there remain just as many unpiloted ships as piloted ones. Because, every time we put a pilot *in* one ship, we first take a pilot *out* of another ship. This is perfectly clear. The ratio of pilots to ships remains constant, overall. Necessarily, taking the entire region into account, that ratio is *fixed*."

"Then," said the colonel, "we've just shown that there are always as many unpiloted as piloted ships or, in other words, two ships for each pilot, or *twice as many* ships as pilots. Yet, with Cantor's method, you say you can 'prove' the number of ships and pilots to be equal. After setting up a procedure to match one pilot to each ship at the head end of the line, and incidentally piling up a lot of empty ships in the other end of the line, then you claim that the non-representative, stacked-deck condition you've set up in the front end *also* holds in the other part—which you have only looted and never counted—and on *this* basis you claim that you have compared the two series as a whole, and thus can 'prove' that they are equal. By matching one pilot to each ship at one end, you 'prove' there are as many pilots as ships. But, all the time, you're getting these extra pilots by emptying hosts of ships, which empty ships accumulate exactly fast enough to maintain the ratio of two ships for each pilot, *but you intentionally don't count these empty ships.* You call this a valid method?"

There was a lengthy silence.

Finally Phipps said hollowly, "I thought when I first heard it that there was something I didn't grasp about this method. But I knew if such an authority as Dr. Cantor used the method, it must be correct. I was puzzled, but—if I'd asked questions, it might have seemed that I didn't understand. I—I wanted to succeed, so I kept my mouth shut. And then—" Suddenly he seemed to hear how all this sounded, and abruptly stopped talking.

The general said curiously, "You 'wanted to succeed,' so you 'kept your mouth shut'?"

The senator cleared his throat, but after a momentary pause Phipps went on more confidently. "Of course, it must just be that Dr. Cantor himself really means some other thing by this method than what we meant here. Yet I'm *certain* that was the sense of it as it was taught us—and as I've seen it elsewhere, many times."

The general said, "Maybe a few other people wanted to succeed, and kept *their* mouths shut when the thing wasn't clear to them either."

"And," said the senator blandly, "in due time got their Ph.D.'s and are now infallible Authorities In The Field."

Phipps winced, then moodily hauled himself erect and looked defiant.

The general shrugged. "Well, the damage is done. Senator, I think we can stop any serious breakout here. Naturally, in normal space, we can use our advantage in manned ships, and as both sides—again in normal space—have only a finite number of ships, we can handle them. But it means we're tied up here to prevent a breakout. And we can't follow them back and finish them until we can send a superior force into Tau-space after them."

The senator nodded pleasantly. "I understand, now, General, and I think you've proved your point convincingly. I'll say so to the committee. Well, we'll be going." The corner of his mouth lifted in an odd smile. "Come along, Binding, my boy. We'll have to tell Marylou all about our adventure when we get back, won't we?"

The two men went out, the one sunk in gloom, the other genial and expansive.

The general glanced at the colonel.

"What the deuce was *he* so happy about? Does he *like* defeats?"

The colonel shook his head.

"I got the impression, sir, that a certain prospective family member has had him a bit up-tight—he thinks he's succeeded in loosening up a Binding relationship."

UPLIFT THE SAVAGE

Darius Henning, Executive Director of the Terrestrial Aid and Development Mission on the planet Sigma, rammed a fresh charge into the stingbolt rifle, squinted at a blur moving in the gathering gloom, and squeezed the trigger.

There was a distant flash, and the high-pitched scream of an agonized Sigman. The scream faded into unconsciousness.

"Got the bastard," growled Henning.

Just to the left in the dimness, there was an indrawn feminine breath, which Henning ignored as he spoke into a little hand communicator.

"Henning speaking. Ralph, how far is that bunch from the wall?"

A faintly tinny voice replied, "No more than forty feet now. They're crawling up that narrow irrigation ditch, shoving oblong bronze shields along over their heads. The plasmoids hit the shields and ground out."

"How many of them are there?"

"Better than two dozen. Of course, we'll knock some off as they come over the wall. But they'll get in."

"You can't stop them?"

"Not a chance. Along here, it's only eight feet from the bank to the top of the wall."

"Who's in the next guard post?"

"George Hazlitt."

"You'd better both pull back to the crosswall. Once they're in, there's too much chance of spoiling the whole crop if you fire at them. And, Ralph, be sure you don't stick your neck out."

There was a sarcastic exclamation at Henning's shoulder. Henning ignored her, but Ralph's comment showed that he'd heard.

"I won't take any foolish chances, Chief. But just incidentally, if we want to get rid of that female spy, now's the time. Why not send her out to interview some Sigmen? This nearest batch has their hot sloth grease and lizard scales right with them. I can smell the stuff from here."

Henning grunted. It took something for an Earthwoman to be disliked so fast on a planet like this. But she had what it took. He spoke warningly into the phone. "Be sure you pull back in time."

"Don't worry, we will. No matter *what* we do, this bunch is going to get away with some groundwheat."

Henning agreed, switched off the communicator, and flipped on the nearby monitor screen. He crouched low by the parapet as the dim red outline showed him the steady approach of a chain of blobs along the dark line of the irrigation ditch. Other blobs surrounded the Aid and Development station, and were now spread out from a hundred to five hundred feet away. Henning flipped off the screen, and squinted into the darkness. Out there about a hundred feet, a deeper shadow slowly glided closer.

The shadow stopped.

Henning cautiously raised his gun.

There was a whir, a rush of air, and the thud of a padded arrow against the wall to his left.

Henning gently squeezed the trigger.

Out in the darkness, there was a brief flash.

A hideous scream told Henning he'd hit his target.

Beside him, there was a sarcastic feminine murmur, "*Got the bastard.*"

Henning straightened, and eyed the nearby shadow. There beside him in the gloom stood a hundred and twenty-eight pounds of delightfully-curved femininity, with a face that showed beauty, character, and intelligence; and the only impulse Henning felt was an urgent desire to slap a length of adhesive plaster across her mouth.

"Oh," came her voice, in itself clear and pleasant, "you *brave* men! And all you have on your side, against these *fierce* natives,

is your own courage, your bare hands, and—an interstellar technology!"

Henning turned away, peered into the darkness, and wondered
why eyes had lids, and ears didn't.

An arrow whizzed past, missing him narrowly.

A quick glance at the monitor screen showed that the Sigmen
were easing in closer, and forming into several loose-knit groups
around the station.

The breeze, which had been shifting and veering since sundown
chose this instant to blow from a new direction, carrying to Henning a trace of the fresh fragrance of the woman's perfume. The
tantalizing scent left him dizzy, but the wind of the passing arrow
snapped him back to reality.

It came to Henning as the arrow thudded against the wall, that
something definite was going to have to be done about her, and
done soon. A pretty unattached woman like this took his men's
minds off their work. She took *his* mind off his work. She was
physically desirable, but with a personality like cider turned to
vinegar. To Henning, it seemed one of the worst possible com-
binations. First his men were attracted, then they were rebuffed,
and to top it off, the woman had a string of academic degrees,
and was out here as the emissary of an independent outfit that
was evaluating the aid and development program. In Henning's
view, she was the exact type, already mentally overstuffed with
ill-digested knowledge, that found it impossible to assimilate a new
idea. There was just no place to fit a new idea *in*. For this very
reason, she was also the exact type that could turn in a ruinous
report with an air of overpowering authority. That Darius Henning's
superiors had foreseen this exact possibility was shown by the
letter that had arrive for him on the same ship as the woman:

Darius:

I don't know if you've heard of the Brumbacher
Foundation, but, believe me, it has a lot of prestige.
The stated purpose of this foundation is to "combine
liberal social aims with conservative fiscal practices, thus
to attain sound governmental policies." I won't try to
guess whether this aim is wise or even possible. My
worries are on a somewhat lower level.

You have doubtless long since received our notification

that one P. L. Forsythe, B.A., B.S., M.S., Ph.D., Ph.D. (Intem.), Soc.D. (Sr.), F.S.I.S., F.T.S.S., F.C.I.A.S., is on the way to carry out for the Brumbacher Foundation an analysis of our practices on Sigma. What we did not care to put into the communications record is the fact that the Appropriations Committee looks on a Brumbacher Report as the next thing to Gospel Truth. This could be awkward, to put it mildly.

As you know, long and painful experience has shown the field men of the Terrestrial Aid and Development Administration that doing good and extending a helping hand is not quite as easy and simple as it looks. Even when the inhabitants of a planet are to all intents and purposes human, little complications can tie our beneficent intentions in knots. It can be an expensive proposition to cram culture down the throats of several hundred million violently-resisting savages. When we try it, our ideas remain our ideas, not theirs. To get them to act as we want, we are, therefore, reduced either to bribing them or to sticking guns in their ribs. The cooperation we get by either method lacks enthusiasm. We end up putting props under a stooge government with no local support, and wind up with a burdensome liability instead of an asset.

Past experience shows that if we should try, for instance, to introduce groundwheat on Sigma by the obvious method of handing out free seed plants, it would be a matter of centuries before we get the groundwheat established. The Sigmen are primitive but intelligent. Their chiefs are bound to suspect such generosity, since their past experience shows that there must be an ulterior motive. The only way to get the groundwheat established fast would seem to be to throw out the chiefs and put in people chosen by us.

But, if we do that, for that very reason they will lack local support. There will *still* be no enthusiasm for the groundwheat. The idea of planting it will remain ours, not theirs. Operating on a limited budget, with limited time to get results, we can't use such backward methods. What we want is for these planets to be well-disposed to us, and to have something to trade when our frontiers are advanced far enough so that we are ready to trade with them.

In order to accomplish this, we have to use methods that will work. What this boils down to is that the ideas for progress have to end up as *theirs*. That is the only known practical way to get them to put their full force behind the work.

This is a very simple fact, but I am afraid that P. L. Forsythe, Soc.D. (Sr.) will not get it. Her liberal aims will lead her to think we should hand the inhabitants the means of progress on a platter; her conservative economics will tell her it would be cheaper to do it that way. She lacks the experience to see that this simple-minded method would cost us a hundred times as much in the end, and still wouldn't work. When a man wants a woman, the obvious, simple, straightforward way to get her is: Grab her. Several hundred thousand years of experience have taught the human race that there are less obvious ways that work better.

If our emissary from the Brumbacher Foundation liked a man, I am reasonably sure she wouldn't just strip to show him how desirable she was, and thereby prove that he should embrace her at once. But that is just the level the conventional aid and development approach operates on: "Here is something obviously great. You've got to want it—even you can see that. And we'll help you get it, out of the kindness of our hearts. All right, now. Here it is. *Want* it. Embrace it!"

Well, now, back to our specific problem. I won't presume to tell you how to handle this woman. As a matter of fact I wouldn't know what to say. I see from her identification photo that she is not at all bad-looking, and the accompanying medical height-weight et cetera, will bear that out, so at least she may prove to be decorative. But with her lack of first-hand knowledge of how we operate and why, she could unintentionally do a great deal of damage.

Dar, this woman and her Brumbacher Report could set human aid-and-development procedures back several hundred years.

I am relying on you to find some way to stop her.
Count on me to back you up.

Bill

Henning had read this letter half-a-dozen times. "Bill" was William S. Able, Chief of Bureau. Able had the reputation of being as good as his word. But before Able could back up Henning, Henning had to figure out what to do.

From down the wall in the gloom came the weird blast of an alien hunting horn. That signaled the arrival of the raiding party.

Immediately the rest of the Sigmen, facing the station on all sides, let out a hideous yell. The thud of padded arrows, and worse yet, the heavy *thunk* of dull-pointed javelins, gave warning of the covering attack that might or might not be driven home. Henning stepped back behind a high masonry shield, and yanked the whistle that hung on a cord around his neck, gripped it between his teeth, and blew a long blast.

To Henning's left front, a dim shadow moved.

With a shock, he realized that the woman was still by the parapet, exposed to the arrows, javelins, and hooked wooden burrs that were flying through the night. Angrily, he shouted, "Get down!"

The dim shadow turned, to say in a sweet voice: "I *do* hope you survive this dreadful attack. You must be heroic to face up to these pathetic children and their toy weapons."

It dawned on Henning that the fool thought anything primitive must be ineffectual.

He let the whistle drop on its cord, and moving in a crouch, so as to stay as much as possible behind the protecting parapet, he quickly pinned her knees with one arm, swung her off her feet, caught her upper body with his other arm, and dropped her flat.

There was a *whoosh* as a spear passed overhead, a jarring thud as it hit the shield, then a clatter and rattle as it dropped to the stone floor.

Then, in delayed response to his whistle, the lights dimly lit up.

The glow briefly showed Henning a vision of perfect femininity. She was apparently dazed, one arm raised as if to shield herself, and, for a change, her mouth was shut.

He reached out and jerked the spear across the floor. The shaft was of rough, heavy dark wood, the end wrapped in a pad the size of a baseball, covered with hide drawn tight around the shaft by shrunken rawhide thongs.

Her eyes followed his movement. She stared at the heavy spear.

"If you'd been standing," he said, "this would have hit you. It would have knocked you off your feet. Very possibly your head would have slammed into the floor or the shield, and cracked like an eggshell. Now either stay *low*, and close to the parapet, or else get back behind the shield."

He twisted away, crawled behind the shield, found his loophole, and began picking off the sprinting figures as they came racing through the dim glow toward the station.

From somewhere came the second blast of the Sigmen's horn, signaling their success in getting over the wall. The attackers faded back into the darkness.

Henning gave a blast on his whistle.

The lights faded, saving the feeble reserve power of the batteries. Somewhere, a *bang-bang* started up as the pathetic low-compression piston-engine got started, and began to turn over the pitiful generator.

"What a place," muttered Henning.

Stooping low to avoid getting flattened by a stray arrow or javelin, he snapped on the monitor screen. The Sigmen were retreating to a safe distance. Since there was no longer any need to cover the raiding party, they were now being very sparing of their weapons. Even without points, and left completely rough, the things took time and labor to make.

The woman's voice murmured, "Is it over?"

"Not yet. This is like the eye of a storm. The raiding party will take as many of the groundwheat plants as they can stuff into their leather bags. Then they'll give a blast on the horn and go over the wall. The ones on the outside will fling in spears and arrows to cover the withdrawal. We'll pick off a few of them. The majority will get away. *Then* it will *probably* be over. You can't be sure, but that's the usual pattern."

"But it's so *silly*. You were *sent* here to *distribute* the ground-wheat plants. Instead, you're fighting to keep the natives from getting them. It's . . ."

While she sought for a word to describe the situation, Henning raised the whistle, and stepped back behind the masonry shield. The Sigmen usually worked fast, and it was almost time.

Sure enough, the blast of a horn cut through the quiet.

"Stay down," he warned. He put the whistle between his teeth and blew hard.

A dim glow lit the shrubs and rolling grassy fields below. A single warrior was running in to launch a spear, but the rest were now content to keep farther back and use their bows.

A storm of arrows streaked through the pale light. A heavy spear rose toward him, and Henning took a shot at the solitary bold figure that had launched it. He narrowly missed, and didn't fire again till the warrior had sprinted nearly back to safety. Then he sent a sizzling bolt close behind him. A yell and a roar of laughter told him that he had gauged the shot to a nicety.

From the distance came a fresh blast on the horn, and a few victorious yells, silenced quickly by low gruff voices, and Henning again blew his whistle.

The already dim light faded out entirely. The generator labored on.

The woman said, "It's over?"

"Except for taking slaves."

"*Slaves!*"

"That's right," said Henning. "These tribes aren't rich. They generally live a little above subsistence. They're *intelligent*, but technologically backward."

"I know that. But what does that have to do with slavery?"

Henning squinted at her in the dimness. Very patiently, he said, "Where a race is technologically backward, the typical labor-saving devices are domesticated animals and slaves. Slaves are valuable."

"Oh." She sounded relieved. "You mean *they*, the *natives*, will take slaves."

"No," he growled, "not if *I* can help it. We will take the slaves." He listened in disgust to her horrified indrawing of breath, and added, "Obviously, we have to, because *they* value slaves, and believe in the system."

She sat up in a sudden angry motion, but Henning noticed that she stayed behind the parapet, "It's all so *confusing*! After all, I was sent out here to evaluate the methods and results on this planet. I find that in a little under twelve years, a hostile, very backward people, ruled by diehard ultraconservative chieftains, has made unprecedented progress. Agriculture has been introduced, schools opened, rudimentary commercial relations established—despite the fact that by and large, the same chiefs retain power. But the method! Here *you* are, actually putting *walls* around the very things you want to give them! And not only that, you *fight them off!*"

Henning's hand communicator buzzed. A quiet voice said, "Chief, there's a party of three Sigmen creeping up on a little knot of unconscious warriors, down here near the setback by the gate. Bill, Mike, and I can sneak out the sally port and get them from behind when they start back, loaded down with their wounded. What do you say?"

"Let me get Arnold and Joe to cover you first. Those 'unconscious warriors' could be part of a trap." Henning got the other two men in position, then murmured into the communicator. "O.K. Whenever you're ready."

The woman now said dully, "Are you *really* planning to take those poor people slaves?"

"Sure," said Henning defiantly.

"That's . . ."

"We need purchasing power," said Henning. "Slaves are valuable on this planet. These people also have very sharp eyes. We *never* force them to tend the plants. We rarely allow them to. But they *sneak every minute off that they can manage in order to steal a look at how we do it.* And they remember what they see. Believe me, their minds are concentrated, and they *learn.*"

From somewhere down below came a murmur of voices, a sudden bloodchilling yell, startled shouts, then the crack of two stingbolt rifles, followed by screams and silence.

Henning spoke into his hand communicator, and learned that it *had* been a trap. The "unconscious warriors" had thrown short padded clubs at the technicians.

"That," he said "was close. We almost lost three technicians. If we'd lost them, they'd have been spirited away and forced to tend plants, train Sigmen to make machines, and on threat of torture compelled to yield up all sorts of secrets. Almost certainly, to keep the captives reasonably content, and to tie them down, the crafty chiefs would have forced them to marry pretty tribal maidens.

They're so much like us, you know, that such a marriage would produce offspring."

"Of course," she said. "After all, there's a theory that Sigma was originally populated by the crew and passengers of a crashed Terran spaceship."

Henning laughed.

She said angrily, "Now what have I done?"

"Oh, nothing," he said. "Here we have a race with copper-colored skin, blond hair, and gray eyes, that speaks a tongue no one ever heard of, and that gave two 6122 linguistic computers irreversible breakdowns, and this race of gray-eyed, copper-skinned blonds, speaking this unheard-of-tongue, has a complete set of bronze-age and stone-age type tribes, scattered widely over the surface of the planet, and some scholar doing research out of a library light-years away deduces that we put them here ourselves in a spaceship maybe a hundred years ago. Excuse me for laughing. Maybe I'm wrong. After all, I missed the important point, didn't I?"

He paused, grinning sarcastically in the darkness.

She waited a moment, then said curiously, "What's the important point?"

"Did he," said Henning, leaning forward, "have his doctorate?"

She jerked back as if she'd been slapped.

Henning grinned, then heard the distant order, spoken so emphatically in the Sigman tongue that it carried in the still night air. There was no time to warn her. They were both standing comparatively exposed behind the parapet. Henning dropped low, snapped her off her feet for the second time, and said urgently, "Keep down!"

This time, she struggled. And she struggled with an urgency that told him that somehow she had totally misinterpreted the situation. It was a relief to Henning when the thud and rattle of primitive missile weapons unmistakably explained his motives, and abruptly she lay still.

For a few minutes, he was busy with his communicator, then he heard her draw a deep breath.

"I'm sorry."

"For protecting yourself?"

"For—" She stopped, then went on angrily, "For thinking I *had* to protect myself."

"Stay close to the base of that parapet. I don't want you smashed up after I've spent all this time trying to educate you."

She made a low angry sound, but she moved closer to the parapet.

Henning took a look at the monitor screen, then blew a blast on his whistle and crawled behind the masonry shield.

The next few minutes were the hottest he'd experienced in some time.

The trouble seemed to be that the Sigman chief now had half-a-dozen of his own unconscious men, plus three valuable outlander potential slaves, at stake. He couldn't give them up without a fight. Henning in turn had three of his carefully-trained technicians, plus six valuable Sigmen slaves, at stake. He couldn't give *them* up without a fight. The thing ended with the Sigmen getting away with four of their own men and, at first, two technicians; while Hanning managed to get half-a-dozen Sigmen, including one that was lugging off one of the technicians. It was an expensive evening for everyone, and meanwhile, around on the other side of the station, the raiding party had quietly made its getaway with the precious groundwheat plants. Those, plus the one valuable technician he got completely away with, enabled the chief to show a profit for the transaction. Henning himself was bound to win, one way or the other, since practically everything that happened in such a raid could be turned to advantage; but he was angry over the loss of the technician, and swore savagely into the phone. For a moment, he considered leading a raiding force out himself; but that was suicide. The Sigmen's advantage in numbers was too great. Snarling angrily, Henning gave it up. He'd just have to make the best of it.

"But," said the woman exasperatedly, "won't the captured technician actually be doing what he *volunteered to do anyway*? I mean, he'll be teaching them to plant, training them in how to care for the plants—even the intermarriage has its advantages in allying the races, and spreading our customs. True, it's very difficult for *him*, but he did volunteer, knowing the risk, so—"

"You don't get it," said Henning shortly. "He *wanted* to get captured."

There was a blank silence, then she said, "What?"

"These technicians," said Henning irritatedly, "are a long way from home. The indescribable cretins back on Earth figure everything on the basis of strength, qualifications, weight-distance allowance and shipping charges. Every extra ounce has to be carried light-years. About the only time we get a woman out here is when it happens to fit advantageously into the shipping schedule. If there were enough accredited female technicians, no doubt they'd send them, in preference to men, till there were all women here, with no men—because, you see," he said savagely, "women technicians weigh less than the corresponding men technicians. That, incidentally, is probably why the foundation sent you here instead of a male Ph.D. with the same specialty. Right now, the big trouble here is, there aren't enough female technicians, so what happens? At least half of these birds, and maybe all of them, are secretly anxious to go over the hill and get pampered by the Sigmen for doing the same job *I* have them do—with a beautiful woman thrown in free! The only catch is, they've first got to somehow get themselves captured fighting hard in honest battle. The Sigmen *despise* traitors and weaklings. If one of our men surrenders, the Sigmen start out by plastering him with hot sloth grease and lizard scales, and then they work up from there. You see what I mean?"

"But," she stammered, "if . . . I mean—" She pressed both hands to her head. "*Everything is backwards!*"

"Sure," he snapped, "according to *theory*. But in actual *fact*, this is the way it works! You can do things strictly on the basis of general principles, and get things more or less done. But you get things done a lot better when you figure out the actual specific detailed properties of the things you're working with. What we're working with here are *people*."

"But surely, the proper way to raise the standard of living of these unfortunate people—"

Henning laughed.

Furiously, she said, "*Now* what is it?"

"In the first place, I'm not interested in raising their standard of living."

"But that's your job!"

His voice grated, "*You* are telling *me* my job?"

"But it's so obvious!"

"And if we raise the standard of living of these people, and train and educate them, and lead them up to a level of material culture comparable to ours, *then* we've succeeded?"

"Why, of course!"

"And if the benevolent social servants we've set up as *leaders*—because they'd *follow* us—get slammed out of their jobs by dictatorial types with dreams of vengeance, then what?"

"Why, they must be carefully guided so that that couldn't happen."

Henning looked at her dim shape in the gloom. In a low cold voice, he said, "Do you know how long you'd last if you came onto the planet with a hundred thousand like-minded followers, armed with every modern device of offense and defense? You'd wind up stripped of power and inside some chief's harem before the third year was out. You no more understand the reality of this planet than a raw recruit knows war after two weeks practice with a broomstick."

Her head jerked as if he had slapped her.

"How can you dare—" she began furiously, stepping toward him with partly-raised hand.

"Because," he said, his voice still low, and colder than ever, "if I so choose, you will accidentally fall over this parapet, and if you're lucky enough to land right, and foolish enough to yell, the Sigmen will have you in a flash. Female Terrans are a valuable curiosity on this planet."

She stood still, and her hand slowly dropped to her side. In a wondering voice, she said, "You *mean* that." There was a little silence, and then she said dazedly, "Why, you must be psychotic."

"Sure," said Henning dryly, "and I'll do you the courtesy of saying that I think you have just barely brains enough to eventually override your own indoctrination, and dimly see the reality here."

"Thanks," she said.

"It's not that I think you're stupid," said Henning. "And it's not just that you're ignorant, although you are. The main trouble is that you're *ignorant and don't know it*, which is just as bad as stupidity, and even worse in a way. A really stupid person couldn't have got into your position, and hence couldn't do the damage *you* can do."

In a toneless voice, she said, "You really must have decided, actually, to turn me over to the natives."

"Why?"

"Otherwise, you would never dare to be so—brutally frank."

Henning snorted. "Wrong again. Somewhere in your extensive education, you doubtless learned that everyone acts for strictly selfish purposes, his *real* reasons, if necessary, being deeply buried in his subconscious. Hence you know that all I'm really interested in is my own advancement—to get higher up in the hierarchy. Right?"

She said stiffly, "My report certainly won't help you reach *that* goal."

Henning laughed. "Then some good may come out of this mess."

There was a silence, and then she said in a small voice, "Well, I guess I was wrong again. But that seems perfectly natural here. Everything I say or do is wrong."

"Which is very irritating," he said quietly, "when you know you are so well *qualified*."

There was an even longer silence, and then she said, "There must be sarcasm in that. You mean I'm *not* well qualified?"

"Who wrote the texts you studied to acquire your 'qualifications'? Who is it that *says* you're qualified? Is a blacksmith qualified because a qualified blacksmith says he's qualified, or is he qualified because he can work in iron? And if he can't work in iron, what is his qualification worth, and what is the qualification of the person who qualified him worth? There are two forms of qualification, you know. One is the *license to practice*. The other is the *ability to do the job*. One qualification is *granted by authority*. The other qualification is *acquired by thought and work*. How closely these two qualifications correspond generally depends on how well the constituted authorities understand the actual conditions. There are many cases where the authorities *don't* understand. You tell me, now that you've seen a little of the situation here, *are you qualified*?"

She let her breath out slowly. Finally, in a low voice, she said, "No. I'm not qualified."

Henning felt a great weight of antagonism dissipate into the thin air. "O.K.," he said. "Now we can talk."

She said wearily, "I've *still* got a report to write. Maybe I should just send in my resignation."

"No," he said. "You've got the *license to practice*. Don't throw that away. Now what you need is the *ability to do the job*. Or, at least, to understand the job. If *you* resign, they may send us some jackass who won't see he's wrong even when he's faced with the facts. Don't quit on us. We need you. That Brumbacher Report carries a lot of weight."

She said wonderingly, "Now we're on the same side?"

"Of course."

"But, I thought you despised me. You said as much."

Henning studied the screen. The natives had pulled so far back into the forest that the screen no longer showed them.

"No," said Henning puzzledly, "I never said that."

"You've certainly been antagonistic. You said I'm stupid, not qualified—"

"Ignorant," Henning corrected.

"Ignorant. All right. And that you'd throw me over the wall and let the savages take me."

The wind changed, and brought Henning the fresh fragrance of her perfume.

Stubbornly, he said, defying the perfume. "I would have. You threatened my work."

There was a lengthy silence, and Henning said, "As a Soc.D. (Sr.), you ought to know that, to a strictly objective observer, women react over strongly to any threat to their children, while men react over strongly to any threat to their work."

"Oh," she said, surprised. "I suppose I knew it, but . . . but it was *theoretical.*" She paused. "That's been the whole trouble, hasn't it?"

Henning nodded. "The aim, you know, is to get an aid and development program that *works*, not one that satisfies theoretical requirements. The aim is to get it to *work in actual fact.*"

"But I can't see why this *does* work. It isn't *logical.*"

Henning said exasperatedly, "Of *course* it isn't logical. It deals with people, doesn't it? Are all people logical? *You can't ignore the properties of the material you're working with!* These Sigmen are tough, hardy, brave, primitive, intelligent, combative, and honorable. If they were soft, weak, cowardly, degenerate, crafty, and dishonorable, do you suppose we could treat them the same way and get anywhere? We'd have to adapt our method."

She said reflectively, "But there's a basic principle in your method, and I haven't been able to find it."

The wind shifted capriciously, and Henning breathed deeply of the tantalizing fragrance of her perfume. The world seemed to reel around him. Deprived of the protection of the woman's detestable unfounded air of superiority, which he had smashed, Henning was now vulnerable to her.

"I *seem* to see it," she was saying, "but I can't . . . can't formulate it. Won't you help me? I *have* to have something definite, something that can be put in my report. I can't simply say—" she paused, as if vaguely aware of some new quality in the darkness. "I *can't* just say the program has to be—suited to the planet." She paused again, began to speak, and stopped.

Henning moved around, trying to get a breath of air free of perfume. The breeze, however, capriciously followed him around, so that he practically drowned in perfume. Then, abruptly, a new thought penetrated to his consciousness: *What was he running from?*

Now that he had beaten the conceit out of her, what was left was a beautiful woman.

True, she had a Soc.D. (Sr.), but he had seen that she could overcome that.

She was a beautiful woman, *who could think.*

The entire situation abruptly changed.

She said, hesitantly, "The . . . There is some general principle, isn't there?"

"Yes," he said finally, "there is. And you can express it in various ways."

There was a brief silence, then Henning said, "For instance, 'easy come, easy go.' If we casually toss our hard-earned methods to people, they won't value them. 'A man truly appreciates only what he has worked to acquire.' The people here have to work to acquire our methods. Having put so much effort into it—having invested their own time and thought—*the knowledge and skill are theirs.*"

She drew her breath in sharply. "Yes, yes. I see it! But don't they suspect? Won't they feel they've been deceived—"

Henning snorted. "Why do you suppose they use padded spears and arrows? Why do they leave off the metal tips of their javelins? Why do they capture our technicians instead of killing them? Do you think they could see our ships come down out of the sky in a blaze of light and not suspect that we have weapons and equipment more powerful than we use? Don't you realize that humans operate on several levels at once, and are readily caught

up in play-acting? Why is a man in mental agony over the loss
of a game of chess? Why is he cheerful over a well-fought win
or draw? Why are sporting contests so heavily attended and the
source of so much gloom or delight?"

In the darkness, she caught her breath. She turned to face
him.

"You mean . . . It's all . . ." She seemed to strangle on the
words.

"It's a game," he said. "It's a delightful manly game, and the
rewards are real."

She seemed to sway, dangerously near the parapet, and Henning caught her.

She struggled, but not nearly so hard as she had struggled
earlier.

Henning drew her close, but with not nearly as much force as
he had used to get her out of the line of fire.

She whispered. "Aren't you going to throw me over the
wall?"

"Not yet."

"First, you want my signature on the report?"

"Obviously."

She murmured something that Henning didn't hear.

He drew her closer.

"What?"

She whispered in his ear, "Games. People play games."

Henning nodded, and looked past her at the horizon slowly
lighting up as the moon began to rise. In just a few minutes it
was going to as private here as on the stage of a theater.

Casually, he said, "Have you ever examined the walls?"

She looked puzzled. "No."

"There's a place here, partly hidden by a screen of foliage, that
we use as a listening post. From a mathematical point of view,
the curve of the walls might interest you. If you'll be quiet—"

She looked at him, first with disappointment, then with suspicion.

"All right," she said finally, and let him take her hand and lead
the way.

Beyond the wall, the moon was rising, lighting up the alien
planet, to show forest and grassland gleaming with dew.

Suddenly it came to her, as actual knowledge, why the people

of this planet, in whatever guise, knowingly or unknowingly, followed Henning's lead.

They *trusted* him.

And why did they trust him?

His actions showed sympathetic insight into their real
nature.

And what textbook or course of study taught insight, or even
recognized its existence?

She thought back over reams of authoritative date. All beside
the point.

She shook her head.

What a lot there was to unlearn!

ODDS

Station Manager Clyde Burgess lowered the sprayer, and resisted the increasingly urgent impulse to breathe. Through the misted lenses of his protective suit, he glanced intently around at the nearly empty racks, lifts, and conveyers of Interstellarcomcorp's Vitalia Depot Number One. Shining brightly in through the large high windows of the warehouse, the morning sun lit up countless squadrons of the intermingled wasps, flies, vrills, grates, snurks, hornets, gnats, shothole beetles and other pests, that drifted and darted through rolling clouds of this latest insecticide.

Burgess looked around at Lew Cassetti, his weirdly masked and suited assistant manager. Cassetti was peering up over a sprayer at the flying, crawling, and hovering pests visible against the ceiling lights.

Burgess tapped Cassetti on the shoulder, and jerked his head toward the door.

Cassetti nodded, and followed Burgess out through the tendrils of vine reaching across the side doorway. Out here, the morning breeze swayed the weeds that filled the vehicle park, and ruffled the leaves of the ivy thickly covering the dozers, grav-wielders, trenchers, and the rest of the shot-holed wreckage of the planet's one large shipment of heavy equipment. The two men tore off caps and face-masks, faced into the breeze, and sniffed lightly.

Noticing none of the head-spinning, sight-graying, hammering-headache sweetness of this latest bug-killer, Burgess breathed deeply. As he breathed, he kept his nostrils dilated, his lips close together, and his tongue warped upward in his mouth, so that none of the innumerable gnats would find clear passage through his mouth down into his lungs.

Beside him, Cassetti stripped off the rest of the protective outer suit, pulled off his sweatshirt, grabbed one of the two buckets nearby, and dipped into a large gray-spotted tub of soapy water. As Burgess, who had gone first into the warehouse, satisfied his need for air, Cassetti scrubbed his hands, face, neck, arms and upper body, then groped blindly for a folded towel by the tub.

Burgess, at last breathing normally, eyes squinted against the nearly level rays of the sun, peeled off the rest of the protective clothing, tossed his sweatshirt near the tub, grabbed the remaining bucket and dipped into the tub.

"Phew," said Cassetti. "Watch out for the soap. It smells like a palace of love, but it stings like acid."

Burgess had just gotten a little of the burning suds in his eyes. Around his head, he could hear a gathering buzz and whine.

"Genuine PDA stuff. It stings *us*, and attracts the bugs."

There was a flapping sound as Cassetti's groping hand found and unfolded a towel. "What did you think of their newest bug-poison?"

Burgess groped for his towel, located the end of the cloth, and used a corner to wipe the suds from his eyes. "What did *I* think? As a war gas, maybe it would work. It sure didn't bother any bugs that I could see."

"It reminds me of that other super-kill."

"The green oil?"

"The purple crystals."

Burgess grunted as if he had been hit, and methodically unfolded the towel. He still couldn't get his eyes open, and he felt the towel cautiously before using it, since there was no telling what might have crawled inside for a little nap.

Cassetti was saying, "I thought my lungs would burst in there. You'd think Planetary Development would realize what would happen on *this* planet to their damned breathing apparatus with its copper fittings. You remember how they sent the crystals?"

"Who could forget it?"

Burgess' memory provided him with a picture of a large black plastic drum with copper plug and pour spout, over which he and the planet's newly arrived branch chemical plant supervisor were bent. On the plastic drum was stuck a big label with skull and crossbones at each corner:

CAUTION
EXTREME
DANGER!
Contents poison to all
Earth–type life–forms!
Avoid contact with skin!
Use in well ventilated area!
Classified insecticide!
Destroy contaminated clothing!
Official use only!
May be absorbed through skin!
Wash repeatedly after use!
In case of contact, seek medical aid at once!
POISON!
EXTREME
DANGER!

Out the shot-holed plug and down across the label crawled a column of small black things like ten-legged ants. The first four legs of each ant were possessively clutching a flat plate-like violet-black crystal.

Looking closer, the two men discovered another column coming empty-clawed up the back of the drum and going inside through another shot-hole.

The branch plant supervisor straightened up, looking dazed.

"I can't believe my eyes!"

Burgess shrugged.

"It's just standard for the planet. The last time, PDA sent us a green oil we were supposed to set out in pans. It was supposed to be harmless to *us*, but the mere vapor would kill the bugs right in the air. Just take a look."

Burgess pointed to a shelf under a nearby window, where bugs alighted on the edge of a wide glass dish, then climbed over each other to swim around in a murky green liquid. Before the eyes of the two men, the bugs clambered out the other side of the dish, to vibrate their wings and preen themselves before taking off.

Burgess said, "We've got a little problem here. You see it. I see it. Everyone on the planet sees it. But Planetary Development still doesn't get it. The problem is, the so-called 'insectoids' on this planet are *different.*"

"Different," said the newly arrived manager, his eyes wide and his voice little more than a croak, "in degree only. All insects and insectoids are derived from the same basic parent stock, spread through space in molecuspore form by radiation pressure." He said this as he might have recited a magic formula to ward off evil spirits.

"M'm," said Burgess, looking at the bugs swimming in the insecticide. "Wait till you've been here a little longer."

The flapping noise as Cassetti reversed the towel came dimly to Burgess. An instant later, Cassetti yelled.

Burgess' eyes were still shut, and he was just starting to dry his face and neck. The yell, for an instant, paralyzed him but his mind moved fast to narrow the possibilities:

Grates, mosquitoes, snurks, and gnats wouldn't give cause for a yell like that.

The quality of the sound was somehow wrong for wasps, green-faced hornets, and redstings.

There had been no clack, rattle, or indignant chatter, so it wasn't a prospector bug.

That left scorpion ants and vrills.

If there were scorpion ants around, considering that Cassetti was only eight to ten feet away, Burgess could count on ants all over the ground, and climbing off the weeds, any second now.

Burgess was already jogging in place, hastily wiping off the soap while his feet mashed down the closest of the weeds and vines, and then Cassetti began to swear lividly, and Burgess, relieved, stopped jogging. It must have been a vrill. Scorpion ants produced the same kind of yell, but there was no leisure afterward for swearing.

Burgess could now get his eyes open. He momentarily scattered a cloud of gnats with a swipe of the towel, bent over, picked up his sweatshirt, examined it carefully, and shook loose a pale-green lacy-winged grate.

Cassette exhaled with a hiss.

"That damned vrill must have delivered twenty thousand volts! How do they *do* it?"

This was one of those questions normally answered only by a

grunt or a murmur. Burgess grunted sympathetically, pulled on his shirt, and heard the dull clatter of the customer bell.

Cassetti went on acidly, "Of course, vrills *can't* do it. PDA said so. 'Insects are no problem on this planet.' —You through with the water?"

"Yes."

They emptied the pails and the tub, then carried the tub, with pails inside, through shoulder-high weeds to the shot-holed cement walk that ran along beside the shot-holed concrete foundation of the warehouse. From under the clapboards of the warehouse, streams of sawdust and bits of wood filtered down, to accumulate in piles along the base of the building.

As Burgess waved off gnats, mosquitoes, and grates, he once again asked himself how he had gotten into this spot. —Why had he picked *this* planet to settle on?

For a moment, his thoughts went back to the intensely real-istic colonization simulator in Space Center XII, where he had breathed the air, felt the gravity, seen the pleasant blue-green sweep of forest, lakes, and plains, enjoyed the warmth of a brilliant sun by day, and the pleasant moonlight by night, while a quiet voice told of a "remarkable similarity to the planet Earth . . . Vitalia is the third planet of a Sol-type sun. It has one moon, which is similar in mass, density, and orbit to Luna . . . The planet's flora is markedly Earth-type . . . Fauna is also analogous to that of Earth, though oddly lacking in cer-tain species. There are no insect-eating birds, while the insects themselves are represented by a thin and sickly population; a few of the species, however, are quite exotic, and might be troublesome if they existed in larger numbers . . . The soil is characterized by great fertility . . . Mineral deposits, however, are anomalous. Save for vast quantities of petroleum, the planet shows few of the usual concentrated ore deposits . . . a surpris-ingly homogeneous distribution of many elements is to be found over the planet's surface . . . A curious feature, at first believed to indicate the past presence of a sentient technologically skilled race, but which has since been proved statistically insignificant, is the occurrence of 'glass mines,' containing huge quantities of both regular and irregular shapes indistinguishable from plates and masses of manufactured glass. No bodily remains, or other indications of a sentient race, have been found, however . . .

Although uranium and other ordinary fission and fusion source materials are rare, the abundant petroleum provides an alternative source of energy, and the planet, situated near a junction of major trade and communications routes, is now being opened both to colonization and to commercial and industrial share-development . . ."

The loud ping-*thud* of a shot-hole beetle striking the metal tub snapped Burgess back to the present.

zzzzZZZ!

There was a second ping-*thud*. Then they passed the end of the warehouse, and walked slowly and carefully, in order to attract no undue attention from the green-faced hornets inhabiting the huge papery gray nest that bulged out from under the eaves.

They put the tub and pails in the equipment shed, and glanced, frowning, at the motionless gray bumps of the two hard-shelled shot-hole beetles on the tub amongst the smaller gray bumps of the compound used to plug previous shot-holes. It was not impossible to get the shot-hole beetles loose. It was just extremely hard—and likely to involve a spattering with the acids the beetles used to dissolve the metal. They shrugged, shut the equipment shed door, and started for the office, some fifty feet away. This building was topped by a huge sign:

—VITALIA—
PLANETARY DEPOT ONE
INTERSTELLARCOMCORP
SHIP–RECEIVE–STORE
OFFICE BELOW

Vines, running wild because of personnel cuts and Burgess' and Cassetti's endless struggle with bugs, twined up this sign, and their tendrils groped for the sky. This visible evidence of neglect usually smote Burgess' conscience, but at the moment he scarcely noticed it. His attention was riveted on a dust-covered motor-scooter leaned against the side of the loading deck beside the office. The rear of this scooter bore a sign:

RAPID
COURIER
CORP.

Cassetti said acidly, "Bad news."

"In person. You missed the last visit."

"What he *brought* was bad enough. What else did he achieve?"

"He rammed that nest of wood ants at the edge of the loading deck, and there were five thousand ants roaming loose in the office. In a way, that beat the time before, when he spun up a fistful of gravel, peppered that nest of redstings, and was gone when the redstings came out to see who did it."

Burgess and Cassetti had stopped, and now hung back, hoping to avoid any lengthy meeting. They waved their hands and stayed out in the open as the desire to escape the countless bugs was outweighed by the repulsion of the courier's personality.

Burgess glanced at the scooter.

"How does he keep that thing running?"

"Cheap construction," said Cassetti. "I looked it over one time he was in the office. They used steel or plastic tubing instead of copper, and pot metal instead of brass or bronze. Shot-hole beetles don't seem to bother much with iron or steel unless there's a little zinc on it—that is, if they've got better stuff to eat." He glanced around the lot at the mounds of fluttering ivy leaves. From time to time, they could hear the "ZZZzzzz" of a departing shot-hole beetle, and the "zzzzzzzZZZ—ping—*thud!*" of arriving shot-hole beetles.

Burgess nodded. "And he has only *short* lengths of tubing to replace. You know, we ought to be able to make equipment that would at least last a little longer."

"Yeah, but how do we make the refineries last? You remember, the idea was to start with fuel oil, then gradually switch over to solar and nuclear power, and meanwhile import manufactured goods in exchange for petroleum-based chemicals. But with bugs that eat metal and take baths in insecticide—"

"I know," said Burgess. "—Watch it. Here he comes."

There was a tinny rattle as the office door came open, and a cord yanked at the shot-holed makeshift bell. Then a heavily swathed figure bolted down the steps, yelled "*Messages!*" jumped on the scooter, and gave the starter pedal half-a-dozen sharp kicks.

Burgess wet a finger and held it up.

Cassetti looked around searchingly.

Burgess said, "Wind will take the smoke back to the warehouse."

"I can't see anything he can hit. —Except possibly that sign post."

"Let's get inside. That stink of gas and dissolved bug-juice . . ."

A cloud of grey-black smoke filled with incandescent streaks and spots poured out the scooter's tailpipe.

BBB-bb-*BBBbbroooom!*

The scooter jolted forward, slowed jerkily, speeded up, then moved so erratically the driver for a moment was over the handlebars. Then the engine suddenly ran evenly again, and the scooter shot ahead, to bang a tall vine-entwined wooden post bearing a sign completely hidden under ivy leaves. The post and its overgrown sign, looming above clouds of rolling black smoke, reeled back, jerkily tilted forward, and then burst in the middle. The upper part toppled in a haze of white powder, carpenter bugs, flourdust beetles, and sawdust. From amongst the leaves of the ivy, there spun out a thing like a small grey basketball done up in unraveling tissue paper.

Burgess grunted. "A nest of redstings! Come on!"

He and Cassetti shot up the steps, shut the door tightly behind them, and stared out the window as the nest hit the ground, and exploded in red and yellow specks.

In the office, for a moment, they could imagine that they heard in the background the smooth whir, the click, and the soft deferent buzz of the scheduling computer, the warehouse indexer, the office communicator, and the other conveniences they'd once been used to. Then the remembered sounds degenerated into the usual noises of flying insects, and wood ants and carpenter bugs at work in their tunnels.

Burgess exhaled, and turned around.

On the sievelike, previously chromed counter that had separated the public from the mysteries of scientific transport, storage, and subspace communication, lay a small stack of papers and envelopes, topped by a yellow slip giving the courier's name, the items delivered, and the time of delivery.

Behind them, as they glanced at the pile of messages, the furious redstings rattled against the windows, then ranged all over the vehicle park, looking for something to sting.

Burgess murmured, "Close."

Cassetti nodded, then they turned back to the messages.

"The last batch," said Cassetti, "had a kindly letter to the effect that she and I wouldn't have made out together, and I should wish her luck with the other guy, along with a mess of service cancellations, customer complaints, price rises, and other kicks in the head. I've got a hunch this is the same."

"Might as well get it over with."

"Watch the ants."

Burgess glanced around. Emerging from a fresh hole in the floor by a chair in the far corner was a black column six or eight ants wide, winding its way across the floor to disappear under the counter. Here and there over the floor, and up and down the walls and across the exposed underside of the roof, could be seen a further scattering of the hurrying pests.

Cassetti nodded at the chair near the hole. "That's where he sits down to check the messages and make out the time-slips. He always gets up like he was going into orbit."

"Hopefully, he took a bootful along with him."

Burgess whacked the messages on the counter to knock any grates or paper weevils loose, handed half to Cassetti, and they walked over to a raised wooden platform whose eight stubby legs rested in eight large glass dishes filled with water. On this platform was a wooden table with a plain wooden chair at each end. Burgess sat down at his end, and Cassetti passed over a folded paper:

—NOTICE—
PURSUANT TO CONTRACT PROVISIONS
RAPID COURIER CORP HEREBY SERVES
NOTICE TO ALL CUSTOMERS
OF TERMINATION OF SERVICE
EFFECTIVE TWENTY-ONE (21) DAYS
FOLLOWING DELIVERY OF THIS NOTICE
—NOTICE—

Burgess exhaled with a hiss, and tore open an envelope printed "Vitalia Teletran, Inc." He read:

Dear Customer—
Owing to conditions beyond our control, we have found it impossible to give you the kind of service we know you have every right to insist upon.

We regret the necessity to close down our facility on this planet, but are compelled by circumstances beyond our control to terminate all our remaining surface transmission services at once. For off-planet transmissions, we will endeavor to continue at least partial service, where possible, for a period of thirty days from date.

We advise customers with urgent messages to transmit them as soon as possible, as our supply of spare parts is severely limited, and insectization of this facility is proceeding rapidly.

Faithfully yours,
G. Bernhardt
Branch Manager

The next letter was headed "Bank of Vitalia," and read:

Dear Customer—

Due to severe insect infestation, our computer records and our printed records have been seriously compromised. Due, however, to a progressive falling off in demand for banking services, we have been able to successfully convert to a system based on leather sacks and stainless steel tokens. Continuing deterioration of the building itself, however, coupled with a large nest of redstings over the door, renders it likely that we will be unable to continue our services.

We, therefore, in accordance with the appropriate provisions of the Banking Code, enclose herewith either a bank check or a debt notice, depending on the overall state of your accounts with us. Anyone wishing to clear up debt or convert a check to Standard Currency should come to our Temporary Offices at 97 Vitalia Street.

We wish to point out, however, to any customer who wishes to cash our check, that these Official Checks are good indefinitely, may be cashed, with proper identification, at any correspondent bank on any planet or in any Space Center, and are printed on special locally fabricated insect-repellent paper incorporating ground-up fibers of Vitalian swamp oak. Grubs, shot-hole beetles, slugs, weevils, grates, and paper wasps have not been known to damage these Official Checks. This is not true of the paper form of Standard Currency.

Very truly yours,
P. Willard Bayne
Vice-President

Cassetti tossed over an envelope.

"We got two of this."

Burgess absently folded the Bank of Vitalia check into his wallet, and tore open the envelope Cassetti had tossed across:

"Dear Friend:

"It is with real regret that we inform you that owing to conditions beyond our control, we are withdrawing our Branch Plant on the planet Vitalia.

"Owing to loss of records, we are unable to write personally to our customers, but wish to thank those of you whose loyalty—"

Burgess ripped open the next message:

INTERSTELLARCOMCORP
EMPLOYEE MEMO

DUE TO FURTHER DECLINING DEMAND, OUR FACILITY ON VITALIA REMAINS UNPROFITABLE.

COMPUTER PROJECTIONS MANDATE EITHER A FIFTY PERCENT CUT IN PERSONNEL OR A FIFTY PERCENT WAGE REDUCTION.

IN ACCORDANCE WITH THE SPIRIT OF OUR EMPLOYEE RELATIONS PROGRAM, WE WILL BE GUIDED IN OUR CHOICE BY YOUR INPUT AS REGARDS YOUR PREFERENCE AS TO THESE ALTERNATIVES.

PLEASE MARK THE ENCLOSED EMPLOYEE INPUT BALLOT AND RETURN IT PROMPTLY.

—C. D. MASHMAKER
PERSONNEL

Burgess exhaled, killed a mosquito, waved away some gnats, and glanced out the front window. Between tendrils closing in from all sides, he had a view across two wheel tracks to the other side of Vitalia Street. Over there were the vine-covered local offices of Sampson, Hodge, Brown, Luce and de Pugh—Stocks, Bonds, Mutual Funds, Options, Lotteries & Planetary Wagers and Hedges.

After staring for a moment at what must be an even worse place to work than where he was, Burgess tore open the last envelope.

> *Dear Sirs:*
>
> *Three months ago, I ordered five (5) Black Marvel pullets and two (2) Black Marvel cockerels from the Farmers' Supply Co-Op at Space Center Twelve.*
>
> *I have received acknowledgment of my order, and the shipment should be in this week. On account of the notorious conditions at your warehouse, and the way every big outfit on this planet is running for cover, I think I should let you know that I do want this shipment. I will pay the shipping charge in cash money, and if you mishandle this shipment, I will take the loss of time and work out of your skin. I don't mean any offense, and you may not be like the bulk of the lackwits and wingless grates who populate Vitalia Center, but I mean what I say.*
>
> *If these birds get in ahead of time, just give them water and keep the bug-killer away from the birds. It won't kill the bugs, and it might kill the birds.*
>
> *Sincerely yours,*
Louisa L. Parnell

Burgess sat back blankly, then read the letter over again. "Lew."

Cassetti looked up.

"What?"

"What is a 'Black Marvel pullet'?"

"A *what?*"

Burgess passed over the letter.

Cassetti read it, and sat back. Finally he shook his head.

"I seem to remember an order to this Co-Op she mentions.

I think the order went out by s-gram from our supply ship. I noticed it, because s-grams are a good buy, but we get hardly any s-gram business. —But that's all I know about it."

Burgess shook his head.

"A mere individual wrote that letter. But it's the only thing I've read that doesn't say, one way or another, 'We're licked.'"

"Take a look at *this* batch."

"I'll trade you."

Burgess sat back, and glanced over what Cassetti passed him. He found a cancelled shipment order, a complaint blaming Burgess and Cassetti personally for insect damage, a notice to Cassetti from Transpatroncorp "to hereby inform you that Transpatroncorp no longer has a future requirement for Electronic Technicians Grades VI through XII on the planet Vitalia," and a wedding announcement originally sent on a chaste white card, transmitted as a message, and reproduced on flimsy yellow message paper.

Across the table, Cassetti groaned.

"Here's one I missed."

Burgess took the sheet of paper, and flattened it on the table:

Evaluations Section
Sector H. Q.
Planetary Development Authority
Space Center XII

to Mr. Clyde Burgess
Station Manager
Interstellarcomcorp
Planetary Depot One.
Vitalia Center
Vitalia (Novo Sol III)
Sector XII

Sir: Your lengthy communication regarding insect infestation, insect characteristics and qualities, insect habits, and communal insect clusters (which you refer to as "bug cities") has been received at this facility and forwarded to me by the Chief, Clerical Staff, HQPDASXII.

As your communication refers to no T-Rating or

Equivalency Grade Rating, I assume that you are non-graded: Etymology T(O)EG(O).

Specialty communications from non-graded personnel are accorded the Status Rating of zero at this facility. Zero-Status communications are not read by the addressee, and are not recorded or filed for future reference. They are routinely scanned by Evaluations Section prior to discard.

In future, refrain from addressing improper personal communications to Planetary Development Authority HQ S XII personnel.

Any communication regarding specialized material which originates with non-rated personnel is improper, as it poses the danger of entry to our data files of non-screened materials.

The name of any person who directs improper communications to this organization is routinely noted, and future communications of whatever character are routinely referred to Evaluations Section.

The fact that your communication contained a threat against the personnel of this Headquarters facility has been noted, and appropriate details forwarded to the Space Police and other proper authorities, including your present employer. —S. Hamway Schrank, Admin T (XI), Etymology EG(2), Office Executive.

Burgess sat back, and silently reread the message. He looked up, frowning.

"What is an equivalency grade of *two* worth?"

Cassetti picked up a short piece of stick, and with a vicious blow flattened a vrill that had just landed on the table. With a growl of satisfaction, he pushed the remains off onto the floor.

"Damned little. It means he took a course in biology in some 'formally recognized educational institution,' and submitted the proper documents to get an equivalency grade credited to him. It's about the next thing to signing your name, 'John Doe, Graduate, Planet of Marshbog Central Kindergarten.'"

"And," said Burgess, looking at the letter, "What is an 'office executive'?"

"A *what*?"

Burgess waved away the gnats, and shoved the letter across the table. He got up, and pulled out a drawer of the plain steel filing case they'd been forced to rely on since the vrills got into the automatic filer.

"H'm," said Cassetti. "I didn't see that. Frankly, I don't know *what* it is. But if my knees are supposed to get weak when I read it after his name, for some reason it doesn't work."

Burgess found what he was looking for, brushed off some ants, shut the file, sat down, killed a mosquito, and reread his letter to PDA:

Dear Sector Chief Paley:

Please excuse my writing directly to you, as many attempts to call attention to the worsening situation on Vitalia (formerly Novo Sol III) by the normal channels have proved futile.

We are faced on this planet with rapidly increasing numbers of insect pests. These include types resembling gnats (of two sizes), mosquitoes, wasps, hornets, and ants, as well as types which burrow in wood, shot-hole metal, and do incredible damage to solid-state, plastic, crystalloid, or molecularized computer and control devices and communications equipment. The only substance these pests do not appear to damage is glass.

Not only do we have a disastrous situation here because our equipment is being destroyed, because the chemical insect-control agents sent us do not work, and because these insects appear to have no natural enemies, but also there is a worse danger:

Space transports have been and are still carrying goods to and from this planet.

What will happen if the actual insects or their eggs should be carried, for instance, to Space Center XII, and from there to other and possibly very distant planets? As the usual insecticides do not work, there is no apparent defense against infestation. If they should, for instance, infest your offices, they could severely damage the central communications facilities and data banks at the very time that the spread of insect infestation began on other planets, and required fast action.

I am not an expert on insects, but for what it may be worth, have observed the following:

1) These insects resist all the usual insecticides. Incredible as it may seem, they seek contact with such insecticides and appear invigorated by them.

2) Their reproductive rate increases enormously in contact with our technology. It is as if the substances present in our technological devices are in some way stimulants to their metabolism.

3) The insects on this planet show a form of group activity such as I have never previously seen or heard of. On the edge of the largest settlement here, Vitalia Center, there are a number of what people here call "bug cities." Many of us have watched the activities in these places through binoculars. If you will imagine a large well branched tree, containing nests of wood ants, hornets, wasps, and other insects—all close together—with all the different kinds of insect pests from miles around carrying the particular substances that they gather to grooves cut in the tree by wood ants, there to deposit these substances in certain grooves, or holes, apparently in trade for other substances deposited in other grooves or holes, by other insects—if you will visualize such a thing, you will have a fairly accurate start for a picture of these "bug cities."

To me, it appears that the facts mentioned above show the existence of a situation that has no known precedent, and that warrants urgent consideration, particularly since time may be short.

> *Truly yours,*
> *Clyde Burgess*
> *Station Manager*

Burgess handed the letter to Cassetti.

"Where do I threaten their personnel?"

Cassetti read the letter through, brushed off sawdust filtering down from overhead, and shrugged.

"Just possibly the guy who answered this can't read."

"Or doesn't think."

Cassetti nodded, eyes narrowed as he weighed the letter in his hand.

"It might be that the best thing *now* is to forget the whole thing. You *can't* write to PDA. If you get in touch with the Space Police, they'll think you're a crank. If you try to get in touch with anyone else, who'll believe you? I've thought of sending messages—but through channels or out of channels, you run into this same wall of morons."

Burgess nodded. "*Anywhere* either of us sends a message, the odds are ten-to-one that they won't believe us."

"Exactly." Cassetti looked relieved. "Those odds are just what I'd say, too. Anyway, they already *have* the facts. Otherwise, why are all the big organizations pulling out? It's the *interpretation* of the facts that they don't have. They each see it just as a situation where they should cut *their* losses."

"Well," said Burgess, "take a look, would you, and see if those Teletran message blanks have been eaten up? Then, just in case a supply ship should come in, I want to get some s-grams ready."

Cassetti stared at him.

"What are you going to do?"

"What *can* I do? There isn't a thing to do *here* that I can think of. All *we* can do is squash gnats and run from redstings. There *ought* to be experiments using birds, anteaters, and so on, but it needs to be done on a large scale and in a hurry. —So, what *can* I do? Naturally, I'm going to send a message to every place I can think of, including another one to PDA."

Cassetti shook his head. "You're up against that standard routine. You'll just make yourself look like a crank! And there are ways for disposing of cranks."

"I know it. But will you tell me what future you or I or anyone else is going to have if every planet we try to escape to, *these bugs have already gotten there first?* —Let's have the message blanks."

It was nearly six weeks later that the Space Force flew in the first twenty crates of insect-eating birds, ranging in size from types smaller than the swallow to a mean-looking monster almost four feet high, with a pointed bill two feet in length, called the banjo-bird. The banjo-bird ate up whole nests of stinging pests at a time, its long narrow seemingly unsuitable bill snapping open and shut so fast it seemed to be run by invisible cogs, while its fine barbed down pierced the wings of insects burrowing in to sting it, broke off at the base, and left the insects spinning on the ground, to be eaten at leisure.

For a time, the air around Vitalia Center was like the aviary at a zoo, as every insect-eating bird that could be collected was thrown into the contest.

Burgess found himself looking around at the half-collapsed buildings, improvised bird-feeders, ranks of bird-houses on poles, and birds building nests over windows, under eaves, and in the shambles of fallen buildings, as the zzzzZZZ-ping-*thud* of the shot-hole beetle was replaced by the chirr, squawk, warble, banjo-twang, and screech of innumerable birds by day, and the silent flitting of countless bats by night.

In the midst of all this, with an oddly high death-rate amongst the birds, but with the bugs clearly beaten, a personal letter arrived for Burgess, delivered by hand by the captain of the ship that brought it. Burgess read:

Dear Mr. Burgess:

This letter will serve to notify you of your appointment as regional director for our Interstellarcomcorp/Second District of Sector XII, effective the date of your receipt of this letter, with pay increase back-dated to the beginning of this present year.

I believe you are already well aware of the accepted explanation for the insect situation on Vitalia. Even Earth, of course, had ruinous insect pests, including types which ate wood, secreted acid, and drilled holes through lead sheathing, but the incredible fit of the Vitalian pests to our technology suggests that they are, in fact, a biological device carefully tailored to destroy the type of technology which we possess, but which we certainly have no patent on. —Others before us may perfectly well have reached the same general type of technology.

The hypothetical sequence we picture as leading to this present situation is as follows:

1) Two opposed sides once faced each other on Vitalia. One relied primarily upon physical-sciences technology. The other on biological sciences technology.

2) The biological side developed insects designed to destroy the basis of the physical-science technology— especially the calculation and control devices. Considering how these insects increased in the vicinity of our one small settlement on Vitalia, the effect, given a number of large cities, can be easily imagined. Moreover, some as-yet-unknown aspect of one or more of these pests is poisonous to the birds which eat them. We, of course, can fly in more and more birds. The Vitalian technological civilization was apparently planet-bound and could not do it.

3) The physical sciences civilization, itself facing destruction, used its own battery of weapons, and evidently destroyed its opponent.

4) The biodevice—Vitalia's metal, plastic, paper, cement, and ceramic-eating insects—continued until no trace of the technological civilization, even the bones of its founders, was left, except for objects made of glass, which the insects were not equipped to destroy.

5) After a long delay, during which these insects were a prey to malnutrition and smaller parasites (this we've found, is why the biodevice insects enjoy our insecticide—it destroys their own parasites), at last we appeared. This was the return of happy days for the insects.

I do not need to tell you that these pests, as you warned, represent a serious danger for human civilization. It is not too much to say that your warning probably saved us the loss of large parts of Sector XII, and possibly much more. It is one thing to destroy these pests by a concentrated attack on a small region of a single newly settled planet. It is something else to contend with them simultaneously on hundreds of developed planets and in countless transports. The shot-hole beetle, for instance, has been found to enclose its eggs in various substances, and can produce a metal-sheathed egg about one-half the diameter of a BB shot, which it glues—"welds" might be a better word—to whatever metal surface suits its taste. It has shown a willingness to lay these eggs on metal shipping-drums, and the hulls of transports.

We have, however, every reason to hope that this infestation can be held to the level of a nuisance nearly everywhere, while we search for an effective insecticide. Obviously, it is more than a nuisance on Vitalia. The planet appears suitable only for agricultural settlement *by sects which prefer, anyway, to have little to do with an advanced technology.*

You may be interested to know how your warning became effective. One place outside Vitalia where these insects are no mere nuisance is Space Center XII, although the cause of the trouble was not yet clear to them. Your s-gram to General Wilforce, however, arrived just as Space Force HQ was experiencing baffling malfunctions in their headquarters battle computer. The master crystal was removed, and found to be infested with shock-generating vrills and wireworm vrill larvae. The General attempted to contact PDA headquarters, and was informed that he was out of his field, and that his communication was "improper."

De-insectization of Space Center XII is now proceeding by sections, under martial law. The luckier sections have such things as chickens to eat up the bugs. The method selected for trial in the PDA section involves the extensive use of such things as spiders, mice, centipedes, and snakes.

I want again to express my appreciation for your timely warning, and the credit it has given Interstellarcomcorp as the one organization on Vitalia that was not completely asleep on its feet.

Sincerely,
Able G. Cox, Col., I. P. (Ret'd) President

Burgess, stunned with surprise, handed the letter to Cassetti, who read it through, and looked up wide-eyed.

"For Pete's sake! I expected you to be strung from the rafters, and you get a promotion! But—I *still* say the odds were ten-to-one against you. You were lucky."

"Yes, but there *are* two ways to look at odds in a situation like that."

"What do you mean?"

"The first way is to figure the situation is unbeatable. —You've got only about a ten-percent chance, wherever you turn."

"I see *that*. What's the other way?"

Burgess began to speak, then paused.

Outside the window, a redsting that had somehow survived

till now whizzed into view. A big yellow bird exploded from the loading dock after it. The redsting blurred aside in a flash of speed. The bird's long bill was waiting when the redsting got there. The bird snapped up the redsting.

Burgess said, "The other way is to figure that *ten times* a ten percent chance is *a hundred percent chance.*"

"Yeah, but—" Cassetti suddenly looked intent. "*If you kept at it,* eventually that ten percent chance was *bound* to turn up?"

Burgess nodded.

"If you can survive long enough to hit the problem often enough, then, even though the odds are small, *they add up in your favor.*"

THE TROUBLE WITH CARGOES

⚜

THE TROUBLEMAKER

12/02/96

Probably the closest thing to hell on a commercial spaceship is to have the gravitor control run wild. Next on the list is what happens when there's a troublemaker in the crew.

Three years ago, we had the first experience. It looks as if we are now about to have the second.

The trouble started when Krotec, our cargo-control man, was killed by a freak meteor at the cut-loose point. We had just thrown the cargo section into hyperdrive and were swinging around to get an empty returned section from the recovery crew when the meteor hit. We all felt bad about Krotec's death. But there was nothing we could do except head back to the loading center as usual.

When we got back to the loading center, word came in that a replacement for Krotec was due on board at 2330.

The captain insists that each new man be greeted as he comes on board. Willis and I, respectively third and second in command, offered to do the greeting. Willis got the job.

Around 0130, Willis woke me up.

"Listen," he said, "that replacement hasn't shown up yet. The transport office says he started out in a little one-man taxi-boat about two hours and twenty minutes ago. Do you suppose he's drunk?"

"I *hope* not."

A cargo-control man has to inspect and approve each cargo before it can be shipped. Because of this, a drunk cargo-control man can cause a long delay. Each delay cuts down the ship's competitive rating. And each cut in the rating means a cut in the bonus given to the officers and crew of the fastest ships.

"Listen," I said. "We're just loading grain, aren't we?"

"We are. Just a few hours more and we'll be full up. If we can get out of here by 0800, we've got a chance to beat *Nova* and get first place for a change. But we've got to get this cretin to start checking cargo before we can even think of leaving."

"How about the transport office? Do they know where this one-man taxi-boat is now?"

"All they can say is that a rough fix shows it's somewhere in B cargo area, and it's sending out an 'unoccupied' signal. That means our replacement has matched locks with some other boat or ship in our area, and left the one-man boat."

It took a few moments to absorb what this meant. Each ship takes its share of fast and slow cargoes. While we were loading grain and leaving tomorrow, other ships were taking on fragile goods that would keep them at the loading center for several days. On some of these ships, roaring parties were now going on. If our wandering cargo-control officer got into one of these parties, it would be no easy job to get him out.

"Well," I said, dressing quickly, "we can't very well start asking where he is."

"No," said Willis sourly. "There are those who would load him up with rum and hide him somewhere just to gain a few points on us."

"That means there's nothing else to do but get another taxi-boat and go hunt for him. One-man boats aren't used much, so we've got a chance."

A couple of hours later, this chance seemed to have gotten pretty thin. I had been staring into the glaring lights and shadows all over B cargo area, and Willis had been calling the transport office at intervals. The transport office insisted the one-man boat was still in B area. But if so, I hadn't seen it. An unpleasant possibility was just beginning to dawn on me when Willis appeared on the little screen, his face white and set.

"Don't bother looking for him any more. He's here."

The screen went blank. I went back to the ship, and saw that the boa-like bulk of the pressure loader had stopped pulsating. Willis was waiting in the control room as I went in.

"You know," he said, "that so-and-so was right here all the time? He was hooked onto the cargo-section's lock, out of sight in the shadow of the ship. That means he has been alone in the cargo-section for a long time, without our knowing it."

"I notice we aren't loading."

"No, we aren't loading. He came in here, and used the screen to get the chief inspector's office. He says there's 'danger of possible weevil infestation' in the cargo, and he's slapped a forty-eight-hour delay on the ship."

"That's ridiculous."

"Is it? Don't forget, the inspector here is a stickler for caution. Any cargo-control man who shows caution gets a pat on the head. And since Krotec got hit before we picked up the empty cargo section, that means we were without a regular cargo-control officer to check the cargo section."

"Yes," I said, "but the captain checked it himself." I was thinking that the captain is a fanatic for efficiency, a rigid teetotaler, an early-to-bed-early-to-rise man, with iron habits and unvarying devotion to duty. It suddenly occurred to me that this would carry no weight whatever with the chief inspector. "Look," I said, "the captain has qualified as a cargo-control man. He's perfectly able to serve as one in a pinch."

Willis smiled. "Sure. But what I am talking about is how it will look on paper. The captain is not a *regular* cargo-control man. The inspector, not knowing the captain, will generously assume that the captain was out of practice and missed something. We will therefore be hung up here till the inspector goes through all his motions. *Nova* will beat us by light-years. But what I am thinking about most is what life on board the same ship as this self-seeking troublemaker is going to be like."

12/03/96

After about three hours sleep, I woke up to find that the captain wanted to see me. Willis was on the way out as I went in. The captain listened intently as I told what little I knew of what had happened the night before. Then he leaned back with his eyes narrowed.

"Well," he said, "we want to be fair to this man. But I don't think we ought to lean over backward so far he can kick our feet out from under us. Suppose you go out there and study his record folder while I get him in here and study him."

I agreed, and in due time started back to the captain's compartment carrying the record folder of one L. Sneat in a portfolio. The captain's door opened up and our new cargo-control man backed out with a slightly glazed look, and both hands spread wide. He was talking in the low earnest voice of the smooth wolf suddenly face-to-face with the girl's father and three tough brothers.

"Why should I, captain?" he was saying. "It wouldn't make sense, would it? Honestly, I *mean* it. Who would do a thing like that? And to the people he has to live with, too?"

"Just bear in mind," came the captain's voice, "if you have several hundred dollars in the bank, you can write quite a few twenty-dollar checks, and nothing happens to you. But write just one check too many and all hell breaks loose."

"Captain, I just don't understand—"

"Then go think it over."

Our new replacement moved away protesting his innocence as I went in and shut the door. The captain was frowning slightly.

"Some people," he said, "are all tactics and no strategy. They are so busy elbowing their way to the head of the line that they never look to see where the line is going." He glanced at me and said, "What did you find out?"

"Our friend was born in '68 on an outpost world called 'Broke.' He passed a company competitive exam, got good grades, and has been a cargo-control man a little less than four years. He has several commendations on his record and no black marks. Our ship is the eighth ship he has been cargo-control man on."

"In four years?"

"Yes, sir. Eight ships in four years."

"Let's see that folder."

I handed it to him.

It may have been imagination, but I thought I saw the captain's back hair rise up as he looked at the names of those ships. He growled, "Go get the latest rating and bonus list."

"Right here, sir."

The captain put it beside the record folder and glanced from one to the other.

Glancing over the captain's shoulder, I could see the names of the seven ships our new cargo-control man had been on before being assigned to ours. They were *Calliope, Derna, Hermes, Orion, Quicksure, Light Lady, Bonanza.*

The lowest seven names on the rating and bonus lists were: *Calliope, Derna, Hermes, Orion, Quicksure, Light Lady, Bonanza.*

Bonanza was in such bad shape that it had a bonus of minus 27.92. That is, the officers and men of *Bonanza* were paying back 27.92 cents out of every dollar they earned, as a fine for inefficiency.

The captain looked at this for a while, then sent for the records tape covering previous rating and bonus lists.

A quick glance at these lists showed us that the month before Sneat boarded *Bonanza,* that ship had a rating of 94.98 out of a possible 100.00.

One month later, *Bonanza's* rating was 76.01.

The captain looked at the record folder again. He had much the same expression as a settler on a new planet, who walks slowly past a tree, ax in hand, while he judges which way the tree will naturally fall, whether it is worth felling, and if so, where to sink the ax in first.

Then he looked up, smiled, and said we'd certainly have to work hard to make up for the delay. That was all he had to say for the moment.

12/04/96

Well, we're moving at last. No weevils were found. But Sneat produced some debris containing what could have been either pieces of bast-weevil wing-covers—or else bits of the brownish semitransparent insulation used on much of the wiring aboard ship. If it was from wiring, of course, it could have been carelessly dropped by anyone. Sneat has tried to get out of a head-on clash with the captain by claiming that this stuff was found, not inside the inner part of the cargo section, but in the outer inspection corridor. This corridor was thoroughly gone over by

Gaites, one of our technicians, before the captain ever went into the cargo section itself. But since Gaites has a reputation for taking life easy, Sneat has succeeded in unloading part of the blame. Meanwhile, Sneat has on his record the inspector's commendation for extreme thoroughness.

12/07/96

Sneat seems to be weathering his unpopularity pretty well, all things considered. For some reason, Gaites is now getting most of the blame for the delay.

12/08/96

Another facet of Sneat's character has come to light. The one officer on the ship with any social standing is Grunwald, the navigator. Grunwald's uncle is governor of New Venus. Grunwald likes chess. Sneat has now taken several tapes on chess out of the ship's library.

12/12/96

In the rec. room tonight were Grunwald and Sneat, playing chess. Afterward, Grunwald expansively pointed out certain fine points of the game. Sneat was all ears—an attentive student eager to learn from the master.

A peculiar thing has turned up lately. On most of our trips, there is a feeling on the ship of well-earned contentment. On this trip, however, there is an undercurrent of rankling dissatisfaction. The original delay, and the charges and countercharges between Sneat and Gaites, seem to have started it. But now that it *is* started, it apparently goes along by itself, one man speaking sharply to another, to produce a vicious circle that is gradually changing the emotional atmosphere of the ship.

What the captain plans to do about it isn't clear. I've remarked on it to him, but it may well be that he doesn't appreciate it. Around him personally, everything is as it was before.

12/15/96

Sneat now seems to be close friends with Grunwald. He is also getting to be friends with Meeres, the medic. Meeres is interested in psychology. Lately, Sneat has been busy with the psychology tapes. Soon he should be able to listen and ask questions intelligently, which should seem fine to Meeres.

12/18/96

If Sneat isn't playing chess with Grunwald, he is likely to be talking psychology with Meeres.

12/19/96

So as to keep Sneat from step-by-step turning the whole ship with the exception of the captain and me, into an "I love Sneat" society, I've pointed out to Willis what is going on. Strange to say, Willis hadn't noticed it. Now that he does notice it, he is once more turning a cold eye on Sneat. The sorry part of this is that the ship is being split into factions.

12/20/96

Willis tells me that Sneat has been needling Ferralli, the drive technician, because Ferralli is overweight. The rest of the crew has also kidded Farralli, but that was good-natured. Sneat's procedure is different. The other day, he asked Ferralli, "Say, boy, are you expecting?" Ferralli smiled dutifully. After a few wisecracks, any other crewman would have let it go. But Sneat harps on the theme: "Say, is it going to be a boy or a girl?" "What are you going to call it?" Sneat has now given this mythical baby a name—"Oswald"—and the whole business is getting on Ferralli's nerves. This is the kind of joke other crewmen will drift into when they can't think of anything better to say, and it is only a matter of time till Ferralli lashes back. Very quickly we may get into a situation where everyone is jabbing everyone else's weak point, and then this ship will be quite a place to live.

12/21/96

I just had a talk with Ferralli. In the less than three weeks since this trip started he has changed from a happy-go-lucky crewman to a mass of bitterness. He says everywhere he turns, someone asks, "How's Oswald?" Everyone, that is, except Sneat. When the going gets rough, Sneat is likely to stop it, saying, "Ah, come on, fellows, break it up. He needs his strength." Ferralli says he knows Sneat starts it; but when Sneat gets the others to leave him alone, Ferralli actually finds himself feeling grateful. The thought goes through his head, "Sneat isn't such a bad guy, after all." I said I supposed this was exactly what Sneat wanted. Ferralli suddenly burst out, "If he doesn't leave me alone, I'll kill him!"

12/22/96

Now, too late, I see why Sneat singled out Ferralli to pick on. Nearly everyone is now afraid of Sneat's tongue. If this were a military ship, we would no doubt so cramp Sneat that his effect would be barely a tenth what it is now. But as it is, it's a civilian ship, with civilian restrictions, and on top of that the captain seems to be patiently waiting for something. What he is waiting for, I don't know. Meanwhile, there is a steadily increasing amount of bad feeling building up, that gives the impression of an open powder keg just waiting for a match. Sneat has begun calculatedly insulting Willis and me, so it seems obvious which way the force of the explosion is supposed to go. So far, Willis and I have had several clashes with Sneat, but he is clever with words, and always wins. Lately I have caught myself wondering how Sneat would react if he found himself stuffed head first into the garbage disposal unit.

12/23/96

Willis suggested that I change shifts at dinner tonight so I could see for myself how Sneat operates during meals. The captain generally switches from shift to shift to check on the quality of the food, and as a rule takes his tray elsewhere at dinner—so that if we lesser ranks want to indulge in horseplay, he won't cramp our style.

But tonight, to my surprise, the captain stayed to eat with the rest of us.

He had hardly sat down, in a general atmosphere of dull brooding apathy, when Willis nudged me, and I heard Sneat make a needling comment to Meeres, to the effect that Ferralli seemed to be "eating for two," didn't he?

I was just starting to wonder how anyone could possibly control that kind of needling when the captain's voice said coldly, "What was that, Sneat?"

For just an instant, Sneat looked jolted. Then he glanced up and said ironically, "Did you say something, Captain?"

In the same cold voice, the captain said, "As you know, Sneat, you just made a comment about someone 'eating for two.' Explain it."

"Just part of a private conversation, Captain."

"You mean it doesn't have anything to do with anyone else here? Just you and Meeres?"

"Did I say that?"

The captain didn't say anything for a moment, and Sneat smiled very faintly. I glanced at the captain, feeling the same frustration I'd felt when arguing with Sneat myself. The captain, however, was looking at Sneat with an expression of intense concentration. Something seemed to rise up in the backs of his eyes as he said, in a very gentle voice, "Do you understand the laws on 'incitement to mutiny,' Sneat?"

A heavy silence settled in the room. Sneat looked jarred for the second time. So was I. It seemed to me that Sneat had skillfully avoided that pitfall.

Before Sneat could say anything, the captain said, looking directly at Sneat, "Why are you so afraid to explain that comment you just made to Meeres?"

"I've already explained to you, captain, that that was part of a private conversation."

"I notice, Sneat, that you avoid the word 'sir' as if you were afraid of it. Just what is it you're afraid of?"

A faint puzzled expression crossed Sneat's face. He opened his mouth and shut it again. Then he stiffened angrily. It occurred to me that somehow the captain had thrown him off-balance.

Again, before Sneat could say anything, the captain spoke.

"You know, Sneat, a private conversation is usually a conversation not many people know about. You don't carry out a private conversation in a loud voice, with other people around, do you?"

Sneat relaxed, and spoke in a drawling voice.

"Well, if you must know, Captain, and if you want to make Ferralli feel bad—go ahead and ask."

"Then you admit that what you said was intended to make Ferralli feel bad?"

"No, but your rubbing it in might make him feel bad. Probably has already, in fact. Why don't you drop it, Captain?"

By now, everybody was glancing tensely from Sneat to the captain. The captain was looking directly into Sneat's eyes as he spoke again.

"You know, you can start trouble, but you can't expect always to drop it and slip out from under, leaving other people to bear the burden."

Sneat started to speak, and the captain added, "There comes a time when the burden lands on *you*."

Sneat sat very still, then casually shoved his chair back.

"You're the first captain I've ever met who tried to badger his crew. I don't think I care to finish this meal."

"People who needle others shouldn't be so sensitive. Just as a cargo-control man who causes a forty-eight hour delay shouldn't try to shift the blame to someone else."

This caused a general stir in the room. The captain made this comment just as Sneat started out, and added, "Naturally, if you have nothing to say in your own defense, you *should* go."

Sneat suddenly swung around and snapped, "That cargo section was filthy!"

Gaites was at the table, and stood up. "The devil it was! It was clean!"

Sneat cast a shrewd calculating glance at Gaites. "Everyone knows you're lazy."

"Yeah? Do you want a punch in the teeth?"

The captain said coldly, "Gaites has been on this ship for a long time, and we never had a delay or a complaint. You no sooner stepped on board than we had a forty-eight-hour delay, for weevils that weren't there. Every previous trip we've taken has been pleasant. Since you've been here there's been nothing but trouble." The captain paused, then added, "Unfortunately, I am forbidden by regulations to reveal anything about the ship or ships you were assigned to before this one."

Sneat opened his mouth, then closed it again. A look of angry indignation crossed his face.

The captain waited politely, and then someone started to laugh. In a moment, everyone would have been laughing, because Sneat was caught in his own traps. Everyone *would* have been laughing, but the instant the first person laughed, Sneat glanced directly at him and said, "Shut up."

This produced another tense silence, and suddenly something in the air of the ship seemed to change.

A tall crewman stood up, and said slowly, "I was laughing, Sneat. Now, with all respect to the captain, I would like to make just one comment. If I may, sir?"

He glanced courteously at the captain.

"Go ahead," said the captain.

Sneat abruptly turned on his heel and started out of the room.

The tall crewman looked at our cargo-control man's retreating back and said clearly, "I am inviting you, Sneat, to tell me 'shut up' just once more, either now or later."

Sneat walked out without replying.

The tall crewman glanced around before sitting down. A set of hard approving glances answered him. Then he looked directly at the captain, and said, "Thank you, *sir*."

The captain smiled. "You're very welcome." He added, "Now, I would like to make a brief announcement." There was an immediate silence, and the captain said, "The base has granted us a Christmas present. We have been given permission to land and spend December 25th and 26th on the planet of New Cornwall."

There was a startled silence, then a roar of cheers. *Planetfall!* How the captain managed to wring that out of Base, I don't know. But all of a sudden we were the same old ship again. The mood and atmosphere that had been missing were back once more. Suddenly the crew began to sing, "For he's a jolly good fellow."

In the midst of all this renewed good will, with everyone feeling like his own self again, I happened to look at the door.

And there was Sneat, looking in.

He was still with us.

12/24/96

I asked the captain today if there was anything we could do to transfer Sneat, or in some way get him off the ship. I suggested that if he happened to stay behind on New Cornwall, that would be fine.

"You mean," said the captain smiling, "if he should by chance get cracked over the head and dumped up some secluded alley, just before we take off?"

"That's what I had in mind, sir."

"Hm-m-m. Well, we can reserve that as a last resort. But I don't think it will be necessary. Do you know much about New Cornwall?"

"No, sir. Of course, we've all been looking it up in the atlas. It's a planet now well into its first stage of industrialization, with a fast-growing population. I don't understand their government system."

"What don't you understand about their government?"

"According to the atlas it's a 'representative absolute monarchy.' There couldn't be such a thing."

"Well," said the captain, smiling, "wait a while. And don't be too hasty about tossing Sneat up an alley with a big bump on his head. Bear in mind how men have always dealt with trouble-some creatures."

"What do you mean, sir?"

"Men bait rattraps with cheese and bacon."

I stared. "But how does this help us with Sneat?"

"Why does Sneat try to terrorize a whole ship? What does he like about this? I'll tell you my opinion: Sneat likes power."

12/26/96

Well, we came down to the planet in the tender, and yesterday was a wonderful Christmas.

To begin with, we no sooner landed than crowds of people welcomed us, and we were all given invitations to spend Christmas with individual families. While we were still overwhelmed from this, we got the additional shock of seeing local officials snap to attention, salute the captain, and call him "Your Highness." This seemed fairly ridiculous, but the captain took it calmly, and pretty soon a white motorcar drove up, there was a blast of trumpets, and everyone fell on his face except the captain and the rest of us from *Starlight*. This incident left us feeling totally out of focus. But that is a small price for having forty-eight hours leave on a real planet. We were willing to overlook the strange local customs.

The next thing we knew, a flunky jumped off the back of the white car, grabbed a polished silver handle and hauled open the rear door. He flattened himself in the dust as a fresh crew of flunkies rushed to unroll a long purple rug about two-and-a-half feet wide. This stretched from the rear door of the car to the captain. This bunch of flunkies then fell in the dust.

While we are staring at this, there stepped out of the car a tall man with a grim enduring look, dressed in several yards of white cloth trimmed in gold and silver, with flashing epaulettes, several rows of medals on each side of his chest, a purple sash, a sword, and a silver and gold baton in his hand.

This mass of flashing color strode up toward the captain, and they stared each other in the eye.

The captain seemed to have a faint smile as he said in a loud clear voice, "How stands the kingdom, Your Royal and Imperial Majesty?"

"It stands well, as you left it, Your Royal Highness."

Just in front of the car, one of the loyal subjects was getting this all down with some kind of camera on a tall tripod. He was doing this while lying flat on his stomach, and staring into a periscope arrangement with a couple of remote-control handles that aimed the camera.

I was beginning to wonder if this wasn't some kind of joke or carnival performance, when somebody nudged my arm. I realized it was Sneat. In a low voice, he said, "Look there."

I looked, and saw, about eighty feet away, an armored car with its gun aimed at us. There was another one nearby, and near that about thirty men carrying long guns and wearing over their left breast pockets an emblem like a silver gunsight.

I glanced around uneasily. "What is this, a trap?"

"No, no," said Sneat, in a low excited voice. "It's the king's guard. See that crown on their left shoulders?"

True enough, that did seem to be it. I looked hard at Sneat in curiosity. It was the first time I had seen him with that eager excited look.

Well, in due time the formalities between the captain and the local king were all concluded, they bowed to each other and the king turned around and started back to the car. The set of flunkies that handled the purple rug sprang into action and rolled it up behind the king as he neared the car. A new set staggered around carrying another rolled-up rug, which they set down in front of the captain. As fast as the first set rolled up the purple rug, the second set unrolled a light pink rug with a purple stripe down each side. Along this, the captain walked.

I glanced around as this procession headed for the car. First the king, then a bunch of flunkies rolling the rug up about two steps behind him, then a new bunch unrolling another rug, then the captain walking along about two steps behind them. All around me were men from *Starlight* with their jaws hanging open, eyes staring, and glancing back and forth from the car to the line of armed guards.

About this time, a third set of flunkies heaved the top off the rear of the royal car, and a fussy individual began rearranging the cushions. The king and the captain got in, all the rugs were rolled up, and car set off to a blast of trumpets.

Sneat said in irritation, "That business with rugs was overdone."

I stared at him, trying to see his viewpoint. But now all the populace, that had been flat on their faces a minute ago, stood up. They seemed to think nothing of having spent all that time flat on the ground, but immediately took up the conversation where they had left off, so that in a few minutes we were each setting out in company with a different family.

Well, we had a morning of sightseeing, many of us went to church, and we all had a big Christmas dinner. The main topic of local conversation was the coming election. I listened in silence as long as I could, but finally was overcome by curiosity.

"*Election?*" I asked.

"Oh, no," said my host. "*Selection*. You see, His Majesty has worked at the job for a decade now. Naturally he's tired. Tomorrow a successor will select himself."

"Select *himself?*"

"Of course. The job is a tremendous burden, you know. It would hardly be fair to *force* it upon anyone."

"You mean, someone *volunteers* to be king?"

"Exactly."

"Well—What if a halfwit—"

"Such people are not qualified."

"All right. But if your kings are *absolute* monarchs, what's to prevent you from ending up under a dictator?"

Everyone laughed. "True," said my host, "in the bad old days back on Earth, such things happened. But here, modern science prevents it. *Our* kings think only of the good of their subjects."

"How does science manage that?"

"I'm sure I couldn't say."

"How do your kings 'select themselves'?"

"Why, we gather in the great arena. The first man to cross the line is king."

I stared. "A sort of race?"

"Oh, no. Not a race. There is never a rush to step over the line. You'll see what I mean."

It developed that the tests we had been required to pass to become spacemen were stiff enough to qualify any of us to become king of New Cornwall if we wanted, and therefore we all ended up the next day with our hosts in a gigantic sports arena hung with silver and gold banners, and with a long straight purple line drawn down the length of the arena.

As we watched, a military band played a march, a line of horsemen in blue uniforms with silver breastplates and drawn swords rode in, there was a blast of trumpets, and the king came in followed by a herald with a big scroll, who walked out to a microphone set almost at the purple line, raised the scroll, and read:

"Be it known, that our illustrious king and emperor, desiring to lay down the heavy burden of his duty, hereby throws open to all you qualified and assembled—be you of native birth or whatever, so long as you be human—the right to ascend the throne.

"With this right, be it well and clearly known, pass the command of all the armed forces of the planet New Cornwall, and the absolute right to command of each citizen what you will, and to be obeyed.

"Whosoever desires to achieve this absolute authority, and whosoever is willing to accept the heavy burden it entails, let him so signify by stepping forward across this line."

There followed a half-hour harangue to point out the nobility of taking up the burden, and the need to give the present king, who had worked hard all this time, a well-earned rest.

At the end of this half-hour, Sneat stepped forward and crossed the line. Sneat is now king of New Cornwall.

12/27/96

This evening, I was busy filling out the necessary forms to account for the disappearance of Sneat, when the captain walked in.

"Well," he said, "that was better than bashing him over the head, wasn't it?"

"Yes, sir," I said. "This really gets him out of the crew for good. A little rough on the planet, though."

"Oh, no. Sneat will make a good king." The captain spoke in the positive manner of one who knows by direct experience. He added, "After all, he hasn't any *choice* in that matter."

I shoved back the forms and turned around to face the captain. He was looking at me with his usual expression, which is a sort of quiet authority. A slight change of the lines around mouth and eyes can shift this expression to one of friendly warmth or arctic chill. It was now necessary to risk the chill.

"Sir," I said, "you realize that this ship is a mass of boiling curiosity?"

"It's good for them," said the captain, with a faint grin. "It will take their minds off their troubles."

"I can't think," I said, "of anyone I'd want to have over me as an absolute monarch. But if I *had* to choose someone for that position, the last person I'd pick would be Sneat."

"And yet," said the captain, "most people you might pick would kick and scream to get out of the job. Sneat *wants* it."

"Yes," I said. "As you remarked earlier, Sneat seems to love power. But does that mean he should *have* power? Human history is overburdened with men who loved power, got it, misused it, made their subjects miserable, and were finally overthrown by some new power-maniac. Then the new man went through the same process as the one before."

"True, but all that is systematized down on New Cornwall. The average king only lasts about eight to ten years. After that, he can't get rid of the power fast enough."

"Then there must be special conditions," I said.

The captain nodded. "There are special conditions. It would be interesting to know why it is that great genius will suddenly appear in one place, and not in another place where conditions look just as favorable. New Cornwall, as you know, is not fully industrialized. But its citizens trade their products with worlds that are industrialized. Advanced electronics equipment is available on the planet, and of course, it has to be kept in repair. Skilled repairmen make an excellent living. It is like this on other worlds, but it was on New Cornwall that the genius appeared."

I listened intently, and the captain went on. "This man became interested in the relationship between the electrical current used in man-made apparatus, and the impulse that passes along a nerve in the body of an animal. The result of his studies was a tiny device called a 'neurister'. A neurister, surgically inserted in the proper place, can receive from outside a signal especially keyed to it. The result of this signal is that the neurister stimulates a nerve nearby. And the result of this is that the person in whom the neurister has been inserted feels a sensation from that part of his body."

A chill traveled up and down my spine. "What kind of sensation?"

"Depending on the circumstances, a sense of uneasiness, a pressure, an itching, a burning, a feeling of pain, or—in the extreme—downright agony. From the king down through the dukes and earls to the lowest squire, the governing authorities on New Cornwall are all liberally supplied with neuristers."

The captain glanced at his watch, and added, "About this time, I imagine, Sneat is stretched out on the operating table."

"Much as I dislike Sneat," I said, "I wouldn't have wished this on him."

"You didn't have to. He chose it himself."

"Who pulls the switch that sends the pain through him if he gets out of line?"

"Each of the nobles has, while he's in office, not only a set of neuristers, but what corresponds to a relay, located within his body cavity. Each of the loyal subjects, on the other hand, has within him a small device corresponding to a transmitter."

Suddenly it dawned on me. "You mean—If, say, some dark night there's a catastrophe like an earthquake or a flood—"

A faint grin crossed the captain's face, and he nodded. "Squires, knights, baronets, barons, viscounts, earls, marquises, dukes, princes, and king—everyone having any authority in the region—suddenly wakes up with a pain in the part of his anatomy that corresponds to the source of the trouble. The king, for instance, is likely to come to at 3:00 a.m. with a peculiar grinding pain in the upper part of the calf of his left leg, whereupon he will jump out of bed shouting, 'Quick! I think another typhoon just hit Bijitoa! Get the disaster crews ready!' The Viscount of Bijitoa, whose whole body is now one living ache, will already be doing everything possible."

"But," I said, "if Sneat has absolute authority, tell me why couldn't he order the neuristers removed?"

"Yes, but here is the real work of genius. A special type of neurister-transmitter responds directly to a triggering impulse from the brain of the king or nobleman who has it. The activating impulse is the thought of evading duty."

"Then what happens?"

"Every neurister in the body is activated. It's like a slow dip in boiling oil.

"It has its compensations," said the captain. "He will have as much authority and respect as he could easily ask for. After the conventional term, a new selection will be held, the neuristers will be removed, he'll have a bonus and a small but steady income. The people will respect him, and whenever he's on the planet he'll have full honors and the courtesy title of 'Your Highness.'"

Suddenly I was alert. "They'll call him 'Your Highness'?"

The captain nodded, then smiled and rolled back his sleeve. Above the wrist, his muscular arm was marked with a number of small fine scars. He said, "I know whereof I speak."

A moment later we had said goodnight, and he was gone.

I sat still, aware of the change that had taken place in the ship in the past few days. Once more everything seemed smooth, efficient, and good-natured.

There could be little doubt that the captain knew how to run things.

No wonder.

BILL FOR DELIVERY

Dear Sam:

I agree about keeping in touch. Old pals should stick together, especially when they're both in the space transports.

Your letter, with quotes from your diary during *Starlight's* trip with the troublemaker, reached me after apparently being forwarded over half the known universe. I promptly slipped the message spool into the viewer, but I can tell you that I slipped it in with trembling fingers, owing to what I've been living through myself. I have to admit that what you went through was pretty awful. But I'll tell you, Sam, what I'm going through is worse yet.

Just as you're first officer on *Starlight*, I'm first on *Whizzeroo*. You will see from that name that our company isn't quite as dignified as the one you're working for, but never mind that. It could be worse. One of our sister ships is TSM *Clunker*. The way these names come about is, the Old Man looks at the records of this or that ship, and all of a sudden he gets red in the face, bangs on the desk, and yells, "Look at this lousy record sheet! They call this the *Star of Space*, hah? Why, they haven't met a schedule in the last ten trips! *Star of Space*, my foot! From now on they're *Muddlehead*!"

And that's that. Next trip to the loading center, out comes a crew to paint out *Star of Space* and paint in *Muddlehead*.

The Old Man judges strictly by results. If you have a streak of

425

bad luck, or even if the whole crew comes down with the green sandpox, through no fault of their own, that's still no excuse. All it wins you from the Old Man is:

"Don't give me your alibis! *Did* you keep the schedule or *didn't* you keep the schedule?"

The answer better be, "Well, yes, chief, *sure* we kept the schedule!"

"O.K. That's all I'm interested in."

You see what I mean. It makes it kind of rough if, through no fault of your own, the gravitor gives out before its triple-clad warranty period is up, or a jump-point slides out of congruity and hangs the ship up in the middle of nowhere for a month. It doesn't matter if you don't have any more control over the trouble than you have over the speed of light. The only thing that counts is, *"Did you keep the schedule?"*

I think you get the picture, Sam. This just isn't an outfit where they study the crew's brain waves after every trip, or send along psychologists, nurses, and free candy bars to keep us happy.

Now as for this trouble I'm in. I think I ought to tell you that the way the Old Man operates is kind of old-fashioned, from some points of view. Now, don't think I'm saying that it's ridiculous. A forty-five automatic is pretty old-fashioned, but when the big lead slugs start coming out, I'll tell you, there's nothing ridiculous about it. That's what you've got to bear in mind when I tell you about this.

One way the Old Man is kind of old-fashioned is the way he operates when somebody double-crosses him. There was a third officer a while back that false-boosted a cargo of first-grade Stiger hides, jumped ship at the next loading center, and collected a neat eighty-thousand profit for the hides and the cargo-section. This bird invested thirty thousand in laying such a long crooked trail that it would cost a mint to track him down and catch him.

Now, the modern, up-to-date space freight executive will not let emotion cloud his reasoning, but will feed this problem to his computer, and will come up with the best answer from a strictly profit-and-loss standpoint.

And what did the Old Man do? Well, they tell me the first thing he did was to rise up behind his desk, spin his chair over his head, and slam it into the wall thirty feet across the room.

"I'll get that crook if it kills me."

Now, as to exactly what happened next, I don't know. I wasn't there. But the bird that stole the hides turned up ten months later orbiting a planet in a space yacht, stone dead with an iron bar wrapped around his neck.

Now, it's a very old-fashioned thing—it's "positively infantile behavior"—to go out and nail the bird that's robbed you, especially when he's laid such a crooked trail that it compounds the loss to locate him and give it to him right between the eyes.

It's old-fashioned. But I'll tell you, Sam, it really discourages the next crook that gets a bright idea.

Double-crossing the boss is rough business in this outfit. Honest but stupid mistakes can be almost as bad. There was, for instance, a cargo-control man on one of our ships—it's named the *Moron's Delight* now—who made three blunders in a row, on the same trip.

First, he missed cold-mold spots on a cargo of hardshell beans. The mold ate into the beans, generated heat and moisture, the beans sprouted, and the cargo-section arrived at the pick-up station split wide open with green slop drifting out.

. Next, he O.K.'d a pressure-plate-type elevator-section filled with a cargo of grain that had cutbug eggs in it. The eggs hatched into maggots, which, eating steadily, grew into armored slugs, and then looked around for some rock to drill into for the next step in their life-cycles. The nearest thing was the wall of the elevator-section, which, as a result, arrived at the pick-up station holed like a sieve, with the grain drifting in a giant cloud around it.

You might think this was enough disaster for anybody, but this cargo-control man was exceptional.

The next cargo was a complete self-contained automatic factory, built for an ore-rich planet with conditions too tough for human comfort. You know how these self-contained factories work. Roughly, one part has diggers, crushers, grinders, and conveyers; another section has separators and furnaces, and the chemical-treatment centers where objectionable impurities are got out, and alloying elements put in; further on there's Special Processing, followed by Manufacturing, where the finished product is made. Another section houses the hydreactor, dynamos, and energy-balance equipment, while yet another has the automatic control center. Outside, there are arrangements to move slowly from place to place, as the factory eats up the ore supply.

There's one more device, that receives the signal by which the factory is controlled from a distance. If you want it to make one thing, you send one signal. If you want it to make something else, you send another signal. The exact nature of these signals is a deep, dark secret, with the control apparatus put together in sections, one contractor knowing one part of the plan, one another, and so on.

But there's a funny thing about these self-contained factories. On recent orders for checking cargo, the cargo-control man is instructed as follows:

WARNING! THIS AUTFAC-62A IS PROTECTED AGAINST SCALE BY SPECIAL CHEMICAL COATING PROCESS. DO *NOT* USE ELECTRONIC PROBE TO TEST FOR SCALE.

The "NOT" in this warning is put in red and underlined three times.

Now, in the first place, no one can buy any chemical coating that will stop scale organisms, despite the terrific demand. Anyone with such a process could make a mint. Therefore, why keep it secret?

And in the second place, why be so desperate to keep the cargo-control man from using his electronic probes? How could they hurt a *chemical coating*?

You see what I mean. There's a screwy aspect to the warning. But there must be *some* reason for it.

Now, what do you suppose this cargo-control man did when he saw the warning?

Right.

He read it over three or four times, growled, "They're nuts," and went ahead and used probes *anyway*. I had this direct from the first officer of the *Moron's Delight* while we were in an entertainment palace on a frontier planet called Snakehell.

The *Moron's Delight*, by the way, makes the run from Snakehell *out*. Personally, this was the first time I ever knew there was anything out beyond that place. But apparently the Old Man found some excuse to open up an outbound run.

Now, as you know, these automatic factories come in different sizes. The biggest come in pieces, with teams of specialists to cluck over them all the way out.

But the particular factory entrusted to *Moron's Delight* —which was named *Recordbreaker* before this happened—was the small model. This is about a hundred feet long by eighty wide in the middle, and has roughly the look, from overhead, of an Earth-type horseshoe crab.

To protect it from damage, the factory has to be put in a cargo section, and the contract specifies a particular kind, specially shaped and padded, and made of thick high-quality alloy steel.

Any spaceman can see that this super-duper cargo-section uses a lot more steel, and everything else, than it needs. But, of course, it was the automatic-factory company's engineers who made up the specifications, and what they know about design-ing cargo sections could be written on the head of a pin. Still, there's no getting out of using the things, since they're specified in the contract.

Now, to get back to the cargo-control man on *Moron's Delight*. Having checked the way the factory was bedded into its gigantic flexwood rests, and having examined all the springs, pneumatic pads, layers of plastic webwork and everything else on his checklist, he duly came to the warning NOT to use his electronic probes, and used them anyway. He didn't find anything wrong, put his O.K. on the necessary papers, and the cargo section was boosted to the cut-loose point. Then the ship started back.

When the deluxe cargo section reached a certain position, it would make a subspace jump. The detectors showed that it did that, so of course it seemed that there was nothing to worry about.

The only trouble was, the cargo section went on through sub-space and *never came out on the other end*.

It's not hard to guess what went wrong.

When this cargo-control man ignored the warning and used his probes on the factory, he was begging for trouble.

Obviously, the wizards who made the factory wouldn't be so illogical without *some* reason. Since they didn't want the electronic probes used near the factory, it must be that the probes would somehow interfere with it. Since the reason they gave wouldn't hold water, there must have been some *other* reason.

Now, just what part of this self-contained factory could the signals from the probe affect? Certainly they wouldn't hurt the digging or initial-processing equipment. But what if, after going through all the elaborate precautions for secrecy, it just happened to turn out that the signals from the probes could activate the supersecret remote-control unit—*by pure accident*?

Sure, they'd make changes. But until then, how to safely ship the almost-finished factories for rush orders they had on hand?

That must have been the reason for the gibberish about the new chemical coating. A cargo-control man with any kind of nose for trouble would read that warning, and you couldn't pay him to put a probe in there.

But, as you remember, this particular cargo-control man did it anyway.

Naturally, life being as it is, he activated the remote-control unit. That started up the factory.

Now, the factory was designed to mine iron ore, and, using its own special process, turn it into iron and steel goods. Well, the whole hundred-foot length of the factory was packed in an alloy steel container. The diggers, crushers, and grinders were designed to handle any ordinary ore, but you can see that an ore of the hardness of this alloy-steel container would pose something of a problem for the factory.

Also, the factory was designed to move under its own power to the nearest ore. But in this case the ore—the alloy steel cargo section—could be detected in all directions, completely surrounding the factory.

Apparently it took time for the factory's computers to work these problems out. So everything seemed peaceful and quiet when factory and cargo section disappeared into subspace.

But not too long after that, the factory apparently worked out the difficulties, slid out some newly-fabricated, specially-tipped drills and magnets, and settled down to business.

When time came for the cargo section to go back into normal space, there wasn't enough left to do the job. It had been eaten up by the factory.

When the alarm on this missing automatic factory came in, naturally nobody had any idea *what* had happened. But it looked like someone had worked out a way to highjack a cargo part way through subspace.

Right away, the Space Force got worried about the possibilities, and put out an All-Sectors alert.

No doubt you heard about that alert, at the time. But you

remember, they called it off, and they never did explain what happened.

Naturally. They were too embarrassed.

They did find the factory, surrounded by a vast number of little metal objects of two kinds. One was a short hollow cylinder closed at one end and slightly flared at the other, about the size of a large inkwell, and with a tiny bouquet-of-roses design on one side. The other objects were little, slightly-arched disks, with a small handle on top of each one. There were literally millions of these things, each one made out of very thin cast-iron.

The Space Force, operating under an All-Sectors alert, was keyed up to the limit to begin with, and at first didn't know what to expect from all these objects. After they got over that, there was the problem of getting the factory into another cargo section, when all the factory was interested in was eating up the cargo section and turning out more millions and millions of these little disks and cylinders. One thing led to another, and since it all took place in subspace, everyone was pretty frazzled by the time they got the factory *out* again, along with some millions of its products.

Meanwhile, anyone with the leisure to stop and think was trying to figure out the function of these small cast-iron cylinders. The disks fit neatly right on top of them, but what was their purpose?

You can imagine their frame of mind when it dawned on them that this miracle of modern science had succeeded in converting an expensive alloy-steel cargo section into a host of worthless undersize cast-iron chamber pots. Worse yet, they couldn't turn the factory off, because the supersecret control-signal generator had been shipped out by a different route, using a competing carrier. And when the special factory representative did arrive, it developed that the factory, in solving the conflicting orders put into it by the accidental signals from the probes, and then in carrying out the mismatched orders by reducing high-quality steel to cast iron, had acquired a "hardnose psychosis," and become "perverse and uncooperative."

In short, the expert couldn't shut it off. Instead, the factory got hold of his control-signal generator and made fifteen or twenty little chamber pots out of it, and he was afraid to go back in there for fear it would try the same thing on him.

You can see, Sam, it was a wild life while it lasted.

Now, the upshot of this, so far as everybody working for the company was concerned, was the renaming of the ex-*Recordbreaker*, its dispatch out beyond Snakehell, the sudden disappearance of the cargo-control man, and a ten per cent cut of all pay clean across the board, including the Old Man's salary, so the company could pay off that cargo section the automatic factory ate up. There was also a big uproar about the psychotic condition the factory had got into, and threats of lawsuit, but the Old Man got it across to the manufacturer just what lousy publicity could come out of this. So everything is now settled except paying for the cargo section.

What I'm trying to get across, Sam, is just how fast you can get flattened if anything goes wrong, and also I want you to get a good clear picture of the trouble-potential of this cargo-control man who disappeared after *Recordbreaker* was renamed *Moron's Delight*. If there was ever anyone who served as a regular magnet for bad luck, he seems to be the one. Of course, he came to us with a wonderful recommendation from Interstellar Rapid Transport, but they're a competitor, if you get what I'm driving at.

Now, Sam, as for my own little difficulties. As I told you, that mess you ran into with the troublemaker was pretty rough, but it looks like a vacation compared to what I've got on my hands.

I think I've told you enough so you'll understand when I say the Old Man has a special way of reacting when anything gets him in a corner. If you think he refers to a computer for the optimum way to maximize profits and minimize losses, I haven't got the picture across. What he does is to cut rates, and speed up schedules, and grab every piece of business he can lay his hands on, practically no-questions-asked.

Ordinarily, we're a little careful about what we contract to deliver. As you know, there's always some zoo eager for a prime specimen of two-hundred-foot live *kangbar*, or some research institute that's just dying to crack the secret of those radioactive cysts that turned up after the big explosion on Cyrene IV. The job the Old Man contracted for wasn't quite as open-and-shut as these two. On the surface, it looked like a borderline case. You'd never touch it if you didn't need the money. But to look at it you'd think you *might* get out of it in one piece. Unfortunately, when this contract came through, our ship—*Whizzeroo*—happened to be between jobs and in a good spot to take it on.

The first I knew of this, "Hook" Fuller, second officer of *Whizzeroo*, walked in and shoved a sheet of message paper under my nose. I looked at it and read:

AM TAKING ORDER FOR DELIVERY FIFTY LIVE BANJO-BIRDS TO HUMAN RESOURCES RESEARCH CENTER ON ULTIMA STP DETAILS FOLLOW STP I AM COUNTING ON WHIZZEROO STP DON'T LET ME DOWN

The Old Man's name was right there at the end of it.

"Fifty live banjo-birds," I said. "What's a banjo-bird?"

Hook may not be grammatical, but he knows his job, and he's tough enough to last in this business.

"Damn if I know," he said, scowling. "But it don't sound so good to me. I been trying to talk the captain into shorting out the gravitors and begging out of it, but the captain's afraid the Old Man might find out."

Pete Snyder, the third officer, spoke up hopefully.

"Maybe we could break off the end of the locking hook. It's already worn down pretty bad. Then they'd have to send us back for a refit and *Spittoon* would get the job."

"That's no good," said Hook, "because this Human Resources outfit is sending their own special cargo section, and it don't hook on. You tow it with cables and spacer bars."

For the next half hour, Hook, Pete, and I sweated over the problem of getting out of this assignment. But we just couldn't find any way out, and in due time we ended up off a pioneer planet that the atlas called "Rastor III" and that the pioneers called "Poverty." The special cargo section was already there, and we seemed to be stuck with the job.

As a last resort, Hook, the captain, and I put it to Barton, our cargo-control man.

"Listen," said the captain, "I'm not eager for this job. There's half-a-dozen subspace jumps between here and cut-loose, and one of these jumps winds us on some new route out beyond Snakehell. We're taking these jumps with a spar-and-cable outfit, we've got to play nursemaid to fifty good-sized birds for the whole trip, and it isn't enough that we certify them now at the start, but they've got to be certified all over again before every jump. We can't just walk down the corridor to take care of them, either, because the cargo section doesn't hook in close. It's just cabled up. Worse yet, the spars are so long the corridor extension won't reach. There's no way to get from the ship to the cargo section without suiting up. Frankly, Barton, this job stinks. Can't you find *something* wrong with the cargo section?"

"Sir," said Barton, "I've turned myself inside out hunting for something wrong with that cargo section. That's the best set-up cargo section I've seen in some years."

"How about scale?"

"No scale in it, and this trip it wouldn't be critical anyway."

"Why not?"

"It's the birds we want to get back. Scale won't hurt the birds. Besides, there's no scale there."

"What about all that freak equipment to keep the birds unconscious? Any flaw in that?"

"Not that I can find. All that stuff is warranted anyway."

"That won't keep it from failing."

"No, but it means we can collect if it does fail. Besides, I can't find anything wrong with it. There's only one thing I can think of."

"What's that?"

"If the cargo section's jump equipment is out of phase with ours, we could refuse to use it."

"No soap. We already checked that."

"Then we're stuck with the job."

Hook and I argued with him, the captain threw his weight behind us, but Barton wouldn't budge.

The next thing we knew, we were ferrying up banjo-birds and loading them into the cargo section, where each bird was supposed to get strapped into his own individual couch, and have an anesthetic tube clapped over his nostrils. This is easy to say, but when you consider that each of these birds stands about three-feet eight-inches high, weighs around sixty pounds, has a set of short powerful wings armed with hooks, has spurs ten inches long on the back of each leg—not to mention the claws—you will see that we had quite a lot of fun getting these things to lie down and breathe the anesthetic. And I haven't even mentioned the best part of this bird yet. That is the bill. You would expects birds built on these lines to have short curved heavy beaks. But not these things. They have a straight slender bill around two feet long, and as sharp on the end as a needle. Since the male birds use the bill like a rapier, it's quite an experience to handle one of them. I almost forgot to mention the male birds' yellow down—if that's what to call it—which is made of innumerable tiny barbs which dig in, break off, work into your skin, and fester.

Thanks to the colonists, who had each bird tied up in a leather bag with its feet strapped together, head sticking out, and a strap on its beak, we were able to load the things into the tender and get them up and into the cargo section. Unfortunately, there was no way to get them strapped onto their individual couches without taking them out of the leather bags. Once we did that, their wings were free. Then the fun started.

I know, you can say, "Why didn't you anesthetize them first?" Well, the anesthetic was intended to keep them under, in a kind of light doze, for the better part of the trip. It was mild, slow-acting stuff, and didn't work unless you could keep the birds' nostrils up tight against the hose for about five minutes. But you had to strap them in to keep their heads still, and to do that, you first had to get them out of the bags. That freed their wings.

Now, the first thing a bird did when his wings were free was to use them to rip the strap off his beak. Now he could stab in a three-hundred-and-sixty-degree arc with that beak.

When he stabs something with it, he puts all his force directly behind the point. The bill will then go through a regulation space-suit, through a man's thigh inside the spacesuit, and stick out the other side, as we discovered from experience.

The only restraint on the bird was the knotted thong holding his legs together. He wasn't strong enough to break the thong, and his bill wasn't made for ripping and tearing. All the same, he was able to hop around after a fashion, and under the light artificial gravity this was bad enough.

Well, you can guess what happened. One thing led to another, and several of the men, jumping back to get out of the way, lost their grip on the leather bags and let more birds loose.

Pretty fast we found out that the birds fight with the bills, not with just us, but each other. The males start up a kind of fencing match, strutting and thrusting, and the females give a *chirr* noise, and sneak kicks at any other females in reach.

Of course, we had this contract, so we had to keep the birds from killing each other. But we had a little handicap we'd never dreamed of.

What seems to set the males off is the yellow down or feathers of the other males. The females, we discovered, have a duller, sand-colored down. Unfortunately, our spacesuits, for visibility, are bright yellow. We had put on our spacesuits to make it safer handling these birds. It didn't work.

As I can think of no words to do justice to the scene in that cargo section, Sam, I'll just have to say that the birds had everything their own way for the first half hour or so.

Then one of us stopped running, jumping, and parrying beakthrusts long enough to realize that that habit of stabbing at anything yellow could come in handy.

The end of the next hour found us looking down on a good dozen of these birds with their bills stuck fast in a yellow-painted two-by-four that we found amongst the dunnage. They were pretty subdued birds, I'll tell you. But now it occurred to us that the birds *still* weren't where we had to put them. And first we had to somehow get their beaks *out* of the two-by-four.

This turned out to be a long, delicate process of tapping the two-by-four with hammers, and once we had it done, we couldn't get anywhere till we painted the spacesuits the exact sand color of the females' down. This put the male birds in a pleasant enough humor so we could strap them down. But handling the female birds, we had to either paint the suits yellow again, or else get kicked senseless at the first opportunity. The female birds don't seem to use their beaks to fight with but they have big clublike spurs, and they don't hesitate to use them.

By the time we got everything done, we were a sorry-looking crew, covered with stab-wounds, bruises, sweat, brown and yellow paint, and raised red splotches where the down hooks had sunk in.

Our medic was afraid the stab wounds might get infected, and since his method of insuring against that was to thrust a swab in to the full depth of the stab, you can see that our misery wasn't over when the birds got through.

I have felt almost that bad at the end of some trips, Sam, but never before at the *beginning*.

"Well," said the captain, flat on his back in a pool of sweat, with the medic just putting his equipment back in his carrying case, "that takes care of 'A.' I'll tell you boys, if 'B,C,D,' and 'E' in this job are like 'A' was, I'll turn in my commission and retire."

We took that, of course, for just so much blowing off steam, but he had a point all right.

Hook gingerly felt a purplish bruise at the calf of his leg. "I think we're over the hump. After all, we've got 'em tied down now."

"I *hate* live cargo," growled the captain, as if he didn't hear. "I particularly hate working for a zoo, a museum, or a research center."

"Why so?" I asked, and he pointed to a copy of the contract lying atop his locker.

"Hand that thing down and I'll show you. I didn't want to show you till we got past this point."

He opened up the contract, searched through it, and read aloud:

"The aforesaid authorized carrier does hereby warrant and agree, in addition, to release from confinement and individually feed and exercise, once each standard Terran forty-eight-hour period, each and every one of the aforesaid units of live cargo, as defined above. The feed and exercise period will be not *less* than forty standard Terran minutes, and not *more* than eighty standard Terran minutes."

Hook clapped his hand to his head, and I sagged against the bulkhead.

"There's fifty of them," said the captain. "If we exercise each of them every forty-eight hours, and do it for forty minutes apiece, that means we're going to be working at it all the time, since it's going to take time to wake them up, and it's going to take time to strap them in afterwards."

"Why," said Hook, looking dizzy, "can't we just forget that part of the contract?"

"Because," growled the captain, "then the birds will die, the contract will fall through, and the Old Man will flatten us."

Well, there was nothing to do but go ahead with it, but before this trip was half up I, for one, found myself wondering which was worse, the Old Man, or the birds.

For one thing, there were just too many of them. It took about a one-hour minimum from start to finish to unstrap, wake-up, feed, exercise, and re-anesthetize, each one of the birds. If there had been fifteen or twenty of them, maybe one or two men could have handled the job, but there were fifty. Then, this one-hour period assumes that nothing went wrong. That was the exception. Nine times out of ten the bird took a crack at a sleeping bird, or it rammed its beak into the man taking care of it, or it bounded up and slugged either him or some bird lying on its back, with both feet.

It wasn't long before we were all either laid up, or else just getting over it. If the birds had gotten weaker or more tractable as time went on, maybe we could have stood it. Instead, contrary to what anyone would think, they just got more cranky and hard to manage. They were wearing us out a lot faster than we were wearing them out.

And, because of the stringent penalties in the contract, we mustn't let any one of the precious beasts be seriously injured.

The reason for the whole trip, according to the captain's information, was that the colonists on the planet, who naturally tried every kind of food they could lay their hands on, had found that the liver of this bird, eaten cooked or raw, created a tremendous sense of well-being, backed up by every outward evidence of health. After about a week, this faded out, leaving whoever had eaten it very sleepy. Aside from the need for twelve to fourteen hours sleep for the next two or three nights, no harmful side-effects resulted, and the treatment could be repeated, again with no visible harm from it. The Human Resources Research Center naturally wanted to find out about this. The obvious way to go about it would have been to cut out and freeze the livers of the birds, and ship *them* for analysis. But the scientists at the Research Center on Ultima had apparently discovered it was easier to get a great big grant for a great big project than to get a little modest grant for a little modest project, so they were going at it in a big way.

That was great for them, but it was ruining us.

Along in the fifth leg, when we were ready to make our next-to-last subspace jump, and Barton, the cargo-control man, had just finished his check, a male bird that was being exercised went past Barton, and spotted the yellow underside of the flap of the open pocket that Barton kept his notebook in. The bird whipped his needle-sharp bill around and rammed it through the flap.

The bill passed through the upper part of Barton's abdomen on the left side, angled slightly upward and came out the back on the right side. Barton collapsed.

The crewman exercising the bird wanted to wring its neck, but no, of course, he couldn't do that, or he'd bring a huge penalty down on our heads.

The medic said there was nothing he could do except ease Barton's pain. The only way to save him was to get him to a hospital. We called a nearby colony planet, and learned that it was an idyllic place to live, but it had no hospital. A Space Force dreadnaught answered our emergency call, and said they had facilities to handle the case. An intent Medical Corps colonel made an examination, and said Barton would recover, but would need plenty of rest and special treatment. The last we saw of Barton was his smiling face above the sheet on a stretcher as he was carried out through the air lock.

Naturally, we were thankful for Barton's sake. But this left us with no cargo-control man.

And under the terms of the contract, a duly-accredited cargo-control man had to check the cargo and certify it before each and every subspace jump, or a massive penalty would be levied, wiping out the profit of the trip.

This seemed bad enough, but this was just the start. Next the captain announced that he had completed his thirty years' service three days ago, and, taking advantage of the retiring captain's privilege, he directed me to set him down, with a list of stores, on that idyllic colony planet we'd turned to for help. We tried every argument we could think of to get him to change his mind, but he said, "No, boys, I'm retiring as captain of the *Whizzeroo*. Damned if I intend to stay on, and then retire as captain of the *Flying Junkheap, Pack of Boobs,* or *Cretinous Jackass.*"

Well, we could see his point all right, and after arguing till we were blue in the face, we finally had no choice but to let him go.

This, of course, made me acting captain, Hook acting first-officer, and so on. But this was the kind of ship—like one on a collision course with a sun—where a raise in rank didn't bring quite the zestful feeling that it ought to.

Since Barton had checked the cargo and certified it, we could now make exactly one more jump. We had to make two to fulfill the contract.

Hook said earnestly, "I wish *I* had thirty years' service behind me."

I nodded glumly, "I know what you mean."

"What do we do now?"

"The only thing I can think of is to send a priority emergency message asking the Old Man for help."

Hook snorted. "What can *he* do? Beside blame us for the whole mess?"

"Cargo-control men retire just like anyone else. But their certificates are still good. If the Old Man can pull enough strings, he may be able to get the Colonization Council, or maybe the Colonists' Protective Association, to run through their recorded files on nearby planets, for a retired cargo-control man."

With no real hope, we settled down to wait for a reply, and kept busy feeding and exercising the birds. The birds kept getting shorter-tempered and nastier and since we had gotten fairly skillful at warding off kicks and stabs from them, they now developed the habit of hitting us with the undersides of their wings. This doesn't sound bad, but the wings are about the only part of these birds that had actual feathers. And along the outer edge of the underside of the wings are several rows of quills that didn't develop into feathers, but end in barbed points. These aren't the hooks I mentioned earlier; these are in addition to the hooks.

By this time, we were all wearing some kind of armor under our spacesuits, and were worrying for fear the birds might break their bills on the armor and thus become 'imperfect specimens' which would incur another of the contract's penalties. Added to all our other worries, this business with the wings almost brought us to the breaking point.

Now, however, to our astonishment, we got the following message from the Old Man:

CARGO CONTROL MAN RECENTLY RETIRED
LOCATED ON HELL STP THAT IS COLONISTS
NAME FOR THE PLANET STP YOU WILL FIND

IT IN THE ATLAS UNDER CASADILLA II STP NO
DETOUR NECESSARY AS THIS IS JUST BEYOND
YOUR NEXT-TO-LAST JUMP STP GET THERE FAST
AND OFFER BONUS KIDNAP HIM OR DO WHAT-
EVER YOU HAVE TO STP ANY COLONIST SHOULD
BE HAPPY TO GET OFF A PLANET WITH THE CLI-
MATE THAT ONE HAS STP COLONIST REPORTED
TO HAVE SETTLED IN PLANETS ONLY CITY WHICH
HAS FIVE HUNDRED INHABITANTS PLUS A SPACE
COMMAND COMBAT-TRAINING HQ STP NAME OF
CITY IS SALT SWEAT STP CARGO MANS NAME IS
JONES STP GO GET HIM AND DONT WASTE ANY
MORE TIME

We read this over several times, then headed for the planet.
The subspace jump was smooth, and we had no trouble of any
kind. The Space Force center on the planet co-operated with us,
located Jones, Jones was eager to get off the planet, and agreed to
end his retirement at once and ship with us at standard wages.

We were dizzy with our good luck, but somewhere a warning
bell was going off. It couldn't be *this* easy.

When this cargo-control man came on board, with hangdog
expression and unwilling to look us in the eyes, we had our
first nasty suspicion. The fellow had a kind of sloppy quickness,
as if he drifted into trouble through lack of method, then tried
to get out by snap decisions. He'd answer without thinking, and
several times shot out lightning replies without waiting for the
whole question. I guess this was supposed to show brilliance,
but since he didn't guess the right questions, the effect sort of
fell flat.

When we'd got him out of the control room, Hook looked
through his record folder and swore.

"This is the same bird that did it to *Moron's Delight*. After
that, the Old Man gave him highest recommendations, and he
transferred to Comet Spacelanes."

Pete Snyder straightened up.

"I wondered what hit them! Remember that double wreck and
explosion?"

"Yeah," said Hook.

"Then what?" I said nervously.

"Well, they juggled him around from ship to ship, and then they gave him highest recommendations and he hired out to Outbeyond Nonscheduled Freight. He lasted one trip with them and it says here he voluntarily chose to retire when the ship reached Casadilla II."

"'*Voluntarily chose to retire*'?"

"That's what it says here."

I'd never heard that one before. I said, "Funny the Old Man didn't do that to him."

"The Old Man had it in for Comet. This fellow damned near wrecked Comet."

"And now," I said, "we've got him."

"Yeah. *We've got him.*"

Like I said at the beginning of this letter, Sam, that mess you had with the troublemaker was rough, but this mess is worse yet.

As I see it, I've got exactly four choices:

1) Watch this cargo-control man day and night, and go the rest of the trip on schedule. But when you've got somebody like this aboard, things go wrong that you never dreamed of.

2) Dump him back on Casadilla II before he has time to wreck anything, and go ahead with no cargo-control man. This will cost us a huge penalty, and the Old Man will tear us to shreds.

3) Break my own contract, forfeit pay for this trip, and settle on Casadilla II. What this involves is pretty clear from the name the colonists have given the planet.

4) Turn pirate.

I don't know what you would do, Sam, but after careful thought I've decided to put this fellow under heavy guard, lock him up till we're ready to make the next jump, bring him out just long enough to let him make his inspection and put his signature on the certificate, and then lock him up again. It doesn't seem like he ought to be able to do too much damage, that way.

After this last jump, we cut the cargo section loose and another line will pick it up and take it the rest of the way to Ultima. We'll be coming back this way, so when we get back here, we'll let our friend "voluntarily choose to retire" all over again, and then we'll head back for a refit. We need a refit.

Now, Sam, here's what I'm going to do. I'm going to leave this letter here, with instructions to hold it unless something happens to *Whizzeroo*, or unless we just disappear and don't show up for a long time. If that happens, they're to forward it to you.

But if we get back all right, I'll go right on from here and let you know just what happened. So you'll know from whether there's any more to this letter whether we got through in one piece, or another one of those fantastic accidents hit us.

I don't think this cargo-control man ought to be able to hurt us too much, if we watch him day and night.

But you never know.

Like I say Sam, this here is a real mess.

As ever,
Al

UNTROPY

Dear Sam:

As you'll see from the return address on the message spool, I am not writing this letter from any place you'd be expecting me to write it from, and as you'll see from the date above, I am writing it a little later than I thought I would. But I'm writing it, Sam, and let me tell you, that's a lot more than I expected to be doing just a little while ago.

As you remember, the last time I wrote was to tell you about that mess we got into trying to deliver fifty live banjo-birds, each of which weighed around sixty pounds, from a frontier planet called Poverty to another carrier who would deliver them to a research outfit on Ultima.

What with their spurs, claws, hooks, bad dispositions, and two-foot long, needle-pointed beaks, these birds proved to be quite a problem. The contract was filled with strict requirements and heavy penalties; one of the birds rammed his beak through our cargo-control man; and then our captain, who had just completed his time, chose to retire onto a nearby colony planet.

This left us stuck with these fifty birds and the contract, with no cargo-control man and no captain, and with the Old Man back at company headquarters breathing fire and impatiently eying the schedule.

Then, when we did manage to locate a retired cargo-control man on a colony planet, he turned out to be a shifty-eyed individual with a long record of disasters, and all told, he scared us worse than the birds.

As for a captain, that, in theory, was duly provided for in the regulations. I was first officer, so the captain's retirement automatically made me acting captain. Unfortunately, so far as having an *actual* captain was concerned—

Well, most of the men we have for officers and crew got recruited from colony planets, where they grow up rough, tough, and independent. You don't impress them much with little brass insignia. They look to the man behind the symbol. And they all knew I was *really* Al, the first officer and not the captain.

The result was, I still got the same respect as before, with a little bit added because on paper I was now top dog, and with a sizable chunk taken away, because the captain, the *real* captain, wasn't here now to back me up.

If you've ever been in this spot, Sam, you know it doesn't take long to get pretty tired of it.

Well, one thing led to another, till it dawned on me that we were right next to running the boat on a committee basis, with each and every committee member having his own private veto. There's not too much first-hand information on how this committee system of running a ship turns out, because it's not too often any survivors of it ever come back alive. It's sort of like the question whether you feel any pain when you blow your brains out. There's not much really reliable first-hand information on the subject.

Before we found out the answer for ourselves, it happened one day that "Hook" Fuller, now acting first officer, was in my cabin with me, resting up after a bout with the birds. Pete Snyder, acting second officer, and Ace Bartry, acting third officer, were there, too, everybody sprawled around wondering how we were ever going to get out of this mess in one piece. Now, as it happened, I had this unreliable cargo-control man locked up in the captain's cabin, because it was roomy and had its own toilet, and the fact of this Jonah having the captain's cabin grated.

Pretty soon, right there before my eyes, the committee system went to work to decide where to stick the cargo-control man, and in the process, good old Ace said things it was O.K. for him to say to his pal, Al, but that weren't so hot for a third officer to say to any ship's captain anywhere, acting or otherwise.

I don't know, Sam, if you ever heard of Iron Fist Karmak, but I served under him once, and I made the mistake one time of arguing a point when the right thing was to say "Yes, sir," and go do it.

Iron Fist Karmak then made a little speech. It was one of those that burns itself into your memory in letters of fire, and that you can really remember afterward, because you wake up nights with it running itself over in your head. Even yet, I still wake up sometimes in a cold sweat, saying "Yes, sir. I will, sir." Then it takes a little while to get unstuck from that speech and come back to the present.

What I'm driving at, Sam, is that I didn't have any trouble remembering that speech. It presented itself to me, ready-made, when Ace Bartry disputed my arrangements for running things, and then, since there was not another thing I could have done to straighten the mess out, I let Ace have that speech, right between the eyes."

When the smoke and dust cleared away, and Ace swallowed hard, and said "Yes, sir. I will, sir," and saluted and stumbled out of there, the overall ricochet, fragmentation, and general shock-effect of that speech brought Pete Snyder to his feet as if he'd been lifted up by the back of his neck, and he excused himself and cleared out, too.

This only left "Hook" Fuller, the acting first officer. I was afraid maybe I'd overdone the thing, and now I wouldn't have anyone to talk to, but Hook only grinned, and wanted to know where that speech came from.

Well, I was telling him, and we were congratulating ourselves that maybe things would run smoother now, when a crewman came rushing in and said the cargo-control man was in the cargo section, and had ordered all the birds unstrapped so he could carry out an inspection of the anesthetizing equipment.

Sam, nobody could describe the scene in that cargo section. Luckily, only about a dozen of the birds were actually unstrapped before the first one woke up and took off after the cargo-control man. By the time we got there, there were eight of them after him, and he had the interstellar sprint record sewed up tight. I could tell you, I suppose, how we finally got the birds off him, how we distracted them while we stuck the boob in the space-suit locker to keep him out of the way, how we finally got the precious birds strapped back in their anesthetic couches, and then how—drenched in sweat, and with the deck seeming to rise and fall around us in waves—we stood there and heard the insane raving of this cargo-control man, who was having some kind of megalomaniac seizure right there in the suit locker, and was threatening us with all kinds of punishments because we'd interrupted his inspection.

I *could* tell you, Sam, but you already know all about those birds, anyway. And every time I think about that scene in the cargo section I can hear the blood start to roar in my ears, and see the incandescent spots dance before my eyes, and I'm not so sure I want to relive that part of it for a while yet.

Just take it from me, we were in a rare frame of mind by the time we got this raving cargo-control man crammed into a suit that was free of beak-holes. We got the face plate on, then we bundled him out through the cargo-section air lock and onto the net. This sobered him up pretty fast, maybe because it occurred to him that all we had to do to get rid of one of our troubles was to give him one good shove. In any case, when we got him inside the ship and dragged him out of the suit, he'd stopped raging, and we had the shifty-eyed hangdog boob who'd signed on in the first place.

After this experience, we naturally expected every imaginable kind of trouble getting past that one subspace jump that remained between us and transfer of the cargo. So we put a couple of big bolts on the outside of the cabin door, and kept the cargo-control man locked up tight in there, with a guard outside keeping track of him, and didn't let him back into the cargo section until just before the jump.

Hook and I got him alone before he went in, and we put it to him in little words just what would happen if he tried what he'd done the time before. We went into the cargo section with him, along with the better part of the crew, which was split up into squads and all set for anything.

While we were all on our toes, set for the worst, the cargo-control man carried out a kind of half-hearted inspection, shrugged, and signed the necessary papers. The instant he finished signing the papers, Hook, who was taking no chances, reached over with a length of pipe and laid him senseless on the deck. We got him out of the cargo section, back into the ship, and locked in his cabin. Then we stared at each other.

This seemed to end our problem.

We felt like people who'd been all set to lift the three-hundred pound weight, and it turns out to be just hollowed-out balsa wood, weighing six ounces.

We should have been relieved. Instead, things seemed to get out of proportion, and we had to remind ourselves that the business wasn't over yet. We still had to make the actual subspace jump, and then connect up with the other carrier.

The jump was no trouble. And when we finished it, there was the steady beep of one of the other ship's signal beacons, telling us everything was in order. In a little while, we'd be in contact with this other ship, which was named *Starbright*. It all seemed too easy.

About this time, Pete Snyder came in carrying a little flat brown bottle, and showed it to Hook. After he'd questioned Pete for a while, Hook handed me the bottle.

"Ace is with the cargo-control boob in the library. While the cabin was empty, Pete went through it and found this."

The crisp, neatly-printed label on the bottle read: "o-Amino-p-sugadeine(2,3,4-tribaloate)-quinquigesimophenoleine." While I was mentally groping around, trying to figure out what this might be, it dawned on me that under this were a couple of other words, in very fine type. I took the bottle over to the control console, where there was a better light, and managed to read it:

(Purified Hopweed)

I looked around. "Pete found this—"

"In the cargo-control man's stuff."

"And he's where?"

"Library."

On this trip, the ship's library had gotten so little use I'd forgotten we had one.

"What's he doing in there?"

"He says he wants to change his specialty. He's studying up on navigation. He says that being a cargo-control officer has led him astray and he wants to return to the true path."

I got hung up for a few seconds trying to figure out the reasoning behind this, but finally managed to get loose. "And where was the bottle?"

"His bunk mattress was cut open at the top, along the edge. Pete says there were half-a-dozen of these in there."

Hook and I stared at the powder in the bottle. Hook looked up.

"What do we do?"

"Better have Pete put this stuff back with the rest. Have him try to fix the place it was in so it won't look like anyone's gotten into it. We'll figure this out later, after we get rid of the cargo section."

Hook nodded, and the communications man said, "Sir, the captain of *Starbright* wants to talk to you."

Naturally, he would. The cargo remained technically our responsibility till *Starbright* had the cargo section. While *Starbright* couldn't actually escape the terms of the contract through this technicality, they could stretch them considerably. If any of the birds, for instance, were a trifle sickly, *Starbright* could suffer a series of unfortunate accidents that would so delay transfer of the cargo section that the sickly birds would have time to weaken and die—with us. Then *we* would get hit with the penalty, not *Starbright*. There were quite a few variations on this idea.

"O.K." I said, "but let's have a short-focus transmission." Nearly everyone on the ship was bandaged up, and it seemed just as well not to advertise this fact.

The communications man said, "Short-focus transmission. Here you go, sir."

The screen lit up to show a sleek-looking officer with every hair in place, uniform fresh and crisp, and insignia glittering. "Omark, Captain, T. S. M. *Starbright*, Central Transportation Lines, Incorporated." There was that about his smooth tone of voice that suggested the purr of a large fat cat eying a canary.

Across the control room, Hook shut his eyes.

Starbright's captain came to the end of his introduction, and stood there looking superior, smug, and completely in control of the situation.

Well, as you know, Sam, in our outfit, we don't go for this superior-attitude stuff. We have *other* methods.

I looked at him on the screen for a while, as if I were looking at some weird kind of bug. Then I said, "Do you know what you're getting into, Omak?"

"What's that?"

"This is a tough cargo."

"What's wrong with it?"

"I don't know as there's anything wrong with the *cargo*. I'm just wondering if *you* can handle it."

This brought him halfway down off his perch, but he was back up on it in a flash.

"An inspection crew will be alongside your boat in twenty minutes. See that the cargo doors are opened at once, or you may suffer some unexpected delays."

His face registered untouchable superiority, but he already had one foot in a trap. I looked at him, and he sighted down his nose at me. Then I let him have it.

"Before you dish out the next threat to hold us up, Omak, remember that the Commission frowns on these artificial delays. This conversation is being recorded." Of course, he should have avoided this obvious mess. But he had gotten irritated.

His expression showed that he knew trouble when he saw it. To paste over the hesitation, while he groped for a way out, he said, "My name is *Omark*."

Naturally, I knew his name. But the idea was to get him mad.

"I'm not worried about your name, Omak. I'm wondering if you can handle the cargo. Do you know what it is?"

"Certainly. It—"

"And no inspection crew is coming aboard this ship, Omak. You can send a cargo-control man and one other into the cargo section. Or you can look yourself."

The look of anger that went over his face was real now. He glared out of the screen.

"Listen, you—"

"Have you considered subcontracting this job? We might run it the rest of the way in, for a price."

The last of his air of superiority evaporated into raw anger. "Listen, you outplanet junk-jockey, we've handled tougher cargoes than you ever heard of. No, we *won't* hire you to run it through for us." He turned away from the screen to bark orders, then looked back, "Cast it off, and get out of our way."

He had now said the words. But it wouldn't hurt to reinforce them.

"If you want it that way—"

"That's the way it's going to be."

I let a look of imitation respect seep onto my face. "As you say, Captain Omark." I turned to Hook, who was out of range of the screen and grinning from ear to ear. "Cast loose the cargo section!"

Hook left the control room in a streak.

I turned back to the screen, where *Starbright's* captain now had a faintly bemused look on his face. It had evidently just occurred to him that there was a price on his having the last word. He was accepting the cargo section as it was, with no inspection at all.

"Ah—" he said, "the cargo—"

I tried to look friendly and considerate. If I remembered correctly, he had said, "Cast it loose," not "Cast the cargo section loose." If he thought of this, he might worm out of it yet. But once his men actually took charge of the thing, he was stuck with it.

"Captain," I said considerately, to get him off on another track and pass a little time, "to the best of my knowledge, one of the birds may be slightly lame. You may want to check the contract, but I believe—"

Hook's yell echoed up the corridor.

"Cargo section loose!"

To get rid of it that fast, they must have cut the cables, and left the crew men in the cargo section to get back on hand-jets.

I said, "Captain, my crew is very experienced in handling this sort of thing. They've already cast the cargo section loose for you. However, if you'd like to reconsider, and want to change your mind about contracting with us to take it back for you—"

He had now been formally told that the cargo section was his. Failure to object to this would constitute "tacit acceptance of responsibility" for the cargo section.

He said irritatedly, "No, we can handle it."

The thing was now officially his.

There would be no point trying to describe my feeling of relief, but Omark plainly caught it. He was now completely down off his pedestal, and wide awake.

He said shortly, "What's wrong with the cargo?"

"I haven't said there was anything wrong with it. I've been trying to tell you, it's tough."

"What do you mean?"

It was easy enough to answer that. As I described the birds' build, their hooks, claws, spurs, bristly down, rough quills and long sharp beaks, a look of comprehension began to dawn on the face in the screen.

"Maybe we *should* have subcontracted with you."

I smiled. "That offer is now officially withdrawn."

"I'll bet." He laughed suddenly, then shrugged. "Send a man over with the papers, and we'll get started. This is the kind of haul where we'll want to break speed records."

Half-an-hour later, all the formalities had been gone through and we were congratulating ourselves that, at last, we were completely free of the birds. We'd been in a nasty spot, but we'd come through.

We were so relieved we felt dizzy, and went around cheerfully hammering each other on the back.

I don't know just what it is, Sam, that makes a man forget when things are going well, the fly in the ointment that was obvious enough beforehand.

Anyway, Hook and me, along with Pete, wound up in my cabin, shaking each other's hands, congratulating ourselves that our troubles were over, and passing around a flask of Supernova Bottled Food Drink. They make this, you know, on Hyperion, where they have a strict prohibitionist government, and about fifty per cent of the planetary revenue comes out of "condensed high-energy liquid food-products." I guess if you run an acre of New Venusian rockwheat through a still and bottle it, you could call it that, all right. Anyway, we had several cases of it on board.

Well, the Supernova Bottled Food Drink was running pretty low, and the ship's officers present were worth around two cents a hundredweight, when there came a pound of feet outside, and Ace bolted in.

"Al . . . I mean Captain . . . the Jonah's taken over the control room!"

Iron Fist Karmak would have ended this in about fifteen seconds. But then, Iron Fist Karmak would never have filled up on Bottled Food Drink with the trip unfinished. While I was cursing myself for forgetting I was supposed to be captain, and struggling to get some idea through the haze of Food Drink, Pete rose slowly up off the deck, looked at Ace gravely, and fell forward on his face.

Ace said anxiously, "What do we do?"

"How'd it happen?"

"He came in with his uniform all neat and his brass polished, and a fusion gun in one hand, and told us he was taking over under Article 66, Captain Disabled or Lost Overboard, and said, on top of that, this was now a cargo section under Article 17, Definition of Relative Terminology, and to prove it he showed us two things like oversize duck eggs and said they'd hatch out into banjo-birds, and under the contract they had to be transported in a cargo section, so therefore this was a cargo section, and he was in charge of the cargo section."

Hook was lying flat on his back on the bunk, and had hold of it with both hands to steady himself. He was listening with an intent look except that now and then the pupils of his eyes took off and went around in circles and he almost fell off the bunk. He cleared his throat.

"Doped up. Hopweed."

I nodded. Obviously, that must be it. I glanced at Ace.

"He make any change in course?"

"Sure he did!"

"How? What did he do?"

"I don't know. I was face up against a bulkhead with my hands back of my neck."

"How'd you get loose?"

"He decided it was time for me to go off-duty."

Time was passing. I still hadn't thought of anything to do, but just then the tail-end of an idea went past, and if it hadn't been for the food-drink, I could probably have ended the mess right there. As it was, I could only grope for the idea.

Ace said urgently, "What are we going to do? We can't leave him there! He's setting us up for a jump."

Hook swung to a sitting position. "Can't jump here! This is uncharted!"

"What do you mean, he can't? He's going to! You can jump anywhere. The only difference is, we don't know where we'll come out!"

"Well, that's it! You could come out in a sun, or in some God-forsaken place. Only a madman or a hopped-up dope-fiend would—"

"What do you think this guy *is*?"

There was a silence during which we should have been thinking. Again, I almost had it, but then the food drink went to work, and about all that came to me was that this was unfair, it wasn't right, it—

Before I started babbling about this, and maybe getting out a handkerchief to cry into, I said, "Take hold of my arm, Ace, and lead me down the corridor to this bird's cabin."

Ace did as told, and we caromed off the bulkheads to the boob's cabin.

"O.K." I said, "see if the stuff is where he had it before. That powder in bottles."

Ace got on the bunk, yanked back the pillow and the covers, and felt around the side of the mattress. "It's here."

"Get the bottles out of there and hide them. Then wait in here, and when he comes back in, knock him senseless."

"O.K. But—"

"Before you do that, aim me down the corridor toward the control room. Just get me headed in the right direction."

"He'll kill you, Al."

"Never mind. That's my worry." I still didn't have any idea what to do about this mess, but I had to do something.

"What are you going to do?"

"How should I know?"

"But—"

"If I stay here, I'll pass out. Come on. Move."

"I don't know. It seems to me he'll just shoot you."

I let Ace have a few selected lines from the little speech I'd given him before, and his face changed color.

"O.K., then, I mean, yes, sir." He aimed me toward the control room. "I *still* don't see what you can do."

"Never mind that. This is what Iron Fist Karmak would do."

Ace said, in a peculiar voice, "Who is—" Then he gave it up. Anyone can stand only so much in any given length of time.

On the way past my cabin, I shoved the door open and spotted Hook, who'd evidently just finished dousing himself with cold water.

"Next time," he said dizzily, reeling across the deck toward me, "let's get some better brand. There's something about this Liquid Food Drink—"

"Like what?"

"I don't know. Wormwood, maybe."

I dragged my mind back onto the subject. Abruptly the idea came to me.

"Reach into my locker beside the bunk there, and get out the hypo gun we used for that load of zoo specimens. It's in the corner, on the right."

"That's too good for him. We ought to blow his head off."

"The trouble is, right now we might miss him. Then where'd we be? Get that gun."

Hook nodded. "This boat has a fairly thin hull, doesn't it?" The door of the locker clattered back, and in only two or three grabs, he had the gun. "Here it is. I hope it's loaded with—"

Just then, with both of us just starting to come back to our senses, there was a kind of twitch, a sort of sudden readjustment, and although everything looked the same, something was different.

" . . . Cyanide," said Hook. He handed me the gun, and said bleakly, "He did it."

I took the gun. One thing about this outfit, the Old Man insists on the best equipment for making sub-space jumps. There was just a trace of that queasy nauseous sensation.

"Come on," I said. "The two of us ought to be able to take him."

"Sure," said Hook. "I feel like half a man, anyway."

We groped our way down the corridor, and were almost there when there was a sort of twitch, a kind of unexpected readjustment, and the consciousness of a sudden change.

Hook caught his breath, and I stood paralyzed for an instant.

He had done it again. Now, had he jumped us back to where we started from, or—

Around and through us, there was a kind of twitch in the fabric of things, an unexpected rearrangement, and a sense of displacement in some indescribable direction.

A *third* jump!

Before anything else happened, I stepped into the control room, already squeezing the trigger of the hypo gun.

On about the fourth or fifth shot, I got him.

As the cargo-control man landed full-length on the deck, Hook staggered in, cursing.

"That last one was a long one."

"He was all set for another. Now, I wonder just where the Sam Hill he's landed us."

I hit the Astroposit button, and there was a long silence as the device compared local stellar patterns with known stellar patterns, and tried to find a match. At length, a strip of paper tape unreeled, and I tore it off anxiously.

POSITION UNKNOWN. SITUATION HIGHLY ANOMALOUS.

Hook swore. "I didn't even know it knew that word."

"Probably it never had reason to use it before." I glanced at the outside screen, and hit the wide-angle button. For just an instant, I stared at it, and couldn't believe what I saw.

"No," said Hook. "It can't be. It's the liquor."

"No, it isn't." Not even Supernova Liquid Food Drink could have done that. We had to find out, so I hit the Tridem Visual Display switch.

The control-room lights faded out. Around us, like shining points of light, appeared the three-dimensional image of the stars outside.

These stars were all of the same brightness, evenly spaced, in a regularly-repeated pattern.

In about half-an-hour, Hook and I had the cargo-control maniac strapped to the bunk in his cabin. Ace, tense with the knowledge of the number of jumps that had been made, almost brained us as we came in, but that seemed like a small matter. Hook and I were cold sober now, and when we brought Pete Snyder around long enough to see that stellar pattern, all of a sudden he was cold sober, too.

"My God," he said. "What is this," he demanded. "A joke?"

Nobody said anything, and Pete burst out, "There isn't any place like this!"

Hook said, "Think back. We've got a Jonah on board. He got control of the ship, and took three jumps."

"We've got to backtrack!"

We snapped the lights back on, and looked at the console. There were the subspace-jump master-control levers:

Recon. OFF
A.C.C. OFF

```
Monitor OFF
Memory OFF
Manual ON
```

Pete said in a whisper. "There's no record." An instant later, he said, "Maybe he just repeated."

"Nuts," said Hook. "The first two were different from that last one."

"If we could figure back from what he's got on the board—"

"No," I said, pointing to the automatic-reset switch. "That doesn't prove a thing. The board cleared itself after each jump, and he was setting it up for another jump just as I got in here."

Pete was staring into the outside screen. "There's no place where the stars are spaced that regular. There *couldn't* be."

Ace was looking at it, too, not saying anything. Then Pete said, in a shaky voice, "This place is different."

That sounded like the number one moronic comment of the year, but he had a point. There was something different in the feel of things—but it was hard to pin down just what it was. On an Earth-type planet, there's a different feel on a warm spring morning than there is on a crisp fall day. It's possible to pin down the reasons for that difference. This feeling was harder to pin down, but it was there just the same.

Ace nodded. "Something . . . something different. Let's turn that screen off."

I switched it off, but the peculiar sensation remained.

Hook snorted. "Between the local absinthe, the cargo boob, and that sight outside, it would be a wonder if we didn't feel funny. Let's get some sleep. At least the boob didn't land us inside a sun. Come on, tomorrow's a big day."

Hook's voice sounded a little strained, but he was moving in the right direction.

"Good idea," I said. "Let's go."

I started for the corridor, and the others followed.

We muttered dazed good nights to each other, and headed for our separate cabins. I didn't know about Hook and Pete and Ace, but I could feel those regularly-spaced stars looking at me right through the hull of the ship. I lay there for a while, face-to-face with the impossible, then rolled over and tried lying on my side, then on my back. It didn't help. I had such a vivid mental picture of those stars that we might as well have had a transparent hull. I glanced at my watch, and saw it was 0245, shiptime. Just then, there was a quiet tap, and I sat up.

"Who is it?"

"Hook."

"Just a minute."

I got up, snapped on the lights, and Hook came in, lugging the mattress off his cot and a pile of blankets, which he unloaded onto the deck. He said apologetically, "I keep seeing those damn stars, lined up for parade. There's something else, too." He flattened out the mattress and got the blankets where he wanted them. Then he whacked the pillow with his fist and lay down. "That cargo-control moron. Did you see how he landed, Al?"

"What do you mean?"

"When you shot him and he fell."

"He went down the way you'd expect if he was somebody kidding around. As if someone were to keep his feet together, lean, and start to fall. Only he wasn't kidding, so he went all the way, full length."

"Did he look natural to you?"

I put the light off and settled back into my bunk. Now that Hook mentioned it, there *had* been something weird about the way he fell. Then I shrugged. "To begin with, he was doped up. Then I shot him with a hypo gun. Naturally he didn't fall the way you might expect."

Hook sighed. "Turn the light on, Al." There was a tinkle of coins.

By now, I'd forgotten my own uneasiness, and was beginning to feel puzzled. I snapped the light on, and looked around.

Hook tossed a small a handful of coins into the air.

I watched exasperatedly, "What's the idea? Are you out of your—"

But by then, all the coins had hit the deck, and formed a nice neat pattern, the largest coin in the center, and the smaller ones alternated in a circle around the outside.

When I stared at this, Hook said, "When this cargo-control man fell, he started to reach back with his hands to break his fall, but then he passed out completely. He ended up flat on his back, with his body in a straight line, both arms out and the fingers spread wide. You could have run an upright mirror down the center of his body, and never have noticed the difference. One side was exactly the same position as the other."

Scowling, I said, "Let's see those coins."

Hook gathered them up, and handed them to me. I shook them up, and tossed them. They came down with the largest one in the center, and the others spread alternately around it, larger and smaller, to form the outline of a stylized, sharp-pointed star.

I looked at this for a while, then stared off into the distance.

I looked back, and there the coins were, still in the same pattern.

I took the coins in one hand, and instead of tossing them up, swung my arm slightly down, so as to scatter them in a rough line.

There was a clink and clatter as they hit, and then there they were.

The large coin was in the center, the others alternated in a long ellipse around it.

I shut my eyes, looked again, then got up and felt of the coins. Next I had Hook describe their position. It was exactly as it seemed to be. The coins, of themselves, had fallen into another regular pattern.

Hook said, "The odds against a thing like this are—" His face took on a peculiar expression. I guess he was trying to figure the odds, and couldn't keep track of all the zeros. "Well," he said, "the thing is *impossible*, that's all. When improbability reaches a certain point—"

"No," I said, "that's where you're wrong. No matter how improbable a thing is, that doesn't make it impossible. If you've got a hundred billion white marbles, and one blue marble, you might still reach in some time and come out with the blue marble."

"Yeah, but if you've got a hundred trillion trillion to the quintillionth power to the—" He went on adding powers and multiplying till he had to take a fresh breath. "If you've got *that* many white marbles, and just one blue one, *then*—"

I shook my head. "I sure wouldn't want to bet on getting it out of there. But as long as that one blue marble is in there, there's nothing impossible about reaching in and coming out with it."

"But the odds—"

"The odds are for betting, so you can judge what's likely over a long period, when everything averages out. The odds don't mean a thing on one single throw."

Hook looked unconvinced. I said, "There's a casino on Tiamaz, where one of the tables has a game played with seven wheels. Each wheel has sixty-four numbers, plus a zero. The numbers are alternating red and green. The zero is black. The rules of the game hold that if the little silver balls, and the golden ball of the master wheel in the center, all settle on zero, the player loses not only what he's bet, but everything he owns. Now, you figure the odds on *that* happening. But that's the rule, and on that planet, gambling losses are legal. Well, I was in there one night, just watching, when a married shipmate of mine, with a big ship-savings account, got into the game, just so he could say he'd played it. He no sooner got started then the number one wheel came to a stop and the little ball settled on zero. Then the next wheel stopped, and the little ball rolled on to sixty-four, then fell over onto zero. The another wheel stopped and the little ball settled on zero. Then another wheel stopped, and the little ball tipped off of number one, rolled onto zero, rocked back and forth and settled down there.

"Well, my shipmate was sitting there, gripping the table edge, moving his lips in silence, and dripping sweat onto the green cloth, as one by one the little balls stopped on zero. Then the last wheel came to a stop, and the last little ball rolled slowly around, and settled on number two. My shipmate shut his eyes, got up, slowly walked out, and I'd like to ask you the odds on what he'd tell you if you told him something can't happen because *the odds are against it.*"

"H'm-m-m," said Hook, and thought that over.

The saying has it that "Seeing's believing," but I don't know. The stars were right out there to look at, and there lay the coins on the deck in front of us; but here we were, arguing about whether it was *possible*, because it didn't seem *reasonable*. And it didn't seem reasonable because we hadn't ever seen it before. Maybe that saying ought to be, "*Habitual* seeing is believing."

"Well," said Hook. "I . . . I see you've got a point. But how do you explain a thing like this?"

I looked at those coins lying in a nice regular ellipse, and wondered how anyone could possibly explain a thing like that. On the other hand, it *had* to be done. If we couldn't explain it, we were going to be in a first-class mess tomorrow, as soon as the crew discovered what was outside.

Well, the wispy end of a thought occurred to me, and I started reeling it in, talking all the while to see how Hook reacted to the idea. He lay on his mattress with one elbow on his pillow, listening intently, while disbelief and hope flickered alternately across his face. Then suddenly he began to nod.

"That's it. You've got it, Al!"

The explanation satisfied him so well that he grinned, got up, and said, "Now I can sleep." He agreed when I insisted that he keep quiet about the coins, then went off down the corridor with his mattress and blankets, and I turned out the lights, lay back down on my bunk, and fell asleep. My last conscious thought was that I was going to have to give that explanation to the entire crew tomorrow, and somehow convince them.

Otherwise, we might have a mutiny.

Well, the ship's chronometer crawled around to what would have to serve us as dawn, and one thing led straight to another till there I was, talking into the ship's public address system. Word had gotten around pretty fast after the first glimpse at what was outside that thin hull.

"Men," I said, "as you've doubtless learned, we have a unique scene outside. Few if any other crews have ever had the chance to see this. What we see out there is nothing less than a complete reversal of the usual rule of Nature. The stars out there are not strewn around in random disorder. In this region of space, disorder is *not* the rule. You have only to look to see the proof of this."

"Experience," I went on, "teaches us that whatever a man tries to do, Nature will try to undo. If he builds a house, Nature will immediately go to work to level it. The natural tendency is for everything to be brought, ultimately, to the same low level of random disorder. We call this the tendency toward increasing 'entropy.' It is the tendency for all material things eventually to reach a vanishingly low level of available energy."

"What does this have to do with what we see outside?"

There was murmur of agreement. That was what they wanted to know, too.

"Why, it has *everything* to do with it. The *only* reason that what we see out there surprises us is—*we're used to the disorder of nature.*"

There was a tense silence while they grappled with this explanation. Happily, this part was apparently true. Later on, things got more doubtful.

"What we're used to seeing in Nature is *disorder*, stars scattered around at random, different sizes and types of stars mingled together without any apparent plan. Throughout history, man has stood for order, and has had to fight against Nature's disorder."

"But now, men," I added, "at last we're in a place where Nature does things *our* way.

"So you see," I said, speaking fast into the intense silence, "some people may say, 'It can't be,' but we know better. Overall, it may be that the increase in entropy, the general decrease in available energy, is the rule. Overall, a tendency for random disorder may be the rule. But there is nevertheless a distinct small chance of exactly the opposite behavior. And the universe is a big place. Well, men, we've been lucky enough to hit it! Maybe we're just getting paid back for what we went through with those birds. Whatever the reason, when that cargo-control man got at the jump lever, we didn't land inside of a sun. Instead, we were lucky enough to come out in a place where *order is the rule*."

There was a confused murmuring, because naturally they failed to see the advantage of the thing.

"And to prove it," I said triumphantly, "take a handful of coins, and just toss them on the deck, and see what happens. In this place, *random chance produces order infallibly*. We *can't* lose. Try it."

Hook was listening, with the air of a connoisseur, and now shook his head exasperatedly. He couldn't quite follow the last part of that argument, and he didn't think the crew would follow it, either.

From all over the ship, however, there now came the sound of coins clattering on the deck. A rising murmur of amazement suggested the proper time to say triumphantly, "So, you see, men, there's nothing to worry about. The tendency of this place is to increase its own order by helping us get away. We'll be out of here as soon as we have time to check the jump equipment. Meanwhile, I suggest that all men not on duty experiment with this condition of reversed-entropy. It's a rare opportunity, and one that few crews have ever had before."

There was a brief cheer from some of the men. I snapped off the public-address system, and took a deep breath.

"*Phew*," said Hook, looking dazed, "Well, it looks like that will hold them for now, anyway."

"How long to check that jump equipment?"

"Not long. If nothing goes wrong, maybe half-an-hour. But then what?"

"Then we get out of here."

"*Another* random jump?"

"Can you think of anything worse than this? Or can you figure out how to calculate our way out of this?"

"No. But—"

"How long is our explanation going to hold the crew?"

Hook nodded. "We better get out of here before the novelty wears off."

"That's what I figure."

"But how do we know we won't wind up inside a sun? And how do we get back on course?"

"I could explain that to you," I said. "And it's a very logical explanation. The only thing is, Nature and logic don't always agree."

Hook, squirming, looked surprised for just an instant, as if he saw what I was driving at. "Yeah," he said, "Well, let's hope this is *one* place where they *do*."

Thirty-two minutes later, I reached out like somebody working a Ouija board, set up the jump, snapped the automatic reset forward to clear the board right after the jump, and pulled the lever.

What I'd been basing my hopes on, and it seemed like a pretty weak reed, was the thought that in this place we had order, not disorder. At least, it looked like *our* idea of order. And it was, you might say, improbable almost, but not quite, to the point of impossibility. This was, in other words, a place where the next-to-impossible was established as the order of nature. In such a place, what would happen when we pulled the jump lever?

Anywhere else, the odds were astronomically against our getting back on course. But how was it here, where the order of nature was reversed?

This was one of those arguments that sounds good, but when you bet on it, you get flattened. Unfortunately, there was nothing else we could do *but* bet on it.

I don't doubt that other people have prayed harder than I did when I pulled that lever, but I was pretty near the top of my own form. Then there was that sense of a twitch, a sort of sudden readjustment that told of the jump, and then all of a sudden Hook, Pete, and Ace were banging me on the back.

"You *did* it, Al! You did it!"

"Did what? Are we back on course?"

"On course, my foot! Look at that screen!"

I wiped the sweat out of my eyes, and looked at it, then I shut my eyes, and looked again.

Centered on the screen in front of us was a loading-center, where ships like ours pick up and transfer cargo. Near the loading center, a huge beacon sent out its visual identification signal, which you might still pick up even if radio, radar, snap-beams, and everything else failed you. As the big beacon swung around, there was a dazzling multiple flash that we couldn't help interpreting.

And when we did, it was an inescapable fact that the almost-impossible had happened. This loading center was our home base. The central office was right there in front of us.

Well, as you can imagine, Sam, the Old Man was really surprised to see us. He wanted the whole story, so I told him all about it—birds, cargo-control man, liquid food drink, non-entropy region of space and all.

Naturally, I expected skepticism, pointed questions, close examination of the evidence, and finally reluctant acceptance of the facts for what they were.

Instead, the Old Man started to laugh. He got back away from the desk in order to have room to double up, and almost laughed his head off. Then with his face still red, with a grin from ear to ear, what did he do but say, " 'Volcanic Bottled Food drink,' eh? Is that the name of it?"

"No, sir." I could see this wasn't going to work out quite the way I expected. "Supernova Bottled Food Drink."

That sent him off again, and several times when I thought he'd come to the end, he'd bang his fist on the desk, and mutter "Supernova," or "Bottled Food Drink," and then he was off again.

This can get sort of wearisome after a while, but he was the Boss, and it didn't bother him. Finally he came out around his desk, squeezed my hand in a painful grip, banged me on the back so hard I almost went out through the wall, and said, "Good work! That cargo went through on time, no complaints, and I heard how you put the squeeze on *Starbright*. That's the stuff! Keep it up!"

"But—Ah—But—What about the stars? What about—"

He let out a laugh that bounced all around the room. "You want to change your brand, boy. You want to keep away from that Volcano Bottled Food Drink."

When I went out of there, he was still laughing, and they tell me he'd start off again for no apparent reason for days afterward. Meanwhile, he didn't lose any time showing his approval of the fact that we'd got the cargo through. I hadn't gotten back to the ship before there was a crew out there painting out *Whizeroo*, which was the name of the ship, and painting in *The Champ*, which was our new name. Personally, I liked *Whizeroo* better, but we didn't have any time to croak about that. Orders came through confirming us all in the rank we had after the captain retired, so now I was a *real* captain, Hook was a *real* first officer, and so on, instead of our just holding the rank more or less by accident. Right after we got word of this, our back pay came through, and since this was partly based on our new rank, it fairly blew the tops of our heads off.

After you've borne up under bad luck long enough, when it does turn and run good for a while, it's easy to confuse the change with a permanent improvement. If we'd had much more praise and good luck, I don't think Hook and the rest of us could have stood it.

Just as we were settling back to admire all the new stripes, and as we were wondering what to do with all that accumulated pay, a message came through from the Old Man, who had gone off to tie up some deal, and wasn't expected back for a while. This message was to us, and it went as follows:

HUMAN RESOURCES RESEARCH CENTER ON ULTIMA WANTS TO EXPERIMENT WITH CARGO OF LIVE NATURAL FOOD FOR BANJO-BIRDS STP HAVE CONTACTED COLONISTS ON BIRDS HOME PLANET AND MADE ALL ARRANGEMENTS STP DETAILS FOLLOW STP I AM COUNTING ON THE CHAMP AND KNOW YOU WONT LET ME DOWN

It took a second to realize *The Champ* was the new name for our ship. Then the details started to come in. It seemed that these banjo-birds, in their natural state, lived on a diet of "web-scorpions," "flying slints," and "double-ended greevils." In turn, these things, in order to stay in good health, required a steady diet of a variety of *other* things, equally outlandish, all of which had to be housed in a "pseudo-arboreal habitat." The idea was not just to transport the greevils, slints, and so on, preferably frozen or canned, but to lug around the whole "pseudo-arboreal habitat," with all these things in it. Alive.

The contract, as expected, specified that the greevils, web-scorpions, et cetera, had to be certified by a cargo-control man before each subspace jump, but after what we'd lived through, that was no surprise. What did give us sort of a jolt was the provision reading:

" . . . The aforesaid carrier does hereby warrant and agree that in no event will the food supply of the aforesaid units of live cargo be contaminated by permitting these aforesaid units of live cargo, voluntarily or involuntarily, to ingest human flesh, or extract from officers, crew, passengers, or others, blood and/or other nutrient materials whatever, in any quantity, manner, or under any condition or conditions whatever, foreseeable or not foreseeable . . ."

There are several other clauses in this contract along these same lines—namely, that we won't contaminate these specimens by letting them eat us up.

Well, Sam, it doesn't exactly sound *good*, and I don't know just what we'll run into, but I don't see how it could possibly be any worse than those birds.

Anyway, it isn't this new assignment that bothers us right now. What sort of burns us up is the reaction we get every time we try to explain about those stars. They don't call it a "mass-hallucination," which would be maddening enough. They call it, a "mass delirium tremens," and I never heard of anything like that.

I know, Sam, we should have kept some record of how to get back there, but then, a lot of people would have gone to look, wouldn't they? And that would have created *dis*order, right? And that, in other words, would have made our safe return a condition leading to increased entropy and *decreased* order, wouldn't it? But everything about that place showed that it favored *increased* order, not decreased order, so what do you suppose would have happened to us if we'd tried to keep a record of how to get back?

I tell you, Sam, there are a lot of people around today that you can't convince without a notarized statement, even when you've got a perfectly clear case, and unarguable good reasons such as I just mentioned.

Well, that's life.

Anyway, Sam, you believe me, don't you?

As ever,
Al

THE LOW ROAD

Dear Sam:

I'm not sure what order my letters have been reaching you in, but this one comes after we had that mess with the banjo-birds, finally got them delivered, and then the Old Man renamed our ship *The Champ*. I got promoted to captain, Hook got promoted to first officer, and so on. As you remember, the Old Man then sent us out to get a cargo of the things these banjo-birds *eat*.

Let me tell you, Sam, when we started that trip, we were really sitting on top of the universe. We had our accumulated back pay, our new stripes, the Old Man's praise, and our ship had a new name. In a transport outfit where the boss names the ships according to their performance, and where *Spitoon* is not the worse name, you can see how it would be to be captain of *The Champ*.

As for our cargo, that didn't worry us too much. After all, we'd lived through the banjo-birds with their needle-pointed two-foot beaks and vicious dispositions. We ought to be able to handle the web-scorpions, *slints*, *greevils*, *night-robbers*, and so on, that the banjo-birds lived on.

Well, Sam, what we overlooked was that the banjo-birds were *specialists* in *slints* and *greevils*, and we weren't.

I know, you haven't had any letter from me about that trip. I just haven't been able to bring myself to talk about it. You can get some idea when I tell you we no sooner limped back into the loading center, when out came a crew to paint out *The Champ*,

469

and put a new name on the ship. We were too beat up to care much, but we figured we'd got off easy when we found out the new name was *Bunglers All.*

What we didn't know was that the Old Man had just got started. Next came an order demoting the lot of us. Instead of being captain, I was now first officer. Hook went down to second officer, and so on. Pretty soon, we got our pay, and another jolt. The demotions were *back-dated.* Next came word that we were fined for various offenses, and out of our cut pay we had to hand over good-sized chunks for the fines. Believe me, there wasn't much left of us when the dust settled.

I know, you might wonder—couldn't we have fought it? In the shape we were in, we couldn't have fought our way out of a paper sack. And we would have run head-on into the Old Man's standard reasoning: "You do the job, and you get the pay. Don't do the job, and you get the axe." The Old Man judges strictly by results.

There *are* outfits where, if you come back a hundred eighty days late, doped to the eyeballs on bootleg hopweed and awash in home brew, with the cargo lost or forgotten, and then after you're back you shoot up the front office just for fun, why, the corporation will send a lot of headshrinkers out to dig up the 'deep underlying causes,' and vice-presidents will moan and wring their hands because somehow *they've* failed *you.* But, as I say, this isn't how our outfit works.

Well, when everything settled down, we were still alive, and we hadn't been fired, and we were starting to think some day we'd get over it, when we got word the new captain was on his way out in a taxi-boat. That really heaped the coals of fire on us. Changing captains is bad enough. But to be demoted, and have a new man put in over you—Let me tell you, Sam, that takes some getting used to.

Hook, now back to second officer, said gloomily, "I wonder what boob they're sticking on us?"

Pete Snyder groaned. "Sure as anything, we'll get one of the ramrods."

That made sense. What Pete meant by "ramrods" was the pair of ex-Space-Force Officers the Old Man uses to straighten out the worst ships and crews. One of the ramrods stands about six foot ten and likes to travel on half-gravity, because the deck bending underfoot irritates him. The other isn't as tall, and he's as spare as a colonist's horsewhip. But regardless of their appearance, one is about as bad as the other. They're both solid poison.

"Ace" Barty, his voice dull, said, "I wonder which one we'll get, Upper Jaw or Lower Jaw?"

They got those nicknames when the Old Man bounced the captain and first officer of *Worst Yet*, and put *both* ramrods in, the bigger one for captain, the other for first officer. *Worst Yet* had a crew that thought it was tougher than any combination of officers—but that was before they shipped out on that trip.

You know, Sam, when something's only half-bad, a man's eager to talk about it. When it's *real* bad, you have to wait and let it come out, a sliver at a time.

You can take one of the tough crewmen who shipped out on *Worst Yet*, with Upper Jaw for captain and Lower Jaw for first officer, and go to the most wide-open joint in the easiest-run space center you can find, and pour double shots of super-nova down his throat as long as the place stays open; about 0200, he'll stare into his empty glass and growl, "The bastards." That's it, Sam. That's all he'll say about it.

Pete Snyder must have been thinking about the same thing, because he said, "Just be thankful it isn't *both* of them."

Ace said bitterly, "Whichever it is, we can make it plenty tough for him."

Hook gave Ace a flat look. "You say anything to him but 'Yes, sir,' and I'll brain you myself."

Ace muttered, "We got to stick together."

"Are you nuts?"

I said, "Anything we might think up, he's already had happen to him. We'd better just endure it."

Ace said grudgingly, "Yes, sir," which was his indirect way of telling me he still regarded *me* as captain. This was one of the first things either Upper Jaw or Lower Jaw would spot, and naturally Ace and I would *both* get flattened for it.

All told, this was shaping up to be an unforgettable experience. I was mentally groping for some way out when a crewman called, "Taxi-boat at the main hatch!"

Hook glanced at me. "Now what?"

"Both of us had better meet him. Whichever one it is."

We trudged down to the airlock, and matched lock pressures

with the taxi-boat. I don't know what Hook was thinking, but I was wishing I could do as our previous captain had done when this banjo-bird business first started, and just retire off the ship onto a convenient colony world, and have done with the mess. But that was a daydream. There was nothing to do but face up to Upper Jaw or Lower Jaw, whichever one came through.

We swung the hatch back, and stood paralyzed as a big white-haired man looked us over, beamed, stepped in carrying a space bag, said, "Come to my cabin when you get done here," and walked out of sight.

That was our *former* captain. —The one who had *retired*.

Well, we closed the hatch, made sure the taxi-boat cast itself loose and started back to its cove, and then we headed for the captain's cabin. On the way, we ran into Ace and Pete, staring as if they'd seen a ghost.

We knocked, and a familiar gruff voice called, "Come in."

The captain was lying back on his bunk, hands clasped behind his head, smiling.

"Boys," he said, "never retire onto a new planet that has winters like *that* one."

"You *hired* on again?"

"Which would you choose, forty-foot snow drifts and a fifty-mile wind, or this cabin? Believe me, boys, space is *soft*. I got out of that place on the first supply ship this spring, got in touch with the Old Man, and he said, 'Sure, come on back.' When I got here he was cursing about 'flying slints.' He didn't get into a good mood till I described the time on that planet when I got stuck in the cabin for four days with only one day's wood, and the snow-wolves padding over the roof trying to pry up the shakes. Let me tell you, boys, this ship is the finest sight I've seen for a long time."

Hook looked dazed, then grinned. What a relief to have our regular captain back! Just then, a crewman brought word that a cargo section was ready, and we were to deliver it to Tarmag II. That was short notice, but nobody complained. We loaded up on supplies, got the cargo section hooked in tight, and started for Tarmag.

Well, Sam, believe it or not, we had *no* trouble on the trip to Tarmag, and we got there well ahead of schedule. Tarmag II turned out to be a planet that was about 99.9% wild. The other

0.1% or so had been settled by a bunch of one-track-minded superspecialists. As near as we could figure it out, there wasn't a real all-around colonist among them. They'd tried to settle on the mainland first, but it hadn't taken long to find out the planet was going to wipe them out, so they tried an island off the coast, blasted it clean of vegetation and wildlife, and practically made it over. Whenever they needed a source of raw materials on the mainland, they burned away the vegetation, put up a wall, sank their shaft or dug their pit, and so far as possible blocked out the rest of the planet. They've got it set up so they transport by air, or in coastwise robot barges, live in a few modest-sized cities, and as much as possible spend their time in the laboratories.

Think of it, Sam. Here's a planet that's earth-type, with luxuriant vegetation, all kinds of animals, room enough for everyone, and what do these colonists do? They turn their backs on all that, and settle in for a lifetime of *research*.

Now, that's unusual, but believe me, there's more to it. While we were down on that planet—in the city they call Lab I—what do you suppose *we* thought about?

Before we started down, Ace was saying, "I wonder what kind of girls they got in this place?"

Once we were down there, Ace started saying, "You know, Al, these guys have got something. I mean, research is the thing. You *learn* something. You *get* somewhere. Otherwise, what's life add up to? You're born, grow up, fight, grab your share, have kids, die, and the kids grow up, fight, grab their share, have kids, die, their kids grow up, fight, grab their share, have kids—what's the *point*?"

Did this tough crew of ours spend their precious leave-time whistling at the girl research-workers, or smuggling out bootleg 200-proof absolute alcohol?

No. They burrowed into libraries, and took special tours of the research facilities. We had to *drag* them out.

"Whew," said Hook, when we started back up in the tender, "it hurts to leave an opportunity like *that* behind."

Ace nodded. "I haven't hardly cracked a book since I got my papers. But down in that library, I could see, for the first time—oh, a lot of things. Like just how fascinating an equation really is. There's a beauty there that—"

Pete Snyder interrupted. "The *best* way to learn is in the Simumodel. Take the body, for instance. You can drift right down into the muscles, follow the nerves, see the blood go rushing by—not *really* see it, of course but you *seem* to see it, and—"

"The thing is," said Ace, "you get the *integral* so what do you do then? You've got the original integrand in the integral. *Now* where are you? Well—"

"This is all kid stuff," said Hook. "Integrals. Muscles. Listen, Al and me—"

There was a kind of funny change in the atmosphere, and then one-by-one we started looking at each other blankly.

Just how the others felt, I didn't know. But suddenly I couldn't care less about the libraries and the Simumodels.

"Now," said Hook, scowling, "what was *that*?"

"Drop back down," I said. "That's the first time I ever ran into a thing like that."

We went down about five hundred feet, and, somewhere during the descent, Ace said, "That's funny. For an instant there, I thought I'd gone nuts. You transpose, then you've got—"

Now, again, libraries and simumodels meant something.

Hook scowled, and started the tender up again.

There was that funny change in the atmosphere.

Ace looked around blankly.

"Down slow," I said.

We eased down, and I could tell from the fascinated expression on Ace's face that he was again thinking about his equations.

Hook said, "That's roughly it, Al. Above that level, liquor and women. Below that level, calculus and anatomy."

As we went up, Pete said dazedly, "We were sabotaged!"

Groping for an explanation, we got up to the ship—somehow I can't bring myself to call it by name—and found the captain and the cargo-control officer had finished checking the cargo.

"Damned queer cargo," growled the captain.

The cargo-control officer, a man by the name of Fisher, was studying a thick sheaf of papers, and murmured, "Maybe none of this will happen."

"Maybe. But the sooner we get this load to cut-loose, the better."

Hook and I glanced at each other. So far as we knew, the cargo was just some electronics equipment in crushproof boxes. What was wrong with that?

The captain went off, plainly thinking hard, toward the control room, and Hook and I wasted no time cornering Fisher, the cargo-control man.

"Say, Fish," said Hook. "What's the matter with this load? I can see the *planet's* peculiar enough. But what's wrong with the cargo?"

Fisher held out a thick sheaf of papers marked:

WARNING!
Read Carefully
Instructions for Shippers, INSTIM Mark IV.

"INSTIM," said Hook. "What's that?"

"That," said Fisher, "is the thing we're shipping. While you guys were down there taking it easy, the automatic loaders were stacking them in by the thousands."

"Yeah, but what *is* it?" said Hook.

"That," said Fisher angrily, "is something I would hate to make any bets on. Remember, we're just the *shippers*. But if you'll leaf through that wad of instructions, you'll see why I'd rather we'd hooked onto a tank with a couple hundred feet of *kangbar* inside."

Well, that didn't sound good. But it looked worse when we got the thick sheaf of instructions opened up, and started looking through it:

" . . . extreme caution at all times to avoid undue jarring of the units . . .

" . . . accidental activation of any given unit is extremely unlikely; but when shipped in large consignments the possibility becomes a definite consideration, and due care must be exercised . . .

" . . . mutual interaction of the units. This triggering-and-reset characteristic is important in transporting large numbers of units . . .

" . . . similar to a chain reaction . . .

" . . . what happens in extreme cases is not known, as no survivors have yet returned . . .

" . . . any unusual pattern of thought on the part of one or more of the crew members is a warning signal . . ."

Hook and I looked at each other.

Fisher said, "You see what I mean?"

"We're starting to."

Pretty soon we hit the following:

" . . . If, for instance, a crew member, who normally dislikes nucleonics, finds himself unexpectedly wishing to study nucleonics, this may be classified as a Tentative Warning Symptom (TWS). If, in addition, other crew members now find themselves wishing to study nucleonics, again for no known reason, then this mass-interest may be classified as a Definitive Warning Symptom (DWS). If, then, *all* crew members find themselves earnestly wishing to study nucleonics, this phase may be classified as an Urgent Warning Symptom (UWS). Any otherwise unexplainable increment in the desire to study nucleonics presupposes the activation of more units. The usual progression from TWS to DWS to UWS is not reversible except in the initial phases, as the activation of additional units is cumulative, selective, and mutually reinforcing, and presumably eventuates in mass-activation of all units. The subjective nature of such an experience is as yet unknown, but, objectively, it is presumed to be fatal . . ."

" 'Objectively,' " growled Hook, " 'it is *presumed to be fatal.*' "

Fisher said, "That's the part that counts, all right. There's also something in there about how, in large consignments, the possibility becomes a definite probability. This is a large consignment we've got."

"What do we do," I said, "if it *does* happen? Is that in the instructions?"

Fisher thumbed through the papers, to read:

"In the event of a TWS, locate and manually reset any triggered unit to zero immediately. This will negate the possibility of accidental activations leading to a DWS and the consequent necessity of resetting large numbers of units, with the accompanying risk that the units will set each other more rapidly than they can be neutralized."

The instructions then moved on to a discussion of how to handle the sensitive units.

"Hold on," said Hook. "There's a little item they left out."

"Where," I said, "does it tell us *how to locate* the unit that's making the trouble?"

Fisher smiled sourly. "It doesn't bother with that. But it does tell us—let's see—here we are: 'Deactivation of the activated units will be signaled by cessation of the anomalous mental response.' "

"So you know when you've found the activated units because then you won't want to study nucleonics, for instance?"

"Correct."

"But the instructions don't tell you *how* to find the activated units?"

"Nope."

"And just how many units are there?"

"Well, let's see. To begin with, twelve dozen units, each unit packed inside its own protective covers, fit into a special carton about two feet wide by a foot-and-a-half high by three feet long. These cartons are stacked up and packed in shock grids. The shock grids are racked, and all but fill the cargo section. You want to take a look?"

Hook and I glanced at each other.

"Lead the way."

Fisher headed down the corridor to the connecting door, shoved it open, and we followed him into the cargo section.

As far as the eye could reach, cartons a foot-and-a-half by two feet on the end were stacked up in shock grids—open frames with specially designed coil springs and dampers—each grid holding what looked like about thirty-two cartons. The grids locked into stacking racks, and the whole works filled up the cargo-section, leaving just room enough for horizontal and vertical access spaces.

"Just suppose," I said, "that you knew which one of those units was making the trouble? How long would it take to get it out?"

"Well," said Fisher, squinting at the frames, "first we'd have to pull out the right grid. That could take us ten hours, depending on where the grid's located. Then we'd have to disassemble the grid. With the special equipment they use at terminals, that would take about two seconds. But we don't have that special equipment, so we'd be lucky if we got it done in an hour. Then we'd have to separate the cartons, and they're bound together with interlocked Crushflex strips. Say ten minutes to get through that and get out the right carton. Next you have to get into the carton. Each carton has twelve dozen units in it. Each of these units has two protective covers. Well, to be optimistic about it, it would take us maybe twelve hours to get at the right unit, *assuming* we knew just where it was to start with."

We stood there thinking that over.

Fisher added, "But if these instructions tell how to locate the activated unit, *I* haven't been able to find it."

"But even if we could, we couldn't reset it immediately?"

"Nope."

Hook swore. "Another disaster-cargo."

"It *might* be all right," I said, trying to generate a little hope. "There are only two jumps between here and cut-loose."

"Yeah, but that second run is a long one. We better think of something to do pretty fast, because you know what kind of luck we had the last trip."

Just then, the captain swung us out from Tarmag II. We were on our way.

For the first few days, everything seemed fine. We made our first jump, and then we were into that long second leg of the trip. Still there was no trouble. If anything, everybody was more normal than usual. I think this was because we were all afraid *not* to be normal. If anyone had an unusual thought, he kept it strictly to himself.

Every time we had a chance, we got together, to try to figure out what to do if trouble started. It was the captain who got the first idea.

"Boys," he said, squinting at the contract, "it doesn't say anything here about our delivering these things *unactivated*."

Hook scowled, "Still, if we don't want the first unit to activate another one, and those two to activate more, we've got to locate that first unit."

"Yes, but the important thing is, the contract *does not so state*. That gives us a choice. Either we locate any activated unit, *or* we find some way to live with it."

"It," I said, "and the thousands of others it will turn on."

The captain nodded, and glanced at Fisher. "Do those instructions make any mention of anything that shields out the effect?"

"Not a thing."

Hook said, "Wait a minute. *Distance*, at least, shields it out." We told the captain what had happened to us down on Tarmag II, and on our way up from the planet, and he quizzed us on it.

"That sounds," he said finally, "as if it's got a definite limit. If we have to, we could treat this as a normal-space haul of explosive cargo, and let it out on the long-reach extension cable."

"If," said Hook, "it waits till after our next jump to act up."

The captain nodded. "Otherwise, we'll have to reel the cargo section in to make the jump, and that will bring us in range of all those units. Well, possibly by the time this thing starts to make trouble, we'll—"

Ace said, his voice somewhat feverish, "We could *probably* work it out by integral calculus."

There was a silence, as everyone turned to take a good look at Ace.

Ace's eyes were shining. He had that fascinated look we'd seen before.

"Let's see," he said. "The cross-section is probably a circle, but it *could* be an ellipse, or even—where's some paper? Boy, integration is the most wonderful—"

We glanced from Ace to the captain, who said, "Lay him out. There could be a feedback between him and the cargo."

Hook and I both laid him out, and Pete Snyder did the same thing at the same time, so poor Ace didn't get much integration done, and if he hadn't been pretty tough, we'd probably have killed him.

"Okay," said the captain, "connect the long-reach and let that cargo-section out all the way. Make sure the cable sensor is linked up with the drive-control. I'll get some men suited up and outside to help you."

We started aft, but halfway there Hook stopped and backed up.

Beads of perspiration stood out on his forehead.

Pete Snyder clenched his fist, "What's *wrong*, old buddy?"

"Before I stepped back, for just a second, I started thinking about calculus."

"Hold it!" I said, before Pete could do anything. "Listen, Hook, can you fight it off and help us with the long-reach?"

"I can try." He took a step forward, then stepped back. "I wouldn't be any use to you."

"Put a mark on that bulkhead, go back and send somebody to help us, then try it with a suit on, and see if you get any further."

Hook took out a marking pencil, drew two vertical lines on the bulkhead, and sprinted back down the corridor. Pete and I went on to the cargo door.

Well, Sam, we didn't have any trouble hooking the cargo section on the long-reach, and we made sure the cable sensor was connected to the drive-control, so any overstrain would cut the drive. We got _that_ part done all right.

The trouble was that as the weight came on the long-reach and helper cables, and as the drive cut back thrust to ease the strain, and as Pete called, "Drive-g into the orange! Low tone from the sensor box!" and as I said into the microphone, "Ease off _slow_ all helper cables—slow, now, _slow_!" and as the men let the helpers out further and the full strain came on the long-reach, and the sensor-box audible-warning climbed up to a wail and slid down as the drive cut back further—as these things happened and the ship pulled gradually ahead of the cargo-section, it occurred to me that Ace was right. When you integrate e sin x dx and get minus e sin x dx in the answer, that _is_ beautiful. It's so neat, so—

Pete, for an instant, stopped calling out the distance in yards, then resumed with a note of strain in his voice, and then the overpowering desire to work integrations was gone, and after a while Pete called out, "Full length on the long-reach! Standby tone from the sensor box!"

I locked up the emergency disconnect, and got everyone back inside. Letting the cargo section out on the long cable can turn into a tricky operation, but that didn't account for the men's pale nervous look as they got out of their suits.

Pete and I checked to make sure the helper cables were in place, and that there were no leaks around the ship's cargo-section space-door. Everything seemed okay, so we went forward and reported to the captain.

The captain studied our faces.

"Boys," he said, "from the way you look, you're leaving out something."

"e sin x dx," I said.

"It hit you, too?"

"For maybe ten seconds."

"How far out was the cable?"

Pete said, "Maybe a fifth of the way."

I said, "This 'activation of new units' is cumulative, isn't it?"

The captain glanced at the Instructions for Shippers, and quoted: " ' . . . cumulative, selective, and mutually reinforcing, and presumably eventuates in mass-activation of all units.' "

Pete said hesitantly, "Sir, maybe we could abandon the cargo under Section XIV—'Cargo imminent hazard to life and limb.'"

The captain didn't bother to answer. The Old Man doesn't recognize Section XIV.

Pete said insistently, "If not, we've still got to make this next subspace jump between us and cut-loose. With this rig, we've got to get that cargo-section in close."

"Then we'll do it," said the captain.

"Yeah, but—"

The captain reached around and took down an expensive-looking blue-and-gold miniaturized book box lettered "Library of Universal Knowledge, 1062 Volumes." He carefully folded out the viewing lenses, pressed a set of little buttons, and handed it to me. "Read this aloud."

A sizeable book seemed to open up as I glanced into the lenses, to read: "Thought Intensifier—A device capable of selectively intensifying intellectual activity in those exposed to its action.

"The thought intensifier, or intellectual stimulator, as a hypothetical device, presently outlawed on several planets, which is believed capable of stimulating known human intellectual interests of many kinds, and maintaining them for long periods, even, with consequent uneasiness, when the intellectual activity runs counter to the exposed individual's natural tendencies. The device cannot, of course, stimulate mental activity that the target is incapable of. A rock, insect, or a man unconscious or in a stupor, is a poor subject for mental stimulation. The device is said to operate by precise activation of selected nerve-tracts or patterns, and obviously such tracts can be affected only if they exist. However, provided nerve-tracts are capable of functioning, this device is said to be capable of activating them.

"While theoretically considered to be potentially useful, in proper hands, and while a large and authoritative body of opinion holds that such devices, if they exist, could and should be used openly to stimulate desirable forms of mental activity, it has also been strongly urged that intellectual stimulators are essentially immoral, and restrict a fundamental 'freedom of thought' (see FREEDOMS, Varieties of).

"Whatever the reality or unreality of these views, the use of thought intensifiers, if it has actually taken place, has been accompanied by such secrecy and indirection that the existence of the devices remains problematical.

"Other names sometimes used in referring to these devices include: 'thought stimulator,' 'thought simulator,' and 'INSTIM,' the latter a supposed *trade-name* for a particularly unstable type of intellectual stimulator (see SHIPWRECKS, Famous) reputed to be of small size, high power, and great sensitivity to shock with resulting random activation.

"Authoritative opinion currently holds that such devices, in the present state of the art, are impossible, and that persistent rumors concerning their use are only examples of folklore-in-the-making (see FOLKLORE, Recent, SPACE SAUCERS, and MYTHS and RUMORS)."

I handed the box back to the captain, and Pete said doggedly, "How does that help us? We've got to hook the cargo section in close to make the jump, and when we do, there will probably be enough of those units activated so the whole ship will be in range. There won't be a thing we can do except calculus. Food won't interest us. Maintenance won't interest us. We'll work calculus till we drop." He looked around, as if to see from our expressions whether maybe *he* was nuts; but, believe me, we agreed with him. I never heard of anyone dying of math before, but that didn't help us. Either we found some way to get that cargo to cut-loose without being mentally swamped by it—or it would kill us.

Pete looked worriedly at the captain.

I've seen the captain bothered more by a comma in a contract.

"Well," he said, "we don't know how fast the range of those units is extending. The first thing to do is send a man on a line back along that long-reach, and meanwhile rig the spider lines. We may have to let this cargo section out further."

That made sense, but it was another headache. With the long-reach, we had *some* acceleration. The spider lines are strong for their thickness, all right. But whatever the stuff is they're made of, it's not only strong, it's *elastic*. Under tension, the thin shiny strands dwindle down so you can only see the reflection of an angled light on them. They don't hang in a true line, once the waves of expansion and contraction start traveling up and down them, and any particular line can loop around maddeningly. The only way to get them to hang right is to put them under heavy tension, and then, without warning, they *stretch*. You can get in quite a mess with these lines, but we had no choice. Hook, easing back along the long-reach, discovered that the field of the units was working forward in jumps that would probably put the whole ship deep inside the field sometime tomorrow.

The obvious alternative was to find a way to shield out the effect.

Using metal stocks from the storeroom, and everything else we could think of, we still found nothing that shielded out or modified the field.

To be on the safe side, we had no choice but to rig the spider lines to the long-reach, and ease further ahead of the cargo section. We had to cut our acceleration, and that lengthened the delay to the jump-point, which allowed more time for things to go wrong.

The captain, meanwhile, stayed calm and cheerful. He even gave orders for the cook to brew up a batch of his special-formula potjack, to celebrate when we hit the jump-point. It seemed a funny time to have a celebration, but we didn't have time to think about that. We were too busy trying to work out some kind of protective cage of current-carrying wires. The idea was that the variations in the electromagnetic field might disrupt the field generated by the INSTIM units. It sounded good, but nothing we were able to send through the wires worked.

Meanwhile, the INSTIM field was creeping out. By sending the tender through it on remote control, with a volunteer inside, we were able to plot the edge of the field and estimate its strength. We discovered it was now roughly spherical, and so strong that, once in it, a man had no slightest choice what to do. He thought, worked, and lived calculus, and that was all. We were in no danger from this, *yet*, but if we reeled that cargo section close to the ship to make the jump, the whole ship would be deep inside it.

The only hope seemed to be to work out some kind of automatic device to reel in the cargo section before the jump, and let it out again afterward. We might have worked this, if it hadn't been for the spider lines. No matter what we did, we couldn't figure any way to make the handling of those lines fully automatic.

Hook and I took it up with the captain.

"Sir," I said, "I don't like to say it, but it seems to me this is one cargo we *have* to dump."

The captain sat back and looked at us, benevolent and unconvinced.

I said, "We can't shield out the effect. We can't moderate it. We can't vary it at all. This model cargo section has to be hooked in tight when we make that jump. At the jump-point, then, we've got to work inside of the field. But we *can't* work inside the field. All we can do inside of it is what *it* dictates."

The captain clasped his hands behind his neck.

"We haven't hit this problem a good low blow yet. We've only tried to solve it on a high level."

Hook said grimly, "I'll hit it as low as I *can* hit it. But *how*?"

The captain took down his little book box, and read aloud, " . . . The device cannot, of course, stimulate mental activity that the target is incapable of. A rock, insect, or a man unconscious or in a stupor is a poor subject for mental stimulation . . ."

He then looked at us.

Hook smote his forehead and swore.

I stood there too dazed to speak.

"There are generally two ways," said the captain, "to take care of a problem. One is to solve it on its own terms, satisfy its requirements. That, you might say, is the *high road* to a solution. The other way is to unhinge the problem—rearrange matters so it doesn't *have* to be solved. That, you might say, is the *low road*. Either way, you take care of the problem.

"Say your girl springs it on you that to prove you love her you've got to go out and bring back the head of a wild *kangbar* you've killed, all by yourself, just for her. The high-road solution of that problem is to go out, find and somehow kill the monster single-handed, and freight back the head.

"The low-road solution is to get her to change her mind, or else find a different girl. That doesn't solve the problem on its own terms. But it takes care of it, all right.

"Now, this cargo of activated INSTIM units puts us in a spot where, to deliver the cargo, we've got to work inside the field generated by the units. But the units are so set that no-one with the *capacity* to be interested in moderately advanced mathematics can help but be interested in mathematics—to the degree that he can't think of anything else. The field therefore presents us with the problem of somehow finding a technological means to shield out the effect, so that we can work inside the field. This solution is the *high road*. But that doesn't mean it's the *only* road."

The captain reached into his desk drawer, and set on the desk a small neatly-stoppered jug.

"I hoped," he said, "that we *could* figure out a way to shield out the effect. It might be a handy thing to know. But, since we can't, it's worth considering that a man can be in pretty sorry shape and still carry out a routine he's used to, especially if he's drilled at it until it's second nature. But he's not going to work out too many abstruse problems when he's in the particular state *I'm* thinking of.

"Just what grip can this field get on us *if the nerve-tracts necessary to work mathematics problems can't function?*"

Well, Sam, I think you get the picture. We drilled day and night from then till we neared the end of that leg of the trip. When the time came the spider lines were a nightmare, but even seeing double from the captain's potjack, we still had the routine down so solid that we were able to reel in the cargo section, make the sub-space jump, and then cut the section loose on the far side. As for the INSTIM units, believe me, there was no handle for them to get hold of us by. That mental lever was out of action.

As for how we felt *afterward*, let's not even think about that. We were still hung over when we got back to the loading center, but the captain explained it to the Old Man, and everything was okay. We'd met the contract, and that was all he cared about.

The ship even got renamed, and I suppose it's an improvement. But *Bunglers All* was bad enough to have to explain to curious outsiders. How are we supposed to explain *Drunk in Line of Duty?*

There's got to be a way around this somehow. Anything you might suggest, Sam, would be welcome.

As ever, Al

TRIAL BY SILK

After almost a hundred days on a space transport, we were naturally happy to land on an Earth-type planet. —Any Earth-type planet.

Our captain this trip was a burly New Venusian named Engstrom. On the big screen over the forward loudspeaker of the public address system, his image showed a discomfort hard to explain. His hemming, hawing, and fidgeting added nothing worth having, either.

Beside me, Willis murmured fervently, "I wish we had the Captain back."

When anyone on *Starlight* spoke the word "captain" with such reverence, he meant, not Engstrom, but our previous captain, who'd recently been transferred to one of the company's newer and faster ships.

I murmured, "Engstrom's a good man. Moreover, he's captain now, so we have to stand up for him."

As Willis and I were respectively third and second in command of the ship, there was no escaping our duty to back up the captain.

Willis growled, "He's not making it easy for us."

On the screen, Engstrom mopped his forehead, hesitated, and cleared his throat.

The crewmen were starting to make ironical comments.

"Now, men," said Engstrom. He coughed, adjusted his tie, rattled a piece of paper, and cleared his throat again.

Willis groaned. "This is pathetic."

"Shut up," I said.

"H'r'm!" said Engstrom, moving around on the screen. "Men, I—ah—It— At this point, I'd like to say a few words—"

"Damn it," muttered Willis, "say them!"

Instead, Engstrom hesitated.

The crewmen were now grinning and joking, and several of the technicians were trying to decide what the captain most resembled as he struggled on the screen. The two leading comparisons were: a) a bachelor trying to change a baby's diaper; b) a perspiring father trying to explain the facts of life to someone who already knew them.

Willis growled, "What's the *matter* with him, anyway?"

"I don't know. He's used the P.A. system before without all this. What's he trying to say?"

"I don't know. But I wish he'd say it and get it over with."

From Engstrom's red face and damp forehead, it was possible to make a shrewd deduction. We could only hope that wasn't it.

Engstrom cleared his throat again, "Men—ah—This is very difficult. I don't know quite how—But it's my duty to tell you, as a captain, that the—er—women—ah—on this planet—are—"

Willis pressed his palm to his forehead.

The men hooted.

Around us stood the grinning crew, tough, competent, obviously well able to take care of themselves.

"—not," said Engstrom, struggling on grimly, "quite the way they seem. I—ah—ah—speak from—ah—experience—and—"

The men burst into laughter. Willis pivoted on his heel and rested his brow against the bulkhead. The air filled with ribald comments.

"—and so," said Engstrom. "I have got to warn you . . . And let me go further. The drink here is not quite the same as the drink on other worlds. Except water. Their water is safe. And watch out for their so-called 'barbecues,' and feasts of all kinds. There isn't a pleasure on this planet, except to look at their scenery—with due care—and drink their water—that isn't in some way—ah—'funny.'"

The laughter had now faded out. Everyone was listening. No one wants to get mugged, blackjacked, or rolled, and there are planets with very cute arrangements for doing these and other things.

"It's a hard thing," said Engstrom, "to get across. There is no *coercion* on this planet. —None at least, that an outsider might see. You won't be knocked over the head, held up, or in any other way *roughly* treated. There isn't a thing we can object to. There's nothing here contrary to the Interstellar Trade Association's standard Code of Conduct. This planet rates AAA in the Bluebook. But, men—" Again there was that urgent expression, like a man looking for a place to put a hot rivet—"watch out for them. Be on your best behavior. —Ah—Be *careful*— Whatever you do, *don't enjoy yourself!* —I mean—you *know* what I mean! —Anyway—That's it."

The captain's little talk came to an end.

The screen went blank.

The laughter of the crewmen was like ripples on a pool during a steadily-strengthening rainstorm. The whole place seemed to dissolve into laughter.

Willis and I felt our way out, to meet Schmidt coming down the corridor from the direction of the mess hall, where there was another P.A. speaker. Schmidt had the look of a man with sinus trouble, on a ship with a faulty pressure control.

The three of us huddled together in a funereal atmosphere, while laughter reached us from both directions, up and down the corridor.

Schmidt groaned, "What do we do now?"

Willis looked at me. "What do we do about this, sir?" He slightly emphasized the "sir," subtly reminding me that I had the rank and was therefore stuck with the problem.

On these civilian space transports, there's sometimes a tendency for first, second, and third officers to form a cheerful little club, devoid of outward display of rank. This happy democracy falls apart when the buck has to be passed, either down or up.

Willis and Schmidt watched me attentively. The captain's talk had us all punch-drunk, but it was now *my* duty to pull out of the stupor and get us moving in some direction.

Schmidt said hesitantly, "I suppose we ought to put an end to that laughter—"

"No," I said. "We'd make ourselves look like fools trying to stop them from laughing. We probably *couldn't* stop them. Did *you* ever try to stop anyone from laughing? We'd be laughing ourselves before we got through. And on top of that, the end of that little talk was the signal that the men could get off the ship. Any minute now, they'll start piling into the tender. We'd better just let them laugh. If there's anything to what the captain says, they won't be laughing on the return trip."

"What," said Schmidt, "*could* there be? He said himself that there's no *coercion*."

Willis quoted, "'*You won't be knocked over the head, held up, or in any other way* roughly *treated.*' —Just exactly what can go wrong?"

Just then a couple of crewmen, obviously on their way to the tender, walked briskly by. One grinned at us, and held up a pair of spiked shoes.

Schmidt fell for it. "What do you want *track* shoes for?"

"To run away from the girls with, sir." The crewman made his face very serious.

His friend added gravely, "The one that caught the captain might still be around down there, sir. We don't want to take any chances." He produced a small tear-gas gun, and looked grim.

Schmidt was speechless. Willis growled in an undertone. "What the devil did you give him an opening for?"

Now, down the corridors came more of our shining-faced crew, all capable spacemen, most of them the masters of skills and techniques that required long thought, practice, and hard discipline, but each one possessed by that ironical humor that rises spontaneously when a crewman sees an officer—theoretically wiser than the crewman—make a total unmitigated ass of himself.

One of the crewmen carried a black thread, on the end of which bobbed an imitation soft-plastic tarantula. One carried a wire cage inside of which, its many teeth bared, lurked a *shreat*. —That is a kind of vicious ratlike animal used in laboratory work. Another crewman had a large-fanged snake's head stuck out of his jacket pocket. Each of these crewmen earnestly reassured his friends that, yes, the planet's predatory girls were *sure* to be scared off by tarantula, *shreat*, or snake.

"I mean," said a crewman briskly carrying a small stuffed alligator under his arm, "what if some beautiful wench comes after me and this *doesn't* scare her off? Eh? *Then* what?"

A technician wearing a set of one-man rocket wings said earnestly, "You fellows are crazy to rely on psychological stuff. We may have to run."

There were plenty of suppressed snickering and gagging sounds, but it was impossible to spot a crewman who didn't have his face set in lines of honest worry.

Willis spat out a low curse as one clumped by wearing body armor and a jack-suit, and carrying across his shoulder a three hundred pound Hellwein dissipator, complete with pronged flaring tripod mount, loops of thick black cable, and power pack.

Schmidt, red-faced, obviously didn't trust himself to say anything. Willis looked away and snarled, "How did they get all this stuff together so damned fast?"

"In a situation like this," I said, "they're inspired. Ordinary human limitations don't count."

"But where did that stuffed alligator come from? What fool would waste his weight allowance on a thing like that?"

"It's made of stiff lightweight plastic with a zipper up the underside. It's got compartments on the inside for razor, socks, underwear, and so on, and the tongue reels out to snap into a socket near the left hind leg and make a carrying handle. It's an overnight bag. A thing as conspicuous as that helps in striking up a conversation on a strange planet."

"I suppose," said Willis, "that there's nothing illegal about *that*. But what do we do about that bird in body armor?"

Just then, half-a-dozen more men staggered by, clinging to the carrying handle of a fusion gun big enough to use in a siege.

There was no way out of it. "We'll have to stop them," I said. "We can't let anything like that go down with them."

But when we stopped them, the six crewmen with the fusion gun earnestly insisted that it was "Captain's order, sir. The captain wants us to protect ourselves against the women down there, sir."

By the time we got the fusion gun back in the heavy weapons locker, the dissipator back in the repair shop, the jack suit, rocket wings, and body armor in the suit rack, and the *shreat* and its cage returned to the medic's lab, we were the maddest collection of ships' officers for light-years in all directions. The crewmen, meanwhile, leaned against the walls of the corridor, red-faced, hands clasped to their mouths and sides, shaking silently.

As the last of them piled into the tender, and just before the hatch completely shut, there was one big roar of laughter that rang in our heads long after the tender was on its way down.

"Well," said Willis, "thank God *that's* over with."

There was a scrape and a clang up the corridor, and Engstrom stepped into view. He was a big, blond, red-faced man with, at the moment, a somewhat haggard look.

"Did they understand?" he asked. "Did I get it across to them?" He spoke in earnest tones, obviously appealing for reassurance.

Schmidt glanced at Willis, and Willis glanced at me. Schmidt then studied his shoes while Willis directed his gaze toward outer space.

Mentally damning Schmidt and Willis, I tried to somehow reconcile that last roar of laughter with the earnest appeal on Engstrom's face.

"Well, sir—ah—it seemed to me that they weren't quite clear how there could be any danger, if they aren't going to be attacked or robbed, and if force was not going to be used on them in any way."

Engstrom groaned. "I was afraid of that. But damn it, how do you *tell* them? If I'd had time enough to think it out—but the cancel on that load at Calfax only just came through, and then the wait-and-liberty order got to us at the last possible moment—how could I *know*?"

Willis said, at first exasperatedly, "Yes, but just what the—ah—I mean—Sir—Why *is* there likely to be danger—down there, sir?"

While Willis was speaking, Engstrom's ineffectual embarrassment had given way to a direct blue gaze that held Willis as if he were in the grip of a vice. Engstrom had clearly detected something in Willis's tone that he didn't like, and Willis was at pains to get what was objectionable out of the way before the captain found it necessary to do the job himself.

"Then," said the captain, looking flatly at Willis, "you don't consider that there *is* any danger on this planet?"

"Oh, no, sir," said Willis, then paused. The captain was looking straight at him and Willis started over, this time with a certain determination in his voice. "Sir, *you've* been there and we haven't. I can't—I can't picture the *nature* of the danger."

Willis' voice had started to climb toward the end, but abruptly he finished in a dead level tone.

The captain looked at him a moment, his gaze hard and intent, then suddenly smiled.

"All I can say is that this is no easy thing to describe without sounding foolish, but if you go down there, remember this: There are supposed to be certain 'trials' or 'ordeals,' as for instance the 'trial by fire.' What you will experience if you go down on that planet is what might be called the 'trial by silk.' Let me tell you, it's tougher than you think."

The captain then nodded, closing the subject, and left us.

It may be that the wisest thing for the three of us to have done would have been to stay on board and catch up on sleep and unread technical manuals.

But between our own curiosity and the captain's uncommunicativeness, we naturally got into a frame of mind that sent us down to the planet as soon as we'd made our final checks on a few items of the ship's equipment.

On the way down in the tender, Schmidt said, frowning, "What, exactly, is a 'trial by fire'?"

Willis said, "It's a—well, an ordeal."

"And what's an 'ordeal'?"

"H'm. Well, I think, in the old days back on Earth, well before space-flight, they used to decide whether a person was guilty or innocent by putting him through a 'trial by ordeal.' I suppose a trial by fire would mean you had to go through the fire and come out unhurt."

"Trial by silk—what would *that* be?"

"I don't know. Silk is soft, with a slick surface, and it's expensive stuff. We had some in a cargo on *Quicksure* one time."

We puzzled over this—without finding an answer—till we finally stepped out at the spaceport, and looked around warily, not knowing what to expect.

A pleasant blue sky looked down upon us. One or two small fluffy clouds drifted past. There were low green hills on three sides in the distance, and a mathematically straight road led from the spaceport toward the city we could see off on the horizon. The only unusual feature was a cluster of rusty space ships and tenders that formed a kind of junkyard stretching over about twenty acres of ground near the spaceport.

A groundcar, with the distinctive throb of an internal-combustion engine, pulled up beside us.

"Taxi, mates?"

"How much to the city?"

"Four-fifty for the three of you. And I'll take you anywhere in town you want to go. That is, if you all want to go to the same place."

"Fair enough." We piled in. Schmidt glanced out at the expanse of rusty ships. "Is that some kind of junkyard?"

"No. Nobody ever claimed them, so they just moved them back to get them out of the way."

Willis looked puzzled. "What do you mean, nobody ever *claimed* them?"

"Just like I said. They landed 'em. They left 'em. And nobody ever come back for 'em."

"Where did the crew *go*?"

"Into town."

The taxi was now speeding down the road.

There was a little silence, then Willis cleared his throat. "The same town we're headed for?"

"Yep." The driver shook a little white cylinder out of a rumpled pack, stuck it in his mouth, held a lighter to it, blew out a cloud of smoke, and snapped a switch on the dash. A powerful *whir* started up somewhere, and the smoke trailed up through a large round grille in the ceiling.

A silence had developed in the car, and it seemed to me that somebody ought to break it. "What—ah—what happened to the people who didn't come back to their ships?"

"Guess they stayed in the city."

"Why would they do that?"

The driver turned briefly to give a knowing leer. "Maybe they *liked* it there."

This produced another silence.

Schmidt had been eyeing the smoke whirling into the overhead grille. "What," he said, "is the purpose of this grille?"

"Why, it's the law, mate. Maybe smoke ain't your dish, see? Why should you have to take it just because I do?" He seemed amazed at the question. "Same reason you have to cap the fumes, even if you're a breather."

Schmidt opened his mouth and shut it again.

The driver seemed to have a sudden thought, and handed back his pack. "Help yourself, mate. I'm a slow one to take a hint."

We all looked at the pack, which had a white skull and crossbones against a black border that went around all sides, and on the front was a drawing of a city seen through a thick haze. In an arc over the city was the name, "SMOGS," and under that the words:

"SMOGS Specially-Treated Smokes. A blend of the finest tobaccos exquisitely flavored with a delicate tinge of sulfur, marijuana, cocaine, hashish, carbolic acid, and other ingredients listed in detail on the back."

Schmidt had started to pull out one of the whitish tubes, but let go of it as if he had a knife by the wrong end.

"Thanks a lot," he said, handing the pack back, "but I—ah—I don't feel too much like a smoke right now."

"Maybe," said the driver, "you like 'Nippers' better. They got more bite. I used to like them myself, but they loosen your teeth too much."

This comment generated another considerable silence. There were more silences on that trip to town than anything else, despite the fact that we were all curious, and eager to learn all we could about this new planet.

The next time, it was the driver who broke the silence.

"Well, mates, what's your dish? Man was made for pleasure, and we got every kind of pleasure there is, right here for the taking. You name it and I'll take you there. What'll you have? Girls? Drinks? Combos? Whips? Feasts? Sizzlers? Dreams? —Or do you like the *stronger* stuff? We got good recoup palaces all over the city, mates. Makes no difference there. What'll you have?"

Doubtless this was supposed to disperse the gathering air of constraint, but it took about twenty seconds before any of us could speak. By this time, Willis had tried on a set of wrought-iron knuckles that he favored for such trips as this, smashed them lightly against his palm, and slid them back into his pocket. I saw Schmidt pat the center of his chest, where under his shirt the thin flat knife hung in its sheath, suspended by a slender chain around his neck. As for myself, I have to admit to fingering with one hand the somewhat narrow thick belt I'd selected after hearing the captain's speech and later warning, while my other hand assured me that I had worn the right pair of shoes for the place we were getting into.

Schmidt cleared his throat. In a somewhat tight voice, he said, "Maybe you'd better just let us out in the shopping district. We can look around for ourselves afterward."

The driver sounded puzzled. "Why, mate, that's where I'm *going* to let you out. In the shopping district. But what do you want to shop *for?* Like I say, we got everything."

Willis' mind was apparently functioning faster than Schmidt or I could take credit for. "Did you by any chance take anyone from *Starlight* anywhere?"

"Why, yes, mate, I did. Three trips."

"What did *they* want? Where did *they* go?"

This could be an important thing for us to know, later on. We might have to do quite a bit of hunting to collect the crew, and it wouldn't hurt to know where to start.

"Well," said the driver, "I'm not supposed to tell, but— Wait a minute. Are you asking about individuals, or just about the bunch as a whole—the most of them?"

"Just the bunch as a whole." Willis had his eyes narrowed. "Not any particular individual."

"Well, I guess I can tell you that." He blew out a puff of thick gray smoke, which was promptly whirled up into the grille. "The most of them—I don't say 'all' and I don't say *not*-all, either, but the most of them *I* brought in were combo men."

This produced another of those generous silences that punctuated the trip.

Willis glanced at me, and I shrugged. Schmidt looked blank. We were mentally running through the list of human frailties, wondering what "combo" might be. According to the driver, most of our crew were "combo" men. Here we had shipped with them over a considerable stretch of universe and never even guessed it. It seemed to show that you might live with people, sleep and eat with them, for months and months, and never really know them. Just what was *combo?* Evidently they preferred it to girls, drinks, whips, feasts, dreams, and sizzlers. Somehow it didn't sound good. Schmidt and Willis became glum and silent, and I was almost afraid to speak, myself. But we had to find out.

"Ah," I said finally, "this—this '*combo*' you speak of—"

"Yes, mate?" The driver sounded hopeful.

"Well—ah—*What is it?*"

We sat there in a state of paralyzed suspense. We *had* to find out what it was. Yet we were none too eager to find out, either. If you will just imagine that you and a few friends suddenly discovered that you had unsuspectingly shipped out for a long trip with almost a whole shipload of "combo-men," you will see what I mean. You would rather find out a thing like that at the beginning or the end than halfway through the trip.

The driver meanwhile stopped the car and looked back. "Are you serious, mate?"

"Yes."

Schmidt said tightly, "We'd like to know."

The driver stared at us, cleared his throat, and scarcely seemed to know how to approach the subject. Finally he said, "You must be *real* high-flyers."

Willis said sharply, "What *is* it?"

"Well, mate—" The driver cleared his throat again—"No need to get excited. It's just what it sounds like. A 'combo' is a—Well, it's a combo, that's what it is—A *combination*. Drinks *and* girls, with some feasts and smokes on the side, and maybe a little something extra later on. A combo is a—a combo, if you see what I mean."

Willis sighed.

Schmidt sat there with a blank expression.

Willis began to laugh.

I told the driver to take us to the same place most of our men had gone to. He nodded, and started up the car again.

The rest of the trip was one long silence. We got out, the driver accepted his pay, scratched his head, and drove off. We looked around. Willis had one hand in his pocket, and Schmidt had idly unbuttoned the third button of his shirt. As for myself, I was wishing that I'd brought along something with larger caliber than the cobra belt and persuader shoes. The three of us were now, of course, wideawake, looking around intently.

Willis said, "This place must be the worst sinkhole in this end of the universe, but it doesn't *look* it."

We were looking across a wide street, with a moderate amount of traffic moving in the street, with granite buildings six to ten stories high across the street, and, behind us, a park with neatly-mowed green lawn, tall flowering shrubs, an artificial lake in which a few people were swimming, and a sandy beach on which lay a host of people.

Schmidt growled, "Offhand, this place *looks* like some kind of utopia."

Willis nodded but stuck his hand in his pocket. "We'd better stick close together."

I happened to glance across the street. "Look there."

Gaites, one of our crewmen, was strolling blissfully along with his arm around a gorgeous blonde.

Schmidt let out a low involuntary whistle.

Willis said wonderingly, "That's one of the most beautiful girls I've ever seen."

Schmidt shook himself. "We better watch out. There's a trap around here somewhere."

Down the sidewalk from the other direction, clasping and unclasping hands with a very warm-looking brunette, came Ferralli, another crewman.

Schmidt whistled again. Willis swore in low fervent tones.

Somewhere, there was a peculiar rumble, and after glancing around futilely for the source, a shadow passed across the street, and I looked up.

A kind of metal bridge passed overhead, apparently supporting a moving walkway. Two extremely shrewd-looking men glided past, talking in low tones, and plainly oblivious to everything below.

I glanced down, and there, right in front of me, was a honey-blonde girl with a beautiful figure, wearing a knitted tan dress, and brushing back a lock of hair that fell over her forehead. She said, smiling, "You seem to be a stranger here. May I show you our city?"

Willis and Schmidt were looking on enviously.

Anyone might suppose that, after the captain's warning, the taxi driver's comments, and the suspiciously utopian look of this place, the three of us would have been on guard and well able to take care of ourselves. Yet here we were like three bugs jostling each other for the first chance to fall into the cyanide bottle.

"Ah—ah—" I said stupidly. Willis slid his knuckles back in his pocket and ran a hand over his hair. Schmidt straightened up and put a look of charm on his face. The girl kept her warm gaze focused on me, and, promptly forgetting the graveyard of rusty ships out by the spaceport, I eagerly accepted. The two of us wandered off, enveloped in a delightful haze.

As we strolled down the street, the girl, true to her word, showed me the fountains, pools, lakes, theatres, wine shops, a communal feast and barbecue center, free communal dwellings, drug shops, fume dispensaries, sizzle palaces—

"Look," I asked, "what happens in the 'sizzle palace'?" The "sizzle palace" had an exceptionally conspicuous skull and crossbones over the entrance.

She kept a gentle grip on my arm, and shivered. "It's terrible. I—I can't talk about it."

Another traveling walk carried a superior-looking individual who glanced down to favor me with a brief pitying look. I looked up at the walk.

"What's that?"

The girl glanced up, and looked embarrassed. "Some people don't know how to live. The walks are for them, to cross over this part of the city. Poor people."

"From the expressions of the ones I've seen, they seem satisfied with themselves."

"Sh-h. Of course they are. That's how we keep them happy."

"You keep them happy by letting them feel superior?"

"Yes, and then we let them do the work of running the city." She shrugged prettily. "It's their dish."

I looked around. With the solitary exception of those overhead traveling walkways, just about everything in sight seemed to be for the purpose of giving pleasure. Now I noticed something else. There were plenty of attractive people around, but the cut-off age seemed to be about thirty-five. Even on the rougher frontier planets, you see people who have managed to survive for more than thirty-five years.

"How is it everyone seems fairly young?"

"Why, when they're worn out, they take a recoup."

"A what?"

"Recoup. They get into the recuperator and it renews them."

"Forever?"

"Oh, no. Sometime or other, they won't make it, and then the bottom drops out." She shrugged. "They never know it."

"So they only live to about thirty-five?"

"Oh, no. That's frightfully old." She giggled. "Who would want to live *that* long?"

I guess I must have looked blank. I'd kind of hoped to make it past that barrier myself.

"Then," I said, "the 'recoup' *wears them out?*"

She looked amused. "No, silly. Man was made for *pleasure,* and it's the *pleasure* that wears him out, not the recoup. But the recoup recharges him, and sometimes he's not in good enough shape to recharge. That's all."

"How long do people last?"

"Oh, twenty-five, twenty-eight, twenty-nine. Who wants to talk about *that?*" She looked faintly puzzled, then murmured, "I *am* forgetful," and removed from her small handbag a little bottle. It mustn't have been over an inch long, and possibly three-eights of an inch thick, with a tiny gold cap. She withdrew the cap, which had a slender glass rod attached, and touched the tip of the rod to her wrists, the hollow of her throat and her forehead.

There was a faint, indescribably delicious fragrance. I had a brief glimpse of a golden skull and crossbones on the bottle, and the word, "CAPTURE."

Two superior-looking men in their forties slid by overhead. One of them looked down, nudged his companion, said something, and the two of them laughed.

There's nothing to bring a man out of the fog quite like a certain kind of laughter. But it doesn't bring him out in a pleasant frame of mind. I looked at the girl and said roughly, "What's your price?"

She looked puzzled. "*Price?*"

"After we have our pleasant little dream together, how do I pay you?"

"Pay? You mean money? But I have an allowance! Everyone has! Why should I want *money?*"

"Who pays the allowance?"

"The government, of course! Oh, I keep forgetting you're a stranger."

"On any planet I've ever been on, people needed more money than they had."

"Yes, but those are *backward* planets. Here we understand all that. Money is only good to buy *pleasure.* The greatest pleasures are the pleasures of the senses. When those are available in full measure, *what good is more money?*"

It began to be clear just what the captain was up against trying to describe this place.

"Listen," I said doggedly, "you can't have that without paying for it *some* way. Here, you evidently pay by being finished off in your twenties. You lose better than half your life in the process."

"But shouldn't a life be measured by the total amount of pleasure received; not by the years it lasts?"

This stopped me for a few seconds, though there was plainly *something* wrong with it.

"Life," I said, groping around for the answer, "is too complicated to measure *either* way. Besides, what about accomplishment? How can you *do* anything if you're smothered in sense-pleasures all the time? And speaking of 'pleasures,' what—"

"Oh," she said angrily, "why do I waste my time with *you?* You belong up there with *them!*" She pointed up at the walkway, turned on her heel and started across the park.

The natural response, of course, was to rush off after the girl. But as she turned, for the first time I really saw the small, jeweled clip she used to hold back her long honey-blonde hair. In color, it matched her dress. Its shape was that same skull and crossbones found on bottles of poison, and across the street on the "sizzle palace."

It occurred to me that there are other girls on other worlds, and it doesn't chop thirty or forty years off a man's life to know them.

Across the park, from the direction of the building marked "Sizzle Palace" in glowing letters three yards high, came a man carrying in one hand a thing like a papier-mâché mock-up of an iron maiden, with an electric cord draped over one arm and disappearing into the battery pack he carried in his other hand.

"Hop in, pal. I'll give you a sample right here. One shot and you'll never be the same again."

"What do *you* get out of it?"

"Well, of course," he said defensively, "I've got my quota to fill. But that's *my* lookout, pal, not yours. Hop in, now."

"No, thanks."

"Come on. I've only got one more to go today."

"I said 'No.'"

"I don't want any trouble with you, pal, but you're going to get in. You don't know what you're missing."

I slid off the cobra belt, and waited for his next move.

He stood eyeing that long length of narrow strap with its peculiar flexible movement and the glittering metal tongue on the end.

He licked his lips, and said, "Guess you're really *not* interested. Well, better luck next time." He backed off with his portable case and battery pack.

No sooner had I turned from him than a brisk little man stepped forward to thrust out a long length of tubing with a pipe-stem on one end.

"Congratulations on escaping that vulture, sir. Here, take a puff of Dreams at my expense."

A wisp of smoke was trailing out the end of the pipe-stem. The faintest hint of it drifted in my direction, creating a brief fantasy of jeweled palaces, slave girls, huge turbaned guards armed with curved swords—

"Here you are, sir."

Through an elaborately-figured bright-hued drape, I could see the smoking pipe-stem thrust forward, and had just sense enough to squeeze the grip of the cobra belt.

The belt rose up with a sinuous swaying motion, and the smoldering pipe stem retreated in a hurry. My head cleared.

"It certainly is disgraceful," said a new voice, "how these people *will* strain the law. Why, the way they try to force their interior pleasures on one!"

About ten feet away stood a man holding a contraption suggesting an overgrown underfed centipede standing upright on its tail. The thing was about six feet tall, with a spine like a length of iron pipe, and curving wires averaging about two feet long reaching out and forward from either side. It was evidently designed to reach around the happy victim. Just what happened next was something I wasn't anxious to find out.

"No, thanks."

"You never know till you try."

"And then it's too late."

"Ah, just a little whip won't—"

He was advancing with this happy-suicide device thrust out in front of him when the cobra belt lengthened out and thrust its metal snout in his face.

The whip salesman beat a hasty retreat. I turned with a sigh of relief, and there was a small crowd offering doped poison cigarettes, liquor doubtless made with wood alcohol, kits containing exotic drugs, syringes, instruction books, and a map to use when the veins got hard to find. None of them asked money for this stuff. All you had to do was sign up with them, and let them supply the goods in the future. On the fringes of this crew, watching sadly and looking like an angel of light by contrast, was the honey-blonde girl. She kept shaking her head to the importunities of the dope and poison salesmen around her, but the one with the pipe-stem on its long hose was now sneaking up from behind. A wisp of smoke trailed toward her.

I shouted, "Look out!" Almost simultaneously, there was the blast of a whistle.

"Watch it," came a stern voice from above. "A little more of that and I'll have you for grabhandling."

A tall, powerfully-built figure in blue uniform was looking down from the edge of the overhead walk.

The crowd muttered, grumbled, and opened up a little. I lost no time in thrusting through to the girl's side. She looked up in surprise, then gave a happy sigh, caught my arm, and clung to it tightly.

The stern voice spoke again from above.

"Did any of these split dish on you?"

"No," called the girl, looking up, "we just—got separated by accident."

"All right."

The crowd now broke up, one or two of them kicking their display cases ill-temperedly.

It was just starting to get dark. The girl hummed happily to herself, took out her little bottle, and dabbed lightly at her wrists, behind her earlobes, and to either side of her neck. This slow vaporizing rapture enveloped us in an enchanted cloud, and we wandered around for a while with our feet scarcely touching the ground. Fortunately, it wore off about an hour later, and the girl then announced she was hungry. I agreed, and we soon wound up at a public feast-site.

Now, I see no objection to a good meal. But, looking around, it was pretty obvious that what we had here was something else.

Stretched out before us were rows of tables, with slanted leather couches on one side of each row of tables. Halfway down the nearest table a crewman was stretched out on a couch with a strikingly-beautiful exotic-looking girl beside him. The table itself was laden with what looked like roast chicken, ham, piles of steaks, and big flagons that were constantly being refilled. As fast as the diners finished one dish, waiters came over with more food and drink on electric carts and replenished the supply.

I looked around. *Starlight* was generously represented at the feast. The crewman I'd seen first was now lying back cozily as his girl dropped delicacies in his mouth. At another table was Ferralli, the drive technician. Ferralli was working with both hands at what looked like the equivalent of about half a ham. At another table lay Meeres, the medic, his head in a dish of some kind of stuffing, eating ravenously and not bothering with the knives and forks. Across on the other side of the place, the familiar face of Grunwald, the navigator, beamed like a pink moon as he raised a two-quart goblet of some pale-yellowish drink, and with the stuff spurting out both corners of his mouth, gulped steadily as he tried to finish off the whole half-gallon in one draught.

An involuntary curse escaped me as it dawned on me just what it was going to be like to crack the crew loose from this pesthole.

About halfway down the aisle between two rows of tables, a man in a white coat bent with a stethoscope over a motionless red-faced, open-mouthed male figure clutching a steak bone in one hand. The doctor listened judiciously, nodded, then someone pried loose the steak bone, two attendants rolled the figure off onto a stretcher and threw a sheet over it, and a man in a gray coat cheerfully put a mark in a record book he was carrying, and looked around hopefully at the other tables.

To tell the truth, this planet was getting a little hard to take. Every time you turned around, someone was right there to help you kill yourself. On other planets, the inhabitants would bash you over the head, rob you, and dump the carcass off a cliff. Here they expected you to jump off yourself, and somebody earned ten credits for it if you jumped off *his* end of the cliff. The obvious thing for us to do was to get out of this place as fast as possible.

Beside me, the gorgeous blonde was dabbing droplets of liquid enchantment on her forehead, wrists, and behind her ears. As she turned her head, that skull-and-crossbones clasp in her hair came into view again.

Down the aisle, three of *Starlight's* crew staggered off toward one of the small blocky buildings that dotted the grounds. Remembering the Roman arrangements for repeated feasting, the whole business looked even worse. The only good thing about it was that a night like this was bound to be followed by a terrific hangover. During the hangover, the men would doubtless be too sick and weak to resist when we loaded them on board the tender.

To one side of me as I was thinking this, busy cooks were working over the meat as it traveled over the hot coals on revolving spits hung from an endless metal belt that moved along steadily. One of these cooks seemed to have the job of shaking on a greenish powder as the meat went past. The box had the familiar skull and crossbones symbol, with the word, "ADDICTEEN" in an arc over it.

There was no doubt at all that we had to get out of this hole, and just as soon as possible.

From one side came a familiar voice, and I turned to see a crewman, a big chunk of meat clutched in both hands.

"Hey, sir," he yelled, "the captain was all wet about this place, wasn't he?"

Before I could think what to say, he ravenously tore off a fresh chunk of meat, looked up, and shouted, "Guess what? I'm *settling* here! I always wanted to be a pioneer!"

I stared around. "A *what?*"

"*Pioneer!*" He beamed. The sultry brunette beside him turned down a mug of steaming drink, and sank her dainty white teeth into what looked like an oversize turkey leg. She gave a quick twist of the head as she tore off the meat, then sat back and chewed demurely.

Just then we came to the end of the line, and the cooks thrust out trays loaded with meat, gravy, and what looked like some kind of stuffing and mashed potatoes, and then we were at one of the feast tables, and an immaculately-dressed waiter was pouring out a sparkling drink that frosted the goblet as it filled it.

There was something about climbing onto the slanted leather-covered platform beside the table that finished off my appetite, but the gorgeous blonde didn't hesitate. She daintily positioned herself on this slanted couch, and eyed the feast.

"What happens," I said, "when you *eat* this stuff? Can you eat other food afterward?"

"You don't *want* to."

Before I had added up all the trouble that was going to cause us, she said, "You just can't *ever* get enough of this. And it's the *eating* of the food that's pleasurable, not the *having* eaten it."

"What happens when the feast is *over?*"

She blushed. "I shouldn't tell you, but—" She brought out, cupped in her hand, a tiny bottle, with a gold and black label reading "Ravage." There was no skull-and-crossbones on the label. The whole bottle was in the shape of a skull and crossbones. On the back was superimposed a representation of what looked like some kind of spider.

It occurred to me again, with considerable force, that there were *other* girls.

She said sweetly, "Is there anything *else* you want to know?"

"Not just now."

She tore into the nearest tray, while I meditated on what to do next. I glanced around, picked up one of several bones lying around on the table, rolled over on my back, clutching the bone in my hand, and bared my teeth.

About five minutes crept past.

"H'm," said a voice from the direction of my feet. "*Here's* an odd case."

I gave a long rasping inhalation, and the voice murmured, "*Interesting.*"

A cool hand rested on my forehead and a thumb peeled back my left eyelid.

"Put this one on a stretcher, and take him into the waiting room. I'll want to examine this a little more closely."

We wound up in a dim-lit grisly place behind a screen of evergreens, with moaning bodies, covered with perspiration, strewn around on the ground.

As the doctor carried out his examination, I said, "I'm from off-planet. What's the purpose of this pleasure set up?"

"Why, to let the unfit pleasure-lovers eliminate themselves! If you let them have their own way, they will wreck any civilization ever built—unless you make allowance to get *rid* of them . . . Now, open your mouth, and let's see your tongue . . . H'm . . . *Cough* . . . That's enough. Roll over . . . Yes, you see, rot and corruption set into every civilization ever built, unless an iron discipline is imposed, or some means is provided to exterminate the hedonists who spread the corruption. The best way to get rid of them, obviously, is to provide them with exactly what they want. It is the genius of our planet that we have worked out how to do it. The expense is really very modest, as long as you let them finish themselves off fast, so their numbers don't become too great."

As he talked, he probed with his fingers, apparently feeling of this and that internal organ.

I said, "What about their—ah—souls?"

"That's not *my* responsibility."

"What happens," I said, "when I try to get our crew out of here?"

He frowned, peering into my eye again. "You're a ship captain?"

"First officer."

"Is your crew something of a—er—dead-end outfit—"

"They're good men."

"Then the majority of them are running wild because of deprivation, not a natural greed for compounded sensations. By tomorrow morning, they'll have had the equivalent of a two-week binge, all in one night. Sanity will reassert itself over what's left of them. All you have to do is collect them from the gutters."

"What happens when we lug them back onto the ship, and they can't eat anything without 'addicteen' in it?"

"Well— You can keep them alive on sugar-water, lemonade— things of that sort, till the desire for food returns. After about six weeks, I should say, they'll start to recover. In three or four years, they may even look back on their experience as pleasurable. In ten years, they may think it was idyllic. Twenty years from now, some of them may wonder why they didn't stay. It's hard to remember a hangover with real accuracy for twenty years." He straightened.

"Whatever *your* trouble is, I think it's temporary."

"Good," I said. "Thanks."

He nodded, and moved away.

One of the corpses lying nearby rolled over and spoke in Willis' voice. "Quite a planet. Now I know why the captain couldn't give us a straight warning. *He* was here about ten years ago."

"Whoever listed this place AAA must have been here twenty years ago."

"At least."

"Where's Schmidt?"

"The last I saw of him, he was wandering around with a terrific brunette. But he kept giving her hair-clasp a funny look, if you follow me."

"I know what you mean." I got to my feet, and looked out.

He wasn't at any of the nearby tables, and I glanced at the line of people entering.

There was Schmidt, giving the cook with the "Addicteen" box a worried look. The brunette standing in line with him was enough to double a man's pulse at a hundred feet. She favored him with a sweltering look, and ran her hand lightly up and down his arm. He, in turn, darted swift glances in all directions, and suddenly spotted us.

A few minutes later, they left with trays. Shortly after that, he joined us.

"I may kick myself later, but this stuff has more voltage than *I'm* used to."

"Before you start kicking yourself, take a look in here."

Schmidt glanced around, and swore in low fervent tones. Then we told him what the doctor had said.

He shook his head. "We better get all the crew loose from here that we can. Otherwise, we're going to have a sweet time handling the ship."

"And what kind of a time will we have when they sober up and remember what we broke up for them."

"If they aren't nuts, they'll be grateful."

Willis shook his head.

Schmidt said, "They aren't stupid. If *we* can see it, why can't they?"

"It's our job to get everybody back on time. If it was *their* job to get *us* back, the situation might be different."

"Truth in that," growled Schmidt. "Well— What do we do?"

I said, "Let's circulate around, and see if anyone looks like he *wants* help."

Not all the crew was there, but those who were obviously did not want help. We then looked around the city, fighting off sizzle, whip, and dream salesmen, and trailed by pretty girls. None of the rest of the crew was visible anywhere. We went back to the feast grounds, and most of the crew had disappeared. We came out in none too happy a frame of mind, and abruptly Schmidt said, "What a *hell* of a liberty!"

Willis growled something unintelligible, and I snarled, "Let's take one more look through that hole in there."

We went back inside the grisly dim-lit place back of the trees, and moved slowly amongst the apparent bodies. One sodden swollen form groaned, and the voice of Ferralli, the drive-technicians, croaked, "My God, sir . . . Get me out of here."

No miserable ruin ever got a more fervent welcome. Here, at least, was proof we were doing some good. As the three of us were carefully lugging him toward the exit, a dim figure weakly raised its hand. The voice of Meeres, the medic, was barely recognizable.

"Help . . . don't leave me . . . drugged . . . please . . ."

We stopped.

This wasn't so good. Three men can handle one fairly easily. They may not be able to handle two at all—especially with whip and sizzle salesmen around, and sellers of dreams working to windward.

We put Ferralli beside Meeres, and searched the place carefully. We recognized one more face, and Willis said roughly, "What'll *you* have? Back to the ship, or more fun here?"

The voice said weakly, "Back to the ship, sir—but not yet, please . . . *Don't go, sir!*"

Willis had turned away. "Make up your mind."

"I *want* to go back—but I can't move. My insides are all floating around loose, sir."

This seemed like something in Meeres' line, and we figured we ought to get some use out of him, so we lugged him over. Then we put Ferralli down on the other side of Meeres, so if he needed medical help, he'd have it, too. We promised them we'd be around, and moved off a little distance.

Schmidt glanced back at them dubiously, "That's after the *beginning* of *one night* in this place. What's it going to be like tomorrow morning?"

"Let's not even think about it. Let's just hope no one gets into one of those 'sizzle palaces.'"

We spent most of the night alternately checking the three sick crewmen, and hunting for others outside. We didn't see another crewman, so we took turns getting some sleep, and let the patrolling lapse till around dawn, then we went out again.

There in the gutter lay a wreck with a snake's head sticking out of its pocket. Nearby lay another with one hand clutching the tail of an imitation alligator. They looked as if they had been connected up with a vacuum hose, and everything inside had been sucked out.

Our other three crewmen had now come to enough to stagger around, so we put them to work.

Around noon, we finally got the whole sorry lot ferried back up to *Starlight*. Engstrom piloted the tender, and helped care for the men, but he flatly refused to even set foot on the planet.

Since the ship had to be run somehow, we put everybody capable of standing back on the job. It was a demonstration of the power of pure habit and believe me, we were nervous for fear it would give way, and land us in a still worse mess.

"Well," said Engstrom soberly, "let's hope we don't go by *that* planet again for a while."

Even after everything that had happened, the memory of that gorgeous blonde still bothered me. Half-joking, I said, "If I'd thought of it in time, I'd have taken a memento along with me. That place shouldn't object to a little kidnapping."

Engstrom gave me a brief sharp suspicious look, then he shook his head. "It wouldn't work." He added, "If you think you've done the right thing, be grateful for that."

"Unfortunately, I don't feel that sense of achievement that should follow doing the right thing."

"Well, remember, you've just been through a trial by silk. An *ordeal*. You don't feel good after undergoing an ordeal."

I shrugged. "Silk is soft."

"Do you think everything soft is necessarily harmless?" He nodded toward a kind of human shambles drifting past in the corridor. "What's the difference whether an enemy disables you by attack, or by leading you to dissipate your strength?"

I frowned. "I've heard of trial by fire, trial by water, and of trial by combat. I never heard of *trial by silk*."

Engstrom nodded. "What they wanted in the old days was to test some individual's supposed merit, and do it fast. Naturally, they weren't interested in this method. Trial by silk applies to whole civilizations even better than to individuals, it takes a surplus of ease and luxury to carry it out, and it's usually slow.

"However," he said, "never underestimate it. Whatever method beats you, the result is the same. You're beat. And if it happens pleasantly enough, you don't even realize what's happening, so you aren't warned."

Another wreck shambled past in the corridor, there was a crash and a yell, and Meeres hurried by with a hypo-gun in one hand.

"I think I see what you mean," I said slowly.

Engstrom nodded. "Enough pleasure is like so many wet sheets wrapped around a man. He generally can't even do anything to get loose."

Then Engstrom's face reddened slightly, and he cleared his throat.

"However," he said, "this is no easy thing to explain."

THE TROUBLE WITH COLONIES

⚜

THE OPERATOR

The rats and greevils were gnawing in their burrows as Jim Fielding, his teeth chattering, joined Dave Hunsacker at the cast-iron stove.

"Shove over," said Fielding. "Don't hog the whole thing."

Hunsacker coughed, and spat phlegm in a basin on a high split-log stool. He shifted grips on the pole that ran crosswise of the cabin, and rested his head on his hands as the blessed heat flowed up from the stove. From near his ear, came a *sqrueek-creeq-greak* noise that set his teeth on edge.

"Damn the pests," he growled, and was sorry he'd spoken. His voice came out in a half-whisper that reminded him how he felt.

Fielding drew a shuddering breath, and murmured, "Thank God we've finally got a foundry, anyway. We needed this stove, and the freight by supply ship would have sunk us."

Hunsacker, afraid to try his voice again, gave a grunt of assent.

"Snow's melting out there," said Fielding. "The air can't be below freezing, can it?"

"Unh," said Hunsacker, turning to get the heat from another angle. It was impossible to get enough, but too much would make his skin tender, even though too much wasn't enough, either.

"Well," said Fielding, "I had on my fur boots, wool socks under that, long johns, fleece undervest, fur vest, and fur jacket, long fur leggings, two wool hoods and a fur hat, and I was shaking all over before I got halfway to Pete's. Seemed like around forty below to me. There wasn't any wind, either."

Hunsacker grunted, and with an effort cleared his throat. "While you were at it, you should have heated a stone—put it in your pocket."

"You're right. I didn't think of it."

"How's Pete?"

"He's got it, too."

"Bad?"

"He says it's nothing. You know Pete. He was shaking too bad to go out to his woodpile. I carried in enough to last him through tomorrow. I think that's where I got this headache."

"He should have got a stove. He can't keep that fireplace in wood."

"He claims you can put in bigger pieces."

"How far did you go?"

"Out to the overlook."

"No wonder you're shaking."

"That isn't any distance."

"It is when you've got the grakes. Ease back, you've taken half the space already."

"Sorry. Well, I was curious."

Hunsacker roasted some more, then Fielding's last comment penetrated to his consciousness. It reminded him of a little quirk in his friend's makeup.

Hunsacker cleared his throat again. "Curious about *what*?"

"Unh?" said Fielding. He changed position and swore. "Do we have to stand and bake like lizards on rocks? I've got work to do."

"Go do it, then. Before you leave, what was it you were curious about?"

"I just saw it out of the corner of my eye."

Hunsacker waited. Fielding said no more. Hunsacker swore mentally, but saved his vocal cords for harder work.

"Saw *what* out of the corner of your eye?"

"That was just after I left Terrill's."

"After you *left* Terrill's."

"Yeah."

"I didn't know you *stopped* at Terrill's."

"Abe was having a fight with his wife."

Hunsacker started to turn his head, but a hammering headache burst into consciousness. He coughed, and spat up a quantity of phlegm. Then he had to blow his nose. He put his head back in place, eyes shut, and the *greak-sqrueek-creeq-sqreek* noise came through clearly.

"You stopped at Terrill's?" said Hunsacker.

"Not for long. Abe and his wife were embarrassed. Thought I might have overheard them." Fielding snorted. "You could have heard them half-a-mile away. One of the logs of their cabin powdered, a bunch of pack-badgers came in while they were asleep, and got into their stores."

Greak-sqreek, went the greevils by Hunsacker's ear, *sqrueek-greak*, as they reduced the hard wood to tunnels of dust. From a corner of the room came a *grak-grak-grak* noise as a rat ate its way along the join of the log.

Hunsacker shivered, started to speak, then concentrated on a more important fact: He had started to shake, despite the fact that he was practically on top of the stove.

He worked the leather glove from the hip pocket of his leggings, opened his eyes cautiously, and crouched, to turn the stove-door handle, and look in. He was greeted by a white powdering of ash over a bed of glowing coals. He reached out to the stack of dry wood heaped against the wall, selected some small pieces, put them in side-by-side on the coals, laid others crosswise atop them, and put some medium-sized pieces on top of that.

Fielding murmured, "Heat seems to be letting up. What kind of apprentice firemen we got, anyway?"

"I've been too busy trying to find out what it was you saw after you left Terrill's."

"Didn't I mention that? There is some kind of camp down there."

Hunsacker growled, "Down *where*?"

"You can see it from the overlook."

Hunsacker noted the small flames spurting from the smaller pieces laid atop the coals, and shut the stove door. Cautiously, he straightened.

Fielding said, "Watch it!" and steadied Hunsacker by the elbow.

A spell of reeling dizziness passed over.

"Thanks." Hunsacker got his grip on the pole, waited a moment, and said, "How come you saw something from Terrill's that led you to go to the overlook? Terrill's is a half-mile this side, anyway, with big woods in between."

Fielding's manner was carefully offhand.

"There was a girl looking down from the trail when I came out of Terrill's."

Hunsacker didn't move.

Greak-sqrueek went the greevils in the pole by his ear.

"A girl," said Hunsacker cautiously.

"Yeah. Just at the head of the trail, where it bends downhill. She turned when I came out, and went back into the woods."

Methodically, Hunsacker considered whether Fielding might be a lot sicker than he seemed. But, in that case, he wouldn't have made it back.

Fielding cleared his throat. "She was wearing some kind of form-fitting one-piece outfit, with a . . . like a bubble over it. I stared at her, and took a step in that direction. Well, you see the picture. I had on all that fur and leather, and some of it isn't exactly in the best of condition. Anyway, she got out of there. Pretty little thing."

Fielding's voice thickened slightly, and he coughed and spat, and was silent.

Hunsacker asked himself whether his friend had gone stumbling and shouting after her. It would be interesting to go out and check the tracks—if he dared to leave the stove.

Fielding, apparently realizing the mental picture he had created, said, "I already had the shakes. Terrill's cabin was cold as ice; worse than outdoors, because the sun hadn't warmed it up. I plodded after the girl, but I tell you, I didn't rush. I was too busy checking to see if the trees kept their shape. I thought maybe I'd gone through the fever and hit the delirium ahead of schedule."

"Did you see her again?"

"Not once. Her tracks were funny, too—as if she walked *on* the snow. But of course it was too soft to support her weight."

"Not in the woods, necessarily. Where the sun didn't hit it, it might still be hard—provided it was compacted to start with."

"Then this wasn't compacted too much, because I went right through it."

"When she turned away, did she have any kind of pack on?"

"I don't know. She turned out of the sun into the shade, and I'd just come out of Terrill's so I didn't see that any too clearly."

"Did you tell Terrill about it?"

Fielding snorted.

"What for? He's *got* a woman."

Hunsacker considered the situation. Since the pack-bears had got Barrow, Hunsacker was theoretically the settlement's leader. The fact was occasionally acknowledged when a colonist, stuck with a problem he couldn't work out himself, brought it to Hunsacker. There was also an occasional deference, or an air of defiance, traceable to the fact that in a vague kind of way Hunsacker represented authority. To try to assert the authority would have been too ludicrous to think about, but nevertheless it imposed on him some obligations.

"Where she comes from," he said carefully, "that may not matter."

"It matters to me. That's what I care about."

"I mean," said Hunsacker warily, "this woman may represent as much of a threat to us as anything else."

Fielding started to object, then gave a grunt of assent. "Could be. Pretty, though."

"Could you see the camp from the overlook?"

"Easy. Just the ship, and two tents maybe fifty feet from its base. They were small tents."

"What kind of ship?"

"One of these base-standers. I guess they call it a yacht."

"Any hatch open in it?"

"Not that I could see from where I stood. I was shaking too bad to think about going around to the other side. This camp was down in that big clearing below the overlook. Not the one at a distance, but right below."

Hunsacker cleared his throat. "Nice spot. The pack-bears hole up for the winter at the base of the bluff."

"Sure. When the melt hits, they'll come out."

"And they'll be famished."

"Right. That makes it nice when they smell flesh."

Hunsacker thought it over. Obviously, he had yet to extract the full story from Fielding. He spat phlegm, and eased his head around into a position that served to minimize the headache.

"What happened when you looked down on this camp?"

"Nothing, at first. I was shaking all over, thinking about this spot they'd picked to camp in, when one of the tents opened up. Another girl, wearing some kind of skimpy two-piece outfit, came out, saw me, went back in for a second, came out, and knocked about a quarter-ton of snow out of the trees onto my head."

"You mean she fired at you?"

"At me, or over me. I didn't stick around to make sure."

Hunsacker considered it from various angles.

"So there are *two* girls?"

Fielding said dryly, "That's the only reason I'm telling *you* about this, friend."

"What did the second one look like?"

"Beautiful. The first was pretty, so far as you can judge at a glance. The second was beautiful, so far as you can tell in one brief look."

"You saw her *twice*."

"I'm not talking about the second time. Anybody that fires at me is ugly. I figure you can have the second one, and I'll take the first one. Just as a rough start to the negotiations."

"See any men around?"

"Nope."

"Anything we might decide, these girls could chop into mince-meat."

"I know that. We found *that* out back before the pox."

"We were green. Spoiled by civilization, and didn't know it."

Sqrueek-greak went the greevils at Hunsacker's ear, as if adding their bit to the conversation.

"What," said Hunsacker, to get his mind off his memories, "were Terrill and his wife fighting about?"

"About which one was responsible for the pack-badgers getting in. That was the standby. They threw all kinds of other stuff in, too. You could hear them way down the trail. They should have treenailed some sticks and leather over that hole first, and stuffed some hay inside, and they could have had the fight in private. As it was, their voices came right out the opening. Their kids were crying, and she was grabbing up this one and that one, and tell-ing them to look at their father and see who was responsible for their being stuck in this godforsaken place, and he was telling her to shut up, he could only take so much, and one of them was smashing up furniture—there's another of those logs they better take a look at, because when they hit it, dust spurted out onto the snow. Anyway, they put things together fast when I came up coughing and clearing my throat. When they opened up, the place looked about as neat as any." Fielding paused, then added, "If they'd fixed that log first, they probably wouldn't have *had* a fight. The sight of that would drive anyone nuts."

"Probably so cold in there from that hole that they didn't get up to start the fire, so the kids started whimpering, and then they found the hole, and the provisions missing, and that did it."

"Whatever started it, they've got the fight to add to what the badgers did. It's a simple question of survival to avoid that."

"You think back before the pox, and tell me how many of us avoided it."

"Not many. And a lot didn't survive, either."

Hunsacker again struggled to get off the subject.

"Both of these girls had on bubble outfits, eh?"

"The first one did. I could see it reflect—glint—in the sun. The second one I don't know about. Why?"

"Unless they've changed them since we've been out here, there's just a thin plastic layer filled with warm air by a backpack heater. That's fine as long as the plastic is all right. But what happens if she steps too close to a needle bush?"

"Rip the plastic."

"And the only protection under this bubble was a little thin cloth?"

Fielding grinned. "Protection? Decoration."

The stove suddenly popped and snapped as the wood caught.

Hunsacker nodded sourly.

"Green. They're as green as we were when we got here, maybe worse. They've paid their money for some dude-camping outfit, and they think they're as safe as in a park on their home planet. Meanwhile, they're going around eighty percent naked on a part of the planet where the women have been cut by a third for two years; but, of course, they're enlightened, so *that* doesn't matter. Those two girls could be the worst disaster to hit this place since the pox."

That night, after the fire had been left to gnaw its way through the big dry chunk he had worked in atop the coals, Dave Hunsacker lay awake, lying on his side, the packbear robe and a down comforter over him, and heat flowing around him from the cloth-wrapped rock at his feet, and the cloth-wrapped rock that he lay curled around. Despite the heat, he shivered involuntarily, but that didn't stop his thoughts.

Two girls camped alone on the packbear flats. Two girls from *civilization*. Two girls who fired on crude unkempt colonists, or fled at the sight of them. Then weird pictures began to flit before his eyes, so he knew the delirium had started. Across the room, he could hear the frame of Fielding's bunk rattle, and knew that he had it even worse. After all that exposure, the grakes would speed up, and Fielding would go through the whole sequence in a day and a night, where Hunsacker had done his best to stretch the thing out for two days. It wasn't the headache, the shaking, and the chills that bothered him the worst. It was the delirium. It had a tendency to focus on some strong emotional experience, and stay with it, to work variations and contrasts that became so intense as to threaten a man's power of endurance. Afterward, the memory faded, which was fine afterward, but no consolation beforehand. Hunsacker held his mind on the two girls, struggling to make the delirium take some new track, to force it to yield him pictures of the packbear flats, or Terrill's cabin, from which Fielding had seen the first girl.

Just then, the picture came clear. The low fern tree, green against the white of the snow, and green against the grayish brown of the slightly weathered logs, sifted down snow as the wind blew around Terrill's, and Lila Terrill, her pretty face framed in the white fur hood, called out, "Dave! Lou! Hey, don't you dare go by until you see this slinky new fur outfit Abe made for me!" She laughed, and breathed out a cloud of frosty breath. "Oh, isn't everything wonderful?" Eyes sparkling, she looked up at the trees, at the sky bright-blue through the green branches edged in white, at the white snowflakes drifting gently down. "And they told us we were crazy to risk a new planet! *They* were the crazy ones!"

The scene vanished.

The lump of dirt landed on Lou's upturned face, the spots half-hidden by the flour she used to conceal from Dave the fact that she had it, so that he would let her go on working with him as the cold settled its teeth in and the fireplace sucked the cold through every track where the pack badgers nightly dug out the clay in search of a gap big enough to get through.

"There is no help available," crackled the communicator, and the voice came through clear and sharp. "We can't risk personnel.

We suggest that you simply avoid exposure, rest in bed in a warm room, avoid all exertion, take frequent hot, sweet, citrus drinks, and see to it that the patients have plenty of fresh air and sunshine, but are not directly exposed to the cold. A steam or electrically heated solar shelter will be ideal. Regular records of body temperature, taken orally, should be kept for future reference, and—"

The snow blasted through the hole where the window had been torn out, sifting down the slope of the drift like a fast-shifting living curtain, scattering across the floor, to be picked up and whirled around the cabin by the hurricane blast that came in under the door where he had shoveled it clear when the snow stopped yesterday, and the sun came out, and they knew the storm was over.

"Lou," he cried, "why didn't you wake me up! You've got to rest!"

"You were so tired," she said. "You worked so hard yesterday."

Then the clump of dirt landed on Lou's upturned face, where she had put the flour to hide the fact that she was sick.

Abe Terrill said, "Lila's got it. I could see the spots yesterday. And now today she's got this awful cold, too. She shakes all the time, and I can't get it hot enough for her. I can't get through the snow to get the wood back fast enough. You and Jim have both lost . . . I mean, you're both *alone*. If you could move in together, and split the work, would it be all right if I took the extra wood you've got piled? I was so busy working on other things last fall I got behind cutting firewood. I never thought we could have a storm like this. I've got to get wood somehow! I'll carry it up myself. Look, it'll be good for you, too, it'll keep you from going crazy thinking about it, and the work will be lighter."

Hunsacker groaned and turned over, and his forearm touched a corner of the rock where his tossing had pulled the cloth away. He struggled out of the delirium.

"Lou?" he murmured, and there was no answer. He sat up in darkness dimly lit by moonlight. From across the cold cabin came racking sobs. But it was a man sobbing.

Hunsacker groped backwards and forward, trying to locate himself in time. The whole sequence mentally unreeled to the end, and he lay back, the pain as fresh and new as when it had happened. He shivered, and the snow whirled, and he looked dizzily around, resting the saw on the log.

Lou was there laughing.

"Come on," she said. "Stop cutting wood for a while. A little more, and you'll be a registered termite, just like we've got in our walls."

"Did you ever see snow, woman? I want to cut wood now, while I can get it. And those aren't termites. They're greevils. Learn the *patois* of the planet if you want to communicate with me."

"Why should I communicate with a termite? Abe Terrill has time enough to make his wife a fur outfit, no less. Now, *that's* what I call adaptation to the environment."

The clump of dirt landed on Lou's upturned face. The bitter cold sapped his strength and made him regret every minute wasted in the pleasant days of fall, when the snow was a mere ornament.

Dave turned over, and the delirium shifted its grip, and came at him from a new angle, bringing a fresh memory before him as, across the dimly moonlit room, Jim Fielding cried out, and neither man heard the other.

Toward morning, it began to let up.

Dazed, Hunsacker struggled awake, to rest dizzily on his elbows amongst the tangled covers.

"Merciful God!" said Hunsacker.

The memories flooded his mind, and then at once began to fade.

From across the cabin, Fielding spoke in a croaking voice.

"You alive?"

"I guess so."

"That's the last time I concentrate it all in one day."

The memories of the delirium were evaporating fast, and suddenly Hunsacker felt ravenous.

"Pretty bad?" he said.

Fielding said grimly, "I got contrasts and ironies this time I never dreamed of before. There was even one—" He paused. "Good. I can't remember it."

"It's not dawn, but I'm getting up. You?"

"Yeah. I'd be afraid to go back to sleep after that. Besides, I'm a little hungry."

"You light the lamp. I'll take care of the fire."

"O.K."

✤   ✤   ✤

Roughly two hours later, the sun was just casting shadows across the gray surface of the snow. Hunsacker and Fielding, heavily dressed against the cold, lay stretched out in the snow, looking down on the silent camp below the bluff.

"Late risers," murmured Fielding.

"Where they come from, this could be the middle of the night." Hunsacker eased slightly to his left, so that his gun, inside its long fur case, didn't press into his side.

"What's that?" murmured Fielding.

From down below came the faintly echoing sound of light footsteps crunching through the snow.

In the dim shadows, a small figure, heavily dressed, and carrying something large and long on its shoulders, came into sight at the edge of the clearing. There was a sound somewhat like sand dumped from a sack as the figure dropped what it was carrying, and it sank in grainy snow.

Fielding murmured, "What's that?"

"Looks like a log."

"Too big."

"Could be pithwood. That's light enough."

"I think you're right. What would they want with that stuff?"

The light, reaching into the woods, showed it more clearly, and Hunsacker corrected himself.

"*Rotten* pithwood."

"Maybe they know more than we think. You suppose they're planning to smoke out the bears?"

"Don't ask me. Which one is this?"

The two men watched the small figure, carrying what looked like a double-bitted ax in one hand, slowly start up a sloping slender ramp extruded from the yacht. The surface of the ramp was free of snow, but whoever it was slipped on stepping onto the ramp, and nearly fell.

Fielding murmured, "I *think* it's the one I saw first. Is that ax sheathed?"

"Not that I can see."

A beam of sunlight was now streaming through the trees, to light the tops of the tents, and the lower half of the yacht. The figure, wearily climbing the ramp, passed through the light, which flashed on the blades of the ax.

Fielding grunted. "Where she slipped, I could have lost my half of this bargain. What's she carrying the thing bare for?"

Hunsacker watched the girl lean the ax against the side of the ship while she felt in her pockets. The way she leaned the ax against the ship was to set the end of the ax handle on the sloping ramp, and rest the head of the upright ax against the side of the ship.

Fielding muttered to himself.

She paid no further attention to the ax, but paused to blow on her cupped hands and work her fingers. Again she felt through her pockets.

She stamped her feet, as if to start the circulation.

The ax head began to slide, along the hull of the ship, picked up speed, then the ax flipped over the side of the ramp, to vanish in the snow below.

Fielding let his breath out with a hiss.

She had some kind of small box in her hand now. She turned an intensely bright light on the side of the ship, then held something cylindrical against the ship. A sizable door slowly opened out at the head of the ramp, the door swinging wide against the ship.

The girl started slowly in, paused, came back, looked blankly around on the ramp, looked at the door, and then turned wearily and went inside. As the door started to close, a feminine voice called, "Where have *you* been?"

"Lost."

The door shut, and Fielding uttered pungent profanity.

Hunsacker rested his head on his forearm, and shook with silent laughter.

"Lost," growled Fielding. He stared at the track lit in the snow by the sun, and that was bound to be visible by the girl's hand-lamp, or by moonlight.

"Well," growled Fielding, "I guess they *don't* know what they're doing."

"Probably panicked," said Hunsacker, keeping his voice low. He paused, studying the tents.

A faint vibration sent a very light powdering of snow sifting down the slope of the nearer tent. Some sort of fastening in the front opened up, and a tall girl wearing, apparently, a two-piece bathing suit, stepped out and looked around. She sent an intent glance over the heads of the two men, who lay motionless in the confusion of light and shade.

"That one," growled Fielding, "is yours. But now, this totals up to *three*."

The girl turned away, and saw the log.

"Good! Phyl *did* get some wood!"

A shapely blond girl looked out of the tent, and gave a scream of delight. "Now we can have a cookout!"

"Four," grunted Fielding.

There was a drumming sound, and snow flew from the other tent. Gales of girlish laughter echoed around the clearing. Two more girls burst out and rolled in the snow, pounding each other with handfuls of snow. The laughter abruptly changed to cries of dismay.

"Oh! It's *cold!* Stop, Stacey. Please stop."

These latest two plunged through the snow to the base of the ramp, and ran up, to bang on the side of the ship.

"Open up! We're *freezing!*"

Fielding growled, "*Six* of them."

"So far," said Hunsacker.

From somewhere down below came a whistle, then a masculine voice called, "Hey, *hey!*"

Fielding and Hunsacker, moving only their eyes, glanced around.

Floating over the clearing at the extreme end, from the direction of the more distant clearing, came a dish-shaped grav-skimmer, that now swooped forward, to hover over the ramp. In the grav-skimmer were four men in their early twenties. One was wearing a loincloth, one a kind of old-fashioned bathing suit, one a pair of green form-fitting trousers creased up the front, and imitation deerskin jacket fringed on the bottom and along the cuffs. One was wearing a set of brief silver trunks, and gold paint apparently intended to show off his large muscles.

The two girls on the ramp screamed in mock panic. One of them shouted, "The pirates are after us! Help!"

Fielding belched, and muttered profanity.

Hunsacker alertly studied the reactions of the girls, noting that the tall girl had an unreadable expression. The shapely blonde looking out of the tent went back inside without saying anything. The door of the ship opened, and a neat intelligent-looking brunette glanced out coolly, wearing what appeared to be some sort of dark lounging pajamas.

Hunsacker, still not moving his head, glanced back at the grav-skimmer, noting, as it idly turned, the snout of some kind of weapon that jutted up at an angle.

Fielding growled, "How much younger than us is this crew?"

"Four or five years, I think. Why?"

"For just a minute there, I felt about ninety years old."

On the grav-skimmer, the male figure wearing the breech clout pointed at the girl in the doorway of the space yacht. He half-crouched, and clapped his hand on his knee.

"Ha, ha, ha," he shouted, his voice creating a peculiar crowing sound that reverberated around the clearing. "Ha, ha, hee, hee, hee, ho-*ho*-ha. Look at that, fellers, a *lay* dee!"

The girl stepped inside and the two girls on the ramp ran in. The door swung shut.

From the direction of the other, more distant, clearing, came a loud croaking sound, rapidly repeated. A second grav-skimmer floated into view. This one carried five more men, two heavily dressed and silent, the other three dressed as for a masquerade. One of the latter called out jubilantly.

"Hey, we got fun later! This planet's got *col*onists!" He pronounced "colonists" with a peculiar jeering emphasis.

"*Col*onists," shouted one of the occupants of the first skimmer, mimicking the tone.

Hunsacker studied the angled gun on this second skimmer.

Fielding murmured, "This looks nice, doesn't it?"

"Doesn't it?" With no extra motion, Hunsacker undid the fastenings of his gun-cover.

"*Colonists! Colonists!*" the men were chanting in the clearing, with the exception of the silent two in the second skimmer.

The tall girl went back into her tent.

Hunsacker said, his voice low: "It looks to me as if that gun has a target-seeking sight—the gun on that skimmer turned toward us."

"I see it."

Hunsacker left the wrapper just covering his gun, and carefully pressed the carrying straps back out of reach in the snow, lest he forget and try to pick it up by the straps out of habit.

Down below, the chanting had reached a pitch and volume

that strained the voices of the chanters. Their voices cracked, and then there was a sudden silence.

From somewhere came a low muffled questioning bark.

Hunsacker squinted at the sky. The sun, now above the horizon, was warming the snow-covered landscape with a burning heat that was undiluted by any cloud cover, wind, or really cold air. Down in the clearing below the bluff, the heat was bound to become more intense as the day went on, since the bluff would reflect the heat of the sun back into the clearing.

There was a soft *shush* of snow behind them, instantly followed by Terrill's voice, pitched low.

"It's me . . . Abe."

Hunsacker, who had tensed himself, relaxed at the familiar voice.

Terrill gave a low laugh. There were further *shush-shush* sounds, and he lay down full length, and crawled up beside Hunsacker.

"If I'd been a bear, I'd have eaten you both."

Fielding, his voice low, said, "Take a look at this gun, Abe, but keep your head down."

Terrill squirmed around, and gave a low fervent grunt.

Hunsacker glanced aside, to see Fielding flip the cover back over his gun. The gun was reversed inside its wrapping, the snout aiming back down the trail, the butt lightly depressed in the snow; a squeeze of the trigger would have sent the bullet waist-high over the place where the trail began to level out behind them.

Fielding murmured, "I hate things creeping up on me from behind."

Terrill murmured, "I was going to bear-bark at you for the fun of it. I'm glad I didn't follow *that* whim. What have we got here, anyway?"

Hunsacker said, "Take a look. Maybe you can tell us."

Fielding said, "It's a little hard to explain."

Terrill peered down at the clearing, where the two skimmers had set down, and the occupants, still standing in the skimmers, were talking to one another with expansive gestures. There seemed to be some kind of disagreement between those dressed as if for a masquerade, and the two wearing heavy winter clothing.

"Well," said the one wearing a heavy coat, "*you* do it if you want. Count me out."

"Scared? Of washouts?"

"I keep seeing that woman's face when she picked up the baby. She looked straight at me."

"So what?"

"I'm not getting in that spot again."

"That was an accident."

"I'm not getting in a spot where that accident can happen again."

"That baby would have died anyway."

"How do *you* know?"

"Colonist mortality is better than eighty percent."

"That's overall. We don't know about *that* baby."

"What's the difference? They don't relate. They're out of the socio-economic system. They're washouts. Hell, they're only human by courtesy. We don't have to worry about what happens to them."

"It's all yours. I don't get anything out of it but nightmares."

"It's like if you crack up anything. You want to do it again right away. That makes it all right."

"Not me. That woman said something with her eyes, and I can't forget it."

"We *could* take you, whether you want to go or not. We could . . . kind of . . . make you do it, whether you want to do it or not."

There was an ugly silence, then the first voice carried, very low.

"*You'll* make me?"

The silence stretched out, then broke in a nervous laugh.

"I was just kidding, Barn. But—"

"I'm not going."

"O.K. So, O.K."

"Hack feels the same way. We both aren't going. We all agreed before we came, we wouldn't tell each other what to do. We're sticking by it."

"O.K., Barn. I was just kidding. Look, here we are arguing about *what?* A bunch of mudfeet. You do what you want. But there're nine of us, and only eight girls. So how do we work that out?"

"Leave it up to the girls. They'll figure it out some way."

"O.K., Barn. Hey, who's got the battlewagons?"

The collision broke up in nervous laughter, and shouts of, "Who's got the battlewagons?" Someone began handing out something too small to make out as they milled around in the two skimmers, bending over to pick up small pipes with curved stems and small bowls, into which they put whatever it was that had been handed out, and then lit the pipes.

From somewhere came a gruff peremptory questioning bark, muffled but insistent, with overtones of ill temper.

Terrill murmured, "The damned fools are in the middle of packbear flats, and it's a warm day."

Fielding looked around at Hunsacker and murmured, "Well, Dave, what do we do?"

Hunsacker kept his mouth shut.

Terrill twisted toward him, to murmur, "You're the Settlement Leader, Dave."

Hunsacker growled, "Where's the problem?"

Fielding murmured, "We need women, and there are *eight* of them. Right under us in the bluff, there's a whole pack of bears, and you can hear the sentinels getting short-tempered. When the day gets warmer, those packbears will come out. They'll eat anything in sight, plant or animal. When they come out, they'll spot the girls."

Hunsacker grunted. "They've got their protectors down there. Look at the armament on those skimmers."

"Will it stop a rushing bear?"

"How would I know if it will stop him? But it will *kill* him."

"What do we do about the girls?"

Terrill put in, "A few well-placed shots while that bunch is doping themselves up, and we will end the thing."

"Don't kid yourself," said Hunsacker. "The racket from a few well-placed shots will bring those bears out of there in a rage. On top of that, that yacht probably has an automatic device recording—and maybe broadcasting to a satellite—everything that happens around it. And, on top of *that*, what do the girls do while we're picking off this bunch?"

Terrill said, "Where *are* these girls you're talking about? I don't see any girls."

Fielding said, "There are two of them in that tent nearer to the ship. And from what's been said, there must be half-a-dozen more in the ship. We've only seen four of those."

"Good lookers?"

"What?"

"Are the girls pretty?"

"Yes, but green."

"They'll get over that."

"Say," said Fielding in a low drawl, "I thought you were married."

Terrill didn't answer for a moment. "I was thinking of Pete. He's over at our place helping out so much lately, I . . . well, I'm glad to see some more women around here."

Hunsacker said dryly, his voice low, "I don't think they came here to settle."

Fielding said, "Well, what do we *do*, Dave?"

Hunsacker said nothing. He was still trying to fit the pieces together.

Terrill murmured, without conviction, "We could warn them about where they are."

Hunsacker squinted at the clearing.

"How?" said Fielding, his voice low and sarcastic.

"Stand up and yell to them."

Fielding growled, "I almost got my head split yesterday, because one of the *girls* saw me. We're supposed to warn *this* bunch?"

Down below, the men were sprawled in odd positions, in the skimmers and on blankets stretched on the snow, the sun now plainly glinting from the bubbles of their warm-suits. Each was drawing on his pipe, his face blissful, save for the one who'd been called Hack, who had a look of horror. The one wearing silver trunks and gilt, played with the controls of the gun with his toes, twitching his biceps and admiring it sidewise as he let smoke drift out his nose.

"O.K.," said someone, his voice now strong and assured. "Now, I say, let's take a look at the local washouts."

Terrill said, "Where do they get this 'washout' business?"

"Give a dog a bad name," murmured Fielding, "and kill him."

Someone else spoke in the clearing, his voice flat. "And I say Hack and Barney Baby come with us. Or we break their heads."

"Yeah. Maybe *Barney* wants to be a washout. How about it, Barn-head?"

The cold voice answered, "Anybody wants to force me gets it in the guts. Who's first?"

"Yeah? Tough, huh? *Jump him!*"

Half-a-dozen of the masquerade figures sprang up, and a violent struggle began.

Hunsacker watched intently, his mind a maze of calculations.

Fielding growled, "Do we stand by while this goes on?"

Just then, it all fit together. Hunsacker growled, "Spread out to either side, and stay *low*. Don't fire until they shoot first, then aim to get any at those guns. I think those are automatic guns. If the bears come out, kill any that start toward that tent nearest the ship."

Terrill and Fielding wormed backwards, and eased rapidly to either side.

Hunsacker studied the scene below.

The flailing knot was still struggling. "Barney" was plainly putting up a formidable resistance, and now "Hack," throwing the pipe away, stood up.

The gilded figure by the gun breathed out a cloud of smoke, and came easily to his feet, swaying slightly. He reached out, gripped Hack around the throat, and jerked him backwards.

Hunsacker wormed sidewise, leaving his gun where it was, and stood up, unarmed.

He shouted, "You down there! Look up! Look up here!"

From somewhere in the bluff below him came a short-tempered muffled ugly bark.

Up off the snow, the day felt hot already, and a current of heated air seemed to be rising up the face of the bluff.

Studying the guns on the skimmers, Hunsacker was sure now they were automatic.

"Hey!" shouted someone below. "A *mudfoot*!"

"Look, a *col*onist!"

Hunsacker, without turning his head, glanced sidewise, to fix the location of his gun.

The gilded figure dropped the motionless Hack, stood up, faced the bluff, and flexed his muscles.

Barney, staggering to his feet as the others turned, stood breathing fast and deeply.

The door of the space yacht started to come open, and then shut again.

Hunsacker instantly shouted, "I want to warn you! You're in danger!"

"*You're* in danger, washout!"

Hunsacker kept his mind on what he had to do.

"I'm in no danger here. You've landed in the wrong place! *Listen* to me!"

Barney was now breathing a little more evenly.

"Listen to the guy," he said. "He's trying to tell you something." His voice was low, and his words came out between breaths. As he spoke, he was looking directly at Hunsacker, his gaze intense.

Hunsacker seemed to catch some significance in the look, and without conscious intent, his glance as he looked back showed approval.

One of the masquerade figures glanced around to say jeeringly, "You don't sound so tough, any more, Barnhead. Better start doubling up on the wagons. O.K., *gun the slob down!*"

The heat rising up the face of the bluff made Hunsacker, in his heavy furs, almost faint. He noted the masquerade figures diving for the guns of the skimmers, saw Barney plant his booted foot in the belly of the gilded giant, and then Hunsacker dove for cover.

There was a sizzling *crack* like a lightning bolt passing over his head, and then the heavy double *boom* as Fielding and Terrill opened up.

Hunsacker eased his gun out of its wrapping, aimed carefully, and fired from one side of a small low evergreen growing near the edge of the bluff. The roar of the gun all but deafened him as the charge, meant to throw a slug that could stop packbears, sledgehammered his shoulder through the heavy clothing.

Below, two of the opposition were down, but one of the two guns was swinging around by itself. Having been once aimed more or less correctly, it would seek the target, using heat and metal-detectors.

Hunsacker fired at the center of the detector.

There was a blinding flash, a deafening *crack*!

He lay dazed, vaguely conscious that that one had been meant for him alone.

He seemed to spiral through a kind of blackness to see the night sky, and then the blaze of sun on snow through his eyelids. He opened his eyes, and peered down. Through the dullness of deafened ears came what sounded like the squealing of many pigs.

Then the scene came into focus.

Huge bearlike forms eight to ten feet high at the shoulder, with

teeth like daggers, boiled across the clearing directly into the murderous fire, reached the skimmers, to rip and smash and crush,
and then fall dead. Behind them, more poured from the burrows.
There was, as Hunsacker's hearing started to return, the hideous
rumbling snort of famished packbears rending their prey.

Hunsacker felt in his pocket, and got out earplugs made of
a corklike bark. He twisted the plugs into his ears, and then
methodically began to pick off any bears that ambled away from
the shambles toward the tent nearest the ship.

The bears, bloodied and snorting, looked around, and suddenly
realized they were being hit from somewhere out of reach. With
grunts and snorts, they surged across the clearing, in their haste
gathering momentum in the direction that would normally have
got them clear in the shortest possible time, but that now took
them straight to where the space yacht stood.

With a series of clangs and crashes, the bears caromed off the
yacht. One apparently stepped on the double-bitted ax under the
snow. It let out a bellow of rage, tore a chunk of the outer metal
off the ship, and waded into the complications within.

Hunsacker studied the guns on the skimmers warily. One was
twisted into a pretzel. The other had the detector smashed, and
wasn't moving. He got up cautiously. Nothing happened. He glanced
around. Fielding and Terrill were out of sight, but holding their
fire. Hunsacker glanced down the sheer face of the bluff. It was
possible to go down that sheer drop. He had done it when they
were first here. Alertly, he noted the tough-rooted fern bushes
growing out here and there from crevices, little ledges, and invisible places of attachment. He looked again at the clearing below,
where nothing now moved, looked again at the fern bushes, put
his gun in its wrappings, put the earplugs in his pocket, and
swung over the edge.

His whole perspective changed abruptly. Heat seemed to billow
past him in waves. The clearing seemed a thousand feet below.
The ledge above was a comforting nest of safety. The bluff was
suddenly peopled with additional hibernating packbears that had
yet to awaken, and were rousing themselves as he slipped and
scrambled by, seizing the bushes, and working awkwardly but
rapidly lower, as with ripping popping sounds the tough rootlets
tore loose, and he shot past to the next handhold.

All he had to do, he knew, was to gather too much momentum,

and he would plummet to the bottom and smash on the rock rubble piled at the base of the bluff, behind which the packbears had excavated their caves in the soft layer some twelve feet thick that was slantingly exposed to the weather there, and toward which Hunsacker seemed now to have been dropping forever, and yet getting no closer.

And then suddenly it was only three more slips and grabs, two more, one more—and with a thud and a desperate dance over the rocks and through the fern brush that sprouted up through them, he stumbled out into the clearing, to plunge awkwardly through the snow.

A cold feminine voice said, "Stop right there."

He tripped, went down in the snow, head first, and lay still for a few moments thinking through what he had planned, and finding it still solid and sound as far as he could make it solid and sound. Then he sat up, but did not rise. He would look more helpless sitting in the snow.

The taller of the two girls, dressed in a skiing outfit that covered her from head to foot, sighted the rifle at him. The blond girl, also well covered, stood with her hand at her mouth beside the tall girl.

Dave said exasperatedly, "Why did you have to camp *here*? There are packbear dens at the base of that bluff, and for all you or I know, there are still a few hibernating bears in there just waking up." The likelihood of this was small, but it wouldn't hurt to mention it. "On top of that, once they quench their thirst, those bears are likely to be back here."

Her grip on the gun didn't waver. In a cold, deadly voice, she said, "You turned them on us."

Dave wondered uneasily just how shrewd this girl might be. But he allowed his face to show only indignation and the beginnings of anger.

"I *what*? Were you in that tent when they were snorting and rumbling around out here, or weren't you?"

She didn't answer, and she didn't shift her aim. The blond girl glanced at her nervously. Dave glanced at the blond.

"Were you in the tent, or weren't you? Maybe I was wasting time picking the bears off when they got near the tent."

The blond girl swallowed, and glanced again at the tall girl with the gun.

Dave ignored the girl with the gun, and spoke to the blond girl, "Keep out of the line of fire. Don't get between your friend and me—but go take a look at some of those bears near the tent."

"I'm afraid."

"They won't hurt you. They never play dead. They either run, or fight to the finish. Go close enough to see their backs, and tell your friend if there isn't a hole blown through the fur at the base of each one of their necks."

The blond girl hesitated, glanced at the tall girl, glanced back at Dave, then turned, and waded through the snow toward the tent. The tall girl reluctantly lowered the gun, but continued to watch Dave with a look of cold alertness. Dave looked away at the base of the bluff, then searched the woods behind the battered yacht. The tall girl glanced up at the sky searchingly, and then sharply back at Dave.

The blond girl called, "He's telling the truth, Chloe. There's a lot of . . . of fur and flesh blown away at the back of their necks."

The tall girl looked directly at Dave, the gun lowered but still ready.

"You turned them loose on us, and then killed the ones that went near the tent, in order to get rid . . . of—"

She glanced at the remains of bodies around the two skimmers.

Dave again wondered how shrewd this girl might be.

"*If* I had done that, I think I could make a case that it was in self-defense; but will you kindly tell me how I, or anyone else, could control these man-eaters?"

"They didn't hurt *you*."

"I wasn't there to be hurt."

She half-raised the gun.

"I saw you come out of there right behind them."

For an instant, Dave was left groping. Then it dawned on him that it was *not* pure shrewdness on her part that had led her to the right answer, but partly ignorance. She thought he had been in the caves with the bears, because she had seen him come from the same direction. Still, she seemed alert and intelligent.

He glanced up at the face of the bluff.

"Look at that bush, halfway down the bluff. See how it hangs off-center? Now look up at the top, almost above it, but at the top of the bluff. See where the snow is broken. It's smooth to either side, but just there it's broken. What do you suppose made that? Now, look down between those two places, and do you see how there's a slightly zigzag line of bushes at different slants—nearly every one pulled slightly out of line. There, below, near the bottom, there's one with a limb broken. The underside is lighter than the upper side. See how it's broken off? What do you suppose did that? Now, at the base of the bluff, I don't know if you can recognize it, but— No, too many bears have been through there. See, the top of that bush below the line down the face of the bluff. It's been broken. But I doubt, with all that trampling—"

"I see it," she said. She looked at him curiously, and glanced again at the sky. She looked back at him quickly, with a wondering look.

"Are you saying you *didn't* turn them loose on us?"

"I'm saying I was at the top of that bluff when they came out, and nothing you could give me, or pay me, would have put me inside those dens with them. Do you know what it would be like in there? You seem to think they're some kind of domestic animal. They aren't. As far as they're concerned, a human being is food."

"But—what made them come out?"

"This is a warm day. They only hibernate during the cold weather. Any loud noise on a day like this will make them restless. There was a lot of loud noise down here."

"But . . . but . . . If you knew this, why didn't you *warn* us? To just *leave* us here, knowing that, was the same thing as turning them loose on us!"

Dave ignored the illogic in this, and noted her changing attitude. He said, letting his voice show hurt, "We *tried* to. And got shot at for our pains."

"'We,'" she said. She looked alertly around.

Dave reminded himself that the girl *was* shrewd.

He said with a trace of sarcasm, "Were you under the impression that I'm all alone on this planet?"

"Why don't your friends show themselves?"

She half-raised the gun, and looked around searchingly.

The blond girl said nervously, "Chloe—"

Dave said shortly, "You fired at *him* yesterday." Cautiously, Dave stood up. If Fielding thought life with this girl would be pleasant, *he* could try it. But, at any rate she wasn't aiming the gun at him. Again she looked at him alertly, then glanced at the sky. He decided to waste no time putting the next part of his plan in action, and swayed slightly on his feet.

The blond girl gave a little cry, and started toward him.

"Keep back," he warned. "Don't . . . don't come near me. I've been sick." He took a wavering step, then fell in the snow.

An instant later, someone turned him on his back, and was cradling him gently, as another voice shouted—and this was a masculine voice, tense and authoritative.

"Leave *him* alone. We won't shoot him. Get everyone out of that ship!"

Dave let himself fall back, then someone planted a kiss on his forehead.

There, *that* was more like it. But this wasn't over yet. He kept his face blank, and lay slackly motionless. He could hear the tall girl explaining what had happened to someone, and then there were a series of short sharp authoritative questions. When she explained how Dave had come down the bluff, whoever was doing the questioning dismissed the possibility brusquely. The girl angrily restated it. Again, whoever was doing the questioning brushed the idea aside. Sarcastically, the girl pointed out each individual bent branch, twisted bush, and mark in the snow at the bluff top that Dave had pointed out. There was a silence at the end, then Dave could hear the sound of feminine voices, from the direction of the yacht.

Dave opened his eyes. Someone said sharply, "He's awake, Captain!"

Dave slowly sat up.

Poised in midair before him were two more dish-shaped grav-skimmers, these somewhat larger than the others, marked with a blue stripe around the rim, and bearing a yellow shield at intervals. In white letters on the blue were the words. SPACE POLICE. In the skimmers were heavily armed men in uniforms roughly similar to those of the Space Force, but with different insignia.

Dave could have done without this complication, but he had taken the possibility into account. Now he readied his defenses.

The second skimmer was already starting to lower itself as the girls looked up, some supporting others who were apparently faint from the grisly scene around them. To jar things into motion, Dave turned and started to walk unsteadily away.

"Halt!" came the shouted order. "Turn around! Where do you think *you're* going?"

Dave turned and held his hands at his mouth to make a megaphone.

"We've been sick! I didn't want you to get it."

"*Sick?*" The man with captain's insignia stared at him.

Dave glanced at the girls.

"I tried to warn them."

The captain glanced around. The blond girl was right in the middle of the others. The only one standing aside, looking at Dave with a very peculiar expression, was the tall girl with the gun.

The captain looked back.

"Sick with *what?*"

"Well, we've had the pox, but—"

"*Pox,*" shouted the captain. He whirled. "Raise that—" He reached out and seized a power megaphone.

"LIFT THAT SKIMMER! LIFT SKIMMER, I SAY! *THIS PLANET HAS THE POX!*"

Dave shouted, "We're over it now! We've . . . We're over it!"

The captain made a signal, palm upward, sweeping his hand sharply up, and both skimmers rose fast. As if remembering something, he looked back down at Dave, and spoke through the megaphone, his voice already faint because of the speed with which the skimmers were rising.

"Take plenty of liquids—citrus fruit—avoid exposure—keep the patients warm—keep complete records. Good luck. Bury those rats there. Other visitors are permanently restricted to the planet. Ship salvage to the first claimer. Impound log and . . ."

His voice faded out, and Dave waved, slipped in the snow, let himself fall to one knee, then got up and looked up again, careful to keep his face free of any expression but a look of anxiousness. The skimmers were too small now to be seen except as dots, but it didn't follow that their scanners could not record his every motion and every line of his face. There, now they dwindled off to the south, and vanished entirely. He was over *that* hurdle. But there were still the possible recorders on the yacht itself.

He looked around to see the tall girl standing directly before him, studying him with a wondering look. He glanced around at the bluff and the forest, and then back at the girl.

"Those packbears may be back anytime. It might be a good idea to—"

From the top of the bluff came the warning crack of a rifle. Apparently the bears were already coming back.

"Get into that skimmer," he said, getting into the other—which had the workable gun. "Stay right behind me. You don't want to set down in the wrong place again. You take half of the girls, and I'll take the other half."

The tall girl glanced back at the forest, and motioned the girls into the skimmers. Dave briefly studied the simplified controls, experimented with them for a moment, then swung the skimmer swiftly up, the sheer face of the bluff dropping down and falling back fast as he streaked along the face toward the east. He glanced back, saw that the other skimmer was no longer following but was starting to swing away from the face of the bluff. He whipped his controls around, and shot for the trees between here and the more distant clearing. The second skimmer whirled to race him, as the girls looked urgently around, gaining altitude as forest and small clearings flashed past below, and then Dave began to gently lower the skimmer as a hole through the snow-laden trees appeared. The skimmer behind instantly followed his example. He glanced at the girls clinging to the handholds, then whipped his skimmer up and slashed through the treetops, sending a shower of snow flying out behind him.

Directly in front of him, another space yacht appeared, sitting upright on its base. From behind and below came shrieks, and a short burst of anger. Dave landed beside the space yacht, put his hand on its cold flank, and said, "By the interstellar laws of salvage, I claim this abandoned ship and its effects for my settlement, to be held in common, and disposed of in accord with the decision of the settlement's duly-appointed leader or his successor, or in whatever lawful way may be duly determined by the members of the settlement."

He glanced up, and saw the second skimmer, heaped with snow, settle slowly to the ground. He glanced at the still paralyzed girls in his own skimmer, stepped out, put his hand again on the yacht, and repeated what he had just said.

The tall girl looked at him with smoldering eyes.

"You don't miss a bet, do you?"

"Ma'am," said Dave politely, "I've done my best to keep the bears from killing you. As far as I know, I haven't hurt you, or threatened you. But if you want to be angry with me, there is nothing I can do about it, I guess."

"Very neat." She smiled, bit her lip, and said, "All right, take us to your settlement's duly-appointed leader." She turned away. "Phyl, for the love of *Pete*, will you shovel some of this snow out, but— Watch it! Just the *snow*! Here, I'll hover. You'd better reach out and get that."

As she turned, Dave had the leisure to observe that the girl *was* attractive, as Fielding had said.

He looked all around, saw nothing that should pose any threat, considered the location of this second clearing, then looked around the interior of the skimmer. It was bloody, with several holes torn through it, but by pure luck nothing important seemed to have been hit. As he looked searchingly around, he noted a thing like a little cylinder—something like a hand-held microphone. He picked it up, examined it curiously, and noted a small nearly round lens at the end, with a button at the side. He remembered the girl who had set down the ax awkwardly, and felt in her pocket for something small, that she had then held against the ship, after which the door had opened out. He glanced at the side of this ship, and spotted what looked like a small lens, about the size of the end of a man's thumb.

He glanced at the tall girl, and said, "Could you come here a minute?"

She hesitated. "You'd better take me to whoever's in charge of your settlement."

He nodded. "Just come over here, and in theory you'll be talking to him."

She waded through the snow. "What do you mean, 'in theory'?"

"Things are pretty informal unless there's trouble."

She glanced thoughtfully at the girls.

"If you're the settlement's leader, you've *got* trouble."

"I was thinking the same thing. Now, I take it you're pretty familiar with this ship, so maybe you can—"

Her eyes glinted.

"*They* followed *us*," she said. "There were fifteen yachts on this excursion, but after what happened the last time, we broke up. We didn't want anything to do with them."

"After the heroes smoked battlewagons, and proved how tough they were?"

She nodded. "It was all right up to that point. It was a pleasure trip. We have been trying to get back to the same viewpoint, but I'm afraid we would never have made it."

"You realize you're marooned here."

"You misrepresented what you'd had. I was watching you."

"*If* I misrepresented, you said nothing to correct me."

She reddened slightly, then said, "There's such a thing as watching a very cool operator, and wondering just what he has in mind. And then finding out too late."

"The point is, the Space Police have you down as exposed to pox. Try and leave here, and there's a good chance they'll pick you up on their screen and put you right back down."

"What do we lose by that?"

"Time and energy. And, it would be illegal for you to take this yacht."

She nodded. "Since you've claimed it. And, of course, it's all down in the automatic log. Well, what do you want to do? We *can't* take the other one. Your bears tore the aft section to pieces."

"Not ours. The bears are wild."

"The results are the same."

"That's what I'm trying to explain," he said. "You're marooned. Naturally, we'll try to help you—"

"Why can't you get in touch with these Space Police, using the communicator in this ship, and explain that we haven't been exposed to this pox, whatever it is."

"Because," he said seriously, "I'm not certain you haven't been."

"Is that what you just had?"

"No. I didn't say it *was* what we *just* had."

"But you knew that blockheaded captain would jump to conclusions."

"He may have been right. I hope not."

"No matter what I say or do, you keep right on going," she said exasperatedly. "And you're always one step ahead. All right, we're marooned here. Doesn't that create something of a problem for you?"

"I was about to suggest that we open up the settlement's new ship, here, so you can all go in and have shelter, at least. Then we can figure out what to do next."

"All right. Let's do it." She was watching him curiously.

Hunsacker cast a brief glance at the yacht, and nodded. He floated up in his skimmer, and she promptly followed in the other skimmer. He studied the key, held it against the lens-like depression in the side of the yacht, worked the small recessed button in the side of the key, and stepped back to give the girls a good view of whatever this nest might have to offer.

The door swung slowly back.

Around him, there was a gasp.

From the interior, there loomed through thick smoke a kind of huge brassy motionless toad with redly-glowing eyes. Chains with weird attachments dangled through the murk from some overhead hook. There was an overpowering stench of filth and incense.

The skimmers swayed as their passengers sat down.

Dave glanced around at the tall girl, and now his gaze caught a trace of motion from the distant block the colonists called Iceberg Mountain. From here could be seen what seemed to be specks traveling across the distant snowfields, the specks enlarging and shrinking one after the other.

He said, "If you'd rather stay with us, instead of here, we'd be glad to have you."

There was a murmur of eager agreement.

Dave shut the door of the yacht, studied the sky overhead, and turned to the girl, still watching him alertly from the other skimmer.

"Keep your eyes open. If you look around at that mountain, you can see what looks like specks. That's a flock of a kind of giant bird that winters in the south. They stick together when they're flying north, but they have scouts at a distance that watch for food. Any one of us would do."

She looked intently at the distant mountain, and nodded.

Dave said, "Stay right behind me, and be ready to go into the thickest part of the forest if you see one of them diving. And stay low. Don't go *above* any of those taller trees, back in the thick forest. There's a thing in some of them that will try to knock down anything that flies above it."

Dave took a careful look all around, then led the way low and fast across the open ground, dotted with clumps of small trees, that connected the two clearings.

As they emerged into the clearing below the bluff, where the smashed space yacht stood, there was a gruff warning bark.

Dave saw the bears, glanced up, and there, far overhead, was a speck, drifting in the blue sky.

"Hang on," he warned, and the bluff, with its tough shrubs clinging to cracks and crevices, dropped past as they climbed.

From below came a weird cough and whistle that the bears used as a signal. The purpose of this noise was a source of controversy amongst the colonists, but as the lip of the bluff dropped past, Dave lost no time getting the skimmer back into thick forest. He landed amongst the thick-boled trees with their dead lower limbs radiating like spokes, and looked around searchingly.

The second skimmer set down nearby, and he gestured to the tall girl to come closer yet.

"We'll have to switch the load around. If that thing comes in here, one of these skimmers has to be able to fight, and move fast. The only way to do that is for the two of us to be in one skimmer, and everyone else in the other."

She nodded, and a few moments later the change was made. A dazzling line that sprang out as he squeezed the trigger demonstrated that the gun still worked.

A quick check near the edge of the bluff showed no sign of danger, and Dave recovered his gun, apparently left there in its wrapping by Fielding and Terrill in case he should need it. Their tracks led back down the trail toward the loose cluster of cabins that made up the settlement.

She watched alertly. "You were telling the truth. But there were *three* of you, not two."

He eased back into the forest.

"I didn't say there were only two of us."

"You tried to lead me to think it."

He glanced at her, noting again that she was pretty and well made, though dressed to conceal the fact. But while he noted this, he was conscious of something else, that had more impact in this part of the universe:

She used her head.

He tried to scan the sky, wondering where that speck had gone, but the trees blocked his view.

"All is fair," he said casually, "in love and war."

She started to speak, stopped, colored slightly, and looked exasperated.

"Do you ever stop thinking?"

From far downhill, the sound echoed through the forest.

FLACK!

There was a distant scream, an urgent shout. Belatedly, a shot ran out.

He eased the skimmer carefully through the trees.

She looked around. "What was that?"

"That's what happens here when you stop thinking."

"What—"

"The flit . . . the bird that was overhead." He glanced around. "The only time you dare stop thinking is inside the cabin with the window shuttered and the door barred, your gun cleaned, loaded, and ready at hand, and either a good fire or the chimney stone down to block the flue. There *are* places where not thinking is a way of life. It's a luxury here."

"What *happened*?"

"My friends were probably telling what had happened up here. The flit . . . the bird, that is . . . was dropping after us, saw it couldn't make it, saw the crowd, and changed its angle of descent. That 'flack' noise is what you hear when it opens its wings after a long plunge from practically out of sight overhead."

They were far back in the trees now, following the direction of the downhill trail, and the second skimmer swung carefully around a bristling tree trunk to follow them.

She looked all around, then said suddenly, "It must be that you need women in your settlement."

He smiled. "An accurate deduction. How did you know that?"

"When I see someone use bears to eliminate pirates, germs to frighten Space Police, and the pirates' bad housekeeping to move the women into his settlement, it's natural to think he *needs* them there. Otherwise, we'd be far away by now."

"We do need you. But what you just saw was ninety percent luck."

She glanced alertly around, then looked at him with a smile.

"You can tell a real operator by the fact that what he does

creates a bigger effect than anyone would expect. He sneezes, and a bridge falls down."

Dave sneezed, and looked around. The forest looked back blandly. He glanced at her.

"Nothing happened."

She nodded. "A top-rank operator often *conceals* the fact."

"If you see it, it's not concealed."

She looked around at the forest. "The real proof is that you borrowed strength when you needed it. You smashed the pirates using the strength of the bears, and in effect you gave the Space Police orders by borrowing the authority of their blockheaded captain. And you didn't *tell* us to come here, and so make us resentful; you put us in a place where we were *glad* to come, due to the force of our own reactions."

"Ninety percent luck."

"It's the other ten percent that makes the difference. It takes a score of ninety-nine to get some things done."

He noted a slender sapling that climbed between two larger neighboring trees. The interlocked branches of the larger trees sagged under the weight of snow.

Carefully, he eased the skimmer into the confined space between the outthrust dead lower branches of the largest tree, and the sapling.

"As for borrowing strength," he said, "tell me some other way to get anything done. When a man fells a tree, does *he* drag that huge mass of wood, bark, and foliage to the earth? No. *Gravity* does the work. When he wants people to cooperate, can *he* compel them to be cooperative? Of course not. He appeals to some interest that will move them. The *interest* does the work. If he flies a spaceship, is it *his* muscle that moves the ship? Why, no, he had to find a way to get some atoms to cooperate, and it's *their* power that moves the ship. The strength that helps him, as you say, is borrowed strength. But what else can he use? He *has* to borrow strength. The fun starts when he forgets, and imagines it's his."

She thought a moment.

"But at least, you don't deny that you *are* an operator?"

He bumped the sapling lightly. A clump of snow plummeted down to the side, distracting her attention.

"Not me," he smiled, and brought the new colonist to the settlement.

WHILE THE NORTH WIND BLOWS

Dave Hunsacker, the early-morning air cold on his face, looked down from above on the dark tops of the big trees he was used to seeing from below. Not since the colonization ship had first brought the colonists to the planet had Dave enjoyed this particular view, and in fact, he was not enjoying it very much right now. Leaning out the open viewport as the space yacht slowly descended, he intently scanned the sea of shadowy treetops, where stray wisps of fog trailed up, and a little of the winter's snow still lay on the branches. Suddenly, near the top of a towering fern tree, a bright yellow glow appeared.

Dave cleared his throat.

"The pests are awake. There's the first blast."

He noted the location of the tree, near a large oblong clearing where the snow still lay in heaps.

In the forest just to the east of the clearing, a dozen more bright dots sprang to life.

He said urgently, "There's more of them! Better lift!"

The space yacht slowed its descent, paused, hovered—

Down below, the first glow blossomed into a climbing foot-thick pillar of fire that lit the surrounding treetops like the rising sun, and was reflected brightly on the snow of the nearby clearing.

The yacht continued to hover.

Dave pulled himself inside, and glanced around.

At the yacht's controls, Jim Fielding, the sweat running down

549

his face, was using both hands to heave upward on the chrome-plated control-stick.

"Something's wrong," said Fielding. "I tried for maximum lift and got nothing."

"Let go, and try it again. If we don't get out of here fast, we're going to get cooked in flaming pitch."

Fielding let go of the control stick, and lifted gently.

Dave looked back out the viewport.

Now the other dots of light had lengthened into climbing lines of flame.

A mechanical voice spoke in soothing tones from a grille over the control board.

"This is your Stand-By Pilot speaking."

Dave, at the viewport, noted the sharply defined edges of the climbing streams of fire. Within the bright glow, shadows seemed to whirl and spin, appear and vanish. Like curving fingers, the dazzling streams were beginning to tilt toward the hovering yacht.

He slammed shut the viewport.

The mechanical voice was saying, " . . . detect no near physical obstacle below, and no approach of other spacecraft which would justify extreme acceleration. Your Helth-Gard System is countermanding, for your protection and the comfort of your guests, an overly extreme control-signal. Always be sure that you use your Convenience Control with care, and that small children do not obtain access to . . ."

With a feeling of unreality, Dave watched the bright curving fingertips dip toward him. Down below, fresh dots of light were blossoming into climbing streams of fire. He kept his voice level.

"Be gentle, and *try to lift again!*"

Fielding very cautiously lifted up on the shiny chrome stick.

The yacht began to climb.

Dave tensely watched the arcs of flame converge.

Fielding said, "*Will we make it?*"

"Not at this rate!"

Fielding with desperate caution lifted the stick further.

The yacht was rising with increasing speed, but the streams of flame were coming faster. Already he seemed to feel the heat of the flame on his face.

The yacht abruptly stopped rising, and again hovered.

"This is your Stand-By Pilot speaking. Advanced instruments detect no physical obstacle below, and no approach of other spacecraft which—"

A bell went off with a clang that vibrated the whole ship. The deck leaped underfoot like an express elevator hit from below by a giant's sledgehammer. There was a roar and a scream of tortured metal, a sense of unbearable pressure, and the world went black.

He came to to the sound of occasional spaced hammer-like blows, and a new and different mechanical voice:

" . . . your Emergency Safewatch Monitor Systems. We regret the momentary inconvenience of Interlock Maxiboost Acceleration, which was necessary to prevent severe equipment and personnel damage due to . . ." There was a pause, then the voice concluded " . . . excessive *heat.*"

Dave Hunsacker, flat on the deck, opened his eyes to see Jim Fielding pull himself to a sitting position, then stagger to his feet to look at the shining chromium-plated stick, and then at the grille over the control panel.

Dave became aware of a severe headache, and of a need for profanity that no profanity he could think of would fill. The day before, the loud and boisterous people who had brought this yacht to the planet had set down near a place locally known as "Packbear Flats," and had rudely interrupted the end of the bears' winter sleep. When the bears finished relieving their irritation, Hunsacker and his settlement had inherited the yacht, and also, due to the earlier landing of a different yacht, they found themselves the delighted hosts for a number of attractive young women. The girls had been led to land because of the look of the spring sun on the winter snow, and the men in the other yacht had been attracted by the presence there of the girls' yacht. It seemed reasonable to Dave and his friends that two yachts, sitting upright in the open sunlight, and pulse-reflection-coated around their spire-like snouts, might attract any number of unwanted guests. The obvious thing to do was to get the yachts out of sight. And the obvious place to put them was under the trees near the clearing, where Dave and Jim Fielding had just tried to go.

Fielding let his breath out with a hiss.

"Well, the slags are sure through hibernating, just like the rest of the pests. But we've still got to get these things out of sight, somehow. *Now* what do we do?"

Dave got carefully to his feet.

"The obvious place is still the same."

"Under the big steelwood trees, just back from the edge of the clearing?"

"Right. The trees are big, well-spaced, clear of limbs for most of their height, and then the branches interlace thickly overhead. Also, they're close to the settlement. The spot is ideal."

"How do we get past the slags?"

Dave opened the viewport and peered down, where a single intensely bright line was still climbing up from the dark forest.

Fielding looked out beside him, watching as the bright line seemed to waver, and suddenly vanished. Fielding said exasperatedly, "Can you tell me how a thing like a giant caterpillar can generate, much less *aim*, a stream of flame?"

Dave shook his head. He said dryly, "However, they *can*."

Fielding nodded. "That time Abe and I decided there were getting to be too many of the things, and we tried to cut down a fern tree to get one of them—you remember that?"

Hunsacker grinned. "I remember it."

"That son-of-a-gun took a shot at me from his hole eighty feet up, and the flaming pitch was right behind me for a hundred yards. It was like trying to sneak off with their prey. The thing *could* have cooked me alive anytime, but it just didn't choose to do it. They only grill *flying* creatures."

"Unfortunately," said Dave, "as far as the slags are concerned, that now includes *us*. I wonder if there's any way we could come in from out of their range, near ground level, so they'd class us as *ground* animals."

Fielding thought a moment, then shook his head.

"The trees are too thick. It would take us forever to chop a way through."

From the grille over the control panel came a polite mechanical voice:

"This is your RoBoButler Service. A Type-3 light gravitor vessel of the skimmer class is again circling the ship, apparently endeavoring to gain your attention."

Dave glanced out the viewport, but saw nothing.

From somewhere came a hammering noise, as if someone reached out and pounded hard on the hull.

Fielding snapped on the communicator.

"Who's there?"

There was no reply, and he tried again, using the outside loudspeaker.

Dave glanced back out the viewport.

Around from his left, twelve-foot leathery wings stiffly outspread, kite-like tail slightly arched, and the big-beaked head on its long neck tilted to regard the yacht, came another of the planet's prime pests. As he watched, it moved its wings briefly with a *flick-flick-flick* sound, spun its tail and head, and reversed its course. It disappeared climbing to the left, and Hunsacker sucked in his breath and slammed shut the viewport.

"*Now* what?" said Fielding.

"We've had *slags*. Now we've got *flits*."

The creature suddenly reappeared in the viewport, circling back from the right. Its beak flashed out on its long neck, and banged against the viewport. Then for an instant its head was pressed against the transparent surface, the big eye peering in intently. Then it was gone.

The two men stood frozen, and it went through Dave's mind that one twist of that curved beak could rip out a man's throat, or strip his flesh from the thigh to the knee. Of course, the flits, for some reason, preferred to first soften up their prey by dropping it a hundred feet or so onto bare rock.

Hunsacker let his breath out slowly. Fielding cleared his throat.

"They don't come much closer than that, old buddy. If the port had been open, that thing could have run its extension-tongs neck in here and snaked one or the other of us right out for the long dive."

From the direction of the control panel there came again the polite mechanical voice:

"This is your RoBoButler Service. We repeat that a Type-3 light gravitor-vessel of the skimmer class is circling the ship, attempting to gain your attention."

"It's gained it," said Fielding, looking over the control panel. "I'd like to know the I.Q. of the computer that runs this luxury pot."

"Somewhere in the high teens or low twenties," said Dave, looking around and fixing in his mind, in case a quick retreat should be in order, the location of the shaft down to the next level. "It seems to me we ought to have some kind of a reply for that bird, before it tries again, knocks the port off its hinges, and climbs in."

"I'm looking for something sharp on this panel . . . Here, this looks promising." Fielding threw a switch, and a recorded voice boomed outside:

"Your attention, please. This vessel is fully protected by appropriate devices of the Advanced Synodic Products Corporation. It will retaliate automatically against any aggressive or hostile action."

The two men glanced at each other.

"*That's* more like it."

A shadow drifted across the viewport. From somewhere overhead, on the yacht's nose, came a faint rumble.

Hunsacker warily glanced out the viewport, to see the flying creature twist sharply to one side.

There was a blast of pink radiance, that narrowly missed it.

The flit shot down around the opposite side of the yacht, there was a violent scratching scrabbling noise, then a loud booming note, a sizzling sound, and a shriek.

Fielding, adjusting the viewscreen, said, "This yacht seems to have some kind of energy cannon mounted on it. —There goes the flit, diving straight down!"

Dave glanced at the screen, to see a burst of bright lines rise up from the forest to form a net around the creature, which abruptly spread its huge wings, twisted in the fiery lines and slammed wildly into the treetops.

The two men watched the screen thoughtfully.

Dave said, "What was that scratching sound after the energy cannon took a crack at the flit the first time?"

Fielding shook his head. "There must be some way to get a better look than I got. It seemed to me the flit tried to run up the side of the yacht to get at the cannon."

Hunsacker thought it over. "And what was the *booming* noise?"

"I don't know. Everything happened fast just then. I didn't *see* anything that ought to have made that noise." He glanced at the viewscreen, and worked its control switches. "The side of the ship seems to be okay."

Dave looked out the closed viewport.

"Rotate the ship, why don't you, and let's take a look around."

Fielding turned the chrome-plated control-stick, and the ship slowly rotated.

Peering out through the viewport, Dave Hunsacker saw a pair of dots approaching from the direction of the lightening sky to the east, and several more to the northeast. In the other directions, the sky was still too dark to make out anything in the distance.

"What do *you* see?" he asked.

"Flits," said Fielding. "Of course, we'd expect to see them. They're migrating north with the spring. And we're right on the main route."

"These don't look like they're migrating north right now. They're headed towards us."

Fielding nodded. "I see it, but I don't understand it. Well . . . Now what do we do?"

Dave tried to get a mental grip on the situation, but couldn't do it.

Fielding suggested, "Set down again?"

"We might as well, I suppose."

Fielding nodded moodily.

"Flits and slags; slags and flits . . . That's the story of this planet. If it isn't one miserable thing, it's another."

Dave nodded, and stared out the viewport. "They *are* headed this way, and coming fast."

"I'll set down." Fielding swung the ship back over the bluff, there was a brief dazzling flash from below, and he lowered the ship to a gentle landing beside the other yacht, in the clearing known as Packbear Flats. The two men dropped down the grav shaft, lowered the ramp, and got out.

There was a small crowd at the base of the second yacht, but Dave stopped beside a tall girl standing a little back from the crowd. He said nothing, looking at the working colonists and the watching girls, then glanced uneasily at the sky.

She followed his gaze. "Trouble?"

He noted that the flits he could still see from here were considerably closer, and still apparently headed for the same spot, as before.

He nodded. "Trouble, with wings."

"The kind of bird that stalked us yesterday? —That was coming north in a big flock?"

"The same. Apparently the flock has paused and spread out to hunt. They do that sometimes, when there's bad weather further north."

"I can't see them."

"Look for a dot that seems not quite stationery, or a kind of dust particle with a slow waving motion. With practice, unless there's one inside a cloud, or coming at you with the sun behind it—you can spot them a long way off. —Especially after they drop down after you once or twice."

She smiled wryly.

"Did all these things turn out just for us? The bears, these flying things, and these things you mentioned that live in big trees, and knock down the flying things?"

"It's just that the weather's changing. The slags—the things in the trees—hibernate like the bears. The flits winter in the south. A week or two ago, all these things were out of sight." He glanced at the other space yacht. "Is it flyable?"

"The fuel line and some of the wiring had been ripped loose. That's nearly fixed. But the plates in the base section have been so badly battered that it would leak air no matter what we might do. It's flyable, I think, as long as it doesn't leave the planet. But we should get it out of sight. You'd be surprised how visible one of these yachts is from high up."

He nodded, but for a moment didn't say anything. Her presence affected him like cool water after a long hot day. Then he smiled, checked the sky again, and described what had happened. As he finished, he was conscious of someone else, and turned to see several men, and a strongly built woman of about medium height, a wrench in one hand, listening intently to him. This was Phyllis Laffert, about whom the colony's men, their egos rubbed raw by her abrasive tongue, often said, "If she was a man, you'd have to break her neck. Since she's a woman—well, what *can* you do?"

She said now, "Well, that's nice. The slags *are* awake, then?"

"Wide awake," said Dave. "There's one, just back from the edge of the clearing, that erupts like a volcano."

She narrowed her eyes.

"You'd say there are more around the clearing than last year?"

Dave nodded. "A lot more. Before we got away from there, there were dozens of them, and from where I was, only part of the forest was visible. On top of that, it's just turned warm, and the youngest ones will still be in torpor, so we didn't run into all of them."

"They have to be cut down," she said to the men, "or thinned out. It's getting so that if a dead leaf blows over that field, it's like an aerial barrage."

The men standing around looked profoundly uncomfortable, and said nothing.

She said, "We can't keep planting that field if those slags aren't thinned out somehow."

One of the men said hesitantly, "Maybe a little later in the year—"

She looked at him angrily.

"A little later, nothing. This should have been taken care of in the winter, while they were asleep. They have no *natural* enemies. It's up to *us* to control their numbers."

"Yes, but Phyl— To climb one of those trees at twenty below zero with your hands numb, and not a branch from the ground up for eighty feet—"

"They should be cut down."

"What? In a howling gale, trees that size, with the wood froze like rock?"

There was a brief twanging sound before she could reply and they all looked around, to see the other space yacht slowly and majestically rise up until it was at the height of the bluff, then pause, and climb slowly higher. It was perhaps one hundred and fifty feet above the height of the top of the bluff when a brilliant line of fire reached up toward the yacht from somewhere back in the forest.

Phyllis Laffert, in a tone of disgust, said, "Now they're *there*, too. —*Scatter!*"

Dave saw one of the disk-shaped skimmers sitting not far off. Since everyone else at once headed for the base of the bluff, and the caves there, he caught the girl's hand, and led her quickly to the skimmer.

From overhead came a loud clanging, but he didn't spare the time to glance up. He shot the skimmer off flat and fast, away from the bluff. When he glanced back, no one was in sight, the yacht was a mere speck high in the sky, and steam was rising from patches of snow on the flat land near the other yacht.

She glanced around, looked at him, and smiled suddenly, but said nothing.

He hovered briefly above some low trees below the bluff, his mind a maze of calculations.

He studied the sky, and the flits. They were still high up, and they were still coming. From his present angle of vision he could see no less than six of them.

She followed his gaze. "*Now* I see them. What are they doing?"

"That's what I want to find out."

He swung the skimmer up, and the morning sun, just lighting the treetops, seemed to lift over the horizon as he rose. Still below the top of the bluff, he passed above the yacht left standing below, and as the sun struck its upright bow, a piercing green flash half-blinded him.

He said, "That's the pulse-reflection coating?"

She nodded. "It stores up light-energy—however feeble the light may be—and releases it almost straight up when the stored energy reaches a certain level. You can see the flash a long distance up. Since it emits only the wave-length coded for that particular yacht, to a certain extent you can identify the yacht by eye—by the color of the flash."

"You can see it *very* well?"

"Yes. It's like a beacon."

"Can you scrape this coating off?"

"You have to somehow dismount the cannon first. The coating is a safety feature, and as I remember the service manual, the cannon is hooked up to protect the coating from damage by life-forms attracted by the radiation pulses."

He nodded.

"And you say there were *fifteen* yachts in the party you started out with?"

She nodded. "We broke up after the trouble on one of the colony planets. That was when it dawned on us that some of the others were using a kind of drug, and raiding the colonists."

"All we need is another crew like that last one. —Hang on!"

She took a strong grip on the handholds.

He glanced around, noted the yacht overhead had moved off to the side, and shot up above the edge of the bluff. As the forest atop the bluff dropped below, he slowed, and watched.

A lance of flame about an inch thick started climbing from below. It arched up like a fusion beam warping through a dense gravitic field, and it was headed so nearly straight for them that Dave could only judge its height by the foreshortened glowing curve he could make out. He started climbing again.

She crouched low, peering over the edge.

There was a sort of wavering of the bright curve, and then it broke, and as far as could be seen, there was nothing.

They were now high up, and the wind was beginning to buffet the skimmer. Dave glanced around, but not down. He hadn't been in the open at such a height in years, and an attack of vertigo was all he needed.

She said, "That was just *one* of them?"

He nodded. "Usually there's a bunch of them, so anything passing overhead runs the risk of getting grilled in the pattern put up by the colony. The only way to avoid being attacked is to get well below tree level; but you can still get hit when anything else gets attacked. If you happen to be down there when the hot pitch comes down, that's not much fun."

The skimmer's communicator buzzed and crackled. Jim Fielding's voice said, "Nice fireworks. You okay?"

"Yeah. This thing has a good rate of climb."

"Don't shake hands with yourself too soon. Another batch of flits are out."

Dave looked around. "That makes sense. Where did you see them?"

"To the west. They're headed north, and there must be fifty or sixty at least in this part of the main body. How high are you now?"

"High enough so I'm afraid to look over the edge. Why?"

"Then you're about their height. Watch out the flankers don't get diving room above you."

Dave looked around, and saw nothing in the cloudy gloom to the west.

"This wasn't a flock of young ones, was it?"

"The smallest one *I* saw looked about twenty feet across the wingtips."

"How were they flying?"

"Beat. But hungry. They weren't making a sound, apart from a slow creak of their wings. We got a good look. This yacht is nice for sightseeing."

"Did they attack?"

"They ignored us. But they may not ignore you."

Dave looked to the west and again saw nothing.

"Thanks," he said.

"Glad to bring the happy tidings," said Fielding.

Dave was now gradually starting to freeze. He felt for the communicator's shut-off, and said, "See you, Jim, I hope."

"Yeah. Good luck, Dave."

He found some kind of a switch, the communicator clicked, and he looked around. To the east, he spotted the flits he had seen before.

The huge creatures were close now, coming together as if drawn from half of a circle miles across. As he watched, one-by-one they came together, and swung around each other, a total of nine huge predators with their outstretched heads turning first this way, then that.

Dave cautiously looked over the edge of the skimmer. Far below, almost directly beneath the circling flits, was the oblong clearing.

They seemed to be at about the same height, and directly over the same part of the forest, where the yacht had been attacked by the first flit.

He frowned. What had brought all these predators together? Particularly at just the spot where one of their number had attacked the ship—which had since moved on?

"Fish around in that compartment," he said, "and see if you can find a blanket, robe, or something."

She drew out a large plaid blanket, and passed it to him. As he took it, it grew warm to the touch.

From somewhere came a *flick-flick-flick* sound, and he glanced up.

A huge creature, big beak outstretched, hurried past some sixty feet overhead, dropped down, and joined the other circling monsters.

Dave gave brief silent thanks that they were still alive, and glanced at the girl. Her pale expression as she searched the sky reaffirmed his estimate of her sense. But the fact remained that they had both missed that one, and it could have had them if it hadn't been on more urgent business.

There were now ten gigantic flits circling slowly, turning their heads alertly in all directions.

Dave looked around.

She said, "There."

From the vague gray background to the west emerged another one.

Eleven flits circled patiently, looking earnestly all around.

She pointed toward the northwest.

"Here's another."

As Dave glanced around, he faintly heard something coming from a different direction. Then, it was clearer:

Flick-flick-flick.

He looked down.

Below the level of the skimmer, neck outstretched, head tilted, came another one—this time from the southwest.

There were now thirteen of the gigantic creatures circling, necks outstretched, tilting their heads this way and that.

He glanced around, and saw, due west, an unusually big one flapping its way in against the wind.

Now fourteen of the monsters circled, grimly patient.

Dave's mind was a boiling turmoil as he tried to join disconnected bits and pieces of information to make some sense of what was happening. One after another the thoughts flashed into his mind, to be examined like the separate pieces of a puzzle:

The flits were coming north.

They were hungry.

They were at or close to the spot where one had attacked the yacht.

The yacht, at that time, had just barely escaped the slags.

The slags lived in resinous trees, could digest the cellulose of the trees, but seemed to also need a small amount of protein. The slags got protein by knocking down flying creatures that passed overhead, the huge flits making particularly desired targets.

Except for the slags, the flits had no known natural enemies.

The slags themselves had no known natural enemies at all.

The flits, except when migrating lived separated, each pair apparently having their own territory, and adjusting the borders according to their numbers.

The slags lived in colonies, which increased fast.

The slags apparently made their raw material from the resin of the trees in which they lived, but how they made it in such quantities, projected it to such heights—and particularly how they lit it in the first place—were mysteries none of the colonists had yet solved. About all that was definitely known was that the slags were very free with their fiery blast in wet weather, and cautiously sparing in times of drought.

Dave thought it over in bafflement, and two more pieces of information occurred to him:

The slags were far more numerous now than when the colonists had first arrived.

The flits, too, were clearly more numerous.

—And then, as he watched the circling flits, the scattered pieces of information suddenly began to fit together. He glanced around, aware that he had fallen into a dangerous reverie, and then he saw that the girl was alertly keeping watch, one hand on the skimmer's gun.

Dave glanced at the flits in momentary puzzlement. The day before, he'd been certain that one of them was stalking the skimmer—getting in position for an attack. Today, they acted almost as if the skimmer were a fellow creature.

Frowning, he said, "Chloe?"

She smiled.

He said, "I want to try something. Keep an eye on these flits, and let me know if any of them makes any motion as if to attack us. I'm going to be watching the forest."

She nodded, and glanced carefully all around.

He swung the skimmer past the huge monotonously circling creatures, and one or two of the monsters glanced at him with what appeared to be an approving friendly gaze. For a moment, he had a weird sense of circling with his fellows, high in the sky, wings spread, the world stretched out below. He told himself that he needed sleep, recovered the thread of his thoughts, and started to drop the skimmer down.

After a moment, she caught her breath, started to speak, then remained tensely silent. Then she glanced at him.

"They don't seem to be going to *attack* us—but *they're follow-ing us down.*"

He looked up, to see that several of the huge creatures had left the circle, and were spiraling down, following the skimmer.

"Hang on," he said. "Apparently, there has never been anything on this planet roughly their size and shape that could fly, except themselves—so they *seem* to accept us as being one of them. In case they change their minds, though, we want to be ready to get out of here in a hurry."

She watched them alertly. "I hope they don't change their minds."

"The *slags*, of course, will also take us for flits."

Dave, looking down at the forest a little later, thought that they were almost as low now as the yacht had been when the slags had gone to work on it. But, so far, there was no response from below, and he continued to drop down.

Then, near the edge of the clearing, a yellow glow burst into life, and another, and another. Dozens of glowing lines began to climb up out of the still dark forest into the sunlight.

From above came a sudden booming, a noise such as Dave and Jim Fielding had heard earlier, but far louder, and growing louder yet. The separate notes seemed to reinforce, resonate, gather power—

"Hang on!" said Dave. He checked to see that she had a firm grip, then shot the skimmer fast to the side. The forest and the rising streams of fire blurred, the booming died away, he peered ahead, and up, and sent the skimmer into a steep climb.

The forest dropped away below, until they were looking down on scattered clouds, sunlit treetops, and two curving arcs of gray specks that converged toward the gray-and-white rectangle of snow-filled clearing atop the bluff. Even here, in the whistle of an icy wind, he could hear a faint booming note, and see a cross-hatching of bright lines against the darker background of the forest.

She looked all around. "Is it safe here?"

He glanced around dubiously. "If your friends on the other yachts don't show up. If the skimmer doesn't quit on us."

"What happened back there? Did you figure out what they were doing?"

"Something Jim Fielding said occurred to me. He said it looked as if the flit that attacked us had tried to *run up the side of the ship to get at the energy cannon*. Now, the energy cannon used *heat*-energy as a weapon. To one of these flying monsters, what would that mean that an energy cannon *is*?"

"A slag?"

"Exactly. And the yacht—a vertical cylinder—what can that be but a very tall tree? Now, if the flit tries to run up the side of the ship, which it thinks is a tree, to get the energy-cannon, which it *thinks* is a slag, what will it do with a real slag?"

She looked over the edge, where the gray specks were vanishing, and the bright lines were no longer visible.

"Then," she said, "that booming was a call, and the flits that hear it go to the spot where they heard the call given. But why should they prey on the slags now and not ordinarily?"

"Ordinarily, they're spread out in pairs. What can one or two of them do against a whole colony of slags? But now they're migrating, and they're in large numbers. What they live on when they're migrating, I don't know, but I imagine they welcome a nice juicy slag when they can get it—and there's a big colony of them down there. The possibility should have dawned on us before. *Something* must keep down the numbers of the slags, or they'd overrun the planet."

He glanced around, looked down, and saw a cloud of steam drifting from the forest near the clearing.

He snapped on the communicator.

"Jim?"

"Dave?" answered Jim Fielding's voice. "You still with us?"

"So far. Why?"

"A hurricane of flits went by, headed in your direction. I thought maybe they were taking turns dropping you on the rocks."

"No, we're friends with them. We showed them where your pals the slags hang out, and the flits went down for a visit."

There was a silence and a murmur of voices, then Fielding said, "Abe's in touch with us from the other skimmer, near the cabins. He says there was a noise like the sky had turned into a washtub, and someone was pounding on it, and then there was a terrific uproar, with screams, breaking branches, streaks of fire in all directions, sizzling snow, shrieks, bellows, and clutching noises. Do you mean to tell me the *flits went after the slags?*"

Dave glanced all around, just in case, then said, "It seems reasonable to me. But I don't *know* what happened. We got out of there. You can go take a good close look if you want to."

"If there weren't quite so many holes in this tub, we would. Where are you now?"

"Roughly over the clearing. It seems to me that we're about three miles up. You know, it *might* be possible to get those yachts into the forest now without getting cooked. The slags have something else to think about."

"That's a thought. Maybe we *could*." There was a tense pause. "We won't get another chance like this. Okay, we're going to try it."

"Good luck."

"Thanks. Same to you, Dave . . . I hope."

"See you, Jim." He snapped off the communicator, and glanced at the girl, who, the blanket tight around her shoulders, and her hands gripping the edge of the skimmer, was looking over the rim to see beneath the skimmer. She turned, and glanced around overhead.

Dave watched approvingly, not only struck by her looks, but by her alertness. He glanced quickly around, then started down.

"You seem," he said, "to catch onto the spirit of this place unusually fast."

She nodded. "In some ways, it's just like home. Only there should be more snow, and a lot of salt water."

"A colony planet?"

She said ironically, "Just a planet to get rich quick on, and get off of in three years."

He grinned. "I suppose a person could learn a lot in those three years."

She nodded. "Such as 'Keep looking ahead, or you may go through where it's thin, and come up where it's thick.' That is, under the ice."

He considered it, and glanced briefly around. "No wonder this place seems almost like home to you. The spirit's the same. It's just the details that are different. But we have a poet here, to immortalize the details. Can you equal this:

"'Do your dreaming while at home in bed.
Our stranglebush makes walking sleepers dead.'"

"H'm," she said, "'stranglebush.'" She grinned and glanced around. "Yes, I think we had something almost as nice:

"'Stay on-trail
That's the law.
Snowtrapper has
A one meter jaw.'"

They looked at each other, and suddenly they were both laughing.

He said, "There was something I wanted to ask you, but I've been hesitating. For one thing, there's something about this place which—while at least it's not civilization—still, it falls short of perfection. Moreover—"

"Do you," she said, smiling, "always make these long speeches before you say something?"

"I was afraid you might not appreciate what it's actually *like* here."

She glanced around alertly. "That's true, but I *do* know what civilization is like. We found that out after Daddy found the ore-body, and all of a sudden we had money." She said this as she might have said, "Then I slipped in a hole and got a broken leg."

Dave glanced around, and studied a large dark cloud about half-a-mile away. He glanced down, where the treetops swayed, and steam and wet smoke boiled up.

"This," he said looking back at her, "encourages me to offer you a way to escape from all that."

"Some day, if you ever get around to actually making the offer, maybe I'll tell you what happened. You want to know in case you ever should land in the same spot."

"The way things are here, the danger of *that* is slight. However, there are other things, and I'm trying to remember . . . yes, I think I've got it, now. You should know at least this much before I say anything else. Just keep an eye on that big dark cloud while I recite this."

She cast a quick look around, and watched the cloud. He thought a moment, then slowly recited:

> "'Welcome, Friend, to our planet of ease.
> In winter here, you will sneeze and freeze;
> But don't complain without good reason;
> Save your curse for a still worse season.
> When sweet summer's sun the snows doth warm,
> The pests pour forth in a hideous swarm:
> Bears and badgers, slags and flits,
> Bugs to drive you out of your wits;
> Stung you'll be, and frequently bit.
> Just name it, Friend; we've got it.'"

She laughed, and he said, "That doesn't cover it, but you should have *some* idea."

She glanced at him shyly, then spoke in a soft voice. "I think I follow your reasoning; but you're so cagey about actually *saying* anything that I'm having a little trouble springing the trap." She glanced at the cloud. "However, there's still time, if you hurry. Perhaps it will help if *I* recite a verse:

"'While the icy northwind still doth blow,
Hasten your travelings o'er the snow.
Brethren, sweet springtime's cozy hush
Will sink you deep in bottomless mush.'

"And," she said, looking around, "this is going to be a warm day."

He took a quick glance around, then, alternately glancing at the approaching cloud and at the space yacht slowly descending toward the clearing, he proposed.

She accepted.

During that instant when neither was watching, there burst from the cloud, wings folded and claws outstretched, a large flit, followed by a second, a third, and a fourth. They shot past the yacht, directly between it and the skimmer, and headed for the forest. Atop the yacht, the energy cannon loomed out of its housing.

Dave shouted, "*Hang on.*"

She gripped the holds, he glanced back, and snapped the skimmer sharply to the north.

The blaze of pink radiance shot past, the flits vanished through a hole in the treetops, a slag below was already taking a shot, and as Dave swerved sharply, another flit dropped out of the cloud and went past like a boulder.

He got more height, then went over the edge of the bluff high enough to avoid the slag nested in the trees somewhere down there, and at once was almost blinded by the glare from the nose of the yacht below. He glanced through the afterimages to observe that she had shut her eyes in time, and as he dropped down toward the yacht, he wondered briefly just what this planet she had come from had actually been like, to breed such alertness and mental control.

Sometime soon, he thought, he'd have to ask her—sometime when the door was triple-barred and braced, his gun loaded and handy, the shutters barred from within, and either a roaring fire in the fireplace, or the chimney-stone lowered solidly into its rests, and the lift-pole jammed in place.

But not just now.

He glanced around intently.

It didn't pay to let the mind wander.

LEVERAGE

Dave Morgan squinted out the doorway of the communications shack at the plowed field baking in the midday sun. Dave glanced past a row of log cabins to a big tracked machine that sat near the edge of the thick intertwining forest. Beside the machine, a knot of men waved their hands around their heads, slapped, scratched, and scrubbed their shirts against their chests. Around them, over them, and on either side, long thick stalks arched out from the forest and dipped in toward the bare soil of the clearing.

On the ground near the men lay a long jointed metal arm with a buzz saw blade on a shaft at its end. Dave noted that this arm sat in the same spot as yesterday, the day before, and the day before that.

A dull clang, and the screech of a rusty nut turning on its stud, carried across the clearing.

Behind Dave, inside the communications shack, Al Weber slapped and growled. "How are they coming on the dozer?"

"Slow as mud."

"They got the arm bolted on yet?"

"They haven't touched the arm."

Weber swore and slapped again.

A droning whine drifted past Dave's ear, and there was a faint breeze on the back of his neck. He gave the gnat time to get settled, then slapped.

Weber said angrily, "That forest will walk right in and take root again if they don't hurry with the dozer."

"Sure," said Dave, "but it's hard to work when you're getting eaten alive." He scowled as a gray blur drifted over the line of cabins and faded toward the dozer.

The men there suddenly slapped, scratched, and waved their hands with a more desperate vigor.

"Funny," said Weber ironically. "We generally get our work done." He slapped, there was a crash, and Weber let out a bellow of sizzling profanity. Before he was through, he damned the men who found the planet, the advisors that led him, Dave, and the others, to it, and their present leader who consistently failed to untangle the mess.

Dave heard this as a familiar background noise, like the spatter and splash of rain streaming through the roof, or the grating creak of beetles shot-holing the beams. He made vague sympathetic noises, and squinted to look up at the glare of the sky. He thought he saw a tiny dot overhead.

Weber was silent a moment, then said, "I don't know if this will work or not. But it's that or crank the generator, and that would mean one of us couldn't do anything during transmission but heave up and down on the plunger."

Dave glanced around. Stacked in a pile near Weber were a number of flat squares about a yard on an edge. Weber said, "We might as well put them back on the roof now. Then we'll know if it was just an accident, or not."

Dave squinted up at the sky. He could see the dot clearly now. "We'd better wait a while."

"Why? Lunch time?"

"Yes, and not only for us, either."

Weber grunted. He came over and peered up, then squeezed his eyes shut, looked away, and tried again. "Right you are."

The dot was growing to a black ball.

Dave took out a whistle on a cord around his neck. He drew a deep breath.

In the field, two of the men were on top of the dozer. Several others were starting toward the long jointed arm.

Dave put the whistle to his lips and blew hard.

His ears hurt.

The two men on top of the dozer jumped over the side.

The men headed for the arm, spun around and streaked for the dozer.

They all dove under it.

A bristle of gun-barrels poked out from underneath.

Dave stepped back and slammed the door shut. Weber heaved a wooden bar across it. Dave grabbed a heavy pole, thrust one end into a notch in an overhead beam, and jammed the other end against the bottom of the door. Weber jammed a second pole against the top of the door. Weber snatched up a long, thin-barreled gun. Dave grabbed an ax leaning against the wall.

Outside, someone yelled.

There was a whistling shriek and a booming clap, as of huge leathery wings, abruptly filled with air. The door jumped as if struck with a club. It jumped, and jumped again. The pole at the top clattered down.

Light rapping sounds pattered on the door. There was a high-pitched scream close by.

The door jolted. The hinge at the top wrenched loose. The bar bent back. One of its brackets snapped off. The bar fell down. The door jerked inward. The bottom hinge squealed.

Weber flattened against the wall beside the door.

Dave stepped toward the hinge side of the door.

A set of big claws slid around the top of the door and jerked it inward.

Dave swung his ax and chopped off the claws.

A light rapping sound tapped on the door. Something whizzed past the leaning top of the door and stuck in the wall inside the cabin.

Weber thrust his gun around the edge of the door and pulled the trigger. He pulled the trigger again and again.

Dave raised his ax.

There was a scream outside. A blast of dirt and pebbles flew in. A scrambling noise dwindled fast into the distance, followed by the spaced flap of big wings, then an intense silence.

Dave and Weber glanced at each other soberly.

Weber took a deep breath, unsnapped a lever that fit tightly against the barrel of his gun, and worked it up and down. The lever moved a rod that thrust down into the stock of the gun. There was a sound like the sucking, pumping noise of an air compressor.

Dave glanced at the lever, started to turn away, then looked back sharply. For an instant, his gaze grew glazed and distant.

He blinked, then turned away frowning. He got a pair of needle-nose pliers and dropped the chopped-off claws in an empty parts box.

Weber took down the pole still braced against the bottom of the door, and pulled the door open. The other side was studded with darts. Outside, the men were streaming back from the dozer, carrying their guns, and waving their free hands in front of their faces. Their faces were set, and their eyes slitted.

"Time to eat," said Weber.

"Yeah," said Dave.

They started for the cook shack.

Dave walked in the cook's end of the cabin, and tossed the claws in the fire.

The cook whistled. "He get you?"

"No, he just got hold of the door. How's Abe coming?"

"Out of his head part of the time. But his arm's going down."

Dave nodded, and walked around a split-log partition into a room with a long rough table. On the far end of the table, near an open door, were set a number of compartmented trays with food and steaming mugs on them. The air in this room danced with tiny black specks.

Dave shut his mouth, closed one eye, and squinted out of the other. A gnat promptly got in it. Gnats landed all over him. They crawled down his neck and up his wrists. He began to itch all over. He picked up a tray, carried it in one hand and his gun in the other, dodged around someone coming in, and walked outside along the line of cabins. He kept close to the cabins in case he should have to jump inside in a hurry. He kept his mind firmly on the simple business of walking to the doorway just ahead, and tried to ignore the hordes of biting crawling gnats.

There was the shrill blast of a whistle.

Dave stepped in through the doorway, and put the tray on a bench.

There was a whistling noise that shot closer fast.

A man dove headlong through the doorway. A shadow spread fast over the ground behind him. Dave realized there would be no time to shut the door, and jerked up his gun. He blinked, but the gnats were in his eyes and half-blinded him. There was a booming clap. The doorway went black.

Dave fired at the blackness.

There was an excited squeak-squeak-squeak, a clatter, and a hoarse human cry.

The blackness was gone. There was a *whoosh!* and a blur of huge wings outside. Dave fired without effect. He saw a black form in the air just off the ground, then a smaller form higher up, then yet a smaller one still higher, then it vanished beyond the trees at the end of the clearing.

Dave put his gun down, and for several moments did nothing but kill gnats.

Outside, someone said in a flat voice, "It got him. Damn it, it *got* him."

Dave now saw that his tray was upside down on the dirt floor, the food spread out in a long smear and the drink nothing but a blot in the dirt. Dave salvaged a half-box of dry D-rations, ate them, and was still hungry.

He picked up the tray, went to the door, glanced overhead, and started for the cookshack. On the way, he passed little groups of men, their eyes looking sidewise toward the last cabin in the row.

Someone said, "It wasn't him that should have been killed."

Dave put the tray in the cookshack, got some more darts for his gun, and pumped the lever of the gun. As he worked, he thought bitterly of the gap between theory and practice. In theory, this gun was ideal. Its light, reusable enzyme-tipped darts, fired by simple air pressure, would, he had been told, set off an irreversible reaction in the blood stream of the animal struck by the darts. The hunter need merely recoat the tip of the dart to use it again. Only small light containers of enzyme need be shipped in.

But in practice, the slightest breeze blew the darts away from the birds. The shock effect was nil. The darts glanced off the leathery skin unless they hit at just the right angle, and then the enzyme never troubled the creature's blood. The net result, Dave told himself, angrily, was that what an antique .45 caliber revolver would have settled in one blast, was never really ever ended by any number of the tricky darts.

Dave finished pumping the gun, went back outside, and automatically glanced overhead.

Someone said, "No need to worry now. It's *full* now."

Dave looked around. Nearly everyone had a sullen waiting

look. The only movement seemed to be an automatic brushing at gnats.

A man with an expression of ingrained resentment said, "The bird got him because he never had a chance. Just like we don't have a chance. Not a chance in the world."

The men looked intent.

The man went on. "But just a few light-years from here, they're flying home in their big helicars right now."

It occurred to Dave that nothing good was likely to come out of this. He listened alertly.

"Yeah," said the man. "They've got their big helicars, all of them. They'll all float down, right on the beam, smooth and easy, and land right outside their apartments. No danger for them. No trouble. The dome will slide down easy over the landing shelf. They'll go in. It's cool inside. They'll go in and mix a cool drink..."

Dave glanced around. Everyone was listening.

"...Then they snap on the trideo and stretch out on the smooth soft sofa. The girl loosens her jacket. The man— But we left all that. We left it. We—"

Dave looked up at the clear hot sky, and raised his hand to shade his eyes. He squinted, saw nothing, but looked anyway. He glanced down, blinked hard, and looked up again.

The voice stopped.

Dave glanced around.

Everyone was squinting at the sky except the man who had been talking. He was looking hard at Dave.

"Go on," said Dave. "Don't stop there. What happens next?"

The man's eyes narrowed.

"Go on," said Dave impatiently. "The girl was loosening her jacket. The man was coming across the room at her. Then what?"

Someone snickered.

The bitter-faced man glanced around. He said, "*We'll* never see a woman again. We—"

"That's right," said Dave. "The ship will bring the women in ten months. But the forest will grow up around us and the gnats will carry us off for souvenirs while we wait for you to tell us what happened after the girl—"

"Yeah," said a new voice. "What happened to the girl?"

Plainly anxious to forget all about the girl, the man snapped,

"They went out to the synchrotherm and put on a steak. That's something else we'll never see again. Steak. We'll never—"

"Were you talking to the hunting party?" said Dave. "I didn't know they were back yet."

Someone else said, in a tone of surprise, "They *might* bring back meat, at that."

The mention of this possible good fortune seemed too much for the bitter-faced man to bear. He burst out angrily, "We'll never see a helicar again, never fly, never see another woman, never eat a steak—"

The men now turned to glance at each other. One of them said roughly, "Go eat some darts if you're hungry. We got troubles enough without all that croaking."

There was a growl of agreement, and a string of sarcastic comments:

"Say, boy, if you want to fly, go stand out in the middle of the field and wait. Maybe the bird will take you for a ride."

"No, no. The guy is really suffering, fellows. Let's take up a collection."

"If he's suffering that much, maybe we ought to ease his pain."

"Not till I hear what happened to the girl."

"Yeah, what about the girl?"

There was a burst of laughter. Several of the men grinned and spat on the ground.

The bitter-faced man looked directly at Dave and said, "You won't live. The bird will take you next."

Dave saw the leader of the colony, a strongly-built man named Daniels, watching from the doorway of the last cabin in line. Daniels beckoned to Dave.

Dave stood still a moment, then brushed some gnats away from his face, glanced up at the sky, and went down to Daniels' cabin.

It took Dave a moment to see in the comparative gloom of the cabin.

Daniels, looking at him thoughtfully, said, "Thanks."

"What for?"

"In the spot we're in, a trouble-maker is a luxury. I was about to go out there and ram his teeth down his throat. You turned it into a joke. That's a better way to end it."

"I doubt it's ended."

"Ended for today. If we get from one day to the next, that's something. Each little advantage may give us room to get a little more." He glared out the door. "At least, if it weren't for these gnats, it would work that way."

Dave suddenly thought of the idea that had occurred to him as he saw Weber work the lever of the dart gun.

Daniels gave a heavy sigh. "Well, we didn't have to come out here. We made the choice, so we take the risk." He glanced at Dave. "How's Weber coming?"

"He wants to try the plates again."

"O.K. Any time he wants to. But tell him to just try a few at first." Daniels hesitated. "Tell Weber I appreciate the job he's doing. Patching those plates isn't easy."

Dave nodded. "Will you want me this afternoon?"

"No. Stay with Weber. And keep an eye on the sky for me. With all those gnats out in the field, we're lucky if we can see to raise a hammer." Daniels smiled. "And thanks again."

"That's O.K.," said Dave. He started to leave, then hesitated.

Daniels said, "What is it?"

Dave shrugged, "I've got an idea."

"God knows," said Daniels fervently, "we could use an idea. What is it?"

"When I was about fourteen," said Dave, "I helped my grandfather move a heavy rock. We each had a big crowbar. He'd lift and hold, and I'd slide my crowbar in and lift a little further, and hold while he slid his crowbar further in and lifted it, and then the rock would roll over. When we got through, he said, 'Boy, if you have a long enough lever, and a place to rest it, and a place to press against, you can move most anything. A great man said that once. You remember it.' It came back to me this morning when I saw Weber pump the lever on his gun."

Daniels listened closely.

Dave said, "About the same time, I remembered seeing a swarm of gnats drift over the cabins, ignore the cook, ignore Weber and me, and join the swarm of gnats around you and the men out in the field."

"They're worse out in the field. You and Weber and the cook were inside."

"After you came back to eat, I was inside the cookshack and they did everything but fly off with me."

Daniels frowned. "That's true. What's your idea?"

"I think the gnats, as a regular routine, gang up in one big swarm. Maybe they regularly prey on some kind of large animal, harass it to death, then feed on the carcass."

Daniels waved his hand in front of his face. "There are always a few around, wherever you go."

"Scouts," said Dave. "The main horde stays with the victim till he drops. At least, it looks like it to me. And if so—"

"I didn't think of that," said Daniels. "Earth gnats are a little more flexible, and I've just been assuming these are the same." He thought a moment. "But if they *do* stick together like that, maybe we can pry them loose enough so we can fix that dozer."

"That's what I was thinking."

"Come on," said Daniels. "Let's try it."

Dave, Daniels, and the rest of the men—save only Weber, who was putting his plates on the communications shack roof—started out in a group across the field. The gnats swarmed all over them. Lips pressed shut, eyes squinted, waving their hands in front of their faces, the men headed for the dozer.

When they got there, Daniels and a man with arms like a blacksmith stayed by the dozer. The rest trudged on with the gnats whining around them, and the big drooping shoots from the forest dangling in their faces.

When they reached the end of the field, two burly men stepped into the intertwining tangle of the forest. The rest of the men made a quarter-turn and stumbled across the end of the field, slapping fiercely.

When they reached the opposite side of the field, two more men slid into the forest. The tormented remainder, Dave included, turned in the opposite direction and shambled back across the field.

From the direction of the dozer came the scrape of metal, then:

CLANG! CLANG! CLANG!

For the next few minutes, the air resounded with the sounds of hard heavy work.

The men halted and devoted themselves to mere existence in the middle of a horde of gnats.

Time passed.

There was a whine that drowned out the whine of the gnats, followed by the grinding buzz of a saw cutting through wood.

A voice spoke from a short distance away.

"Relief for Dave Morgan and Jack O'Neill."

Dave started across the field. Someone said, "Daniels wants to see you. He's over at the cabins."

Dave stopped to get rid of the gnats that crawled over him from head to foot. When he got through, he discovered that he was still waving one hand automatically. He stopped, and glanced all around carefully.

He was free of them. Only an occasional gnat whined past.

A great weight seemed to lift, leaving him light-headed.

He took a glance overhead, then looked around. The dozer was working its way steadily down the field. The air resounded with the whine-*buzz*-whine-*buzz* of the saw cutting off the big shoots, and the chop and clatter as men cut them into lengths and tossed them in heaps.

Dave started for the cabins.

Daniels was looking at the communications shack with an expression of deep thought on his face. When Dave came up to him, he grinned. "It worked. It seems like a miracle."

"It sure does," said Dave, who had phantom images of innumerable gnats flitting around his head.

"I wonder," said Daniels. "How far can we carry this? If there are ten men on one side of the field, and one by one they walk over to the other side, at what point will the gnats go over, too?"

"That's a good question. We could try it and see."

Daniels nodded. "It seems to me there's some kind of pattern emerging here. While we were out on the field, Weber got some of his solar plates up on the roof. One of those crows, starlings, or whatever passes for them on this planet flew past, looked, flew back, and took a flying dive at the plates. Pretty soon the air was full of them. They practically tore the plates to pieces."

Dave scowled. "First there was one? Then a whole bunch of them?"

"First one went over, flew back, took a closer look, and dove on the plate. Next, three or four flew in from various directions. Pretty soon, they were coming in from all points of the compass."

Dave looked away, scowling.

Daniels said, "Funny, isn't it?"

"Yeah," said Dave. "The gnats fly together in clouds. The trees twine together and send shoots in together from all sides at once. The birds attack in a group. This is a regular planet of together-ness."

"Don't forget the big bird."

"There don't seem to be too many of them yet," said Dave. "But for all we know, there's a hundred others flapping in from thousands of miles away."

"God forbid," said Daniels, alarmed.

Dave scowled and thought for a while. Finally, he said, "There's an advantage to concentrating all available force on your prey or your enemy, but the creatures on this planet seem to do it by reflex action. That's not so good. It's predictable. Did Weber have any idea *why* they dove on the plates?"

"He thought maybe they saw faint reflected images in the plates, and the images didn't act right, so the birds attacked."

"Makes sense," said Dave dryly. "Obviously, the birds in this place are conformists. The images don't react like other birds. Ergo, tear them to pieces. Hm-m-m."

"Well," said Daniels, "it doesn't help us much. The plates have to be exposed to light, or they won't store any energy. But if they *are* exposed to light, some bird will fly past and see his image. Bang! And before we can get out there, the plates will be in shreds. Of course, if we had something we could pull over them in a hurry—"

Dave grinned faintly.

Daniels scowled. "What are you thinking of?"

"Does the cook have any pans?"

"Pans? What do we want with pans?"

"Never mind. Let's go see."

They went toward the cookshack, glanced uneasily overhead, then went inside.

Dave came out grinning, and yelled across to Weber in the communications shack.

Weber looked out and stared at him as if he were crazy.

Daniels came out of the cookshack and bawled out orders.

Weber shrugged, went into the communications shack, came out with a three-foot square plate, put a rough ladder against the roof, and started up.

Daniels helped boost Dave up onto the roof of the cookshack, and Dave put a big bright pan flat on the roof, then shoved one prong of a meat fork through a hole in the pan's rim and into the wood of the roof.

Dave climbed down off the roof and waited.

Overhead, there was a squawk.

A small black streak dropped down near the dishpan, and flew around inspecting it from all angles. There was a loud indignant squawk. Suddenly the bird landed a peck on the shiny pan. Where the bird's bill hit, could be seen the darting visual image of the reflection of the bill. The bird immediately shot around to the other side of the pan and tried to take the reflection by surprise.

The reflection was not fooled, and got there just as fast as the bird did.

There was a mighty clatter as the bird attacked the image.

More birds flew over, stared, dropped down, squawked, and dove for the pan.

The sky grew thick with birds flying in from all directions. The space around the pan erupted with flying feathers. There was a deafening clatter and squawk. Birds with their beaks open and their eyes shut rolled down the roof and fell off onto the ground.

Dave glanced around at Weber on the roof of the communications shack. Weber was bent forward with his eyes wide, his arms dangling, and his jaw hanging open. The big square plate lay on the roof beside him, but the birds were rushing past without the slightest notice.

Daniels choked, and burst out laughing. He shouted at the birds, "Get that nonconformist! Tear him to shreds! You may be a little beat-up yourselves at the end, but—Rip into him! Peck him! Kick him! Bite him! Yank his feathers out!" He turned to Dave. "Which side are you betting on?"

But now Dave was staring at the growing heap of upended birds piling up under the roof, with fresh squadrons rushing to the slaughter overhead. Suddenly he was reminded of a runaway nuclear pile. He turned around, and sprinted to the communications shack, got the pole used to brace the door, ran back to the cookshack and knocked the pan off the roof.

The birds rolled off in a big knot which broke into several struggling heaps.

"Get that pan out of here," said Dave. He kicked the swarms of fighting birds apart.

Daniels tossed the pan into the cookshack and helped kick apart the heaps of birds.

Dave finished pulling apart a little knot of diehards with their beaks in each other's feathers.

"A little more of this," he said, "might upset the balance of nature. Who knows what these birds may eat and keep in check?"

Daniels nodded.

The birds now straggled around and flew up in little groups to roost on the ridges of the cabins. They ran their beaks through their ruffled feathers, and sat on one foot to scratch at the sides of their heads. Then several of them looked fixedly out toward the field. The whole flock, save for those still heaped on the ground, took off for the field in a cloud. This cloud of birds headed for the end of the field where the men stood doggedly waving their hands around their heads. The birds swirled and dove above the men.

Daniels said, "They're eating the gnats! We've solved it!"

The cook came out of the cookshack with a cloth bag in one hand, and a sharp knife in the other. He tested the knife with his thumb as he headed for the heaps of birds.

Daniels grinned. "Yes, sir, we've got it. Look at that. Meat."

The cook put down his knife and shoveled birds into the bag with both hands.

Dave frowned, and picked up the pole he'd taken from the communications shack.

"I don't know," he said, scowling. "It seems to me that in all the uproar we've lost track of something."

"Nonsense. Listen, without the gnats bothering us— Oh, I know, life may not be *perfect*. But this means, we've licked the *big* problems, so—"

The loud blast of a whistle cut across the field.

Dave saw Weber streak for the communications shack. Dave glanced swiftly up, then sprinted after him. He helped shove the door shut, then thrust the pole in a notch in the overhead beam, and jammed the other end of it against the bottom of the door.

Weber picked up the wooden bar, and dropped it in place. One end caught in its bracket, and the other end swung past the broken bracket, so the bar fell on the floor.

"My God," said Weber. "I forgot."

"I thought you did," said Dave. He jammed another pole in place to brace the top of the door, then picked up his ax. He looked at the door. The hinge side leaned slightly in at the top. "If that thing hits the door, he'll get in. The guns will only sting him. Is there another ax in here?"

"I think so. I'll look."

While Weber looked, Dave could hear a whistling shriek that grew rapidly louder. He stepped to the wall on the hinge side of the door, and raised his ax. There was a loud clap. The door jumped inward. The top pole fell down. The door jumped again. There was a scream from the hinge and it leaned in.

Dave flattened against the wall.

The door sagged as a big set of claws shoved it in.

There was a flapping noise and the bend of a thick leathery wing shoved in the door.

Dave raised his ax a little higher.

Weber cried out, "I can't find one!"

Dave glanced quickly at the overhead beams to see if he had room enough.

A huge recurved beak on a long neck shot in the doorway, straight for Weber.

Dave swung the ax. He hit the long neck, stepped out and swung at the place where neck joined leathery shoulder. The huge wings jerked forward. A big set of claws reached up. Dave chopped savagely at the neck. He chopped again and again, through tendons, gristle and bone. He chopped till the sweat ran in his eyes and his arms couldn't lift the ax.

The whole huge mass of leather leaned over and sagged backwards. Dave turned around, breathing hard, leaned against the doorframe and wiped the sweat out of his eyes. He saw Weber with one arm and both legs wrapped around the long neck just back of the head. In Weber's free hand was a knife. The knife was sunk to the hilt in one of the creature's big eyes. As Dave watched, the huge beak opened, the neck twitched, then the beak half-closed and lay still.

Outside, Dave could hear the sound of running feet. Someone looked in, and sucked his breath in sharply.

A familiar voice cried out in the distance. "I told you. One-by-one it will take us. We don't have a chance. Not a chance."

"Ah, shut up," said someone else. "They killed it."

Dave straightened up, still breathing hard, and looked around.

The inside of the cabin looked like a backwoods slaughterhouse after a busy day.

Daniels looked in, an expression of awe on his face. He said apologetically, "Maybe my victory proclamation was a little premature. I completely forgot about these things."

Dave said, "It just occurred to me . . . while I was chopping through that thing . . . why couldn't we have a deadfall? They always try to get in the place where they see us go in. Put a heavy rock in a frame over the door. Jerk out the pins that hold it just as they break down the door. Meat for dinner."

"Hm-m-m," said Daniels.

A new voice said, "We could even bait them down on purpose. Why not? I'm getting sick of waiting for these things to grab us. Why not decoy them in?"

The cook said, "Let me through. Watch the knife, please."

A familiar bitter voice remarked, "All the same, by the time the women get here, there'll be nothing waiting for them but a pile of bones, that's all. Nothing but—"

There was a solid crunching sound.

In the quiet that followed, the men gathered around to watch the cook, a big knife in his hand, bend over to study the bird.

Ten months later, in early spring, a ship came down with a cargo of supplies and highly nervous women. The crew of the ship looked out, squinted, looked away, blinked their eyes, looked back hard, and stared.

Big piles of firewood were already stacked amongst solid, weather-bleached cabins. From the side, fresh wood grew conveniently in toward the clearing, where it was apparently cut off by a man on a dozer.

Around the edge of the clearing sat a number of giant cages with huge sullen-looking birds peering out between thick wooden bars. A man dressed like a chef ignored the ship to thoughtfully probe the ribs of one of these birds with a long stick.

Flights of smaller birds wheeled and dove overhead.

The crewmen scowled down and the colonists looked up impatiently.

"Where," said one of the crewmen in a low voice to another, "are the graves?"

"I don't know. I only see one."

"Well, they just don't get through the first winter without losing around fifty per cent. It never fails."

"We'll ask them. But we'd better hurry and unload. We don't have much time on this schedule."

"Let's go, then. I'm curious."

The colonists, however, acted for some reason as if they were more interested in greeting their women than in chatting with the crewmen.

The crew blasted off in a bad frame of mind. The colonists, they growled, could at least have told them a little more than one word.

"What does it *mean*?" the crewmen demanded.

" 'Leverage'!"

THE SIEVE

Benton squinted narrowly at the green leaf Dave Ander was experimentally rolling in his hand.

"I don't know, Dave," said Benton. "Maybe it's none of my business. Still—" He looked around at the trees, some of them six feet through the butt, that surrounded the clearing. The carcass of the dead roller was still sprawled over a heap of fallen logs at the edge of the clearing. The wrecked dozer was still upside down, and was already rusting where the roller's claws had ripped off the protective coating. Benton took a deep breath. "All the same, we've got to get going again. Summer won't last forever."

Ander broke up several more pieces of dried gray leaf, then tipped his hand to let the small pieces sift out onto the green leaf. He rolled the leaf up again, bound it carefully with the pliable stalk of a small vine, then tied it and broke off the rest of the vine. He turned it this way and that.

"Ah," he said.

"Dave," said Benton, "are you going to smoke the thing now?"

"Why not?" Ander felt through his pockets and came out with a pack of matches. He struck one.

"Dave—" said Benton. He hesitated, and again looked over the clearing. Of the row of cabins, only the "Administrative Center" was undamaged. And on the porch of the Administrative Center sat four men and three women, their backs against the wall. Their legs were outstretched, and their heads tilted back. A wisp of white smoke drifted out away from them toward the south.

Ander touched the match to the gray flecks protruding from his rolled leaf. The match blew out. Ander swore, and hastily struck another. Eagerly he sucked on the leaf.

"Dave," said Benton. "For the love of Heaven. Look. It doesn't do any *good*. Nothing's *changed*. When you get through with that, where are you? You're no better off than when you started."

"Ah-h-h," said Ander. His eyes closed and opened again dreamily. He sat down on the ground, sucked hard, blew out a cloud of white smoke, then lay back in the earth that had been plowed and was already growing up again in weeds.

Benton looked down at Ander for a moment, looked at the four men and three women leaning against the Administrative Center. He looked at the dead and slowly decomposing roller, whose stench, once the wind shifted, would be carried this way to make the place practically uninhabitable. He glanced at the burned earth where the supply rocket had landed tools, medical supplies, and seed, and to which it would not return until next spring. He looked again at Ander, lying comfortably in the sun and rolling his head from side to side as he blew out white smoke. Ander's face wore a look of complete contentment.

Benton looked at Ander's face, looked at the weeds and ruins, and found no words suitable to express his feelings. He turned on his heel and started back toward the cabins.

The sun, sliding down toward the west, was hot on Benton's back and shoulders as he crossed the furrows. His shirt clung to his skin. He was thirsty. He felt slightly light-headed from hunger. He was aware that his mind was functioning with the same degree of efficiency as a dismasted sailing vessel.

He passed a log cabin with the roof smashed in, the chimney knocked full length on the ground, and the logs at one corner mashed down like a child's toy under an adult's foot. On the half-ruined porch of this cabin sat a girl. The girl had blond hair and high cheekbones. Her head was tilted back, and her shirt open at the throat to show smooth white skin.

Benton stopped. "Dr. Forbes?"

The girl blew twin jets of white smoke out her nostrils. She tilted her head forward and regarded him dreamily. She opened her mouth, and moved her lips soundlessly. After a moment, words came. "Yes, Ben?"

Benton walked over to look down at her. "Ander, Stephenson, Ginetti, Muller, and Greenbaum are all smoking the stuff."

She looked up at him with a faint smile. "Are they, Ben?"

The way she said it made him feel foolish. "Also," he said, "Shirley, Tac, Lou-Ann, and you."

"I see, Ben." She nodded wisely and drew on the rolled leaf. A submerged hint of some other emotion crossed her face. "What about Gina?"

"I haven't seen Gina since the rollers went through."

She smiled faintly. "Have you looked?"

"I've looked all over the place."

"Why, Ben?"

"*Why?*" He stared at her. "A rocketship," he said, "puts down at a spaceport. One of the landing legs collapses. Fourteen injured passengers are carried off. The passenger list shows there were fifteen on board. The spaceport officials search the ship for the last passenger. Why?"

The blond girl shook her head and smiled lazily. She picked up and held out toward him an unsmoked rolled leaf with a few gray flecks protruding from one end. She smiled with her head tilted back. "Sit down, Ben."

"No, thanks," said Ben.

"We might share a dream, Ben."

"Wouldn't that be nice?" he said sourly. "And sooner or later, we'd wake up."

"What of it, Ben?" She patted the rough floor beside her. "Sit."

He didn't move. "Thanks," he growled, "but I'll stand."

She smiled dreamily. "Afraid, Ben?"

He said, "When the rollers came through, were you afraid?"

"I was," she said. "Oh, I was afraid. But I'm not now."

"Aren't you? I'm more afraid now. Exactly what do we do when *winter* comes?"

"Winter?" she said. She frowned as if she could not quite place the word.

"Winter," he said. "This isn't Earth. We can't shove a half-credit in the slot and walk off with dinner on a tray. We've got to have the food *stored*. To store it, we've got to raise it. To raise it, we've got to plant it. To plant it, we've got to work the ground. Nine people sitting around blowing smoke out their noses don't get much *work* done."

She started to giggle, choked, coughed, then held out the rolled leaf. "Ben," she said, "never condemn without knowledge. That was my mistake. I tried to stop people from using this. I was very righteous, Ben. You see, I only saw it from the *outside*. But then, I experienced it myself. Now I have a much broader viewpoint. I can see it from the inside, too. I'm in a position to judge both sides of the question, Ben, and you're not. You can't judge me so long as you remain lofty and superior—and ignorant—looking at me from without."

"I'm not trying to judge you," said Ben grimly. "I just want to get the dozer fixed, the field plowed, and the seed in. Once we do that, you can smoke the stuff all you want."

At some point while he was talking, the girl began to smile. She giggled, spluttered, and sat shaking silently. "Ben—" she said, her voice soft and low, her head tilted back, her lips parted, and the mass of smoldering poison clenched in her fingers. "Ben, dear, don't be so superior."

Benton turned away, started toward the Administrative Center, took a long look at the row of people on the porch, blowing out smoke and lolling with their heads back, and decided that he would go somewhere else.

He turned around. His gaze took in the wrecked cabins, the dead roller, the overturned dozer, the weeds in the field, and the immense trees of the forest. He thought he saw something move in the deep shadows of the trees. He walked to the second cabin from the Administrative Center, ducked under the broken logs, and felt his way around the gloomy interior. On the mantel of the fireplace was a pair of binoculars. He took them down, went outside, studied the forest a minute, then raised the binoculars. At last he made out, in the shadows of the trees, a human figure carrying something that he couldn't quite see, but which appeared long and slender, like a dart gun.

Ben studied this figure for a long while, then swung the glasses slowly right and left and saw nothing moving in the forest. The forest, he told himself, was understandably quiet after the rollers went through. The hunting party wasn't due back yet for another day or two. Gina was missing, true, yet the hunters had taken all the dart guns but one, and that one, Ben knew, was in this cabin right over the fireplace. Therefore, how was it that someone carrying a dart gun was walking through the forest?

Ben got down his own dart gun and stepped outside.

He went around the side of the cabin to the back, crossed a narrow strip of plowed earth, wormed through a barricade of overturned tree stumps, and trotted to the nearest corner of the clearing. He ran along the edge of the clearing, and swung into the forest as he approached the far side, where he had seen the figure moving.

By this time, a cloud of fire gnats had located him. Ben threaded his way through the forest while these gnats worked him over like so many red-hot knitting needles. By the time Ben spotted the figure moving through the trees ahead of him, he had a number of welts the size of a man's thumbnail. He studied the figure for an instant, noting the green gum smeared on face and hands to keep bugs away, and, held in one hand, the metal pole with short, angled rods at the top.

Ben called out, "Gina?" He kept the gun centered as he walked closer.

The figure stopped and turned to look at him. In a weary voice, the girl said, "Now what?"

Ben lowered the gun. "I saw you from the cabin. The way you were carrying that thing, I took it for a dart gun. I wondered who it was."

"Oh."

Ben waved the cloud of gnats away from his face. "Let's not stand here all day."

They started toward the clearing. Ben said, "What is that thing?"

"The top of the uniwave mast," said Gina. "I had just set it up when the rollers came through. When I dug myself out again, it was gone. I followed their path and finally found it."

He frowned. "When did you leave?"

"I helped get the leaf-smokers out of their ruins first. I guess about an hour after the rollers came through."

"You slept out?"

She laughed. "There's no hotel out there."

"What was it like?"

"Heaven until around midnight, and purgatory from then on.

I was so tired I fell asleep the first soft place I came to. When I woke up, it was cold, damp, and too dark to go anywhere else. But anyway, I had the antenna." She glanced at him. "Has anything happened here?"

He said, "Ander, Tac, Genetti, and Dr. Forbes are on the weed with the rest."

After a moment, the girl took a deep breath and said, "Forbes gave us all those lectures against it, too."

"Well," said Ben, "now she's approached it with real scientific detachment, and she can lecture us from either side."

"How about you?"

"No thanks," said Ben sourly. "I'd like to be alive next spring."

"So would I. But I have my doubts."

"It's simple enough," said Ben angrily. "We've got to have water, food, fuel, and shelter to get through the winter. The supply ship drilled the well while it was here, so that's done. We've got wood all around us, and all we've got to do is cut it up. We've got food to last us till after harvest, but that's all. So either we plant more now or we starve this winter. What could be simpler than that?"

"My brother," said Gina, "is an engineer. He and two friends went to work on New Mars when New Mars was begging for engineers. The three of them were getting triple pay, tax-free, and double for overtime, plus a big bonus if they stayed for thirty-six months. Now, of those three, two of them stayed the full time and came back with ninety thousand credits; the other one got to drinking a kind of fermented cactus juice, got fired, ended up working as a laborer, drank up his pay, and got killed in a landslide."

They were walking across the fields toward the cabins, and it suddenly occurred to Ben that there might be a tricky situation as he and Gina passed Dr. Forbes' cabin. Already he could see the sun slanting on her blond hair and motionless figure. As Ben was trying to think what to do, Gina went on:

"The two friends that came back said it was a matter of simple logic: The three years would go by no matter what they did. The only question was, where would they be at the end of it?"

"True," said Ben. They were getting closer to the cabins, and he had yet to think of anything.

"They also said that they had gone blank in the face talking simple logic, and it didn't do any good."

"Yes," said Ben.

"And," said Gina, "I'm afraid logic isn't going to help us much here, either."

"Hm-m-m," said Ben. They were almost in front of Dr. Forbes' cabin.

"Well," came the musical voice of the blond girl, the sun shining on her hair, "I see you found her, Ben."

"Yeah," said Ben, moving on.

"Attractive, isn't she, Ben?"

Ben looked at Gina, her face and hands smeared with thick green gum, her hair matted, and dressed in work clothes that had as much shape as a sack thrown over a post.

Gina glanced at Ben with a look of surprise, then looked back at Dr. Forbes angrily.

Ben wished sincerely that he were somewhere else.

Dr. Forbes said, "He was looking for you, Gina."

"Thanks," said Gina.

Dr. Forbes said, "Oh, she's a fine animal, Ben, no doubt. But will she share your dreams?"

Ben tried to get his feet working, and failed.

Dr. Forbes leaned her head back lazily, and drew on a rolled leaf. The sun, now slanting across her tilted head, accentuated the hollow of her cheeks.

"Will you," Ben burst out, "kindly put that thing down for a minute and get something to eat?"

She smiled contentedly. "If you'll smoke it, Ben, I'll stop. We can talk and dream together."

"No, thank you," said Ben.

"Who knows, you might save me, Ben."

"Sure, I can get you out of the quicksand by jumping in with you."

"Ooh," said the blond girl, "you are so righteous, Ben."

Gina bowed her head and walked away without saying anything.

Dr. Forbes shut her eyes and smiled lazily.

Ben turned away angrily, went to his cabin and put the dart gun away. He went back out and found Gina by the communications shack. With her face smeared with the green gum, Ben couldn't see her expression. She said, in a perfectly ordinary tone, "She never did like me. I don't know why. Maybe because I am a mere technician and she has her doctor's degree."

"Maybe," said Ben. "I doubt it."

Gina shrugged. "Will you help me fix the antenna?"

"Sure," said Ben.

It took them the rest of the day to get the antenna fixed, and all the following day to straighten out the shambles in the communications shack. The next afternoon, Ben spotted the hunting party coming through the woods. He went out to meet them.

The hunting party consisted of a man named Becket, tall and rangy, and with hard eyes; two men carrying the carcass of a medium-sized animal on a pole slung over their shoulders; three tall girls with grim expressions; and a grinning man with a piece of grass dangling out of one corner of his mouth, who was called Potter.

Ben looked at their faces and said nothing. Becket glanced around and whistled. "What hit this place?"

"Rollers," said Ben.

"Which?"

Ben pointed. "There's a dead one over there, if you want to look at it. They put their heads on their tails, and roll like hoops."

Potter said, "You're out of your head, man. You've been smoking too much of that good weed."

Ben said, ignoring Potter, "They rolled out of the forest from the north, mashed down the cabins, flipped the dozer out of their way and disappeared into the forest on this side."

Becket said, "How did you kill it?"

"With a dart gun."

"Where did you aim?"

"The head rests on top of the tail when they're rolling. I shot when the neck was exposed."

Potter said, "It's coming out your ears, man."

Becket said, "Use an enzyme-tipped dart?"

Ben nodded. "Nothing else would even have made them itch."

Potter said, "You boys can blow off the gas, if you want to. It's me for that little old weed." He turned to look over the three girls and said, "Anybody want to come along?"

Two of the three tall girls looked pointedly away from Potter.

The third idly shifted her gun so it aimed directly at him. She toyed with the trigger mechanism.

Potter jumped aside. There was a *puff*, and something whined past him.

Potter yelled, "Becket, did you see that? Did you? I got something coming for that!"

Becket turned to look at the girl and said, "Don't waste ammunition." He glanced back at Ben. "Where is everybody?"

"Smoking the weed."

Becket winced. "All of them?"

"All but Gina."

Becket scowled. "We've *got* to get this place planted."

"Sure," said Ben agreeably.

"Damn it," said Becket, "it's all right to smoke that stuff *if they do their work*. Who's in charge here now?"

"What do you mean?" said Ben. "Muller's conscious. He's colony administrator. He isn't dead, or disabled under the terms of the Code."

Potter said, "Is that little blond doctor on the weed?"

Becket was looking over the weeds flourishing in the field. "This has got to be planted," he said. "Haven't you done anything to get the dozer fixed?"

Ben said grimly, "Maybe I didn't get it across to you. I'll try again."

Potter said, "Why, he's trying to make you look like a fool, Becket."

Ben said, "Excuse me just a minute, Becket." He turned and walked over toward Potter, who raised his gun and said, grinning, "Walk easy, Boy. I might just decide to put a little enzyme in your blood, Boy. How you think you'd like that?"

The girl who had fired the dart toward Potter snapped back the bolt and swung up her gun.

Potter whirled, his own gun coming up.

Ben sprang forward, and struck Potter on the chin. As Potter tried to struggle, Ben jerked the gun away from him, smashed the butt into his head, and stepped back. Potter collapsed on the ground.

Ben looked at the girl who had raised her gun and distracted Potter. "Thanks."

The girl said, "Is he dead?"

Ben felt Potter's pulse. "No."

"Then," said the girl, "it isn't over yet."

Ben frowned and walked back to Becket. "I was saying," said Ben, "Muller is still in control of his senses. They all are. Are you asking me why I don't *make* them put down the weed, get up, and do what they're supposed to?"

Becket frowned, but didn't answer for a moment.

Ben said, "I know, seeing this mess comes as a shock. I'll do anything I can to straighten it out. You just tell me, though, *what am I going to do?*"

Becket looked around at the half-crushed cabins, and the weeds in the fields. He said, "You can't talk sense with them?"

"Oh, they'll talk sense. They just won't *do* anything."

"Well, why not take the weed away from them?"

"Because they can walk north, south, east, or west, and get more anytime they feel like it. There are nine of them and one of me. Figure it out."

Becket shook his head. "I see what you mean. I'm sorry I jumped on you. But I can tell you one thing. We're going to have to figure something out, and soon." He motioned to the rest of his party. "Let's go." He walked beside Ben on the way back. As the party split up on approaching the cabins, Ben saw Gina watching him from the door of the communications shack. She cupped her hands and called out:

"The set's working. West Three is on the screen."

The face on the screen was that of a man with a heavy beard, narrowed eyes, and a carefully blank expression. He said roughly, "What do you want?"

Ben stared at him for an instant, then said, "Well, a bunch of rollers went through here several days ago, and knocked out our transmitter—"

"Working now, ain't it?"

"Yes," Ben said, "it is, but—"

"Then what do you want?"

Ben could feel pressure building up, as if his head were about to explode. He leaned forward and said slowly and distinctly, "We would like to *use* it."

The man stared back at him, then his bristly face split into a gap-toothed grin. "New here, are you?"

"We haven't been here a month yet."

"Hm-m-m." The man turned away. They could hear his voice as he asked. "How does their bearing check?"

Another voice said, "It fits with what they say. But they could be a lot closer, using a damp-down on the beam power."

"I don't figure them carrying that much equipment around with them." The bearded man turned around. "Just landed, eh? Are these 'rollers' you talk about pretty big, tuck their tails under their heads and roll along giving a shove with their feet every now and then?"

"That's it," said Ben.

"Tell me something," said the bearded man. "How do they see so they never hit a tree?"

Ben blinked. "I don't know."

"You wouldn't believe it, but we had a man killed deciding that question. They can see because their eyes stick out on stalks, like a snail's. Whether it's true, I don't know; but that's it, we've decided. You want to kind of decide things, so in the middle of winter, when the snow's six feet deep outside, and the wind's been blowing steady for three weeks, you won't have too many unsettled questions laying around."

The possibilities this comment seemed to open up left Ben speechless for a moment. He swallowed and nodded.

"Another thing. How many are there in your party?"

"Eighteen," said Ben. "There were twenty, but two of the women got sick just after we landed, and died."

"Funny," said the bearded man, "the women generally die in the winter. Late winter."

"Oh."

"Well," he said, "how many of these eighteen are boobs?"

Ben leaned toward the screen and cupped his ear. "What? I didn't hear you."

"How many of these eighteen are boobs? You know, jerks, deadheads. Fools."

Ben blinked. "Well—" He thought a moment. "One, maybe."

"Then you're in heaven and don't know it. All right, tell me this. How many of your people are absolutely, one-hundred per cent trustworthy?"

Ben thought a moment. "Maybe eight."

"Then you've got too big a proportion of people you can't trust. Kill the rest."

Ben clenched his hands. "Wait a minute."

The bearded man leaned forward and said earnestly, "You kill them, or they will kill you and themselves both. We aren't on the home planet. You're still on ship rations, so you don't know what you're up against yet. You think you plant your seed and work your crop and harvest your crop and the horn of plenty runs over. You think you'll do your work and get your pay. That isn't how it goes.

"The first year we were here, we felled, cleared, burned, plowed, planted, and raised a fine crop. A little animal no bigger than your hand came out of the forest by the tens of thousands one night, while we were sitting around telling each other what a fine new life we were building here, and these little animals stripped every grain of corn off almost every ear in the field, and we sat there and heard the corn rustle and never knew anything was going on until it dawned on somebody that there wasn't any wind. Don't plant corn. Plant potatoes."

Ben shut his eyes a minute. "We planned to put in a lot of corn."

"Put in a lot of potatoes instead."

"We don't have that many."

The bearded man shrugged. "Tough. Leave word with the supply ship next time it comes."

Ben turned aside and glanced at Gina for a moment. In that moment, Ben saw Gina as sturdy, sound, and hard-working. This moment passed in a flash; when it was gone, Ben was left with the solid impression that he could *rely* on Gina. A part of Ben's mind that had clung with concern to Dr. Forbes let go for that moment, much as Ben would have let go of a clump of poison ivy.

The bearded man was looking at him. "*We* didn't do it right," he said. "*We* did it slow and messy. We had a woman liked to make men jealous of each other. Took us almost a year to get rid of her. It's a plain miracle we didn't all kill each other off first. Then we had a man wouldn't pull his own weight. We lugged *him* along for a year-and-a-half. He had an accident through sheer carelessness, and then it was up to us to give him a blood transfusion. We had the equipment. But we didn't do it. We needed the blood ourselves. That wasn't all, either. We even had one that figured he'd be king and we'd work for him. He had a talent for it, I'll admit that. It took us three weeks to evolve through that mess, and when the end came, we had a grand finale that wakes me up with the shakes even yet."

He looked at Ben shrewdly. "You see what I mean, boy. Don't go through all that. Do it fast. Do it neat. And don't put it off either. I've thought this over a lot, now that it's too late for us to do it. I think the thing to do is to get the lot of them drunk some night, and add a little something to the liquor. Or, you could set up a night guard that incidentally looks in on everybody, now and then as they sleep. Naturally, none of *them* is going to volunteer for night guard. When they get used to the routine, they won't even wake up when you look in. Then some dark night, bash their brains in while they sleep. Or—"

He went on this way detailing with relish plan after plan, while Ben's thoughts grew numb and his brain froze over. Ben heard someone move behind him, and glanced around.

Becket was staring open-mouthed looking at the screen. He tore his gaze away and looked at Ben.

"Potter's smoking the weed," he said. "With Dr. Forbes."

Ben shook his head wearily.

Becket said, "I see what you mean about their being logical. She almost convinced me she was sane and I am crazy."

Ben nodded, and started to turn away.

Becket cleared his throat unhappily. He said, "She said to tell you—if you don't come to see her soon, she'll make her dream with Potter."

Ben shut his eyes and stood perfectly still.

"She said," Becket went on unhappily, "that in her dream, she can call him Ben, and never know the difference."

Something seemed to rise up inside of Ben, and hammer to be let loose. When it died away, he heard himself say, in a voice that sounded calm, "Well, I can't stop her."

"She's going to kill herself with that weed," said Becket miserably. "She's skin and bones."

"All she's got to do is put the weed down, open some concentrate, and work her jaws."

"But, Ben—" cried Becket.

Ben glanced around and saw that Gina was crying. For some reason, this made him mad. "Listen," he said to Becket, "when she started on that stuff it turned me inside out. The way she talked and acted, I could see the whole sequence of events stretched out into the future. We aren't at the end yet. You and I are going to suffer the agonies of hell while she floats around in dreamland. It's going to take *time*.

"But *she* won't suffer," said Ben angrily. "You tell me. You've looked at her face. Is she in any pain?"

Becket drew a deep shuddering breath. "No," he said finally. "But we've got to *do* something!"

"You're perfectly free to think on it," said Ben. "If you think of any way we can nurse ten grown-up babies through spring, summer, fall, and winter and still have time to do the work we've got to do, you let me know."

From Becket's expression, it was plain that he was thinking hard.

Ben glanced at the screen and saw that the bearded man was watching with a puzzled intentness. "Well," he said, and nodded his head wisely, "it sounds like you have your troubles. But there'll be more. And you're too far away to count on anyone but yourself. You just remember what I—" He stopped and said, in a different tone of voice, "But you won't. It isn't human nature."

"No," said Ben wearily. "We won't. But then, we won't *have* to."

When the supply rocket landed next spring, the crew found eight healthy men and women, three babies, and on the edge of the clearing, ten neat graves with flowers growing around them.

As the ship lifted after unloading its supplies, one of the crewmen turned and said to another, "It seldom fails. You come back after the first winter, and there's only half the people left. It's like a sieve. Some get through, and some don't. But what happens?"

"Who knows? They don't talk about it much. All I know is, *I* don't want to be a pioneer."

"No, nor me either."

They shook hands on it. Fervently.

MATING PROBLEMS

Bart leaned his weight against the length of tough vine while Ed slid the pole under it again and heaved up. There was a snapping, popping sound as a few more tendrils parted. Ed grunted, straightened up, mopped his neck and forehead.

"Rest a minute."

Bart nodded, and the two men stood beside the vine, breathing hard. Across the clearing from them was an L-shaped row of log cabins. Three cabins near the middle of the L were fire-blackened on the side facing the clearing. The center cabin had its door charred through, and its roof burnt partway off. In the field, a little beyond the burned group of cabins, stood a big red dozer. The protective coating on the side of the dozer toward the forest was blistered and peeling.

Bart saw this without really being aware of it. He even glanced over the third of the three cabins without noticing the shape in lighter brown outlined against the charred black. A stranger would have been struck by this shape, which looked like a life-sized, child's drawing of a woman. The legs and trunk were much lighter than the black wood, with a darker outline of coat and skirt, and a faint, arm-length blur reaching toward the blackened cabin door. Bart was used to this, and vaguely noticed it only when Ed said, "I wonder how they'll make out?"

Bart looked around, noticed a little group of men around and under the dozer, and two others slowly walking back from the far end of the field, where there was a row of low rectangular mounds with fresh evergreen boughs laid on them like flowers. Opposite the cabins was a thing that Bart looked at only briefly. He glanced at Ed, and realized that was what Ed was looking at. Ordinarily, Bart avoided the sight of this thing, but he looked at it now.

Across from the cabins, looking unreal and foreign against the trees, was a tall, silvery cylinder about fifteen feet through the base, and tapering to a slender rod at the top. Up the side of this cylinder, and in a ring around the top third of it were big pink letters spelling out:

HI THERE! III

At the base of the cylinder, looking up at it, were three men. Two were carrying a long rough ladder made of poles. The other had a coil of rope and a crowbar.

Bart looked away from the *Hi There! III*, and spat on the bare dirt. He said, "If you want the truth, Ed, they've got about as much chance to get in there with that crowbar, as you and I have to cultivate this field with our fingernails."

"I'll bet there's a lot of stuff in there, if we *could* get it open."

"Sure," said Bart. "As I said the middle of last winter."

Ed looked uncomfortable. Bart said, "We could have chopped him out of the bush in a day, if we'd all worked at it. While the body was intact, we could have held his hands to the lockplate, opened that ship's hatch, and now we'd have it done and over with."

"We had to bury the women."

"Will you kindly tell me why we couldn't have waited a day longer?"

Ed's eyes glinted. He said evenly, "My Nan had a hard life here."

Bart shut his eyes a moment. He said carefully, "I know that, Ed. She was a hard-working woman."

"She was. A good woman."

"That's right."

"It is."

"But we could have waited one day."

"It wouldn't have shown respect. If heavy snow came it might have been spring before we—"

A throaty female call interrupted them.

They looked around. A tall shapely woman wearing a thin dress stood away from the end cabin and called, "*Sup-per!* Come and get it, boys!"

She repeated this call several times. Bart and Ed glanced at each other. Bart thought of the conversation just past, and said, "I'm sorry, Ed. I don't know how I got onto that again."

Ed's face creased into a slow smile. "That's all right. You may be right, for all I know. I just couldn't have done it that way, that's all."

They started across the field, the raw earth lumpy underfoot. In front of them the woman who had called turned and started back toward the cabin. It would have required great preoccupation not to see that the dress she was wearing tightly molded her figure. This wasn't ideal in a colony where four men had lost their wives in the last six months; but then, this was just one of her ways of stirring up trouble.

Ed squinted at the woman, and growled, "Maybe I shouldn't say it, seeing I'm his brother, but it seems to me Sam could have found a better wife to bring out here than her."

Bart nodded. "If you could persuade him to tone her down a little, it would be a big help."

Ed grunted. "I've tried to warn him what's going to happen. Look what I got for my pains." He put his finger to his lip, to show a badly chipped front tooth.

Bart shook his head. They walked in silence to the cabin, and pushed open the door.

A long table was set up inside the cabin, and two attractive, plainly-dressed women with severe facial expressions were putting stewed meat and potatoes on the table. A tall well-built man had his back turned and was laughing and talking to Sam's wife, who said, "That's simply fascinating, Lonny. You tell me the rest after supper, now."

Ed shut the door hard, and Lonny turned around. He was about six feet tall, and had wavy black hair which he managed to trim short and neat. He was clean-shaven, and smiled with a flash of white teeth.

Ed said, "Sam's coming."

"That so?" said Lonny. He laughed and looked at Sam's wife, who smiled.

Bart said, "Any news?"

Lonny glanced at Bart, and said, "Oh, on the uniwave?"

Bart nodded, and ladled some of the steaming hot stew into his bowl.

Lonny said, "I was just telling Linda. We've got visitors coming. Women."

Bart spilled some of the stew. "Women?"

"Yeah."

The door opened and several bearded, tired-looking men filed in. One was a powerfully-built man with a pugnacious look. Sam's wife gave a little throaty cry as he came in. He strode over to her with a possessive look, and bent to kiss her. She tilted her head back, and leaned close to him. The room was silent as they kissed. Bart glanced around and saw that every male eye in the room except his own was fixed on this kiss.

The door came open again, and some more men came in. These were the three from the ship. They were talking as they came in, but stopped as they saw Sam and his wife. In the silence that followed their closing of the door, the kiss went on. One of the men who'd come in glanced around and grinned. "Why so quiet? This a library or something. Hey, Lonny, what's the news?"

Lonny turned around, his face flat and pale.

Sam's wife was now making little noises in her throat. One of the other women stamped her foot, set a tray down hard, and went through an inner door to the other room of the cabin. As she went out, she slammed the door behind her.

The kiss was now gradually starting to break up. The grand finale came as Linda broke away from Sam, her gaze fixed on his, lips tremulous, and a promise plain and clear in every motion. In just a moment now, she would give a shaky half-moan, half-sigh, then turn away and leave the room. Bart was waiting for this moment. So were the rest of the men in the room. Just before it came, Bart said clearly, "Lonny says we're getting some visitors—a bunch of new *women*."

The men at the table and standing by the door blinked and glanced at Bart. Bart was watching Linda, and saw her eyes narrow. Bart grinned and said, "You said that, didn't you, Lonny? About the women?"

Lonny took a deep breath. "Yeah."

Every male in the room except Bart and Sam was now watching

Lonny, who glanced down frowning at his hands clenched white-knuckled at the edge of the table. Bart was still watching Sam's wife, who cast a venomous glance at him, and went out, closing the door a little harder than usual. Sam blinked, then turned around with a puzzled look.

Somebody said, "Snap out of it, Lonny. What's this about women coming? Is that the truth?"

Lonny nodded.

There was an eager silence, and Lonny said, "It isn't what you think. You know what ship they're coming on?"

"No. It's not time yet for the supply ship."

Lonny said bitterly, "Well, then, brace yourself. They're coming on the *Hi There! IV.*"

There was a moment of silence. In this silence, there went through Bart's mind the whole chain of events that had come about after the *Hi There! III* had come down. He remembered the surprise of the colony as the shining space yacht set down during the first real flurries of winter. He remembered the eagerness with which everyone greeted the stranger. After all, he would have news. Anything seemed welcome that would vary the dull monotony of winter. Bart could still remember the big hatch swinging open and the stranger floating out on a fair-sized dish-shaped grav-skimmer, glancing down and aiming a glittering contraption with a multitude of knobs and lenses at them, and saying:

"Stay just like that, there. That's it. Ah." There was a clicking and a flashing, then the skimmer drifted down to a little above their level. The stranger, nattily dressed, leaned over the side. "Any sport round-about?"

"Sport?" said someone, blank-faced.

"Sport. Hunting. Fishing. You know."

Bart said, "You're a little late. Most of the meat animals on this planet either hibernate or go south for the winter. You'd better leave the fish alone. We lost a man eating fish when we first got here."

The visitor's eyebrows climbed. "Really?"

"Yes. Some of the fish are poisonous. We don't know which are and which aren't."

"Is that so? Fascinating." He glanced away, then looked back. "Do you bury your people?"

"What?"

"When they die. Do you bury them?"

Bart frowned. "Of course. Why?"

"Where's this chap buried? The one who ate the fish."

Bart glanced across to the far edge of the field, where snow was heaped on the arms of a rough wooden cross.

The visitor followed Bart's gaze. "Oh, yes. Fine." He raised his complexity of knobs and multiple lenses. Snap! Whir. "Splendid," he said. He glanced at Bart. "Any more graves handy?"

"No," said Bart.

"Do you have any scenery? Anything worth looking at?"

Bart didn't say anything for a moment, and the visitor said, "Well, I'll look around. Don't let me keep you." The skimmer rose and paused. The lenses swung across the clearing toward the cabins. Snap! Whir. Snap! Whir. Snap! Whir. The skimmer swung off toward the south and vanished over the trees. The crowd remained standing at the base of the ship. Up above, the big hatch swung silently shut.

Someone turned to Bart. "Too bad you didn't tell him the fish were good to eat."

Before the coming of the *Hi There! III*, Bart could remember that the colony had been troubled with grudges, misunderstandings, poor crops, lean hunts, insects, wild animals, a lack of tools, equipment and conveniences, and all the things that plague the first isolated colonies on new worlds. But they had never before felt quite the way they felt after the *Hi There! III* came.

This chain of thought ran on through Bart's head as he looked at Lonny and the other silent men around the table. One of them said thickly, "Who's on the *Hi There! IV*?"

Lonny said, "I don't know if I got the name right. I think it was Mrs. Sidney Siddleigh-Varnov. That would be his wife . . . I mean widow. And her three daughters."

"When are they coming?"

"Tonight."

Bart said, "Did you talk to her yourself?"

"No. Brewster at South Two called me up. They came down there yesterday. The woman wanted to know what happened to her husband. Brewster was sympathetic, at first. He told her her husband had landed here. When he tried to tell her what happened later, she got mad. Brewster said she instructed him to inform us that she was coming here immediately and would demand a satisfactory explanation. I think that was how it was worded."

A noise of disgust went around the table.

Bart said, "Well, let's eat."

After supper, Bart and Ed went back across the field to the root. The sun had set, but it was still light. Ed picked up his pole and slid it under the root. Bart took hold of the length of vine. They heaved. There was a light snapping noise, like the ripping of cloth. They looked at each other.

Bart said, "It's rooted again."

Ed nodded. "I wish we had the dozer going. The dozer could dig this out in no time now."

They heaved, and pried. Occasionally, there was the loud snap and pop of sizable rootlets parting. When they could get no further prying at it, they dug. Finally they stopped to rest.

Ed said, "At least, *he* came in the winter."

Bart blinked, then saw that Ed was looking toward the three men working on the *Hi There! III.*

"Yeah."

"Then," said Ed, "at least we had our work done. She's going to get here just when we've *got* to put everything we've got into our work. Otherwise, we starve this winter."

Bart nodded. "But I will bet we *don't* get much work done while she's here."

Ed glanced down at the root, and said stubbornly, "We're going to get this out."

Bart glanced down at the thing and nodded. He looked up at the chopped-off dead vine dangling overhead. It was thick and tough-looking, just as the vine attached to the live root was thick and tough. Bart noticed a trace of green on the root. "We aren't going to have much time to do it. That thing is putting out shoots already."

"We can't let it get into its second year!"

"I know." He glanced at Ed. "You want to work all night? We can get it out by morning."

Ed nodded. They built a small fire not far away, piled up plenty of extra wood to have on hand, and went on working. Gradually, it got dark.

It was late at night when they came to a place where the root had a head-sized bulge in it, then narrowed down and divided into two parts, each no bigger than a man's thumb.

"Ahh," said Bart, "here we are." He felt along the roots and carefully dug away the dirt around them. He tugged carefully, then dug some more. He felt Ed's hand on his shoulder. The hand tightened. Bart stood still.

Ed growled, "Wind's shifted. Listen."

Bart straightened up slowly. There was a light breeze on his face, from the direction of the cabins. He heard a low masculine voice, and a higher-pitched woman's voice. The sounds of the woman's voice reached him distinctly, "Lonny, dear, what if Sam should wake up?"

Ed swore in a strangled voice, and started to move forward. Bart grabbed his arm. "Wait a minute. She's going to make trouble no matter what we do. If we stop her tonight, we'll have trouble tomorrow night. But if we get this root out now, we're through with it. If we don't there'll be no end of trouble."

"She's my brother's wife."

Bart groaned. "Yes, but look, Ed, you can't *stop* her. We *can* stop this root."

"I've got to do it. Let go my arm."

Bart let go. Ed disappeared into the darkness.

Bart swallowed. He bent down and felt the root. He took a deep breath, and worked slowly. The root was only the thickness of his thumb, but it remained that way as he dug. He tugged at it gently, but it stayed firm.

From across the field as he worked came a low giggling. Then there was a gruff voice and a sort of indrawn scream. Next came a thudding and grunting noise. Bart listened to it for a while, then went back to work on the root. After a while, there was a louder thud, and he heard Ed's voice saying what sounded like, "You stay right here."

"Good," thought Bart. He consoled himself that at least Ed had won. Not that he could see what good it would do. He was thinking this several minutes later, when there was a thunderous roar, a blaze of light, and a slim silver shape dropped toward the clearing.

Bart jumped out of the hole, and dove into the nearby forest. It had suddenly occurred to him that the ship might land right on top of him. But when he looked around, he saw that it had settled farther down the field. The outside of the ship was a blaze of floodlights. Bart saw the words *Hi There! IV.* Then he saw something else.

The ship's lights lit brightly the cabins and the people staring out. They also lit Ed, his face bruised and his clothing torn. In addition, the light lit Sam's wife, who was standing as if frozen in a torn and fairly skimpy nightdress.

The door of Sam's cabin came open. Sam came out and glanced around. "Linda! Where are you? *Linda!*"

Sam stopped, looking at Ed with his face bruised, and Linda in her nightdress. Next, Sam looked at the people in the doorways, looking at Linda and Ed. Sam stepped back into the cabin and came out with a wrench in one hand. He walked steadily toward Linda and Ed.

Linda said, "Sam, it isn't—" Her voice trailed off, then she tried again. "Sam, dearest . . . you don't . . . understand."

Ed didn't say anything, but merely looked grim as his brother came toward them.

Bart fought off a sense of paralysis and got to his feet. He shouted, "It wasn't Ed, Sam! Look at his face! He just fought for you! *It wasn't Ed!*"

This had no more visible effect on Sam than shouting at a tornado would have had.

Bart started to run, then he saw something else.

At the door of Lonny's cabin, at the far end of the L-shaped row of cabins, Lonny was looking out, one hand on the door frame. Lonny's face was bruised, with one eye swollen shut and the other half-shut. His cheek was cut, and his nose bloody.

Sam stopped, looking from Lonny to Ed. Suddenly, he said, "Now I see it!" He threw down the wrench.

There was a sharp *whack*, the noise from a motion so fast Bart missed it. Then Linda was stretched out flat on the ground. Sam bent down, gripped her roughly, and threw her over his shoulder like a sack of grain. He started back to his cabin.

Ed bent over and picked up the wrench. He looked around uncertainly, then glanced at the ship. Bart glanced at the ship. The hatch was open, the four women were staring out. Bart started toward them, thinking this was something else that might as well be gotten out of the way as quickly as possible. Ed came along, and several other men apparently had the same idea.

The women stared out the hatch as if paralyzed. Suddenly one of them said, "Don't . . . don't you come near us! Keep back!"

Slam! The hatch was shut.

Bart looked at Ed, then suddenly laughed. "Something tells me they don't think we treat women very well on this planet."

Together, the two men went back to digging out the root. By six o'clock in the morning, they were exhausted, but they had dug up the root. They piled the last remaining sticks on the coals, and hunched close to the fire as the sticks caught with little spurts of flame.

Ed said, "Now what? Carry it off into the forest?"

"Well," said Bart, "if we can, we want to fix it so it stays fixed. No matter how far we carry it, it'll take root where we set it down, and go to seed. Some of the seeds will scatter, some will root, and we may have this all over again."

There were footsteps behind them, and they turned around. Sam was standing there. He smiled, and said, "I'm sorry, Ed. You tried to tell me."

Ed said, "That's all right."

"I'm sorry about your tooth. I shouldn't have hit my own brother."

"Can't be helped. You have to do what you think's right."

Bart was trying to understand Sam's cheerful look. As far as Bart could see, Sam should look anything but cheerful.

Ed said, "About Linda, Sam—"

Sam said, "She'll be all right. If she tries anything again, I'll brain her. She knows it."

Ed nodded. Bart stared into the fire. Sam said, "You fellows been working pretty hard. Thought I'd come out to help."

Ed said, "We got it dug up. We're figuring what to do with it."

"Burn it?" said Sam. "No, I see that's no good. The first warmth would set it going, same as a heavy rain."

Ed nodded. "We can't chop into its roots, either. That'd start it, too."

Bart said, "If we could sling a rope over a high limb and haul it up into a tree, could it root from there?"

"It'd send stalks down," said Ed. "The thing is, we should have gotten it last fall. Then we could have chopped it up during the cold weather, and burned it a piece at a time."

"Well, we've got to think of something."

Ed said, "Only, we've got to do it soon. See those buds?"

In the gray light of dawn, it was evident that the green buds were swelling. The three men hunched around the thing, considering where to go. Their thoughts were interrupted by a loud *clang*.

The hatch of *Hi There! IV* was opened out. A rather handsome woman in her late thirties looked out, with a couple of girls of eighteen or nineteen peering out behind her. The woman's nose looked pinched. She said, "I am going to lift ship and set down in a clearing to the north of here. I don't want my girls exposed to such—indecency—as they were forced to witness last night. But you are going to explain to me very clearly and fully, precisely what happened to my husband. I have a mobile turret on board this yacht. There may be no law on this planet, but I shall see to it that you—animals—pay your legal debts in full."

The hatch slammed shut. Bart, Ed, and Sam glanced at each other. They carried the root into the woods, where they watched the take-off.

Ed said angrily, "A mobile turret."

Sam said, "With her interfering we'll *never* get our work done. Almost got the dozer fixed, too."

Bart said, "About where to put this root, now."

The three of them looked at each other. A little glint seemed to pass from eye to eye.

Ed said, "There's only one clearing to the north of here that I know of. That's got a stream running through it. Where they tried to start a colony once before."

"I know the place."

They chopped down some saplings, made a rough frame, got strips of hide to bind it together, and put the big root on it. Then they started out through the woods.

When they were almost at the clearing, they paused to peer through some bushes on a low hill overlooking the clearing. The ship was near a gully that had a stream trickling along the bottom of it now, and when the spring rains came would be a roaring river.

Sam said, "Looks like she wanted to stock up on water."

Ed said, "If we sneak down that gully, what's the chance she'll see us?"

Bart nodded. "Good idea. I'll go out and distract them. Suppose you work around out of sight, and I give you fifteen minutes to get to the gully. Then I'll go out and talk to them, and you whistle like a nightbird when you get the thing in place."

"All right," said Ed. "But when we whistle, run! When this root feels the water, it'll think the spring rains have come for sure."

Bart nodded. "Don't worry. I'll run, all right."

He waited fifteen minutes after the others had left, then got up, and went well to his right so he wouldn't get caught between ship and gully when the root was set down. He dropped into the gully, stepped across the water, climbed out, and started toward the ship.

The woman looked out the hatch, pinch-nosed. Various attractive girls peered out behind her. Now that there seemed to be no danger they had a bold look Bart found irritating. None of them said anything, but they all looked him over from head to foot, as if he were a display in a window.

Bart looked at the woman. "I'd like to tell you what happened to your husband."

She looked at him coldly, "It's fortunate for you that you've decided to see reason. I am not bluffing when I say that I have a turret."

"In the ship with you?"

"In the ship with me. Now get on with your explanations."

"Your husband landed here," said Bart, "around the beginning of winter. He took a great number of what I suppose were photographs with some kind of elaborate camera. We warned him about certain dangers on the planet. We tried to tell him this isn't Earth. But your husband was not exactly approachable, and he didn't come to us for advice about what to avoid. Possibly all his equipment gave him a false sense of security. He blundered into a sawtooth plant—"

"A what?"

"Sawtooth plant. It has a spray of long wiry stalks radiating from a large, urn-like cup in the center. These stalks have big thorns, that angle sharply back toward the cup. If you get caught in it and struggle, you no sooner get free of one set of thorns on stalks than you're caught in another—and closer to the cup. The only way to get loose from the thorns is to move forward. Then if you try to pull back, they catch you again. Eventually, you end up in the cup. The cup secretes a digestive fluid. The plant is carnivorous."

The woman turned pale. "Did Sidney—?"

"He got in it. He put up quite a struggle."

"And you didn't help him?"

"He had a sort of cylinder," said Bart. "A fusion pistol, I think it's called. We shouted to him to stand still. It was winter, you see, and the plant wasn't active. If he had stood still, he'd have been all right. But instead, he pulled out this gun and tried to fight the plant. He was like a man caught in a barbed-wire fence who tries to shoot his way free. In the process, he burned away part of the plant; but his aim was a little off, and he also set three of our cabins on fire, killed two of our women outright, and burned another so badly she died later. One of the women he killed was a doctor. Because of her death and the loss of medicines in the fire, we couldn't care properly for another woman who got sick. She died, too."

"That's dreadful. What—Where is Sid now?"

"In the plant."

The woman's hand rose to her mouth. "You mean, you *left* him there?"

"Personally," said Bart, "I was in favor of getting him out. The rest of the men didn't go along. We buried the women, and then a blizzard came along and covered everything up. By spring, we were too worn out to go down and wrestle the sawtooth plant for him. Besides, we had other work to do."

"Poor Sidney. Did he—" She frowned. "Just a moment, now. You say the plant was inactive. In that event, it might entangle a person, but it could hardly kill him."

"No," said Bart. "One of us shot him with an enzyme-tipped dart before he burned us all to a crisp."

"You *shot* him? But he didn't kill those people intentionally. He would have paid for every bit of damage. Gladly."

Bart took a deep breath. "Try and tell that to a man who's just seen his wife burned alive. Your husband was still letting out blasts from that gun. He *had* to be stopped."

The woman's nostrils grew pinched again. "I can't save him now," she said, "but I certainly intend to see to it that he has a decent funeral, at least. You are going to get him out of that dreadful plant, and you will construct a—a—"

"Casket," said Bart in disgust. "Not right now, we won't. We have to cultivate, plant, clear, cut wood, hunt—"

"You will do what I say first. Then you can do whatever you want."

"It will be too late, then. We have to do it in season, or it's no good. Then we'll starve."

"That's unfortunate. You shouldn't have killed my husband."

There was a clear warbling note. A thin tendril snaked up over the bank of the gully, and started to cast around in various directions.

Bart said sharply, "Do you have plenty of food and water in there, and a good supply of air?"

The woman looked startled. "Of course. What—"

"Lock the hatch!" yelled Bart. He turned and sprinted. He ran till he was out of breath. He leaned against a tree till he recovered, then he went to find Ed and Sam, and the three of them watched from a low hill.

Where the middle of the clearing had been was a low jungle of broad green leaves. There was a higher mound in the center, with long stalks swinging slowly around from the top of it, groping for attachment. From under this mound came a blast of dirt and flame. The mound strained upward and dropped back. There was a loud roar. Big leaves blew away to show a net of tangled vines gripping the *Hi There! IV*. In a blaze of light, the vines nearest the center withered away. Those further out began to glow red, smoke, and burst into flame.

The three men watched intently.

The stalks on top of the mound dove to the ground in long arcs. New tendrils rose from the foliage on all sides and twined around the ship. The ship heaved and dropped back. Big leaves blew away. New tendrils snaked in and grew thick. There was a series of short blasts from the ship. The roar of the rockets and whine of the gravitors alternated with the sizzle and pop of roasting vegetation. Through clouds of steam and smoke the three men could see a fist of big vines gripping the middle and upper sections of the ship.

Ed said, "She may or may not kill it. But I doubt it'll have much strength left to make seed."

"What's more," said Bart, "since that vine is wound around the hatch, we should be able to work in peace for a while."

Sam nodded. "We'll come back later on. See how things are. I imagine a few weeks fighting that vine will tame them women down some."

Bart was checking the cargo list with a crewman from a supply ship later on that year. The crewman was looking around with an expression of puzzlement. "Say," he said, "I was sorry to hear about your—your bad luck last winter. But don't I see some new women here that weren't here before?"

"Volunteers," said Bart. "They came out to join us."

The crewman looked as if he were seeing a river that flowed uphill. He said weakly. "How did you manage that?"

"Well," said Bart, "we had two problems. Either one alone was too tough for us. They both had to be settled fast, like the problem of two mad dogs coming at you from opposite directions."

"Yeah? What did you do?"

"We got out from in between," said Bart. "We combined them. Then they settled each other."

HUNGER

Able Andrews stepped out of the forest into the clearing. He set down the heavy sack of seed potatoes, and, after ten days of life-or-death vigilance, glanced with relief around the settlement that for four years had been his home on this brutal world.

Ahead of him, through the intervals in the row of cabins that lined the edge of the clearing, he could see the sunlit, partly-plowed field. He could hear, far to his left, the low rumble that meant that Bart Henderson had somehow, single-handed, fixed the dozer. Now they could plow, cultivate, haul timber and saw up firewood. A wail from a nearby cabin gave proof that his sister's eleven-month-old son had survived his absence, and that Bart had somehow managed to care for the boy while preoccupied with the dozer. And this thought brought back the memory that had been mercifully blotted out by his cat-and-mouse existence in the forest.

To Able's right, he could see part of the double row of rough crosses and stars that marked the low fresh mounds of dirt, all in line with the other older mounds of dirt that stretched across the width of the field to the far side. With sledgehammer force came mental pictures of the endless digging, carrying out of bodies, prying at rocks, chopping at roots, and shoveling back of dirt, and this all blended into one agony with the sickness, the howling wind, the deep drifting snow, and the cold that couldn't be kept out.

Able shut his eyes, then forced himself to look straight ahead at the field, and think of the summer ahead, when they had to do what they could before winter settled in again. He forced himself not to think of all they'd expected to accomplish by now, when actually they were reduced to two grown men, an infant, and a long double row of mounds of dirt.

Able picked up the sack of precious seed potatoes, and started toward the gap between two of the cabins. If they could do well enough with these potatoes and their other crops, they'd have something to offer when fall came. They could strike a bargain, and join up with another settlement where young Bobby could be raised decently—

It was then, while he struggled to patch together a new plan that, as Able's angle of vision shifted, he saw the pool of swamplike useless muck spreading out from the far edge of the clearing, reaching well out into the field to make a heavy blot where the water stood in puddles.

"Merciful God," said Able.

Another step showed him, further to the left, a glint of bluish metal where there should have been trees.

Able's dart gun, which had been slung at his shoulder, abruptly was in his hands.

Above the approaching rumble of the dozer, and the crying of the baby, came a man's unfamiliar voice, carrying a well-developed grown-up whine which Able hadn't heard since he'd left civilization. The words, sloppily formed, were spoken with a strange emphasis, so that all Able could make out was the final, "I *won't!*"

A shrill female voice, edged with hysteria, cried, "If *you* won't, I *will!*"

Able glanced swiftly around. For an instant, he thought he must somehow have reached the wrong settlement. But there to the right was the trail to the river, and beside it, the same greenberry bush he'd tended for years. There on the bottom log of the cabin nearby was the same light-brown, arrow-pointed slash, where his foot had slipped while he was chopping, and he'd narrowly escaped losing the foot. Overhead were the broad leaves of the staplenut tree that always lashed the roof of his cabin in a windstorm, and in the distance, over the trees straight ahead, was the familiar pale-blue summit of Carraboon Peak.

This was the settlement, all right. But these were the wrong voices.

He picked up the sack, slipped back to the edge of the clearing, and, gun partly raised, watched the weathered orange bulk of the dozer detour the soggy section, and pass by on the far side of the field.

From somewhere came a low feminine murmur, all but drowned out by the clank and rumble as the dozer, hidden by a cabin, crossed the field, then came into view again on the near side.

The worn canvas side-curtains neatly strapped up, the dozer ground past with Bart Henderson in the cab, leaning back to watch the big plows smoothly turn over the soil.

Able lowered his gun, sucked in his breath, and gave a whistle that began high, shrill, and penetrating, then wavered, and very gradually descended by eerie stages.

The dozer stopped with a clank.

There was the thud of feet hitting the ground, then silence.

Able watched alertly.

A slender figure, gun in hand, slipped around a corner of a cabin, to vanish in a clump of brush.

In a low voice, Able called, *"Bart."*

"Abe!"

"Over here."

The slender figure stepped out in the open, glanced around, then, grinning, walked swiftly closer.

"Abe, you son-of-a-gun! You whistled like a wire bird?"

"I wanted to get your attention without going out in the open. Listen—"

Bart saw the sack. "What did you get?"

Able frowned, then bent to undo the thong at the neck of the sack.

"Ah," said Bart, crouching to look over the seed potatoes. "You did well."

From somewhere, Able could hear a murmur of voices.

Bart stood up and grinned. "That's better than grinding up staplenut meats and filtering the meal a dozen times to get the sting out. Or guarding the cornfield day and night to keep away the pests. Boy, I'm glad you made it! I was afraid you were finished."

"Yeah," said Able, frowning. "But, listen—"

"How were things at Six?"

Able blinked. "Not good." He pinched the right sleeve of his leather shirt, to show two small punctures that fit over each other as if a thin, very sharp nail had been driven through. "There was enough poison on the end of that dart to finish a dozen settlements. All they had to do was come an inch closer."

Bart swore. "They shot at you?"

Able nodded. "They think any stranger must be a carrier of the sickness. They haven't had that yet."

"But then, where'd you get the seed potatoes?" Bart asked.

"I went another twenty miles to West Seven."

"All that way through the forest?"

"I don't know any other way to get there."

"How were they there?"

Able shook his head. "They're in a mess. They were down to twelve couples last summer. And the fools had left a belt of wire trees on three sides of the clearing. They claimed it kept the carraboons out of the crops. Well, a hunting party was late getting back a few weeks ago, a thick fog came down, the men lost the trail, and wire trees polished off four of them. Last winter, the sickness had carried off four of the women."

Bart shook his head. "Well, that leaves them eight couples. And they're immune, now, so—"

"They're immune to the sickness. But they don't have eight couples."

"They were down to twelve last summer. They've lost four men and four women. Four from twelve leaves eight."

"The four men the wire trees got weren't the husbands of the women the sickness killed. They were *other* men. That makes eight unattached men and women."

"Well—"

"Sally," said Able dryly, "has a yen for Bill. Bill likes Greta. Greta's trying to get Mike's eye. Mike always did like Bernice. Bernice is mourning for Dave. Meanwhile, Edna—"

Bart shut his eyes.

Able said, "If I looked at any one of those women for more than about ten seconds, someone started loading his gun. There were eight women there, and one of them made it a point to be friendly. I tell you, I made the trade and cleared out fast."

Bart grinned. "Why didn't you bring one back? The friendly one?"

"What, loaded down with a sack of potatoes? In strange country, with eight of their men to one of me? And forty miles of wire trees between me and home?"

Bart laughed. "Well, you could have—"

The unfamiliar male voice, that had startled Able earlier, again rose over the clearing, the words slurred so that it took an instant to make out the meaning:

"But, Lennie, the doctor *told* me to get a change of scene! My nerves are gone, absolutely *gone*, I tell you! A man's system can stand just so much! Really, we've hardly *gotten* here, and now *she* wants to go back. How am I supposed to—"

Able glanced around, his gun ready.

Bart shook his head wearily. "I forgot. Step over here a little further to the right."

Able picked up the sack and followed Bart to a spot where they could look out at an angle between the two end cabins. Across the clearing to their left was a glittering metallic structure, shining in shades of blue, pink, and violet, with a dazzling strip of yellow, that Able for a moment couldn't get into focus. Then the thing resolved into a variety of shapes he could recognize, and involuntarily, he swore.

Like a forty-foot-square chunk of luxury vacation resort, sat a raised swimming pool with diving board, a fifteen foot strip of dazzling sand, a screened-in porch that jutted out at an angle part way over the pool, and, visible on a sort of outthrust metal terrace beside the pool, several beach chairs, a chaise lounge, a round table with big candy-stripped umbrella, and a stand bearing a frosted carafe and three full glasses.

"Where in hell—" said Able, and then bit off the rest as he saw in the background, with multicolored pennants fluttering in the breeze, the space yacht out of which this collapsible paradise must have everted itself.

"How long has this been here?"

"It came down the day after you left. A man's voice called, 'O.K. if we set up here?' and I said 'Sure.' I was glad to hear a human voice. There was a kind of grunt, and that was all they had to say. A set of slits appeared in the side of the space yacht, the side opened out, and then the damnedest collection of rods, metal plates, screens, tubes, and loops of wire, pushed out from inside, thrust into various positions, there was a series of loud clicks and snaps, and a continuous sliding noise, with more stuff pushing out from inside, and in about twenty minutes, there it sat, just as you see it now."

Able studied the yacht.

"What potentate could afford a thing like that?"

"Oh," said Bart dryly, "the guy's a circuit element."

"A *what*?"

"On the left side of his head, and in one or two other places, there are half-inch circular spots where the hair doesn't grow, with two or three small, dead-white dots, forming regular patterns in the centers of these half-inch spots."

Able frowned, trying to pin down an elusive memory.

Bart said, "When we were shipping out, they were advertising for volunteers to test for 'brain-circuit characteristics,' remember?"

"Vaguely."

"The idea was that certain characteristics of the human brain were useful in computer construction, but very expensive to duplicate artificially. So they were trying what I think they called a 'hybrid linkage.' If the characteristics of a volunteer's brain happened to be right, he signed a waiver, they in effect plugged him into the circuit, and then they used him until either his contract ran out, his brain characteristics slid out of adjustment, or their needs changed. In return, he got a huge payment, and a pension for life."

Able studied the space-yacht as the meaning of this sank in.

Bart said, "Naturally, they didn't pick those people for intelligence, any more than you select a transistor or a vacuum tube because the thing is smart."

Able looked at the soggy muck spreading out from the base of the pool.

Bart said, "This boob has a yacht equipped with nuclear reactors, forcescreens, heat-rays, and heaven only knows what other little necessities of life, that he can misuse at our expense any time. Look there!"

Able saw a little blue-and-white skimmer, its slender legs holding its gliding-membrane taut, streak almost horizontally toward the roof of the porch that jutted out at an angle over the pool.

There was a dazzling flash, the skimmer's fur burst into flame, and its forward motion slowed so rapidly that it dropped almost vertically, to splash into a marshlike puddle.

"Now," said Bart, "brace yourself."

There was a metallic rattle, then a recorded voice boomed across the field:

"Your attention please. This vessel is fully protected by appropriate devices of the Advanced Synodic Products Corporation. It will retaliate automatically against any aggressive or hostile action."

Able stared at the remains of the little skimmer lying in a puddle of water.

Atop the nose of the towering space-yacht, a variable-beam energy-cannon retracted into its housing.

Able glanced around wonderingly, and for the first time saw around the yacht's pool and porch, the thin long and thick short rods of a noise-suppressor. Whatever happened out here, it wouldn't disturb their sleep in there. A mirage-like, white fluffy cloud, drifting apparently between the yacht and the trees behind it, told of another device that created, at the owner's pleasure, the illusion of a different outside scene.

Able glanced at the dead skimmer. "What's next?"

"I don't know. This business has happened dozens of times, but it's never gone any further."

Able's attention was caught by a blur of blue and white.

A second skimmer, this one gliding considerably higher, streaked across the clearing.

There was a dazzling flash.

The skimmer's fur burst into flame, and so, too, did a chunk of knobby, irregular, pale-blue tree trunk in the line of fire, across the clearing.

"Watch out," said Bart. "If that seed-knot cooks off—"

By the edge of the pool, a flabbily-built man wearing purple shorts, sun-glasses, a green sport shirt with violet pattern, knee-length socks and bedroom slippers, walked out onto the outthrust terrace, and flopped down in a beach chair.

Bart murmured, "If only it could have hit any tree but a dead bitchwood."

Following the man, face flushed and angry, came a woman with the build of a starved model, wearing a two-piece bathing suit.

The man waved his hand at her as if brushing away gnats, and picked up a glass.

The woman leaned forward to say something.

"*New*," said the man loudly, apparently meaning "No." He looked away.

She said, "Won't you let me—"

"I *won't*."

"At least listen—"

"*New!*"

"But—"

"Go away! Shut up!"

She straightened angrily. "You can go to hell!"

The man's body remained in the same position, but his head turned around. He threw the glass in her face.

The yacht's loud-speaker gave its metallic rattle.

The energy cannon loomed out of its housing.

The burning tree hissed, and a plume of white vapor spurted out from a pineapple-size bump faced toward the space-yacht.

Bart swore. "Sure as rats and blizzards, that seed-knot is going to blow."

"Your attention," said a loud, recorded voice. "Any further provocation—"

A menacing hiss came from the section of burning tree. The flames climbed higher up the trunk, reaching for new bumps and protrusions.

"Grab that sack," said Bart. "Get further back in the woods!"

"The baby—"

There was a loud *bang* from the tree. A shotgun-like blast of nut-size seeds sprayed across the clearing.

The cannon swiveled in a blur of motion. There were a dozen bright flashes.

"No time!" yelled Bart. "He's safe inside. Once those other knots cook off—"

Able swiftly measured the distance with his eyes. He shook his head, grabbed the sack and ran at an angle away from the burning tree.

Whoom!

A shaft of pink radiance lit the burning tree and a dozen others around it. A moment later, they were all on fire.

The recorded voice went on " . . . If this molestation does not cease within three minutes, strong measures will be . . ."

Bang! Another seed-knot cooked off. Bang! *Bang!*

Small, hard, nut-sized objects whizzed and droned overhead, hit tree trunks with a sharp cracking noise, and bounced and ricocheted in all directions.

Able landed hard and rolled behind a big tree. It was by far the best cover in sight, and Bart was already there.

Whoom!

Flaming branches dropped all around them.

A machine gun banging and hammering opened up as fresh bitchwood trees caught fire and put their emergency reproductive method into action.

Somewhere near, there was a hissing, sizzling, noise

"That does it," said Bart. "They've got a staplenut on fire."

Able peered cautiously around, and sniffed. "Which way is the wind?"

"Straight for us. Once that green sap starts to boil—"

Able glanced behind him, where the seeds flashed through the air, tearing up the leaves and dirt when they hit.

"We can't go back there—"

A pale-green foglike cloud drifted forward, the first faint wisps charged with a stinging odor that brought white flashes and a flood of tears to the eyes, a searing sensation to mouth and nose, a hot tight thickness to the lungs, and a general sense of being trapped in a constricted hole, unable to move or breathe or—

Able was running headlong, flying objects whizzing around him. Something rapped the back of his head like a hammer. He lost his balance, plunged down a steep slope, barely missing slamming head-first into a tree trunk, then something twisted crosswise under his feet, and he threw himself forward with every ounce of strength he had.

There was a singing, creaking noise. The air filled with a cloud of dead leaves and dust, and there was a multiple crack like the lash of a dozen whips.

Able sucked in a ragged breath. "*Wire tree!* Look out! *Wire tree!*"

A peculiar shrill high-pitched whistle sounded overhead, carried over the hiss, bang, and *whoom* from behind them, wavered, and descended by slow eerie stages.

Able wiped his eyes and looked up.

Some forty feet away, the veined green bole of a wire tree rose from the forest floor, its many tiny leaflets casting a pattern of flickering hypnotic shadows on the ground. Around the trunk was a wide circle where the dirt boiled, and small pebbles danced in the air. Overhead a large bird with big claws and curving red beak dropped from limb to limb, head turned sidewise to peer hopefully into the blur of the thrashing trap roots.

"That was *close*," said Bart, clinging to a nearby tree trunk and gasping for breath.

"Don't move," said Able. "Look behind you."

Thirty feet away in the other direction stood a veined green trunk, flickering shadows moving hypnotically over the ground nearby.

Bart looked, turned and said suddenly, "Where are the seed potatoes?"

Able looked at him. "If you think you could have carried them through that—"

"It isn't that. Listen."

Above the sizzling and banging, and the boom of a loud-speaker back at the clearing, came the chortle of a skimmer calling its fellows to a feast.

Able stared at the interlacing streaks, and the black objects bouncing over the edge of the slope. To go up there now would be suicide.

He shook his head. "I left the sack by the big tree. I couldn't have carried it through that."

"It isn't your fault, Abe. I should have helped carry it."

"You couldn't have. It would have been too slow. We'd have been pelted to death in the first twenty seconds."

Bart stared up the hill.

Able, thinking back, could think of nothing he might have done differently. Taking the one choice open to him at each turn, he was inevitably led into this mess.

From up the hill, apparently in the shelter of the big tree, came the chatter and chortle of a horde of feasting skimmers.

Bart said, "If I can run fast enough—"

"Look at that haze blowing past up there. The skimmers evolved in this place. That boiling sap just makes their eyes water a little. If either of us goes up there, we'll strangle on the first breath."

"That's true," said Bart. A moment later, he said tensely, "But, do we have to just stand here while we lose our last chance—"

A distant, carrying voice boomed. "Any future hostile action on your part will be crushed with a severity equal to that you have just experienced. Let this warning be sufficient."

Able shut his eyes. He took a slow quiet breath. When he looked around again, the trap roots were burying themselves in the dirt for the next try.

From the direction of the clearing came the wail of a terrified baby.

Able said, "I've got to try to get back. Maybe I can work around the worst of this. When that smoke and seeds let up—if you could get back to that tree—"

Bart nodded. "Be careful. Some of those wire trees we finished off after we landed are sprouting from the stump. Sometimes you don't see them till you're on top of them. The trap roots are only thick as threads, but they're ugly to get free of."

"I'll be careful."

"Good luck."

Five hours later, Able and Bart stood amongst the bare clay-mortared stone chimneys, their faces red from the heat of the glowing coals and smoking ends of logs that had been cabins. Nearby, plastered with steaming mud, stood the one remaining building, the thick-walled and heavy-roofed storage cabin. On three sides of the clearing stood the charred sticks of bitchwood trees, and here and there a smoldering staplenut spat green foam that boiled away in clouds.

Able glanced at the dozer, its paint seared off on top and side, the roof of the cab melted down, and the metal mud-shield on one side welded to the track.

Behind them, the baby was crying. Able had gotten him out just before the tree fell on the burning cabin roof.

Bart said, "What a mess. We've got only a few potatoes. The dozer won't go anywhere till we fix the track. We don't have the equipment to do that right, so whatever we grow, we'll have to raise it by hand. But there's only two of us to cultivate and guard the crop, so we won't have enough, even if everything works out, to join up with another settlement. We've got nothing to offer except three hungry mouths."

Able was studying the space-yacht, noting the late afternoon sun slanting on the fluttering sunshade. On the diving board stood a shapely girl in a two-piece swimsuit and white bathing cap. Her intelligent features showed a slight wrinkling of the nose as she posed on the board.

"The wind," said Bart, "let up just then."

Able glanced at the curving line of dead animals in the muddy water outside the base of the pool.

"Where," said Able, "does that water come from?"

"The pool. The first few days, the water was recirculated, but apparently a filter gave out. The boob there..."

Able noticed the man in the chaise lounge, making expansive gestures as the thin woman nodded hasty agreement.

"...The boob there," said Bart, "threw a fit, and blamed the woman, but the girl said maybe they could drain off some of the water to keep it clean. She set the mechanism so a trickle came off. The boob reset it so a flood came out."

"There are just the three of them?"

"That's all I've seen."

"What relation are they?"

"The thin woman is the cretin's wife. The girl is the wife's kid sister. They had a sisterly talk one night, and it sounded as though life was never any bed of roses for them, but since Mort—the husband—made his windfall, they've been loaded with money, and the husband has been threatening to go nuts. He's got all kinds of luxuries, doesn't have to lift a finger, isn't happy, and just naturally blames the wife."

Able studied the two. "Is the wife sick?"

"I don't think so," said Bart. "Why?"

"She's so thin."

"What would your digestion be like if you were a woman married to that?"

Able nodded. Across the way, an argument had sprung up, making him wish the focused compression-waves of the noise-suppressors worked on outgoing as well as incoming sounds.

The girl, scowling, climbed out of the pool, and said, "Lana—"

Trembling, the woman looked at her. "What is it, Helen?"

The man, frowning, glanced at the girl. His bad humor evaporated. "What's the trouble, Lennie?"

"Did you notice that smell?"

The woman shook her head.

"Yeah," said the man. "I got a whiff of it. Something dead."

The girl frowned. "Do you suppose we'd better take a look?"

Able glanced at Bart. "Can they see anything at all out here?"

Bart shrugged. "I yelled my head off when the water started pouring out. I was as close as I could get without getting cooked by that cannon. They didn't hear me or see me, even though they looked through me half-a-dozen times."

On the terrace, the man was saying, "Why bother? It's just the gobbies. They don't live very sanitary, you know."

Able said, "'Gobbies.' What's that?"

"His name for 'mud-footed settlers.'"

The girl said stubbornly, "They might need help."

The woman glanced at her husband.

The man stiffened. "Nuts to that. What am I, a settler's aid fund? If they want to lay around in their own filth, that's their look-out."

The woman said, "Please, Helen—"

"They may need help."

The man's voice rose in pitch. "For Pete's sake, Lennie, can't a guy relax? So what if they butchered a dog and they're too lazy to bury the guts. Most of these gobbies are criminals and defectives, anyway. You want to load all that on me? I say it is none of our business."

Bart passed a hand over his face.

Able was studying the energy-cannon in its housing atop the nose of the ship. He looked down at the big doors where the porch and pool thrust out of the yacht, looked hard at the fluttering sunshade and the long shadows cast on the side of the ship, then studied the dozer.

"*Please*, Helen," the woman was saying, "Don't . . . Don't make him . . ."

The man shouted, "Don't make me *what*?"

The girl frowned and sniffed. That the air now seemed fresh to her appeared likely, since the stench was now blowing full in the faces of Bart and Able, the wind carrying it away from the ship.

Able glanced at Bart. "Did you notice that the rear power take-off on that dozer is clear of the wreckage, and the big flat metal plate over the converter housing is undamaged? What's to prevent us from connecting the grinder attachment to the take-off, and reaching in through that shambles to work the control-lever?"

"What's the use? We can't go anywhere till we fix the track."

"I was thinking we could fix it if we had that ship. And by simple right of self-defense—"

Bart stared at him. "But how? We can't *touch* that yacht. We could have a dozen rocket-launchers and an old-style army division here. It wouldn't do more than set off a red light on a board somewhere, which the boob would ignore. The only thing that could get past that force-screen and the energy-cannon would be another energy-cannon. Assuming, that is, they don't have a beam deflector, in which case we'd get the whole works right back in our faces."

"If they had a deflector," said Able, "would they use a shade to keep the sun off?"

Bart frowned at the sunshade. "What are you driving at?"

"The yacht has the advantage in weapons, but a pure-routine computer is running them. It strikes me intelligence still ought to count for something."

"Maybe. But what?"

"Help me bolt on that fine grinder, take the hatch off, find some kind of straight edge and improvise a protractor—and we'll find out."

Both moons—the little distant one, and the big Earth-style one—were up that night, and the big one was full, which helped the work.

They worked most of the night, got a few hours sleep, were up by early dawn, and late afternoon of the next day found them in a deep narrow trench, the baby squalling under cover of a flat rock laid across one end of the trench and heaped with dirt. Two long poles stretched up to a frame of charred wood between two charred trees. The frame held the big metal plate from the dozer, polished mirror-bright and pivoted to turn when Able pulled one of the poles. Two carefully-positioned wooden rests determined the extreme angle the metal plate could turn to. Upright in front of the plate was a dry billet of bitchwood, its explosive seed-knot aimed toward the space-yacht. The second pole held a briskly-burning torch.

"O.K." said Bart. "The women are safe in the pool. He's inside."

Able moved the torch over, setting the seed-knot ablaze. "O.K. Fire the gun."

Bart bent at a dart gun already armed, wedged in place, and heaped over with dirt. He squeezed the trigger, worked the loading mechanism, squeezed the trigger, again, worked the loading mechanism—

The loud-speaker boomed. "Your attention. This is the only warning you will receive. This vessel is fully protected by—"

Bart squeezed the trigger and worked the loading mechanism.

Able eased farther down behind the thick bank of earth.

WHOOM!

The air lit up pinkly. The bank of earth steamed, particles of dirt at the top jumped like popcorn.

Bang!

The knot let fly its seeds.

The radiance lifted, to shine on the polished metal plate. The charred wood frame caught fire but held its shape.

Able counted seconds.

From across the field came a male yell.

Able pulled back the pole. The plate pivoted.

A choking and coughing drifted across the field.

Able counted slowly, then picked up a long stick lying nearby and knocked loose the smoking rest that held the plate from turning farther. The metal, pivoted slightly off-balance, swung around under its own weight, presenting its narrow edge to the energy beam.

The burning frame began to sag.

Able said, "Quick! Get under cover. When that plate catches the beam and reflects it at random—"

From across the field came choking, gagging, male curses and female screams.

"Shut everything off!" cried the girl's voice. "We've got to get out!"

Abruptly the radiance was gone.

The blazing frame crashed to the ground.

The choking and coughing grew worse.

Bart said, "We must have had the angle right. It sounds like we hit that staplenut dead on."

"Just pray the wind doesn't shift." Able peered out cautiously.

Across the field, a big staplenut tree was on fire, clouds of greenish fumes boiling off to wreathe the yacht. The nearest of the yacht's big cargo doors, where the porch and pool had been thrust out, was discolored, and so buckled as to jam it open. Through the opening, choking fumes swirled in, the gap incidentally posing air-loss problems if the yacht tried to leave the planet.

Stumbling across the field came the woman, then the girl carrying a kind of light-weight rifle, then the man, apparently unarmed.

"O.K.," said Able, picking up little Bobby. "Don't show yourself, but keep him in your sights."

"I still think you need a gun."

"Honey's better than vinegar." Able cradled the baby in his arms, and walked slowly out into the field. The baby let out a scream of discontent.

The girl, her eyes streaming, raised the gun.

Able turned the baby so that it gave a piercing wail that carried across the field.

The woman cried, "Don't shoot, Helen! It's a baby!"

The girl wiped her eyes and stared. She lowered the gun.

Able tried to look friendly, and took pains to keep the baby prominently in view

The baby kicked and squalled.

The two women came closer, as if drawn despite themselves by some powerful magnet.

Able, his male incompetence glaringly obvious, shifted the baby around as if looking for some handle to get hold of it by.

The baby swung wildly with both fists.

The women, reassured by all this obvious helplessness, came straight for the baby. The girl took the baby, handing the rifle to the thin woman, cuddled the baby and talked to him. The baby stared at her. The thin woman looked longingly at the baby, and shifted the gun around in a way that made Able's back hair tingle.

Able said in a humble, bashful voice, "If you want, ma'am, I'll hold that while you look at the baby."

"Yes," she said, brightening, and Able had the gun.

He recognized it as a Model XX Superlight, firing explosive pellets charged with quick-acting poison. The selector lever was set at "A" for "automatic," and Able promptly thumbed it back to "S" for "safe."

Across the field, the man from the yacht was wiping his eyes. He saw Able, patted all his pockets in rapid succession, then suddenly jerked a flat oblong thing from a small belt case.

To Able, this thing had the appearance of a hand-communicator. It had a speaker, a telescoping antenna, and he could see a switch at the side. Then, too late, he realized it was too big for a communicator, and might well double as a hand-launcher for acorn grenades.

The man had the telescoping antenna aimed at Able. A sudden realization kept Able from trying to use the gun.

The girl cried, "Why does *he* have the gun? *What's Mort—*" She screamed.

Across the field, there was a dazzling bluish flash that left a hideous after image.

"*Did he shoot Mort?*" cried the woman.

Able kept the gun down.

The girl said, "Mort shot himself with the hand-launcher, Lana! I saw him!"

"Oh!" said the woman, and began very quietly to sob.

Bart walked up, carrying the dart-gun inconspicuously, barrel down and stock out of sight under his arm.

Able glanced at the distraught woman. "Don't hurt the baby."

"Oh, yes, the baby." The woman cuddled it. "I'm sorry, honey, I'm sorry. Oh, Helen, Mort was *so* unhappy."

Able said, "There's staplenut milk over there in the cabin, if the baby is hungry." He glanced at the girl, who was studying him curiously. "But," he said, "whatever you do, don't go in the forest. There are trees on this planet that have contractile false roots that can whip and squeeze you to death, and crush you into fertilizer in no time."

The girl put her hand out for the gun.

Able held the gun out to her. "Keep it on 'Safe.' It won't hurt the trees, and we're the only people left in this settlement."

She smiled and let her hand drop. "Keep it. I guess you know what you're doing."

Able blinked. The two women went toward the cabin, carrying the baby, which was making gurgling noises instead of the usual screams.

Bart and Able cautiously approached the space-yacht. Able tossed a rock, which landed, unharmed, near the base of the pool.

Bart said, "I would never have expected him to shoot *himself.* I fired at him, and missed. I thought he was going to shoot you, and incidentally blow up the women and the baby."

"He was," said Able. "He forgot the launcher was dual purpose, the top part all communicator. *He aimed the wrong end.*"

Bart shut his eyes.

"Look," said Able, "the wind's veered around. We can go up that ramp without getting gassed."

An hour later, they'd explored the ship, locked the control board, stopped the flood of water pouring out on the field, and were standing on the terrace by the edge of the pool. Around them they saw, not the clearing, but a moonlit beach scene, with couples lying on blankets, bonfires in the distance, radios playing softly, and white foam swirling far up a long smooth beach. Able, studying the console that stood under the porch, finally spotted a lighted button marked "Local." He pushed it, the beach scene disappeared, and there was the clearing.

Bart said softly, "Look at that water. What's to prevent our taking a swim?"

"Nothing I can think of."

"Look, there's a *shower.* Over there, in the corner under the porch."

"I see it."

"Ye gods, think of it—the ship has a machine-shop, three or four book-viewers, dozens of library cubes, soft beds with real sheets, a kitchen, enough food concentrates, staples, and luxuries to last years, medicines of all kinds, electricity, hot and cold running water, plus all this out here—*and he wasn't happy!*"

Able nodded.

Bart said, "How could anyone have all this and *not be happy?*"

"I suppose happiness doesn't come in one piece, like a rock. It has parts—like an axe, with a head and a handle. And generally either part alone isn't enough."

"What are the parts?"

"Well, look how miserable we were, for lack of material things. And look how miserable he was, for lack of self-control."

"Hm-m-m," said Bart, staring off across the field where a soft glow showed that the women had discovered the lamp. "I never thought of that. But, say material advantages make up the head of the axe, and self-control is the handle. There's still something missing. What about that little wedge that's driven in to keep the head of the axe from coming loose?"

"Well, that's clear enough," said Able, glancing at the lighted cabin. "Life is full of these little tricks. What happens when somebody *does* get happiness? As likely as not, the handle of self-control shrinks up, the head of material goods flies off and sinks itself in his foot, he lets out a yell, throws the handle fifty feet, and there's the end of it.

"But take the people who have found happiness and seem to keep it. How do they do it? It appears that, regardless of their means, *they think and work hard*. The thought and work, in turn, generate hunger—a need for food, rest, comfort. I'd say the little wedge that holds happiness together is *hunger*. Without that, the biggest feast is just so much grease and indigestion."

Bart thought it over, then nodded. "Back home," he said, "they're always talking about 'abolishing hunger.' They might think about it some more."

Bart and Able took another glance at the pool, the terrace, and the treasure-laden ship, then started back across the field.

"Thanksgiving dinner," said Bart thoughtfully, "isn't worth much unless you work up an appetite."

"True enough," said Able. Then his mind abruptly descended to details. "Watch it. We don't want to land in that crater where the acorn-grenade went off."

They veered sharply to one side. "Glad you remembered *that*," said Bart.

Able glanced at the softly-lighted cabin ahead, and considered another little detail. He and Bart were two men, and, in the cabin there, were two women. He remembered the mess at West Seven, and winced. Philosophy, such as he and Bart had been talking about, was strong stuff—but if there was anything to turn it inside out, it was women.

Still, he told himself, there were only *two* of them.

Maybe they'd get through this alive yet.

Able and Bart crossed the field, and gently—warily—rapped on the cabin door.

CONTRAST

Hale Armbuster watched intently as the forty-foot long constrictor glided toward him along the edge of the narrow path. The huge snake looked at him with the calculating gaze of a carnivore moving in on its kill.

Hale glanced up. The big tree-spider had its dropnet nearly spun, and was gazing down at him with cool speculation. And across the grassy strip between the cave and the edge of the ravine, what looked like a rotten stump crept a few inches closer every time he turned the other way.

For the thousandth time, he damned himself for getting into this mess in the first place. He wasn't a colonist, but here he was on a colony planet; and not in a settlement but out in the untouched wilds. He'd never expected to spend his life in a fool trap, but he'd put in a year and a half in this place already. Worse yet, he was beginning to have doubts that he would ever get out of it. For one thing, it looked today as if everything might come to a head at the same moment.

The constrictor now had reached the place where the path widened, so that it could, if it chose, glide behind a tilted boulder and up a steep embankment to disappear into the brush, and come back at him later from his left and rear.

He watched tensely.

The snake chose instead to glide steadily up the path, past the rock, and directly toward him.

He bent, and pulled on a vine that lay near his feet. The vine

635

tightened and came up into the air, and he yanked hard. At the other end of the vine, near the boulder, the trigger stick jerked loose. The boulder tilted forward and slammed down on the middle of the snake. The front end of the snake whipped around to attack the boulder.

Hale breathed a little more easily and glanced around.

The rotted stump was now about a yard closer.

The tree-spider had fished up a number of stones on a long strand hung with sticky globules, and was methodically placing the stones so as to weight the edge of its dropnet.

The front end of the snake was struggling violently to get free of the boulder, but so far was having no success.

Hale selected a spear from the pile near the mouth of the cave, and waited till the tree-spider had its net weighted. Then he walked to one side.

The tree-spider lowered its dropnet, and followed, twirling the net gently on a strand guided by one leg as it sprang from limb to limb to get more directly above him.

Hale glanced up at the spider, then darted aside and back.

The stump bunched itself as he moved to avoid the spider. A set of small eyes rose on stalks to study his movements. Out of the corner of his eye Hale could see the stump tense and start to change its appearance as it braced for the spring.

Hale whirled and slammed his spear into the stump.

The stump bounded up with an explosion of short thick legs that lengthened out to wind around the spear.

The spider was now directly overhead, and dropped its net.

Hale gripped the spear by the end of the shaft, and slammed it up into the dropnet. The stones whipped the net tight around stump and spear. The spider hauled its prize up and spun it around, adding new strands.

Hale, the sweat running into his eyes and blinding him, wiped his arm across his forehead. He drew a deep breath. Then the watchword of the colonists on this planet came to him: "Look out. There's another one around somewhere."

He glanced around.

The giant snake now had its nose under the edge of the boulder, trying to pry it up. The snake's tail end was lying motionless, which seemed to show that its back was broken. The spider was cheerfully hauling the "stump" further up into the tree, along with the spear. Later, Hale would get the spear back, along with more grisly trophies, when the spider cleaned house.

But right now, he felt a prickly uneasiness, and realized it was because he had no weapon in hand. He got his gun, walked back with it, and took another look around. Everything *seemed* to be in order.

There was a faint clatter of falling bits of stone. Behind him.

He took a flying dive for the nearest tree.

There was a *squish* sound. A spatter of droplets landed all around him as he hugged the dirt between two big roots of the tree. Where the droplets landed, grass, ferns, and moss turned black and withered away.

Groundrunner, Hale thought. In his mind's eye he could see the low, many-legged body gliding toward him, its tail-section raised up to let fly another blast of poison. Hale held the gun ready, listening for the soft clack of the groundrunner's segments.

From the direction of the cave, came a low, earth-shaking rumble, then a thud like a ton of rock hitting the earth. There was a thin, high-pitched scream, then a violent clacking and thrashing. Blasts of droplets hit ground and tree trunks in all directions, leaving patches of blackened moss and bark. When this passed, he risked a glance.

The groundrunner was in front of the mouth of the cave, its long flat body twisted on itself, its head end pinned under a boulder the size of a space-yacht's power unit.

Behind it, deep inside the cave, there was the glint of big eyes spaced several yards apart.

Hale stepped out from behind the big tree, glanced up, and saw that the tree-spider was intent on sucking the juice out of the imitation stump. For the moment he was safe from that direction. He looked around warily. Nothing seemed to be creeping up on him. Then a swiftly-moving shadow caught his eye, and he looked up again at the tree-spider, to see a flat snakelike form with stiffly-outstretched transparent wings alight gently on a limb, around on the other side of the tree from the spider. A glide cobra. The cobra folded its membranes, moved quietly along the limb, and eased out on the trunk. Clinging to the thick rough bark, it worked its way out above the preoccupied spider, eyed the spider calculatingly, brought forward another length of its body, and poised to strike.

Hale aimed carefully, and shot its head off.

The cobra fell twisting from the tree. The spider jerked, watched the cobra fall, then looked at Hale. Hale couldn't say if the look actually expressed gratitude, but it seemed to.

Hale looked around, saw nothing new, and shifted his position to see if anything else was trying to sneak up on the spider. So long as the spider was overhead, the likelihood was very small that anything else would move in. Thinking of the things that might set up housekeeping in the nearby trees, the spider seemed almost like an old friend. It occurred to Hale that it was probably for the same reason that the monster tunneler had come out and heaved the rock onto the groundrunner. Hale was the tunneler's assurance that giant snakes, grabs, and hooks would not move into the cave.

He looked back at the dead groundrunner uneasily. Somehow, he had to drag that thing to the edge of the ravine and shove it over. Otherwise, its scent would bring nocturnal predators right up to the mouth of the cave. But he couldn't move the ground-runner until he got the boulder off of it. The boulder was too big to move by hand, so he would need tools. The big poles and crowbars, and the jackscrews from some spaceship's emergency tool kit were hidden under a shelving rock close to the deadfall where the forty-foot constrictor was pinned.

This snake was now lying with its bloody head stretched straight out, eying Hale with a look of cold calculation. It was plain to be seen that Hale would not get the tools till the snake died, and the snake was far from dead.

Uneasily, he glanced up, to gauge the height of the sun by the light filtering through the leaves. He saw that he didn't have much time.

He was starting to look away when, high overhead, something glinted. There was a flash of reflected sunlight.

Hale squinted, recognized the thing, and let his breath out in a groan. How could he fight this? Snakes, spiders, hooks, ground-runners, tunnelers—he could fight them or make his peace with them. But this thing overhead was different.

He sprinted to the cave, put the spears out of sight inside, and stayed inside, waiting doggedly. Maybe, just possibly, the fool would go away.

Whir!

No, he thought. No such luck.

Whir! Whoom!

Whir!

The disk-shaped grav-skimmer dropped to hover near the cave. A face that would have been considered intelligent on quite a few civilized planets peered over the edge of the skimmer.

To Hale, as to the hundreds of colonists on this planet, this face looking out over the edge of the skimmer was the living embodiment of full-blown imbecility. That look of breathless curiosity, the darting eyes, the sudden flash and *snap* as the glittering array of knobs and lenses swung around, all signified an eager desire for things that the people on this planet earnestly wished to be rid of.

The sightseer now spotted the tree-spider.

Hale watched warily. There were various degrees of fools, and no one could predict just what this one might do next. The skimmer was obviously safe from the spider, which was trying to make itself inconspicuous. But that did not prevent the sightseer from slamming the emergency switch for a violent power-lift. The skimmer rose in a burst of speed, straight for a high overhead limb. Just before it hit, some kind of automatic force field, or stepped-up high-power antigravity beam, came into operation, slowed the skimmer and sheared the massive limb completely off the tree.

Hale shut his eyes. He could hear the scream as the big nest in the fork of the high limb plunged for the ground. Three fluffy yellow balls the size of turkeys rolled out. Two lay dead or unconscious, but the third instantly flung back its head. There was a high-pitched trill, that rose rapidly out of Hale's range of hearing.

Whir!

The skimmer came down again, and before Hale could move, the sightseer leaned out of the ship, spotted Hale, pointed at the tree spider hugging the bark.

"Hey, feller, you're in danger! Look at that giant crab there!"

Hale sucked in a deep breath. There was nothing to do now but try to live through the mess.

The sightseer shouted, "I'll fix him for you!"

He swung around a four-foot long gun with a complex sight almost as big as the gun barrel.

"NO!" shouted Hale. "Leave it alone! Don't—"

A dazzling beam issued from the mouth of the gun. Bits and fragments of the tree-spider's legs fell twitching to the ground. The bark of the tree burst into flame. Where the spider's body had been, there wasn't even smoke.

Hale opened his mouth, then clamped it shut. Now there was no telling *what* might move in. Tree-rats. Fire hornets. Nests of glide-cobras. Anything.

The sightseer leaned out of the skimmer, grinned widely, and clasped both hands over his head in the boxer's gesture of triumph.

"I fixed that crab for you, didn't I?"

"Yeah," said Hale. He let his breath out slowly and eyed the skimmer. He put the gun inside the cave, reached up, felt along a wide rock shelf, and took down a long supple leathery cord. He went back outside, and studied the skimmer, which had three barlike handles thrust out from its rim. They were, he remembered, used for guiding an idling skimmer from the ground, carrying it with power off, or for strapping large game and trophies to the underside.

The sightseer, scowling at his cool reception, was now looking Hale over from head to foot, noting the leather clothing, beard, and long, roughly trimmed hair. The skimmer rose a little.

"Say, no offense, boy, but are you really civilized?"

Hale pointedly ignored the question, and started for the giant snake, which was lying stretched out, both eyes turned up to watch the skimmer. The skimmer followed right along, its occupant plainly unaware that: 1) the unmoving snake was far from dead; and 2) the crawling and flying things on this planet had a deep and mutual hatred for each other.

When Hale was about as close to the snake as he dared to go, he glanced and gestured to the sightseer. He said in a loud, purposely authoritative voice. "You're in danger here. Go away."

The sightseer said haughtily, "You don't order me, feller. I bought my travel permit, and I go where I feel like."

"Suit yourself. But it's dangerous here." Hale did not speak quite so loudly this time. The sightseer came a little lower, naturally doing exactly the opposite of what Hale told him to do. He was now studying Hale curiously.

"How do you *live*, feller?"

Hale pointed to the cache of tools, "I keep crowbars and a jack in there. This rock here is a trap—a deadfall. A pole props it up, and a vine runs out so I can jerk the trigger stick and drop the rock when I need to. Then the boulder slams down. See how it works?"

The sightseer had a small microphone thrust out, and was taking everything down in sound as well as on film.

"Real primitive stuff," he said, looking pleased. "You sleep in that cave?"

"That's right. There's a big animal called a tunneler that lives in the back. He doesn't bother me as long as I don't go back too far. There are spears and a couple of guns on a rock shelf near the entrance. There's a pile of furs on that shelf, where it widens out further back. I sleep there."

"Hey, this is good," said the sightseer. "Speak right into the mike, now." He swung the skimmer forward and around, to get a better angle as Hale continued to keep his back partly turned and to talk in a low voice.

Nearby, the giant snake lay tensely still. Its gaze, the eyeballs turned up toward the skimmer, grew intently fixated.

"By the way," said Hale, still turning, "you wouldn't be willing to help me move that rock near the cave, would you? Just so that I can get the groundrunner out of there? It would only take a few minutes."

The sightseer put his camera and microphone away. "Sorry, boy, I'd love to, but I'm in kind of a hurry." True to form, the sightseer wouldn't help.

The monster snake was now looking almost directly up, where the skimmer floated overhead.

Hale readied the loop in his hand.

Wham! The big head of the snake came up in a fluid blur, and hit the skimmer like a battering ram. The impact threw the sightseer out into the air. The skimmer shot up and sidewise, then readjusted downward to its set altitude. Hale gauged the distance, shot the rope out, caught one of the handles, and jerked the skimmer to the side.

The sightseer slammed heavily to the ground. The snake looked on with an air of quiet satisfaction.

Hale kept a wary eye on the snake, got the skimmer well to one side, and hauled himself up. The cutting of the slender slippery strand was painful, but then he grabbed a handle, reached up, took a fresh grip, and levered himself over the edge.

He found himself in a world of unbelievable luxury, surrounded by red leather cushions and softly-glowing control panels. The huge fusion gun rested on a flexible power-assisted mount, so that he needn't exert himself as he loosed overpowering blasts of energy in any direction he chose. A multiple ultrarange 6-V receiver and recorder with built-in library of records awaited his touch on a button. Recessed into the edge of the skimmer beside the 6-V was a Dispenser capable of materializing anything from a bottle of orange pop to a full-size dinner. The interior of the skimmer was softly cushioned and padded, so that the occupant need suffer no discomfort from sharp corners or a hard surface.

Hale recognized all these things as of old, but the sudden contrast between poverty and luxury accentuated both. And the prospect of actually escaping from the hell down below left him almost dizzy.

The rope still trailing out, he guided the skimmer toward the sightseer, who was standing white-faced, half-crouched in a kind of terrified paralysis.

There was a roar and a rush. A shadow passed over the skimmer, and a huge form smashed into the snake; its giant wings thrashed, and its talons sank into the tough flesh back of the snake's head. The snake reared back, twisted its huge head. Its jaws opened and seized a taloned claw.

Clouds of dust and feathers flew out. The sightseer sprinted for the cave.

Hale swung the skimmer closer, and called, "Climb in!"

The sightseer blinked, and abruptly his face cleared. He straightened, to shout peremptorily, "Get out of that skimmer!"

Hale shouted, "I can't lower the skimmer. So long as it's in the air, that bird won't bother us. You knocked its nest down, but it thinks the snake did it. The birds on this planet don't harm each other's young. This skimmer classifies as a bird as long as it's up in the air. Just climb up the rope. Don't argue. It's getting late, and its no fun to be out after dark on this planet."

The sightseer, white-faced with rage, pointed at Hale. "Out, I said." He tapped a small wrist-communicator. "I'll have the Planetary Police here in five minutes. Get out of that skimmer now and I won't prefer charges."

Hale glanced uneasily at the sky. It was starting to get dark. And once it started to get dark here, it got dark fast.

"Look," he said. "Argue about it later. Not now. Climb in. I'll help you."

The sightseer, face white and lips compressed to a thin line, snapped his forefinger up to point at Hale, then down at the ground.

"*Out!*"

Hale shook his head. "I want a ride to the nearest settlement. You owe me that, at the least, for the damage you've done. Climb in and let's go."

"You don't invite me into my own skimmer, fella. I said, *Out* and I mean it. Now, get out!"

Hale shook his head in disgust. He glanced around the interior of the skimmer, spotted the little bookcase with its inexpensive novels, and the standard volume titled "Survival."

He tossed out "Survival," untied his rope and dropped it over. He pointed, and shouted, "When you need water, the spring's back there! Watch the tree-rats and the glide-cobras!" He hit the Dispenser's selector buttons, threw down a dozen packets of emergency rations, dropped firelighter, knife and ammunition pouch on the pile of rations, and slammed forward the skimmer's controls.

The sightseer's angry threats of arrest and imprisonment faded into the background.

The skimmer streaked through the trees, rising at a shallow angle as Hale guided it with remembered skill between the huge trunks, and up through a break in the limbs. He punched the destination control to settle into a long straight run for North 2, the nearest settlement.

On the way, he knocked down three huge night-gliders with the fusion gun. Then, having at last gotten over a stretch of open country which was a little safer, it occurred to Hale to turn on the communicator. Before he could speak, a fragment of conversation came out the speaker.

"Hello," snapped the sightseer's angry voice, "is this Planetary Central?"

"Well," murmured a voice with a patient, unhurried drawl, "I suppose you *could* call it that. What we call it is North 1."

"It doesn't matter to me what *you* call it. I want a squad of the Planetary Police out here on the double. One of these natives just stole my skimmer!"

"That so?" drawled the voice, sounding vaguely interested. "You mean this happened at a settlement?"

"No, no. Not a settlement. Some kind of one-man hovel out in the sticks. I'll describe the whole thing plainly enough when the Police get here. They can home in on my signal. Now, snap it up."

Hale shook his head, and punched the Dispenser for steak, French fries lightly salted, and a large, chilled, chocolate milk-shake. For months he had dreamed of this exact menu, to awaken dry-mouthed. As he pressed the buttons, the Dispenser hummed obediently.

"Well," came the unhurried voice from the communicator, "I sure am sorry. You see, there's no Planetary Police *on* this planet. If we had them, they couldn't get to you. We got no skimmer except a few private ones. And if we had skimmers, we probably wouldn't use them anyway. Everybody's too busy working. This is a new planet. You sightseers are always telling us how quaint and primitive we are. Well, we are for a fact." After a pause, he added, "You got my sympathy, though."

There was a silence.

The bell on the Dispenser gonged in respectful tones, and the Dispenser produced steak, French fries, and a chilled milk-shake.

Hale cast an habitually watchful glance around the moonlit horizon, swerved and blasted a flight of hooks diving in at him. In doing so, he made the mistake of passing over a lake, and had to take violent evasive action to escape the scores of hungry grapples that shot up on jets of phosphorescent spray. Through it all the grav-field held his meal so that not the slightest bit was spilled. He ate, looking warily around.

"B-But," stammered the voice from the communicator, "what will I *do*? I can't stay *here*."

There was a jovial chuckle from the communicator. "Oh, I'd stay there if I were you. You got maybe three hundred miles of jungle between you and the nearest settlement. That's nothing in a skimmer. But it's a long way on foot. And you'd be eat up before you got here."

There was a string of violent curses and threats, to which North 1 replied blandly, "Nope. Sorry. Can't do it . . . Sure. Too bad. It's a pity . . . Oh, you got our sympathy all right. We're more scared than you are. *We* know what you're up against, and you don't. Course, you'll find out, starting any time now."

Hale took a sip of the milkshake, then spotted a small fast bird diving on him. Then another and another. He looked all around, and made out a large dim form coming in from another direction. Decoy bird, he thought. He shot the big one and the small ones dropped at the same instant.

Below, the dimly-lit cabins of North 2 appeared before him. He snapped on the landing-light of the grav-skimmer so that no one would mistake him for a night bird, turned off the communicator, and carefully settled down.

To one side, looking just as he had left it, was his space yacht.

Hale paused to ask the tall brawny settler who came out of a cabin if he would help put the skimmer under cover so it could be used the next day to rescue the sightseer.

"Nope," said the colonist. "I won't. I'd help *you*, mister, because you lived out there a long while, and here you are, still alive. I can talk your language, and you can talk mine. But I wouldn't touch that sightseer with a twenty-foot stick, and if you're smart, neither will you."

"Why?"

"Well, I'll tell you. You go out there tomorrow morning and rescue him and the odds are that at first he'll fall all over you. Then he'll get back to his space yacht, climb in the Recuperator, and come out the same boob he was when he came down here. He'll think things over and get indignant. He'll report you to the Space Police. He'll report us to the Space Police. He'll charge robbery, assault, attempted murder, piracy, and everything else he can think of. He'll blow up like a volcano. When the dust settles down, we'll all be coated with tar, and that fool will go off in a blaze of righteous indignation. Is it worth it?"

"Hm-m-m," said Hale, thinking it over. After all the time he had spent out there, he was not anxious to spend a new chunk of his life being dragged through law courts, and in and out of jails and prisons.

"And then," said the colonists, "there's another reason."

"What's that?"

"How would you find him? For him to get there in the first

place, we had to tell him just the right co-ordinates, so the fool could set his destination control for them and go out there to get some 'real primitive scenes.' We don't aim to tell you or anyone else where the place is till he's been out there long enough to have either been killed or got some sense beat into his head."

"I could follow the signal from his communicator."

"Ten-to-one the fool has lost his temper and smashed it by now."

"Hm-m-m," said Hale. He had slammed his own against the wall of the cave before the first hour was finished. "How long will you leave him out there before you send somebody out?"

"Depends on how long he lasts, how many of these sightseers we get in our hair, and how ugly we feel. After a man's survived a year or so of it out there, we send the sightseers out to him on a regular schedule. In order to last that long, even with all the game there is out there, his viewpoint in that length of time has *had* to change. Well, the sightseers don't help him, they just bother him. Before long he feels the same way about them that we do, and then he ropes one in and gets out of there. It's the only way to live with them. They waste our time, spoil our work, and sour our disposition. They come out here because they 'want excitement.' Well, we give it to them."

Hale relaxed on the cushioned surface of the skimmer. An odd thought came to him. About eighteen months ago, he had set out in a skimmer just about like this one. He had been impatient, dissatisfied, and in a bad mood. Since then, he had been tricked, trapped, and attacked by beasts of all descriptions.

Now he was back in the same spot he'd been in to start with. But now he felt contented. He mentioned this to the colonist, who nodded, and said, "That's how it works. People come out here because they aren't satisfied. They don't actually *know* why they come out here, but they sense it. We've got something in great supply, and they need a little of it."

"What's that?" asked Hale.

"Contrast," said the colonist.

"Contrast?"

The colonist nodded. "It's hard to appreciate anything unless you've got something—or some memory—to contrast it against. A good friend never stands out so well as when everyone else is a traitor. Green doesn't stand out against a green background, but it practically jumps out against a red background. It's the same way with civilization. The new devices and unheard-of luxuries are wasted against an unvaried background of advanced technology and unheard-of luxury. Most of the value of such things goes unappreciated because there's no contrasting background, either real or remembered, to judge them against."

"Then," said Hale, "when some sightseer comes out here, vaguely dissatisfied with everything—"

"We figure," said the colonist, "he needs a contrast. It just isn't humanly possible to really appreciate something smooth unless you've experienced something rough."

Hale smiled. "And so, you—"

The colonist grinned. "And so, we do our best to help. Once a man has been here, he's equipped to put up with years of new devices and civilized luxuries.

"He can appreciate the smooth, because he's really experienced the rough."

AFTERWORD

Christopher Anvil is best known as a science fiction writer for his Pandora's Planet sequence and the various stories placed in his Colonization series, primarily those involving the Interstellar Patrol. With this volume, the third in Baen Books' reissue of Anvil's writings, those stories are now back in print.

But Anvil has written a large number of other space adventures, unconnected to either Pandora's Planet or the Interstellar Patrol. Many of them deal with the various ways in which the human race interacted with aliens, and it's those stories that will be featured in the fourth volume of this reissue, *The Trouble With Aliens*.

At the center of the volume will be the various stories that are part of Anvil's "The War With the Outs" series, including such well-known ones as "The Prisoner" and "Seller's Market." So if you enjoyed this volume and its predecessors, there's plenty more to come.

And now I need to publicly thank a number of people whose efforts have played an important role in making this multi-volume Anvil reissue possible. First and foremost, Henry Cate, who first urged me to start an Anvil reissue and who has been extremely helpful in tracking down the multitude of stories scattered across many magazines over a period of decades. Actually, I should specify Henry Cate III, because his father Henry Cate, Jr., was also very helpful.

In addition, I'd like to thank Jim Budler, Matthew Class, Dave Gerecke, Robert Klein, Dave Lampe, Mary Qualls, Mark Rubinstein, Peter Sims, Simon Slavin, Mark Stackpole and Joe Webster.

—Eric Flint
September 2004